If Where You're Going Isn't Home

Book 3

Not into Night

Max Zimmer

demands of the faith as Shake and his young friends take their first steps into adulthood. But the great craft of this book is that it neither demonizes nor sanctifies its characters. And it neither demonizes nor sanctifies the Mormon church and faith. Zimmer presents his wonderful, quirky, and often hilarious cast with affection for all their foibles and strengths."
> — *Rolf Yngve, author,* Dog Watches: Stories from the Sea

"As a musician, I felt that the pulse of music in Shake's life, as well as his whole world as created by Zimmer, were so compelling—so real, I forgot I was reading fiction. There's such delight in the details, it was impossible to look away."
> — *Fred Simpson,* Just Another Sunrise: Poems to the Sun

"This is it my friends, what we have all been waiting for, magic, brilliance, humanity, compassion, wonder, imagery, no more searching, this is a must read that as soon as I completed it I couldn't wait to begin again, for I know I will be reading this book repeatedly and every time I pick it up, even if I only have time for a page or two, I will be sent soaring....Thank you Mr. Zimmer for restoring my faith that great literature is still being written. Mr. Steinbeck would be so proud, for as his brilliant work, you have truly captured the human spirit. "
> — *Melba, Amazon reviewer*

"I read the first chapter and was hooked. It felt like a movie. Huck Finn and James Dean in one brave and amazing kid. The voice is true. The writing is out of this world. A pillow mint on every page."
> — *George Goetz, writer*

"Journey won a place in my heart as one of the books that I will not only read twice (I already have), but three times, four times, five times and perhaps even more. Zimmer has created a character in Shake Tauffler that I really care about. Shake's story is told in the second person so we see what he sees; we experience what he experiences and we feel what he feels. His friends are funny, his friends are tragic. His friends stand up for him and one betrays him. He has a crush on one girl but by the time he finally gets to talk to her he finds her vapid and shallow. He stands up to bullies and pays the price. He is everyman."
> — *J. Eastman, Amazon reviewer*

"Even if you don't care about Salt Lake City in the '50s, the LDS church, jazz, racism or the post-war immigrant experience, you will care about Shake Tauffler."
> — *R. Hadfield, Amazon reviewer*

"Shake is all of us, and we all have had to decide at some point to stay home as are or accept the quest away from places we thought at the time were bountiful."

— *John H. Gill, Amazon reviewer*

"Journey is a poignant coming of age story of Shake, the son of Swiss immigrants who came to Utah to practice their Mormon faith, it rings true emotionally. And his descriptions of the dry, desolate-but-beautiful landscape around Bountiful reminded me greatly of my home state of New Mexico. He makes us love Shake right away, and we root for him as he questions his religion, tries to navigate the emotional terrain of a complicated family, and discovers his strengths and deep interests . . .This is not "Big Love" or "Book of Mormon." Just fabulously crafted fiction (based on real people)."

— *Audrey, Amazon reviewer*

"I was late for work because of this book. I neglected my family because of this book. This guy, Max Zimmer, is the real deal — an author with great gifts and an authentic voice and vision. I know "I couldn't put it down" is cliché, but I couldn't . . . .This is a great American story, like *To Kill a Mockingbird*. I can't wait to read books two and three. "

— *Edd Franz, Amazon reviewer*

If Where You're Going Isn't Home

Book 3

Not into Night

This work of fiction is modeled in various ways on the author's youth and on true events. As in all fiction, while the perceptions and insights are based on experience, the names, characters, places, and incidents portrayed in this work are either products of the author's imagination or used in a fictitious way. No reference to any real person should be taken as literal or factual.

Cover execution by David J. High, highdzn.com
Composition by Kevin Callahan, BNGObooks.com

The religious beliefs, customs, practices, rites, and processes portrayed in this book are accurate for their time period. This authenticity also holds true for the missionary experience described herein. Based on actual experience, verified where necessary by research, it is true to the doctrine and authentic in rendering the experience and culture of a foreign Mormon mission as taught, practiced, and lived in the 1960s.

The events of the civil and voting rights turmoil portrayed in this book, and the movement's leaders, opponents, victims, heroes, atrocities, defeats, and victories are taken from historical accounts and national and international newspaper and magazine articles and accounts written in real time, as they happened and were printed. Every effort was made to keep this hallowed material as true to place and time as possible.

In remembering and portraying the cities, towns, and villages of Austria that serve as the settings for this novel, the author was fortunate to reunite with Edi Goller, a lifelong native of Austria who served as a deep resource of recollection and historical, geographical, and cultural illumination to authenticate these portrayals.

The songs "I Loves You Porgy" and "Someone to Watch over Me," lyrics from which are cited in this book, were composed and written by George and Ira Gershwin.

The song "One Hand, One Heart," lyrics from which are cited in this book, was composed and written by Leonard Bernstein and Stephen Sondheim.

ISBN: 978-0-9997975-3-2

The Story and its Making

Not into Night is the third novel of the series *If Where You're Going Isn't Home*, a story that chronicles the growth of a boy caught between his dream to play jazz trumpet and the strictures of his father's Mormon faith.

Journey, the first book of the series, takes him from almost twelve to fifteen. The second book, *Of the World*, takes him from there to nineteen. In *Not into Night* he reaches the age of twenty-one. The fourth and final book, currently in progress, takes him deep into his twenties.

The genesis of what has evolved into this project is a love story I wrote in the summer of 1978. The story haunted me for several years. What I eventually came to recognize was that its psychic and dramatic setting—what it was like to grow up Mormon in America—had never been put on the map of our collective consciousness in a universal way that readers everywhere, from all walks of life, all religions, all cultures, could reach and experience from the familiar territory of their own lives. To create that setting, I put the original story aside, and began where the story needed to begin—with a boy at the beginning of his duty to his father's faith and his dream to play jazz trumpet. His story—the four-book chronicle of his odyssey—is a story still guided and informed by the love story that gave it life that summer.

FOR EDITH

Who gives this book its heart.

Contents

PART 1

IF YOU CAN KEEP HER

CHAPTER 1

IT WILL BE your duty to live righteously, to keep the commandments of the Lord, to honor the holy Priesthood which you bear, to increase your testimony of the divinity of the Restored Gospel of Jesus Christ, to be an exemplar in your life of all the Christian virtues, and so to conduct yourself as a devoted servant of the Lord that you may be an effective advocate and messenger of the Truth.

Cissy.

The night in the grove in the park in San Jose where the trees were low and close and held the red steel body of Yenchik's 40 Ford in the cradle of a million summer leaves while you held each other naked in its naugahyde interior and learned from each other how it was done. In the dark you could barely tell her skin from yours. On the sleepless drive home, at night along the coast and then inland through Sacramento and up into the Sierras, it was like she was there with you, across from you in the passenger seat, crying out when you crested the summit at the sudden incandescent shock of a billion stars.

Oh my God. Shake. Look. All the stars. I've never seen so many up so close.

Yeah.

It's like we're out in space with them.

And then the line of the sunrise far across the desert as you came down off the mountains into Reno and knew without looking that she wasn't there in the Ford with you, but where you'd left her, looking back at you one last time before closing the front door of her house the rest of the way. You rode alone across the desert, always toward the illusion of a silver shoreline that kept receding ahead of you, through the desert towns across Nevada. Somewhere along the way the faceless man was there in the passenger seat, the stale shit smell of reproach where he should have had a face, silence where his face should have had a mouth when you talked to him. And then the quiet way he started burning. The way the almost transparent spreading flame licked its way along the rim of his ear and flickered across the backs of his withered hands. The way he never moved while the whirling stench of him burning filled the Ford and barely let you breathe. When the last of him was burned away, and the wind cleared the last of the smoke out through the open windows, the desert air made you cry for how fresh and sweet and cool it was. In the distance ahead of you as you crossed into Utah the wall of the Wasatch Front began to stand up black from the lake of liquid chrome the sun made of the desert floor. When you saw them you knew. The mountains were where the road would end. That was okay now. You'd ended it your way. You knew the way back. Now you could consecrate yourself to your mission call to serve the Lord in Austria.

If you can keep her.

On the runway, waiting for takeoff, the plane is still except for the whistling rush of air through the idling engines. The morning sun sets white fire to the scratches and streaks in the hazed window at your shoulder when you look out at the city. The dome of the State Capitol nested on the hill. The Temple just down from it. The four blocks of downtown buildings that rise from the neighborhoods around them. From there you have to go on memory because from the runway, from your seat, you can't see them. The long straight aqueduct of State Street. The Sojourner, Manhattan, Indigo, other clubs in the city and up and down the outskirts towns along the foothills where your band played. The Music Building up on campus. The night yards at Hiller where you taught the miner kids from Magna how to play their instruments through the chainlink fence that protected the heavy equipment you guarded. Up on the back side of the city, where neighborhoods of expensive houses crawl up into the foothills of the East Bench where the rich kids live, the mountains shoulder up into the pale haze trapped by the stagnant summer weather in the valley. A million years ago the valley was the bed of a prehistoric lake called Bonneville. Now it feels like a lake again, pale yellow water closing over everything, ancient water taking back the space and time that your life here occupied.

Cissy.

Stay here forever.

The way she appeared in the terminal to say goodbye. Breathe in deep, through your nose, she's still there. Perfume. Breath. What she washed her hair with. Her own long ride across the desert yesterday with her brother Jeff. A hint of sweat in her pink church dress. It had to make her nervous coming here. You look away, from the window, at the small steel ashtray with its steel lid set flush into the end of the armrest. You look at the Triple Combination Lieutenant Tanner gave you in your lap, at the titles Book of Mormon, Doctrine and Covenants, and Pearl of Great Price stamped one under another in gold into the cover, at the gold letters of your whole name set like babyteeth into the black leather.

Shake Wilford Tauffler.

Hatch and Wissom and Clayton, the other missionaries headed for Austria with you, are scattered around the plane because you're not supposed to sit together, but with strangers, strangers you can share the message of the Gospel with because you're missionaries now, because your mission kicked off as soon as you took your seat. The man in the seat next to you is a big man maybe your father's age. The three pearl buttons in the ironed cuff of his green cowboy shirt make you think of the caps on the valves of your trumpet. The sunburn in his face was deep and permanent while his forehead and scalp were milk white when he took off his new straw cowboy hat to put in the rack above you. The way he looked down at you before he took his seat you could tell he was Mormon and knew what you were headed for. You could tell he expected to talk and have you listen. For a minute you could smell dust made sweet with deodorant.

Karl and Molly and Roy and Maggie.

Earlier, before they pulled in and locked the door and the plane turned and then taxied on its whining engines out to the head of the runway, you could pick out your family, standing with their faces against the mammoth wall of glass that formed the front of the terminal. In the blazing morning light you could see Molly and Roy and Maggie waving. In the long row of windows that ran the length of the plane you knew they couldn't tell which one was yours. But they stood there waving anyway, waving blind into the blazing sunlight, waving on faith that you could see them. Karl's hand was up but just to shield his eyes. Your father and mother stood there. They were lined along the sill of the glass wall with the waving families of other missionaries. Nobody knew them. The way they stood there you could see where they could almost be seen for just another family. Another American family among all the other families lined up waving. But then a negro girl had appeared across the terminal. A negro girl in a pink church dress and white church shoes, flush with negro blood, flush with the way she loved you, flush with her drive from San Jose with her brother Jeff, your army buddy Jeff in his Airborne uniform, just to let you know. She let you walk her across the mirrored sunlight of the polished stone floor. In her pink church dress and white church shoes she let you introduce her to each member of your family. Your father and mother and Karl and Molly and Roy and Maggie.

Cissy.

What your mother will do with the news that your sweetheart's negro. What price she might make Molly pay. What your father will do with a girl you can't marry in the Temple. What Karl will do. If he'll tear the head off the doll of Molly's memory of the beautiful girl who took her hand and smiled at her to let her know that she was beautiful too. That she was someone who could be seen.

Roy and Maggie.

They'd be fine.

In the idling plane, waiting at the head of the runway, you look again through the sun-crazed scratches and streaks of the window at the city you won't see for two and a half years. You thought you'd closed things down. Closed all the doors. Let the roads go dark behind you. Left things where you thought was the place where things were left, in the desert, where Lieutenant Tanner handed you off to God while the sunset turned the dirt floor of the desert silver blue like a lake of steel and rimmed the low black silhouettes of the distant mountains with fire. And then there she was, just minutes ago in the terminal, in her pink church dress and white church shoes and the deep rose glow of her honey coffee colored skin. And every door behind you suddenly stood open again like a wind had torn through all the things you'd closed. And every road left dark, every road you'd ended, became as endless again as the desert highway that continuously parted the lake of shimmering silver in the distance ahead of you on the sleepless drive home from San Jose.

Jesus god Cissy I love you

Oh god Shake help me help me

Loose now, her first time here, a tourist in the city outside your hazed window, a city that has already begun to fill in the space and time you once took up. Her and her brother Jeff. What they'll take in. The state capitol building. Main Street. Liberty Park. The university. Fort Douglas. Hogle Zoo. The collapsing shipwreck of Saltair Resort. Temple Square where they'll walk along its promenade of continuously exploding flowerbeds and maybe take a tour. See the inside of the Tabernacle. Listen to the history of the big organ and its arsenal of tall gold pipes. Stand in the right acoustic place in back while someone drops a pin on the pulpit and the sound it makes when it hits the wood takes off across the domed ceiling and rains down in a single raindrop on their ears. Wander through Assembly Hall. Stop at the black bronze statue of the handcart family and hear about the pioneers. Stop at the seagull monument and hear about the miracle of the gulls. Stop at the gray stone walls of the Temple and listen to the guide, Cissy's face turned up so that sunlight glows this deep gold rose in the honey coffee color of her skin, the color of her curse, skin whose astonishing color is meant to let people know she's not allowed inside. People walking by, people seeing her in her pink church dress and white church shoes, wondering what she thinks she's dressed up for, what she thinks she's looking at, what business she even has looking.

We repose in you our confidence and extend to you our prayers that the Lord will help you thus to meet your responsibilities.

Cissy.

In the harness of your seat, the plane trembling at the head of the runway, you close your eyes and see her there again, across the terminal, a mirage at first in the trick sunlight across the mirror of the stone floor. And then you'd taken her by the hand and shown everyone there, every other family, every other girlfriend, every other missionary heading for a mission field somewhere, that you could kiss a negro girl and live. Shown your father and mother that you could kiss a negro girl and survive the venom of her negro blood. Shown them how to do it. How to love a negro girl when you didn't know how not to love her.

Thank you, she'd said, to your gathered family, when she thought it was her time to go. Thank you all so much.

Tears shining in her eyes.

The big man next to you is restless. He's leaning over you now to see out the window himself, so close you can hear him breathing and smell dust and aftershave again, his arm across the armrest to where his big hand is almost in your lap, to where the three pearl buttons on the cuff of his cowboy shirt make you think of your trumpet again, tucked away in Robbie's basement. You pull back to give him more looking room.

"That's some haze out there," he says.

His voice isn't weathered the way his face is. It's a church voice. Even quiet it's a pulpit voice. The voice of someone used to being treated like he's always right. Someone expecting to always be respected and obeyed. You wonder if he saw you with Cissy. If you've got some kind of lesson coming.

"Yeah."

And leave it there for later. Six hours to New York will be long enough to talk to where things will get long past stale. You close your eyes. Cissy's there, her smile quiet, and you smile in secret back at her, knowing she can close her eyes and see it. The engines finally start coming up. The brakes hold the plane in place against their pull. The long fuselage sways and twists and arches as the power builds. There were guys on State, rich guys pulling up at a light next to Yenchik's Ford or Quigley's Hudson looking to race, who did this. Stood on the brakes and ran their engines up, building this unforgiving hydraulic power in the torque converters of their automatics, eager to let it go the instant the light went green. Back deep in the tunnel of the fuselage you can't see what the pilot sees. A clean runway. A long blade of concrete. A drag strip. Lights going green. The brakes come off and the plane starts to rocket forward. The steady hand of the force that thrusts you back into your seat is absolute. Force you can't question. You're going. Cissy. You let it push you back into the cradle of her naked arms. Cissy. Form your hands to feel her face and everything else the way you memorized each other blind, by feel, in the dark in San Jose. Cissy. The plane lifts off the runway in a hard steep howling reach for altitude. As it rises through the summer haze, breaks its dirty surface, you can feel the haze close back over down below you. Cissy. Somewhere north of Ogden, high enough to clear the yellow shoulders of the summer mountains, the plane heels to the right to set its heading east for New York City.

Cissy.

The Lord will reward the goodness of your life, and greater blessings and more happiness than you have yet experienced await you as you serve Him humbly and prayerfully in this labor of love among His children.

Lilly. Keller. Jasperson. West.

Load. Lock. Aim. Fire when ready. Your neighborhood buddies. The guys you've known since the first Sunday you lived here. The guys you came through seven years of the priesthood with. One by one, as they turned nineteen ahead of you the last few months and got letters of their own from President MacKay, their own mission calls, you looked at them like the gray steel warheads of 90 millimeter tank rounds, tall rounds lifted out of their racks on the turret floor, slid into the breech of the big gun, locked in place, aimed at one or another mission field, then fired through the long recoiling barrel of a tank you ran around Fort Knox and the Mojave Desert. Lilly to Mexico. Keller to England. Jasperson to West Virginia. West to British Columbia. And now you. And in two weeks Doby. Yenchik the only one not going. Because his mother was dying and his father wanted to keep him home. And now his 40 Ford at the bottom of Pineview Reservoir. And him nowhere. No sign of him. Just gone. Where he could be.

Your father.

The plane still climbing. The peaks and canyons of the Rockies crawling past below you. This is it. What has always been there, waiting for you, where you take that step alone off level ground and onto the whistling uprush of open air. You've earned every church award along the way. You were expected to get them. The Army didn't matter either. This is it. Where you take your father's name, the famous name of your dead grandfather, back to where it came from, to find the son he wants and bring him home. Home with a man's wrists, finally, wrists with some hair on them, wrists too big for your thumb and finger to touch when you reach around them.

Cissy.

The letter she said was already on its way to Austria. Already there maybe. Waiting for you. You fly into the teeth of the afternoon and coming night as they move across the country toward you.

CHAPTER 2

"WHAT IS THIS?" says Wissom. "Every airline's got its own building?"

"Looks that way," says Hatch.

At Idlewild Airport you and Hatch and Wissom and Clayton catch an airport bus to the TWA terminal for your flight to Paris. Through the windows of the growling bus the lights and signs and roadways and the separate buildings for different airlines make the airport feel like some space age city. You come off the bus to the deep raw whistling hum of highways out there somewhere in the late afternoon. You enter the terminal and come to a stop together. The white span of all the space. The huge bowed wings of the ceiling. How they lift high overhead toward archways made of vast windows. How every line and surface is a curve, curve after sweeping curve, one continuous warped and blended curve. Hundreds of voices mingle in flight like frenzied birds across the sky this place can hold. You look at each other. Hatch and his year round swimming and skiing tan that burns deep red in the pockets of his acne scars. Wissom and the small arrowhead of black hair that points down into the forehead of the ghost mask of his sharp Count Dracula face. Clayton the Pillsbury Doughboy. And you. Lost the same way they look. Light on your feet on the unfamiliar floor beneath your shoes like you could lift off and fly too in this place where you can't feel gravity.

"Wow," says Clayton.

"I didn't know a building could do this," says Hatch.

You've thought of it too. The Tabernacle, the only other building you know with a high domed ceiling, looks crude next to this place. Homemade. The belly of a whale instead of the white sky of these colossal wings.

"It's like a monster bird," says Clayton.

"Forget a plane. This place could fly us there."

"Lot of foreigners," says Hatch. Looking at people now.

"Yeah." Wissom looking too. "Weird clothes."

"See that woman?" Hatch pointing. "I say she's French."

"How do you know?"

"Jackson Hole's full of foreigners. You get a feel. You look at someone and know what accent's gonna come out of their mouth."

You realize you're standing with your suitcases in the river of people flooding through the doors behind you.

"Come on. Let's check in."

"I'm hungry," says Clayton. "Can you guys check me in?"

"No," says Wissom. "They need your passport. You can't go off on your own anyway. You're on your mission."

"I forgot."

After checking in you say you'll go with Clayton. Tell Hatch and Wissom you'll meet them at the gate. Find a place that looks like a coffee shop, open to the terminal, a space age counter and a field of round white tables and space age chairs. Maybe half the tables are occupied. Couples, people by themselves, foreign looking families, suitcases and bags around their feet.

"I'll wait out here," you tell Clayton. "Just go to the counter. Order something you can take. We need to get back."

"Like what?"

"I don't know. A doughnut. A burger. Ask for a menu."

"But I'm not supposed to leave your sight."

"I can see you from here."

"Okay."

You remember the Coke you got from an airport shop in Los Angeles while you were waiting to be flown to Knox.

"It's probably gonna cost you."

From the edge of the coffee shop, out past the last of the tables and empty space age chairs, you watch Clayton take a seat on one of the counter stools and look around for a waitress or someone to smile at and say hello to. A couple of guys your age are standing a few feet off. A big guy with a broad and placid face and a blond flattop haircut wearing a green bow tie, white shirt, wrinkled brown and blue plaid sport coat, glasses whose big plastic frames are the color of caramel. Under his sport coat his shoulders look like anvils. He's big enough to have played high school football except that he doesn't strike you as a jock. There were big guys back home, like Paul Wendell, who never went out for sports. The other guy's maybe half the size of the big guy, thin, a boy's round face, a head that could use a bigger body, crazy black hair like Robbie had. Over his light blue shirt he's wearing a dark blue blazer like the Key Club guys in high school, Levis, black sneakers. Like Robbie, he can't stand still, his sneakers restless, his big eyes on the move, his hands balled in fists in his levi pockets. College guys. Like you just were. They look rumpled. Like they haven't shaved or maybe even showered in a while. In your dark charcoal suit, silver and blue striped tie, new Florsheim shoes, the way they're dressed makes you feel slick, rich, someone you're not, never been before. If they're musicians. What they play. The big guy could do standup bass. From the way they look around they look like they've never been here either.

"How you doing?" the big guy saying, in a gentle voice.

You were thinking Cissy. The whole United States between you now. Kansas. Iowa. Pennsylvania. Soon an ocean. You didn't know you were looking in their direction. You weren't looking anywhere.

"Okay," you say. "You guys?"

"Cool." He crosses a few feet of floor and swings his big hand out. "I'm Bill."

The little guy steps forward, takes his right hand out, and it's warm and damp when you shake it. "I'm Jerry," he says.

"I'm Shake."

"Shake?"

"Yeah. I know. But that's it."

"This place is nuts," says Bill. "Science fiction."

"Where you from?" you say.

"Minneapolis. Jerry's from Racine. You?"

"Salt Lake."

"Utah," says Bill.

"Where you guys headed?"

Jerry shakes a bent cigarette out of a crushed pack of Camels and lights it with a paper match. Slides an ashtray out to the edge of a nearby table where he can reach it.

"We're just waiting for a flight to come in," says Bill. "Couple of buddies flying in from Paris. They been hitching around Europe. We're headed south soon as they get here."

Jerry exhales a long straight pipe of white smoke that flares out toward the end like the bell of a ghost horn.

"They're late," he says. "We need to be on the road already."

"They're not late," says Bill. "Their plane is."

"Either way," says Jerry. "We're standing here."

"Driving?" you say.

"Yeah," says Bill. "We drove here. Jerry's Volkswagen bus."

"Started acting up too," says Jerry.

"I told you," says Bill. "That gas filter you never changed."

"Where'd you drive from?" you say.

"Ohio State. We both go there."

"What's that fancy book?" says Jerry.

"Just a book a friend gave me."

"A Bible?"

"No."

"Looks like one."

"Where south you headed?" you say.

"All the way, man," says Bill. "Mississippi."

"Jackson," says Jerry.

"What's down there?"

"A shitstorm," says Bill.

"The movement," says Jerry. "We're joining up for the summer."

"Civil rights?"

"SNCC," says Jerry. "Heard of 'em?"

"Yeah."

"That's who we're hooking up with," says Bill. "Hope to, anyway. If they'll take us."

The liquid metal voice of a woman keeps announcing flights over the terminal's speakers. A stewardess walks by. Bill's eyes are calm as they follow her weaving dark blue skirt through the tables. Jerry sets his cigarette on the table edge so that the butt burns in the air, pulls folded pieces of paper out of an inside pocket of his blazer, opens one, holds it out to you.

"Here. This is what keeps me fired up."

You tuck your Triple Combination under your arm to take it. A photo clipped out of a newspaper. In the middle of an intersection a cop faces off a young negro with the slim build of a high school kid. Negroes are crossing behind them. Some looking. The sidewalks crowded. On a corner building behind them a tin sign that says Jockey Boy Restaurant hangs above the doorway. The cop wears one of those Nazi officer hats with a shiny black visor and a high crown tall enough to serve as a mounting face for his badge. A belt rigged with holsters for clubs, pistols, handcuffs. Sunglasses black out his eyes. The negro kid's in a light shirt and open sweater and thin leather shoes more suited to dancing than being on the street. The cop's got a German Shepherd on a leash. The shepherd's on its hind legs, lunging, ears back flat, teeth buried in the kid's stomach. The cop's one fist holds the leash while his other fist has the kid by the collar of his shirt and sweater. Knees bent, one shoe off the ground, the negro kid's just stumbling back, scared, not knowing what you do when a Shepherd has your stomach in its teeth and a cop has your shirt and sweater in his fist. Which way you go.

"I hate cops," says Jerry. "They're bad enough in Wisconsin. They get worse in Ohio. Down south they're just fuckin' thugs. Klan in uniform."

"Yeah," you say. "I've seen this."

Late at night at Hiller, in the small office, reading the newspapers and magazines that someone always brought in, waiting for the night mechanics to show up, coffee going, the sharp fresh sawdust smell from the burbling cough of the percolator. Staring at the photo. Staring hard to see the dog's teeth. How much of his stomach they've got the kid by. The photo was black and white. You wondered then what color the kid's clothes were. If there was blood you could have seen.

"This was the Children's Crusade," says Jerry. "In Birmingham. Back in May. When kids from all the negro high schools cut class to march through town singing freedom songs. The cops turned police dogs and firehoses on 'em. This kid's only fuckin' seventeen."

"I read that," you say.

"But it worked," says Bill. "They got a deal from the city to stop segregating small shit like water fountains and lunch counters."

"Yeah," says Jerry. "But it didn't hold. The Klan ended up bombing a black owned motel thinking Doctor King was there. And the house of his brother. Someone saw the cops do the house. That set off a riot."

You've read the story. Bill and Jerry toss it back and forth like they're playing catch. Bill stays calm but you can see the fire deep in his eyes.

"The state troopers came in," he says. "With submachine guns. Even a tank showed up. Kennedy finally had to send the Army in. Called it Operation Oak Tree."

"A tank?" you say.

"Yeah," says Bill. "A tank."

Jerry unfolds and hands you another photo. "Here's another reason I'm going," he says.

A burning Greyhound bus stopped on a road somewhere. The busted windows like a row of open furnace doors while fire roars out of them and smoke rises in a black roiling thunderhead out of the ragged metal crater where the roof is burned away. You've seen this one too.

"Freedom Riders," you say.

Negroes and whites together. You looked at it and remembered riding a Greyhound shoulder to shoulder with Cissy's brother Jeff from Monterey to San Jose before you knew he had a sister. Black and white again so that the fire was this dirty white cut with gray.

"A mob firebombed 'em." Jerry's eager bitter voice brings you back from Hiller's and the last night you cleaned your trumpet there. "Then they held the door shut when the riders tried to get out. When they finally let 'em out they were burned and choking." He picks up his cigarette, takes a deep hit, sets it down. "I mean fuckin' ready to die." Smoke bursts from his mouth on the consonants. "The mob didn't give a shit. They lit into 'em with bike chains and rocks and bats and pipes. The cops just stood around in case someone started talking about lynching."

"I'm going for Medgar Evers," says Bill. "Heard of him?"

"Yeah."

"They killed him. Not even a month ago. Shot him in the back in his front yard coming home from a meeting. He was a hero. A World War vet. They buried him in Arlington."

"The soldier cemetery?"

"Yeah," says Bill. "Full honors. That had to give the Klan a shit hemorrhage."

"Here's another one," says Jerry.

The jet of water from a firehose trained on her broad back reaches across a downtown street and holds a middle-aged negro woman bent over and clutching a railing. You can tell she came out dressed for church. That what she had planned and where she was going deserved the attention of doing her hair and pinning a Sunday hat in place and choosing a Sunday dress and purse and shoes. Now her hat's this rag that barely holds to the whipping ropes of her soaked hair and her purse swings crazy off her arm in the blast of water roving back and forth across her back. Where they grip the railing her dark wet hands are the hands of the women bearing their trays and bowls of food into the sunlight of the back yard where you fell in love with Cissy. The photo black and white again. What color her soaked dress was. How she matched the color of her shoes and her thrashing purse to it.

"Jesus," you say.

"Birmingham motherfuckers."

Jerry takes and folds the clippings together again, puts them away, picks up his cigarette where the ember has reached the table edge, takes a drag that burns the ember deep into what's left of the butt while he gives you this quick glance and then looks hard off to the side. You try to square his young round face with saying motherfucker. With pulling on a cigarette that hard. Smoke from his mouth and nostrils punctuates his breath again.

"The mayor's this redneck asshole named Bull Connor. Real vicious cocksucker. Used fire hoses on high school kids and women like her. When they kept coming he had the water pressure turned up. When they still kept coming he used monitor guns. On school kids and women. Know what a monitor gun is? Know what it's for?"

While the ember burns bright from another pull you go back in your head to the Army. Through all the guns you learned and heard of.

"No."

He exhales another long white bitter blade of smoke. "It's this special high power nozzle. It can knock bricks out of a wall at a hundred feet. Think what it can do to skin. Shred it. I mean it busts bricks. It could break ribs. Rip your fucking face off."

"Take it easy," says Bill.

The soft warm medicine of the skin of Mrs. Taylor's hands when she took your windburned face in them the night you showed up at her door in Yenchik's 40 Ford. And then all of Cissy. The curve of every surface of her honey coffee skin. You couldn't see it in the dark. But you could feel its color in your hands.

"Here's the one I keep for inspiration," says Bill, pulling his own clipping out of his plaid sport coat, unfolding it, handing it to you. "Case I ever forget who the enemy is."

Through the window of a bus a mob of men stand along the dirt bank of a roadside. White guys. All white. Pale like they live where the light of day can't reach them. Fists cocked back with rocks and chains. Bats and pipes slapped against palms in the steady malevolent cadence of waiting. You think of the parking lot fights you and Porter and Snook went looking for at the rich kid high schools. You feel the slow crawl of their inbred hate across the bottom of your stomach. Their lips so snarled and twisted and gnawed away they could never get what was left of them together over their busted and stunted teeth to fit the mouthpiece of a trumpet.

"Klan," you say.

"What you're looking at," says Bill, "are the deformities of the inbred. Generations of screwing among themselves."

The men you saw on the dark street of some village deep in Europe the time you got baptized for the dead. The decomposing dead who came out to thank you for taking on and washing off their sins. Using your body to do it.

"What're you guys gonna do down there?" you finally say.

"I just wanna kill some of them Klan chickenshits," says Jerry.

You hand the clipping back to Bill. Take the Triple Combination out from under your arm to hold it again.

"We're gonna help people register to vote," says Bill. "Not these guys. Negroes. Blacks. They've been getting the crap kicked out of 'em for trying. We're gonna be marching too. There's a big one to DC next month."

"With Martin Luther King," says Jerry. "You read his letter from the Birmingham jail? I got a lot of it memorized. Maybe he'll let me work for him."

"Not if you keep yapping about killing people," Bill says. "Nonviolence. That's what he says. That's what works. You gotta take it and just keep coming."

Clayton comes back. Whatever he ordered was wolfed down on his walk back through the tables. He's wiping his mouth with a paper napkin, looking into it, checking what might be coming off his face. You watch Jerry figure out he's harmless.

"No," says Jerry. "Bill's right. Those high school kids, they didn't care if a Shepherd tore their guts out or a monitor gun tore up their skin. They just kept coming. Fifty at a time. They didn't raise a hand. They had every siren and fire hose in the city going. They got every reporter and tv camera in the world there. That was the cool part. They got that fuckin' mayor to cave. The kids did. Cuz they just kept coming. The Freedom Riders too."

Jerry stops, glances at Clayton's smiling face and shining eyes, decides that along with being harmless he's clueless too. "I know it's the right way," he says. "It sucks to watch 'em have to take it is all. I don't know if I'll be able to."

"They'll train us," says Bill. "Stuff like sitting at lunch counters. You get dirty cigarette smoke blown in your face on breath so foul you got to keep from breathing or you'll puke. And when you puke they got you. You get your head slapped from behind but you got to always know it's coming so you can keep from flinching. You flinch, they got you. You get your chair rocked but you got to stay loose enough to ride it cuz if you use your feet to keep from falling they'll say you were standing up to face 'em down. Bam. They got you. You get coffee spilled in your crotch so hot it feels like ice at first but you need to know it's coming so you can hold still for it. Or else they got you. You get whacked with a rolled newspaper. You got to let it happen. Let 'em call you niggerlover and your girlfriend black bitch. Let 'em pour pancake syrup on her head. Or they got you. They got your hate. Got you raising a hand or looking at 'em wrong. Got you calling 'em cracker. So you gotta learn to take it."

"Is this about negroes?" says Clayton.

"Yeah," says Bill, and in his eyes you can see the shine of the quiet fire burning deep inside his own chest. Then, quiet, his head down, he says it again. "Yeah."

"You call them blacks?" you say.

He brings his face back up. "Black. Yeah. That's what they've started saying."

"Instead of negro?"

"No difference. Negro means black in Spanish. Why not use English."

Black. If Cissy would call herself that. Black. Just that stark naked word. If you'd think of her that way. And now negro feels stupid. Black makes sense with white. You white. Her black. Even though you're this weird light beige and she's this coffee rose.

"You've done this before," you say to Bill. "What you're doing now."

"Back during spring break," Bill says. "South Carolina. Greenwood."

You look at Clayton. "They're headed south. Mississippi. Driving down as soon as their friends get here."

"If they ever do," says Jerry.

"For what?" says Clayton.

"They're gonna help the negroes. Blacks. Help 'em vote. Knock on doors. Like us."

"Oh!" Clayton's instantaneous cheerleader grin lights up his farmboy face like the sign in front of the Frostop at dusk. "Elder Tauffler's girl-friend's a negro!"

Bill and Jerry stare at Clayton. Clayton glances at you. He keeps his grin in place but panic starts its black shine in the pupils of his eyes.

"Who's Elder Tauffler?" says Bill.

"Him!" says Clayton.

Bill looks at you. "What's this elder thing? Now he's saying it."

Clayton's panic keeps him going. "We're missionaries for the Church of Jesus Christ of Latter Day Saints," he says. "We're on our way to Austria!"

"What?"

"Mormons," Jerry says. "They had 'em in Racine. Guys in suits on bikes." Then he says, "So that's gotta be that Book of Mormon."

Bill ignores him. "Your chick's black?"

You look at Bill. Wonder if they know the rest of it. Descendants of Cain. Men who can't be trusted with the priesthood. Women not worthy of the Temple. Everything they've taught you to believe that makes you one of the inbred. That puts a rock or bike chain in your hand while you wait for a Greyhound full of Freedom Riders.

"Last time I checked she was."

"She's beautiful too!" says Clayton.

Bill gives you a long hard serious look. Like maybe wondering what it's like with a negro girl. Then he grins. "Well, shit, Elder Tauffler, if your chick's black, the heck with Australia. You got more skin in this game than we do. Come with us!"

"Everyone says Australia," says Clayton. "It's not. It's Austria."

"Your girlfriend," says Jerry, suddenly in your face. "For real. She's black."

Here it comes, you think, in your slick new suit and tie, your polished Florsheims, your Triple Combination with your name in gold.

"Yeah."

"You gotta come, then. They're your people."

And then, for an instant, looking down at the white rubber toes of his black sneakers, you're thinking you could change that gas filter in a flash and keep his Volkswagen bus on the road all the way to Jackson. Thinking if you could live on sixty bucks a month in Mississippi like they said you could in Austria. But there was Jeff and San Jose. Professor Fowler and Los Angeles. Cissy. Offers you've already walked away from so you could go where you were always going, dressed the way you're dressed up now.

"I can't."

"What does your girl think about everything going on?" says Bill.

"She lives in San Jose."

"So she's far from all this stuff."

"Yeah."

You watch Bill look down, twist the toe of his right shoe like he's stubbing out a cigarette or snuffing out a bug too tired or lost to run, look back up at you.

"I think it might behoove you to come up to speed on this stuff. Since your girl's what she is."

"Maybe I need to."

"Just come with us," says Jerry. "That's the quickest way. On the job, man."

"I can't."

"Sure you can. Let's go find your luggage."

"I'd have to bring him."

Jerry takes a quick sideways glance at Clayton.

"I'm serious," he says. "We got room for one more."

Bill looks past you, steps out, starts waving both his arms.

"They're here, man. Hey! Frankie!"

You turn around and look. Two guys your age again, duffle bags slung off their shoulders, their free arms in the air, walking across the terminal floor.

"Wish I coulda talked you into it," says Jerry, and turns and waves back.

"Take care," you tell him.

"Last chance," says Bill. "Wanna come?"

"I can't."

"I understand. Good meeting you then. Elder."

"You too. Freedom Rider."

"Good luck in Australia. Go get 'em."

"You too. Be careful. Look out for Jerry."

Jerry swings the mop of his black curls around. "Fuck you, Elder!"

"For sure," says Bill. "I will."

Clayton stays quiet on the long walk to your gate along the red carpet of a sleek white oval tunnel. In your stomach there's this raw cold hollow fear you can't name. Cissy. The whole United States between you now. Along with everything else.

"I shouldn't of said that about your girlfriend," he finally says. "I'm sorry."

You're thinking if this bright white quiet tunnel is what it's like when you die. If this red carpet is meant for you. If Jesus and your ancestors are waiting at the end.

"It's okay," you tell Clayton.

"I can't keep my mouth shut. I never could."

"Don't worry."

"You wouldn't believe what that burger cost. I think I just ate a whole week of my food money."

"Nobody's gonna let you starve."

Come up to speed some. At Hiller, where you guarded the big construction and roadbuilding machines through the night, you used to wait till after midnight, after the kids who came to the fence got back in the Pontiac and Walt idled it dark across the field to the road that would take them home to Magna where the miners and their families lived. You used to wait till after you got your homework done for your harmony and composition classes. Till after you took your last walk along the fenceline and checked doors and locks and other points around the sheds and buildings. Till after you wandered the yards and played your trumpet one last time to the big machines while the high running lights of the night semis went roaring past above you on the high dike of the Interstate and the sound of your trumpet would chase and try to follow them. And then till after you blew out your trumpet and put it in its case and got coffee ready for the night mechanics when they started coming in from their overnight repair jobs in the field. After that was when you used to do it. Come up to speed. Tuscaloosa. Selma. Gather the papers and magazines scattered around the small office and pick the ones that talked about it. Cambridge. Baltimore. And after that, with the smell of coffee boiling off the percolator, was when you finally took a seat in the busted office chair at the desk to learn what it was all about. Danville. Jackson. And after you learned, after you got it, after you knew most everything, kept going. Winona. To keep up. Albany. Birmingham. To see what was new. Always Birmingham.

You weren't with her then. You hadn't seen your face in a drawing crosshatched by the wires of a chainlink fence. You hadn't taken Yenchik's 40 Ford to San Jose. You kept up to speed then out of the longing ache of having had to give her up. Out of your usual vigilance. To guard her. To know her. You don't know. You just did.

You board your flight and find your seat, alone again, Hatch and Wissom and Clayton elsewhere in the plane, by themselves too. A thin man with a briefcase and a balding head and a long slim cigar in his shirt pocket folds the brown coat of his suit and lays it in the overhead rack before he looks at you and sits down. You look out the window to your right. This place you're leaving. Where everything is from here. Jackson. Salt Lake. San Jose. Without a compass in the rising dark wind of this slowly exploding place you don't even know which way. Cissy. Black. This new word. What will happen.

At the head of the runway the engines go full throttle and drown out the ache of the nameless fear still in your stomach. The pilot releases the trembling plane. You lift off the edge of level ground, rise off the million early lights of New York, and fly out into the coming dusk and over the bottomless night of the Atlantic Ocean.

CHAPTER 3

BY THE TIME you see them they've already zeroed in on the four of you. Two grinning American guys in short-sleeved white shirts and dark ties, they come striding across the floor of the airport, call you elder when they shake your hand, help you claim your suitcases, take you out through the airport across a parking lot where the damp hot steamy feel of the air brings Fort Ord to mind. They load you into a faded blue Volkswagen bus. Inside the stifling hotbox of the bus, once you're moving, none of you talk. You make the ride instead with your faces pasted to windows that don't roll down. Sweat runs out of your hair into your forehead and tickles where it cuts down the sides of your face and into your ears. In your new suit you smell the dry stale stink of old cigar smoke from the skinny almost bald man who sat next to you till you reached Paris. The tired little engine hammers in the steel floor under your shoes. All the traffic signs use pictures. The highway from the airport lacks the sense a highway had back home that you could follow it forever. All the cars look stunted. None of them look like they could even start to cross Nevada.

Close your eyes and you can see Jerry and Bill and their buddies in another Volkswagen bus on the road to Mississippi. From there you can feel the nameless fear you brought across the ocean. If you were with them. On your way south to knock on the doors of negro shanties. Careful not to let the thought take on the hot dimension of desire. Because God could smell desire a long way off. He could see its raw red glow inside you.

Cissy.

In Vienna the narrow streets are walled with buildings and the buildings keep going on forever. Sometimes open plazas full of manic little cars. The machine gun drumbeats of cobblestones under the wheels. A woman in a sleeveless yellow dress with long brown hair and shoulders that gleam almost gold in the sunlight steps off a curb and glances at your window. You can't tell if she sees you.

You remember coming in over the roofs of Paris. How the streets were still flooded in the late dawn with this astonishing rose gold light that had vanished by the time you switched planes and took off again. In full daylight now, in the neighborhoods of Vienna, the streets are lined with large stone colored houses, some with their doors framed with columns, houses that stand like waiting ships behind low walls and wrought iron fences. You remember your mother asking for a shot of Beethoven's house. If this is where he lived.

Finally the bus pulls over and parks on a narrow street in front of a stately house that reminds you of the rich old mansions along South Temple in Salt Lake. Stone steps rise from the sidewalk to the porch of the front door. Two tall stories of pale yellow masonry and high windows rise up to tall roofs angled against each other and shingled with tiles the color of salmon. Windows set into the roofs give away a third and maybe fourth floor. You're soaked with sweat. Hatch and Clayton too. The elders who brought you in from the airport let the four of you sort your suitcases out. Wissom asks where you are. The Austrian Mission Home. You carry your Samsonite up the steps through the front door. Other elders drift into the lobby to introduce themselves. Everyone's face American. Everyone's grin the grin on your own face. Everyone's handshake firm.

"Welcome to Austria. I'm Elder Halbertson."

"I'm Elder Peterson."

"Elder Jensen."

"Elder Gerhardt. Welcome. There's the head if you need it."

You take turns in a small bathroom off the lobby. You didn't know how bad you had to go. That it could feel this good. When you come back out another elder joins you.

"I'm Elder Cannon. You can leave your bags here."

He holds open the door to a room off the lobby. One end of the room holds a long chestnut colored conference table surrounded by wooden office chairs. The table is long enough to land model airplanes on. The other end of the room is empty except for twenty or thirty metal folding chairs that lean folded in rows against the back wall. The room is a study in shades of cream. The carpet, the walls, the ceiling, the long drapes that belly out and drift aside when air from the tall open windows across the room moves through them. The numb cream shades of a blank dream. You wonder what goes on in here. What important things get the chairs unfolded. What things give this blank dream of a room its holy feel. Elder Cannon motions you to take chairs around the near end of the table. He walks up front to the other end. From the chestnut surface of the table where your Triple Combination lies you can smell wax worked into wood.

You're here. From how quiet they are, you can tell that Hatch and Clayton and Wissom feel the gravity too, in this hushed room where the only thing each of you has this far from home is the other three of you. For the first time since your room back in the Salt Lake Mission Home you're face to face again where you can look at each other and talk.

Wissom's got his leatherbound pocket notebook open on the table and his blue and silver Schaeffer fountain pen ready in his left hand. Clayton runs his handkerchief across his round wet gleaming face.

"Welcome to the Austrian Mission. President Smith asked me to welcome you today. He apologizes for not being here, but he's looking forward to meeting you."

Standing at the other end of the table, Elder Cannon is blond, pale, the Mona Lisa smile of a saint in his long soft oval face. In his plain brown suit he looks thin. The collar of his shirt hangs loose around his neck. The tips of his long fingers rest on the surface of the table like piano keys are built into the polished wood and he's holding down two chords.

"How are you doing?" he says. "How was your flight?"

"It was great!" says Clayton, with his happy cheerleader bark.

"It was okay," says Hatch.

"Boring. Long."

Wissom. You wonder if he's nuts just coming out and saying it. Not quite noon. Birds chirp outside the open window but deep in your ears you can still hear the whining roar of the engines that pulled you through the night. No toothbrush. No sleep. You were vigilant. Vigilant the way you've always been a passenger. Watching the dark through the pale ghost of your face on the window. Doing your part to get where you were going. The smell of the flight mixed with sweat and stale deodorant rises in a stale sweet cloud from inside your suit coat.

"Elder Tauffler? How about yours?"

He looks amused. Asking like you were on a different plane from Wissom and Hatch and Clayton. But you hear what your father said. Be obedient and humble. A mission isn't a popularity contest. The less they know about you the better.

"It got us here," you say, with a smile.

"That was the idea." Elder Cannon smiles back, looks down, contemplates his hands, shifts his fingers to another set of chords, looks up again. "I'll just take a few minutes to go over some things and answer any questions you might have. Each of you will be leaving here today with a new senior companion. We've tried to pick one for each one of you that we think will suit you best, based on what we knew about you before you got here. Any questions before we get started?"

Cannon. A name you can't say without saying Elder first. One of those names where the roots of the Church reach down through the older cemeteries into the bones of the pioneers. Everything about him has the inherited spiritual composure a name like Cannon carries. Born holy. In a house like this. Modesty in the cut of his straight blond hair. Serenity in the calm pool of his face. The soft glow of mercy in his smile. Reverence in the way his fingers move when they touch the wood of the table. Like a prelude or hymn is playing. Like he's playing it in his mind. And there's his voice, soft and kind and fluid, a voice that could sell trumpets to a race of people without the lips to play them, like the roadside mob in Bill's photo. Even his brown suit looks holy. Like he bought it in some consecrated store and God was there to help him pick it out. This is it, you realize, the son your father wants you to bring back home.

Across the table Wissom's hand is up.

"Yes."

"Who are you?"

"I'm Elder Cannon. I didn't mention that? I'm sorry."

"I know your name. I mean are you someone important. How come the mission president picked you to talk to us?"

"I'm his second counselor," Elder Cannon says, and his smile goes a little bashful, like he's shy about admitting his position.

"Where's his first counselor?" says Wissom.

"His first counselor is always an Austrian member of the Church." He looks at the silver watch strapped by its tiny belt to his thin wrist. "Right now, I imagine he's at work." He pauses. "The first counselor takes care of the local members. I'm responsible for the missionaries."

"So what did you know about us?"

"What do you mean?"

"As far as matching us up with seniors."

"Not much, really. Some information from your bishops."

"What did my bishop tell you?"

"I'm sorry. I'm not at liberty to tell you that. But I know you'd be happy with what he said."

"So from what he said," says Wissom, "You figured out who you'd match me with."

"We also prayed for guidance."

He stands there, his quiet smile on Wissom, waiting to field the next thing Wissom wants to know. You're thinking Bishop Wacker. What they asked him about you. What he told them. If anyone at the airport reported Cissy. Elder Cannon lets Wissom go.

"Okay. So I'll start with companions. Remember that your senior's always in charge. Don't question him. You may not always agree with him, but you should always obey him. If you don't like his way of doing things, don't complain. Ask the Lord for patience. Your turn will come when you're a senior. You should only question him when he's doing something you know is wrong. Ask if you can pray about it. Never let him out of your sight. Make sure he never loses sight of you."

"Even in the john?" Wissom says.

Clayton's the only one who laughs. One loud bark before a wild look around the table tells him he's on his own. Elder Cannon smiles. Goes on to talk about learning German. Letting your senior do the talking the first six months to give you time to learn to talk yourself. Occasional voices from the sidewalk come through the open window. Women, a couple of men, the foreign words too soft and thin and fast to understand. The chatter of passing kids in a language you'll never speak with their native ease. But chatter that reaches deep and sudden into your memory and finds the imprint of a kid in Switzerland.

"Okay," Elder Cannon says. "You'll each get a set of saddlebags and a pocket looseleaf of the six lessons in German. Your first six months are also to give you time to memorize them. Now. You're not expected to work seven days a week. You get Friday off to do your laundry, go to the bathhouse, write letters, rest, and have some fun. We call it Diversion Day. Yes, Elder Clayton."

"How come not Saturday?"

"Saturday's the one day most Austrians are home. So it's a good day to be out working. A lot of your return appointments will be on Saturday. Sunday, of course, you'll be busy with meetings. Elder Wissom?"

"What's a bathhouse?"

"Where you'll take a weekly shower."

"We have to go somewhere?"

"Most of you will be living in single rooms. You'll have access to a toilet and washbasin but probably not a tub. Or permission to use it if there is."

Wissom looks at the table. Taps the head of his pen on the wood.

"What kind of stuff can we do for fun?" says Clayton.

"Go to a movie, a concert, a play, a museum. It's a time to recharge your batteries. Go hiking. Austria's beautiful. You're not allowed to leave the country, and we don't want you taking trips out of your assigned area. But aside from that, you're free to do what you'd like, as long as you know the Lord would feel comfortable doing it. Elder Hatch?"

"How about sports?"

"We encourage you to get involved in sports, because it's a great missionary tool. Team sports. You're not allowed to swim, but everything else is okay."

Hatch sits up. "We can't swim?"

"No. I'm afraid not."

"Why not?"

"Well, the position of the Church comes from the Gospel, which tells us the Devil rides the waters. So there's the possibility of temptation. But it's also about your safety."

"What did you say the Devil does?"

Elder Cannon smiles at him with this awkward apology in his face. "He rides the waters. According to scripture."

"You mean the ocean."

"Do you swim, Elder Hatch?"

"I was All State three straight years. You're talking about the ocean, right?"

"I'm afraid not."

"What else? Lakes?"

"All swimming. Any swimming."

"Pools?"

"I'm afraid so."

"The Devil rides swimming pools?"

How Hatch can get rattled this easy. Give so much away.

"I'm just here to tell you the rules," Elder Cannon says. "We're not allowed to swim. Period. Elder Wissom?"

"Wait," Hatch says. "You're saying we can't swim at all."

"That's right. No swimming. I'm sorry."

"Okay. Maybe you mean regular missionaries. I've got a swimming scholarship when I get back. I gotta stay in shape."

"We've all made sacrifices to be here. Two years ago I gave up a scholarship in mathematics."

You want to help Hatch out. Tell him about Professor Fisher's offer the last day of class to do the summer in Los Angeles as a studio musician. The way Fisher thought a mission was something you did in Africa. The way Fisher got up when you said no and left you on the bench like you were nothing more than air or light or a line of music somewhere or the distant backfire of a truck down in the city.

"This isn't math," Hatch says. "It's swimming. It takes conditioning."

"Well," Elder Cannon says, "All I can tell you is that the Lord's work has meant a great deal more to me than that scholarship did."

Tell Hatch what will happen to your own chops. How in two and a half years your lips will end up soft, like a baby's fumbling for a nipple, even if you use your mouthpiece every day. How jazz will have changed. Moved on while you were here.

And then Hatch sits back and says, "So is mathematics against the rules?"

Elder Cannon smiles and waits him out. You wonder if he brought his slide rule on his mission. To keep his math chops up. Hatch finally looks down at the table. The acne scars in his sunburned cheeks go this bright almost shining red.

"Sorry," he says.

Wissom's hand goes up again.

"Yes."

"What's a typical day like?"

Wissom's pen still hovers unused above his leather notebook in the crook of his left hand. Now he cocks it.

"Okay." Elder Cannon puts the flats of his hands together, looks up, touches his fingertips to his chin. "When I was still in the field, we'd get up around six, pray, get dressed, and study till seven or so. Then we'd stop for breakfast at a milchgeschaeft. We'd have a buttered roll and milk and head for our tracting area that day. By eight or so we'd be knocking on doors. We'd stop at noon for lunch and then usually tract till six and then stop for dinner. Then — yes."

Clayton brings his hand down.

"What did you call the place where you had breakfast?"

"A milchgeschaeft. A dairy shop. They sell rolls, milk, newspapers, things people need in the morning. They're all over. You'll find one in your neighborhood."

"What did you do for lunch and dinner?" Clayton asks.

"Lunch was usually another roll and some fruit. An apple or banana. Dinner was home. Sometimes a small neighborhood restaurant."

"Restaurant?"

Elder Cannon looks at Wissom.

"Yes. Sometimes. Where else?"

"On sixty dollars a month?" Wissom says, almost derisive, like he's saying Elder Cannon's lying.

"I know it's hard to believe," says Elder Cannon. "But you'll see."

"You're saying sixty dollars covers rent and everything else and restaurants too."

"It's surprising. But it does."

Wissom reaches forward. Elder Cannon watches him put his Schaeffer pen to his notebook. Wondering, maybe, why anyone would need a pen like that. What it would matter to what he wrote down.

"Anyway," he says, "after dinner we'd get ready for the evening. If we had appointments we kept them. If we didn't we'd go tracting again till around eight. Then we'd come home, tend to personal things, study and pray and go to bed."

"How much tracting are we supposed to do?" asks Wissom.

"We like to see you put in seventy to eighty hours a week. Not all tracting. Time spent with investigators and other activities where you feel like you're doing the Lord's work. Your seniors will show you." Then he says, "Time you spend with members is important, but if an investigator isn't present, it doesn't necessarily count as missionary work."

Investigator. A word you learned back in the Salt Lake Mission Home had a meaning other than someone looking to solve a crime. A mission meaning. Someone looking to possibly join the Church. Someone who answered your knock and let you in the door.

"What do you mean," says Wissom, "what you like to see?"

"Your weekly report. You'll fill one out every Sunday. It covers every hour of the week. You'll write down how many hours you spent studying, eating, tracting, meeting with investigators, associating with members, even sleeping."

A big beige tape recorder stands with its coiled cords and reels and two microphones on a gray steel cart in a corner behind Elder Cannon. A Tandberg. Expensive. Swedish. You know because you used one once in the Music Building to tape Good Morning Heartache with Sandy singing and Lenny on piano. You wonder what they use this Tandberg for.

"Seventy to eighty hours?" says Clayton.

"It adds up quickly. I think you'll be surprised."

"How many hours are there in a week?"

"A hundred sixty eight," says Wissom the accountant. Then he says, "We write down when we sleep?"

"Not when. Just how long. Elder Clayton?"

"Can we get packages from home?"

"Of course."

"How about visitors?"

"In what way?"

"My parents. They've never been to Europe. They want to bring my sister too."

"We don't encourage family visits, but if they're coming anyway, I think that would be okay. I'm sure they'll be allowed to spend time with you."

"Do I have to be here for a while first? Like a year or something?"

"I wouldn't think so. We don't have special limits. I just wouldn't have them come tomorrow. Elder Hatch?"

"How about girlfriends?"

"We really discourage visits from girlfriends. We need you to stay focused on the Lord's work. Elder Wissom?"

"We're getting married," says Hatch.

"Even then," says Elder Cannon. "I'm sorry."

You're staring at Hatch, seeing his girl, knowing from the clubs you've played what kind she is, that she'll have a new last name and a kid by the time he knocks on her door again.

"What are the rules about garments?" says Wissom. "Taking them off?"

"Well, your garments are a protective shield, not only against disease, but against evil spirits and temptations of the flesh. So yes, you should sleep in them, if that's what you're asking. But you can take them off to bathe, of course. Elder Hatch?"

"Skiing's okay, though."

"No. I'm afraid that's another sport we don't allow."

"We can't ski," says Hatch, like he can't believe he's saying it.

"Are you a skier?"

"Does it matter?" says Hatch.

The room goes dead. You watch Hatch shake his head and look across the table out the open window. You watch one of the heavy drapes lift on the slow strength of an air current. You hear the recurrent barking of a dog outside and remember Rufus, leashed to the tire in the bed of Manny's pickup, barking in the dust rising behind the tailgate while you stood there waving him goodbye. In the home movie your father took you couldn't hear Rufus barking. Only see the repeating recoil of his head. You could use the Tandberg now to record the dog outside so the movie your father took could have a sound track.

"I was on the ski patrol at Jackson Hole," Hatch finally says. Then he says, "I didn't mean that. It does matter."

"No need to apologize," Elder Cannon says. "Any more questions? Elder Tauffler, you must have something to ask."

You look back at him. If there's a rule that says no jazz. If the Devil rides the steel bird of your trumpet. If a trumpet is a devil horn like Cissy's uncle called it when you tried to hand it back to him. Why Hatch and Wissom and Clayton can get away with letting him know who they are. Why for you, here to fill your grandfather's shoes and harvest Austria, it's the less they know the better. Questions that want to be answered so bad they feel like they're written in tattoos on your face.

"No," you say. "Not so far."

"You sure?"

"How far are we from home?" you say.

"Salt Lake? About five and a half thousand miles."

"That's all?" says Clayton. "That's not that far."

"Far enough for me," says Hatch.

"What kinds of things do you like to do?"

The question comes off Elder Cannon light and easy. But it's meant for you. You hold Elder Cannon's look. Whatever you give him will be the start of what you are from here on out. Something you'll wear like a shirt you can't take off to wash.

"They're not important," you say. And then you say, "Not while I'm here."

"I wouldn't say that."

And now you've got everyone's face your way.

"Then I guess music," you say.

"What kind?"

"Classical."

It just comes out. Your face goes hot, for betraying Mr. Selby, the musicians you learned from, everyone who knows you. From your armpits lines of sweat cut the skin inside your arms down to your elbows.

"That's interesting," Elder Cannon says. "Any favorite composers?"

"Beethoven."

"He's my favorite too," he says.

And now you can tell your lie has walked you straight into looking to Wissom and Clayton and Hatch like your nose is two feet up Elder Cannon's butt.

"I like Sibelius too," you say.

"Did you know Beethoven lived in Vienna?" Elder Cannon says.

"Yes."

One of Elder Cannon's front teeth is shorter than the other one. Chipped or broken. He doesn't try to hide it. Why you couldn't say jazz when he probably knows already. Why you couldn't say trumpet when Bishop Wacker probably drew him a picture of one. Where his suit coat hangs open his shirt is limp like it's been washed a thousand times.

"I've got a question," says Hatch.

Elder Cannon turns his way.

"Yes."

"They're having the Winter Olympics here next year."

"Yes. I've heard," says Elder Cannon. "What's your question?"

You look away while Hatch searches for one.

"Nothing," he finally says.

"Let me know if you think of one." Then he says, "Do you Elders know what transfers are?"

"You move us around," says Wissom.

"Now and then we'll rotate you to a new senior companion in another town or area. We usually schedule them every three to six months. They don't always include everyone, so it doesn't mean you'll be transferred every time, but you can count on working with several different companions all across Austria."

"When do we get to be seniors?" Hatch says.

"That depends. When the Lord thinks you're ready. Or we need new seniors to replace the ones going home. Elder Wissom?"

"How many people will we be baptizing? Say in a month?"

"We try not to put too much importance on numbers."

"I've got a friend on a mission in California. He says he's baptizing about ten people a month. I just wanted an idea."

"California's a little more fertile than Austria right now. We've been averaging about one baptism per missionary."

"One a month?"

"No. Per mission."

"A whole mission? Two and a half years?"

Elder Cannon looks down, comes up with his apologetic smile, looks back at Wissom. You glance down at your Triple Combination.

"Some of us go home without having baptized anyone. That doesn't mean we didn't work hard, or weren't good missionaries, or were any less successful than your friend in California. Austria's a hard mission. The people here are content. They have their families, their lives, and they live in a beautiful country. They think they have everything they'll ever need. They're complacent. That's our challenge. To take that complacency away from them."

Elder Cannon glances down at his hands. And then his pale smile follows his slow gaze across your faces again. Everyone's got the same question on his face. If he's had his one baptism. You shift your arms.

"Do you know why we need to do that, Elder Clayton?"

"Because of the Catholic Church?"

"Well, most Austrians are Catholic, and yes, that's a big part of our challenge. Elder Wissom?"

"Are you saying they're lazy?"

"No. Not at all. They're just happy with the way things are."

"So people in California aren't happy?"

"I'm not getting my point across. Austrians aren't as curious as Americans are. Not as open to opportunity. As long as they're content they're not interested in the Gospel. That's how Satan works. It's one of the tools he uses. He tells them it's fine to be content. That they don't need more than what they have. We know better, of course. Elder Wissom?"

"You're saying that being complacent is one of the Devil's tools."

Elder Cannon looks at Wissom's Schaeffer. The way it's ready to snare his answer.

"I'm saying that the Devil knows how to use their complacency against them. There's a big difference."

"So how do we take this complacent thing away from them?"

"We need to let them know, however we can, that there's more to life than what they already have. There's the fullness of the Gospel. There's eternal progression. Godhood. We need to keep sowing that seed."

Hatch and Wissom and Clayton. None of them look like they get what Elder Cannon means. You do. How content you were with simple melodies, the easy standards, three-chord rock and roll. And then along came Mr. Selby and the musicians whose photographs hung on his wall. And then you knew how far from content you really were. And then you never played those songs that way again. That's what you want to tell them. Tell Hatch how content he'd still be with wooden skis if someone hadn't come along and let him know they made them out of steel and fiberglass. Wissom how happy he'd be with a bottle of ink and a feather if he'd never seen a fountain pen. Clayton how happy he'd be with a baked potato if he'd never heard of a French fry.

"Just remember," Elder Cannon says. "The Lord has promised all his children that they'll have the opportunity to find their way back to Him. The only way they can do that is through the Gospel. Nobody can be missed. Nobody can be overlooked. You may be someone's only chance to hear the Gospel."

You think back to the Salt Lake Mission Home. The speaker who told you not to go out of your way to seek out negroes. Let them come to you. So Elder Cannon's wrong. Negroes can be missed. The door to Cissy's house can be skipped. Dirt road rows of small flimsy wood shanties in photos you've seen from Mississippi. White guys your age with clipboards talking to negro women standing on their board porches holding babies. Leave guys like Bill and Jerry to knock on the flimsy board doors of their shanties. You keep your eyes on the table in front of you where your Triple Combination lies.

"So what I'd like you to remember is this. There'll be times when you're tired. When you won't feel like knocking on that last door. When you'll think that a small alley or side street isn't worth exploring. When you won't feel like going around an apartment building to see if anyone might live in back."

He sweeps his soft eyes across your faces. You don't look away this time. Negroes who live down an alley or side street. Negroes who live around back.

"When that happens," he says, "I'd like you to ask yourselves this. What if my sister lives down that side street? Or my brother behind that building? Or a future prophet of the Church is waiting right now for the knock on his door? Or someone lonely or sick who could use a prayer?"

What you do if it's a negro. From outside, the sudden laughter of children exploding like a string of firecrackers makes Elder Cannon glance at the window and smile.

"So yes. Some of us go home without having baptized anyone. We've spent our mission planting the seed of the Gospel. And we've made sure we didn't miss a single soul. Sometimes that's what a mission is."

Someone's stomach gives off a long hollow winding rattle. Wissom jumps and clears his throat. Elder Cannon smiles.

"I'm almost finished." He looks down, at his hands, looks up again. "We believe that Austria's on the verge of breaking open. That the work done by the missionaries before you is about to bear fruit. That the mission field here is ripe and ready for the harvest. We keep waiting for that special missionary who'll show us how to deliver Austria to the Lord. We know one day he'll be here. Who knows? It could be one of you."

Hatch looks lost on some ski slope. Clayton sits there smiling from the dream seat of a John Deere tractor while the sunset leaves its light on a field of corn. Wissom studies the tip of his pen like it holds a speared insect. You've heard the California stories too. Seen missionaries come home with suntans out of magazines and three hundred baptisms. In your grandfather's shoes you're here to harvest Austria. You'd be done then. You could take off his shoes and head for San Jose. That special missionary. Deep in your chest you feel fire catch in the kindling of the possibility while shame burns deep in your skin in the face of the thought that it could be you.

"We're bringing you some lunch," says Elder Cannon. "Your seniors should start showing up soon. The bathroom's just down the hall." He spreads out the palms of his hands and smiles. "So welcome to Austria," he says. The four of you say thanks. You look away. How easy it is, you're thinking, being this cool, this modest, with a name like Cannon and your father's army at his command. He heads for the door and stops. "I almost forgot." He reaches inside his jacket, comes out with a couple of envelopes, hands them to Hatch.

"Sorry," he says. "If you could please hand these out for me."

CHAPTER 4

HATCH SLIDES one envelope across the table to Clayton and hands the other one to you. Still warm from being in the pocket over Elder Cannon's heart, from the burning in his bosom, it's an airmail envelope, blue and red stripes around the edges, your name and your foreign address in Cissy's handwriting.

"From Joy!" Clayton cries.

He rips the envelope apart. Fishes out the letter, unfolds it, waves it in the air. He takes it in both hands the way a kid holds a children's book while he dives into reading it. Hatch and Wissom watch while you tuck your letter into the pocket inside your suit coat and feel sweat in the damp cloth of your shirt. They don't say anything. They saw her. Clayton finishes his letter and heads off for the bathroom. Soon after he returns a dark-haired girl with a pretty face comes in with a platter loaded with sandwich halves. She's wearing a black and white uniform and humming some melody meant for little kids to sing. She's followed by an unsteady old man carrying a shaking tray of Seven Up and Fresca cans, a can opener, paper plates, napkins. Still humming, she sets the platter on the table, keeps her face low while she waits for the man to put his tray down. Clayton waits till they leave. Then he's up off his chair so fast you wonder if he goosed himself, a paper plate in one hand, leafing through the stack of sandwich halves with his other one.

"Hey!" says Wissom. "Stop touching everything."

"Nothing but ham and tuna," Clayton says. His first two sandwich halves are gone in a warmup. He polishes off a Fresca in two long chugs, puts the empty can aside, takes four more sandwich halves. While they eat, Hatch talks about getting back to Jackson Hole not knowing how to swim or ski, and Wissom talks about the impossible math of eating at restaurants on sixty bucks a month. In one of the ham sandwich halves on the platter you can see mustard and mayonnaise along the pink line of the meat where a knife cut the sandwich open. You finally take half a tuna sandwich and a Seven Up.

"So who's yours from?"

You come alert. Look at Wissom. You know what he's asking. What you've been waiting for since the airport yesterday morning. Sweat breaks out of your armpits again.

"Her name's Cissy," you tell him.

Wissom leaves his pen on the table.

"When do you plan on reading it?" he says.

"Later."

"Must be burning a hole in your pocket," Hatch says.

Your chest blazing where the letter rides. Your heart pumping liquid fire.

"It's a slow burn," you say.

You look at your watch. And then across the table, past Wissom, past the drapes at the play of sunlight on the leaves outside, then back at Wissom. He's still looking at you. Like you figured.

"She was beautiful," he says.

It leaves you staring.

"What?"

"Your girl," he says. His lips drawn thin in a smile you can't read. "Cissy."

"Heck," says Hatch. "She was amazing."

That she comes up for conversation in this room that echoes the cream godliness of the Celestial Room in the Temple, the room where God lives, the room that her curse keeps her from entering except as a servant.

"She sure was," says Clayton, his big face glowing.

"Yours weren't bad either," you say.

"Where's she from?" Hatch says. "She looked Hawaiian."

"Hawaiian," Wissom says, humored. "I don't think so."

Clayton lays his letter down, takes a napkin, wipes his mouth clean of mayonnaise and bread crumbs.

"The Amazon maybe," says Hatch.

"Amazon," says Wissom, mocking now. "Guess again."

"Okay." Hatch looks hard at Wissom. "Then we'll say Tahiti."

Across the table Wissom's face changes. Wissom takes a long considered look at his pen before he looks back up at Hatch.

"Yeah," he says. "Maybe not Tahiti. But definitely Polynesian. South Pacific."

"I know!" Clayton says. "Bali Hai!"

"Bali Hai," says Hatch. "That's it."

"Yeah," says Wissom. "Bali Hai. I couldn't think of it either."

You look from Clayton to Hatch to Wissom. They're watching you. Letting you know. She's safe with them. Buddies now, no matter how far across Austria they scatter the four of you, letting you know they'll protect you from the way your girlfriend's a negro.

"Thanks," you say. "I'd just as soon just leave her who she is."

Under his black eyebrows, deep in their white sockets, Wissom's eyes burn dark with disbelief. Hatch drops his eyes to the table where his open right hand lies on its palm. The sunburn in his scarred cheeks goes this almost savage red again. Clayton fiddles with an empty Fresca can.

"You know what we're saying," says Wissom.

"Yeah," you say. "I just can't do that."

Wissom's eyes relax. "You mean beautiful," he finally says.

"Yeah," says Hatch. "Beautiful. That's good."

"Yeah," says Clayton. "Like I told them."

This far from home. This long to go. Your buddies now. Emotion floods your throat and makes you look down and ride it out. When you look back up they haven't looked away.

"I'll tell her." How she looked when she thought it was time to leave. How she looked at your family. If you can keep her. "She'll be happy. She'll tell me to thank you."

The elder who comes for Wissom is an outdoor looking guy, athletic and tan, a crewcut fringe of blond hair that fits like a halo around the sides and back of his scalp. Big shoulders ride under his suit coat. You can smell the mission field on him. So this is who they thought Wissom would be suited to. He waits for Wissom to put away his Schaeffer pen and leather notebook. They're off to a place called Leoben.

Clayton draws an elder half his size, a skinny guy, maybe from South High, with tousled thin brown hair and red ears and a smallboned face that makes him look like he was born resentful. He asks which one of you is Clayton. He grabs half a tuna sandwich off the platter and wolfs it down while he watches Clayton sleep. So this is who they thought Clayton would be suited to. He finishes the sandwich half and wakes Clayton up. They're headed for Innsbruck.

You and Hatch move to the other side of the table where you can watch the door.

"Read your letter," he says. "Heck, if you want privacy, there's that little john just down the hall."

"I can wait. Thanks."

"No. Go on. I'll come knock if your senior shows up."

"What if yours shows up first?" you tell Hatch. "I wanna see who he is."

"Suit yourself," says Hatch. Then he says, "You get any sleep on the plane?"

"No."

"Me neither."

"You sit next to anyone?" you ask.

"Some foreign woman in this weird dress."

"What was weird about it?"

"Like this sheet she'd just wrapped around herself. This weird orange pinkish color. Like crepe paper. How about you?"

"Some skinny business guy with a bald head and a beard. He smoked these thin cigars."

"That's what that smell is."

"You can smell it?"

"Yeah," says Hatch. "A little."

If Elder Cannon smelled it. The possibility is a line of lightning touching a point in the valley out beyond you, beyond the hillside, out beyond the brass bell of your trumpet. That special missionary. Shame runs hot deep in your skin again.

"Did you talk to the woman?" you say.

"I said hello. She just smiled. Fine with me. She was eating these stinky black things. I figured if she opened her mouth they'd be on her breath."

"What were they?"

"I don't know. Figs. Something weird. I couldn't read the can. How about your guy? You try to convert him?"

"I said hello too. He just gave me this look like who was I. That was it."

Hatch nods like he gets it.

"This guy in front of me though," he says. "He had his seat leaned back so far it was in my lap. There was his head. Right there. I coulda given him the priesthood."

You smile. "You should of."

"Yeah. In his sleep."

Then Hatch goes slowly serious.

"What's wrong?"

"One baptism," he says. "For a whole mission."

Here to harvest Austria. Fear stirs restless deep in your stomach again.

"Yeah. Kind of grim."

"I'm supposed to give up swimming and skiing for two and a half years for one freaking baptism." He sits up. "You think Cannon was trying to scare us?"

"Why would he want to?"

"That stuff about the water. The Devil. He had to be making that up."

"I don't know." You remember the Army. The simplicity of obedience. "They're just rules," you say. "Just follow them for now. You'll be okay."

Hatch stares at you for a minute.

"And skiing," he says. "Man, we're in Austria. The freaking Olympics."

"You play an instrument?"

"Some piano when I was a kid," he says. "I couldn't sit still for it. Why?"

You remember how Eddie always wanted a keyboard player. Then you tell Hatch about your trumpet, about jazz, about the offer Professor

Fisher made the last day of class on the bench in the park across the drive from the Music Building, about what happened. You leave out last night's offer to go down to Mississippi in a Volkswagen bus you could keep on the road.

"Los Angeles? You mean you could be doing records?"

"Yeah. Pretty sure."

Hatch contemplates you.

"It's okay," you tell him. "Otherwise I wouldn't be here."

"Tough choice."

"Yeah." And then you think of Yenchik. The afternoon he opened the hood of his hot rod 40 Ford to show you the supercharged new engine where his father had put his mission money. "It's gonna be okay for you too."

"Guess I could exercise. Stay in shape. They must have gyms here."

"They gotta."

Hatch looks at you. "I thought you told Cannon classical."

"I trained classical." Thinking of Professor Arban's big red book. "I play jazz."

"Man. I love jazz. It's a lot like skiing."

Hatch takes half a ham sandwich off the platter, looks at the mayonnaise where it's gone this half transparent pale yellow color, puts it back.

"So your professor thought you meant Africa when you said a mission."

"Guess that's where most people think missionaries go."

"That's funny," he says. "Africa's the last place they'd send us."

"Yeah."

"Your girl," he says. "I didn't mean it like that."

"I know." And then you say, "Bali Hai. Good old Clayton."

"Glad he's the one going to Innsbruck," he says. "I'd go nuts."

"Maybe it's because snow's made out of water," you say. "Maybe that's why they won't let you ski."

Hatch laughs. "Sure. The Devil rides the slopes. I wonder what kind of skis he uses. Blizzards maybe. Heads." And then he frowns. "Shit. I don't know."

And then, head down and still frowning, he raps the fingers of his right hand on the table, then stops and sits there staring at his hand.

"I gotta ask you something," he finally says.

"What's that?"

All he moves when he looks up at you are his eyes.

"You seem like a cool guy."

"Thanks."

"No. That's not it."

And now he cranes his head and his glance ricochets all around the room before he looks at you again.

"What?"

"It's about fornication," he says. "You know. How they excommunicate you for it."

The muscles in your crotch go tight.

"It's about the worst thing you can do, I guess."

"That story they told us back in Salt Lake. About the mother who'd rather see her son come home in a coffin than excommunicated."

"Glad she's not my mother."

"But that's just if you do it on your mission, right? Getting excommunicated for it?"

"Were you just looking for bugs?"

"When?"

"Just now. When you looked around."

"No. Not that I know of." And then he says, "I don't know. Maybe I was."

"I think we're okay."

"Yeah. Anyway, what I was asking. Getting excommunicated. That's just if you fornicate on your mission, right?"

You feel sweat cut rivulets from your armpits down across your ribs again.

"I think so," you say. "Yeah. Pretty sure."

"I know while we're here our puds are supposed to be sacred. Like they belong to God or something. But how about before or after?"

"Before or after your mission?"

"Yeah." Then he says, "Just wondering."

When Cissy cried out help me in the dark of Yenchik's Ford in the shelter of a million leaves.

"I think before is okay." You smile at Hatch. "Unless you think she's pregnant."

"I'm not thinking anything," Hatch says. "Just wondering."

The elder who comes for Hatch is a tall guy, a broad worn comfortable face that makes him look forty, glasses, brown hair brushed back off his creased forehead, a homey attitude that makes you think of your family dentist. They're headed for a town called Spittal.

"Catch you later," says Hatch, shaking your hand.

"You too."

His new senior gives you a grin.

"Have a good mission," he says.

CHAPTER 5

DOWN TO YOU. You give Hatch and his senior plenty of time to leave. Then stand up, stretch, walk around the end of the table to the air of the open window. Leaves hang still in the calm July afternoon but somehow air moves into the room. You hold open your coat to let it through to your shirt. You check your watch. If you'll have time to read her letter. And then read it again. You sit back down and give it ten more minutes while you leave the envelope where it rides, in the pocket of your suit coat, against your heart. Keep yourself alert for the arrival of your own companion. A dog bark. The explosive flight of a startled bird. Leather soles on stone. The gate latch. The front door. An uptick in the voices that come occasionally from the lobby. The last time you went without sleep like this was when you followed the blazing supercharger of Yenchik's Ford across the Nevada desert home. Home from San Jose. The room feels like a room where people come to watch each other die. The folding chairs are for them. Now you feel the invitation to fall asleep again, the ruthless pull of the blank dream of the room, the way you felt it from the endless lull of the desert highway, the way the seat of the Ford kept wanting to hold you like the cradle of her arms. You finally head out the door for the little bathroom down the hall.

You open the envelope. Her handwriting. You haven't seen it since Fort Knox. In your suit you sit on the closed lid of the toilet seat and let the memory come rushing forward. A trail of small green flowers spills down the left side of the paper.

Dear Shake,

I hope you had a safe trip back home when you left here, and then on to Austria to start your mission. It seems like a million years have gone by since the starry night we spent on campus. I just want to let you know that after we made love in the car that night, it was really hard for me to face my family. I felt like Mommy and Daddy would be able to tell that something was different about me, something seriously different, and I didn't feel comfortable facing

them. But most of all, I didn't want anything to take my mind and heart away from how wonderful and special I felt at the time either. So, when you dropped me home, I went straight upstairs to my room and laid in bed thinking about our time together over and over, until I finally fell asleep. It was the most beautiful night of my life, Shake. You're always on my mind. I'm in love with you, Shake, and I always will be.
Cissy

The bathroom wall in front of you is patterned with small blue tulips on wavy stems like the tails of kites. Against their light brown background they don't move. You sit there in your suit and stare till your legs go numb. Against their light brown sky they never move. You ride out wave on wave of stark numbing longing to never have ever left her and the tulips and their kite tails never move. You lower your eyes to the letter but leave them out of focus and her writing blurred. How she was with you. How you kept her with you. From San Jose up the coast through Vallejo and then Sacramento and then across the Sierras. When you crested the summit at Donner Pass how the stars amazed her. So close. How you kept her with you almost all the way to Reno. How by then the sun was coming up and you had to let her go. Home for breakfast. For what she was planning to do that day. Let her go because you had to cross the sleepless desert home alone. And then come here. But how you kept her with you all night long. How you kept her with you all the way to sunrise over Reno. Over the exhausted look of its neon lights.

If she's pregnant.

You'll go home. Put on your own shoes. Be with her.

If you can keep her.

Wild horses thunder through your head. But you can hear her voice like a crying violin. The soft mute of your trumpet drifts in and out when she pauses and reaches for breath.

If you can keep me
I want to stay here
with you forever
and I'll be glad

You bring her letter up and hold it to your face with both your hands. Then bring it down and read it one more time. You hear the front door open and then close. And then two voices from the lobby through the panels of the bathroom door.

"How was your trip?"

A voice you know is Elder Cannon's.

"It was interesting."

A voice you don't recognize. Said through a smile.

"How are things in Knittelfeld?"

"It's good to be back in Vienna."

"Congratulations on making senior."

"Well, we'll hope so. But thank you."

You can hear the smile, the music of a small laugh, in his voice.

"I'll get your new junior."

"I'm eager to meet him."

This far from home, in the still life of this little room and the fixed kites of its stemmed tulips in their pale brown sky, you put the letter back in its envelope and tuck the envelope away. Everything they'll know about you will start from here. The rules are rough but simple. The penalties hard but clear. You flush the toilet, run water over your hands to fake the reason you were in here, dry them, step out into the lobby to meet the guy they thought you'd be suited to.

Part 2

Instead of Bombingham

CHAPTER 6

"HERE HE IS." Elder Cannon smiles and extends his hand in your direction. "Elder Tauffler, this is Elder Will Morgan. You'll be working with him here in Vienna."

About your size. Light brown hair that doesn't look like it gets much attention takes a low rake across his forehead and the top of his glasses. A herringbone suit with the shoulders round and the knees and pockets bagged out. His face the same neglected dusty look as the rest of him. But it's a young face. This almost sad but curious intelligence in his eyes. His hand fine-boned and firm when you shake it. You had him pictured taller. Wiser. Older. The steel of a testimony in his face. But the possibility that they were right. That they knew what they were doing.

"Hi. Nice to meet you."

"Nice to meet you."

"Sorry I'm late."

"Sorry my hand's damp. I just washed it."

"Elder Tauffler's a musician too," Elder Cannon says.

So this is what Bishop Wacker told them. And Wacker would have told them jazz. But in Elder Cannon's face there's just his smile, the one tooth shorter, like there's more to you than some lie you told about classical music.

"What do you play?" says your senior.

"Trumpet." Wondering how this is supposed to go. Your father's territory. His rules of conduct. "How about you?"

"Piano," he says. "Organ too. But mostly piano."

On the carpet next to his wrinkled brown shoes stand a leather briefcase and an old cloth suitcase. You peg him for classical. He rubs his hands together like there's a piano waiting out the door behind him.

"So are you ready?"

"Sure am. Just need to grab my book."

You come out of the conference room with your Triple Combination. Elder Cannon hands Morgan a slip of paper and a key ring with an old-fashioned silver key the size of a little fork you've seen people in clubs eat lobsters with.

"Do you know how to get there?"

Morgan studies the slip of paper. "It's close to Prater," he says. "We'll find it." He gives you an easy smile that says he's figured you out too.

Elder Cannon turns to you and puts his hand out.

"Good luck, Elder Tauffler. We're looking forward to great things from you."

You step out the front door of the Mission Home into the late afternoon. On the sidewalk, on foot, your ticket home to Utah two and a half years away, you feel your mission start the same irreversible and permanent way you could feel the Army start when they shaved your head at Ord. Behind the low wrought iron fences, flanked and sheltered by tall trees, stand the solid hulls of the houses you saw earlier. Houses behind whose doors and windows people who live in Vienna live. Whose language you'll be learning. Whose doors you'll be knocking on. You lug your big gray Samsonite and carry your Triple Combination down the hill behind Elder Morgan. You draw on warm air fresh from the soft humid musk of old trees and thick grass. There's not a street like this in Salt Lake. The houses and trees around you feel like they were here a hundred years before it dawned on Brigham Young to make the desert blossom like a rose. At the bottom of the hill the polished iron spines of railroad tracks are set in cobblestones. Elder Cannon told you he was a musician when he introduced you. Like you.

"So you play keyboards," you say, still not sure of the rules, especially now that you're alone with him.

He looks at you. "Keyboards?"

"Piano and organ."

"You call them keyboards?"

In his tone this trace of a scolding teacher, maybe mocking, that makes you smile.

"Yeah."

He smiles too. "Well, then I suppose the answer's yes."

"Classical?"

"Mostly. How about you?"

You already told him, back in the lobby where you were introduced, that you played trumpet. This time you keep faith with everyone who always kept faith with you.

"Jazz."

He looks at you like you're a statue of someone he's never seen before. Like you can't look back.

"I'm afraid I don't know a thing about jazz," he says.

"I can show you anything you'd like."

"We'll have to see."

"Did Beethoven live around here somewhere?"

"No. He lived in the old part of town. Why?"

"My mother wants a photo."

In the shade of the tram stop he studies you again. Slow smile. Anticipation at the edge of some adventure.

When the tram arrives, its bell dinging, you haul your Samsonite up the steps. He pays your fare to a man in a uniform. The tram is empty. Overhead, on advertising placards, the letters are familiar, but the words they form mean nothing. Through the floor you can hear the hum of the motors and the grind and whine of the steel wheels on the steel rails. In the shadows of the late afternoon people at stops come forward in answer to the dinging bell and climb aboard and look for places to sit. Solitary old men lose themselves in papers they look like they've been carrying around for a while. Stout old gray-haired women with net bags filled with groceries keep their faces turned toward the windows. Young couples, couples your age, catch you looking at them and lower their voices to murmurs like you could even understand what you might overhear. Morgan is lost in some brochure he's pulled from an inside pocket of his suit coat.

Long, rickety, mazelike, the ride takes you deep into the heart of Vienna. More and more people get on. You give up your seat so you can stand and look out the window. You've never seen a more elaborate and endless city. Not Louisville. Not San Jose. Salt Lake feels like some town the desert would claim if its lawns stopped being watered or the Tabernacle stopped holding concerts or guys stopped dragging State.

"We need to transfer here," says Morgan.

You muscle your Samsonite through and off the crowded tram, cross a cobblestone street, board another tram when it appears. Vienna wells around you, chaotic and somber together, an armada of stone ships, colossal and intricate, bright shops and sidewalk cafes on the cobblestone floor of a foreign ocean. Finally, away from downtown, you get off the tram, stand there with the strange feel of cobblestones under your shoes while Morgan checks the slip of paper Elder Cannon handed him.

You can tell from watching him look for a street sign that you've ridden your last tram. That somewhere in this neighborhood is where you'll live. Music plays off speakers behind you. You turn around. You're outside the open gate of an amusement park. An enormous Ferris wheel lifts little boxcars on the long spokes of its wheel maybe twenty stories high above the shadow of the jumbled ragtag music of the park into the late afternoon sunlight. It's a Ferris wheel you've seen in photographs. Now you're seeing it for real. Real enough to go inside and buy a ticket for a ride.

You follow him across the street and down another street while he looks at numbers painted on metal plaques or chiseled into the stone of buildings. Then he stops and pulls a door back. You step into the damp dark immense stone vault of a lobby. Shallow basins that could pool water are worn into the broad stones of stairs as you make your way to the second floor. Morgan stops in front of a door and knocks. You hear the long slow heavy shuffling of old feet and then the clatter of the locks laid into the battered wood along the door jamb. The door pulls back and leaves a woman standing there. Framed by a tousled burst of wild white hair, her heavy face is contemptuous, indignant, close to furious. You think of Beethoven. She looks like she's wearing five different nightgowns. Morgan exchanges words with her you don't understand. Still frowning, she pulls back the door, stands back to let you and your luggage in, points down a dark hallway. You follow Morgan while she closes and locks the door behind you. At the end of the hallway he sets down his suitcase, opens a door, takes a glance inside where light from a window somewhere catches the side of his face, turns back to you.

"Welcome home," he says, smiling, his voice at the bright edge of an adventure again.

It's a large room that looks like it was furnished with pieces hauled out of houses laid open by bombs or by the clawed buckets of steam shovels the way Mrs. Harding's was. Nothing matches. A huge dresser. An upholstered brown chair in a back corner. A small desk with a wooden chair and metal lamp. A tall free-standing two-door closet big enough if you laid it on its back to be a coffin for a family. Worn and overlapping rugs whose elaborate unmatched patterns make them look like they were collected one by one. The room has the smell of another century. There's a bed. A double bed. The fact that it's double and can hold two people doesn't change the way it's the one bed in the room.

Morgan goes through the room, opens and closes the drawers of the dresser, the doors of the standing closet. You put your Samsonite down on the floor and work the stiffness out of your curled fingers.

"You take the drawers on the left. I'll take the ones on the right. We'll each take half the armoire. Is that okay?"

"You mean that closet thing?"

"Yes."

"Sure. That's fine."

Back in the Mission Home, in the lobby, you checked him out while Cannon introduced you. Between Morgan's suit and Elder Cannon's suit you felt cheap in the brand new charcoal suit you were so proud of wearing. Cheap and reeking from having worn it since yesterday morning. You thought maybe you should have bought a couple of used ones from Deseret Industries or some other used clothes place.

Morgan hauls up and lays his suitcase on a bedspread made out of lace like a tablecloth, snaps it open, lifts and lets the lid fall back. You watch him. See a whole new guy. A guy you'll be sleeping with. When he leans over and starts to pull things out, shake them loose, lay them on the bed, there's a stoop in his upper back and his coat hangs off his sides like a worn saddle blanket off a skinny horse. He keeps pushing the sweep of dusty light brown hair across his forehead back up above his glasses. It's long around his ears too, and on his neck, where it's started to curl forward toward his ears.

You think of Cissy. The way you saw her when you thought of a place with her, dividing the drawers, leaving you half the closet, your pillow and side of the bed reserved for you while she slept on her own side. Morgan starts carrying clothes to the dresser. Filling the drawers he took for himself.

"You might as well unpack too," he says. "I'll move my suitcase over."

"I guess the bed's for both of us," you say.

"Looks like we don't have much choice." Then he says, "I don't bite. Do you?"

Chapter 7

T HAT   NIGHT   HE takes you down the street away from the Ferris wheel, where its spokes and boxcars are lighted now against the blue steel of the twilight, to a small corner restaurant. The place has a few square wooden tables and a short bar with five stools. Cigarette smoke cuts the thick smell of seasoned meat and vegetables boiled in vinegar. At the one occupied table two old men play some card game in the company of two almost empty beer mugs. A woman with her dark hair pinned up in a rooster tail sits smoking at the bar. She nods to let you know that you can pick a table on your own. Morgan takes one by the window. You look outside. Around the restaurant again. A place to stay. A place to eat. This is where you live. A street called Wolfgang Schmaeltzlgasse. This endless city. The woman lifts herself off her stool, weaves through a couple of tables, drops handwritten menus on the yellow tablecloth in front of you, asks a question.

"Zwei wasser, bitte," Morgan tells her, and she leaves.

You think you heard wine or beer in her question. You think of asking Morgan if you heard right. See if you can get him to give you that quick strict teacher look again. Except you're not sure yet how this is supposed to go between you.

"I can tell you what these dishes are," he says.

"I know bratwurst," you say. "And wiener schnitzel."

"Wiener schnitzel's pricey on our budget," Morgan says. "Schweinsbraten too. We'd be fasting the last week of the month."

"What's this knoedel thing?"

"Just a big dumpling in broth." He works his hands like he's making a snowball out of the air between you. "Like a baseball."

"How about goulash?"

"Meat in this thick brown spicy sauce. Don't ask me what kind. They cook it forever. It's pretty strong stuff."

"I'll have that."

"Gulasch bitte," he says. "That's what you'll tell the kellnerin."

"The waitress?"

"Yes."

"Kellnerin. Okay."

"She wants to know if you'd like bread or nockerln with it."

"What's nockerln?"

"Do you know what spaetzli are?"

"My mom makes them."

"They're the same thing. Spaetzli is Swiss."

"That's what I'll have, then. Spaetzli."

Morgan orders bratwurst with boiled red cabbage. In a couple of minutes the woman sets your plates in front of you and heads for her stool again. Deep brown, almost purple, the sauce rich with little rivulets and pools of grease, filled with rags of meat and veined with onion slices, your goulash looks like an injury ladled onto a pile of spaetzli. The taste is meaty, spicy, lush. Its slow explosive heat reaches deep enough to where you can feel it back in the corners of your jaw. Behind the bar, the woman fills a small glass from a bottle, sets it next to her ashtray, comes back around, takes her stool again and sits there, her only customer. Shreds of the melodies of songs reach you from a tinny radio somewhere deep inside the place. You figure the kitchen.

"So how is it?" says Morgan.

"Really good. What did she just say?"

"Mahlzeit. Like bon apetit. Everybody says it." Then he says, "Did they tell you you're my first junior?"

"You're my first senior."

"Guess we'll learn as we go."

"How long have you been here?"

"About fourteen months."

"How's it been?"

"So far?" he says, and you realize that the flash of mild surprise is just the way he starts things out. "Well, I guess you could say interesting. I started out in Vienna. Like you. Since then I've worked in Graz, Klagenfurt, Wels, and until yesterday in Knittelfeld." Then he says, "Where are you from?"

"You mean home? Bountiful."

"You grew up there?"

"Through high school. How about you?"

"I went to East." He looks at you. Measures how much he should tell you. So he's not sure how this goes either. "Not legally. Our house was in South High territory, just three blocks off State Street, but my mom taught English at East and got me transferred there."

You remember the East High girls you and Quigley picked up on State one night in his Hudson. If Morgan would know them.

"Did you ever drag State? Living that close?"

He looks at you. The surprise in his eyes and mouth not mild but hard this time.

"No," he says. "I never dragged State."

"Sorry."

"That doesn't mean I didn't want to," he says.

Learning how to anticipate him, where he's safe, you ask about his family. He tells you his older brother played high school baseball and works in a shoe store in Pocatello. His older sister goes to nursing school. He cuts a slice of bratwurst. You take a fork of goulash, chase it with a bite of bread.

"What does your dad do?"

"My dad? He left us when I was in third grade." He looks up from his plate. "So I don't know what he does."

"Left you?"

"Another woman and her kids. In fourth grade I got rheumatic fever. For a long time I thought he left because he liked her kids better than us. Because they weren't sick like me. But then we heard he left her too. And her kids."

"Rheumatic fever. That's serious."

"It wasn't bad. It just kept me from having, you know, a regular childhood. I didn't do what other kids did. I hated sports. Mostly because I couldn't play."

"Sorry."

"Don't be. I got to stay inside and learn piano. That's pretty much what I did all day." He smiles and says, "Want to know my claim to fame?"

"Sure."

"It's a well kept secret."

"It can't be a claim to fame if it's a secret."

"Well." He smiles again. Liking the way you caught him. "Between me and you."

"Okay."

"I've never owned a pair of sneakers."

"Not even for gym?"

"I was excused from gym."

"You must be pretty good," you say. "All that practice. I'd like to hear you play."

"Oh, I'm sure that will happen. But tell me about you."

You're not sure what to tell him. Your father's words cross your mind. The less they know the better. But then he's been open. You figure he'll let you know if you go too far.

"I've got two brothers and two sisters. I'm the oldest. My father's a bookkeeper. He teaches the Adult Gospel class at church. My mother's the ward organist. That's it."

"How did you happen to get called to Austria?"

"I was born in Switzerland. I'm still a citizen. If I showed up, they'd draft me. So Austria was the next best place." And then you say, "How about you?"

"That's easy. Vienna. City of Music." Then he says, "If your mother's an organist, how come you picked a trumpet?"

"I heard one once," you tell him. "That was it."

The cattle truck coming off Soldier Summit. Seated almost eye level in front of the radio speaker. You gave up long ago trying to decipher the song it was playing. You could never match it to any melody you knew. It was obviously a solo. And you didn't understand then about chord changes, about the signature they gave a song, so you didn't know to listen for them. But none of that mattered. It was the sound. You can still hear it, more than seven years ago, five and a half thousand miles away, clear as it was then. That clear bright ringing sound whose notes took flight across the sky out through the windshield. Morgan has the look of dust in his face too. Like his hair and shoes. Road dust. The button-down tips of his collar frayed. This guy from East High who really lived in South High territory. The sad but curious intelligence in his eyes again. Waiting for an answer.

He asks how old you were when you started playing. How you learned. Away from the subject of your family you just let go. Tell him about the winter in the sandpit where you taught yourself to play. But not about the wild fear whose wind tore cold across the bottom of your stomach with all the names of everything you were doing wrong. You tell him about Mr. Selby. About the records you learned from. About the international jazz ensemble called How Should I Know, Eddie and Robbie and Jimmy and Santos and you, and about the Indigo, but not about the night the lady in the red dress opened the back door of her old Ford and reached into everything she owned and came out with a lamp she gave you. About the Music Building but not about Professor Fowler's offer. About jamming at Sammy's. You leave out Katy. About watching the yards at night at Hiller and playing to the big machines, but not about the Magna kids, the kids whose fathers worked the copper pit, who came to the chainlink fence at night to hear you play and be taught how to play themselves. About the Army but not about Cissy. About the desert where you left the things you had to leave but not about Lieutenant Tanner handing you off to God.

"Gosh," he says. "I know the Indigo. Where it is, anyway."

"You must have done some performing too."

"Some. Mostly solo and small chamber groups." He grins and suddenly there's mischief in his eyes. "I did an organ recital once at the Cathedral of the Madeleine."

"The Catholic one? On South Temple?"

He nods. Still grinning. "The Church of the Devil."

"That's as bad as the Indigo."

"You should see their organ. Not the Indigo. The cathedral." Smiling. Then he says, "I'd like to do a recital here in Vienna."

"At a cathedral?"

"Oh yes. The main cathedral. The mother cathedral of Austria. I'll show it to you."

"Here in Vienna?"

"It's called Stephansdom. Saint Stephen's Cathedral. I've already played a smaller organ there."

"They let you?"

"It was an audition. For the main organ."

"Did they know you were a missionary?"

"Of course."

"A Mormon one?"

"Not in so many words. No."

It's one word, you're thinking. A baby's cry comes from the back of the restaurant. The bark of a man's voice from the kitchen makes the woman crush out her cigarette and get off her stool and hurry out of the dining room. The two old men playing cards heave themselves around to see what's going on. Out the window, in the dusk of the street, two guys walk by without looking in, lost in talk of their own.

"So can I ask how many baptisms you've had so far?"

"One," he says. "Just after I got here."

"That's pretty cool. Right off the bat."

"I didn't do much. My senior had already taken her through the lessons. She was ready." Then he says, "Looks like you liked the goulash."

"All the way through."

"So why a sandpit? Especially in winter?"

"So I wouldn't bother anyone." And then you say, "How come piano?" He smiles again.

"It was just there. In the way. This huge piece of furniture in the living room that made music. I couldn't just ignore it." He shrugs and laughs. "I don't know. If there had been a cello there, maybe I'd be a cellist. Or a kettle drum. Good heavens. It could have been that accidental."

Your turn to laugh.

"Playing that piano was the one thing that made me feel powerful. I wanted to be better at it than any other kid around."

The woman comes over and picks up your plates and utensils. She asks you something in German.

"She wants to know if you'd like dessert," says Morgan. "Do you?"

"Can we afford it?"

"We'll split one. Next time." He looks at the woman. "Er sagt nein danke."

Curved lines like gills cut deep into her cheeks when she smiles at you. She leaves a slip of paper on the tablecloth.

"I did a year in the Music Building," Morgan says. "I was probably already here when you were there."

"What'd you do about the draft?"

"I have flat feet. So they didn't want me." He laughs. "My gosh. Between rheumatic fever and flat feet, you must think I'm a wreck."

"I'd just like to hear you play."

"In the morning we'll get you a bike." Morgan picks up the slip. Lifts his glasses off his eyes and reads it. "Then we'll go get mine." he says. "It's at the Sudbahnhof. You brought bike money, right?"

"Yes. Let me pay my share of that."

"It takes Austrian money. Do you have any?"

Your face goes hot.

"No."

"We'll get you some tomorrow. You'll need it for your bike." He pulls a billfold out of the inside pocket of his coat and counts out some strange looking pastel bills. "You'll have to tell me about jazz sometime."

"Anytime. I'm buying dinner tomorrow."

"You don't have to tip here," he says. "In Austria. It's included."

"Okay."

"What would you like to do now?"

"I need to write a letter."

Morgan's face goes alert.

"Not to your father."

"No. My girlfriend. Just to let her know I'm here."

"Your girlfriend."

"Is that okay?"

And now his face goes grave, and he's quick to look away, out the window, like he can't look at you or has to hide whatever's going through him. What you said wrong. It lasts an instant. But it leaves you restless. Why he said your father.

"Of course," he says, looking back at you. "That's something else I've never had."

"A girlfriend?"

"Like sneakers," he says. And then he says, "No. I didn't mean that. I know they're not like sneakers."

CHAPTER 8

"THAT WAS QUICK," says Morgan, and hands you an envelope he picked off the little table coming in the door. It's from Cissy. The address she sent it to is crossed out. Someone at the Mission Home wrote in your real address. You decide to read it before you write to her. The same trail of small green flowers frames the left side of the page.

> Dear Shake,
>   This letter is short, because I have an appointment to see my college counselor about some class choices. I can't begin to tell you how excited I was when Jeff told me he would come with me to Utah to see you off at the airport. It was his idea to keep it a "secret," but I was so nervous about it. Anyway, that all disappeared when we got there and I spotted you in the distance with your family. I just wanted to run across the terminal floor as fast as I could, without saying a word, and just give you the biggest hug and the longest kiss possible. But I had to mind my manners. I have to tell you, Shake, you looked so handsome standing there in that suit. Gosh. I didn't want to ever say goodbye. Please write to me soon. I miss and love you so much.
> Your girl,
> Cissy

And then, at the small desk, in the light of the metal lamp, you take out the earlier letter you got from her that day, and read it too. And then you write Dear Cissy. And then, for a long moment, just look at her name. And then write her about coming to the airport. How at first she seemed like a mirage, a dream, because you never expected to see her there. About how beautiful she was in her new pink dress. About how kind she was to your family. About how good it felt to kiss and hold her.

And then you bring her up to date. You write her about Morgan but not about the way you have to sleep with him. About the goulash. About the baby crying from in back. About the huge Ferris wheel with its little boxcars. About the elaborate immensity of the city. About the briefing at the Mission Home. About Wissom and Hatch and Clayton telling you she's beautiful. About the flight but not about Bill and Jerry, on the road now for Jackson, because you don't know how to talk to her about what's going on down south, or tell her why you're here instead of there.

And then, toward the end, you look at the window for Morgan's reflection, where he occupies the upholstered chair across the room behind you, and when you see him lost in a stack of sheet music, you write this to her.

You were with me on the drive home from San Jose. I made sure. I kept you with me. I didn't want to go. I wanted to turn around too. Every mile. But instead I kept you with me. When we went over Donner Pass you were amazed at how close we were to all the stars. Like we were out in space with them, you said. Like we could reach out and touch them. I kept you with me all the way till sunrise. I wish I could have kept you longer. But you had to go home for breakfast.

And then you write I love you. Shake.

You wake up in darkness to the first day of your mission. The radium hands on the little travel clock on the nightstand tell you it's almost four. You're way too charged for sleep. You lie there at the edge of the sagging mattress where you've managed not to roll into the dark valley between the two of you. You listen to Morgan breathe behind you, enough to touch now and then on the light growl of a snore, and soon you're hooked, listening for it, waiting for it to happen. By ten after five you've had it. And you need the bathroom bad. You kill the alarm on your clock so it won't go off at six. Make your way in your garments in the dark behind the kitchen where the bathroom is. Close the door, find the knob of the switch, wince when the tiny room explodes in light, unbutton the long vertical crack in the back of your garments, spread it wide, sit down, let go. You listen for the splash. There isn't one. You wipe, stand, button up again, turn to look. There it sits, a coiled brown pile in a shallow puddle of pee, on a porcelain ledge in the white bowl. You look for the flush tank. Find it mounted high on the wall. A handle hangs from a chain. You pull it. Water comes charging down the pipe from the tank, blasts what you've left on the ledge in a furious slurry against the back of the bowl and down a white hole, and leaves the porcelain clean again. The force of the water astonishes you.

You wait and listen for the noise to bring the landlady running. Then feel your way back to your room. Take the chair at the small desk by the window. Listen to Morgan's breathing rise now and then to a snore against the hurried tick of his alarm clock. Watch windows light up in the dark wall of the stone building across the street from you. Slowly daylight comes to the deep canal of the street. The window catches the slow gold rose of the sunrise. You get up to watch your first morning come and open the window for some morning air. Two tall panes of glass, framed in old wood, hinged, are fixed with handles where they meet. You turn the handles slow. Careful to be quiet. The panes swing inward back against the wall. Noise from the street turns more distinct. Across a space of maybe a foot stands another window like the first one. This time the panes swing outward and the noise from the street comes raw. You pull them closed. Hear the rattle of Morgan's alarm and the rolling groan of the bed as he reaches out to kill it.

"Go ahead," he says. "Leave them open."

Thinking how you could sit out there between the windows open, on the ledge, bring your feet up, lean back, play your trumpet to the open street.

"Okay."

"In winter," he says, "we keep milk and food out there to keep it cold."

Like suddenly he's lived here before.

"It stays cold?"

"Between the windows," he says. Then, like he's read your mind, he says, "All the old windows in Austria are like that."

"I didn't know."

"How long have you been up?" he says.

"Just a while."

"Okay," he says. He pulls the covers back and kicks his legs out. Sits there. "Let's pray," he finally says, looking your way, his hair crazed, on his feet now next to the bed in the gray bag of his own garments.

You kneel on the floor next to him with your elbows on the mattress. He showed you last night how to pray together, first out loud, a common prayer, and then again, silent and in private. This morning it's your turn for the common prayer. In your private prayer you talk to God in imagined words to an imagined face. Talk to your missing buddy Yenchik. Talk to Cissy. When you're done, on your feet again, Morgan translates what the landlady said yesterday when she led the two of you around the place. You can use her stove and fridge but you can't use her dishes or the big tub in the kitchen. The white porcelain bowl on the big doily on the dresser is your washbasin. The pitcher next to it is to get warm water from the kitchen. The towels and washcloths next to the pitcher are for you. On Friday leave them in the kitchen. She'll give you clean ones.

Morgan pulls on his pants and throws on his shirt and leaves it untucked and unbuttoned.

"I'll be right back," he says.

"I'll get you some water."

"Thank you."

From the way he answers you wonder if fetching his water is a permanent job. When he's done washing you rinse the bowl and get water for yourself. Shave and wash your face and crotch and armpits in the corroded silver of the mirror. Water hasn't felt this good since the Mojave. You use your new travel iron with the hinged foldaway handle to do your shirt on a towel you lay across the desk. You get out the saddlebags they gave you, two cloth pouches, big enough for schoolbooks, held together with straps that go over your shoulders and across your back so that the pouches ride underneath your suit coat, below your armpits, against your ribs where detectives carry holsters. You load one pouch with the little notebook with the lesson plans in German. The other pouch with brochures that talk in German you can barely read about Temple Square, the Tabernacle Choir, the Handcart Pioneers, things you've grown up with.

Morgan ties his tie while he tells you about your tracting area. A piece of the city assigned to you like you're a mailman or a cop. The old apartment buildings you live among. He hands you a ragged notebook the size of a wallet. The black cover is worn down to cardboard gray around the edges.

"It's the tracting book. It was left here by the elders we just replaced. You're in charge of it."

You open its stiff worn pages. They're divided into crowded handdrawn rows and columns.

"The rows are addresses and apartments in our tracting area. The columns are the dates the elders knocked on their doors."

Most all the rows have names. Janda. Mocharitsch. Loidl. Voglreiter. Hein. Salzgeber. Handwritten dates head the columns. Below each date, for each apartment, the letter R or N, written with different pens in different colors. You catch on. The record of every time that every door in your tracting area was knocked on. You flip to the front. The oldest dates go back four years. You were fifteen. In tenth grade. Not a priest yet. Still looking forward to your driver's license. The latest dates are two days old. When you said goodbye to Cissy and Jeff and your family. While you were on the plane.

"What do these Rs and Ns mean?"

"What Rs and Ns?" says Morgan from across the room.

"In this book. Next to the addresses."

"R means reject. N means no. They mean the same thing."

"That's all there is. Rs and Ns."

"I'm sorry," he says. "We're not in California."

It dawns on you. How the notebook isn't as much a record of knocking on doors as a record of being told to go away. One baptism per mission. This is what it means. This is how it happens. Thousands of knocks. Thousands of times of being told to go away and going back and being told to go away again. Guys who did their time, shared the double bed before you and Morgan came along, and then moved on, and then went home. The work of the Lord. Here in this notebook. Guys who feel to you like giants. In the crowded formation of rows and columns the letters feel almost sacred. The ink that wrote them sanctified. The latest column lets you know where you'll add your own new column headed with a new date.

After a glass of milk and a buttered roll called a semmel at a dairy shop, he takes you to change your dollars to schillings, send your letter to Cissy off in a streetside mailbox, then buy a bike from the shop the mission has an arrangement with. It's a three speed bike with a rack over the back fender like the rack you used to lash your trumpet to on your bike back home. The one they've set aside for you is blue. They have you sit on it to get the seat adjusted. You carry it on a tram to a vast train station called the Sudbahnhof where Morgan gets his own bike out of storage. Then ride them home. Your first time on a bike in a suit on the streets of a city, in a pair of garments, your pud and balls loose, absorbing the beat of the cobblestones. Whatever Morgan led you to think about his athletic skills is history. He can fly on a bike. Riding high, head and shoulders up above the roofs of cars, his suit coat sailing on the wind, he slices through traffic like Zorro, runs sideways through red lights and slaloms through pedestrians, never looks back for you. If he got his speed from wanting to outrun God, outrun names, outrun things the way you did. If he learned to ride on State and the other city streets of Salt Lake. You keep up with him by knowing how lost you'd be if you lost him. In the dim lobby where you live you find a thick pipe behind the stairs to lock your bikes to.

"You don't need those sneakers you never had," you tell him. "You can ride."

"Practice."

And then you're ready. The tracting book tucked within easy reach in the inside pocket of your suit. A new pen ready to draw rows and columns and then fill them in. It's almost noon. Outside again, on foot, the sun burns hot on your head and back.

"I had another question," you say.

Morgan stops and turns to you on the sidewalk.

"Yes?"

"I was looking through the six lessons this morning. The German version."

"Is this a German question?"

"No. The first lesson calls the investigator Herr Braun. The rest of the lessons call him Bruder Braun. You know why?"

"If he makes it through the first lesson," Morgan says, "you've got him hooked. Calling him Brother after that is just reeling him in. That's what the Church thinks happens."

"Do you fish?"

Morgan laughs. "No. My first companion did. I asked him the same question."

And then you laugh too.

"Come with me," Morgan says. "I've got some things to show you."

And he takes off walking in the direction of the park where the Ferris wheel stands idle and its boxcars hang empty in the noon heat.

CHAPTER 9

MORGAN SPENDS the rest of the day acquainting you with places
all across Vienna. Sweat from your armpits soaks your shirt where your
saddlebags ride. That night he takes you to a place called the Wiener
Konzerthaus for a piano concerto. The vast elaborate beauty of the place
takes your breath away. On Thursday he takes you to a church called
Mariahilferkirche where you're astonished again at the intricate and ornate
wealth of the interior and the vault of the painted ceilings. Then to an art
museum. Then on a tour of a palace called Schloss Belvedere. A walk that
night along what he calls the Donaukanal to an outdoor concert in a park.
The next day is Friday. Diversion Day. You put on your Levis and sport
shirt and sneakers, leave your saddlebags home, stuff your dirty missionary clothes in a pillowcase. In a light rain under a low overcast you take
them to the cleaners down the street and spill them on the counter to be
tallied. Morgan's wearing an old pair of penny loafers.

From there you head for the bathhouse. At the tram stop Morgan tells
you that guys can shower either in a private bath or in the company of a
hundred other Austrian guys. You're fine with a hundred other guys. It's
the way you showered in the Army.

"It's a mission rule to rent a private bath," he says.

You already sleep with him. Now you imagine being in a private bath
with him. In the gray rain his brown hair looks defeated and his face raw.

"Are they big enough?"

"For what?"

"For both of us."

He studies you. Smiles when he figures out you're serious.

"We each rent one. I like you, Elder, but not that much."

Not knowing what to say, riding out the flash of shame and anger, you
look away, up the street.

"All I was thinking was we're not supposed to be out of each other's sight."

"It's okay. It's just for a shower."

You look at him again. Then down at his loafers where rain has given
them a shine.

"Long as it's okay."

"It is. It's fine."

"Isn't it cheaper out in the open?"

"What?" he says.

"The shower. The bathhouse."

"That doesn't matter."

"Why not?"

"Because you're an Instrument of the Lord."

"Yeah?"

"Because there are men there who might look at you and see some other kind of instrument," he says.

You look away again. Out the window at a statue of some saint carved into an alcove in the stone wall of some building.

"You don't even want to tempt them," he says.

"Nobody's trying to tempt anyone. In the Army we—"

"It just happens."

The bathhouse is a big gray building called Dianabad. You pay your fee and take a towel from a scowling woman in a white uniform. Your private bath is an actual room. A small room with a locking door and a small white reclining couch like Freud could have used for his patients. Everything that isn't furniture or a fixture is tiled in white. The floor, the walls, the raised altar of the deep tub in the center of the tile floor. It reminds you of the room in the Temple basement where old men reached their oiled fingers underneath the sheet that was the only thing you were wearing. The room could be a holy place if it didn't have the feel of an asylum. A room for the insane. A flexible steel tube holds a shower nozzle.

It's the first time you've been on your own and naked in a while. Now it dawns on you. You can lock the door and have your way. Take your garments off and stand there naked. Turn the water hot and then aim the blazing needles of the shower nozzle at your crotch. Wrestle with the Devil to keep him from putting your hand around your pud. Beg the Lord for the will to let it go untouched. But it has to be washed. And it comes to where your mind reaches into the toybox of the girls who've caught your eye the last few days. The chesty woman at the dairy shop whose freckled cleavage makes you look away in shame and then sneak another look. Or slips back home. To Katy. Who said you had Russian hands and Roman fingers. To girls earlier, up and down the orchard towns, in the back of Quigley's Hudson or Snook's Chevy. To the Scoutmaster's wife and her mohair sweater. Just never Cissy. And then you end up pounding yourself raw. It's never felt better. Maybe because you've gone a while. Or because it's your first time standing. Or because you're alone in this white temple designed to celebrate you naked. Or because the Lord is watching. Or everything. But for sure the water. When it comes, it comes from the soles of your feet, in quakes that turn the bones in your legs and knees to rubber, quakes that radiate in raw heat up your back into your head and leave you shuddering, face to face with God, back all the way to the first time you learned what it was, the night your father stood watching from the silhouette of his head in your doorway, the waves of his black hair crested with fire from the light of the hallway behind him, the knob to your bedroom door in his hand.

Are you all right.

Afterward you feel weak. Humiliated. Painted red with shame. Defiant. You comb your hair without the mirror. You look at the small white couch and wonder what Freud would tell you. You drop your towel in a big wheeled hamper back out where you bought your ticket and avoid looking at the woman who must have known from the start what you'd end up doing. Outside again, liberated, you can't avoid the signs that Morgan did it too. The way his wet hair looks like he combed it blind. Like you did yours. His more relaxed and footloose walk. Like he feels like dancing. Like you do. The long thought he has to put into looking you in the face. The way he looks a little dazed like he's having trouble remembering what comes next. Like you must look. If he does it standing up or sitting down. If he made up the mission rule himself about using a private stall.

"So what do you want to do now?" Morgan says.

You think of the tracting book in the inside pocket of your suit. It's been since Tuesday morning. You haven't drawn your first column yet. Written your first R or N into a little box. There's no way you can write anything into it right now. Not where your writing hand has been.

"I don't know."

"Just want to walk?"

"Sure," you say. "Sounds good."

The sense of home you first heard in the chatter of kids outside the open window of the Mission Home. Everywhere Morgan takes you. Home. Deep in your memory. Deeper than Utah. The Avenues, Brewery Hill, Rose Park. Deeper than the ranch. Home before any home you ever had. Elusive but real. The memory deep where things find their imprints. Where you first must have experienced European buildings in the feel of this air under this kind of sky. First must have seen the European windows of a bakery shop filled with fat gold magical loaves and buns and cookies and then gone inside on your mother's hand and smelled everything. First must have seen how a light quick summer rain leaves a wet varnish on the gray and brown and red of cobblestones. This deep yearning pull that this is your life. This is its beginning. It was the country next door, and you were only there till you were four, but this could be Basel. This is where you started. Where you first experienced cold and heat and rain and sun and snow and touch. Where your mother fed you a soft boiled egg on a balcony and ran you and your buggy to a shelter when the Americans flew overhead and dropped their leftover bombs. Where you first knew who your father was.

On Saturday, back in your suit and tie and saddlebags again for what Elder Cannon said was the best day of the week, the day when most everyone's home, Morgan takes you to places where plaques next to doorways tell you where Mozart and Beethoven and other composers lived. Narrow meandering cobblestone streets and dwarfish pastel blue and pink buildings in the old part of Vienna with doorways that only come up to your face. He uses your camera to take a photo of you next to Beethoven's door.

"That should make your mom happy," he says.

He hands you back your camera. Studies you in the sunlight of this miniature street.

"What's the matter?"

Beethoven's door is the closest you've come all week to a door where someone lived. A door you could knock on. You're restless to ask what's going on. The tourist stuff all week. When you'll be knocking on doors for real. But it hasn't even been a week. And so you let it ride.

"Thanks for the photo."

"Oh." He sends a quick smile down the street. "Anytime."

"So where are we going now?"

"There's someone I'd like you to meet. An old friend."

Her name is Frau Kettler. She's a retired music librarian. A woman Morgan and his senior befriended when he worked Vienna at the start of his own mission. On a tram on the way to her place he fills you in.

"She's a good friend. She's really cosmopolitan. I wouldn't take just anyone to see her. But I think she'll like you. Just leave the conversation to me."

"So she's an investigator?"

"She was at first. Elder Banford tried teaching her the Gospel. She seemed interested. Then we realized she was mostly just being polite. To keep us coming back."

"So she's not really interested."

"She may be. Someday. She's not someone you can rush." And then he says, "So let's try to not mention religion."

In her building you climb four flights of stairs to reach her door. She's small, plump, cherub faced, dark haired, with a librarian's patient smile lodged in her heart shaped lips. Her kind silver eyes are the first you've ever seen that actually twinkle when she drops her rhinestone glasses and lets them ride on their gold chain on the high slopes of her full breasts. She and Morgan talk excitedly and happily across a small coffee table set with doilies, little spoons, teacups in saucers, a teapot, and a little sugar bowl, all painted with the same intricate flowers. You drink this light sweet tea she calls Kamillentee. Heavy burgundy drapes make the room impervious to the light and heat and noise of the afternoon. Light comes from an orchestrated medley of floor and table lamps. The time of day comes from a jeweled clock on an end table. Your mind goes back to Molly and Maggie sipping pretend tea from painted tin cups on their bedroom rug. You wonder if this was the kind of place they were imagining between themselves. A place impervious to their mother. A safe and pretty place. After an hour or so, Morgan gets up, takes off his suit coat, hands it to Frau Kettler. She hangs it in a closet down the hall while he seats himself on the round stool at the huge upright piano that dwarfs the heavily furnished room.

"Your coat too?" she asks, her English timid.

You tell her thanks but no. You need to hide your saddlebags. Keep them from scaring her off. Hide the sweat that soaks your shirt where they ride. Hide where the colors of the brochures have bled through the wet canvas and stained your shirt. From the pillows of the sofa you hold your cup and watch and listen to Morgan attack her piano. You don't know much of what he plays but you recognize Debussy. Brahms. Rachmaninoff. His playing amazes you the way Lenny's playing did. Except Lenny could play Rachmaninoff and move into Cole Porter without you even feeling it. Like the cut of a razor blade. Morgan can only play what's in front of him. Frau Kettler's face takes on a glow that looks like it comes from some rose-colored bulb inside her head. Occasionally she looks your way with a smile you try to give her back.

He plays for a couple of hours. Sits up and stops only to look through the shelves of sheet music Frau Kettler keeps in a glass-fronted hutch in the corner. When he's done he's thirsty. Frau Kettler has a glass of water and a fresh pot of Kamillentee waiting. He drains the glass in one long chug of swallows while she pours him a cup of steaming tea.

You sit there in the damp harness of your saddlebags itching for your trumpet. If she'd like what you can do. What Morgan would say. But you understand, well before it's time to leave, that this is a ritual, something that's been done before, time after time, Morgan here with someone else. That your trumpet would be out of place. That there wouldn't be room or sky for its steel bird sound. But you can feel it in your hands. The residue of Morgan's playing.

When you leave, the street outside her building is caught in the transitional early evening light that belongs half to the fading sky and half to the muted streetlights. It's the kind of light that is the closest light can come to being music. The light you aim for when you play.

"What did you think?"

"Pretty amazing. You play like you ride your bike."

"Thank you. I mean Frau Kettler."

The way her sweater and glasses and the perfect innocence of her smile made you remember the Scoutmaster's wife.

"She's a sweet lady."

"Sweet." He smiles openly. "She is, isn't she."

"What was that piece you said was Brahms?"

"The intermezzo?"

"The one that started with those big arpeggios."

"Oh. The rhapsody. G minor."

"Not having a childhood paid off," you say.

"Thanks. I like to hope so."

You round a corner. Well down the street you can see the lighted stop for the tram you took to get here. Now you'll take it home with a guy who plays classical piano as well as anyone you've ever heard. Morgan looks down the street toward the tram stop. You look at him and see longing. This weary gray you've seen before in the skin around his eyes like he's tired of wondering what everything is for.

"Did I tell you opera season starts in September?" he says.

"No."

"Hopefully we'll still be together. I'd like to take you to some."

You look at Morgan. "We can afford operas?" you say.

"If we use stehparterre. Standing room. Do you like opera?"

"What's standing room?"

"It's an open place at the back of the hall. Where you stand to watch the opera."

To keep from lying you think of the one opera from your father's record collection that you like. Rigoletto. Where the clown learns at the end that he's killed his daughter.

"Sure," you say. "Opera's fine."

Morgan smiles. "Let's not go home yet," he says. "There's a neat little gasthaus around here we used to use. Let's eat first."

CHAPTER 10

ON SUNDAY, five days into your mission, a long walk through the length of Prater gets you to the churchhouse. When you see it from across the street it's an ultramodern box two stories high that makes no sense among the older architecture of the buildings that surround it. The bottom half is glass. The top half is faced with tall white concrete panels separated by thin black inset stripes. A white steeple that looks like a chimney made of cinder blocks rises off the sidewalk and thrusts a tall white needle into the sky. Morgan tells you it's brand new. They just finished it last year. Missionaries stand talking on the sidewalk around the glass door. Their grins are steel when they shake your hand. More missionaries stand around the back of the chapel. Men and boys you can tell aren't American have started to fill the front benches for Priesthood Meeting. Morgan leads you up one of the aisles. Chandeliers that look like flying saucers hang from the ceiling. To the left, down off the podium, stands a long black concert grand piano. Up behind the podium and the pulpit, two rows of silver organ pipes, staggered by height and size, reach out across the front wall of the chapel like a pair of open silver wings. Morgan tells you the organ is a tracker organ.

"A what?"

"Tracker. The keys are manually connected to the pipes with a complicated system of cords. Nothing electronic. So the keyboards and pedals have to be built into the front of the organ case. See? Up there. Just below the pipes."

You follow him forward where you can see the two keyboards and the white knobs of the organ stops on either side.

"So you play it facing the wall?"

"Yes. That's why it has that big rearview mirror. See? To the left there. So the organist can see what's going on behind him."

A mirror the size of the Jeep windshield you shattered with your forehead. The taste of Brylcreem.

"Yeah."

"Most untrained organists hate trackers. I love them. The more stops you pull out, the more pressure the keys need. You can feel it. It gives you the feeling of being directly connected to the pipes. Like it must be to drive a powerful sports car."

Carburetor linkage. Shift and clutch linkage. And then the simple linkage of the valves inside your trumpet.

"The three best organs in Salt Lake are all trackers. The Cathedral of the Madeleine, the Episcopal Cathedral, and the Assembly Hall on Temple Square."

Madeleine. Where he played. The big sand-colored Roman Catholic cathedral that rises high off the north side of South Temple just up from downtown. The Church of the Devil. The one church Salt Lake had that came close to the churches in Vienna. You always wondered how it lasted. Why nobody ever burned it down or bombed it.

"Have you played this one?"

"I did the last time I was here." Then he says, "When they built this church, the members wanted the organ so bad they skimped on the heating system. Last winter the ice got an inch thick on the windows. They put heaters in this summer."

"That's some piano," you say.

"A Boesendorfer," Morgan says. "The Steinway of Europe. I heard it was a gift. I'm not sure."

For Priesthood Meeting a boy whose face in the rearview mirror looks maybe fourteen plays the organ. Men and boys sit alone and in loose groups across the front few rows of benches. Austrians. It dawns on you. Austrians you could talk to. Austrians who believe in Joseph Smith and the First Vision and the Word of Wisdom like you do. Who hold the priesthood. The lyrics are German but they sing the opening and closing hymns with the same full throated force as your father's friends back home. After the meeting the chapel doors are opened to women and girls and families. For Sunday School the organist is a small woman with a long braid of dust brown hair coiled on her head.

You expected more. Maybe not the shoulder-to-shoulder congregation that packed the chapel back home. But more than the gathering scattered across the field of the benches here. Many of them are women, old, without men, hair bunned up like balls of gray yarn, women who come alone with colorless shawls across their broad round backs and with the angel smiles of grandmothers. They gather in the benches right in front. Families take up a few of the rows behind them. Teenagers and guys and girls in their twenties collect along the outside rows. Some girls your age. Some pretty. Some coupled off. There aren't enough of them to call a ward. So you figure they're a branch. Like the people who came to the long green tin-roofed shed that stood in the sagebrush up behind the schoolhouse in La Sal.

"How many branches does Vienna have?"

Morgan stares at you. His mouth opens and closes a couple of times before he decides how to tell you what he has to say.

"This is it."

"You're kidding."

He looks at you. "I'm not," he says.

"All of Vienna?"

"Yes. So far."

You look around again. This endless city. The harvest so far. Suddenly they have the feel of people drawn together by some hobby like collecting bottlecaps or being fans of some dead actress. The missionaries sit a few empty rows behind them, in the middle rows of the chapel, like Secret Service guys doing their job without looking like they're meddling. Behind them the benches are empty. Rows of benches that would look to your father like they're waiting for you to get around to filling them. Pity floods your chest. There were more people when you played at the Indigo. There was the lady in the red dress. You could probably go stand outside and give popcorn balls away and bring more people in than years of missionaries have.

In the breaks between meetings you trade smiles and handshakes with some of them. They're used to guys like you not knowing how to hold a conversation. It's how things are. They get it. And so you hang in the rear of the chapel with the missionaries. Introduce yourself. Hands look to shake yours. Guys ask if you're new or just a transfer. Some of them remind you of Jasperson and Lilly, sacrament water in their veins, old before their time, guys who talk like all they do is knock on doors and all they care about is nobody going missing. You wonder if they rent private showers too. Others are there to talk about anything else. American stuff. Stuff about being home and going home again.

"Hendrick's folks are buying him a Porsche. He's picking it up in Stuttgart. You fuzzin' believe that?"

"Yeah. His dad's the president of some bank in Idaho Falls."

"He oughta wait till he gets home and get a fuzzin' Vette."

It's a big guy with broad shoulders under his black suit, thick black brushed back shining hair, this quiet contempt in his smooth round face, the small almost malicious eyes of the rich guys who came down off the East Bench to drag State.

"An XKE, man."

"An XKE looks like a stepped-on cigar."

"You think a Porsche could beat a Vette up Little Cottonwood?"

"Are you fuzzin' serious."

"What about you, Vance?"

"I got my El Camino. I'm hoping my girl's still there."

"You got long?"

"Four months."

"Sobchak's got this Austrian chick he's talking about taking home."

Back home, where they held it off till seven at night, Sacrament Meeting had the feel of something special, a concert or assembly, something you had to get dressed up for again. Here they hold it half an hour after Sunday School. So the members only have to make the trip once, you figure. Because god knows how long the way is. How complicated the tram connections. How much it costs to get from where they live to where they come to worship with their angel smiles in the presence of missionaries from America. By one o'clock it's over. You step out into the afternoon sunlight with the feel of coming out of a matinee. When you're home again, your suit coat and saddlebags off, Morgan shows you how to fill out your weekly report.

"It has to count every hour of the week. No matter what you spent it doing. You don't have to start yours till Tuesday. When you got here."

"Okay."

"Then from Tuesday afternoon when we left the Mission Home, our numbers all have to match, to show that we spent every hour since then together."

You're face to face on opposite sides of the small desk in your room. He spins his report around and slides it toward you where you can see his numbers.

"How'd you count the bathhouse?"

"In here. Personal."

"How'd you count Frau Kettler?"

"I told you. She's an investigator. Look at Saturday."

"When did we do the rest of this? Where was I?"

"We did it every day. Everywhere we went. You were right there."

"I don't remember knocking on any doors."

"No. Because we didn't. But do you remember me talking to people?"

The concerts you attended. On occasion to a stranger while you stood in line for tickets or took an intermission. Striking up a conversation maybe long enough to do the weather. You don't know. You couldn't tell what they were saying.

"Yes."

"If I tell someone we're missionaries," he says, "it counts as tracting time. If we spend time with them after that, that counts as time spent with investigators."

You try to remember hearing the words missionare or Kirche Jesu Christi.

"Even if we don't talk to them again."

"That's right."

"Even if we're just watching a concert with them."

"Yes. We start the conversation. It's up to them to take us up on it."

You look for him to let you know he's kidding. He just looks back at you.

"Okay," you say.

"You don't sound convinced."

"No," you say. "I'm fine."

He studies you. In the light from the window the skin around his eyes and mouth goes tense and then loose again.

"From now on," he says, "always have a couple of brochures ready."

"Tell me something," you say.

"Okay."

"The missionaries." And then you say, "Everyone says fuzz. What's that about?"

He gives you that sharp look you've figured out how to provoke and when to anticipate. A couple of zits in his chin are at the end of their lifespan.

"You know exactly what it is," he says. "Don't play dumb."

So you were right. A way of saying the real word and dodging the price of saying it for real. A way of ending it if the real word is the word you started out to say.

"How do they get away with it?"

"That's something you don't need to know."

"No? Why?"

"Because you're never going to use it. That's why."

Clouds darken the street out the window. You turn on the lights in the room. Rain keeps you in the rest of the day. You write Cissy. Later on your family. Keep it about your bike and the photo of Beethoven's house and your day at church. Dodge the question your father will want an answer to. How the Work of the Lord is going. At bedtime, next to Morgan on your knees, you pray in silence for tomorrow, the start of your second week, for Morgan to be finished getting reacquainted with the city.

On Monday, the sky blue and the air fresh and the streets washed by the overnight rain, you stop at the dairy shop for a roll and milk and the post office to mail your letters and send the report of your first week to the Mission Home. You know where to start from the tracting book. The street and the building. The end of the hall on the top floor where someone named Lischka lives. Your saddlebags ride cool and easy under your armpits against your sides. Morgan's got his old brown briefcase. You don't know why. Coming out of the post office you're ready to tell him where your first door is. He doesn't ask. He heads across the street instead. You follow him into Prater, under the vacant boxcars of the idle Ferris wheel, along the path you used yesterday to get across the park and out the other side. He's walking fast. All business.

"Where are we going?"

"The church."

"Sunday was yesterday."

He raises his face to the trees. Pushes his hair back off his glasses. Looks ahead again.

"Did you forget something?" you say.

"I need to look at some new pieces."

And now you know what's in his briefcase.

"You mean piano."

"Organ too."

"Isn't it locked up?"

"I have a key from the last time I was here. Sister Rindlisbacher gave it to me."

"Who's she?"

"The organist."

His own key. You let it register that this walk across the park could be permanent.

"What do I do while you're playing?"

"Gosh. I don't know. Work on the lesson plans. Whatever you'd like." Then he says, "You're always welcome to listen if you want."

And now you look down the street while a sick wind starts to send its feelers across the floor of your stomach. The letter you wrote your father two nights ago. How busy your companion's keeping you. How he'll be the first to know about that first baptism. The letter Cissy writes you almost every day. The more doors you knock on, she writes, the sooner you'll be home with her. The letters you write back to her. The letters from here. Vienna. Here instead of a place called Jackson down in Mississippi. Here instead of a place in Georgia called Americus. Here instead of a place called Selma down in Alabama.

If you can keep her.

Chapter 11

In closing, just let me say that you have a wonderful opportunity. To work in the mission field to bring souls to the Lord. It's a once-in-a-lifetime opportunity I was never fortunate enough to have. But I can have it now, second hand, through you. I imagine the doors you knock on and almost feel like I'm there, filled with the Lord's spirit, thrilled to bear my testimony. I hope you don't mind your "old man" horning in and piggybacking along. Let's make the most of it, by golly!
Your loving Father

NEVER LEAVE his sight. That Monday morning in the chapel you stayed at first where he could see you in the rearview mirror of the organ. A bench toward the back. He could play. Like there was no tomorrow. You finally opened the pocket-sized looseleaf and picked up the German script of the lesson plan where you last left off. The draw of the organ was too powerful. Your head kept coming in on your trumpet. You kept catching your fingers playing the valves. And Morgan kept breaking rhythm. Stopping, repeating passages, trying different phrasings out. You knew you weren't supposed to be out of his sight but you asked him anyway. If you could use a classroom down the hall.

"Just away from the music," you said. "So I can study."

He looked at you in the rearview mirror with his glasses off. From the back of the chapel you watched his eyes fish for you. He couldn't see what was on your face. And so you left it there while he thought your question over.

"Okay."

You took a classroom at the end of the hall. Closed the door. In the plain room with its blackboard and white walls and bare linoleum floor and single window, you took one of the metal folding chairs, started memorizing the lines again, reading them at first, then closing your eyes to recite them. There were words you didn't understand. That was okay. As long as you could say them. You learned both parts, yours and Herr Braun's, so that you could anticipate his answers. All you could hear of the organ were the dull throbs of the low notes. You kept reciting the call and response of your questions and Herr Braun's answers as you led him toward the unescapable admission that his church was false. It didn't matter what church. When you got there it stunned you how easily he caved. How quick he was to cough up his religion to a guy from Utah in his living room. Then my church must be false. You wondered if it really worked that way. If they tested the questions and answers and this was how they worked on real people. You didn't know.

When you looked up again, and checked your watch, two hours had passed. Piano music came through the closed door now. You followed it. Morgan was hunched over the keyboard of the big black grand he called the Steinway of Europe. The wing of the lid was angled up on its stick to ricochet the notes out across the chapel. His hands were furious. Off the bare walls the music was huge. Insane. You didn't know the piece, but you could tell he was ending it, bringing it home. You waited till he got there.

"How's it going?"

How he started and looked around. How with his glasses off again it took him time to find you. How he couldn't see what you couldn't keep off your face.

"Fine," him saying. "I'm almost done."

"Mind if I wait outside?"

Half turned on the piano bench, looking at you, how his eyes had that weary look of sad intelligence. How he lowered them to look at his hands and think for a minute.

"No," him finally saying. "Go ahead. I'll be out soon."

Into your second week you could see Morgan start to settle in. Put together his routine. Lay the things he liked doing out across the hours and days of the week. Into your third week you pretty much figured that going door to door in the buildings of your tracting area wasn't on his list. Going into August, when your check for the month came in one of your father's bundles of magazines and clippings, you knew from the quick pang of shame behind your eyes that the tracting book with its tiny hieroglyphic Rs and Ns was an ancient record, a closed book you might never open.

You carried it with you anyway. But you were catching on that this would be it instead. The churchhouse most every morning when it wasn't being used for something else for two to sometimes four hours of piano and organ practice. Music performances in the afternoons and evenings. In parks where couples lay on blankets in the grass back in the shadows. In elaborate jewel boxes of rooms in places hidden throughout the city where you sat on straightbacked chairs in dead air and watched men and women dressed in black play their way on violins and clavichords and cellos through chamber pieces by Schubert and Chopin. In cathedrals where the lunatic notes of organ recitals came shrieking off the high stone cliffs and the painted heavens of the ceilings. Back alley music shops where Morgan bought sheet music by composers with names like Hovhaness while you killed time in the aisles looking for anything resembling jazz. Not to buy it. Just look for it. The bathhouse every Friday where you stood trembling in the hot rain of the shower wanting to puke with shame while the thunder of your orgasm rocketed through your body. And a couple of afternoons a week in Frau Kettler's living room where you drank Kamillentee while Morgan played the pieces he'd practiced at the churchhouse.

The shame you felt when you looked at that August check. The way it blurred your sight. Money from working Mrs. Harding's yard to picking beans and peas and apricots to washing dishes at Servus Drug to guarding the equipment yards at Hiller. The way mission money had to be earned twice. The way you'd earned it once already but weren't doing anything now to earn again. Stealing it instead. Your own money. How you felt like a thief.

"Take your time," you telling Morgan, that first Monday, on your way out of the chapel to look for a place to study.

In the grass of the back yard of the churchhouse stood an old round picnic table with two curved benches. You wondered how it ended up out here behind the ultramodern architecture of the churchhouse. If the workers used it for lunch. The planks were warped. The decomposing wood soft and in places streaked with moss. The bolted joints wobbly. On the table a crusted old flowerpot held a crooked red geranium. Two trees reached up to make a closed arch of morning shade.

You made it your place. That first morning, while birds scolded each other in the leaves of the trees, you memorized a few more lines of dialogue with Herr Braun till they started to sound like lines from a fairy tale between two wide-eyed child angels. Then you wrote Cissy on one of the fold-up airmail envelopes you'd started carrying in a saddlebag. Over the next few mornings you wrote letters home to Karl and Molly and Roy and Maggie. You knew your mother would intercept them before handing them over opened. And so you wrote them careful to avoid what she would look for. What would make her voice go singsong at the edge of some nasty accusation she couldn't keep herself from making.

You wrote Doby and West and Keller and Jasperson and Lilly. Asked if they've heard anything new about Yenchik. You wrote Lieutenant Tanner and remembered the bite of the tiny rock in the bone of your knee in the vast dusk on the steel floor of the Mojave. And you wrote Cissy. Almost every morning now the way you'd been writing her almost every night.

You never thought it was possible to write anyone that often. But it came easy. There was always something to tell her. Always another way, like a solo, to let her know you loved her. Almost every day but Sunday there was a letter back from her on the rickety little table inside the front door when you got back home.

> Jeff came home on leave. We had a block party. I missed you. Everybody says hi. Daddy asked for his song again. That was when I missed you most.

That Friday, the ninth of August, you put the first month of your mission behind you. One month. It wasn't worth telling anyone. And by the following Monday, except for Cissy, you were out of people to tell anyway. You'd written everyone. People needed to write you back before you felt cool about writing them again. While you waited for letters back you looked for something else to do. Tried the dialogue of the lesson plan again and ran into the same arrogance of your questions and the same fairy tale innocence of Herr Braun's answers. But you finished the first lesson and earned enough of Herr Braun's trust to call him Bruder Braun as you started on the second. Read through the brochures in your saddle-bags. Watched people going by out front. Wondered what you looked like when they looked and saw you there.

And you remembered Hiller. The same long waiting after you were finished practicing, after your last round along the fenceline and across the yard, after the coffee was made, the hour or two left before the night mechanics started coming in again. The way it felt then like it did now. The slow crawl of that early morning dark. What you did back then. The stories you found to read. And then at Idlewild. What the big blond guy named Bill had said. How it would behoove you to come up to speed on this stuff. This negro stuff. Since your girl was what she was.

In the dairy shop where you ate breakfast there was a newspaper rack. And down the street a newsstand with racks of magazines. Time and Life and Newsweek were in English. Magazines like Stern and papers like the Arbeiter-Zeitung were in German. You could use them to learn to read and from there to learn to talk. On your weekly report you could write them up as study time. And there were photos. Photos that didn't need a language. Photos in whose faces despair and hope and fear and rage and heartbreak and everything else were wordless and instantaneous.

"You're buying that?" Morgan asked you the first time you took a copy of the Arbeiter-Zeitung off the rack in the dairy shop and laid it on the counter for the woman whose freckles ran deep into her cleavage to ring up on her register.

"Yes." You handed the woman your Austrian money and let her drop your Austrian change into your palm.

"Why?"

"To read while you're playing." And then saying, "Learn German. Study time."

Morgan had something to say again when you stopped and had the man at the newsstand take a copy of Newsweek off the rack behind him.

"That's in English."

"Yeah."

Morgan waited while you paid for it.

"Do you plan to count learning English as study time?"

"You tell me."

"You know that kind of reading is discouraged."

Taking the magazine and holding out your palm for change. Thinking of all the sheet music he bought. His briefcase fat with it. If sight reading was discouraged too. Thinking of the closed record of the tracting book in the inside pocket of your suit coat.

"So is playing Hindemith," you told him.

How he whipped around so quick his sand-colored hair came down across his glasses. How he pushed it back and peered at you with his eyes narrowed and his jaw set. How you were ready for him. Smiling. Your kidding smile. How he looked hard to make sure.

How he finally smiled himself and said, "You're probably right."

At the table, the fallen red geranium petals wilting to flakes of shriveled rust around the base of the flowerpot, birds going, the soft shade dappled with sunlight flickering through the leaves, organ or piano music coming muted from inside the churchhouse to scatter on the noise of traffic from the street, you started coming up to speed again, catching up on all the stories, all the names and all the places. A place called Americus. A theater called the Northwood. A place called Gadsen.

Back in the office at Hiller, where you'd read from the battered old desk, a story would sometimes take you so far away that the sudden scratch and yowl of the CB radio or the honk of one of the night mechanics would make you jump and look up and see the smoking headlights waiting through the restless dust and the blazing chainlink wires of the locked gate. You'd be in one or another Southern town or city. A place called Greensboro. A place called Saint Augustine.

Back then you'd read from the vantage point of what you'd lost. Cissy. There were times where she would ambush you. Where you'd be reading about the Children's Crusade or the Freedom Riders and a memory would cut right through you like the blade of a ghost knife, but instead of blood leave shame behind, shame for what you'd done to make her let you go, shame you'd have to stop and just ride out.

Back then you'd read like an outsider. A spectator. Like you were reading through a chainlink fence like the fence that ran the dirt perimeter of the yards you guarded. Your run to San Jose in Yenchik's Ford took care of that. Just to tell her what you'd done. How wrong you'd been. Now the fence is gone. Now, in the stories you read, you're on the street. Her appearance at the airport, out of the mirage of a pink dress against the coffee honey color of her face, took care of that.

Now, in this city that crowds around you when you remember the spread of the desert towns across Nevada, you read from the vantage point of what you have. Her love again. Her skin. The feel of muscle and bone just under it. The quick shock of her smile. The way her eyes skate sideways when you make her suddenly shy.

At the table you keep reading out of the instinct you've always had. To stay vigilant. Somehow watch over her. Know what might come her way. Be ready. The trained blast of water from the nozzle of a fire hose against the small of his back holds a tall young negro and two children pinned with their faces against the window of a shop as they try to keep from being blasted through the glass. Sometimes just the naked instantaneous force of a photo makes you lift and turn your head and look away to keep from seeing her. And when you do you can't make sense at first of where you are.

And you write in answer to your father's letter where, at the end, in a postscript, the line lurks that always makes you glance away. His closing postscript. Still waiting to hear the wonderful news of that first baptism.

> I'm sorry you never had this opportunity, Papa, because it's wonderful. I'm grateful for everything you've done so I could have it. And you're not horning in or piggybacking along. I'm doing this for both of us. I feel you with me every day. Every door I knock on.

And in your own postcript you write him back the line that the son he wanted would have written. Still waiting to share the news with you.

CHAPTER 12

YOU MOVE through the rest of August. In the walls of your room the heat builds to where you have to sleep uncovered, in your garments, braced against the pull of the dark sagging valley of the mattress where you might meet Morgan. The only apartment buildings whose stairs you've climbed are Frau Kettler's and the worn stone stairs to the floor where your room is. You've climbed her stairs two and sometimes three afternoons a week to sip Kamillentee and watch Morgan play himself insane. And then on Sunday count the hours.

To make them count he strikes up conversations everywhere you go. A woman at a concert. A music shop clerk. A man sitting next to him on a wall using a child's umbrella to shade his bald head while a string quartet plays in a garden at the Schoenbrunn. You learn how to act like you understand. Listen for the word Missionare while you stand there, smile in place, ready to go for your saddlebag and whip out a couple of brochures when Morgan signals you. Sometimes you hear it. Sometimes you don't. Sometimes you've drifted off. A tune running through your head. Your mouth and tongue and lips and fingers playing the shadow of a trumpet.

"I don't know if these brochures work," you telling Morgan once.

"What do you mean?"

"It gives people a way out. You know. A polite one. Like hey. Thanks for the brochure. Wow. Look at that. I'll read it and get back to you. Auf Wiedersehen."

Morgan thinking it over.

"Maybe a polite way out's not a bad thing. For people who want a way out."

You looking off. Just over his shoulder. Just for a minute. To ride out this feeling you didn't know was coming and didn't want him to see.

"Yeah. Maybe you're right."

"If you're tired of carrying them, well, that's another story."

At the backyard table, while Morgan plays away inside, you take out the other stuff you carry in your saddlebags. The real stuff. The negroes

Bill talked about at Idlewild. The negroes who planted themselves on stools at lunch counters across the South. How white guys and girls were joining them. White college kids like you.

Bill said they had to be trained. You wondered how you'd do if you sat with them. You imagined dirty cigarette smoke blown into your face so foul with the breath it rode you had to keep from breathing or you'd puke. If Bill was right. If once you puked they had you. You imagined your head slapped from behind. Imagined how you had to be prepared, always know that it was coming, keep your neck loose so that you could kill the reflex, keep from flinching. If Bill was right then once you flinched they had you. Coffee spilled in your crotch so hot it felt like ice at first. How you had to know the sting of the burn was coming and steel yourself to hold still for it. If once you cringed or winced they had you.

If you could let it happen. If it was Cissy sitting next to you. If you could let them call you nigger lover and your girl nigger bitch. If you acted like you heard them then they had you. If they poured pancake syrup and coffee creamer in her hair and you let them see a muscle twitch while it ran into her forehead then they had you. They had your hate. They had you calling them cracker mouthbreather. Redneck motherfucker. They had you cracking a ketchup bottle on the counter and grinding the glass teeth of its jagged rim into the nearest mouth. They had you. And then they had their way with you. Because you never cared how hurt you got. You always knew it wouldn't last. It would get better. That was why they'd have to train you.

Nonviolence. If you could learn it. In Vienna, in the back yard of a churchhouse thousands of miles away from the stories you keep reading, where sunlight through the trembling leaves plays on your hands and your open magazine and the soft weathered surface of the table, it's hard to know. You think back to the fights under the yellow lights in the parking lots of high schools. The curly-haired kid on the pavement with his fingers crushed in the loops of his brass knuckles. The back of your head laid open bleeding. If you could have walked away. The State Street fights. If you could have let yourself be hit and not hit some stranger back. Just take it. It felt stupid. It felt crazy. You'd have to have a reason. They'd have to train a reason into you for sitting still. Because you never cared how hurt you got as long as you hurt someone back.

From the table you've learned to tell when Morgan exhausts his practice session. A break at the end of a piece goes on too long to just be looking through his music for the next piece. A minute later he comes walking across the grass around the side of the churchhouse with his briefcase. By then you're always packed up too. Your magazines and papers in your saddlebags. The looseleaf with the lesson plans still on the table. In plain sight. He always looks stunned in the sudden daylight. Stunned by where he finds himself. His bathhouse look.

"I don't think it's a good idea for you to wait outside."

"You said I could."

"What if someone came by and saw you here alone?"

"People see me all the time."

"I mean missionaries. Like the District Leaders."

You look away. The two days two weeks ago that you climbed the stairs and walked the hallways of buildings besides Frau Kettler's and your own. The District Leaders were coming. Morgan told you how they'd split you up and take you tracting. The first day was practice. So you'd look experienced. Like knocking on doors was nothing new. Despite the reason you were doing it you felt good. Check the names in the tracting book against the mailbox names. Make changes where you found them. Climb to the top floor. Start from one end of the hallway. Work your way down to the next floor. This was what a missionary did.

It took Morgan three buildings to teach you the ropes. Then he was done. But by then you had fresh pages of your own. Your own columns headed with your dates and with your tiny R in every box. In the dim hallways with the doors set deep like crypts into the flaking walls you could feel the Spirit. You could pray that night. The second day was when they came. You went tracting with a guy named Elder Richardson. Knocking on doors, introducing yourselves and what you wanted, hearing Keine Zeit through the battered panels, writing another tiny R into the tracting book, you fooled him into thinking that you knew what you were doing. In your grandfather's shoes, here to harvest Austria, you lied about all the doors you were knocking on each day, hoping he wouldn't ask for the tracting book to check the back dates. The way you were on your own. The way Morgan had taught you to synchronize your lies. This cut of rage goes through you. You ride it out and let it keep on going, to Birmingham, to the mouthbreathers of the South where it belonged, before you look back at him.

"They wouldn't see me doing anything wrong," you say.

"What would you tell them you were doing?"

"Studying."

"What if they saw you reading a magazine? Or that newspaper?"

"They'd see the lesson book right there."

He narrows his eyes and looks toward the street.

"What if they asked you where I was?"

"Inside practicing."

"You're never supposed to be out of my sight. That's the rule."

"So you want me to come inside? Where you can keep an eye on me? You've got that big rearview mirror."

He searches your face.

"I don't know," he finally says. "It might be smart."

"I can't."

It surprises him. And then his face goes stern.

"You certainly can," he says. "If I tell you to."

If you could take it. If you could sit still. Not this time.

"If I was on a mission," you say, "sure. You could tell me anything. But I'm not."

In the grim set of his eyes and mouth there's hesitation. Maybe fear. Hurt. The way he's always been alone. It makes you look away again.

"There are seniors who would report you for saying what you just said."

Thinking of the hardworking ones at church. Dust on their shoes. Elders who would take you tracting and make your hours count for real.

"Got it."

"Right now you're on my mission. And you're lucky to have me."

You meet and hold his eyes.

"You're right. Sorry. I was out of line."

CHAPTER 13

ONE AFTERNOON he takes you to the massive stone battleship of a cathedral called Stephansdom. Saint Stephen's Cathedral. The mother cathedral of the Catholic Church in Vienna. He wants to renew his acquaintance with the organist he got to know the last time he was in Vienna.

"He said yes?"

"He had me audition on a smaller organ. Then he said yes to the main organ."

"Wow. How was it?"

"I was transferred out of Vienna before I had the chance to play."

"So you're hoping he remembers you."

"And hasn't changed his mind. Wait here. I'll be back."

You've been inside cathedrals around Vienna. This is the big one. It takes your breath away. Rows of gray stone columns climb high into beamed arches that make domed chambers of the sky they hold high above your head. That a building could hold this much sky. You think of the chapel back home and the first time you saw how much sky the beamed ceiling could hold. It feels like a toy house now compared to this place. You walk up the center aisle past benches equipped with low shelves for people to kneel on. A circular stone stairway leads to a high pulpit. Carved into the stone face of the pulpit are statues of men dressed like characters from Shakespeare leaning out of open windows cut in stone. At the front of the cathedral stands a high red and gold altar shouldered between tall stained glass windows. To the sides, past the two rows of columns that lead like tall stone trees carved with scrollwork down the center toward the altar, lies even more space, and statues stand along the vast stone walls. Rows of tall paned narrow windows whose tops arch into the beams of the ceiling let muted daylight flood the interior with the pale light of an aquarium.

You turn around and look back. Tourists wander the stone checkerboard of the floor and occupy benches here and there with people who are here to pray, most of them women like the widows at church, some with their heads bowed, some on their knees with their forearms on the bench in front of them, turning beaded necklaces in their hands. All the way back in the rear wall of the cathedral, racked in a stone gallery high above the giant doors you came in through, you finally see the arsenal of tall thin soaring silver pipes, arranged in rows like the skeletal spread wings of a prehistoric metal bird. The instrument Morgan is here to see if he can play.

"It has four keyboards," Morgan says, coming up behind you. "Over a hundred registers. Over ten thousand pipes."

You're wondering how your trumpet would sound in this place. If the steel of its notes could cut stone.

"Where do you sit? When you play?"

"You can't see it from here."

"Like the Wizard of Oz?"

He laughs.

"So what did they say?"

"The organist remembered me." You hear excitement in the quiver in his voice. See it in the worry in his eyes and the uncertainty in his crazy smile. "He said the offer's still good."

"Are you going to play now?"

"Not now. Some afternoon for a half hour or so. He has to check the schedule with another organist. We'll come back."

You go outside into the blazing white sunlight off the plaza. He stops and puts both his hands to his mouth.

"Are you okay?"

"I'll be fine," he says.

You finally ask the question that has troubled you since visiting your first cathedral for an organ recital.

"Is it okay for us to go inside these places?"

He brings his hands down and looks at you. It takes him a minute to know who you are.

"Cathedrals?" he says. "We're not going to mass or anything."

"Yeah. But you know. The Church of the Devil."

"Do you believe that?"

You look out across the plaza where people are eating, talking, reading, sitting there taking things in. If you could pick the tourists out from the people who belonged here.

"It's what they say," you tell Morgan.

"You'll have to trust me. I know what I'm doing. I'm your senior."

"Got it."

"Stop telling me you got it. There's no such thing as a Church of the Devil. The Devil hates churches. He wouldn't be caught dead in one."

And the question you've asked before but can't help asking now.

"So when do we start?"

You meant to catch him off guard.

"Start what?"

"Knocking on some doors."

"I thought you might want to see the city first."

"What's left to see?"

A shallow muscle in the skin at the corner of his eye starts ticking. A zit off the corner of his mouth has gone through the stages of its life. The red spot of a dying star.

"I'll let you know."

You hold his look. Everything you've seen. Everything that hasn't counted. All the hours you've felt like crap about reporting.

"I'm letting you know," you say. "I think I've seen enough."

When he doesn't answer you look off again at the people on the plaza. People you'll never know. The missing. You see Jerry and Bill down south in Mississippi, working a row of shanties, climbing the next plank porch, knocking on another door, persuading a thin young negro mother in a housedress to save herself by letting them help her register to vote. Bringing her the Gospel of the Vote.

"I just need a reason to be here," you say.

He doesn't say anything. You look down at your shoes as if you could see the afternoon heat of the stone steps come up through your soles.

"Look at me," says Morgan.

"I'd rather not."

"You'll find your reason," he finally says. "Like I found mine." Then he says, "It won't be your father's. It'll be your own."

And now you look at him, his face grave, his eyes gentle, and you don't know what to say.

"Promise yourself that. Don't be here for your father. Be here for yourself."

Easy for you to say, you think. A runaway father.

"I don't know how to do that."

"I know. Coming from me it sounds easy. My father wouldn't have cared even if he'd stayed." Then he says, "He built a bar in the basement. Shaped like a pistol. It's still there. He left that too."

You look away in shame. Rheumatic fever. No sneakers. No childhood. A guy whose mother got him into East High when he should have gone to South. How this is maybe all he has. How maybe you should let it be.

"Think of it as your mission," he says, while you watch a kid on a bike weave his way through pedestrians on the sidewalk. "Because that's what it is. Not your father's."

You look back at him. The same grave face. The same earnest kindness in his eyes. Like there's more to what he's saying.

"Maybe that'll help," he says.

"Yeah. Maybe."

"You'll find your reason. I promise."

CHAPTER 14

WHILE HE SHOWS you everything you still have left to see, while you wait for him to let you know you've seen enough, the papers and magazines you buy at the dairy shop and the newsstand and read at the back yard table start to talk about a march on Washington. A big march. The March for Jobs and Freedom. A mostly negro march. Set for August 28th. A Wednesday. You recognize the march that Jerry talked about at Idlewild. You wonder if he'll drive his Volkswagen bus up from Mississippi. If he ever changed his filter. If Bill will come with him. Buses and trains and planes are bringing people in from all across the country. Wednesday. President Kennedy and his brother Bobby won't give them the weekend. Only a single day. And a day that Kennedy limits to its daylight hours. Don't show up till sunrise. Be out of town by dusk.

> I want to go. So bad. My friend Debbie wants to go too. They have buses taking people all the way across the country. I want to see Dr. Martin Luther King speak and hear Mahalia Jackson sing. My great aunt Martha lives there. I know we're supposed to leave Washington the same day but if I wanted I could stay an extra day or two with her just to visit. I'm trying to get my mom and dad to let me go. Would you like to go? I wish you could.

Hunger rises warm into your chest. Hunger to be among them. Hunger that stands in the crossfire of all the questions whose answers stand against your going. Where you'd get the money. What would happen to your mission. If they'd take you back. How you'd pay the rest of what it is you owe your father. If that's even possible. Most of all the fenceline. In but not of the world. The fenceline that sets you apart from the world around you. Apart from the firebombed bus blazing on some Southern roadside. From the woman bracing herself against a railing while a firehose from across the street rakes the back of her Sunday dress and strips away her hat and whips the ropes of her soaked hair. From the high school kid with his stomach in a German Shepherd's teeth. From the negro heroes whose records taught you most everything you know. Apart from a march in Washington. Apart from anything negro.

Here instead of there. That far apart. Sometimes the hunger to go and immerse yourself in them is suddenly so sharp and startling your eyes move off the newsprint to the gray wood still damp with dew where sometimes a small black ant will be picking its way along an eroded line in the grain.

There at dawn. No sooner. Buses and trains and caravans of cars have to stage their departures from places across the country to all reach Washington at sunrise. From the cities of the west coast they start heading east on Saturday. On Sunday they take to highways from the cities of the mountain west. On Monday into Tuesday they roll out of the cities of the heartland. On Tuesday they kick off the trip out of the bloody cities of the South. In the middle of the night on Tuesday into Wednesday they start rolling out of the northeast. At the table you wonder what it must look like from the air. Long snakes of headlights following the arteries of highways from across the country to the waiting heart of a Washington sunrise. All of them loaded up again and gone by nightfall.

The morning after, on the rack in the dairy shop, the march is the front page story in the Arbeiter-Zeitung. The stagnant heat of late August gives way to September before the march starts showing up in American magazines. In the changing air, the sense of expectation as autumn sheds the weight of summer, kids wear the uniforms of their schools. Young couples, couples your age, couples who belong here, are everywhere. And then Newsweek and Time are there with stories. Life with color photos that give the stories faces. Under a blue sky one photo takes in the long reflecting pool all the way from the Lincoln Memorial to the spear of the Washington Monument. Wherever there's room are people. Three hundred thousand. Their faces in the sun. Negro and blanco. Black and white. In a photo of the Lincoln Memorial the luminous white statue of Lincoln seated in his marble armchair rises calm behind the speakers and singers gathered on the steps and around the microphones at his feet.

At the newsstand you've tried to keep the number of magazines you're buying down. Ration them. Spread them out the way you do your letters home to keep from drawing too much of your senior's watchful attention.

"What's going on?" he says, as you cross the street toward the path through the park to the churchhouse.

"There was this march on Washington."

He stops. Squints at you in the bright cut of morning sun across his face.

"You mean the big negro march," he says.

"You know about it?"

"Is that what all this reading is?"

"What do you mean?"

"The negro movement."

Your face burns.

"That and other news. Why?"

"You're lucky to have me for a senior."

"I know. How so this time?"

"I don't mind. But most seniors would."

"Mind what?"

You're not supposed to be interested in that kind of thing. You should know that."

"Now I do."

"Another senior would say that your testimony's not what it should be. You should be reading the scriptures. You could even be reported."

"Thanks for letting me know."

He looks you over.

"Anyway, I hope it does some good."

"What?"

"The march you're reading about."

You know that what you're reading happened days ago. That the faces of three hundred thousand people gathered between the memorial and the monument are gone. Back home again. That Lincoln gazes through marble eyes with their chiseled pupils along the length of the reflecting pool on the grass and concrete of a mall that feels abandoned now. You don't care. *I'm trying to get my mom and dad to let me go,* she wrote. *Would you like to go? I wish you could.* On the Saturday before the march you and Cissy catch a Trailways bus out of San Francisco. Fall in with a convoy of other buses. Head East. Climb the Sierras with everyone singing gospel and freedom songs and the blind engine pushing hard behind you. Cross through Donner Pass and then come down through Reno and from there through the desert towns across Nevada. This time she stays with you. Through Salt Lake. The dark skin of her eyelids closed in sleep. Moonlight on her face. Innocent of the six illuminated spires of the Salt Lake Temple and the gold statue of the Angel Moroni blowing his soundless horn. You keeping watch out the window the way you always do. This time for the mouthbreathers of the Klan waiting in the moonlight of Nebraska with their bats and rocks and the lighted wicks of Molotov cocktails looking to splash fire through the window. This time for Cissy instead of her brother Jeff. But the same ghost your face makes on the glass as you keep watch. The same cigarette smoke from the rows around you. Windows cracked open for air. A woman singing soft, barely above a hum, on her own, ahead of you in the darkened bus. *Sometimes I feel* like a motherless child. In the overhead rack, where Jeff left his mother's bottle of Cornhusker's lotion on the bus back to Monterey, rides the bag of deviled ham and tuna sandwiches Cissy's mother Mrs. Taylor made. Across the country, as you close on Washington, convoys of other buses from other American cities converge and join your growing caravan.

On the fourth morning after leaving you enter the Capitol. The straight dark glistening trunks of the trees stand deep in the sunrise mist. Cissy takes your hand. In the unleashed exuberance of three hundred thousand people, in the shared adventure of the daylight hours, you listen to people speak and sing. Mahalia Jackson. Josephine Baker. John Lewis. Marian Anderson. Martin Luther King. With their fire still burning in your chest, you're out of town by dusk, headed home again.

Out front, across the street from the churchhouse, a jackhammer is going, striking its chisel blade through concrete, the engine that powers its compressor alternately lugging down and running free. From the table you can hear the Austrian voices of the workers when they turn the hammer off. In sunlight alive with the quivering shadows of leaves you turn the page of the magazine and start to read again.

I have a dream today.

Cissy's hand in yours. The voices of the workers fade as you start to hear another voice. The voice you're reading. The engine of his written voice. Even typed, in print, the black words tremble with its power. Even silent, words you don't hear but read, their cadence moves through you like sometimes music does. Resonates in your lungs and bones like Robbie's drumbeats or the deep notes of Jimmy's amplified bass guitar or Morgan's tracker organ. What you're reading. Where you're from. Where you're going. Where it's taking you. Where you live. What your reason is. You don't know.

Part 3

Letters from Home

CHAPTER 15

IN HER SWISS handwriting, on one or two small pages decorated with pale green flowers, your mother sends her own news. Her innocent side, the sweet obedience of a schoolgirl, leaves you restless like it always has, makes you glance away from the memory of a woman lying naked and uncovered on her bed, reading in the lamplight, the bedroom door open in the summer heat while you and Karl look from the dark of the hallway.

> Yesterday we received the postcards you sent from Vienna. Yes, Shakli, it is a beautiful city! One day I would love to see it myself. The opera house is magnificent. And that cathedral organ! I would be afraid to play it! Did you know that they call Vienna the City of Music? Karl is learning the flute now. Molly has given up piano. Roy is taking lessons from Sister Lake. Maggie has little interest in learning. I have no more students now. How I miss the songs that you and I used to play together! You play trumpet with such feeling! Do you need garments and socks? Are you eating right? The sisters at Relief Society always ask me about that handsome young man in Austria!

In defiant print, like the cutting teeth of a rip saw, Karl tells you that a couple of his high school teachers have asked about you, that he's started to play the flute, that his latest stunt to rile the neighborhood was running a gallon of lawnmower gas down the long gutter of the hill and lighting it.

Molly writes from a distance. Mostly about church. Always about we instead of I. We did this. We did that. Or a faceless fact. There was a dance at church last week. There were refreshments. Not if she went or not. Not what she wore. Not if she helped decorate the gym or baked a plate of cookies. Her letters aren't meant to be cold. They're just without emotion. You search her words for any shame her mother might have scorched her heart with. And then you realize. The distance itself is shame. The one emotion she lets you see because she doesn't know that she can't hide it.

Roy writes that he played a Chopin nocturne in Sacrament Meeting. That he's started to play jazz. Brubeck tunes like Strange Meadowlark. That he misses your trumpet.

Maggie sends you a pencil drawing she did in school. A missionary in a suit and tie and a girl in a dress for church, side by side, holding hands. Under the missionary she's written Shake. Maggie under the girl. You didn't know she could draw.

Each letter except Karl's ends with how they pray for you. In their innocent encouragement you can hear your father's instruction. Don't forget. You're writing to a missionary. And you can read your mother's urging. You should write your brother. Each letter you write back is written knowing that she'll intercept and read it. And so you're careful. You look forward to hearing Karl play his flute because in another two years, when you're back home, he should be good enough for the Utah Symphony. You don't ask Molly if she's started dating. You know the answer. You don't ask how her mother's treating her because her mother would peel her open like an artichoke to find what she was telling you. You tell Roy you'll teach him anything you know but you don't say jazz. You tell Maggie the drawing is beautiful but not that you've taped it up on the wall of your room. You still remember what your mother did with the last photo you taped to a wall.

"Who's Maggie?" Morgan wants to know.

"My kid sister. She drew it."

"The one who's nine?" he says. "She's really quite good."

Only your father's letters are regular. Once a week there's an envelope on the rickety table just inside the door. Each letter's a blend of news and scripture. Like the Army, at Ord and then at Knox, there's a remote feel to what and how he writes, a sermon feel, a gentle humble feel, except that it's meant for you, a congregation of one, like he's speaking from the pulpit and you're the one guy in the chapel. Only his letters from home are typed. Reading them, you can sometimes hear the keystrokes of his big Royal typewriter, coming from the furnace room up through the floor of the living room the night you came home from your first date. The way their machine gun clacking paused to listen to your mother call you names so profane they burned themselves deep and permanent into the tissue of your memory. Then cautiously picked up again.

It should go without saying that we include you in our prayers at the dinner table and when we gather around the coffee table at night for family prayer. I know that you're working hard every day with your companion on the harvest. I know that it can be discouraging. Remember that your family and the Lord are with you. Remember to take off some time to enjoy the historic city of Vienna and all its many wonders. Still waiting for the wonderful news!
Your loving Father

Once a month your father's letter comes packaged in a taped and string-tied manila envelope full of articles clipped from the Salt Lake papers and the publications of the Church. Brochures and pamphlets pushing Utah and the Mormon Way. Transcripts of speeches by the General Authorities. You look at his careful wrapping job. More tape this time than he used for his packages to Ord and Knox. This time the string is doubled. This time it has to go a much longer and more hazardous distance. By golly, you can hear him say, it has to hold up. Still waiting for word of that first baptism. His always closing thought has to reach its destination.

Nobody mentions Cissy.

This time when you write her you don't act lame and stupid like you did at Knox when you thought you could walk her backward out of loving you. This time you don't let go of what you want to write. This time, when she writes about going to a movie or to listen to some jazz, you don't let go of what it takes to be with her. This time you write her back like it's you in the seat there next to her, shoulder to shoulder, the color of her fingers laced through the color of your own. This time, when she writes about washing her hair, you write her back about how lush it looks all lathered, pure white froth in her pure black hair, and you're there to wipe away the tendrils of foam that find their way down her dark forehead before they burn her shining eyes. This time you hold still and give her love for you the fixed and quiet target of your love for her. This time you write her back from the longing and powerful heart of your loneliness. This time you try hard not to dodge her. But sometimes, buried in a letter, there's a sleeper, something that leaves you staring at the wall or out the window wondering what to write her back.

My friend Julie says that girls can go on missions too, she writes. Except for us. I didn't know that. I thought you had to have that priesthood only guys can have.

Except for us. You know what she means. Negro girls. Because girls who go on missions have to go to the Temple first. Except for us. What leaves you restless is the way she just accepts it.

"Bad news?" you hear Morgan say, from across the room.

"No," you say. "Just news."

A runaway father doesn't write his son. So you always give Morgan first shot at the reading material your father sends, to give him some mail of his own while you read your father's latest letter. You always read it twice. Search it for anything, some secret code, some reproach in the scripture he chose, that tells you what he thinks of Cissy and her visit to the airport. Nothing's ever there. So either she doesn't exist or what she did was too bad a sin to be forgiven. And if it can't be forgiven then there's nothing to forgive. And if there's nothing to forgive then there's nothing worth discussing.

"I wonder why he sends you all this. Is he trying to make you homesick?"

In the armchair that he's come to own by default, Morgan's leafing through the clippings, stopping to read one now and then before dropping it in his lap.

You have to smile.

"The last thing he wants is me coming home. Especially emptyhanded."

"What do you mean emptyhanded?"

You turn to the window where you can see your face reflected, pale, elusive, ghostlike, half in silhouette, the face of someone just home from another chamber concert instead of a night in Bruder Braun's living room.

"Nothing," you say.

You write her at night from the small desk off the side of the window under the light of the metal lamp. Like her, you use this special airmail paper that folds itself into an envelope around what you've written her, and then carries it all the way to San Jose. From her letters, from her handwriting, Morgan can't tell the color of her skin.

"Is Priscilla your girlfriend?"

Priscilla. Her full first name. You figure he knows it from the return address on her envelopes when he gets to the mail before you do.

"She goes by Cissy."

"What's she like?"

You remember the guys you came to Austria with. What they said that first afternoon in the conference room after Elder Cannon left.

"She's beautiful." Then you say, "She sings."

"What does she sing?"

"Love songs. Standards. I guess anything." And then you remember her in her pale blue robe in the choir of her church. Singling out her voice. "Church songs. Gospel."

"She's from San Jose?"

"Yeah."

"What does she look like?"

Shirt off, shoes off, pants still on, some sheet music in his hand, more music in his lap in the upholstered chair in the corner. What he said about the march. How he hoped it would do some good. Her photo right there in your wallet. And what you promised her. Not to look at it. Not to use it to remember her. Remember her for real.

"Dark hair. Nice smile. Big dark brown eyes."

"She's waiting for you?"

You take a long look at the floor.

"She has this theory," you say. "About a mission. There's a certain number of doors we have to knock on. Like say ten thousand. The more of them we knock on every day, the sooner we'll be done and on our way back home."

He takes his time.

"You know that's not how it works," he says.

"So does she. So she says this too. The more doors I knock on, the faster the time will just feel like it's going. For both of us. The sooner it'll feel like I'm back home."

You wait for Morgan to say something.

"She wants to keep count of the doors for me," you say.

He puts his glasses on to look at you. The light and shadow on their lenses keep you from seeing through them to his eyes. You glance at the letter you're writing Cissy. Yes. How girls can go on missions. How you've heard there are four of them in Austria. How they can knock on doors and convert people. How they just can't baptize the people they convert. How they have to ask a guy. You've let go of what it takes to keep the rest of it from her. How girls have to wait till they're twenty-one to go. How the Church wants to give them a chance to marry first. How that's their real calling. How a mission's like a last resort. An old maid last resort. You already know you'll be throwing what you wrote away.

"Do you have a picture?" you hear him say.

If you could risk it. Take it out of your wallet and hand it right to him. If that would be okay as long as you didn't look at it.

"You said I'm lucky to have you for a senior."

"Yes. I'm pretty lucky too. Why?"

"Can you promise me that?"

"Why?"

"Can I count on staying lucky?"

"What do you have in mind?"

His wary look. And then it strikes you. Not to hide her. Not to be scared. Not the brave way she came to the airport in a new pink dress. Not how proud she was of you.

"You're right," he says, after a minute. "She's very beautiful."

In his armchair, her photo in his hand, his glasses off so you don't have to worry that you'll see her face reflected in their lenses, so your promise to her holds.

"Thanks."

"Do you plan on marrying her?"

"I know."

"Know what?" he says.

"That it wouldn't be in the Temple."

"That's not what I meant." The way he talks sometimes with this reflective and weary sadness. "Until just this year, you couldn't have married her anywhere in Utah."

"What do you mean?"

"There was a state law against it."

"A Utah law?"

"They just got rid of it this spring. They had an ugly word for it. Miscegenation. Now it's legal. For Utah anyway."

"Miss what?"

"Miscegenation."

"What does it mean?"

"Marriage between different races. Usually between white and another race."

Miscegenation. You silently try it. A twisted word that makes your mouth feel ugly. You remember your priesthood teacher Paul Hunt. The Corvette guy with the wife he brought home from Hawaii.

"Like Hawaiian?"

"I think it's just negro," Morgan says. "In the Church anyway."

Miscegenation. You've wondered if there was a name for you and Cissy and what you did in Yenchik's Ford. The leaves so dense in the grove where you parked you couldn't see the difference in your color. The way she cried out for you. The way you weren't struck dead. The way you lived.

"So for a Hawaiian it's not miscegenation."

"I guess it's not."

"So it's like the priesthood. Legal for anyone but negroes."

"She looks kind," says Morgan.

"How about California?"

"Oh, I'm sure it's fine there," he says. "Probably has been for years."

"But it's okay in Utah too. Now."

"Since spring. My mom wrote and told me." Then he says, "I guess this explains your reading material."

"Reading material?"

"All the stuff you're reading. About the South."

"It's more than her."

"How?"

"The musicians who taught me how to play."

"Musicians?"

You name some of them. Clifford Brown. Art Farmer. Coleman Hawkins. Sonny Rollins. Lester Young.

"Heard of them?"

"Not really."

"Louie Armstrong? Miles Davis?"

"Yes."

"They were pretty much all negro."

"Jazz. Of course. They taught you?"

"Their record albums did."

Morgan still holding her photo. Still looking at her.

"Did she really write about counting doors for you?"

"She offers all the time."

"What do you tell her?"

"Different things. Jokes. Lies."

He lays the hand holding the photo of her face on the armrest and looks off across the room. Without his glasses on you're reminded that he doesn't know what it's like to read a letter from his father. Or write a letter to a girl.

"Listen," you finally say.

He looks at you.

"What?"

How shy you were. About the kids with instruments back in junior high. How you never thought you could be one of them. How you could watch them play, like here, like every concert you go to, but not play yourself. And then how Carla got you not to care. How a girl with a violin played Danny Boy and finally touched a match to the waiting campfire in your chest and got you over it.

"A girlfriend," you say.

"Yes?"

"It'll happen. She'll come along." And then you say, "Here. Let me put it back."

"Oh." Surprised to find the photo in his hand. "Sorry."

Chapter 16

YOU WONDER if San Jose has lunch counters. You know it has a bus terminal. Trailways. You stopped in to ask the guy behind the counter the way to the address you showed him. You didn't look around for a waiting mob, topped off and dripping hate like kerosene, with bats and rocks and bicycle chains. You didn't know to look around for restrooms labeled white and colored. But if San Jose has separate water fountains. Hamburger drive-ins with windows off the sides in case you're negro. If she's okay. What she thinks about what's going on. You don't know. You don't ask. Because you wouldn't know when something you'll write by accident will be wrong, and hurt her, and you'll have taken the step where her love falls suddenly away through open air. Instead you keep reading. To stay vigilant. Watch over her.

"What's that?"

Morgan from his armchair behind you.

"A mouthpiece."

Without turning around. Revolving it in your hands. In the open for the first time since you got here.

"For your trumpet?"

You set it on the desk, stand up, look at him. He lowers the copy of The Improvement Era your father sent and puts his glasses on. By the time he focuses on you, your easy smile is there, the smile you always wore on gigs with the band, one you've learned to use to keep Morgan from thinking you're questioning something or complaining.

"You know Martin Luther King?"

"I know who he is."

"You know what he does?"

"Yes."

"He can't have the priesthood."

"I know."

"You know why he can't?"

"Because he's a negro."

Still smiling.

"Because he's not responsible enough."

"What are you after?"

"That's what they tell us. They aren't responsible enough."

"Where is this going?"

"What do they mean? Not responsible enough to pass the sacrament? Afraid they might eat all the bread off the tray before they pass it?" And then you say, "Martin Luther King. Not responsible enough."

"I don't think that's what they mean."

"So what's he not responsible enough to do?"

"I knew this would happen."

"You know what racism is?"

"You've been reading too much again." He looks down and lifts The Improvement Era your father sent you off his lap. "Maybe you should try more of this."

You stare him down. Still smiling while fire blazes in your forehead and lightning runs hot and itchy in your skin. He looks away embarrassed.

"Sorry," he says.

"Are we racists?" you say.

He's quick to look back at you.

"Be careful," he says.

"I'm just asking. We won't let them hold the priesthood. I don't know how that's different from not letting them sit at a lunch counter."

"Racists base it on hate. We base it on the word of God."

"What if it's God's word to not let them sit at a lunch counter?"

"That's nonsense."

"We base it on believing they're less valiant. You think Martin Luther King's less valiant than we are?"

"We base it on what God tells us." Then he says, "You need to be careful."

"It doesn't make sense. A girl holding herself still while pancake syrup's being poured on her head. She's less valiant."

"Of course not."

"So what is it?"

"You're scaring me."

"Do you think God's a racist?"

"Elder!"

You catch yourself. How the smile got lost somewhere. How hard you're breathing.

"Sorry."

"You should be thankful you're having this conversation with me."

"I wouldn't have it with anyone else."

"Maybe you should ask God himself. When you pray tonight."

"Do you think he knows that? King? About the priesthood? That he can't have something we've had since we were twelve years old?"

"I don't know what he knows."

If he would ever march on Salt Lake. Give a speech about the priesthood.

"Sorry," you say.

"There are things we're not supposed to question."

You look down. Turn your head slow side to side. Pick up your mouthpiece and put it to your lips just for the imprint of its steel kiss.

"Did you bring your trumpet too?"

"I need to get out of this room. Can we go somewhere?"

Chapter 17

IN CHURCH YOU sing the German syllables of hymns you know by heart in English. Match the English you know by heart against the German on the page of the hymn book. One Sacrament Meeting, leafing through hymns while a Church Authority from Munich rains his German thunder down on a bareheaded congregation hungry for a late lunch, you look for a hymn you grew up singing. For the Strength of the Hills. It's not in the book. By the end of the speech and then the benediction you've come up with a second missing hymn. O Ye Mountains High. After the meeting Morgan doesn't believe you. Says maybe you missed them because you're not that good at German yet. Looks for himself.

"You're right." Giving you a lost look. "They're not here." Then he says, "Maybe your grandfather missed them."

Your famous hymn translating grandfather. You write your father about them. While you wait for his answer opera season opens. Morgan takes you the second week of September for your two month anniversary. The opera is Die Zauberfloete. The Magic Flute. Mozart. He says to bring a handkerchief. You wonder if the story's sad. Like Rigoletto. You make it to the Opera House in the middle of the afternoon to get a place in line outside, on the plaza, for standing room tickets, the only tickets you can afford. People have already started lining up. You spend three hours waiting in the sun while Morgan strikes up a couple of random conversations where you listen for words like Missionare. Kirche Jesu Christi. When you hear them, twice, you relax, knowing you can write the afternoon and the opera off as time spent with investigators.

Once people get their tickets they take off running. So does Morgan. Running on floors that are slick with what looks like marble, you follow him, to a door that opens on the standing room. The stehparterre. The room is set into the rear of the opera hall, its floor tiered up and back, each tier equipped with a rail upholstered in velvet, the front wall open to the vast and elaborate hall and the orchestra pit and stage at the far end, the room high enough to let you see over the field of cushioned seats. The velvet rail is a place to rest your elbows and mark your spot if you need to leave for the head or for intermission. People around you tie their own rags and neckties and handkerchiefs around the rails to mark where they'll stand. Some bring food. Others small bottles. A heavyset woman brings a footstool and sits down next to you where you can look at the top of her head and smell liverwurst while she eats a biscuit. Well-dressed people fill the seats of the hall in front of you. Listening to songs whose words you can't understand, to an orchestra flecked with muted lights, you watch extravagantly costumed singers act out a story you can't follow. But you know the music. One of the operas your father played in La Sal on the portable record player you later used in the garage to learn jazz from the albums Mr. Selby sent you home with. With the audience spread dark like a night field of cauliflower heads in front of you, the distant stage bright with costumes, you remember the quiet smile of radiant bliss in your father's face at one or another Utah Symphony concert at the Tabernacle. How lost he looked. How you knew not to interrupt him. How he would love this. If you could write him about this place. You know you can't. But if you could.

Afterward, in the crawl of the crowd toward the doors, Morgan asks how you liked it. Mozart. Like always. Music that rarely gave you the breathing room to have it move you.

"My father would have loved it," you say.

Morgan is quick to turn his face to you, grave and gray, and is just as quick to turn away. A look you've seen before but never understood.

"I liked it too," you say. "Thanks."

But he doesn't ask again. The next day, after an early afternoon concert, you're waiting for the tram that will get you within walking range of Frau Kettler's place.

"Two months," says Morgan. "Gosh. I can't remember that far back."

You can. The days you haven't earned your keep. Haven't even earned what you can't keep yourself from doing at the bathhouse.

"Have you started your mission calendar?" he says.

You've heard missionaries talk about keeping them. Not in days but months. Thirty of them. You could cross the first two off if you'd been doing what you came here for.

"Do you keep one?" you say.

"Of course not. That's something prisoners do."

At the dairy shop the Monday morning following your first night at the opera the Arbeiter-Zeitung is sold out. The next morning you pick up the Tuesday edition. Washington untersucht Negermord. Washington investigates Negro Murder. A bombing in the city of Birmingham. Sunday. Two mornings ago. A church. And then what stops you. Cuts through the morning and leaves everything that was the morning altered. Four negro girls killed. You wave off the roll and glass of milk the woman with the spill of freckles down between the valley between her breasts starts to serve up for you. Just buy the paper and take a seat with Morgan and look through the window at the street.

"Are you okay?" Morgan asks.

"Just not hungry."

"What's going on?"

"They bombed a church in Birmingham."

"Birmingham?"

"In Alabama."

"Who's they?"

"I guess the Klan."

"Who?"

"The Ku Klux Klan."

"My goodness."

"Four negro girls were killed."

"Goodness gracious."

The Sixteenth Street Baptist Church. The bomb planted outside the night before and timed to go off Sunday morning during Sunday Service. On the opposite side of the wall against which the bomb is planted, in a basement room, a class of boys and girls meet for Sunday School. In another basement room, a dressing room, four girls get ready for the Adult Service upstairs. The Sunday school kids are reading Christ's teaching to love thine enemies in the Gospel of Matthew when the bomb goes off. The blast blows through the heavy rock foundation of the church. Kills the four girls in the dressing room. Maims and wounds more than twenty Sunday School kids. Adults attending the service upstairs search through the rubble for the ruins of their children.

The missing hymns. Your father's answer comes in a letter you find after coming home one night from a concert where a small orchestra took on the Fifth Symphony. At the end of another night of watching people play instead of playing yourself, at the unearned end of another day, you feel ragged and dirty and useless when you take off your suit coat and saddlebags and open the envelope.

In answer to your question, the Church decided some time ago to remove any hymns that mentioned Utah from its European hymn books. Those hymns encouraged too much emigration from the European branches. The Church wanted its European members to stay where they were and build the Kingdom of God in Europe. There's a hymn you missed. Land of the Mountains High.

And then he writes the expected stuff that lies like the dark ache of some long dead animal in your stomach and sets lightning off inside the long black cloud that turns the sky to iron.

We're still waiting to celebrate the wonderful news of your first baptism. I tell you, while it was one of the supreme pleasures of my life to be able to baptize my own children, I've always regretted that I never had the opportunity to do what you're doing. I understand that Austria is a stony field, so to speak, but sometimes we have to go that extra mile, by golly. I'm sure that if you spend less time pondering the hymn book, and more time applying yourself to your real calling, we'll soon hear the wonderful news.
Your loving Father

You carefully fold and then rip the letter up. Tear the words apart. Shred the bloodless logic. Four girls dead. Twenty others hurt. Your real calling. You put the pieces back in the envelope the letter came from Utah in. Out the window, headlights fire their bright paint along the bleak stone face of the building across the street, leave dark rectangular shadowed holes where you know the sightless windows are.

"What's going on?"

Last time you looked, Morgan was sitting on the bed, in his garments, using the clippers out of the manicure kit you bought while you were at Fort Ord to cut his toenails. In the pale reflection of the room behind you off the window, he's still there, looking your way.

"Tell me again whose mission I'm on."

"Did your father write something?"

"No. I'm okay."

And you see yourself there, reflected on the window, in silhouette with the light of the room behind you, your suit coat off, your saddlebags off, otherwise still dressed, still in your long sleeved shirt, your necktie on, your face dark, your head the shape of your skull, your father's envelope still in your shadowed hand, and what you see is suddenly all you are. If the Utah hymns were still in the book when your father and mother were living back in Switzerland. If their lyrics were what lured them into moving all the way to Utah. For years you've known that you were Mormon before you were American. That if you weren't Mormon you wouldn't be American. That you'd have grown up instead in Switzerland. That instead of buying yourself a trumpet for your birthday you might have bought an alphorn or accordion. That you might be playing polkas instead of jazz. If it was just a hymn. Your mother and father and all your relatives singing Utah We Love Thee in some small churchhouse in Basel. If that's the real reason. If who you are is that much of an accident.

"It's your mission," Morgan finally says.

The members here. People who won't be singing O Ye Mountains High because they don't even know it's there to sing. You take a long breath and turn from the window. Put on your easy smile so what you say won't sound to him like you're complaining. Just wondering.

"You remember those missing hymns?"

"From the hymn book. Yes."

"I asked him about them."

"What did he say?"

Morgan listens. When you're done he doesn't have anything immediate to say. He forgets about his toenails and looks away from you at the chest of drawers in front of him.

"It makes sense," he finally says. "Gosh. In a really terrible way."

"April in Paris doesn't make everyone pick up and move to Paris."

"No."

"Autumn in New York either."

"No."

"It's a pretty cheap way to think of people."

"I wouldn't say that in front of anyone but me."

"Sorry." An easy smile again. And then you say, "So they'll never see those hymns. Not know they exist."

"I guess that's the idea. Unless they see an American hymn book."

"Maybe there's different American hymn books too. Maybe the Church wants members in Kentucky to stay in Kentucky."

"Don't be silly."

You give resentment time to ride through you.

"So how do we look them in the face?" you say.

"What do you mean?"

"The members. How we're supposed to look them in the face."

He looks at you.

"What they don't know won't hurt them."

"But we know."

"Then trust the Lord," he says. "He did this for a reason."

"That doesn't help me look them in the face."

"Then talk to the Lord about it," he says. "I don't know what else to tell you."

Chapter 18

TALK TO THE LORD about it. What Morgan is supposed to tell you. You've been praying all along. But somewhere along the way you've stopped. Stopped talking to God except in your spoken prayers, where you have to, where Morgan's listening, where you kneel in the morning to ask for God's help for the day and then again that night to tell him what you've done with it.

At first, in your silent prayer, you talked openly to God. You asked him for the routine stuff. To help you become a better junior. To help prepare you to fill your grandfather's shoes. To watch over and bless each member of your family. You knew enough to never mention Cissy. You prayed for Cissy at the end, after you said Amen, not to God but to yourself, to stay vigilant for her.

Later still, used to the stubble of the rug beneath your knees, it got hard to ask God for anything. Given that you weren't working. Given that you hadn't earned the right that day to talk to him. You asked anyway. Tried to talk to him about not working. Asked him to forgive you for your lack of patience. For your sometime anger. But you felt shame when you said I'm sorry into the dark where you hoped he would be listening. Because you weren't sorry. Because you just wanted God to fix it. You told him he'd called you here to do his work. To harvest Austria. You asked him to fix it so you could. And then, when nothing happened, when the only thing that changed was the concentration of the fury when you tried to see his face, you stopped asking him.

And later still, with requisite humility, you started to talk to God about the stuff down South. Told him you understood why he looked at negroes as inferior. But wondered why they had to keep on being punished. They went to church. They worshipped him. They wore Sunday suits and dresses. Their powerful voices sang for him. They even wore their suits and dresses when they marched. They might have thought of him as someone else, the wrong God, but they were innocent. You weren't supposed to seek them out and teach them who the real God was. You were supposed to leave them among the missing. And so they had no way of knowing.

You could read God's answer at the rickety backyard table. Nothing.

So you thought there might be a higher purpose to an older woman being firehosed. To a German Shepherd with its teeth in the stomach of a kid. To a firebombed bus of Freedom Riders. To four churchgoing girls slaughtered. To a boy shot off the handlebars of his brother's bike. They'd missed out on the War in Heaven. Maybe they needed a makeup war to learn what war was like. In his answer you could read God's message. Feel his furious rebuke. Tend to your own business.

And then somewhere along the way you stopped praying your silent prayer to God. You pray now to anyone but God because when you look for his face all you see is his withering disappointment. And then you kneel there with your eyes closed, waiting for Morgan, wondering what he was telling God.

What God sees now. Two guys side by side. On their knees in the limp bags of their garments, elbows on the bed they share in a room this far from home. What God sees, looking down on you, your uncombed morning hair, the single button that holds the sagging back flaps of your garments closed in a room whose doilies and rugs and furniture have nothing to do with you, the opera you came home from the night before still in your ears. May thy Spirit guide us to the next opera and give us the strength to stand through it.

You use a knife to cut the fragile light blue paper that folds itself into an airmail envelope.

My darling Shake,
     We had another barbecue last weekend. Everybody was asking about you. It's hard to know what to tell them. You know. Because of what you're doing. Mommy said to just tell them you're doing fine. So that's what I've been doing. Uncle Paul brought his trumpet again. He still talks about how you put the devil in it. He got mad because he had to play it himself. It was just play mad, though. Of course Daddy asked for his song again. That's when I missed you most. When Uncle Paul was playing instead of you. I never knew till I sang it with you who I was singing it for. Now I do. Since I fell for you. I love you so much.
Cissy

You can close your eyes. Still see the fierce curls of black hair on the back of her neck. Hear her voice. I get the blues most every night. Uncle Paul's trumpet in your hands.

The weather from late September into October cools and rejuvenates the city. On the open plaza of the Opera House your garments stop sticking to you like the limp skin of a peeling sunburn. The weather has brought young couples out and made them brazen. You see them making out on the steps of cathedrals and government buildings. Their coffee getting cold between them on the rickety tables of sidewalk cafés. Giggling on trams with schoolbooks in their laps. On blankets under trees in parks. Holding each other's waists on corners and in front of shops. Walking down sidewalks hand in hand while you walk along behind them with the guy you sleep with. When the cobblestones gleam with rain you see them share the intimate and luminous temples of pink and blue and yellow and green and white umbrellas. They belong here. Of this place. Of this world. This is what Earl Bird was after. This is what your father meant. You just in it. Here for now. From some other place. From under the shroud of your own umbrella, ribbed and black, you try not to look at them, try not to feel like an undertaker when they glance your way.

If you can keep her.

Birmingham.

Magazines start showing up at the newsstand with their more seasoned stories of the bombing. Stories in English. American stories. At the picnic table leaves have started floating down through the cool dry October air. Over the next few days you get the picture. All Kennedy wants is to calm down all the marching and rioting because it's an international embarrassment to him. When King and other negro leaders beg him to send in federal troops to control the white retaliation, Kennedy resists, and sends a committee there instead. J. Edgar Hoover sends in the FBI but doesn't like negroes any more than the next night rider does. So nothing much changes. Cops, state troopers, firemen run rampant. In Newsweek you read an article called Case History of a Sick City. How its racial hate and violence and its racist population have been there since its birth as a coal and iron ore and steel town. How it has never pretended to be a Southern city. How defiance and resentment have always been its birthmark. Rootless in a place where roots grow deep. Without tradition in a land proud of its southern way of life. A city that has always been what it is now. A running sore on the powdered pure white skin of the South. An inbred place where little girls can be slaughtered on a Sunday morning. A city that has seen more than fifty bombings since the second World War. Where one negro neighborhood has been bombed so many times they call it Dynamite Hill.

Sometimes a leaf the color of rust or mustard floats down on what you're reading. You get the message. You're here. Here instead of Bombingham.

In the corner restaurant where you and Morgan eat a couple of nights a week, where the woman smoking at the bar brings your plates and takes you for granted like the regulars you've become, the radio plays like a fractured wind through the harsh and heavy voices coming from the kitchen.

You're conscious of the songs. Aware that they're love songs. Some in English. And then one night you listen to one that changes the way your bratwurst tastes. It's a ballad, slow, lazy, one you've heard without paying much attention to. You've come to know it mostly for the sudden melancholy rush of violins between the verses. This time you finally listen to the words. One line gets your attention.

Small town girls. We'd hide from the lights on the village green.

The song goes on. You stay behind. With Cissy in the dark cradle of Yenchik's Ford in the grove of a million shielding leaves. So dark you can't tell her skin from yours. Hide from the lights. On that one line she comes to you so instantaneous and fierce the smell of her hair floods your nostrils and makes the bratwurst in your mouth taste like coconut and chocolate.

"Are you listening?"

Across the table your permanent date is looking you over again. A dumpling the size of a cat's head rests in a big white bowl of oily yellow broth between his elbows. A quarter of it has been sliced away.

"Yeah."

"What did I just say?"

"That your knoedel tasted like it had sand in it."

"How do you do that?"

"Do what?"

"Look like you're a million miles away but still hear everything I say."

"That's what I was doing?"

"It's pretty amazing," he says. "How's your bratwurst?"

"It's good. Want some?"

"That's okay. I'll put up with this thing."

"You don't have to."

"Maybe I do. Just to remember not to order one again."

Sinatra sings it. The one time you paid Sinatra much attention was in high school auto shop when you and Quigley took Polk's truck for a joyride. You wore Polk's hat so you'd look like Polk, just out teaching Quigley how to drive his truck, but the hat made you look like Sinatra instead. Now his song becomes a refuge. Inside the song is your girl. Inside it are the lights you hide from. Sinatra doesn't say where. You make it Vienna. Sinatra doesn't give her a face. You give her Cissy's. Sinatra doesn't give her hair. You give her the lush black hair she washes in the kitchen sink. Inside the temple of the song you take her everywhere. Where she stands next to you at the back of the opera house with your elbows touching on the rail. Where she walks nested up against you under your umbrella and tells you she'd rather go hear some jazz somewhere. At night, at the end of your silent prayer, you say goodnight and watch her walk up the path to her house, turn around smiling in the porchlight and wave at you in the driver's seat of Yenchik's Ford, turn back and go inside.

Chapter 19

Back in May when a tank showed up in Birmingham to crush the riots after the cops and the Klan bombed the Gaston Motel and the house of Martin Luther King's brother. How for the first time Kennedy sent the Army into the South. Bill back at Idlewild calling it Operation Oak Tree. And then back in June when Kennedy called up the Alabama National Guard to escort two negro students through the door of the University of Alabama.

And you're here.

How you've thought about it. If Kennedy called up the Reserve and sent your Armored unit in. What you could do with a tank. Find out where and when the Klan meets. Crush every redneck car and truck around the place. Use the fifty caliber gun on the turret to cut down any cone-headed mouthbreather coming out to save his ride or thinking he could stop you with some peashooter rifle he hunts possum with. Show them what a real bomb can do. A few high explosive rounds. Roll the tank slow through the blazing carnage of the houses. Let it sink easy into the blazing graves of its basements and then give it the gas to come smoking, dripping with fire, climbing up the other side. Swing the cannon around when troopers and cops start showing up with their pistols blazing and the silly dings of their ricocheting bullets ringing off the turret. Flatten their squad cars. Crush their twirling roof lights like the embers of smoked-out cigarettes tossed to the asphalt and stepped on. A renegade tank they can't do a thing to stop till they bring their own tank in. And when they do you'd take it out because you're good. Seventh out of thirty thousand. You'd have the Zippo to prove it. You'd have time. Find where the next meeting is. Find where the bombers live and take down their inbred neighborhood. Then name it Tank Hill. You'd have time. Time to get enough rounds off for the neighborhood to earn the name.

"Remember back in June when they got those two negro students into the University of Alabama?"

At the tram stop, waiting for the tram that will take you in the direction of the outdoor afternoon string concert you're headed for, Morgan looks at you.

Here. Here where he can see you.

"Vaguely," he says. "Why?"

"Remember how Wallace blocked the door and President Kennedy used the National Guard to get them past him?"

"Who's Wallace?"

"The Governor of Alabama."

"I didn't know that part."

"Kennedy could call in the Reserve. That's me."

"You're on a mission."

With the soft heat of the September sunlight on your back you turn to look at the small red boxcars where they hang idle off the struts of the giant Ferris wheel.

"I know."

"You really need to stop reading what you're reading."

"It passes the time."

Instead of being called up, instead of rolling a rogue tank into a Klan neighborhood and wiping it off the sick face of this place called Birmingham, you and Morgan buy fragile collapsible campstools made out of canvas slings and wire frames that you can carry in Morgan's briefcase. That way you can sit instead of stand the three hours you spend waiting on the plaza of the Opera House for the ticket booth to open. Wozzeck. Turandot. The Barber of Seville. Carmen. And one night Rigoletto. The one you remember. Your father's favorite. In La Sal he used to play the big black double sided album on his portable record player. That night, in the stehparterre, while the final scene plays out, you imagine your father at the velvet rail with you instead of Morgan, standing to your left where you could turn and see the rough bliss in the quiet profile of his ridged face while a clown on the stage sings out his broken heart to his dying daughter. And then, too sudden for you to even think of holding back, tears crest your eyelids and run down your face for how much you miss him.

With summer gone, her letters have started to lose their soft unfocused summertime feel, their languid hide from the lights feel. In her letters she always shared with you the places she had been. A movie. A jazz club. The beach. A diner. She always wrote about you being there. So she was doing the same thing. Imagining you there out of her own longing. Giving you form in the refuge of her own imagination. Since starting her sophomore year and her job at the library again her letters have stepped back some and taken on more forward focus. Art History. Economics. English. Biology. Papers. Projects. Classes she can't invite you to attend because you're not a student there. A work study job you can't ask her to leave for the soft October rain of a Vienna afternoon.

In biology lab today we dissected rats. This Asian guy Mark who's my partner wouldn't touch it. It made him gag. He's really smart but he's a baby. I had to do everything myself. Did you ever dissect anything, Shake?

And now, coming home to your room after another day you feel you haven't earned the ending to, you read her latest letter and feel a new fear scuttle like a lone leaf across the floor of your stomach. That she's leaving you behind. Not on purpose. But because things that move leave things behind that don't. You remember the first time you tried to play along with one of Mr. Selby's albums. The way the band kept time. The way it couldn't stop and wait for you but had to keep moving while you fumbled for a note you'd lost. Like a train you'd fallen from. A train that kept pulling farther out of reach while you searched the gravel of the roadbed for your note. It wasn't the band. It was the tempo the song demanded. It isn't Cissy. Just her forward motion into autumn.

You remember the campus sidewalk where you held and memorized each other. If she uses it when she walks from class to class. If she remembers too.

If you can keep her.

Walking through the Stadtpark one fall day you hear what sounds like gypsy music off across the grass. Morgan follows it. A group of musicians dressed like people Shakespeare wrote about are playing mandolins and wooden flutes. Morgan takes a small flute out of his inside suit coat pocket and asks if he can join them. From a painted iron bench, in the stingy shade of a young tree that has shed half its leaves, you watch the guy you sleep with stand in the sun in his tired herringbone suit and lose himself in a shaft of polished wood he plays with his mouth and fingers. The songs they play are happy little things. Mothers gather round and listen with their children. You should be happy too. But you look away. And then, out of nowhere, you feel the crowded weight of this claustrophobic stone and statue city. Feel this reckless longing for the mouthpiece tucked in your Samsonite and the horn that goes with it. For your dirt stage high on the hill behind your house and the long hoarse distant whistle of the afternoon Union Pacific or Rio Grande from the marshland out across the valley. Summertime. You raise your trumpet. Feel its pipes and valves in your hands and its mouthpiece to your lips as you play off the whistle and send the full rich ringing notes like birds made of the shimmering sound of steel across the winter valley. My Funny Valentine. The words that were never meant for you. Maybe this time. Cissy. Wait. Stay little Valentine stay.

"I still need a reason to be here."

Morgan sits next to you in the sling of his collapsible campstool on the plaza of the Opera House. With the sun low you've been tracking the shadows of the buildings to the west as they extend across the plaza. Early in October the air is calm but losing any warmth it held. A color like tea stains the clear blue of the sky. People waiting like you for the ticket booth to open are strung out ahead of you and behind you. Some stand. Others have stools like yours. Some have bags of food and drink from bottles. You've got a copy of Newsweek. Morgan a book of poems by Goethe. He's already made small talk with two women ahead of you and the couple behind you. You heard Missionare. So you're on the clock. Working. He uses a finger to mark the place where you interrupted him.

"To be here?" he says. "You mean at the opera?"

"Here. Austria. Vienna. Yeah. The opera."

"What are you saying?"

"I'm saying what I'm saying."

He glances at the rolled up Newsweek in your hand.

"I still don't think what you're reading is good for you."

You look down to keep him from seeing a flash of anger light your eyes on fire.

"What's not good for me is not doing what I came here for."

Morgan closes his book. Stands up and stretches. You stand up too. He looks at the roof of the Opera House and then at you. In the weak sunlight the sadness and curiosity in his face are flat. A teacher, tired of you, but still attentive.

"I know I'm not supposed to complain," you say.

"You mean your mission."

"This . . . this tourist thing."

"Tourist thing," he says, intent on your face.

"Tell me again," you say, "how this is your mission."

"This is my mission," he says.

You look into the face of the guy with his first date still ahead of him. The guy with his first pair of sneakers out there too.

"There's only one mission my family cares about," you say.

"Yes?"

"It's not yours."

"I didn't think you could be cruel," he finally says.

You look off across the plaza.

"I've never felt more useless."

"Useless," he says.

"There's this jazz professor at the U. Professor Fisher. You know what he offered me at the end of spring quarter?"

"Tell me."

"A summer in Los Angeles as a studio musician."

"I'm sorry. I don't know what that is."

"Someone who does recording sessions with famous jazz musicians. Plays with them on their albums."

"Are you saying you regret your choice?"

You look off again and watch the wind pick up and skate a scrap of paper a few feet across the plaza.

"Here's another one," you say. You look back at him. "I ran into these two guys back at Idlewild Airport. Jerry and Bill. From Ohio. You know where they were headed?"

"Tell me."

"Mississippi. Driving an old Volkswagen bus from New York down to Jackson. You know why?"

"I'm sure you'll tell me."

"To help negroes fight for their rights. Sit at lunch counters with them. Ride buses with them. Get beat up. Knock on doors in negro neighborhoods. Help them register to vote."

"That's not our calling."

You look away again. Two pigeons follow an old woman across the plaza. They stop when she crosses out of the sunlight into shade. You look back at Morgan.

"The knocking on doors part is."

His face goes hard. "Not for the same reason," he finally says.

"I could help them get registered for the priesthood."

"I won't have you talk like that," he says.

You glance down at the canvas slings of your empty campstools. What the two of you look like sitting there in your suits and ties.

"I'm sorry. The guys I met at the airport. They're doing something real. That's all I'm saying."

"Is that what you'd rather be doing?"

"You call what we're doing real?"

"What do you think is real? Tracting? Is that what this is about?"

"I know you have a hard time with it. I'll do all the talking. All you have to do is come along."

"That wouldn't be right."

"I need a reason to be here."

"I told you. You'll find one."

"I need one now," you say. Then you say, "Or I might as well go home."

"Are you threatening me?"

"Somewhere else. Wherever I can feel like what I'm doing is real."

"What about your father?"

"I'll tell him I saw his favorite opera."

And then you're staring each other down. With the sun on his face you can see the torn membranes in the hazel pupils of his eyes. The way a dying zit has spawned the white point of a new zit.

"You can't go home," he says.

"I need a reason not to."

"You want to go tracting. Fine, then. We'll go tracting. We'll start tomorrow."

"You're serious," you finally say.

"Yes. I am. Why wouldn't I be?"

"Okay. Okay. Good."

"Just figure out where we need to start."

"I already know."

"Is that it?"

"Yes."

"Good. Tonight let's just enjoy Tosca."

Chapter 20

AND SO, three months and change into your mission, Morgan takes you tracting. Where you stand in lobbies and check the names in the tracting book against the names on the mailboxes. In the dim dank hallways lit by small caged bulbs the doors are set deep into flaking walls. Wir sind zwei Missionare der Kirche Jesu Christi der Heiligen der Letzten Tage. Wir moechten mit Ihnen sprechen. We'd like to speak with you. You rarely make it that far. Keine Zeit. No time. When the doors have peepholes you stand there smiling like you're being photographed. Nicht interessiert. Not interested. Sometimes nothing but footsteps coming your way, pausing, then turning around and going the other way. Sometimes at your knock a set of locks along the pockmarked edge of the door will successively clack open and the door itself will crack and the weathered strip of an old face with a single eye will appear. A single crazy eye that darts like a lizard back and forth between Morgan's face and yours. Most times you're talking through a battered door. Missionare. You get to add your own columns, your own dates, write in your own R for reject into the tracting book again.

In two to sometimes three hours every morning Morgan's done. And if Morgan's done then so are you. You don't care. You're doing what you're here for. You start to talk to God again. Come out of hiding when you write your father. And Cissy. Like she wrote. Time flies. Your own momentum now. You can start to catch up to her. She can count the doors.

"Okay. That's that."

Looking up and down the street. Shielding his eyes and squinting in sunlight this sudden after six floors of windowless hallways. The gray strain in Morgan's tortured and dusty face.

"One more building," you say.

"I don't know."

"I'll do all the talking."

"Okay. You're right. But we'll take turns."

You leave the rest of the day to him. It's his mission. You'll take what he's giving you. It's enough to keep the burning in your bosom going. Enough to come home at night and start to feel what it must be like to have earned the day. Enough to have the right to ask God to turn his back and give you the minute of solitude you need for what you do in the bathhouse. Enough to ask your father how your mother's treating Molly. To keep reading the papers and magazines that keep you caught up, that let you keep turning your longing into vigilance, that let you know what might come her way so you'll be there if she needs you. Freedom Day in Selma where the Birmingham bombing mobilizes hundreds of negro men and women to brave the Governor's state troopers and the mouth-breathers of the Klan in the fight to register to vote. The traveling Free Southern Theater. The outbreak of Freedom Schools. The harvest coming in. The movement bringing in the harvest all across the South. Thank God Almighty. You working the field too. Like you were called to do. So you can say it too. Thank God Almighty.

The second Sunday in October, during the break after Priesthood Meeting, the news goes around the back of the chapel. The new mission president is coming to Sacrament Meeting. Walter Lindner. All the missionaries are talking. Asking the same questions. Saying the same things. You stand around in air that carries the minted welter of raw aftershave and mouthwash and listen. You think back to last Sunday when President Smith gave his farewell speech. It was the first and last time you would see him. He was headed back to Utah after three years here. Tall, thin, gentle, dignified, a horseshoe of white hair around the back of his head, you looked at him and thought ambassador. He spoke German. Most of his speech was stories. Stories about missionaries. From the way soft laughter kept breaking out you could tell that there were missionaries in the congregation who either recognized the stories or had been in them. You listened but knew you didn't belong to what was going on. President Lindner is your second shot. He's new. The shot you have with him is the same shot every other missionary has.

Word has gone around Austria. The chapel is packed by the time Sunday School starts. Metal folding chairs are set up on the open floor behind the benches. The widows are busy with people they probably rarely see. In the break after Sunday School you hang out in back with a couple of elders.

"I heard he's German."

"From fuzzin' Germany?"

The word still throws you for how it starts out like the real thing and then corrects itself in midair.

"No. Utah. He came over from Germany when he was young."

"He have a German accent?"

You think of your father's accent. "I say he does," you say.

"How much to say he doesn't?" says the one named Sorenson.

"I don't know. A schilling."

"You're on."

"I heard he's a carpenter."

"A retired one."

"So he built houses?"

"I guess. Stairs and furniture and cabinets and stuff."

"I heard he's short. Built though. Like a bulldog."

Across the chapel you see one of the elders you met at the Mission Home your first day here. Gerhardt. Dark blond where he's not bald. Thick hairy wrists and forearms like you keep hoping for. He carries a gray metal stand up the side aisle and sets it on the floor below the pulpit and leaves. A minute later, he's back, carrying a beige machine the size of a small suitcase. You recognize the big Tandberg tape recorder from the conference room back in the Mission Home. So this is what it's used for. Waiting for Morgan that afternoon you wanted to plug it in. Light up the dials. Bring it alive. Use the microphone to make the needles jump. There was no tape. Nothing would have been recorded.

"What about you, Elder Tauffler?"

Your name brings you back to the two guys you've been talking to.

"What?"

"There's a transfer comin' up," says Sorenson.

"When?"

"This month maybe. Couple or three weeks. Got someplace in mind you'd like to go?"

"Vienna's all I know."

"I'm hoping for Innsbruck. Good place to spend the winter. Ski bunnies everywhere."

"I'm hoping for Salzburg," Heywood says. "I went there on a field trip in high school."

Through his Buddy Holly glasses his pale eyes look at you for the response you figure he's used to getting. A field trip? All the way to Austria? Wow. We were lucky to get taken to an apricot orchard. You turn back to Sorenson.

"Who decides?" you ask.

"I guess the Mission Home," says Sorenson. "Guys like Cannon. For us it's just wait till the envelope shows up. A day later you're on a train for a rathole like Linz."

The organist starts off the prelude for Sacrament Meeting watching her rearview mirror. Voices fall off. Gerhardt finds an outlet, turns the Tandberg on, takes a roll of tape and lashes the Tandberg microphone to the gooseneck of the microphone on the pulpit. He opens a wooden folding chair and sets it next to the big machine. Then sits down, facing the congregation, a soldier guarding something nobody plans to steal.

When he comes into the chapel it's with the bishop and first counselor and two other Austrian men and Elder Cannon. He's about your father's height and build. His hair is full, flowing, sculpted white waves that gleam like dunes of snow polished with ice. Under his arched white eyebrows his eyes have the furious look of a hawk's. In the big-chested cleavage of his black suit his shirt is this brilliant white plumage split by a dark tie.

They reach the podium. Show the president his chair. Defer to him with this obedient adoration. You watch him acknowledge them the way you've watched men acknowledge your father. Like he has their worship coming. A carpenter, you want to tell them, just an old carpenter, the way you always wanted to tell your father that Earl Bird was just a hairdresser, Bishop Wacker just a football coach. A retired carpenter. A guy who swung a hammer and used his teeth to hold nails. You put him in coveralls. Put him in a kitchen where he stands there listening to some housewife tell him how she wants her cabinets done. A carpenter with his hair and ears and nostrils full of sawdust. And then you feel like crap for what you're thinking. Cheap for what you're feeling.

The meeting moves through the opening hymn, the invocation, the announcements, the sacrament hymn, the bread and water. His eyes rove back and forth across the congregation with this placid effort at tolerance for the people out in front of him. Below him, on the floor below the pulpit, Gerhardt looks straight ahead. The bishop gives the president a long and reverent introduction. The president scowls at him as they pass each other on the stand. He takes the pulpit in both his carpenter hands like he's testing the strength of the wood it's made of. He looks out across the congregation. Gerhardt turns the Tandberg on, watches the dials, while you wait to see if you'll be a schilling richer.

CHAPTER 21

IT ISN'T LONG before you see what tracting does to Morgan. Not climbing stairs. Not his knuckles. You're doing most of the knocking. But the way his face has gone grim and gray when you're out working. The way he stoops and holds the banisters going up the stairs. Sometimes a harsh Keine Zeit barked through a closed door will make him stand there staring blind at nothing long after you note the reject. Sometimes a watery old bloodshot eye in the crack of a door will leave him standing there bewildered long after the door's slammed shut and the locks ratcheted back into place. Once he stands there lost so long an angry shout comes through the door. Go away! Before I call the police! It isn't long before two and sometimes three hours fall off to less than two and sometimes one. And then, toward the end of October, the morning comes when you see him across the room, at the desk, looking through a stack of sheet music. You stop ironing your shirt and set your travel iron on the towel covering the desk.

"What's going on?"

He turns his head your way.

"Just looking for some pieces."

"Now?"

"Yes. Now. Why?"

You've seen it coming. That last hour. The hour that still gave you enough to talk to God. Letting it go. What you didn't see coming was what it would feel like.

"We're not going tracting," you say.

He lowers his head. Gets up from the chair. He's wearing his shirt and tie and socks for the day but not his pants and shoes. The legs of his garments hang loose and baggy to his knees. He starts to cross the room. Stops and turns toward his armchair. Looks up at the dull dark portrait of the young soldier on the wall. Then turns your way.

"I just . . . I can't do this," he says. You watch his mouth fish for words again like words are insects hovering in the air. "I'm sorry," he says. "I just can't."

"You mean tracting."

"I don't know how to sell things. I just don't. I'm not a salesman."

"You're a missionary. Not a salesman."

"I feel like a salesman. A really horrible one." Then he says, "All I want to do is apologize to people for bothering them."

He looks to the side. Narrows his eyes like the sun's there, bright and burning, instead of a wall in the shadow of the room.

"What about all the people you talk to when we're out somewhere?"

"That's different. I tell them what I'm doing here. If they want to know more, they can ask." Then he says, "I'm not at their door like someone from Avon."

"We're not selling lipstick."

"No. I know. It's just too hard to hear no all the time."

"It's not because of you."

"I wish I could feel that way."

That last hour. Letting go of the last shred of a reason. What you didn't see coming was the way it would make you frantic.

"I could do the tracting on my own," you say. "You could just wait in the lobby. Just an hour."

"You know you can't do that."

"Then maybe you could wait down the hall."

"That wouldn't be right."

"It'd be fine with me. If someone let us in I could signal you."

"That's like an ambush."

"Maybe there's a way you could play for them. That's not selling anything."

"How would we get a piano around? Up and down stairs?"

"No. I mean that flute you played in the park."

"It's called a recorder."

"Right."

"What about your trumpet?"

It stops you cold. That shimmering sound running the length of a half-dark hallway. The insane ricochet of trapped notes off the walls. Old men would come charging out of their doors with bayonets and rifles from the war.

"I left it home. I told you."

"I'm sorry." He looks at you. "I have to say no."

"Just a building. One building a day."

This tired gray sadness takes the muscle and bone out of his face.

"Please," you say.

He breaks off, takes a couple of steps that go nowhere, stops with his face toward the window.

"I know I haven't done right by you. I'm sorry." He turns to you. "If you'd like, I can talk to Elder Cannon about getting you another senior."

You look away. While he learned piano he must have heard kids playing in the street. Kids he could have had for friends. You look down at the ironed front panel of your shirt. You'll be going back to the picnic table. Brushing the dead leaves off. Losing what you've earned. This frenzy of defeat and anger ripples and flickers through the muscles in your chest like heat lightning deep inside a dry overcast you could see from the rim of the sandpit that had made its way across the desert.

"No. It's okay. I'm fine." Then you say, "I didn't mean to make you feel bad."

CHAPTER 22

ON A BRIGHT AFTERNOON in late October Morgan finally gets his chance to play the main organ with its four keyboards and hundred registers and ten thousand pipes in the mother cathedral of Austria. Stephansdom. He's been practicing at the churchhouse while you sat outside and read and waited. Everything he wants to play is memorized. He doesn't need the music. Your first time there you thought of the Church of the Devil. The Great Whore of the Earth. How maybe you shouldn't have come inside. It crosses your mind again as you stand inside the vast soaring space of the cathedral and Morgan goes looking for his organist friend. When he brings him back to meet you his friend shakes your hand but doesn't let you upstairs with them. Morgan seems to be okay with leaving you. You let go of the rule that says not to let each other out of sight.

"Then I'll stay down here," you say.

"Okay. Don't leave the cathedral."

It takes a while before you hear anything. You figure the organist is showing him the ropes. The pipes finally send their hoarse notes rolling across the chambers of the high vaulted ceiling of the cathedral. You recognize the tune. The steady hypnotic lifting and falling throb in the left hand. Brahms. Herzlich Tut Mich Verlangen. My Heart Is Filled with Longing. The haunting cry of the melody. Of all the organ pieces Morgan plays it's your favorite. You can barely see him, and so you imagine him, his back hunched over the keyboards, dwarfed in his round-shouldered herringbone suit by the arsenal of silver pipes at his fingertips. While he plays you wander around the floor of the cathedral. It takes your breath the way it did the first time you were here. Arranged along the side walls are broad shouldered standing wooden cabinets that Morgan told you were confession booths. They look like dark elaborately carved phone booths for a time when there were no phones and maybe not even glass. You decide to check one out. A narrow central closet with a window curtained by purple velvet stands between the dark bookends of two side booths with narrow doors. You choose the door to the booth on the right. The rising cry of the organ as Morgan takes the steady cadence of the prelude toward its climax is suddenly muted as you step inside and close the door behind you.

With the music goes any hope for light. You should have taken time to look around while the door was open. Your knee hits the hard wood of a small bench. Your shoe kicks up against a small shelf on the floor and almost pitches you off balance. You feel for the bench and sit down and look into almost perfect dark. Light shows in thin faint lines around the door of the booth. The air has the stale shoe polish smell of old wood like the air in Mr. Hinkle's store. There's also perfume, heavy and sweet and laced with the smell of armpit sweat. You reach your hand out in front of you. In the dark the wall is so close you think of a coffin lid. Muted voices come from somewhere. Two voices too soft to understand except as a conversation. You wonder where they're coming from. They stop. The cabinet creaks as it moves with some shift in weight. In the dark a door closes. Then the more immediate sound of wood sliding through wood comes from the wall at your shoulder. Faint light comes through a lattice. You can only see pinpoints of presence and motion through it. You catch on. Whatever happens in a confession booth is about to happen to you.

"Gelobt sei Jesus Christus."

Praised be Jesus Christ. The voice that comes through the lattice is gentle, patient, weary. From the voice you imagine a creased forehead, crinkled eyelids, the soft skin of a fleshy lower face, Bishop Byrne's huge paint-spattered hands on the armrests of his chair back home. This time the voice is meant for you. A priest. An Austrian priest. A Catholic priest in the house of the Great Whore. Praised be Jesus Christ. He says it once. And then goes silent. If he's waiting for you. What you're supposed to say back to him.

You don't know. And so you say, "Gelobt sei Jesus Christus."

And then you stare into the dark and wait.

"Nein," he finally says. "In Ewigkeit. Amen."

No. In eternity. Amen.

"In Ewigkeit. Amen. Sorry."

Sorry. Stupid. You sit and wait again in the dark while Morgan fires the pipes through the climax and starts to bring the prelude home again.

"You can kneel if you feel more comfortable. And we can hear each other better. There's a place to kneel below the window."

His English surprises you. And how he knew you were sitting. You move to your knees on the small shelf. With your face against the lattice there's enough light to see that it's carved from a single slab of wood. Through the small holes, like pieces of a jigsaw puzzle, you can see part of his ear and the polished red skin of his shaved cheek.

"Do you have something to confess?" he says.

"I don't know."

"How old are you?" he asks.

If God has given him the power to see everything. If there's a trick mirror somewhere that lets him look inside your closet. What he knows just from your voice. And so you tell him.

"Forty."

"I forgive you for telling me a lie," he says. "But remember that you are confessing to God. I am just his representative."

Your face goes hot.

"Nineteen."

"Amerikaner?"

"Yes."

"And what are you doing so young and so far from home?"

"Just on vacation."

"By yourself?"

You think of Morgan, high in the back of the cathedral, playing out his dream. How you could ruin it for him if you told the priest who the organ player was.

"Yes."

"I forgive you again, my son. But you must try to be truthful."

"I'm sorry."

"So tell me what you would like to confess to God today."

Not to God because God already knows it all. But to a Catholic priest in whose gentle way you remember Bishop Byrne. You panic. Run through the possibilities. They flash across your mind and fill the dark booth with their changing light. About being in love with Cissy but not about how her naked skin looked next to yours in a borrowed 40 Ford in a grove of trees on a summer night in San Jose. About the dusk ride on a Ferris wheel where the high leaves were black against the red sky of the sunset on your first date to the State Fair but not about your ride that night across the desert after your mother called you the indelible name of a beast that fucks while you heard the keystrokes of your father's typewriter from the basement hesitate and wait. About the parking lot and State Street fights but not about the kid who got his fingers crushed in the rings of his brass knuckles. About all the girls who let you slip a hand inside their bras and up inside their thighs but not about smelling Katy's perfumed pubic hair the night before your mission farewell. About taking care of Mrs. Harding's yard but not about her maid Lupe bringing you lemonade that would sparkle in the captured sunlight. About being the seventh soldier to score a hundred on the tanker test but not about your father throwing out the Zippo they awarded you. About being baptized for nineteen dead men but not about Yenchik peeing in the water of the font. About buying your trumpet from Mr. Hinkle but not about lying to him when you tried to get a refund. About the lady in the red dress at the Indigo who gave you a stained glass nightstand lamp out of everything she owned but not about your mother telling Molly it was the lamp a whore would have. About the faceless man in the dark suit who always haunted you but not about the Stetson he bought in Elko or the way he smelled while fire burned him away to smoke in the passenger seat. About your father looking forward to your first baptism but not about being here to harvest Austria in your grandfather's shoes. If the priest knows all of this already too. If God can show him what you're thinking. He's already caught you in two lies. If you have to outrun thinking, outrun the names of everything the way you had to when you were a kid, so that not even God could find you.

The organ pipes go quiet as Morgan ends the prelude and prepares the organ for his next piece. And in the echoes of footsteps and hushed but brittle voices you can hear from the stone cliffs of the cathedral again, in the dead air of this dark booth the size of your grandfather's coffin, you remember the one confession that immediately ends most any conversation. The one confession that will set you free. Let you off your knees and out the door.

"I'm a missionary," you finally say.

"Oh," he says. "But not Catholic."

"No."

"Is that what you're here to confess?"

How you're more of a tourist than a missionary. How your father keeps waiting for the news of your first baptism. How you have to lie to him about how you spend your time. How you have to match your weekly report to Morgan's inventive ways of coming up with hours worked.

"I don't know."

"Being a missionary isn't a sin."

How you don't know why you're here if you're not here to knock on doors. How you could be in Mississippi.

"I know."

"You're still a child of God."

"I know."

"So what do you really wish to confess today?"

How nervous you and your buddies were about the big question when you faced your annual interviews with Bishop Byrne and then Wacker. If you'd molested yourself. How you always had to lie and hope you could get away with it. How Bishop Byrne rarely asked, and if he did, left you a way to slip out of answering. How Wacker always came right out with it. Have you played with yourself. Like you didn't count for anything. So it was easy to look him in the face and lie to him. Now, on your knees in this booth this far from home, you wonder what it would be like to tell the truth for once. If it would lift the long shame. The guilty overcast of that iron sky. If this priest in his gentle way can forgive you. If he'll condemn you to hell. You could be gone in a flash out the small door if he did. Wearing the dress priests wear he couldn't run fast enough to catch you. He wouldn't even know what you looked like.

The high cries of the organ pipes fill the vast cavern of the cathedral with the reeling of a thousand shrieking birds. Both of you have been drawn toward the lattice that separates you just to hear each other. You're close enough now that if they took away the lattice you could stick your tongue into his ear. What you'll say. What you'll call it. Jacking off sounds sacrilegious even in a Catholic church.

"I masturbate."

"Ah. Masturbieren."

Almost the same word. Through the holes in the lattice you watch quick tiny ripples move through the muscles under the red skin of his cheek.

"Yes."

"Well," he says, "at least you've brought me a real sin."

A sin that nobody has ever persuaded you to confess. Not Bishop Byrne or Bishop Wacker. On your knees in the dark you feel naked.

"Okay."

"Tell me more," he says.

"Like what?"

"I don't know. How often?"

"Once a week."

"Once a week? When and where?"

How you've started shivering. How you'll get dressed again in a booth this tight. How you'll even find the leg holes of your garments in this almost pitch black dark.

"When I go to the bathhouse," you finally say.

"In Vienna?"

"Yes."

"Not in the open, I hope."

"No."

"Then where?"

"A private bath."

"I'm relieved," says the priest. "There are bad men in bathhouses."

"I heard."

"Have you examined your conscience?"

You lower your eyes to the recess where your bare knees stand in the dark on the small hard wooden bench where people kneel.

"Yes."

"Are you truly sorry?"

"Yes."

"I can hear that you are. But can you apologize to God?"

"I tell him every time I do it that I'm sorry."

"I mean now. I'm his representative. He'll hear you through me."

"I'm sorry."

"Can you promise him that you'll stop this grave sin?"

"I keep breaking it."

"Is it something you want to stop?"

The music from the organ calms and comes slow and soft now from the pipes. Different voices, some harmonic, some dissonant, enter and start threading their way through the song in the first few measures. And so it takes a minute but you recognize the core melody. Come Come Ye Saints. The hymn the pioneers sang while they crossed the Great Plains and the Rockies with their handcarts and covered wagons, while they endured tribulation, while they fought off Indians, while they buried babies and wives and husbands along the way, while they kept each other going, escaping persecution for the place far in the west where they could settle in peace. Come come ye saints, no toil nor labor fear, but with joy wend your way. The lines that thread through the song become increasingly dissonant. In their dissonance they become human. You hear gnawing doubt. You hear aching fear. You hear anguish. You hear irreversible madness. You hear inconsolable grief. You hear desperation. You hear hunger and thirst. The savagery of weather. A mother being pulled away from the crossed sticks and the mound of rocks and the bouquet of sagebrush that mark her child's fresh grave. And should we die before our journey's through, happy day, all is well. We then are free from toil and sorrow too, with the just we shall dwell. You've sung this song. You've belted it out with your congregation. Everyone the same. You've never heard individual voices pulled out of its melody. Never heard the song this nakedly human. The dissonance of emotion. How in the dissonance of their individual voices the pioneers become real. How maybe a guy like you, a pioneer your age, would sneak away from his wagon at night sometimes to jack off in the sagebrush.

"Son?"

In the dark coffin of your booth the single word comes soft through the lattice at your face. And it's not till then that you realize you just heard a Mormon hymn in a Catholic cathedral.

"I'm sorry."

"You were listening," he says. Then he says, "So was I. A beautiful terrible piece."

"Yes."

"I asked if this was something you wanted to stop."

Morgan's arrangement still has you astonished.

"Yes."

"Do you think you can?"

"I don't know."

How you're crying. How you don't know when you started. In the silence while Morgan prepares the organ for his next piece you can feel tears cut paths down the skin of your cheeks. Feel the ache in your throat.

"Is this why you came to me?"

"I didn't know you'd be here."

"Well, now that I'm here, how would you like me to help you?"

"Help me stop?"

"Keep your thoughts clean. Keep God with you. As a missionary you know that. Don't let Satan draw you into temptation. Understand that you have a higher purpose than gratifying the unholy urges of your body. Look at women as children of God and not objects of carnal desire."

"Is that how you do it?"

In the long silence your face goes hot with shame.

"I'm sorry."

"I'm . . . verwirrt," he finally says. "I can't think of the word."

"Confused?"

"Confused. Yes. You're not Catholic. And yet you come to a Catholic priest to ask to be forgiven for the mortal sin of self gratification."

How to tell him you didn't mean to come to him. How you just stumbled into this.

"I can't give you the penance and forgiveness that Catholicism offers."

"I understand."

"I can't tell you to say the rosary and then receive the Eucharist. Those are meaningless to you."

"I understand."

"Don't you have your own God? Doesn't your faith offer a pathway to penance?"

If you confessed it to Morgan. Who did it too. If you confessed it to Elder Cannon. If the pathway to penance would lead from there to the punishment of a plane ride home.

"Yes."

"Then all I can tell you is this. Gehe hin und suendige nicht mehr. Do you understand that?"

"Go my way and sin no more?"

"Yes. I forgive you."

"Thank you."

And inches from your face he draws down the wooden blind that turns the lattice black again. For the minute you stay there on your knees, unable to move, you hear the blind slide up on the other side of the booth. Hear him say Gelobt sei Jesus Christus. Hear a voice answer. In Ewigkeit. Amen. You get off your knees and turn and find the door and step out squinting into the diffusion of daylight, tinted like tea where it comes through the stained glass windows that flank the altar, of the vast vaulted interior of the cathedral. You leave the booth door open for an old woman waiting there and walk away. Every line, every statue, every stone, every painting, every arch that reaches bold as a cliff for the chambered sky of the ceiling is sharply drawn. The echo of every whisper and murmur and footstep is crisp. The rack of silver pipes high in the rear wall is quiet. Morgan must be looking for you. You wipe your eyes and cheeks. You inhale the clear air while you walk. Forgiven. So this is what it feels like. You remember riding with Porter and Snook coming home on one or another highway after a night out. The rush of asphalt or concrete in the headlights. In the dark behind you all the unforgiven things. All the nameless sins just out of reach in the dark mystery deep in the back of your head. All the things you were moving too fast to be forgiven for. You suddenly regret leaving the booth after only confessing one of them. It was the only one whose name you knew. Masturbation. You want to go back now. Name the rest of them. Wait for the old woman. The priest could help you name them. And then forgive you for them one by one. But it's too late. From the front of the cathedral you look back toward the rear. You see Morgan talking to the organist behind the rows of benches near the giant doors. How light can taste, you think. How sound can fly. How your trumpet would sound inside this place.

"Where were you?"

Coming out of the cathedral into the blazing white sunlight off the plaza.

"Just wandering around."

"What did you think?"

"What you played?"

"Yes."

"Come Come Ye Saints. Is that your arrangement?"

"Why?"

"Is it?"

"Did you like it?"

"I could hear their voices. The pioneers."

"Is that a yes?"

"Yes."

"You really liked it?"

"It was incredible."

"I wrote it back home. I wanted to play it in church. They wouldn't let me. They said it was too creative." Then he says, "So you liked it."

Like the first time you were here, you look away, out across the plaza where people are sitting, strolling, posing for photos, taking in the October sunlight and its uncertain almost false warmth. The missing. His mission. You let go of what it takes to wear your grandfather's shoes while your father waits for your first baptism. Let go of what it takes to have Cissy want to count your make believe doors for you. On Sunday, with God watching, you'll be expected to write this hour down as time spent with investigators, and you'll let go of what it takes to justify the hour by having told a priest you'd never recognize on the street or in the stehparterre of the Opera House that you were a missionary. Let go of what it takes to feel forgiven for every time you've masturbated. Let go of what it takes to hear in Morgan's voice your own appetite to be told how well you play. So you liked it. Let go. Let the wind catch it like a kite whose string burns a line in your skin as it sings loose through your hand.

"Yeah." Looking back at his waiting face. "I didn't know you could do that."

CHAPTER 23

THE MORNING of the bombing a negro girl has breakfast with her father. Bacon and eggs and coffee. After breakfast he drives her to the 16th Street Baptist Church where he drops her off.

You go on in, honey. I'm going to get some gas and I'll be back in a minute.

A minute later, at a gas station two blocks from the church, he stands by his car watching an attendant fill the tank when the morning explodes. Rocks and glass clatter down the street and rattle through the trees. He hears screams. He leaves his car and runs. People are pouring out of the church into the cold street when he gets there. Women and children are shrieking in the debris. Men are shouting. A girl named Sarah Collins staggers blind out of the hole the explosion opened in the wall of the church, blood pouring from her face, her arms stretched out in front of her sightless eyes, her screaming incoherent, while you sit there reading in the terrifying calm of this decomposing picnic table in the back yard.

At the end of October word comes down the mission grapevine about a new approach to getting into people's doors. The city's newer and younger neighborhoods are these tall vast apartment complexes where young families live. Families with little kids. You've got a couple of them in your tracting area. The approach is this. You put together some games and songs. Then hit a playground, gather up the kids, play some games, sing some songs. Become their friends. Their American friends. Learn their first names. When you're done, ask for their last names too, because you'd like to come back later on and play some more, meet their parents. You and Morgan talk it over one night at the corner restaurant.

"This is from the Church?"

"They call it Primary," says Morgan. "You can't get more Church than that."

Primary. The name's as familiar to you as toothpaste, soap, anything you grew up with. Going to the churchhouse every Wednesday when you were kids yourselves to spend a couple of hours making things out of colored paper, playing games, listening to some religious story, singing

Jesus Wants Me for a Sunbeam. Where Molly learned how to make paper angels for the Christmas tree and then taught Maggie how.

"You want to try it?" Morgan says.

"I'm game for anything."

"How do we gather up these kids?"

Morgan looks at you surprised.

"Gosh. They didn't say. I guess we'll just start with some songs and see what happens."

"Do we wear suits or street clothes?"

"I think suits," he says. "After we're done with the kids we could find a gasthaus. Give them time to go home and eat and get their homework done."

"It feels bad."

"I know."

"Like we're fooling the kids. Using them against their parents."

"You know the answer to that, don't you?"

"It's the Lord's work?"

"That's right, Elder."

"I guess kids can be his instruments too."

"We don't have to do it."

"So do you know any games?"

"I was never a kid," says Morgan. "Don't you know any?"

"Not in German."

"Let's just do songs. This first time."

"You know any?"

"We can find some. I could play my recorder and you could sing."

"I think we should stay away from church songs."

"Of course."

"I know one," you say. "About turning a frowning face upside down."

"I think I remember it."

"I just need German lyrics. Paper and crayons so kids can do their own faces."

You use a marker to draw a simple reversible face on a square of yellow cardboard, a face that frowns when you hold it right side up, then smiles when you turn it over. You buy construction paper and crayons. Morgan gets some songs from a music store. You stake out a playground. In the half hour after Sunday School one of the widows helps you translate the frowning face song into German. You make your move on a windy October afternoon. The playground is a clamoring jumbling chaos of kids in coats and jackets playing on slides and swings and jungle gyms and toy horses mounted on car springs and rotating platforms like lazy Susans big enough to ride. The dry rags of dead leaves dance wild at the ends of their stems while the wind tries to break their hold on the thin branches of young trees. Two mothers in plain scarves look your way from a green bench across the hard sand floor of the playground. You stay on the wide concrete path back off the playground. Morgan starts to play. The notes are hoarse torn whistles on the wind. His hair floats out and whips around his head. It starts out slow, halting, just a few kids coming over, their little faces curious. The mothers across the playground look skeptical and alert. They're right. In your suits, one of you with a briefcase and the other with a two-foot flute, you've got a lot to prove. One, two, three at a time, other kids stop swinging and chasing around, drop out of the jungle gyms, come down the slides, stumble off the turning platforms, dismount the toy horses, bunch up in front of you. One of them breaks the ice.

"Bruder Jakob! Spielen Sie Bruder Jakob!"

Play Brother Jacob. Are you sleeping. Are you sleeping. You grin and wink at the godsend of a dark-haired kid in a brown cloth jacket who calls for a song you know. The German version of Frere Jacques. You look at Morgan. He nods. You raise your arms. Feel the wind whip up your back. A couple of kids jump the gun. You give them time to recover. Maurice Abravenel, you're thinking, conductor of the Utah Symphony five and a half thousand miles away, the way he sweeps his hands. Morgan hits the opening note and the playground slowly explodes as the kids catch the contagious little song.

Bruder Jakob! Bruder Jakob!

Schlafst du noch? Schlafst du noch?

Horst du nicht die Glocken! Horst du nicht die Glocken!

Ding dang dong! Ding dang dong!

Are you sleeping, are you sleeping, Brother John? Brother John? Morning bells are ringing! Morning bells are ringing! Ding ding dong! They take it through again, their faces turned up, their eyes on you and Morgan, some of them singing to each other now, face to face, the song this screaming match between them. You keep conducting. When they get to the end again you stop conducting and raise your hands. When you've got their quiet attention you start marching in place in front of them. You don't need to look at the mothers to feel stupid. This young undertaker. Morgan gets the cue. Starts marching in place himself and playing.

"Eins! Zwei! Polizei!" you holler. One! Two! Police!

You use your hands to beckon them to start marching and sing along.

"Eins! Zwei! Polizei!" some of the bolder and quicker kids repeat.

"Drei! Vier! Offizier!" you holler, marching harder. Three! Four! Officer!

"Drei! Vier! Offizier!" And now, marching, mouths wide open, eyes on you, they've all got it.

"Funf! Sechs! Alte Hex!" Five Six! Old witch!

"Funf! Sechs! Alte Hex!"

"Sieben! Acht! Gute Nacht!" Seven! Eight! Good night!

"Sieben! Acht! Gute Nacht!"

"Neun! Zehn! Auf Wiedersehen!" Nine! Ten! See you again!

"Neun! Zehn! Auf Wiedersehen!"

Morgan plays a little turnaround and ends it. The kids won't have it.

"Nochmal! Nochmal!" they shriek. Again! Again!

"Eins! Zwei! Polizei!"

The mothers on the bench are wearing smiles now. And so you take your improvised choir through the song again. This time you throw a couple of jumps and twirls in with the marching. The kids follow you, bumping off each other, stumbling and shrieking. And then a song called Gruen Sind Alle Meine Kleider. And then one called Gretel Pastetel. And then Hopp Hopp Hopp! Der Sandmann Ist Da! Der Kuckuck und der Esel. Hansel und Gretel. The kids sing along in shrill sometimes shrieking voices while Morgan's fingers dance up and down the wooden spine of the flute. You think of the Pied Piper. He shoots a periodic glance in your direction. With his mouth around the thick knob of the mouthpiece and his hair crazy in the wind it's hard to tell what he wants. When it's suppertime, at the end, Morgan plays a little love song called Muss I Denn, one the kids falter through and finally stop and listen to because they don't know all the words, but across the playground the mothers sing quietly along. From there you bring out the main act, the yellow cardboard drawing of the reversible face, and hold it up so the frown shows, with the smile hidden in a crease across the forehead. You nod at Morgan. He starts playing while you kick off your translation of the lyrics.

"Wenn du jemand boese siehst, hilf ihn zu versteh'n, dass wenn er ein laecheln hat," turning the cardboard over quick so the smile shows and the frown disappears into another forehead wrinkle, "wird alles besser geh'n!"

They want to be the ones to hold and turn the cardboard. They want to know how the face works. They want to know the song. After they've learned it you break out the paper and crayons and show them how to draw the reversible face. They work on the concrete. The mothers come over to watch. Morgan keeps playing. You move among the kids, helping them, telling them your name is Shake, asking them theirs. Katya. Walter. Marie Therese. Oskar. Gretchen. Kartik. Heidi. Tomas. Max. Gabriele. Name after name. As the kids finish, they get up, try the face and the song out on one another. You help them remember the words. When to turn their faces over. The mothers cross the playground back to the bench. Other mothers have started calling down from the high windows of the tall buildings. You take out your notebook and start collecting last names. The kids are eager to tell you. Watch while you write them down. Make sure you get them right.

Cynthia Wesley, the girl whose father dropped her off to go up the street for gas, was one of the four girls killed by the bomb. That night, at supper in a nearby restaurant, sharing a big round wooden table with Morgan and four strangers, you eat knackwurst and watery red cabbage off a chipped white plate. Across the table an ancient woman with a red face and collapsed lips and scarved and wiry white hair scowls bitterly at the big white knoedel she's cutting up and wolfing down, like she's eating it alive, showing it who's boss. While you eat you look back and forth through the tracting book for the address of the complex. It isn't there. Neither are the names you scribbled in your notebook while kids pulled at your arms to see that you had them right.

"I can't find this place in the tracting book," you tell Morgan.

"It's new," he says. "I guess it's never been done before."

"Want me to start a new page?"

"I guess you'll have to."

Another new page. Here instead of Birmingham. Out on the playground a little girl with blue hightop shoes and light brown pigtails and cheeks the color of peaches who told you her name was Sophie stole your heart when you had her spell her last name. Shy like Maggie. Flames lick up through the sticks of the campfire inside your chest again. Their heat floods the cage of your ribs. You push your dirty plate forward, into the table, clear the space in front of you, find the first blank page in the tracting book. New last names from the kids. You copy Hannah's from your notebook. You'll get apartment numbers off the mailboxes in the lobbies.

CHAPTER 24

A STEEL ELEVATOR takes you to the fourteenth floor. Morgan lets you knock. Your knuckles hit painted wood. You hear a kid's voice, high and urgent, a woman's answering voice, heels on hardwood, latches, and then the door opens. A woman stands there, one of the little girls you played with at her side, a dark-haired girl in a yellow dress and red jacket who sang her lungs out facing down another girl. Now her grin is shy but reckless with excitement. You try to remember her name. Katya. Her mother's blond, good looking, maybe in her thirties, a question in her smile while she holds the door.

"You know my daughter?" she says, in German.

"We were here earlier today," says Morgan, in German too. "We were playing songs for some of the children in the playground."

"So why are you here now? Who are you?"

"We're missionaries from the Church of Jesus Christ of Latter-Day Saints."

"Amerikaner?"

"Yes. Is your husband home?"

"Ja," she says, the question making her tense up.

"We'd just like to talk to you. For a few minutes."

You look past her, down the hardwood floor of her hallway, into her living room, through to the window she might have opened earlier to call her little girl upstairs for supper. In your line of sight, in the living room, there's a simple end table with a metal lamp. The square brown armrest of a modern sofa. The edge of a white rug. A home. A family. The woman starts making sense of things. You watch her smile glaze and her courtesy harden. Morgan's working to get to the end of one of his tortured Austrian sentences when she shakes her head, takes her daughter's hand, steps back, softly closes the door on the two of you.

You put an R next to her name in the new page of the tracting book. You don't look at Morgan. You saw how quick his face turned red when the door closed on his unfinished sentence.

"So who's next?" he finally says.

"Mueller," you say. "Number 1107."

"Next time," he says, "I want you to have some brochures ready."

"Okay."

"Eleventh floor," he says. "Let's go."

The next eight doors are pretty much the same. A mother or father. A little kid. The hallway out to the living room. Morgan gets more practice. You make sure you've got brochures in hand when the truth of what you're doing comes around. People welcome the brochures as a way to end the conversation.

Then, on the fourth floor, the conversation doesn't end. A little boy starts singing as soon as he sees you standing there.

"Eins zwei Polizei! Drei fier Offizier!"

"Hush, Kartik," his father says. He's a small Indian guy with glasses, somewhere in his early forties maybe, still in his necktie from work. His son takes off skipping and singing down the hall into the apartment.

"Funf! Sechs! Alte Hex! Sieben! Acht! Gute Nacht!"

"Kartik! Hush!" A woman's voice from inside.

"You're American?" the Indian guy asks. His English is British.

"Yes," says Morgan.

"How do you know my son?"

"We taught the kids some songs this afternoon on the playground."

"Come in."

Suddenly you're on a sofa. There's a coffee table with a glass top just past your knees. It happens too fast. You're fresh off the street. Still carry its noise and smell and rush on you.

"Could I get you a drink? Some coffee? Beer?"

"No thanks," says Morgan. "We're fine."

In the corner by the window stands a drafting table. Blueprints are curled out across the top beneath the glowing fluorescent tubes of a white desk lamp. The little boy worms in between you and Morgan. You tousle his dense black hair. He grins up at you. His father takes a cushioned wooden armchair across the small room next to a bookcase with an open back and a tv on one of its shelves. From another room you hear the woman's voice again. You make out English. American English. From the gaps of silence, bursts of laughter, you can tell she's on the phone.

His name is Keshevan. People call him Kesh. He's an architect. He went to school in England and then to college in the States. Stanford. Morgan's never been to California. You've been there, to Disneyland, and then Fort Ord for basic training, and then to San Jose, and so you lead the conversation. Monterey. San Francisco. He drove East once, in a borrowed Ford wagon, to look at some Colorado architecture, and so you talk your way through Sacramento, over the Sierras, and then through Reno and across Nevada. Lovelock. Battle Mountain. Winnemucca. Elko. The desert towns. Morgan takes over when you get him through the border town of Wendover and cross him into Utah. Steers him into Mormonism. Kesh recalls a Mormon family he met in a town called Spanish Fork. They sold him gas and then they fed him supper. You like the guy. You admire him for the way he drove through the heart of Mormon country and came away unfazed.

"Kesh?"

He turns around. You look up. The woman's in the doorway, fat, big-chested, wearing a big pink tent of a housedress splashed with pale green flowers, mouse-colored hair that looks like it hasn't been washed in a month, an oily hubcap of a face so homely you have to catch the reflex to look away.

"Who are these people?" she says.

You and Morgan both stand up. Kesh is on his feet already.

"Excuse me," he says, his arms extended. "Allow me to introduce my wife Sheila. We met at Stanford. Sheila, this . . ." He makes a small apologetic laugh. "You'll have to forgive me," he says. "I got so excited talking about the States again, I forgot to ask your names."

Morgan starts to speak. He stops as the woman comes out of the doorway into the living room and dwarfs the man she sleeps with.

"You're the guys who were playing with the kids today," she says.

"That's right," Morgan says.

"What was that all about?"

Morgan stares at her. She turns to Kesh. "Kartik told me about them. Two Americans. Playing games. Singing songs. One of them played a flute. They had every kid in the complex going. Said they'd come back tonight and play some more."

Kesh just looks at her. She turns back to Morgan.

"What were you up to?"

Morgan shrugs and manages a smile. "Just having some fun."

"What are you doing here?"

"Talking to your husband," says Morgan.

"Why did you come back? How do you know where we live?"

"Kartik told us."

"What are you guys?" She looks at Morgan and then you. "Perverts?"

"Sheila," says Kesh. "Please."

"Actually," says Morgan, "we're missionaries for the Church of Jesus Christ—"

"Mormons? Mormon missionaries?"

"Yes."

"So you tricked my kid into giving you our name. So you could come snooping around tonight with your Joseph Smith bullshit."

"I wouldn't put it like that."

"Tell you what. I don't care how you put it. You should be ashamed. You're worse than perverts. Using my kid to get into my house."

"We'll just leave. We didn't mean—"

"You damned right you'll leave. Right now. I see you around here again, I'll call the cops. Eins zwei Polizei. Kartik, come here. Kesh, get them out of here."

CHAPTER 25

THE THIRTEEN-YEAR-OLD BOY riding the handlebars of his brother's bike was killed by a white kid, sixteen years old, an Eagle Scout, riding shotgun behind his white buddy on a motorbike. They'd just come from a Klan rally at a go kart park. The motorbike was decorated with confederate stickers. The gun was a twenty-two caliber pistol. It fired twice. The name of the boy on the handlebars was Virgil. His brother's name was Jim. Virgil pitched off the handlebars into the street with a bullet in his chest and another in his head.

Jim, I'm shot, he cries, from where he lies in the street.

Over the retreat of the motorbike's hammering engine.

No you aint. You aint shot. Get up, Virg.

Over the pounding heart of the truth that his brother Virg is dead. Virg. Dead. Thirteen. A negro kid around Roy's age. The Eagle Scout who shot him. A kid Karl's age.

"It wasn't just you. She meant both of us. Okay?"

"How's that supposed to make it easier?" says Morgan. "She was right. You know it and so do I."

"What did we think we were doing?"

"What we were told," he says.

"It wasn't our idea."

"It was our choice."

"We didn't know," you say. "Now we do."

The next morning Morgan stays in bed till almost noon. You wash up and dress, hear the doors of neighbors you've never seen open and close, listen to their footsteps in the hall, sit at the little desk, write another letter to Cissy, put more of the lesson plan to memory, read through another couple of wars between the Nephites and Lamanites in the Book of Mormon. You never know when he's awake or sleeping.

"Hey."

He turns on his back and looks at the ceiling.

"Yes," he says.

"I'm going out to get some breakfast."

"You can't go alone."

But he doesn't move.

"Just don't look when I leave," you finally say.

"Straight there and straight back," he says. "I'll time you."

For the first time since you've been here you're on the street alone. There's a naked feel to it. Like the fresh feel of air on the shaved skin behind your ears and down the back of your neck when you first come out of a barbershop. At the dairy shop the woman whose freckles spill off the deep slopes of her breasts smiles when she catches you and asks where your friend is. Sick, you tell her. Krank. She says to wish him better while she cuts your rolls and butters them.

Morgan's up and washed and dressed for going out by early afternoon. You jump a familiar tram and head across Vienna along a familiar route.

He doesn't tell Frau Kettler you've been called perverts. But she gets the message that somehow he needs tending. She helps him get his herringbone suit coat off. Pours his Kamillentee. Lets him decide what they talk about. Touches her consoling fingers to his knee when he falters, goes silent, looks off with sudden melancholy at the wall at something only he can see. Passes concerned little smiles across the room at you when he's at the piano, lost in some sonata, his back turned, like the two of you are in on this nursing thing together. When you return her smile, let her know she's right, delight makes her cherub cheeks rise up and touch the bottoms of her rimless glasses, makes her magnified eyes glitter. She believes you. Actually believes your smile. Believes your little smile while behind it, in your head, you pick up her porcelain teapot and send it flying at the wall. Rip her coffee table off its French legs. Pull her big piano over on its heavy face. Take her lamp and club her glass cabinet and her shelves of little figurines and handpainted dishes to smithereens. Tear her red blouse open. Send its little ruby buttons flying. Fight your way out of this draped and cloistered room where you never know when the sun goes down. Get out of here before you suffocate or drown or whatever kind of death this is. Get air. Get to the street and bare your face to a red sun setting through the dirt-streaked windshield of Robbie's van and the rust haze of the Kennecott smelter out toward Skull Valley. She believes you. Believes this little smile that tastes like you're kissing tin while Morgan plays his anguish out.

In her bathroom you drain yourself of Kamillentee into the same kind of toilet back in your apartment, the same porcelain ledge, the same wall-mounted tank whose explosive release lets everyone above and below and around you know you're done. You keep your head down when you wash your hands in her basin. Keep from looking at the small shelf and all the miniature bottles filled with bewildering little fluids you'd rather eat crap than have to smell. At the little mirror above them. Because you're afraid you'd see her there, the way she sees herself, painting her puckered lips into a rosebud, looking into the swimming pupils of her magnified brown eyes. No, you think. You can't get used to this.

On the fourth day Morgan's fine again. Like being called a pervert was a bad cold that had to run its course. You're up and out for breakfast early. While he practices you sit at the table out back and read about Virg and Jim. You aint shot. You rock back on the bench and open your mouth at the quiet desperate horror of that line. That afternoon, in a crisp wind under a clear blue early November sky, you're back on your campstools again, on the plaza in front of the Opera House, where Morgan talks to a sunburned guy from Australia with a dusty blond beard and a crushed straw hat who's waiting like you to stand through Carmen. He plays violin. Only one of his eyes moves. In the eye that doesn't move the iris is this pale white star like the pearl cap set into each valve of your trumpet.

CHAPTER 26

HEADING INTO NOVEMBER there are mornings where it's cool enough you need to go back in and climb the stone hollows of the stairs again for your London Fog raincoat. The restless couples you saw on the trams and streets and benches look like they're settled in, have places to call home, hole up warm for the winter. Like you, they've started wearing coats, not dark raincoats, but jackets, short jackets, especially the girls, form-fitting jackets that hug their breasts, come down snug around their waists, then end, leaving their butts to take the shape of teardrops, teardrops of soft and boneless flesh, swollen and full in the tight skin of their jeans, like apples or peaches or anything else that takes till this late in the fall to ripen.

My darling Shake,
   Today you stopped me cold on my way to school. But then it wasn't you. I saw it when he turned around on the sidewalk. And I just stood there helplessly and felt sweat on my neck and in my hands. Oh Shake.

For you there's a place too. A place to come home to. Home from the concert. Home from the opera. Home from Frau Kettler's. Home to the smell when you open the door, damp and sharp and thick with things like lard and wurst and cabbage, the smell of the woman you rent from. Home to where you imagine Cissy. Not this room. But back in San Jose or in a house like Lenny had in the Avenues or some other American city. A place with her. A place to hide from the lights. Where the chill of her wool jacket unzips to give off the oven warmth of her breasts. A place where you watch the loose and rolling twitch of her shoulders while she brushes her teeth. A place where she lies on the bedspread in her panties and winter socks and a teeshirt, reading some book or flipping through a magazine or doing homework while you sit on a chair by a window, aware of her, your trumpet muted, softly exploring some ballad.

One night a week into November, the smell of coming home still in your nostrils, you leave your raincoat and saddlebags on while you use your toenail clippers to cut the double string your father used to tie the thick manila envelope, then tear it back along the flap where your father ran scotch tape. The first thing you find when you pull out what it holds is your traveler's check for sixty dollars. Your November check. Morgan looks through the rest of the mail and sets a regular envelope on the dresser next to the washbowl.

"This is yours too," he says.

"Thanks. I'll get to it later."

You hold the packet of clippings and magazines your father always sends out to Morgan.

"Here."

"I can wait till you're done."

"I've got his letter to read."

Morgan takes the packet and heads for the bathroom. You stand there with your father's check and letter in your hand. The fourth check he's drawn from the bank account your mother opened for your twelfth birthday. Money you earned and paid tithing on and put away. Money that came from every job you worked and from the car they wouldn't let you buy. There's a small American Express office in the glass lobby of a downtown building where you'll trade the traveler's check for Austrian cash in the morning. Your money. But when the woman hands you its Austrian equivalent, its feel will be counterfeit, a false feel, not for how you earned it but for how you know you'll spend it. Tickets while the doors of your tracting area go missing. Tram rides while your bike stays chained to a pipe downstairs. Morgan comes back from the bathroom and sets the clippings and magazines down on the dresser.

"Why does your father think you care about Utah's education system?"

"He likes to brag."

"I know. But the education system? That's just odd."

You've never heard anyone call your father odd. You look down at the check again.

"What's the matter?" Morgan says. Behind you, he opens his side of the armoire, hangs his suit coat, closes the door again. "Bad news?"

"Not really."

"You were standing there ten minutes ago. You've still got your coat on."

He's bent over the small desk, the lamp on, sliding the sheet music he bought earlier in the afternoon out of the sheath of a thin paper bag. You watch him open a piece of music, follow the bars with his finger, play them in his head. The pull of the saddlebags on your shoulders feels like a practical joke. Like dirt you've been told to carry around Vienna just to see if you'd be dumb enough to do it. The brochures you filled them with four months ago. Their once sharp corners worn smooth and round from chafing on the canvas. Like the stuff you carry in your wallet.

Cissy's photo. Your license. Things you've put on hold. Things you could be doing. Turned over in your head enough to round their corners too.

"It's just tough," you say. "Getting this money."

"What money?" says Morgan. He doesn't look up. And so he misses the spasm of hate that goes through your jaw. Hate for the way you've had to let your mouthpiece go. Hate for the way a piano player can play and still talk to someone and a trumpet player can't.

"This money I'm not doing anything to earn."

And now he looks up, and his finger stops, and you've got his attention to where he can't play and talk at the same time either.

"I thought you said you earned it."

"I did."

"So then it's yours."

You watch him fold the music closed and leave it on the desk. In the lamplight see the name Alan Hovhaness on the cover.

"I don't feel right about spending it."

While he works his brown tie loose to let it hang unknotted from the ends of his collar, unbuttons the collar button of his shirt, he crosses the few steps of floor to where you're standing, looks into your face.

"You're serious," he says.

"I can't even pray. Talk to God."

For a minute you hold his startled look. Then break away to the buttons that hold the frayed points of his collar down, and then, when that feels too personal, you look down at a faded purple flower the size of a hubcap in the patch of rug between your shoes.

"This is about tracting again."

"It's about doing something," you say.

His eyes go narrow. While he takes the wide end of his tie and pulls its length out through his collar he walks a few steps toward the bed and then turns your way again.

"This is about expecting great things," he says.

"What great things?"

"The harvest."

"What harvest?"

He turns the lamp on the nightstand on, drapes his tie across the back of a chair, and crosses back to where you're standing, your father's letter and check still in your hands.

"You know very well what harvest. Everyone does. President Lindner spoke about it last month. How Austria's ready for the harvest."

You think back to his speech. How the seed had been planted in the wicked and stubborn dirt that was the mission field of Austria. How it had taken root in promiscuity and godlessness. How it had flourished because it was the seed of the Restored Gospel. How he would turn the tide of the mission by December. You remember his withering bombastic rage. How he expected to harvest a place he hated with such fury.

"Yeah. What about it?"

"Is that why you think you're here? What God expects? You to harvest Austria?"

"I didn't come here for this."

He studies you again. The light from the lamp on the nightstand behind him leaves a thread of gold dust in the fine almost invisible hair along the edge of his face.

"I'm going to tell you something. Don't take it wrong. It has nothing to do with you."

"Go ahead."

"There's not going to be a harvest. This is how Austria has always been. This is how it's going to stay. God knows that."

"So we just go to operas and concerts and recitals instead."

It takes him a minute to open his eyes again.

"You and I believe in very different Gods," he says.

"What do you mean?"

"My God always wants to hear from me," he says. "No matter what. He knows I grew up being told that a mission would be the best two and a half years of my life. He wants me to make sure it is."

"I grew up that way too."

"Put that stuff down," he says. "Please. Take off your raincoat so I can stop feeling like you're leaving."

He walks away, pulls the tails of his shirt out of his pants, picks up the letter he left for you on the dresser, turns back to you.

"I'm sorry," he says. "I've never tried to understand jazz. I should have let you teach me something. We should have gone and heard some."

You've read their flyleafs on the papered sides of kiosks. The places that advertised jazz. You've walked past their doors. You've let go of what it took not to go inside.

"They don't play it in concert halls and opera houses," you say.

"I know that," says Morgan. "Don't treat me like I'm stupid either."

"I'm sorry. But it doesn't matter. I left it home."

"Your trumpet. I know. I meant we could have heard some."

"No. I left everything home. Jazz period."

"You didn't need to do that."

The Mojave. Sitting on a dune with the retreating heat of the sunset on your back. Running warm sand through your fingers while Taps played on a bugle over the distant speaker back at camp.

"There's jazz in some of the composers you play. Brahms. Debussy."

"Well," he says. "I wish we could do this over. So you could show me." And then he says, "At least you won't be forced to stand through any more operas."

"What do you mean?"

"You got another letter. We both did. Here."

You put your father's check and letter on the dresser and take the envelope from him. It's from the Mission Home. The letter tells you the Lord has chosen you to continue your labor in a place called Villach. You're supposed to catch a train day after tomorrow.

"So this is how they let you know," you say.

"I'll be staying here," says Morgan. "I'm getting a new junior."

"Who is he?"

"I don't know. Larry Hemingway. Looks like a greenie."

"I'll leave him my campstool."

"Who's your new senior?" Morgan says after a minute.

"Elder Nick Paulson."

"I know him."

"What's he like?"

"I can't say."

"You know this place?"

"It's a village in southern Austria. Almost on the border of Italy. You can see the Alps. It's beautiful."

He crosses the floor to stand in front of the window. You can't tell if he's looking at his own reflection on the glass, a black ghost face with rain-mussed hair in an untucked shirt backlit by the transparent reflection of the ancient room, or across the dark street at the lighted windows of the building that faces him.

After a minute he says, "Let's go eat."

"I thought you weren't hungry."

"I guess I mean celebrate." He opens his pants, tucks his shirt in, buckles his belt again. "There's something I finally need to tell you. I don't want to do it here."

HE HAS YOU take your tie off too. Drop your saddlebags. In the November air outside your neck feels bare and your shoulders light. In the corner restaurant the tables are empty. You take the small table by the window where you ate your first night here. The warm smell of seasoned food in the dining room has always made you hungry. Across the table Morgan takes his suit coat off. Sits there with his shoulders round and the frayed gray cuffs of his long sleeves buttoned the way he plays organ at the church and piano at Frau Kettler's. You've seen him dressed almost every way a guy can be dressed. In just his garments with the top pulled off his arms to down around his waist so he can wash his armpits in the morning. In a suit and tie and overcoat with a black umbrella covering his head. Never like this, out in public without a tie and his collar loose, like you're there to play cards. You shed your suit coat too, hang it over the back of your chair, unbutton your cuffs, roll them back to your elbows.

The first time you've seen your wrists this way since you got here.

The woman at the bar has company. A big guy maybe in his forties in a black turtleneck with a heavy beard and shaggy brown hair as thick as wool. They're facing each other. Their knees touch. She smiles when she exhales through her teeth and aims the plume of smoke away from his face. It's the first time you've seen her dark hair not pinned carelessly on her head but loose and long. On the bar near his hand are a shot glass and half a mug of beer. A knapsack leans against the foot of his stool on the floor. The kitchen is quiet, the tinny radio clear, playing a German love song you don't know. You feel this quiet excitement in your chest. This adventure. A transfer. Someplace new. A step deeper into your mission. A new senior. You look at Morgan and see everything you like about him. Everything you'll miss. You can see the same recognition in his face.

The woman comes over and sets two large glasses of water on beer coasters on the table. Slips two menus out from under her arm and lays them in front of you and Morgan. Then raps her fingers once on the table, turns, heads back to the bar. You and Morgan raise and tap your glasses and take a quick swallow of water.

"Here's to Villach," he says.

You don't know what to say. He's not going anywhere. And so you say, "Here's to Vienna."

"I could spend the rest of my mission here."

"We never did ride that Ferris wheel."

"Would you like to?"

"Isn't it closed now?"

"Maybe. I haven't looked."

The last time you rode a Ferris wheel. You smile remembering. On your first date with Linda Bowen at the State Fair. The sunset ride where you could reach up from the swaying carriage at the top of the wheel and almost touch the high black leaves where they hung trembling against the blood orange of the sky around them.

"What did you want to tell me?"

Morgan's attitude goes solemn. His face muddled. His eyes skittish. He uses both hands to draw his glasses off his face. Looks down and brushes some crumbs aside. Looks up, opens his mouth, closes it, looks away and down again.

"Something I've kept from you," he finally looks up and says.

His voice is soft. His naked eyes and gray face tell you this is something different from rheumatic fever and never having sneakers. More serious. Newer.

"Okay."

"First of all," he says, "you have to promise not to tell anyone. I mean anyone. I could get in real trouble."

"I won't. I promise."

"If certain people knew," he says, "it could mean the end of my mission."

"What's going on?"

"You don't owe your father anything," he says.

You stare at him. He doesn't look away. Keeps his own eyes level and his face more grave than you've ever seen him look.

"What are you talking about?"

"You don't owe him a thing."

"I heard you the first time."

"You remember President Smith," he says.

The mission president when you got here. How the first and last time you saw him was at his farewell speech. How he looked the way you thought an ambassador would look.

"Yes."

"I had to promise him I'd never tell anyone. But I like you and it's something you deserve to know."

"So tell me," you say.

"Just promise me. Not anyone."

"I promise."

"No matter how upset you might get."

"Tell me."

"Did your father tell you he wrote President Smith a letter?"

"A letter?"

"Yes."

"My father wrote him," you say.

"I had a feeling you didn't know," says Morgan.

"When? What kind of letter?"

"You weren't here yet."

"Before I got here?"

"Maybe a week or two before. Calm down. You don't want to get that baby crying."

From the bar the woman looks your way. Stretches her leg to the floor to slide off her stool. Morgan shakes his head to stop her. It wasn't about Cissy. Your father didn't know she existed till you walked her across the polished stone floor of the airport to introduce her. And that was a day before you got here. Morgan holds his glasses by the temples so the lenses are angled down. Below them on the tablecloth they amplify the dim light of the restaurant like the two pale circles of miniature spotlights.

"President Smith told me. When they decided to put us together. You and me."

"He told you?"

"I was still in Knittelfeld. He came through there on his last trip around the mission."

"What'd he write? My father?"

"I didn't see it. President Smith just told me what it said."

"What did he say?"

"That great things were expected of you. Because of your grandfather."

"Tell me something I don't know."

Morgan puts his glasses on again.

"Maybe I should leave it there," he says.

"No. Tell me everything."

"He said that to achieve them you'd need help. These great things expected of you."

"What kind of help?"

Morgan meets your eyes and this time holds them.

"He said you have trouble respecting authority. You could be rebellious. You need special attention. You know. Watching over. Looking after."

"Looking after."

"A good hardworking senior with a firm hand."

Morgan holds still while you do a wild search of his face.

"My father wrote all that."

"Yes."

"Not my bishop. Not . . . someone else."

"No."

You look down at your hands. Ride out the shame raging in your ears, the sudden ache deep in your throat, the cry of the wind through the place where you could always find him. Your father. The way you came here thinking nobody would know you. How you could start out fresh the way you did the Army. Like everyone else. From scratch. How he could beat you here. Tell them what he thinks of you. You didn't know. How what you thought was the place where you could always find him falls suddenly away from the toes of your shoes through thousands of feet of open air. Tears born less of hurt than anger well into your eyes.

Across the room the man at the bar laughs. Soft. Something the woman said. Joanie Sommers singing Johnny Get Angry comes from the radio in the kitchen.

"It was a terrible thing for him to do," says Morgan.

You see him where you've seen him a million times, at his big electric Royal typewriter on its flimsy stand, fingers going, keys clacking in machine gun bursts, him framing his next line in the pauses between the bursts.

"It's who he is," you say, because you don't know what else to say.

"Shake. Listen to me."

The first time you've heard your name since you left Salt Lake. The name nobody here is supposed to use.

"President Smith felt the same way."

"That I'm rebellious."

"No. That it was a terrible thing for your father to do."

"Excuse me," you call, and when the woman at the bar turns your way, you say, "I'd like a beer, please."

She hesitates before she answers. "What kind of beer?"

You point to the three taps that stand on their pipes above the bar.

"A draft beer?" she says, off her stool, going around the bar. "Which one?"

"What do you recommend?"

"Ottakringer?"

"Yes please."

"One? Two?"

You hold one finger up. Her loose dark hair falls off her shoulders down across the sides of her face while she holds the yellow tap and looks down to watch the pour. She carries the mug through the tables and sets it in front of you. You hand her your menu.

"Thank you."

"Not hungry?"

"No. Just thirsty."

She looks at Morgan. He hands her his menu too. She shrugs, takes it, leaves.

"I don't blame you," he says.

You take hold of the handle. Try it on for size. Watch the head of foam start slowly to cave in on itself. Under the foam, through the glass, the beer is the color of pale honey.

"It's not cold," you say.

"I don't think they serve it cold."

You look up at Morgan. His tone is casual but his eyes look worried and his face uncertain. Maybe he doesn't deserve this.

"I came here to work," you say.

"I know."

"Be an Instrument of the Lord."

"I know."

"Who else saw his letter? Elder Cannon? President Lindner? This new guy I'll see tomorrow?"

"I'm sure nobody. President Smith would never pass around something that awful."

"Why'd he tell you?"

"He wanted me to know what you were up against. Your father's letter disgusted him. He said he'd never seen a father betray a son like that."

Betray. The shock of the word cuts the dark behind your eyes like lightning and ricochets and rolls like thunder through your head. You take your hand off the glass handle of the mug. Look around for things to trust. The woman at the bar who brought your beer. The man with her who'll remember to take his knapsack when he leaves. The view out the window. The table that holds your beer. The glass itself. How everything holds. Keeps its true proportions. Does its job. You finally look at Morgan again.

"He used that word?"

"Betray? Yes."

"Did he write my father back?"

"Your father didn't deserve an answer," Morgan says.

"He told me the less they knew about me the better off I'd be."

"Your father told you that?"

"I took him at his word."

For a minute Morgan's eyes look wild at everything but you.

"Sometimes I think I'm better off not having a father," he finally says. This is one of those times."

You look down at the beer in front of you. A few shreds of foam remain like the ragged coastlines of disappearing islands. You don't know how to understand father and betray in the same breath. How to hold both of them in your head. This lonely fear in your stomach when you try. The ache in your throat the way it has always ached since you were a kid.

"You know the part that really made President Smith sick?" says Morgan.

"No."

"That great things were expected of you."

And now you look up at him.

"Why?"

"He said this is Austria. There are no great things. He said your father pretty much set you up to fail."

"Fail."

Morgan watches you. Waits before he answers.

"He said that only God could do what your father says he expects of you. Convert everyone in Austria. And he won't. It violates the free agency he gave them."

You look down again into the beer you ordered. Gene Pitney sings Town Without Pity from the kitchen radio.

"I can't keep you from drinking that," he says. "I can just ask you not to."

You look up. "So all this time you've known." you say.

"I have."

"And I had to wait till now to hear it."

Morgan opens his hands and for a minute looks into his palms. "I have no excuse," he finally says.

"You could have told me the first night we were here."

"You didn't know how to order a beer four months ago. I didn't want to have to order one for you."

You stare at him. Smile and shake your head. That he could be insane enough to think that what he said was funny.

"I'm sorry," he says, subdued, a fingernail nibbling at something in the tablecloth. "The truth is that I didn't know you then. I do now."

He raises his face. Looks at you for a minute.

"What would you have done differently?" he says.

You've already reviewed the possibilities. Caught a flight back home. Before you were in too deep to leave. Before the summer was gone. Told Professor Fisher you'd been wrong. Hoped his offer was still good. Bought a used Porsche with your mission money either way and headed for California. Split the summer between Cissy in San Jose and your trumpet in Los Angeles. Or you could have headed south and gone to work like Bill and Jerry. All the places you've read about where you might have made a difference. Done something. Instead of here. The wind starts to rise up the dark night wall of the cliff again. None of the possibilities were ever possible. Only this one. Where you got here not knowing that your father had already let them know. You look into the dark outside the window.

"I don't know," you say. "It didn't happen."

"Well . . . I'm sorry."

Another stark possibility comes to you.

"Was this all a test?"

"What?"

"The last four months."

"A test for what?"

"To see if I could respect authority."

Morgan studies you. You can tell you've hurt him.

"Sorry."

"Absolutely not."

"So tell me why I'm here."

He shakes his head. Brings up his hand to scratch his nose and rake his hair back off his forehead. Stares cold out the dark window. What that grave look has always meant. You get it now. When he turns to face you his familiar sadness shimmers in his gray eyes.

"I don't know. To hold them to their word. Make sure it's what they promised you. The best time of your life."

For a long time you just look at him.

"I'll miss your playing."

"I'm sorry I missed yours."

Since getting here you've stored your letters from home in manila envelopes. One envelope for Cissy. The other for your family. Most of them from your father.

"I was just thinking," you say.

"What?"

"How many other letters he wrote."

"I don't think so," Morgan says.

"If he wrote one to President Lindner too."

Morgan glances at your beer and looks back up.

"I can't say."

And suddenly you're thinking of the tracting book in the inside pocket of your suit where you've carried it the last four months. You take it out, open it, look at the columns and rows of tiny Rs and Ns written in different hands by nameless missionaries across the stiff and wrinkled pages. Every R and N a knock on a dark door in a dim hallway of doors that was never opened or was quickly closed again. Every R and N a symbol of a ritual that began with a knuckle on wood and ended in the defeat of hope and then the brief renewal of hope that maybe the promised harvest, always just out of reach, was waiting behind the next door. Over and over and over. The definition of insanity. A sadness too incomprehensible to name comes over you.

"What are you doing?" Morgan says.

You close the book and put it away. Look across the table at the guy who's given you this incredible city. This City of Music.

"Wishing I had the last four months to do over again."

"I'm sorry," Morgan says. "I know they weren't what you expected."

"No," you say. "You were right."

"About what?"

"About the best time of my life."

"What do you mean?"

"The operas. The concerts. The cathedrals. The museums. The Imperial Palace. The Belvedere. Everywhere you took me and everything you showed me."

"What about them?"

"I enjoyed every one of them. I want you to know how grateful I am. For all of them. I wish we could do them over again so I could show you what they really meant to me."

Across the table Morgan looks startled and then confused and wary.

"Don't play with me," he finally says.

"I'm not."

He studies you. His face grave.

"I've been a real . . . let's say brat. I'm sorry."

He takes a skittish look out the window.

"You don't need to be," he says.

"You know what I enjoyed the most?"

"No."

"Listening to you play. Those mornings at the churchhouse. Those afternoons at Frau Kettler's."

When you see water shine in his eyes you look down. When you look up again, they're dry, their look steady and penetrating.

"Your arrangement of Come Come Ye Saints? At Stephansdom? It made me cry."

"That bad, huh?"

You don't return the little smile that plays briefly in his lips.

"I've never had a piece of music make me cry."

And while he looks away, while he turns his face away, you look at the frayed and yellowed cuffs of his shirtsleeves.

"Thank you," he finally says.

"Guess where I was when you played it."

He smiles. "Somewhere in the cathedral, I hope."

You tell him about stumbling into the confession booth not knowing what it was. How the voice of the priest surprised you. How the conversation went. Everything but the masturbieren part.

"So he knew you were a missionary?"

"From what he asked and what I answered, he figured it out."

"Is that what you confessed to?" Morgan says, smiling.

"We just talked. Except when you played your arrangement. Then we both just stopped and listened."

"He listened too?"

"Who could do anything else?"

He looks away again.

"I've never set foot in a confession booth," he says, when he looks back at you. "What's it like?"

"Dark. Like a coffin."

"I've never been in a coffin either."

"Me either. So I don't know. A little closet."

The two of you sit in silence across the table. Your father comes back to mind. How he stood in the way the last four months of you and Morgan making friends. How you made friends anyway.

"I need to go," you finally say, rolling the cuffs of your sleeves down, buttoning them.

"Where?"

"Anywhere. Just walk. I don't know."

You push back your chairs and get up. Put your suit coats on again. You reach down for your untouched mug. Morgan follows it with his eyes as you raise it.

"Here's to my father."

PART 4

ONE HAND ONE HEART

Chapter 28

Shake, my darling, today this will be short. I'm going with my mom and dad to visit friends in San Leandro. But not before I write you. So they're waiting outside for their stubborn daughter. Too bad she's so in love with you . . .

IN YOUR SEAT by the window, Cissy's note in your hand, the train heads south through the outskirts of Vienna and the factory and warehouse neighborhoods where distant steeples pierce the bleak haze out beyond the smokestacks. Then the land runs flat. Across the compartment, facing you, an older couple with their overcoats folded on their laps hold hands and watch the window pass the time and distance. A woman next to you sleeps with her scarved head slumped over on her far shoulder and the plump underside of her chin and the knot of her scarf turned your way. In the trembling flesh beneath her chin you can see the rocking of the train. You can see the train too in the faces and hands of the tired old couple across from you. You try to think of a way to introduce yourself. Get them talking. Get them to like you enough to where they might care to hear about a religion out of a place called Utah or have it explained to them why the church they were born into is false. Nothing comes. There's noise anyway. The distant engines and the whistling steel drumbeat of the wheels. You open the lesson book to the page where you left off. But the words lack the traction to hold your eyes, and the scripted answers Bruder Braun is supposed to give are less and less real, more and more childlike, harder and harder to imagine hearing any grownup give in return to the scripted questions.

The questions and answers are written in German. You can hear the cadence of your father's voice as you read. Morgan called it betrayal. What in four months your father never volunteered to tell you. Just kept to himself while every letter repeated what he wanted. That first baptism. From a son who didn't know how to wear his grandfather's shoes. You ride with the always moving target of the son he wants. You ride with this hollow place in your chest where you thought your father was. This abandoned place where his letter to President Smith scuttles across what you thought was the floor of the earth till it reaches the edge where the world falls thousands of feet away and the letter dances on the updraft like a moth just out of reach. You've been here before. Where your clenched throat hurts but your staring eyes stay dry.

Sometime in the afternoon the scenery out the window starts transforming into country so beautiful this deep into the Indian summer of November you can't ignore or trust it. The woman next to you wakes up in time to stand up and arrange herself and get off in a city called Leoben. Wordless, not talking to her husband, the woman across from you puts her coat in the rack above her head, fetches and unties a paper bundle, uses her lap as a table to cut thick pink slices off some kind of sausage and match them to pieces of bread. The smell of heavy meat and garlic makes its way across the compartment. The train sets off again. She puts a sandwich in her husband's hand. He eats while he watches the window. Nested among the fields and forests where the mountains and hills descend in shallow valleys are villages whose houses are clustered loosely around the steeples that seem to shelter them. This hunger for their streets and houses. The deep spontaneous pull of where you came from. You look for trust again. You can't find any. Roads thread themselves through fields that roll green across the hills and then snake into the forests. The dream roads you used to make from your father's Swiss calendars for your dream Porsche.

The couple across from you get off in a town called Klagenfurt. And then you're alone. Questions have found a home in your stomach and started to settle in. Paulson. If this will be where your mission starts. If he's been told, despite what Morgan said, about your father's letter. If it's part of your record. A record you had before you even got here.

In Villach, at the station, your new senior is so clearly American there on the platform you know as soon as you see him that he's there for you.

"Welcome to Villach, Elder."

A quick search of his face for what he knows. Some sign of what your father wrote as a way of introducing you.

"Thanks," you say. "It's beautiful here."

"Yeah."

He's Morgan's opposite. An overcoat and suit that aren't bagged and wrinkled. A steel grin to let you know he has the Spirit. A handshake like you've stepped blind into some kind of gripping contest. A smooth round face with the gloss of aftershave. Brown hair brushed straight back in a way that tells you he never skips a haircut. He's shorter than you and carries himself with the strut of an athlete or a dancer. He takes your bike to push it home for you. You stop occasionally to stretch your cold and curled fingers and switch the Samsonite to your other hand. He holds your bike and waits with his eyes off past you somewhere and a light closed smile that could mean anything.

In the November cold and fading light the winding cobblestone street through the heart of town is lined with pastel-colored buildings, old shops, churches that look like they were built hundreds of years ago. There's a plaque next to the doorway of almost every building, brass or painted wood or stone, old and weathered, like everything important that could ever happen here has already happened. In its perfect beauty the town looks caught in time, posed, ready to photograph, almost counterfeit. You're quick to understand the permanence of being here. How far you are from Vienna. How far Vienna is from home. From the all night truckstops where diesel smoke hangs in the air and mosquitoes and gnats and other insects spin themselves insane in the overhead lights. Above the rooftops and steeples, above the forested hills beyond them, mountains of naked rock vault up with such steep and immediate force you think they're thunderheads at first. Snow covers their flanks. Paulson tells you they're the Alps and they're probably in Italy.

"That's Italy?"

"Some of them could be in Yugoslavia," says Paulson.

"Where's home?" you ask Paulson.

"Still a ways," he says.

"No. I mean where you're from."

"Idaho Falls. You?"

"Bountiful. A town just north of Salt Lake."

Your room's in a finished attic above the two floors of a house where a Fiat dealer lives with his wife and two young daughters. The room is bone simple, the beige walls bare, the furniture plain. The slope of the roof cuts into the ceiling on either side. Your bed's the size of a cot. But this time you're the only one who sleeps in it. There's another bed for Paulson, just like yours, across the room. Between the beds there's floor space for a wooden table and a couple of wooden chairs where you'll sit and do your study time and write your letters. Against the back wall there's a dresser, a wall mirror with a crack that cuts a sharp line down across your face and leaves its two halves slightly skewed, a window you can use for a winter fridge like the window in your room with Morgan. A hot plate and two saucepans sit on top of a small bookcase.

"We're allowed to cook?"

"Small stuff. Soup. Beans. Eggs. Burgers."

He tells you which drawers are yours. Which side of the small closet. Which side of the dresser top you can use for your toiletries. Shows you a cubbyhole where you can store your empty Samsonite. Tells you the bathroom's down on the second floor where the Fiat dealer's daughters have their bedrooms. As long as you clean up, you can use the sink to do your dishes, the bathtub once a week on Friday once the daughters leave for school.

"We don't have to use a bathhouse?"

"What did I just say?"

"Sorry."

You unpack, hang your extra suit and shirts and ties, put your garments and socks away, stash your Samsonite, wash up in the sink in the second floor bathroom. You can't use the tub for what you did in the bathhouse. Not with two young girls using it to bathe. You'll have to use the toilet, learn how to do it sitting down, be quick, flush what you leave on the porcelain shelf in the bowl. Paulson's at the table making some kind of chart in a notebook when you get upstairs again. In his small hand is the fat gold torpedo of a fountain pen like Wissom has. He's using a wooden ruler to lay a thin black shining line across the page.

"Nice pen."

He stops and holds up the pen where he can revolve and admire it.

"Think so?"

"Yeah."

"Thanks. It wasn't cheap."

"Doesn't look like it was."

"It took me over a month to get it."

"What kind is it?"

"It's a Schaeffer." Then he says, "I'd appreciate it if you didn't use it."

You search his face. The kind of thing he might think from what your father's letter told them about you.

"It wouldn't cross my mind," you say.

Paulson's your second brand new senior. Until yesterday he was a junior. He's been in Villach since September. He tells you it's been tracted out. There isn't a door in town that hasn't been hit at least once within a year.

"So we'll be working the villages outside Villach," he says. "There's plenty of them."

We'll be working. You take a new look at him.

"You guys must've worked pretty hard," you say. "To do the whole city."

He looks at you. His smooth face pleased.

"That's what we're here for, Elder."

"So what's next?"

"You mean now? It's Saturday afternoon. Nothing. Settle in. Study if you want. We'll go eat later. Maybe catch a movie."

You take Maggie's drawing out of the manila envelope for family letters and start to tape it to the wall above your cot.

"What are you doing?" Paulson says.

"Putting up this drawing my kid sister did. Of her and me."

"What do you need it on the wall for?"

You turn and look at him.

"It's from my kid sister. It reminds me of my family."

"I don't know if we're allowed to tape things to the walls."

"Did they tell us not to?"

"No," he says. "But I think you should ask."

"I'll let them tell me," you say.

When Paulson has nothing more to say, you turn back to the wall, tape down the last two corners.

"By the way," he finally says, "we run church."

"You mean the meetings."

"Yeah. You and me. How's your German?"

"Not bad."

"Good. You'll be the speaker at Sacrament Meeting tomorrow."

"Anything you'd like me to talk about?"

"Just introduce yourself. The rest is up to you."

"I'll need to write out some notes." Then you say, "Mind if I borrow your pen?"

CHAPTER 29

Early the next morning, the air cold and the sky above the town just taking on the light of sunrise, you take your bike and follow Paulson's flying overcoat through the quiet shadows of the cobblestone streets. Your knuckles ache. You'll need to get gloves like Paulson has. The churchhouse is the ground floor of a small two-story building in the outskirts where houses give way to welding and repair shops. A faded and cracked wood plaque next to the front door says 10 Oktoberstrasse 17. Paulson flips on the lights. In the cold room you blow on your hands. At the front of the room are a portable pulpit and a small wood table with a bread and a water tray on a lace tablecloth. An ancient upright piano stands against the side wall with some hymn books stacked on top. Maybe twenty wooden folding chairs are clustered in loose rows on either side of an aisle down the middle of the room. At the back of the room there's a set of narrow stairs whose bannister disappears into the ceiling. A cast iron stove with a shallow wood box and black coal bucket next to it remind you of the schoolhouse in La Sal. The bucket you filled from the pile of coal out back when your turn came round. Newspapers stacked against the wall let you know how the stove is fired. A thin closet is built out about a foot out from one of the room's back corners. A room in the other back corner is barely big enough for a washbasin and toilet. The floor is wood. The walls and ceiling are light green hazed with dust. All the walls have windows. You figure from there that the room is the size of the building. That it takes up the whole ground floor.

"What happened on October tenth?" you ask Paulson.

"October tenth? Why?"

"The street's named after it."

You wonder if Paulson can look at you without sizing you up. Smile without you feeling somehow stupid.

"I never thought about it. Ask one of the members."

"What's upstairs?" you ask.

"Just another room."

"Is it ours?"

"Yeah. The whole building is."

"What's it used for?"

"Nothing. Just some storage."

"Mind if I look?"

"Go ahead."

The stairs take you up through the ceiling and open out onto the floor of a room the size of the one below. Hollow blocks of gray light stained pink from the sunrise define the windows and show you where the walls are. You find a light switch. A bulb in the ceiling comes alive. The windows go almost black. Some boxes covered with cloth and two broken chairs take up a corner. The tin column of the big black stovepipe from the stove downstairs comes up through a hole in the floor and goes through another hole into the ceiling. The floor is slick with dust. A streaked blackboard hangs on one of the walls without chalk or an eraser. Out one of the windows, using your hand to shield the light reflected from behind you, you look down on the rising dawn of the neighborhood. A couple of one story warehouses. Trucks parked with their tailgates closed against loading docks. A shop surrounded by old farm tractors scavenged for parts. Weeds crushed like pale yellow fossils into the dark November mud. You turn back to the room. You picture where the drums would go, the piano, the standup bass, the amplifiers, where Sandy would want her microphone, the music stands where you and Eddie would put your charts. If they could only see it. Downstairs again, you take off your London Fog raincoat, drop it across the back of a chair.

"Neat room," you tell Paulson.

"Yeah. Too bad there's no heat up there."

"The stovepipe probably keeps it warm. Long as the stove down here is going."

Paulson sizes you up again. "Yeah," he says. Then he says, "I didn't appreciate what you said about borrowing my pen yesterday."

So he took it wrong. And carried it into today.

"It was a joke. I was smiling."

"I wasn't."

"I got that." Then you say, "Want me to fire up the stove?"

"Herbert usually does. He should be here any minute."

"Who's Herbert?"

"This young guy they baptized last summer. He's eighteen. He's got a killer case of acne, man, but he's a good guy." Then he says, "You don't play piano, do you?"

"When I was a kid."

"Can you play hymns?"

"Maybe."

"Nobody in this fuzzin' branch plays piano. We've been doing everything a capella."

You think of the Madrigals back in high school. Their nimble voices chasing each other around like naked angels in the woods while you sat way back in the dark of the auditorium with Robbie or Doby or some other buddy.

"Want me to try?" you say.

"You got time. Priesthood's not for a while."

You open a hymn book to the German version of Come Come Ye Saints. The hymn Morgan played on the Stephansdom organ while you were in the dark of the confession booth. You rack it on the shelf in front of you and lift the long lid off the keyboard. The ivories of some of the keys are gone, leaving bare wood, the wood stained dark where they've been played. The ivories still left are yellow and lined with the thin black grain of tiny cracks. You run a C scale. The action of the keys is slow and heavy. The strings so out of tune that the scale has pieces of minor and blues and half diminished scales. The dampers are gone to where the chaos of sound keeps ringing around the room. Two keys, B and lower E, don't rebound when you use them.

"I thought you said you could play."

You turn around. Paulson's face is more smirk than smile. As if everything's some kind of contest.

"I didn't say what I could play."

"You said piano."

"I said maybe."

You look at the hymn. Four flats. Your fingers hunt the keys for the starting chords. Once you get going the hymn is simple. The changes so basic you feel like you're laying bricks. You run through some others. O My Father. Till We Meet Again. Do What Is Right. The Lord Is My Shepherd. Paulson hums along with some of them. Your forearms burn from the work it takes to drive the stubborn keys. You get used to not having the B and lower E. To the sour arguing of the untuned strings. To the deep and ancient anger of the old instrument.

"Any requests?" you ask.

You turn around. Paulson's at the pulpit reading. Around the room the windows have started taking daylight.

"Know any tunes from West Side Story?" he says.

"I've heard of it. But that's it."

He goes back to what he's reading on the pulpit.

"Shame."

You remember one of the last pieces you learned the summer and fall your trumpet spent hidden in the garage. "How about Slaughter on Tenth Avenue?"

"What's that?"

"Another musical."

"Okay."

"It's kinda sad. Right after someone gets killed. But it's nice."

"West Side Story's that way too," he says.

Your fingers find the opening chord. And then you start coaxing your way into the piece, looking for the changes, dropping back to get a better run at remembering how it moves. You work your way to the end and turn around. Paulson likes it. He's heard the melody. The door opens. A young guy in a brown suit with tousled brown hair and a big grin closes it behind him. You stop playing. With the dampers gone the dominant chord you just played keeps sounding around the room, hankering, looking for movement, hunting for the chord you were moving toward.

Chapter 30

"Herbert," Paulson says. "Gruessdi."

"Gruessdi," he says. And then nothing while he hurriedly fetches coal, fires up the stove, comes back from washing his hands. You get off the bench. Along with the old brown suit he's wearing the thin green blade of a tie and the big brown wingtipped shoes some missionaries wear. You wonder if they're hand me downs. Herbert shakes Paulson's hand.

"Sorry I am late," he says. Still breathing hard. "I am running the whole way."

"Out late with Hilgi again?"

Paulson's eyebrows jump a couple of times and his grin goes sly and Herbert comes up with the half shy smile he knows he's supposed to.

"Nah. We have been playing in Ping Pong . . . tour . . ."

"Tournament?" you say.

"Yes! Tournament!"

Paulson perks up. "Last night?"

"Yah," Herbert says. "We win, too. Are keeping on playing." The grin is back. You can tell from the way he sets it, firm and broad and thrust forward, that he learned it from the elders.

"Where?"

"The Volksgymnasium."

"The public gym," says Paulson. "Man. I'd love to play. I'm a killer player."

"Then you should come!" says Herbert.

"I don't know, man. You might regret that invite." Paulson steps back and fakes a couple of paddle swings at a couple of imagined balls.

"No," says Herbert. "Too much like dancing. Like this." And he goes into a football player crouch, mean, all business, tossing an imagined paddle from one hand to the other.

"Maybe in Austria," Paulson says. "Not where I come from."

"Okay," says Herbert. "We play Austrian Ping Pong against American."

"When?"

"We will play again on Tuesday. At nineteen hundred. But only tournament." Then he says, "Sorry. Seven at night."

"So I can't play?" says Paulson.

"Tuesday only for tournament," says Herbert. "But we are playing soon."

"Okay," Paulson says. "Game on." He extends his arm your way. "This is Elder Tauffler."

His hand is cold when you shake it. His acne is what Paulson said it was. From running, from the morning air, it's probably more raw than usual, charged with blood, but under the ravaged skin his looks and his exuberance break through the bad stuff.

"You were you playing the piano?" he says.

"Yeah. Sort of."

He turns to Paulson, claps his hands together, laughs. "Hey! We have music!"

"Looks that way."

He doesn't catch the shift in Paulson's attitude. You figure Paulson's miffed about having his Ping Pong chops compared to dancing. Herbert turns to you. Wants to know where you're from. How long you've been in Austria. Where you've worked. You want to know about his baptism. What he does. Where he got his shoes. He tells you he got them from Elder Limburg. You tell him you don't know Elder Limburg. He tells you Elder Limburg baptized him and then went home in August. You slip into German. He stays with English.

"Where does he live?"

"Kerrens."

"Kerrens?"

"You have good accent!" he says. "Sound almost Austrian!"

"I had good teachers."

"Like I have good teachers!"

"What was that name again?"

"Kerrens?" he says. "Korrens?"

And then you get it. Kearns. One of the big amorphous outskirts neighborhoods of Salt Lake. One of the neighborhoods that spread their inexpensive houses and country western joints out west across the yellow floor of the valley toward Magna and the Oquirrh Mountains and south toward Point of the Mountain penitentiary.

"Kearns," you say. "Like burns. Kurns."

"Kurns," he says.

"That's it," you say.

His grin shows through the savage creases it leaves in his scarred cheeks.

"Someday I visit Kurns," he says. "Elder Limburg has been inviting me."

With its afternoon sky this dirty yellow from the smokestack of the Kennecott Copper smelter, you're thinking. When he's got this breathtaking place.

"He will taking me skiing. In the Rockies!"

When he's got the Alps right out the window.

"Nice."

"Before he is leaving, I am helping him to buy good Austrian skis. Blizzards."

"You ski?"

"Since four years old." He spreads out his arms and you know he's taking in the town and the mountains that cradle it. "Everyone is doing it." He laughs. "Nothing else to do."

"There's Ping Pong," says Paulson.

"Oh. Yes. Sorry. Ping Pong."

"When are you going?" you say.

"When I am having the money. Maybe in two years. Or three. That's why I am speaking English. I want to be good at it when I go!"

You'll be home by then, you're suddenly thinking.

"Come see me too if you want. I live close to Kearns."

Excitement blazes in his blemished face.

"Sure? You are skiing too?"

"I don't ski, but sure, you can come."

"I can teach you!"

You laugh. "That's okay. We'll do other stuff. Hey. We could even drive up to Idaho Falls. Visit Elder Paulson."

"That would be nice!"

Herbert's grin is open and defenseless as both of you look at Paulson. He's at the pulpit, leaning over the open manual he was reading earlier, writing something down with the fat torpedo of his Schaeffer pen.

"What do you say, Elder Paulson?"

Paulson doesn't look up. "I say we get Priesthood started."

You get this cold feeling. But Herbert holds his grin. "I will check the stove again," he says, and heads down the aisle, his shoulders down like a servant's.

"You don't want to wait for the rest of them?" you say.

"This is it," he says. "Wanna play an opening hymn?"

"You and me and Herbert?"

He finally looks up. His smile is meant to let you know you're one shade deeper into being stupid.

"Yeah," he says. "Just us. You wanna play a hymn or not?"

You listen to Herbert push coal around inside the stove.

"Sure. What would you like?"

"Your choice. You can say the opening prayer too."

"What do you say, Herbert?"

From the back of the room Herbert looks up from the stove at Paulson. Paulson nods. "How Firm a Foundation?" Herbert says.

And so the three of you sing How Firm a Foundation. Paulson's not a bad singer. Herbert's almost as bad as the piano but sings with such gusto it doesn't matter much. You give the prayer in German without asking Paulson how he'd like it. After the hymn, and the prayer, you take one of the front row chairs across the aisle from Herbert to help him give the room some sense that it's occupied.

"You're supposed to sit up here, Elder," Paulson says.

And so you take a chair behind the pulpit. Paulson starts the priesthood lesson out in German. You can't get over the concept of a Priesthood Meeting with only one guy in the audience. Back home there had to be a couple of hundred guys in the chapel. Even in Vienna there was enough of an audience so that it never crossed your mind to wonder why a bunch of guys would put on suits and get together for a meeting early on Sunday morning. Herbert sits there with his back straight and his shoulders in and his hands in his lap like he's crowded in between two other priesthood holders. In the front row he's five feet away from the pulpit. But he's listening to Paulson talk about the role of the priesthood bearer in the home like there are twenty other guys around him.

Paulson reads most of the lesson out of his manual. So Herbert's mostly safe from hearing German words arranged into English sentences. But the way he reads them makes it sound like German never was a European language. Like it's the state language of Idaho. It doesn't seem to bother Herbert. He's listening to an Instrument of the Lord. The only time he moves is when a piece of coal explodes like a rifle crack in the hot belly of the stove. After the lesson you play Ere You Left Your Room this Morning as the closing hymn. Paulson asks Herbert to say the benediction. Herbert steps up behind the pulpit and says a German prayer in front of an empty room.

You've got more than half an hour before Sunday School. You and Paulson walk to a dairy shop up the street for a buttered roll and some milk. You can tell he's peeved. The woman behind the counter is sturdy and robust. Her thick dark blond hair tied in a lazy knot off the back of her head. Wearing one of those farmgirl dresses that spills her cleavage into the framing container of a white blouse. You and Paulson eat at one of the two café tables in the front window. A rusted white Opel is parked outside.

"Herbert's pretty excited about going to Utah," you finally say.

Paulson's looking out the window too. He smiles without turning his polished face from the glass and waits until he swallows what's in his mouth.

"You think he's really going, huh?"

"Sure sounds like he is. Limburg invited him."

"Yeah," says Paulson. "So did you."

You look at him. "Yeah. I did."

Paulson takes a swig of his milk.

"You think Limburg meant it?" he says.

"I don't know Limburg."

"Well, I know him."

"You saying that Limburg just said it?"

"No, he probably meant it, just like you. But he's back home now. He's had his homecoming. He's got his chick. He's back in college. You think he still cares about a kid from Austria?"

"I don't know."

"What's he gonna do with an Austrian kid in Utah? Take him to class? Line him up with some girls? Go out and polka with him?"

The joke is so crude the bite of buttered roll you've got in your mouth starts going sour. Paulson looks at you like he scored a point in this contest he keeps playing.

"America's for Americans," he says. "Like me and you and Limburg. Austria's for Austrians. Even the Church says that. You can be buddies with Herbert all you want, but don't forget that he's gonna be staying here."

The missing hymns, you're thinking. Utah We Love Thee. O Ye Mountains High. With the Alps outside at the edge of town.

"I know all that," you say. "We're just talking about a visit."

"Yeah. Well, I didn't appreciate it when you told him he could come and visit me."

"You're right. Sorry."

"Forget it. He'll get over it. Besides, he's got a girlfriend. She's pretty hot. Wait till you see her."

"So we're going Tuesday?"

"Ping Pong? You bet. I'll show him what's what. Friggin' A."

Six women and a boy show up for Sunday School. Five of the women are old. Herbert greets each one of them with his unleashed exuberance. In his own language he's talkative, animated, sure of himself, makes the women shine with adoring pride. He introduces you to each of them. Sister Gaggl. Sister Rohrer. Sister Schmied. Sister Gottschling. Sister Pichler. The warmth their faces radiate let you know they've already adopted you. The sixth woman, Sister Dietl, is maybe in her thirties. The boy's her son. His name is Heinzi. Paulson tells you he's the outcome of a one night stand. At ten years old he can see the priesthood coming over the horizon. Herbert takes a slice of bread wrapped in a handkerchief out of his pocket. Hands it to you.

"For the sacrament," he says. "There are cups in the bathroom for the water."

Herbert tends the stove and distributes the hymn books. The women take off their coats, leave their shawls on, take chairs in the second row. You drop the slice of bread onto the bread tray, fill the paper cups of the water tray in the bathroom, set up the little table for the sacrament, cover the trays with a cloth. Paulson takes you aside and tells you what your duties are. He'll do all the pulpit stuff. You'll play piano and prepare and bless the sacrament.

"Shouldn't Herbert take care of the sacrament?" you say.

"He's just a deacon," says Paulson. "He'll pass it around."

"A deacon?"

Paulson veils his smirk. "Yeah."

"He's eighteen. He was old enough two years ago to be a priest."

"You don't just get made a priest," says Paulson. "He's got to go through the ranks like everyone else. He needs to be a teacher first."

"So he's not even a teacher yet."

"Not yet."

"Can't prepare the sacrament. That's why he had me do it."

"That's the rule."

"Who decides when he gets to be a teacher?"

"I do."

"Got it."

Paulson formally introduces you and tells the smallest congregation you've ever seen that he's the senior now and that you play piano. They're thrilled. You feel bad about the resistant and sour choiring of the strings but the women sing like angels. Paulson gives the invocation and announces Herbert's Ping Pong tournament. Despite his accent the older women look at Paulson with tender adoration. When his German stumbles into some grammatical snare, their distress for him is real, as real as their relief when he finds his way back out again. While of these Emblems We Partake is the sacrament hymn. You play the congregation through the first verse, and then, with Paulson standing there conducting, you let them sing the second verse a capella while you cross the room to the sacrament table to fold back the cloth and shred the single slice of bread into the single tray. You make it back to the keyboard for the third and then the fourth verse. Then back to the table again where you kneel on the little footstool. The card with the blessing for the bread surprises you. It's in German. O Gott, you read, unser himmlischer Vater, and when you're done you stand back up. Herbert comes forward. You hand him the tray. He turns to the widows. Suddenly, laughing and brash through the thin glass of the window, as startling as a car horn, the voices of two girls pass by outside. The faces of the widows change. They go alarmed. Then cross. Then more ashamed than cross. Sister Rohrer touches her shawl. They take their piece of bread from the tray in Herbert's hand with shy concentration.

It sinks in. Their surrounding attention. The way they sing. The way their worried faces pull for Paulson to get to the end of a German sentence. How much it means to them to come here. Herbert serves the women and the boy. Then Paulson, from his chair behind the pulpit, and then you, and after you've taken your piece, you hold the tray for Herbert. Then you and Herbert do the water. Sister Gaggl gives a Sunday School lesson on obedience. A break after Sunday School allows the women to catch up with each other. Between the day warming and the affection that radiates its warmth off the women the stove becomes unnecessary. Herbert lets it go. Paulson calls for Sacrament Meeting. You take the pulpit when it's time to speak. Your speech is about love. You look at them from where you stand. The women. A boy named Heinzi. Herbert. Their adoring faces. You can feel the radiant warmth of their pride in your chest where your lungs have breathed it in. They're here for this. You didn't know, getting it ready last night with your own cheap ballpoint pen, that a speech about love would be the last speech they would need to hear. But it's all you have. Love. You stand there defenseless in its luminous and unapologetic presence.

CHAPTER 31

ON MONDAY, and then again on Tuesday after your morning prayers, after washing up and getting dressed, after a couple of hours of study, Paulson takes you tracting. He takes his time in front of the mirror and so you start out late. You stop for milk and a buttered roll, then head down Hauptplatz, stop again to buy some gloves, pedal across a long bridge over a river whose slow dark current splits the town, follow Paulson's overcoat along a road that takes you out into the country. The wind through your ankles is cold and your knuckles still ache in your new thin cloth gloves but the November air is lush with the deep fall scent of the pastures beyond the fences and the cows the haybales feed. Your saddlebags rock back and forth against your ribs in cadence with your pedaling. In the morning sunlight your front tire rolls across the dirt and broken asphalt of the roadside and sends pebbles twanging off into the dying grass. Occasional cars approach you from behind. You look at Paulson's overcoat, riding the wind, and know what you look like to their drivers. When they putter by, little Fiats and Peugeots, you look down on their roofs from the perch of your seat the way you did from the passenger seat of Robbie's van. Where a road sign says Sankt Magdalen Paulson stops to compare the tracting book against a mailbox off the roadside. You look at the house that goes with it. It charges you to be this close, to have it be this big, like you've pedaled into the third dimension of one of your father's calendar photos and had it suddenly turn real. Off the side of the house a woman in a green scarf wades through a dying garden. When she holds one up to the sky, turns it in her hand, you can tell she's looking for tomatoes. This late, you think. This warm when you're standing still.

"Get out a couple of brochures," says Paulson.

And that's where you start. You reach inside a saddlebag, pull out a brochure showing Jesus Christ appearing in the woods to Joseph Smith, another one about the Mormon Pioneers. The woman stops and watches you while you push your bikes up the driveway toward her. Her broad red face is bloodshot with the threads of a thousand little veins and her light brown hair is streaked by a summer of sun where it shows from under her scarf.

"Gruess Gott," Paulson says.

"Gruess Gott," she answers.

"How are you today?"

"Good," she says. "Can I help you?"

She's not shy. Faced with two smiling American guys in suits, pushing their bikes, she smiles too, ready to help with directions or a glass of water or whatever else it is you're here for. And then Paulson tells her who you are. You wait for her. Stand there, brochures in your hand like you're bringing her the mail, too charged to keep yourself from looking way too glad to see her. You watch her smile run out. Austrian dust dulls the shine of your polished American shoes.

"Where?" she asks.

"Die Kirche Jesu Christi der Heiligen der Letzten Tage," Paulson says again.

"Missionare?" she says sharply. "Aus Amerika? Nein. Keine Zeit."

"Something to read?" Paulson says. She's already turned her attention around to her garden. You extend the brochures toward her back in case she turns back around.

"Keine Zeit," she tells one of her tomatoes.

"Many thanks," Paulson says.

On the way back out to the road he tells you to put the brochures in her mailbox. You make sure she's not looking. And then you're off again, riding or walking your bikes from one farmhouse to the next, opening gates, getting dogs to like you, knocking on doors, talking to people out working in their yards. All of them go through the same transformation when they get why you're here. A farmer out working on the carburetor of his tractor engine shows you at first what he's fixing and then, when Paulson breaks the news, tells you to get off his property. All of them get postage-free brochures while Paulson marks them off as rejects in the tracting book. Foreign mud starts to crawl up and dry around the soles of your shoes. You start to understand you don't belong here. That your reason for being here is what keeps you from belonging here. That the dead cornfield you and Paulson stop to take a leak in isn't one you'll be harvesting. But this is what you're here for. To knock on doors. God in your knuckles. The rejects only fuel the fire in your chest. Get you closer to the door that may crack open, then pull back, then let you in.

And then Paulson says, "Okay. Time for lunch. Let's head back."

It's been a couple of hours. Ahead of you stand the outlying houses of another village.

"Maybe there's a gasthaus up ahead. We wouldn't have to ride back out here."

Paulson squints down the road.

"Naw. There's one back in town. Let's go."

The farmer repairing his tractor is still outside. The woman gathering tomatoes is gone. The bridge that splits the town is busy with people strolling and hanging out against the railings in the Indian summer warmth of the November sun. You eat fast. Paulson takes his time. He doesn't take you back across the bridge. He takes you shopping. Not big stuff. Stuff he can afford. Airmail envelopes, a notebook, a souvenir patch, stuff you figure he needs by way of preparing himself to be the kind of senior he's meant to be.

On Tuesday night, at the town gym, Herbert introduces you to his girlfriend. Her name is Hilgi. She smiles and puts out her hand to you.

"Gruessdi, Herr Tauffler," she says, with a slyness in her eyes that startles you, until you realize it isn't her, but you, the way you haven't had a girl smile at you that way or felt the clasp of a girl's hand in yours for months, since the airport, since it was Cissy's hand.

"Gruessdi, Hilgi."

Dark brown hair that she wears in bangs and a casual ponytail, dark brown eyes, a full mouth, skin so smooth it makes you think of drinking milk. Not a knockout. But she has looks, the winter kind, the dark and warm and brownhaired kind where you lose yourself in her face and sweater in the deep back seat of a borrowed Buick on a night where it might be snowing. You're more prepared when she introduces you to her two friends. Ilse and Therese.

"It's nice to meet you," Ilse says, in English, her grip light while you feel the fine bones under the warm skin of her hand. "Maybe for Christmas I knit a nice scarf for you."

With Paulson watching, all you can let yourself do is laugh, then say, "It's nice to meet you too, Ilse."

They take seats with Herbert on the lower bench in front of you. The parted top of Ilse's dark blond hair is right there at your knees. While the bleachers fill and the noise rises you look everywhere else. Six green tables are arranged across the big floor. Each table is manned by two guys taking practice shots at one another. Up in the ceiling the overhead lights are caged in wire housings. On the far wall the numbered cards of the scoreboard say 21 to 17. A tall ladder between the opposing scores tells you the numbers have to be changed by hand. There aren't any baskets and backboards. You wonder what kind of game it was. A huge bell somewhere high in the rafters goes off like a fire alarm. Hilgi wishes Herbert luck and reaches up and kisses the ravaged skin of his cheek.

Out on the floor the first heat of guys faces off at opposite ends of the tables and stand there smacking their paddles. You spot Herbert. Each table has a referee. One of them blows a whistle. Balls start flying. Pocks fill the gym. Everyone starts yelling. The players are brutal. They stand way back, swing like fighters, hit the ball like a bullet they want to put through the crotch of the guy across the net. Herbert gets the guy he's playing on the run, lunging side to side, stepping farther back, till he softly tips the ball across the net and it dies before the guy can even think of how to get to it. You yell and turn to Paulson. Paulson's watching Hilgi. Through all the tumult coming off the walls, all the action on the floor, he's fixed on Hilgi, and it chills you the way he looks at her.

You spend the next morning watching him shop for a paddle instead of pedaling out across the long bridge to the road that takes you to the village where you left off yesterday. After he finds the perfect paddle and buys a set of balls, you walk to the churchhouse, follow him up the stairs to the empty room on the second floor, watch him look around.

"This is perfect," he says. "Made for it."

"Made for what?" You look around. You still see a music studio.

"A Ping Pong club," he says.

"You want to play Ping Pong in here?"

"We just gotta get a table."

He takes his paddle out of his shopping bag, takes position against a wall, dances back and forth against an imagined volley more like a fencer than the guys you watched play in the gym last night.

"We can use that blackboard for a scoreboard," he says.

"A scoreboard? Why?"

"We're gonna have our own tournament."

You take another look around the room. This time, you see Hilgi standing against the side wall, watching Herbert whack the ball across the net while Paulson watches her.

"A tournament," you say.

"It's a missionary tool," says Paulson. "Get some young blood interested in the Gospel."

"How do we get from Ping Pong to the Gospel?"

"Leave that to the Lord," says Paulson. "Where's your testimony, Elder?"

"Maybe Herbert knows where we can get a table."

"I got a better idea," says Paulson.

From there you go back to the gym. Paulson finds a guy in an office off the gym and tells him what he wants. Tells him it's for a church. The guy lights up. He takes you out to a storage room and shows you a table there. It's been used to where the green is beat to pieces and the white lines are almost gone. Paulson asks how much. The guy says they'll donate it. They'll even throw in a net. But they won't deliver it. He roots around in a closet and hands you a couple of battered paddles with the rubber loose around the edges. You and Paulson haul half the table through town and wrestle it up the stairs at the churchhouse. Then go back and get the other half. When you get them standing the legs are so rickety and loose the tables wobble and sway like rafts on a river.

"I can fix the legs," you say. "We could bracket the tables together too."

"What do you need?"

"A hardware store."

"We'll get paint there too," says Paulson.

"Some glue too. For the paddles."

"Man," says Paulson. "This is gonna be one fuzzin' clubhouse."

Chapter 32

By the time you're done, the table's painted, the floor mopped, the rubber mats on the paddles fixed, the windows cleaned. You leave them open to air out the smell of the paint. The next morning, instead of heading out to the countryside, you get some paper signs and tickets made up at a printing shop. Ping Pong. 10 Oktoberstrasse 17. Blank lines where you can write in the date and time. Saturday from noon to six. You find a place to buy a blackboard eraser and some chalk, some tape and some thumbtacks, and set out to spread the word. Paulson keeps the receipts for reimbursement by the Mission Home. That afternoon you leave your suit coats down in the meeting room and practice in your shirts and ties. Paulson waxes you. That night you do a movie. On Friday morning, your day off, you put on your Levis, your sweater, your sneakers, and Paulson tells you he's going downstairs to ask the landlady to use her phone.

"What's up?" you say.

"I want to give Sanderson a call," he says. "See if him and Hatch want to play some Ping Pong this afternoon."

"Hatch?"

"Yeah. You know him?"

"I came here with him."

"Yeah?" says Paulson. "Hey. They're in Spittal. Twenty minutes away."

"That'd be cool."

Paulson throws you his derisive little smile. "Yeah. I need some tougher competition if I'm gonna be ready for Saturday."

Sanderson and Hatch show up at the meeting house just after lunch. You remember Sanderson from the afternoon he picked Hatch up in the conference room at the Mission Home. The guy who looked like your family dentist. He comes through the door in a pair of baggy khaki pants and a yellow and red Hawaiian shirt that makes his glasses pink and his face look sunburned. It looks like his Utah head was planted on some California guy's idea of how to dress on Diversion Day. Like the guys who came back from Los Angeles and Vegas after their weekend leave from summer camp in the Mojave.

"Hey!" he says. "You guys ready to get trounced?"

"Hey!" says Paulson. "Good to see you, man!"

"Saw your Ping Pong signs in all the windows just walking here," Sanderson says, shaking Paulson's hand. "You guys plastered the town."

"The only way to do it," says Paulson.

Hatch comes through the door in a gray sweatshirt and an old pair of Levis.

"Hey, Hatch," you say.

"Hey," Paulson says, scolding. "That's Elder Hatch."

"Hey. Tauffler." Hatch grins and shakes your hand. Paulson throws him a scolding look and heads up the stairs with Sanderson. "I'll be darned, man," says Hatch. "You're here?"

It's good to see him. The bright sunburn in his raw face back in July when you got here has aged to a quiet tan.

"I just got transferred a week ago."

"From where?"

"Vienna."

"Man. I've been stuck in friggin' Spittal since we got here."

"I figured when I saw your senior."

"Yeah. He's heading home in a couple of weeks. I'm his last companion."

"Wow. That's close."

"Tell me," says Hatch. "He's been sitting on his trunk since I got here. It's kinda hard, just getting here, and here's this guy who's going home."

You remember the Hawaiian shirt you bought in Louisville. The phony shirt you had on when Cissy first saw you from her porch. The shirt she thought was a uniform for your band.

"Looks like he's going to a luau."

"Yeah," says Hatch. "I keep telling him nobody's wearing those things anymore back home, but man, he's crazy about that fuzzin' shirt."

Down from the stairs and ceiling come the opening pocks of the ball, the skidding and pounding of sneakers, Sanderson's voice deep against Paulson's high-pitched yelling.

"Good to see you keeping up that tan," you say.

"Heck. We're always outside."

"You guys do a lot of tracting?"

"All the time, man," says Hatch. "He's trying to score a baptism before he goes."

"He's never had one?"

"Nope. So we're out banging on doors ten hours a day. We're running out of places. We even started taking the train out to these little dorfs nobody's ever tracted. Strange people out there, man."

"You seen Wissom or Clayton?"

"No. I heard Clayton's in rough shape, though."

"I heard that too. Real homesick."

"How's your girl?" you say.

"Ah, I dunno. Not sure. How's yours?"

"She's good."

"Tell Paulson about her?"

"No way."

"Smart. How you getting along with him?"

"We tracted a couple of days. Then this Ping Pong thing came up." Then you say, "He's a new senior. He's figuring things out. Trying new stuff."

"Yeah."

"What?"

Hatch looks around the room.

"He's a little stuck on himself."

"Yeah?"

"You haven't seen it?"

"Like how?"

"Like how he's in love with mirrors. How long you been with him? A week?"

"Yeah."

Hatch looks toward the stairs. The racket hasn't let up. Hatch drops his voice to where it's almost a whisper anyway.

"His last senior, Bowles," he says. "Just before you got here, I guess. He always had a problem getting him out of the house. Away from the mirror."

"How do you know?"

"Bowles used to tell Sanderson," says Hatch. "Sanderson told me. Then I saw it."

"It's that obvious, huh."

"You notice yet how he's always checking out chicks?"

Herbert's girlfriend, you're thinking. "Tell me."

"It scared Bowles. The whole arm's length thing. But he'd never go near one. Paulson's a tease. He just likes getting them to notice him. Swap a smile. Flirt a little. That's all."

"How're you doing?" you say. "With the swimming and skiing stuff?"

"I try not to think about it. Working all the time helps. Sometimes I think how Sanderson's gonna be skiing two years sooner than me."

"He doesn't ski. He surfs."

Hatch laughs. "Yeah. From that shirt. Heck, every time I look at these mountains, I gotta pretend I got two busted legs."

"Sorry."

"How about you? That mouthpiece you had?"

"I keep it tucked away."

"Why? You got all that time to practice while Paulson's glued to the mirror."

"Maybe one day. See what happens."

"The worst you can do is tick him off. Big friggin' deal."

It's warm enough upstairs that they've got the windows open. Sanderson plays like an Austrian. Whatever it takes to whang the ball back Paulson's way. Sweat comes flying off his head in diamonds when he swings. His Hawaiian shirt is soaked. Paulson doesn't have a prayer. And Hatch can't stand up to anyone. Even you can beat him. He doesn't mind. He just treats it like a game he's lousy at. But you watch Paulson tighten up, get meaner over the run of the afternoon, beat you and Hatch like he's out to punish you for never beating Sanderson. You know what he's thinking. It's his table. He's got the brand new paddle. It's not fair. You think Sanderson would throw him just one game. Make him easier to go home with. Sometime after six, the four of you wash up downstairs, and Sanderson and Hatch head back to the station to catch the train to Spittal.

Saturday's no better. Herbert shows up at noon. Over the next hour, other kids start showing up with their paddles, confused and guarded at first about the church sign by the door outside. You recognize some of them from the tournament last Tuesday. Paulson writes each of their names on the blackboard and starts things off. You play a big mangy kid named Mogy who yells "Achtung!" every time he whacks the ball your way and laughs with a loose-mouthed "huh huh huh" when you can't return it. Hilgi comes by around two. You've already been erased. Paulson waits till she's there before he finally steps up and takes Herbert on. Herbert doesn't get it. That Paulson needs to win. That if he ever wants to get advanced from deacon to teacher, and from there to priest, then Paulson needs to win. But Herbert blindly plays him as hard as he played the first two guys he beat. Halfway through the game the outcome is so grim you have to go downstairs. Sit at the piano. Run a couple of blues scales. Wonder what to play. What comes to mind is the arrangement of Greensleeves Morgan taught you on the Boesendorfer in the Vienna chapel. The song that Mr. Hinkle played on the violin that day you limped into his store to look for the sound you'd heard. His eyes shut and his knees turning small slow circles. Greensleeves. The song Hidalgo strummed on his red guitar on the bunkhouse porch. Big rolling arpeggios in the bass and big chords for the melody while the ceiling hollers and pounds away above your head.

On Sunday it starts to rain. When the women come they leave their wet umbrellas open, back by the stove on the floor, a flock of black sails that brought them here and wait to sail them home again. That afternoon you fill out your reports. Paulson counts everything that had to do with Ping Pong. Time spent with investigators because none of Herbert's friends is Mormon. That's okay with you. The rain is deep and still and lasts into Monday morning. You pull the black rubber overshoes you bought in Vienna over your leather street shoes, button your raincoat up, get your umbrella out. Paulson matches you accessory for accessory. And then some. A big plastic full length poncho with sleeves and a hood.

"Hey," you say, watching him grope for the sleeve holes. "That's cool."

"Yeah. I got it in Leoben."

"Do they sell them here?"

"Nope. Never seen 'em anywhere else."

He shakes out the folds. Wrinkled sheets of dark green plastic keep falling loose until they reach his ankles.

"So? What do you think?"

"Looks like a shower curtain."

"I'll ask you again when we get back."

On your bike, you follow him through town, watch him weave through puddles like a dancer in a garment bag. Rain runs off your hair and down your neck. The wind the speed of your bike creates blows the rain back off your hands where you can feel it crawl up your forearms under your sleeves. By the time you get to the town where you left off almost a week ago your raincoat and shoes and the calves of your pants are soaked. You lock your bike to an iron railing that looks like public property, take your umbrella out of your basket, pop it open. Paulson peels off his poncho inside out, shakes it, wads it into a bundle the size of a sandwich, and clamps it to his bike rack before he opens his own umbrella. Water runs off his lower face. But you're amazed at how dry his pants and tie and hair and raincoat are. Almost like he never left the room.

"Man," you say. "That thing does the job."

Paulson smiles. There's victory in it. "Pays to be prepared."

CHAPTER 33

THE RAIN IS STEADY but light. You love being back to tracting after putting the 10 Oktoberstrasse 17 Ping Pong Club together and holding the opening tournament.

On Tuesday morning, while Paulson prepares himself to go out, the rain comes to an end, the attic window brightens. By the time you're done with your milk and buttered roll at the dairy shop the sky is cloudless. You take a different road out of town. The puddles are fresh. You slalom your bike around them. A road sign tells you you're heading toward a dorf called Heiligengeist.

The village of the Holy Ghost is small. You work through its doors in less than an hour. Then start hitting the houses and farms on the road back to Villach. You're back before noon at a back street restaurant where you hook the handgrips of your bikes on the ledge of the window, where you take the table at the window so you can watch them, where the radio out of the kitchen plays polka music. The cook serves you a greasy schnitzel. Out the window, while you cut through your hard shingle of breaded meat, an old woman with a cane makes her way past, bent forward, a rope over the shoulder of her old overcoat, dragging a cardboard box half full of coal along the sidewalk. Nobody can be missed, you think, watching her. But your workday's done. You've knocked on your last door.

The 10 Oktoberstrasse 17 Ping Pong Club meets under Paulson's direct supervision for one more Saturday. And then, tired of having Hilgi watch Herbert beat him, Paulson loses interest. He turns the table and blackboard over to Herbert and his friends and puts Herbert in immediate charge. Herbert's friends bring friends. Hilgi brings girls. And you figure the girls are why Paulson drops in every Saturday without taking his overcoat off. Stands back and observes like he's the boss of everyone and the president of everything. Gives Herbert orders Herbert doesn't need. His way of beating Herbert. His way of letting Hilgi and the girls know. Ilse comes over sometimes to watch and make small talk with you. Sometimes when you're downstairs she comes down too. Paulson doesn't miss a thing.

"That chick still want to knit you a scarf?"

"She said maybe."

"I think you need to tell her thanks but no thanks."

You look at him. Back home he'd be the last guy you'd want for a friend. He wouldn't even be the guy you'd pick to beat up in a high school parking lot when you and Snook and Porter used to go out looking.

"You want one too?"

"That's not what I'm saying."

"What color?"

You learn that you're not the only Americans in town. There's another one. A white haired bearded old American who retired here and lives on the other side of the bridge. His name is Frank. He calls himself an expatriate. You run into him now and then. If he sees you he hollers. And then you stop if you're walking or swing off your bikes if you're riding. Paulson doesn't seem to want to share him. And so you listen to him and Paulson gab while you take in his lederhosen shorts and all the badges pinned to his Tyroler hat and the fierce profusion of deep intermingled lines in the leather skin of his face. His accent is English but still retains enough American to make you homesick. Expatriate. You wonder if that's how Switzerland would look at you. What it would be like to be retired here yourself. How there would be too much you'd miss. The naked feel of the endless desert. Soldier Summit. Dead Horse Point. The hillside above the sandpit. Raw open places with the space to let the sound of your trumpet soar through an infinite sky. The weather. Where you're headed today. What he's doing. The conversations don't last long. Paulson bumps them up to an hour spent with an investigator in your weekly reports.

You learn that Paulson's smirk, easy and quick and cheap as tin, is a permanent condition. You learn that he never much laughs at anything funny you say. Other elders, elders like Sanderson and Hatch from Spittal and from other towns you visit back and forth with, may be busting up around a restaurant table at some story you tell or joke you crack. Paulson sits there with this small tight pissed off smile looking quietly hurt. You learn that his voice, not deep to start with, goes high and nasal when you get him mad. You learn that he played a Jet in Idaho Falls in a high school production of West Side Story. You learn that you could piss him off if you asked him what a Jet was.

Then there's what Hatch told you. What you already knew. Day after day as you move through November you watch him try an arsenal of different smiles, different ways of cocking his smooth round polished face, different ways of combing his hair in the mirror, while you wait at the table past nine and then past ten to get out of the room, away from the vapor of his aftershave, onto your bike, out into the country, start knocking on doors for the day.

West Side Story. It tells you why he walks with the buoyant strut of the dancer on the sidewalk. Why every shop window you pass is a quick shot to the side to see how he's doing. You learn that when a girl coming toward the two of you starts smiling you can sneak a look at him and find him wearing a smile you've seen him practice. You learn that when a girl smiles at you instead he'll sneak a look across at you. So you smile back. Smile back like you've just played Stormy Weather and it was meant for her. Get her to smile back like she listened and knows what you were doing and liked where you took her. It makes Paulson morose as a kid with nothing to show for Halloween but an empty pillowcase. But he knows he can't say anything. Just has to wait till a new girl comes along and throws him a rescue smile.

"Cute, huh?"

Waiting till she's history and out of earshot.

"Jailbait," you say.

"What's jailbait?"

"Too young."

"Oh. I get it." Turning around for another look. And then he says, "You sure?"

Across the rock upthrust of the Alps the snow line has been coming lower. It won't be long till it reaches the hills and then the valleys and roads you use to ride out to the distant villages. Early one Saturday morning late in November you're following Paulson across the bridge in the center of town when you see Frank across the roadway. He's wearing a brown herringbone overcoat over his lederhosen. His lower legs are bare and hairless from where his coat ends to where the loose tops of his black socks begin. He's always been on the reserved side of friendly. This morning he's out of his mind. He sees you, starts waving, runs hobbling across the bridge to where you're pedaling. You swing off your bikes and haul them up on the sidewalk out of traffic. His eyes are mad. His whiskers amplify the agitation of his creased face. You can see the shiny rose red skin, smooth as scar tissue, along the inside of his trembling bottom lip.

"Did you hear?" Waving a colored newspaper in Paulson's face.

"Hear what?" Paulson says.

"Kennedy's been shot!" He searches Paulson's face. "The President! My God! President Kennedy! He's dead!"

Jesus, you think. Holy crap.

"Sure," says Paulson, and looks at Frank with a smirk that says he's way too cool to fall for a joke from an old American guy who lives in an Austrian town. Frank stares at Paulson. Then steps back, pulls himself together, and he's suddenly tall and calm and formal. But offended more than anything.

"I'm quite serious," he says.

"Wait," you say. "Can I see that?"

You take the paper from his hand. The Arbeiter-Zeitung. Sure enough. Kennedy Ermordet, the headline says, and underneath it there's a photograph, the president and his wife in the back seat of a convertible limo, their smiling faces turned in bright sunlight toward the camera, a crowd on the far side of the limo, a sign held in the air that reads All the Way with JFK. American words in an Austrian newspaper.

"He's dead," you say. "Kennedy's dead." You stare at Frank. "He can't be dead."

"I'm glad one of you understands me," he says.

"That's crazy," you say. "What happened? When?"

"Yesterday. He was in a motorcade in Dallas. Riding in that Lincoln Continental with the top down. A rifle shot to the back of the head. Jackie was right there next to him when his head exploded. This photo had to be shot just before it happened."

In a series of smaller headlines under the Kennedy Murdered headline it says ein Kuba-Politiker.

"What's with Cuba?"

"That's who shot him. Some lunatic Cuban with a rifle. They got the Cuban."

You look at Frank. Staring you in the face. Mouth open. Expecting something from you. A miracle. The bloodshot whites go all the way around his eyes. You feel wild too. You look aside, at the bridge, at the pedestrians, at the rooftops, at the crags of the Alps made smooth with snow, at the suddenly insane calm of this foreign place, back at Frank.

"I can't believe he's dead." You can hear the fear in your voice. "This is nuts."

"I can't believe it either."

He takes his paper back. Looks at you less wild. Brings up his arm and rests his old man hand on your shoulder. Then pats you a couple of times and lets his arm down.

"I'm sorry. I didn't mean to upset you."

"He just got elected again."

"He did."

"It's crazy. President Kennedy was gonna send us to Cuba. I was on active duty at Fort Knox. We were on standby all night."

"Fort Knox," says Frank. "Armor."

"Yeah."

"That's what I did. Second World War. Patton."

If he was one of the seven out of thirty thousand.

"They sure he's dead?" you say. "Papers can make mistakes."

"They raced him to the hospital and tried like hell to save him."

"I can't believe he's gone."

"The whole world loved him. The right people hated him. Khrushchev and Castro."

"Do you ever think of going home?" you hear yourself ask Frank.

"I am home, son. This is where I plan to die."

That pull again. That this was home for you once too. Before all the other homes.

"I can understand," you say.

He looks at you.

"Thanks for telling us. About Kennedy I mean."

"Thanks for listening." He looks at Paulson and his face goes cold. "I'll see you gentlemen around."

He touches the brim of his Tyroler hat and takes the street to get around your bikes. You watch him go. President Kennedy dead. What's going on back home. Karl and Molly and Roy and Maggie. Sandy and Lenny and Robbie and Eddie Santos and everyone. Cissy. San Jose. To be stuck in this Disneyland town this far from home where everything's exploding.

"He wasn't kidding," Paulson finally says.

"No."

"Well," says Paulson. "Guess we better head out."

You stare at him. "You mean knock on doors?"

"Yeah."

"You're kidding."

"Why?"

You look at his placid face. Unbelievable. "Sorry. Knocking on doors is the last thing I can do right now. I don't even know if I can ride a bike."

Paulson smirks. Shakes his head and looks off.

"What'll people think?" you say. "A couple of Americans knocking on their doors with their president dead?"

Paulson's taking a distant look along the bridge behind you. You know from the look that there's a girl there at the end of it, across the bridge, walking in your direction, straight into the teeth of his irresistibility.

"You're right," he says, through the lure of a smile. "I think we need hats."

"Hats?"

"They'd make us look more important," he says. "Yeah. Dignified. Hats. To go with our umbrellas."

"President Kennedy's been killed and you want to buy a hat?"

"Got anything against that, Elder?"

"You don't mean Tyroler hats. Like Frank's."

"I mean real hats."

You think of the faceless man and his Stetson.

"Like cowboy hats?"

"No. Business hats. Like FBI guys wear. You know. Like Sinatra."

How in high school you and Quigley stole your auto shop teacher's pickup truck for a joy ride. How Quigley wanted you to wear your teacher's hat so you'd look like him. How in the side mirror you looked like Sinatra instead.

"Hats make you go bald," you say.

"Yeah. I've heard that too. After forty years maybe." And there's his smirk again. "What are you? Too good to wear a hat?"

You look off for a second or two.

"You can get one. I'll pass."

"That's not gonna look right. We both need them."

"You get one. That way people can tell you're the senior."

"I didn't think of that."

From the way he retracts his smile you can tell the girl looked the other way.

"Maybe we oughta do something Kennedy would of done."

"Like what?" he says. "Invade fuzzin' Cuba?"

"He never wore a hat."

You learn through the course of the morning, mostly from salesmen while Paulson tries their hats on, that when the president's head exploded his wife was close enough to get spattered with his brains. That she held his head in her lap on the race to the hospital. It isn't long before Paulson's got himself his hat. A brown felt hat with a little brim. That afternoon you head for the 10 Oktoberstrasse 17 Ping Pong Club. Paulson wears his hat upstairs. Herbert's and Hilgi's friends don't let Paulson catch them swapping looks and raising eyebrows. That night you write Cissy. Tell her you heard. Feel helpless and useless when you tell her you hope she's okay. The next morning, while the papers blaze with headlines of the assassination, while you read that a Cuban guy named Oswald was caught in a movie theater, while the sun rises into a cloudless sky, you and Paulson walk instead of bike to church. Paulson's carrying his umbrella, working on the swing you've seen English guys in movies use, getting the syncopation right, learning how to hold the handle loose and let it slip to get the metal tip to crack the sidewalk. The Cuban Missile Crisis. You stood ready all night long in the barracks at Knox to be mobilized to take your tank to war. Trucks were parked outside for you. Even after they stood you down that morning you felt like you were in on something. Ready to go to war for President Kennedy. Part of it. Not like this. More than five thousand miles away with a guy learning how to whack the sidewalk with the tip of his umbrella. This hot shot guy in his new hat. People ahead of you turn around at the sharp crack of metal on cement. They look just long enough to see it's him, a guy with an umbrella on a cloudless day, not some crazy Cuban guy behind them shooting off a rifle.

CHAPTER 34

Shake? Do you still know my kisses? When I close my eyes I can feel your lips and taste them. Do you still know? Because I do . . .

LYNDON JOHNSON takes the oath on a plane bearing Kennedy's body in a casket back to the capitol. Once more, the way it did in Vienna, the hunger for home and for purpose fills the vacuum you'd reserved for your mission when you emptied your life of everything it was made of. You start to read again. Keep watch. Resume guard duty. Check the front pages of papers and covers of magazines at a newsstand in town. Mississippi. The fight to register negroes to vote in the election that would have elected Kennedy again a year from now if he hadn't been assassinated.

And now a place somewhere in Asia called Vietnam. Protests in San Francisco and at Berkeley and other schools against what has started taking on the character of war. San Francisco makes you anxious. You remember the highway signs that night. How close it was to San Jose once you crossed the trestle bridge out of Vallejo.

Under a bright December afternoon sky you look at Paulson and then the Newsweek in your hand. Hold out your other hand for change from the man behind the counter of the newsstand. High on the rack behind him are Playboy and other magazines with naked women on their covers.

"You plan on reading that?"

"Nah. I just look at the pictures."

Under the brim of his new hat Paulson smirks and turns away.

Dear Shake,

I still can't believe he's dead. Why would anyone want to do that to him, Shake? Why? Our Philosophy class had just gotten started when the Dean's voice came over the loudspeaker saying he was so sorry to inform us that President Kennedy had been shot in Dallas Texas. What? Professor Stevens told us to stay seated, he was going to the teachers lounge to see if there was news on the TV. We all just got up and followed him out into the hall to go to the teachers

lounge and the hallway was packed with students. As we got closer, I heard the sound from the TV, and then all of a sudden some of the students and teachers started sobbing and a couple of kids were screaming. "Oh my God….he's dead!" My legs got weak, so I just crouched down to sit on the floor in the hallway and cried. I cried until Professor Stevens came over to me and touched my arm. "Cissy," he said, and his voice was shaking. "Cissy, please, get up." I just didn't know what to do with myself, Shake. I went back to the classroom and grabbed my purse and my books, and went outside. I started walking off campus, just wanting to get home. Then I heard Daddy calling me. He and Mommy were in the car, they were there to bring me home, and they were crying too. I'm starting to feel a lot better, but it was a terrible week. Everything about his death, the funeral, all on TV for days. It hurt the most to see Jackie and the kids like that. I love you. I want you here with me. For Christmas. For always.
Cissy

In the middle of December the long Indian summer in the shadow of the Alps runs itself out. You still go tracting almost every morning. Sometimes there's snow and you spend the day in your room. Sometimes there's slush and you have to coast through puddles with your legs pulled up to keep them out of the ice water roostertails of your front tire. Christmas decorations go up on street lamps and doors and in shop windows. You stay home more and more. You hear about the Beatles. A simple little song called I Wanna Hold Your Hand comes from the kitchen radios of the backstreet restaurants you and Paulson sometimes use for supper. You see pictures of their mushroom haircuts on the covers of the papers at the dairy shop where you buy a buttered roll and milk for breakfast from the woman whose breasts in the cradle of her farmgirl blouse is where you put your shamed face on Friday when your turn on the toilet comes around.

Karl and Molly and Roy and Maggie send Christmas cards. Your mother sends socks, two new pairs of garments, a couple of bars of Liszt chocolate. Your father sends you a long letter and newspaper photos of Temple Square lit up with its millions of Christmas lights. Still waiting to hear the good news. You send the family a photo book of Villach and your mother a silk shawl in shimmering browns and golds and silvers. Cissy sends you a pair of fur-lined gloves to shield your knuckles from the wind you generate on your bike. You think of the woman with the Pontiac who gave you two dollars for gloves for the same reason. Cutting the fingertips off your mother's old gardening gloves so you could play while you kept your hands from freezing in the sandpit. You pass the glittering window of a jewelry shop and buy Cissy a necklace of a sparkling heart made out of Austrian crystal. Paulson looks your stuff over. Calculates it against what he got. You're surprised he doesn't have a girlfriend. Neither of you are prepared for what the members do on Christmas Sunday. Hilgi's friend Ilse comes through with a handknit scarf. Paulson chose dark green. You chose red and gray stripes. Your high school colors. Sister Gaggl gives each of you a handknit headband for your ears. Herbert gives each of you a stylishly narrow Austrian tie. Paulson's is blue. Yours is slick green. Word has gotten out that there's a hot plate in your room. And so two of the widows give you pots and pans they've polished to look like they're new again. Some invite you for Sunday dinner. You and Paulson hold out your empty hands. They won't stand for an apology. You do so much for them. This is their turn.

"I didn't know you could pick two colors," Paulson says, in front of the mirror in your attic room in his overcoat and hat, playing with different ways to wear the scarf Ilse knit for him. "You could have told me."

"Sorry."

"If I'd known I would've picked something besides green."

"You could have asked," you say. "That's what I did."

"Next time something like this comes up, you should tell me," he says. Then he says, "You wouldn't be interested in trading, would you?"

Ilse. Hilgi's chubby friend with long dark hair parted down the middle. Knitting him the scarf whose color he asked for. Her happy smile when she gave it to him.

"You'd look like you went to my high school," you say.

"High school. I never thought of that. Orange and black."

"Those were your colors?"

"Yeah. I hated them."

He puts on Sister Gaggl's headband over his ears and tries the scarf with its long ends tucked down inside his overcoat. It gives him the puffed chest of a rooster.

"Guess I'd have picked green too," you say.

"I can't wear my hat with this headband."

"At least your ears'll be warm."

"It itches."

"At least you'll know you still have ears."

"How about trading ties?" he says. "Yours goes with my scarf."

"We can't do that to Herbert."

"Really think he'll care?" says Paulson.

You remember your mother wanting to give away the drugstore statuette of two white angels Molly gave her the Christmas you were home from Knox.

"Yeah. He'll care. But there's something we can do for him."

"What?"

"Something that won't cost us a nickel. And make his Christmas."

"What?"

"Ordain him a teacher."

Paulson stops and looks at your face in the mirror.

"I told you," he says. "When the time's right."

"What's that supposed to mean."

He takes the headband off, smooths his hair, puts his hat back on, and wraps the scarf around his neck again with one long end tossed over his shoulder. He keeps a sly smile on his face while he cocks his head at different angles.

"It means when the time's right," he says.

How the time to ordain him teacher won't be right till Herbert lets him win at Ping Pong in front of his girlfriend Hilgi. Watching him preen makes you want to puke.

"It's Christmas," you say. "He can start the New Year out as a teacher."

"The priesthood's not a Christmas present," he says. "It's something you earn."

"Then how come it's always a birthday present?"

"What do you mean?"

"Didn't they make you a teacher on your birthday? And then a priest?"

"That's the way it's done."

"Not for converts. You know that. I've seen it."

"I'll let you know when he's ready."

"Waiting for the Lord to tell you?"

"I can report you for that, Elder."

"If you don't want to do it now," you say, "then I will."

For a long moment Paulson freezes, the scarf in his raised hands like he's surrendering, his smooth face fixed on yours.

"I don't think so," he finally says.

"I've got the same power of ordination you do."

He stops messing with his scarf and finds your face again.

"You're on thin ice, Elder."

How you'd make Herbert a priest. How you'd take him right through teacher. So he could bless the sacrament too. He could read the German bread and water prayers better than you or Paulson anyway.

"He's past old enough to be a priest."

"You really want me to call the District Leaders."

"I guess I'd have to tell them why he's still a deacon."

Paulson's eyes freeze in the polish of his suddenly wounded face. This isn't how you do it, you're thinking, getting Paulson to make Herbert a priest.

"Look," you say. "I'm sorry. Just think about it. He knows how to prepare the sacrament. A slice of bread and filling some cups with water. You've seen the way he watches over the congregation. Makes them welcome. Keeps the peace. He already visits them. That's it. That's what teachers do."

"They usher too," says Paulson.

"Just think about it. That's all I'm asking. We may never baptize anyone, but at least we could do this one good thing. You know how he'd love it."

Paulson regards you again. Looks back at himself. The scarf is wrapped once around his neck. Its ends hang like green wool waterfalls down the front of his overcoat.

"I think this is it," he says. In his overcoat and hat in your attic room he turns from the mirror to face you. "How do I look?"

"That's it. You got it." You smile to let him know you're kidding. "Just need your umbrella."

"Mind taking a photo?"

"Not at all."

"Let me sleep on Herbert."

In the morning he's got his smirk on. A victory smirk. It's early in the day for any kind of contest. You're both still in your garments. Your hair crazy.

"I came up with a better idea," he says. "For Herbert."

"What?"

"Let's pray first."

You kneel at your chairs across the table from each other. It's his turn for the out loud prayer. He goes through the usual introduction. Asks God to let his Spirit guide you to the doors of those who are eager to hear the message of the Gospel. Asks God to soften and open their hearts to receive the Holy Ghost. Then tells God his idea. That he wants to ordain Herbert a priest. That he's old enough. That he's proven he's worthy. Asks God for his blessing. You say Amen with Paulson. And then you go into your silent prayer knowing what the word rejoice means. That Paulson took your bait.

"Wow," you tell him when you get back off your knees. "A priest. What a great idea. You think it's legal to skip teacher?"

"When I make him a priest he'll automatically get all the teacher stuff."

"Sounds good."

"I'll have to interview him first. Make sure he's not messing around with Hilgi in ways he shouldn't."

You look away.

"I think he'll be fine," you finally say.

"Long as he tells the truth." Then he says, "If he passes, we'll do it Sunday in Priesthood Meeting."

In an empty church, you think, in front of an audience of empty chairs.

"How about Sacrament Meeting.? In front of everyone. Let him invite his friends. Who knows? They might get interested."

You watch him fight a silent contest with himself. "Yeah," he says. "Maybe he'll want to bring Hilgi."

You tell Herbert that Saturday when the 10 Oktoberstrasse 17 Ping Pong Club convenes for an afternoon of smacking the plastic eggshell of a hollow ball back and forth. He starts shaking. Loses his game. He doesn't care. Paulson interviews him downstairs. On Sunday, in Sacrament Meeting, in front of the widows, in front of Sister Dietl and her son Heinzi, in front of Hilgi and Ilse and most of the membership of the 10 Oktoberstrasse 17 Ping Pong Club, you sit Herbert in a chair facing the congregation. The room is full. Most every chair taken. Wearing the ties Herbert gave you, you and Paulson lay your hands on his head, and then, acting as the elders of Israel, in the name of the Holy Ghost and by the power of the holy Melchizedek priesthood, you ordain him a priest and confer upon him all the rights, powers, and authority pertaining to his new office.

The first time you heard applause in church was the night you played in Sacrament Meeting with Sister Avery and Sister Johanson for your Duty to God Award. He Walks with Me in the Garden. Sister Avery with her country western vocals and Sister Johanson on her rain forest harp. You remember how the congregation hesitated and then exploded. The second time you hear applause in church is when you lift your hands off Herbert's head and he stands up slow from his chair under the sacred weight of a brand new priest. Hilgi and Ilse and Mogy and the rest of the 10 Oktoberstrasse 17 Ping Pong Club don't know the rule about no applause in church. Your family of members doesn't care. They join in. The widows. Sister Dietl and her son Heinzi. You look for Mogy to yell "Achtung!" but he doesn't. Herbert turns around to shake Paulson's hand and then yours. His grin so fierce you're scared it will leave his face deformed. Then you stand back while he's mobbed. Hilgi, helpless and bright with pride, can't get enough of holding and kissing him. Everyone crowds around. Your scarves are on the coat rack where Ilse can see that you're wearing them.

"You're a priest?" his Ping Pong buddy Christian saying. "Can I confess my sins to you?"

Herbert laughing. Paulson watching with a benevolent steel smile on his polished face like this has all been his bighearted idea. The regular members holding back, waiting till Hilgi and Ilse and his Ping Pong friends are done with him, knowing that here in this building Herbert is theirs.

"We have a priest!" Sister Gaggl saying. "Our own priest!"

"Our own priest!"

"Yes! For Christmas!"

You and Paulson stand back behind the pulpit watching.

"You did good," you tell him, in English.

He gives you a quick glance and looks back at Hilgi.

"The time was right," he says.

CHAPTER 35

THEY'RE WAITING in front of the churchhouse after the last of the widows has said her affectionate and reluctant goodbye as a lonely week lies ahead of her again, after you've swept the floor and straightened out the chairs and made sure the stove is down to embers, when you and Paulson wrap your Christmas scarves around your necks and Paulson puts on his hat and you step outside. Three of them. The big kid named Mogy. Herbert's buddy Christian. A wiry kid named Rainer whose multicolored wool cap is pulled down over his forehead and ears and hides his thick red hair. Members of the 10 Oktoberstrasse 17 Ping Pong Club. From where they stand in a cluster, off to the side, under a small tree whose bare branches twitch and tremble in a gusty directionless wind, they shuffle forward to form a row across the path that leads from the door to the street. Christian stands between the other two. You sense a problem.

"Hi," you tell them.

Christian and Rainer nod. Mogy lifts his mittened hands out of his coat pockets. The winter sun is low and lays the dark blades of their shadows long across the snow. Paulson, still basking in the benevolence of what he did for Herbert in front of his girlfriend Hilgi, is clueless. When he locks the door, and turns around again, they come a step closer on the shoveled path. Mogy doesn't look happy. He looks dark. Christian and Rainer look awkward and unsure.

"Hey guys," says Paulson, a strut in his voice. "What's up? Where's Herbert?"

"He's celebrating," Christian says. Then he says, "With Hilgi."

The way he says Hilgi puts you on alert.

"He should be," Paulson says. "So what's up?"

"We'd like to talk to you," says Christian.

"Okay. We're listening."

"Just to you."

And now Paulson senses a problem too.

"Okay," he says.

Christian looks down at his shoes. Resolve narrows his eyes and tenses his face when he raises it again.

"We want to ask you to stop messing with Hilgi."

"Messing with who?"

"Herbert's girlfriend."

"Messing with her?" He scoffs. "What are you talking about?"

"You know."

And now his voice tightens and goes higher.

"What do I know?"

"What everybody knows."

From under the brim of his hat Paulson looks at you with a thin smile, sick and helpless, and in his eyes you can see a nervous fear. He finally looks back at Christian.

"Everybody knows I'm messing with Herbert's girlfriend? That's what you're saying?"

Mogy goes to step forward. Christian puts out his arm to stop him.

"What I'm saying is that you need to stop."

"I haven't touched her. I haven't gone near her."

The way Christian's face goes pained you can tell he was hoping this would go easier

"There are other ways to mess with her. Ways that bother her." Then he says, "They bother us too."

"I'm a missionary. I don't mess with girls. That's a rule."

Paulson doesn't seem to remember that none of them is Mormon. Your shoulders tighten. In the pockets of your overcoat your hands start forming fists you haven't used since State Street. If he weren't a missionary, you're thinking, you'd stand back and let them have their way with him.

"All we don't care about is Herbert and Hilgi."

"Did Herbert put you up to this?"

"He's innocent. He doesn't see. He has too much respect for you."

"Does he know you're doing this?"

"No," says Christian. Then he says, "Neither does Hilgi. Nobody does."

"So you just decided—"

"Stop messing with her," Christian says.

"Tell me how I'm supposed to stop doing something I'm not doing."

"How you stop is up to you. We're just telling you to stop."

"Achtung!" Mogy yells.

And then all of you just stand there, still, except for the wind, the way it tousles Christian's and Mogy's hair, the way you feel it through your own. Paulson's looking at you again, the same tight and helpless smile in his polished face, the same paralyzing fear that won't let him look away. You get it. It's cold. Rainer's shivering. Everyone's looking for a way out.

"He didn't mean anyone any harm," you finally say.

Christian and Mogy and Rainer look at you in silence.

"Hilgi's a beautiful girl," you say. "I've looked at her too. I've looked at her and thought what a lucky guy Herbert is. That's all he's done. Maybe more obvious. Now he knows."

Paulson doesn't move. His eyes are locked on you. He looks like he's lost the ability to talk. You imagine the turmoil of humiliation and embarrassment he must be riding out. Christian looks at Mogy and then Rainer.

"That's good enough for us," he finally says, and comes forward with his hand out. Mogy and Rainer follow him. They go to shake Paulson's hand, and when he doesn't look like he sees them, they shrug and tell you goodbye.

They're gone by the time Paulson escapes his trance. You fetch your bikes from behind the churchhouse and follow his hat, his pumping legs, and the flapping tails of his overcoat back home. Christian and Mogy and Rainer, you're thinking. Thank god they waited till after Herbert's promotion to priest or it never would have happened.

It takes a couple of days after the three members of the 10 Oktoberstrasse 17 Ping Pong Club confront him for the wound inflicted by that encounter to heal. He only talks to you when he has to. And when he does he won't look at you. He'll talk to his shoes, to something on the table, to the window. His mirror time drops off to almost nothing. When he comes around to being Paulson again, he does what you've been waiting for. Tells you he didn't need you sticking up for him. He had things under control. He had it figured out. All you did was make him look bad.

"You didn't have anything to do with it, did you?"

You look at him. Shake your head and let it go. A healing wound itches for a while. You're the itch and he's just scratching it.

Dear Shake,

I just realized something that is going to be hard for me when it happens. We can't celebrate the New Year coming in together because of the time difference. When it's 1964 there, it'll still be 1963 here in California. It doesn't seem right. I really wish we could be together. It's just so hard. I really miss you. I'm going to a party and I'm going to wear the necklace with the crystal heart you gave me. People will ask me about it and I'll get to tell them about you. That way you'll be with me.
Cissy

Your father's letter with your January check is a few days late. He held off, he writes, because he wanted to write you about the family Christmas. How your photo book got passed around. How they missed you but understood that you were working hard toward your first baptism. Winter has settled in since Christmas, cold and gray and stubborn, and his letter leaves you restless, haunted, deepens how sick you are of sitting around an attic room. Across the table, Paulson's busy with a ruler and glue and scissors, cutting photos out of The Improvement Era you let him have, pasting them into a looseleaf he's using to make a scrapbook.

Paulson looks up from his scrapbook. Wants to know how long you've been here on your mission.

"What's today?" you say.

"The fourteenth. January."

"Six months," you say. "Back on the ninth."

"You keeping a calendar?"

"No."

He looks at you and whistles. You feel it on your face. Smell the Austrian mouthwash he used when you came back here from lunch.

"You've got six months to mark off," he says. "That's a big bite. You should start one."

"I've thought of it."

"I could never save up that much time."

"When'd you start counting?"

"The first month." He shakes his head. "You gotta start one. Man. Knock off six months all at once."

"Calendars are what guys in prison do," you say, smiling, remembering what Morgan said.

"What?"

"Mark off time."

"That's a real spiritual attitude, Elder."

On this cold bleak afternoon it makes you want to puke to be trapped like this with a guy who never knows you're kidding.

"Soldiers too," you say. "I knew guys in the army who did."

"You were in the army?"

"Reserve."

"What'd you do?"

"I was a tanker."

"A tanker, huh." He watches you sideways. "Oh yeah. I heard you tell Frank." Then he says, "Real tanks?"

"With real bullets."

"You shoot it?"

"Everything."

Sizing you up. You've learned how to hear it in his voice. You think of pushing it. The seventh out of thirty thousand to ace the training test at Knox. The blast it was to run the big machines all over the Mojave. The prayer on the desert floor where Lieutenant Tanner told God to give you good companions.

"Here." Paulson pushes his ruler your way. "Draw a calendar. Thirty months. Thirty boxes. Six columns. Five rows. Then cross the boxes off. Or color them in. Man. Six months. A whole row already."

You try it on the back page of your notebook. Just to see what thirty months looks like. Your mission laid out in thirty boxes. Time served against time left. Paulson watches you measure and draw them. Hands you a box of colored pencils. The top row of six behind you. Ready to color in. You think of black. Then red. You don't know. You take black and draw a corner-to-corner X in the first six boxes. And then you're just left staring while the floor falls out of the bleak winter afternoon that has kept you home. Left staring at the boxes you have left. Twenty-four of them. Two years. You've never seen that much time this starkly drawn. Never so clearly seen the stark impossibility of having Cissy wait for you. Your stomach hurts. You carefully tear the page out of your notebook. Wad it up and toss it in the wastebasket.

"Whoa," he says. "What're you doing?"

"I can't do this."

"Why?"

"This is just waiting to go home."

"What do you mean?"

He wants an answer. Waiting to go home. Sitting around an attic room dressed up in white shirts and ties like a couple of unemployed insurance salesmen while Cissy's life moves her ahead and out of reach.

"I don't know." You look down. "Forget it."

Deeper into January, and then February, with winter hard and raw and permanent, while you wait for your Friday turn in the tub and afterward on the toilet, while you wait for Sunday, you fall into a routine. A late escape from the smell of aftershave in the airless room. A couple of hours tracting. Pedal out to some village in the slush of the roadside. Cissy's fur-lined gloves on the grips of your handlebars. Your knees numb from the cold. Cars pass, with skis racked on their roofs, and you lift your feet to clear the sheet of slush their tires shoot out across the shoulder. Sometimes the blinding sunlight off the skin of the thawed and then frozen snow that covers the fields and mountains takes you back to the winter in the sandpit. White smoke rises from the chimneys of houses whose doors you knock on. Faces go from curious to cold before you get through your introduction. You relish the fugitive heat you feel before a door goes closed. By noon or earlier you're headed back. Where you write letters. Read till you're sick at heart through Cissy's old letters if you haven't come home to a new one. Keep memorizing the lesson dialogues.

Read magazines you pick up. Grind through a few more numbing pages of the Book of Mormon. Try anything to eat through the deepening guilt and despair of the afternoon into the dark. Get stupid. Heat a can of beans for supper and donate a groschen to a fart fund every time you cut one. Trap a spider one day on the dresser under a water glass, name it Helmut, and then don't know what else to do with it till the day it lies there dead. On mornings when snow comes down outside the window you get dressed and then wait till it lets up. Some days you never leave.

You've learned how to do it on the toilet. How to rifle through the girls who've looked or smiled at you that week. How to keep your feet on the floor, how to lean into it, when it happens. How to use a wad of toilet paper instead of pointing your boner down into the bowl. How to let God watch. How to brace yourself for the surge of guilt that follows and washes away the rapture when you flush. How to put on a face for Paulson when you go upstairs again.

Sometimes he takes you out for the afternoon on the whim of a borrowed interest. There's the Sunday morning Herbert tells you the upstairs room has gone abandoned because he and his friends are spending all their free time skiing now. There's the Monday afternoon where Paulson has him take you to a ski shop and the Monday night he starts a ski fund out of his sixty bucks a month. There's the morning you tell him about wanting a Porsche. There's the afternoon you pedal to a dealership in a neighboring town that has nothing but brochures they won't let you take with you. There's the day he decides you need Austrian driver's licenses so he'll be ready when he's asked to be District Leader and handed the keys to a Beetle. There's the three week school you take to learn to drive in German. There's the gymnastics tournament one night where you watch him flirt with a redheaded tumbler named Marie. There's the next afternoon where you watch him model leotards and tights in the mirrors of a sportswear shop. There's the morning you take your mouthpiece out and tell him about your horn. There's the afternoon you spend at a music store watching him talk to a salesman about an English horn and then decide on a harmonica. There's the day he asks what it's like to drive a tank. You tell him. It stumps him. He doesn't know what to do.

Over the desperate crawl of the winter afternoons and nights you become friends. Provisional friends. Friends in a way that both of you know will end the day you're separated by a transfer. Because you'd remind each other too much of the winter days that made you need to be friends to start with. A fart fund. A dying spider. But friends for now.

Dear Shake,
   I forgot to tell you this. Daddy's boss got him three tickets to a concert back in December at the Civic Auditorium to hear a new

young singer perform. I wore the pink dress you like so much. The lady was around my age, 20, but her voice was so different. Strong, yet sweet. Her name is Barbra Streisand and she came here all the way from Brooklyn. Daddy complained because she didn't sing his song. You remember, don't you? From the barbecue? We did his song together.
I love you so.
Cissy

And then one day the movie West Side Story comes to town. He takes you to the matinee. He points out the Jet he played. Baby John. Singing along soundless with his lips. Toward the end comes a scene between Tony and Maria in a bridal shop where they dress up and do their wedding. And sing. Make of our hands one hand. Cissy. The times she's talked of movies she wants to see with you and you've seen your hands together, on the armrest, the color of her fingers laced through the color of yours. Make of our hearts one heart. The night in Yenchik's Ford when you put your hands to each other's naked chests and felt your hearts beat. Make of our vows one last vow. The vow where you marry her not just for time but for all eternity. Make of our lives one life. Now it begins. Now we start. One hand. One heart.

You see six more matinees. Two guys in suits and ties and winter raincoats in their laps in a movie house in the middle of the afternoon. You don't mind. The ache that mingles love and fear and longing in the chambers of your heart. You don't mind that either. Because she's there with you the way you've always seen and felt her. One hand. Because yours has stopped, gone almost dead, you can feel the forward motion of her life. One heart. Feel her leaving you behind without wanting to. Pulling out of reach in the innocence of not knowing that's what's happening. Day after day one life. The ache comes up your throat and sticks there. Tears brim and then crest and cut down your face. Paulson never knows why. He thinks it's the movie. He asks how many times you'll need to see it before it doesn't make you cry. One heart. Where you can cup your hand in the dark and feel her breast and the heartbeat under it. You never tell him. Where his lips mouth the lyrics, yours mouth her soundless name. Cissy.

Chapter 36

There are winter days when you wonder if people shouldn't be left alone. When you wonder what's wrong with their being content. If you just showed up at their doors as Americans you'd be okay. They'd be decent and friendly. If you invited them to church on Sunday but called it something else. They'd be generous and kind. They could bring their kids to Ping Pong. They'd have you for dinner just to ask what you thought about President Kennedy and the negroes and Vietnam. Why that couldn't be enough. Why they had to be led through a lesson whose logic trapped them into having to admit their church was false and their minister a fraud. What it cost Herbert by way of friends when an American guy from Kearns befriended and baptized him. Days when it feels like maybe all the good you're there to do is tend your tiny flock of members. Make the monthly rounds. Let the widows take turns having you for Sunday dinner. Run meetings for them. Visit Frau Schmied in the basement she calls home, too old to make it to 10 Oktoberstrasse 17 on Sunday, her shrunken feet in beige stockings and shoes that used to fit. Thank you, she says, when you get up off your knees next to the chair she spends her days in. For praying for her.

Much of your idle time goes to writing Cissy. Thinking of her. Remembering her. Worrying about her. Toward the end of January you went looking for a Valentine's Day card. It was early yet. The shops didn't have them. But it needed a couple of weeks to get to her in time. More to make sure. And so you settled for a wedding card. Hearts and lace and flowers. Close enough. You crossed out the German words and wrote your own.

Dear Shake,

Thank you for the beautiful Valentine's Day card! I was so excited! The pale pink hearts and white lace were really pretty on the front, with those little pink flowers inside. You even crossed off the Austrian words and wrote Happy Valentine's Day instead. But you know me. I had to know what was crossed out, so I took the card to school and asked our music professor, Dr. Frantzen, if he knew what the words meant. He took the card from me, looked at it, and smiled. He said it's German, Am Tag der Hochzeit, which means On Your Wedding Day. Oh my God. I was so surprised. I never expected him to say that. I was thinking more like Happy Birthday. Anyway, he looked at me and said, "Miss Taylor, you are a lucky young lady to have a beau who would to go to such lengths to send you a card all the way from Europe." I guess I blushed and took the card back. I said thank you and left. Shake, I love you so much! You're so sweet to think of me that way!

So, back down to earth. I'm home today because there are demonstrations on campus. Yesterday one of my professors said that President Clark is an ombudsman at the college now. That's the name for someone who's supposed to try to ease things between the professors and the students. It's a big deal here. We're the first CSU school to have somebody like that. It's been peaceful mostly but Mommy is worried about me going in today. You know how she is. Nothing important is going on that I can't make up next week. I called the library to tell them I wouldn't be in.

What about you? Have you been reading about this stuff in the papers over there? I wasn't sure if you knew about any of it. Everybody's talking about the sit-ins. They're happening everywhere. I was reading in the paper how some students in Nashville were doing a lunch counter sit-in and a group of white teenagers attacked them. The cops came but they let the white kids go and arrested the negro kids for disorderly conduct. The kids got a lawyer but when he started his argument the judge just turned his back and the lawyer just said to the judge's back, "What's the use!"

Anyway, that's what's going on in a lot of places, but it's peaceful here. Nobody's being arrested or anything like that, but there's this feeling in the air, a bad feeling, and I'm so worried it's going to turn out awful. Daddy's always watching it on the news, and he thinks it's going to get worse this summer, that people are going to start fighting and end up getting hurt or maybe killed. I don't think anything like that will happen here. It's different here. Negroes don't need to worry about being told they can't go anywhere or sit in a malt shop if they want to. But still, what's going on down south, it's just not right. I love you so much. I'm so lucky you're mine. Please take care of yourself.
Love always,
Cissy

"Did she get the card?" says Paulson, from his cot across the room, looking up from a letter of his own.

"She got it."

Cissy's card back to you lies on the table with the envelope it came in. Paulson looks back at his letter and then at you again.

"She didn't mind?"

"Mind what?"

"That it wasn't the right card."

"She loved it."

"She send you one back?"

You hold it up. Leave it closed. From across the room he looks it over. The winter in the attic room together has eroded his cocky attitude and dulled its mocking edge. He hasn't mentioned or even looked at Hilgi since the Sunday he was spanked by the members of the 10 Oktoberstrasse 17 Ping Pong club. You've started to feel bad for him.

"Hey," he says. "Look at that. A real one."

You look at him. His jealous smirk looks exhausted of anything but the orchestration of the muscles that hold it in his face. He'd love to know what she looks like. See a photo. Test out his arsenal of smiles on her face. On the sightless eyes of the photo he doesn't know is in your wallet. On the face he doesn't know is a negro face. The face he'll never see.

"Yep," you say, smiling. "Real as they come."

Dear Cissy,

I've been keeping up with everything because I love you and want to be ready in case you need me. Ever since I got here I've been watching over you. I know that sounds stupid this far away. But if anything comes to San Jose I'll be there. If you ever get scared I'll be there. As soon as I'm done I'm coming to be with you. Less than two years now. Unless you need me sooner. I'll know if you do. I love you so much. One hand one heart.
Love, Shake

Dear Shake,

The way you started signing your letters sounded so familiar. It was right on the tip of my tongue but I couldn't think of it. So I asked Mommy and she told me it was from West Side Story. And of course I knew right away. When Maria and Tony are in the bridal shop and they sing together. Oh Shake. That's so sweet. I went out and bought the sound track. I want you here so bad. Make of our lives one life. Day after day one life. See? I learned it. Now I can't stop singing it!
Love, Cissy

Winter starts losing hold in March. Daylight comes earlier through the attic window and lingers deeper into the afternoon. Snow thaws back from the shoulders of roads and from the winter soil and grass of the fields. On your bike the wind's still cold but sometimes you'll ride through a sudden pool of warmer air. Out in the villages the doors aren't as quick to close as they were in the bright cold numbing heart of winter. And then you get the news. It comes from Doby, in Hamburg, on his mission in West Germany. You've been writing back and forth since he got there last July. You still want to get released together. You've made renegade plans for everything you'll do. Get drunk. Buy a Volkswagen from the factory and tour Europe. Take a boat to New York. Drive the Volkswagen cross country home and take the time for every side road that comes along. Get a pad together. Not just a room but a real pad. He doesn't know about Cissy. You never took the chance to tell him. You've just come up from downstairs with the mail the landlady leaves for you. In your room again, on the edge of your bed, you sit there holding Doby's open letter, not knowing what to think or do or feel.

"What's the matter?" says Paulson.

"This buddy of mine. Bobby West."

"What about him?"

"His dad's been killed."

Paulson swings his legs around and sits on the edge of his cot.

"Killed? How?"

"A car accident in Nevada."

"Holy moly," says Paulson.

You remember the big white Caddy. The samples of drugstore stuff West's father kept in its trunk. The sample cases of little Cepacol mouthwash bottles you and West and Doby tried to get drunk off once. His father. His big quick confident salesman grin. His bald head. The way he always wanted to know what you and West were doing when he found you working on the Pontiac. The way he laughed at your wisecracks when your father wouldn't. The big laugh. Like abrupt thunder. Stilled now. Stilled and gone like the lightning that used to flash off your grandfather's little spectacles when he moved his head in the sunlight.

"The other car cut out to pass someone."

"So it was head on?"

"Guess it had to be."

Route 40. The two-lane highway across Nevada that ran through all the desert towns. The highway they were in the process of replacing with the Interstate that would skirt them. The blinding chrome fish of the air scoop on the blower of Yenchik's engine in the unrelenting desert sunlight.

"When?" says Paulson.

"Like a month ago. Back in February."

"Is that letter from your buddy?"

"No. Not West. My buddy in West Germany."

Yenchik. His Ford in Pineview Reservoir. How they never found him. How they figure he wanted to just disappear. Just start a new life as a different guy. In a different city with a different haircut or clothes or place of birth. You see his Swedish mother in a teeshirt. A glancing look on your way to look at something else just to catch the pendulant swing of her loose breasts as she pours you and Yenchik lemonade at her kitchen table. If her heart gave out yet. How his father's doing.

"That sucks."

"Wish I could talk to him. To West."

"Talk to him? From here?"

"I know. My whole check." And then you say, "Wish I could be there." You smile at Paulson. "I could talk to him for free. Work on his car with him."

Paulson comes back with a nervous smirk.

"Well, Elder, we know that can't happen."

You look at him for a minute.

"You ever wonder what you'd be doing if you weren't doing this?"

"You mean my mission?"

"Yeah. If you weren't here." Then you say, "If you were just, you know, Nick Paulson."

The first time he's heard his first name out of you.

"We're not supposed to think like that, Elder."

"We're not thinking. Just imagining."

Paulson mulls it over. And then his smile is real and desire mixed with memory in his eyes.

"New York," he says. "A dance company."

"Yeah?"

"Yeah. I'd like to perform in musicals. You know."

"Broadway."

"Yeah." Then he says, "You'd be playing trumpet somewhere. Right?"

"I guess so."

"San Jose. Where your girlfriend lives."

"Right now I'd just like to keep my buddy company."

Working on his Pontiac at Steed's Texaco. Doing State. You remember the night a pickup pulled up next to you at a light on State. How the driver had a beard that reminded you of Jesus And so you said Hi Jesus. At the next light, he asked you what you'd said, so you said Hi Jesus again. How he went off and chased you through the Avenues and then the West Side and then all through Rose Park, headlights hard on West's bumper the whole time, before he broke off and let you go.

In his letter Doby says West came home from his mission in British Columbia to take care of his mother and little brother and sister. The man of the family now. You write Doby back to thank him. You write your father to ask why he couldn't be the one to tell you. And then you sit down to write West. Sit there in the wooden chair on your side of the wooden table with your Austrian ballpoint and think of West and wait. Try to imagine what it's like to have your father dead. Wait till what you should write him shows itself. Because when you look for it you don't know where to find it. Just this black cry. This cry that could lift you out of this nowhere dark and ride you all the way home to Bountiful to keep your buddy company.

CHAPTER 37

IN EARLY APRIL West heads back to Canada. His father's in his grave. The wrecked Caddy and its trunk of drugstore samples are in a junkyard somewhere on the back side of some desert town. His mother's back to doing hair again in the salon West's father built for her in the garage. His brother and sister back in school with their friends. With the rest of his buddies still on their missions, Doby and Lilly and Keller and Jasperson and you, with the place where Yenchik used to be a vacant place, West didn't have anyone to hang out with, and couldn't find anything worth doing, and started going crazy seeing his father everywhere he'd always seen him. And so the only thing he knew to do was go back and work off what was left of his mission. He had a baptism almost to the finish line anyway. You wonder how the other guys are doing. How many baptisms Lilly's racked up in Mexico. Keller in England. Jasperson in West Virginia.

Your father writes to say he's sorry. Telling you about West's father being killed must have slipped his mind. And then he writes what never slips his mind. Still waiting. You look away, at the wall on Paulson's side, at the blank blue square of sky the open window holds captive. That first baptism. You're waiting too. Knowing what will happen when you get it. How he'll move the target to that second baptism. The bewilderment and hurt of his letter to President Smith gone cold like the empty windswept place in your chest where you used to think you had a father. Like Morgan. And now like your buddy West.

As the slopes start to close, the roofs of passing cars begin to lose their racks of skis, Herbert opens the 10 Oktoberstrasse 17 Ping Pong Club again. Winter did away with Paulson's interest in Hilgi. With it went his interest in Ping Pong. A priest now, Herbert is entrusted with a key to the churchhouse, in possession of the authority to manage the club on his own. The first of April you and Paulson take the train to the city of Graz for a two-day missionary conference. Sanderson and Hatch are both gone, Sanderson home, Hatch to Salzburg, and so you and Paulson make the ride with Rawlins and Daniels, the guys who replaced them in Spittal. Rawlins brings his guitar. You sing three-chord rock and country songs on the train. Everly Brothers. Kingston Trio. Elvis Presley. Johnny Cash. A Beatles tune called She Loves You. Other passengers don't seem to mind. Some clap. Some join in. In Graz you listen to speeches and presentations about new ways of getting into people's houses. Catch up with guys you knew back in Vienna. Hang out with other elders and listen to conversations peppered with fuzz again. You spend the night in a youth hostel with some British and Canadian and American guys bumming their way to Africa. Rawlins tries to get the British guy to admit that the Church of England is false but the guy turns out to be an atheist. He tells Rawlins that Jesus was just another bloke with a beard. It doesn't faze Rawlins. Atheism is just another false religion.

The next afternoon President Lindner speaks. Still with the full head of scalloped snow white hair. The white eagle eyebrows over the commanding fury of his gaze. This time, for an audience of missionaries, he uses English. In his German accent you hear your father's voice. In your father's voice you remember what Morgan said about his letter to President Smith and wonder if he wrote one to President Lindner too. It doesn't feel that way. From the pulpit he doesn't look for you in the audience. But the deadline for his promise to turn Austria around expired last December. It looks like it softened him up to have to watch it pass while Austria kept going. Made him more like one of you. Like there maybe was no harvest. There was just hard work. Now he speaks of fear and courage. How fear makes you look back. How courage turns you forward. It does what you came to the conference looking for. A reason to be here. After the long abandonment of winter new kindling flares up through the cold fire in your chest. The sense that Lieutenant Tanner gave you in the desert. That the Lord has you here to do something nobody else is here to do.

You get home to your room close to three in the morning. Paulson grabs the mail on the way upstairs. He jumps his eyebrows a couple of times and hands you a letter from Cissy. It's a regular white envelope this time, the size a card comes in, stamped air mail and par avion on the back and front. You finish taking off your shoes and then your tie before you open it. The card is for your birthday a month and a half away. There's a letter folded up inside it. A letter several pages long.

Dear Shake,

I hope you're doing okay. I know it's early but I didn't want to miss your birthday. I'm almost done with classes. The summer job I told you about came through. I'll be working part time in Japantown next month. It's a new store called Kay's Shisheido. My job will be to unpack the boxes of makeup that come in, then wrap the little bottles and compact powders up so they look pretty, and then put them on display. I wanted a sales job but they told me they already had ladies for that. So I'll be making two dollars an hour for four hours during the week and on Saturday. It's almost fifty dollars, not too bad compared to waiting tables at the Burger Pit, but at least I could have gotten tips there. But I'm happy with Japantown. It's pretty around there and it will be fun to work in a new shop.

So there doesn't seem to be anything much to say. A lot of times I start to feel like the time just doesn't go by. With us I mean. Like we're standing still almost. It's like you've been gone away so long, but it's not a year yet, and that's only a year with another year and a half to go. How do you feel about it? Do you think about all the time we have to wait for it to be our turn to be together? Do you think about what you'll be like by then? That far from now? I do, about me, I mean, and I can't imagine.

Last night I was watching the Donna Reed Show and it was a repeat. The one where Mary sings "Johnny Angel." Oh, Shake, I just started crying. I felt like I knew how much she loved him and wanted to be with him. And I knew that she had a chance to see it happen. Her mother and father understood too. Especially Donna Reed. She knew her daughter was in love. But I think I was crying because I knew, I know, that we love each other but will never have that. Not the way we should. I don't want to talk about your family, but as sweet as they were to me, I don't think your parents would want me for a daughter in law, and I'm not a bad person. I don't think it's them. Just what they've always been told and the way the people they have to live with would look at them. But it hurts to keep wondering, Shake. It hurts to think I can never fit in, and I really don't want to have to worry about it anymore. Fitting in.

I know that you love me, Shake, but we both know that you can't walk away from your whole life. Like if you would close your eyes and say to yourself, "I want Cissy in my life," and then when you opened your eyes and your wish came true, I would be standing in front of you, but everything else would be gone. Your family, your friends, your church. Everything except for me. You can't do that, Shake. We can't do that. Can you see that it's just too much to ask ourselves to hurt that much and have the pain of a really bad ending? I couldn't take it, Shake. I couldn't. But I can't say the words to end it either. I can't. But Shake, my darling, we're a beautiful dream that could never come true. Do you see that? A beautiful, lovely dream I'll never forget. Please don't hate me, Shake, or be mad at me. I know I don't have the right to ask, but please. I couldn't stand that. I'm so sorry.

I'll always love you, Shake. Goodbye.
Cissy

"Everything all right?"

Still listening to her voice on that night sidewalk on the campus in San Jose. Urgent. Resigned. In the lamplight still seeing all the movement of her face through every sentence she said or listened to. Her eyes down and hooded by their lids. Their quick skate sideways out of pain. The heartbreaking blend of understanding and surrender in her smile. The sudden distress of lines in the honey skin between her glittering wet eyes. Pain as quick as the shadow of a bird across her face. Her shoulders bare. The white headband out of which burst the lush black curls of her hair. Her breath warm. Talking things out before you both fell quiet and in the lamplight closed your eyes and memorized each other with your hands and mouths. And so it startles you to hear Paulson's voice. Look up and you're in this attic room. His polished face. Night out the attic window. The travel clock on your nightstand reads almost three in the morning.

"Yeah. She's fine."

"I mean you."

"Me?"

"You look like you just got slugged in the gut."

"I'm fine. Just tired."

"Someone else die?"

"Nobody died."

He takes the card where you left it on the table and opens it. You tense up.

"It's your birthday?"

"Not till June."

"That's what I thought."

"She wanted to make sure it got here on time."

He thinks about that for a minute.

"She says love always. Sounds sweet."

"Goes both ways," you say.

It takes him another minute to figure out there's nothing else coming. He puts the card back down.

"Well, sack time for me."

A beautiful dream. While Paulson gets ready for bed you write her a quick note back.

Dear Cissy,

Right now I just want you to know I could never hate you or be mad at you. All I could ever do is love you. It's all I know how to do. I don't know how to do anything else. I'll write more later.
Love,
Shake

You fold and seal and address the envelope and from there turn out the light and go to bed too. Not to sleep. You know sleep isn't coming. Just try to think while a thousand birds rise off the floor of your heart to reel round and round inside it in a shrieking whirlwind of black wings. A beautiful dream that could never come true. Yes it can. Let me tell you it can. Just to pace yourself to the black night out the window and its calm infinitely gradual revolution toward the gray of dawn beginning and then the sunrise of the day you can put your note in the mail to her.

You've seen it coming. In the way her letters have thinned out. In your own stark recognition of how infinitely long you were asking her to wait. In the way you could feel the momentum of her life pull her out of reach. In her dawning consciousness of the gulf between the color of her skin and the church you were in Austria for Still, helpless not to, you write her every day without waiting for an answer. Sometimes twice if something comes to mind. How your mother and father would love her because everyone around them would. How when you wished for her and then opened your eyes it wouldn't be just her in front of you. It would be her brother Jeff. It would be her mother and father. It would be her circle of Airborne uncles. It would be her back yard filled with everyone. And it would be your mother and father and Karl and Molly and Roy and Maggie. Because it would be your wedding. How she could have what Donna Reed's daughter had. How she could sing Johnny Angel with her eyes closed and when she got done you'd be standing there in front of her with everyone. Nobody would be missing. How the two of you could have any kind of love you wanted. How you could close your eyes and wish for her and when you open them she's always standing there with everyone. How you were almost a third done with your mission. How in only twice as long as now you'll be there. How you'll come right now if she needs you because without her nothing in your life would matter. How dreams come true. Especially one as beautiful as yours. How all you'll ever need if someone made you choose was her. Her and your trumpet. All you'll need. All you've ever had.

How four days later Paulson catches on.

"That was a Dear John," he says.

Across the table from you there's that light smirk of a cheap victory you've seen him use too often. Like the only way he can win something is by you losing something. What you see there now is payback for Hilgi. You come to your feet. From the abrupt way he sits back you can tell he sees what guys on State Street and in the parking lots of high schools used to see.

"Listen to me," you say. "You need to leave this one alone."

PART 5

WHAT CHILD IS THIS

CHAPTER 38

A FEW DAYS into April, green starting to haze the fields and pastures while the snow line has steadily thawed back up the flanks of the Alps, transfer letters show up in the mail. Paulson's going to a town called Wels. You to a town called Klosterneuburg just outside Vienna to work with a senior named John Novick. You make your rounds to the members to say goodbye. Tell them new elders are showing up the same day you'll be leaving. They want to know if one of them plays piano. In their faces you see the makeshift family whose unapologetic pride gave you haven from isolation through the winter. The family related not by blood but by their faith in Joseph Smith. Herbert and Hilgi and some friends take you by cable car to a mountaintop that overlooks the town. So you can say goodbye from there.

"You're in charge for now," you tell Herbert, at the railing of the overlook.

"Yes. I take good care of everyone."

"The new missionaries will need your help."

"I am ready."

In the sunlight, duty shines through the scarred skin of his eager face, this guy Christian called innocent.

"Here's my phone number when you come see Elder Limburg."

"My English will be good then! I will see the Temple!"

The train takes you back north where you started just over nine months ago. You don't expect much from the transfer. Nine months gone. Not much to show. Cissy. There was the place where you kept her. You try writing her from the train but the ride makes your ballpoint pen jump like a lie detector needle. And so you keep watch again, through the window, feeling her there, writing her that next letter in your head, the buoyant weight of her own head on your shoulder as it sways in sleep with the rocking motion of the train. You'll find a way to keep her. You have to.

Novick meets you on the platform at the Sudbahnhof and helps you fetch your Samsonite and bike. He takes you by tram to Franz Josefs Bahnhof for a short train ride up a river to Klosterneuburg. He's a big guy, easygoing, thick black crewcut hair, a fleshy almost goofy smile, eyes that droop toward the outside so that he smiles like a clown with a broken heart. He's got a wide lumbering knock-kneed walk where his shoes are angled out like he's using them to clear leaves or snow out of his path. He comes from a California town called Bakersfield where he played high school football.

"Southern California. In the valley. Not on the coast."

"Close to San Jose?"

"Not really," he says. "Four to five hours away."

Your room's on the attic floor of a yellow house on a steep uphill street. An older woman and her grown daughter live there. Novick says they're Russian. On your way past a living room crowded with heavy furniture you see an old grand piano. You climb two flights of stairs to find that you're back to sharing a bed. A hot plate sits on the dresser. A kitchen-sized wood table stands against a wall with a couple of old wood chairs. Novick's got his books to one side. Pushed back against the wall, dwarfed by an old cast iron table lamp with a scalloped and tassled pale green shade, stands a small blue plastic radio.

"There's a bathroom on the floor below us," Novick says. "We can use the sink and toilet but not the tub. There's a bathhouse in town we'll use on Friday to shower up."

"Okay."

Through one of two windows in the room you look out over the town you'll be working. At its center stands a massive compound of elaborate buildings with twin bell towers at one end and a big dome the green color of copper rust at the other. On a low rise, the compound of buildings dominate the town like a vast and extravagant stone ship, docked at permanent rest among the shallow roofs of the houses and buildings around it. Here and there you see parts of the wall that surrounds it.

"It's a cloister," says Novick. "Whatever that is. It's where the town gets its name. Everyone just calls it the Stift. The towers are a church. The dome part was for the Kaiser."

"Stift," you say, to remember the word. "So you've seen it."

"Just from outside. I haven't gone in."

"No?"

"Catholic property," he says. "Enemy territory."

Over the rooftops, past the bell towers and through the distant trees, you can see a deep blue blade of water. If it's a lake or river.

Novick comes over to look. "It's the Danube," he says.

The Beautiful Blue Danube. The waltz your mother plays. The river whose city version you saw in the bridged canal that runs through Vienna. Now its country version. Right here. So close this far from home.

"Sorry about the one bed," he says, when you turn away from the window.

"I'm used to it," you tell him.

"Well," he says, "you shouldn't ought to be."

"I guess you either."

"Mind if I write a quick letter? Send my girlfriend the address?"

"Not at all," he says. "I'll do some reading."

With the letter done you unpack. Put your things where he shows you. Then sit down and talk. He's been in Klosterneuburg two months. He's a few days shy of the last four months of his mission. He figures you'll be his last companion and this town the last place whose doors he'll knock on. Coming from Paulson you're struck by his humility. This soft half shrugging way of talking. This look to his smile like he's on the verge of turning what he's saying into an apology.

"What's the radio for?"

He looks at it. The two knobs. The round grate for a small speaker. A chipped corner and a sharp crack halfway across the top.

"Just to listen to music sometimes."

"Is it okay if I tape a picture to the wall?" you say.

"Depends on what it is," he says, with a smile to let you know he's kidding.

"Just a drawing my kid sister did. Of her and me."

"Sure. Go ahead."

The next morning you're on your bikes early, headed through cobblestone streets for your tracting area after breakfast, knocking on doors, looking for the missing. After the first couple of hours, the finish line for the day for Paulson, Novick keeps going, all the way till lunch, and after lunch you're back to pick up where you left off. Walk around every house that has the possibility of a another place to live out back. Down every alley. No time. No thanks. Not interested. He doesn't care. Each reject goes in the tracting book. He carries a big black battered briefcase. Straps it onto the rack over the back wheel of his bike the way you used to tie up your trumpet. You get home late the end of the first day wondering if this will be permanent. But the second day's the same. And then the third.

"What's the briefcase for?"

"My flannel board. A couple of Book of Mormons and other scriptures. Brochures." A trace of apology shows in his smile. "You never know," he says.

Flannel board. Three hinged pieces of cardboard covered with flannel where you stick paper dolls of Jesus, the Angel Moroni, Joseph Smith, other figures to illustrate the story you're here to tell. They gave you one too.

"Did you ever use your flannel board?"

"Just for practice," he says. "But you never know."

And then you know. He's a workhorse. And you're finally on your mission. At the start of each day, from the street in front of the house in the canyon formed by the houses on either side, you can see the town spread out below you. You coast down the hammering cobblestones, Novick's coat and pants cuffs flailing in the wind, and the towers and dome of the Stift are there to remind you who's in charge here. Whose god rules the town. Novick acts like he takes it as a challenge. Like slapping himself in the face. From there he lives to tract. You leave the room by eight and don't come back till eight or sometimes nine when the house is dark and you have to tiptoe up the stairs, take off your shoes and talk softly in your room, hold down your out loud prayer. You rack up tracting hours like an odometer on a long haul semi. You look forward to wearing out the soles of your shoes the way they were made to wear. To patching the holes they told you the seat of your bike would wear in the crotch of your pants. Novick's got a lazy drawl to his voice that carries over and makes his German sloppy. He doesn't care. He'll talk to anyone. It's his job. Your German's good enough to where he soon starts giving you every other door.

And most every night you write Cissy. You haven't heard from her yet. It takes time for letters to get back and forth. But this is how you keep her. Let her feel in your words this new exuberance you feel. Let her feel the way you're moving forward too, along with her, time moving quickly now toward the day when the door you'll knock on will be hers again.

On your mission. Ten months in you can finally start to call yourself an Instrument of the Lord. With Novick at your side you can start to talk to God again in your silent prayers. Fill out a weekly report that doesn't make you sick. Write honest letters home. Start proving your father wrong. Check out the fit of your grandfather's shoes. End each day like you earned instead of stole it or just let its exhausting hours pass. Kneeling next to Novick, listening to the humble way he talks to God, you can let yourself feel like you belong here. Feel the Holy Ghost blow the heat of its breath into the black embers of your campfire.

The names Elder John Novick and Elder Shake Tauffler appear in the mission newsletter for highest hours worked. Novick's immune to being recognized. For him it's the work. You send the newsletter home. I'm proud of you, your father writes, in answer to the first one. Maybe with a little more prayer and dedication we'll soon hear the long awaited news of that first baptism. You ride out the defeat you're left with. Burn through the recharge of betrayal for the letter he wrote to President Smith. You keep mailing the newsletters anyway. Not for your father, but for your mother, for your brothers and sisters, because you're here for them, because you're here to let them know that they can come the distance too, because you're here this far from home to show them how.

At the bathhouse, instead of the private stalls, Novick the jock uses the public showers, out in the open with other guys like you did in high school after gym. Back then, from being born in Switzerland, you were pretty much the only guy who had a foreskin. Now you look like almost every other naked guy while Novick's often the only guy without one. And you're back to using the downstairs toilet once a week on Friday.

You make friends with the mother and daughter who own the house. They're from Russia. Sometimes at night when they're still up you play around on the grand piano in their living room. The mother is short, gray haired, sweet the way she breaks into a smile when she catches your eye. Her daughter Olga is husky without being fat with a sullen dark moon face and thick black hair she wears in a coarse bun. You figure she's somewhere past thirty. Her breasts put her in a league with the scoutmaster's wife back in your home ward. At night she'll listen to you play in a white nightgown sheer enough that when she dances through the lamplight or stands in the curve of the piano you can see through the cloth to the soft full heavy bowls of her breasts where they sway across her chest, half a beat behind your playing, her nipples obscure but visible shadows whose tips are tickled into being hard by the fabric sliding back and forth across them, the shadow of pubic hair in the crotch of her deep thighs. You don't mind looking when you get the chance. Storing away what you see for Friday. You've earned that too.

And back on that first night, after a supper of boiled potatoes and half a bratwurst, from an armchair across the room, there was the way you watched Novick pull his chair around to the front of the table, bring the radio forward, turn it on, and sit there like a big kid, face to face with the music coming out of the little speaker, so low and scratchy you could barely tell it was jazz. Jazz. If you could trust your ears. How he sat there, his coat off and his head low, not moving for a straight hour. How not even his feet moved to the cadence of a tune. How his big black thick-soled shoes stayed quiet on the floor like he wasn't wearing them. With your Triple Combination open in your lap to the Doctrine and Covenants you didn't intrude. How it looked too private. How you weren't so sure you wanted to hear it anyway. You remembered how Porter and Snook and some of your other high school buddies liked to hear you play. How here and there you heard a trumpet or song you used to play and felt the changes in your lips against the mouthpiece, with Robbie and Eddie and Jimmy and Santos there around you, and when you closed your eyes you saw the red and blue spears of light run up and down the brass of the trumpet you'd said goodbye to back in the Mojave sunset. On the fourth night how you finally asked him.

"Mind if I listen too?"

How he turned around surprised. His mouth open.

"Sure."

How you took your chair at the end of the table.

"Thanks."

How he turned the radio half toward you. "Sorry," he said. "I didn't know you liked it."

"I never told you. Don't be sorry."

"My last junior didn't."

"His loss."

"Round Midnight," he says, naming a tune that was unmistakable three or four notes in. The piano player was unmistakable too.

How you said, "Tyner."

"You know that?"

"Listen to his left hand. The voicings. He uses fourths."

How Novick turned the radio up a notch. How the piano lost its tinny quality and the cascade of Tyner's playing went deep and drenching. How you and Novick sat there listening for a while.

"You like hearing it live?" he said.

"Live?"

"You know. Like a jazz club."

"Is it okay?"

"I don't see anything wrong with it. Long as we put in a good week." How he looked at you, smiled his goofy sad-eyed smile, said, "This is cool, man. You like jazz. I got lucky."

"Yeah," you say. "Me too."

Missionary work. Topped by jazz. Whoever in the Mission Home played the chessboard game of transfers got it right this time. From that fourth night on you sit there together, night after night, him in front of the table and you at its side, the radio turned so that you share its speaker. Sonny Rollins. Art Tatum. Clifford Brown. Ornette Coleman. Davis. Coltrane. On and on. All your heroes. All the men you learned from. All the negro giants whose form the clouds would take in the twilight sky around you in the sandpit and then later on the hillside. Constellations where the stars were the rings they wore and the glints of light off their instruments. Sometimes the longing gets out from under you. And then you get up and walk across the room to settle down. Novick turns down the radio.

"No. You don't need to."

"Okay."

One night after the broadcast ends he asks how you got into jazz. You tell him about the sound you heard come out of the radio in the cattle truck.

"You didn't know what kind of music it was?"

"I'd never heard it before."

He wants to know more. And so you tell him about your family. How you came from Switzerland. How you moved around and then spent four years on a Southern Utah ranch. How you were on the move from there to a town called Bountiful when the radio came up with the sound that hooked you. How you later learned it was jazz. You leave out Mr. Hinkle. You don't tell him about your horn.

"How about you?" you say.

It takes him a minute. Sitting there like you in his shirtsleeves and loosened tie with his collar unbuttoned. Toying with the knob without turning the radio on again.

"I had a foster family when I was little," he says. "This black family that lived next door to my real family. My foster dad was a guitarist. He loved to play jazz. He taught me all about it. Played me records. Told me stories about musicians. Even tried to teach me jazz guitar. I just couldn't get it. Improvisation. I could listen to it but not play it. But I fell in love with it."

He smiles to himself. Lays his arm and hand on the table remembering. You can't tell if it's sadness or apology in his face.

"I loved listening to him play," he says. "I called him Pops. Like his real kids did."

"You lived next door to your real family?"

He looks at you surprised.

"Oh no. My real folks came from Oklahoma. They didn't get along with their folks so they packed up and moved to California. They were pretty much free spirits." He looks at you. "You know what that means?"

"Like nonconformists."

"Yeah. Anyway, they got married in California and moved into a house next to this black family. Then they had me." Then he says, "When I was seven they were killed in a car crash."

"Wow. That's rough."

He lets go of the knob. Looks at the back of his hand for a second or two like he's wondering how he should keep going. Takes a slow breath through an apologetic smile.

"I didn't have anyone. They couldn't send me to Oklahoma because they didn't know where in Oklahoma to send me. So the black family next door took me in. I was friends with them anyway. I played with their kids all the time." He sits back in his chair. "The Jamesons." He laughs. "My foster dad and mom enjoyed their marijuana." Then he says, "They were good people. They treated me like I was theirs."

"So they raised you?"

"Just for four years. He was in the military. When I was eleven he got a two year transfer to Guam. Him and his wife didn't think it would be good for their kids. So they left them with their grandmother in LA."

Cissy's brother Jeff in his Airborne uniform at the Salt Lake Airport. On his way to Guam too.

"So you lived in LA for a couple of years?"

"No. They left me there. They were friends with this Mormon family who wanted to adopt me." Then he says, "They baptized me and got me going in church." He looks at you. "You know the rest."

"How about jazz?"

"I took that with me. My new folks didn't mind. I even got one of their sons into it. Tim. I'd buy records with my allowance. Late at night in bed I'd listen to a jazz station."

"Transistor radio?"

"Yeah. With an earphone."

"I did the same thing."

You trade the smiles of buddies now before he goes on.

"When I got older I started going to gigs. Concerts. I couldn't get enough. I read Downbeat and other jazz magazines. I joined a jazz fan club. We'd get together and swap the stories we read or heard about." Then he says, "I couldn't do what I loved. That was okay. I could still love it."

You sit there struck by his modest honesty. You wonder why you kept from telling him about your trumpet. If you were scared or just selfish. It's too late now. Now that he's told you everything.

"Who's your favorite?" he says.

"Wow. I don't know. Usually the last guy I listen to. How about yours?"

"Yeah," he says. "Dumb question. "I like the West Coast guys. But then I'm a West Coast guy too." He shrugs and says, "I don't know. It keeps changing."

"Me too," you say, in case the day comes when you can tell him the truth.

"Yeah." He looks at his watch. "Guess we oughta pray and get to bed."

On Friday morning, Diversion Day, you drop off your laundry and head for the bathhouse. You use the toilet before you leave to get the landlady's daughter off your mind. You pedal home before noon with the early summer wind in your wet hair. You stop at a newsstand where Novick buys a copy of Newsweek. He uses the afternoon to read it lying on the bed. You've never seen anyone read a magazine the way he does. Like a book. From the cover straight through to the end. And on Friday night you sometimes catch the train into Vienna and follow Novick past the concert halls you recognize from Morgan through the unfamiliar streets of places he tells you are Schwedenplatz and the Donaukanal to one of the jazz clubs you didn't know was there. The places are small. Their doorways usually recessed and hidden three or four steps down from the sidewalk. If you couldn't hear the music on the street, or didn't stop and read the notice naming some player or band on the wall, you'd never know what they were.

The musicians are a mix of guys and an occasional singer. Old and young. Negro and white. Jazz and blues. Ashtrays you have no use for and a couple of sweet warm European Cokes occupy the small tables you and Novick share. The rare chatter from other tables dances on the music on air clouded with cigarette smoke hazed red by candles mounted in wax-crusted wine bottles. What strikes you is the way the customers are mostly here to listen. The way they quietly cheer the solos. Applaud as a song comes in for a landing. Most of the bands don't have trumpets. When they do, they take you back, back to junior high, a kid in the dark of the auditorium, watching another kid on stage do what you didn't dare let yourself do back then. You were a kid. Scared of a used trumpet and its power to make your mother crazy and set the combustible air of your house on fire. Now you're a missionary. Not scared this time. Just smart enough to know the fence you keep between what you're doing here and what you did back home. Sit back. Enjoy. Dream of Cissy there with you. Think of what you'll tell her when you write her when you're back in your room again. You'll hear from her. You know you will. Let that steel bird sound fly you forward to the time you'll be back home again. This time with her. One hand one heart. Because time is flying now. Because you're working. Because you've earned that too.

CHAPTER 39

ONE MORNING, the low flatbottom hulls of a fleet of thunderheads moving dark and slow across the sky, you pedal past the rear gate of the grounds of the Stift around which the town is built. Feelers of wind have been snaking through the streets, carrying dirt, rags of loose newspaper like crippled seagulls, leaves that have fallen too early, the scent of rain. Because of the coming rain you're staying close to home. As you pass the arch of the open gate you hear piano music. A piece you know. One your mother always played. You circle back, stop, put your feet down on the cobblestones. Novick circles back and rides around you once before he stops next to you.

"What's up?"

A white stucco house two stories high stands with its back against the wall just inside the arch of the rear gate that leads onto the grounds of the Stift. The music is coming from two open upstairs windows.

"I know that piece," you say.

"That piano music?"

The front of the house has no door. But there's a small wood door set into a high wall that runs maybe fifteen yards from the gate to the corner of the house. Working with Novick has made you good at spotting and exploring doors.

"Mind if we go in?" you ask him.

"Through the gate? I can't."

"Scared?"

"I don't like looking for trouble."

Beyond the house stand the church and the towers that house the bells. Across the way an elegant three-story building with a palace face makes the house where the music is coming from look plain. While you stand there, the door to the building opens, and a man in a black suit follows a man in a monk's robe. They look at you as they start walking toward the cathedral. The man in the suit looks back your way couple of times.

"Nobody can go missing," you say, standing there, your bike between your legs.

"You're serious," says Novick.

"No. Not those guys. Just this house," you say. "Where the music's coming from. That's probably the door there. Through that wall."

"It's on Catholic property," he says.

"Yeah?"

"We gotta cross Catholic property to get there."

"You mean from here to the door?"

"Yeah."

You remember what Morgan said.

"It's not the Church of the Devil. The Devil wouldn't be caught dead in a church."

"Yeah. Maybe I'm being stupid. Let's go."

"Mind if I do the talking?"

"Sure."

The door through the wall opens onto a small grass yard hemmed with the stucco backs of houses. An uneven path of old stone slabs leads between them and branches off to the two shallow steps and small porch and wood door of the house you're looking for. Through the door you can hear the music. You lean your bikes against the house and stand back till the music stops before you knock.

The woman who opens the door surprises you. Maybe you expected a nun. She's just a regular woman dressed in regular clothes. Her soft round face, clean of makeup, has the alert discipline you heard in the music. So it was her. Set in the slightly stained darker skin around them her eyes are kind and also curious. The waves of her brown hair are parted and combed up off her forehead. In a green dress, buttons down the front to her waist, she's maybe your mother's age.

"Gruess Gott," she says.

"Gruess Gott," you say.

"May I help you?"

"We were going by and heard you playing," you say. "Rustle of Spring. My mother plays it. I wanted to say how nice it was to hear it."

Surprise moves into her polite smile.

"Thank you. Who are you?"

"We're missionaries. From America. I'm Herr Tauffler. This is Herr Novick."

You wait for her eyes to go distant, her face cold, the way you've always seen it happen. It doesn't come. Instead she extends her hand.

"I'm Frau Goller. It's nice that you like my playing. What did you call it?"

"Rustle of Spring. Christian Sinding."

"Ah. That's English. We call it Fruehlingsrauschen."

"You play very well," you say.

"Thank you again."

From behind her you hear the rapid slap of shoes down a stone staircase. A girl's face appears around Frau Goller's dress.

"Hello," you say.

She looks at you. And then at Novick.

"The gentleman said hello," her mother says. "They're from America."

Her dark almost black hair is cut short in a lively pageboy with bangs across her forehead. Maybe she's eight. Maybe nine. Her wide eyes blue in the wide field of her clear face. Light freckles across her nose. You're taken by the slight projection of her chin below her mouth. She wears a pale blue dress dotted with white flowers, buttons like her mother's but a child's dress, white socks and black shoes. You put out your hand to her while thunder rolls through the dark clouds above the town.

"My name's Shake. What's yours?"

Expressions play across her face with the dance of moving light on water.

"My daughter's shy," her mother says. "So," she says, to her daughter. "What do you say?"

Her hand comes forward. You feel it in your hand like a skittish chipmunk.

"Tell Herr Tauffler who you are," her mother says. "Have you forgotten?"

She takes back her hand as if she can't both shake your hand and talk.

"Edith."

"Hi, Edith. This is my friend John."

"Now say hello to Herr Novick."

Novick extends his football hand. She stares at it. Her mother nudges her. He barely has time to close his fingers over hers before she takes her hand away.

"Go close the windows," her mother says. "Hurry!"

You can hear her take the stairs two at a time. Lightning cracks the air. And then her footsteps are lost in the sudden thunder that crashes overhead and rockets across the town. You duck. Drops start coming down. Fat and hard. You and Novick look back and forth along the houses for shelter.

"No! Come inside! Quick! Before you're soaking wet! You can wait here!"

A small dark lobby with wooden doors in the paneled walls. The dust smell of polish. Frau Goller leads you up a narrow stone stairwell to a landing where a door stands open onto a dining room with a long table and chairs. She motions you inside. In the entryway, hooks on one wall for coats, another wall is decorated with an arrangement of maybe twenty small animal skulls with miniature antlers. From the dining room she takes you into a neighboring room large enough for a grand piano at one end and space for rugs and chairs and small tables across the rest of the floor. Two short brown leather couches take up a corner. Shelves and small recesses built into the walls hold books, stacks of sheet music, religious statues and ornaments and special glasses. Across the room you recognize the windows you saw from the street, closed now, a stone fireplace between them. The wind drives the rain in explosive whipping bursts across the glass. Edith comes running in.

"That's all of them?" her mother says.

"Yes, Mama," she says, breathless, the house barricaded against the assault of the storm.

You realize where you are. Surrounded by the enemy. A dark portrait of a furious old man lets you know you have no business here. Frau Goller invites you to take the leather couches. Lightning flashes just outside the windows. The thunder is instantaneous, huge, violent. It shocks the air and sets things rattling all around the room. It knows who you are. Instruments of the real Lord. It wants to shake the house till it shakes you and Novick loose, down the stairs and out the door, where it can reach you.

"There," Frau Goller says, once you're seated. "Would you like something to drink? Tea? Coffee? Something to eat?"

"Thanks, but not for me," says Novick, and looks at you. Inside his open suit coat you can see a saddlebag under his arm.

"I'd like a glass of water, please."

She excuses herself, puts her palms together, leaves the room. You're inside. You wonder what Novick will do. If he'll try to lead her to admit that the church on whose property she lives is false. He knows you're not supposed to talk to her too much about the Church without her husband here. Frau Goller comes back to hand you a tall glass of water.

"Thank you."

She smiles at your accidental use of English.

"You're welcome," she says, in English too.

She takes a wooden chair with a high back from the wall and sets it across the coffee table from you and Novick. Her daughter sits on the flowered rug beside her. The violent head of the storm has moved on, taking the lightning and thunder and wind, leaving a steady summer rain. What you're doing here in Klosterneuburg. What church you're missionaries for. Novick pulls his Book of Mormon out of a saddlebag to show her. She listens at first and then brings the conversation back to the two of you. Where in America you're from. How many of you there are. Novick lays the Book of Mormon on the coffee table. She leads the conversation gently but with this persistent eagerness. Like she really wants to know what she's asking you to tell her. What interests her most is what makes two young Americans give up so much of their lives to be missionaries for a church she's never heard of.

Novick tries to tell her. Keeps picking up the Book of Mormon. She keeps letting him know to put it down again. Keeps coming back to the two of you. Novick tells her about Bakersfield. He's reluctant at first because he's supposed to be telling her about the Gospel. But she listens with this attentive smile and kindness in her eyes. She softly pulls stories out of him he hasn't told even you. He explains football. He keeps trying to pull the conversation back to church. How grateful he is that he was raised Mormon. She tells him she understands because she was raised Catholic. You tell her about growing up in Utah. She wants to know if you play piano too. Novick interrupts you when you skip the part about being born in Switzerland. She raises her eyebrows while Novick tells her how your grandfather translated the book he's holding into German. How your family moved to Utah to live in the Zion of the Mormon Church.

"Maybe that's why you speak German with a Swiss accent," she says.

"I do?"

"Did your parents speak it at home?"

The swear words they threw around in Swiss. The names they would call each other.

"Sometimes. Yes."

Edith jumps to her knees to whisper into her mother's ear.

"You have a voice," her mother says. "You can ask him."

She shakes her head. Her bangs dance and her short hair whips back and forth.

"She wants to know how old you were when you left Switzerland."

The girl looks at you expectant. Like it was her who asked the question.

"I was four," you say. "How old are you?"

She looks at her mother for permission.

"Eight." Then on her own she says, "I'll be nine in June."

"When?"

"The sixteenth."

"June sixteenth."

She watches you laugh.

"Yes," she says. "Why?"

"No school today?"

"She didn't feel well this morning." Her mother looks at her. "Better now though."

"What's so funny about my birthday?"

"Nothing. What grade are you in?"

"Three," she says.

"Another year of Volkschule." Her mother looks at you. "You must not remember much of Switzerland."

Your mother feeding you a soft boiled egg in a high chair on a second floor balcony above a courtyard where kids played games and rode their bikes. The sunlight on your mother's face. The one memory.

"No." Then, seeing her wait for more, you say, "It's what I feel more than remember."

"What you feel," she says.

"Like home."

She looks at you. Affection makes a brief home in her eyes.

"Because Austria reminds you of Switzerland." she says. "Your native country."

"I think so."

"So close to home," she says. "I can understand."

And then it's your turn to do the asking. You ask about the house. While Novick keeps touching the Book of Mormon, nudging it around, she tells you it was built around five hundred years ago. How it has the charm of not a single straight doorway or ceiling or wall or floor or any other surface meant to be straight. How it was built as a convent for the nuns who tended to the Stift. How the ground floor below you consists of utility rooms. How the house stands on five cellars and subcellars connected by stairs and tunnels. She winks when she tells you the tunnels also used to connect to the monastery across the way where the monks and students live. You try to imagine the rooms of the house filled with nuns. The best you can do is the Lion House in Salt Lake where Brigham Young kept his wives. You wonder what happened to them. Where all the nuns went. If their skulls and skeletons are piled in bins in one of the cellars below you.

You ask about her. While Novick folds his hands and keeps them still she tells you she teaches school. Kids who back in Utah would be in junior high. Her husband's name is Hubert. He wanted to be an organ maker. Then the war came. When it ended he didn't have the money to make organs. So he began making harmonicas. And then musical tops. And then other instruments. Before long he started working in injection molding. And from there he started designing and making toys as well. Now he has a factory where he makes plastic parts for instruments but mostly toys. Farm animals. Cartoon characters. Dolls. Houses for them to live in. Furniture for them. Edith leaves. Comes back with a yellow cartoon duck and a brown cartoon cow. She hands you the cow and Novick the duck. The rubber is firm and solid. The cow so comic you have to laugh. It pleases her. She laughs too. Delight shows her small teeth and ignites her face and pushes her cheeks into her eyes. You ask what their names are. Alfonso? Pedro? She laughs again. The shyness gone like smoke on wind.

"They're both girls. Those are boy names." She points at the cow. "That's Caroline." Then the duck. "That's Monika."

Sunlight floods through the window now.

"You should both meet my husband," Frau Goller says. And then she says, "You can't talk to Hubert about religion. The war killed his belief in God."

"Was he in the army?"

"There was no army. We were occupied. He fought in the Resistance."

"How long have you lived here?"

"Before Edith was born."

On the rug again, the cow and duck at her knees, she whispers to her mother again.

"She wants to know if you have brothers and sisters," her mother says.

"I have two of each. The youngest one is a girl about your age."

"Are you her big brother?"

"I'm the biggest," you say, smiling.

She darts her eyes back down.

"What are they named?" she says.

"Karl, Molly, Roy, Maggie." Then you say, to get her to raise her face again, "How about you?"

"Yes," her mother says. "Edith's our only child. So she gets all of our attention. Don't you, sweetheart."

This time, in the sunlight that brightens the room, her shyness is real and she doesn't know what to do with it.

"Do you have plans for Sunday?" her mother says.

"Just church," says Novick.

"Do you have time for lunch?"

"We're not done with church till one."

"Then could I invite you and Herr Tauffler to have Sunday dinner with us?"

You look at each other.

"I want Hubert to meet you. He likes to meet new people. Especially two nice young men from America."

"We'd like to meet him too," says Novick. "What time should we come?"

"Around four?"

"Okay," says Novick. "We'll be here."

On your way to the door you turn around and take your passport out of its pocket inside your suit.

"Edith? I have something to show you."

"What?"

You open your passport to the photo page. Point to your date of birth. She follows your finger. Then steps back. Covers her lower face with both hands. Looks up at you with eyes so big they show white all the way around the blue.

"That's what was funny about your birthday."

"What?" says her mother.

"It's the same as mine."

The sun is out, the sky clear of the storm, but you walk your bikes because the cobblestones are still too wet and slick to hold the tires. Novick looks back to make sure you're out of range and then grins and sticks out his hand to you. You grin too. What you feel is brand new. This exuberance for this crazy thing you've just pulled off. This is what it's like.

"We did it," he says. "We did it."

"We did. We got inside."

"The Lord meant for you to hear that music. For her to play it right then."

"He did. He knew."

"Mind if we pray?" he says. "Right now?"

"Okay."

And while you close your eyes and bow your head, while steam rises off the cobblestones in the sunlight, while you feel people walk by, Novick quietly thanks the Lord for leading you to her open windows. You say Amen together.

"A whole family," you say.

"She wants us back. She knows what we are but she wants us back."

"That's the best part."

"Maybe we should just ride around town listening for piano music."

"We could."

"That little girl took to you," says Novick.

"I liked her."

"So what do you think? Think we can baptize them?"

You remember Frau Kettler. What Morgan said.

"If we take our time," you say. "Don't forget her husband."

"I got less than three months," says Novick. "Maybe that's enough time."

"She said she wouldn't mind it when he's not around."

"Okay. We'll do that then."

"I wonder what he's like."

"I don't know. A resistance fighter. Maybe a big guy."

"Gary Cooper."

"But he makes toys too. And plays clarinet."

"Yeah. I don't know."

"You know, if we baptized them, they'd have to move," you say.

"What do you mean?"

You're walking your bikes again.

"They'd be Mormons. They couldn't live on Catholic property."

After a few steps, Novick says, "I didn't think of that."

Chapter 40

IF YOU'RE THE jazz musician then Novick's the joker and historian of jazz. If you can play then he can reel out endless jokes and stories about the players. You already know from Mr. Selby the reason Charlie Parker was nicknamed Bird. But that's just a drop in Novick's deep bucket of material. It doesn't matter where you are. At breakfast. Out tracting, between doors, making your way from one rejection to the next. At supper in the backstreet restaurant you sometimes use. At night where you divide the soup you heated on the hot plate. One morning while you're working the hallways of a big apartment building.

"You know Lester Young?"

"Yeah. Of course."

"They called him the President."

"I heard."

You raise your hand and knock three times on the wood face of the door.

"Prez for short," says Novick. "He hired a drummer who wasn't playing what he wanted to hear. During a break the drummer tried to make conversation. So he says hey, Prez, when was the last time we played together? And you know what Lester says?"

"No."

"Tonight." His face breaks into its big brokenhearted clown smile. "Get it?"

"Tonight. Yeah. cool."

You see the usual giveaway flash of a floating eyeball through the peephole. If people ever worry about getting shot in the eye. Or stabbed with an ice pick.

"Ja?" comes the voice.

"Wir sind zwei missionare der Kirche Jesu –"

"Missionare?"

"Ja. Wir moechten mit Ihnen —"

"Keine Zeit."

You check the apartment off in the tracting book. Move on to the next door.

"That's how he fired the guy," says Novick.

"Yeah. Good one."

At night, between tunes, listening to the disk jockey say names like Coleman Hawkins and Dizzy Gillespie and Cab Calloway in an Austrian accent.

"You know Gene Quill?" says Novick, turning the radio down for a commercial break.

"No."

"I don't either. Just this story. He's a sax player. One night he's coming off the bandstand and this young jerk stops him and says All you're doing is playing just like Charlie Parker. And you know what Gene Quill does?"

"Tell me."

"He holds out his sax to the jerk and says Here. You play just like Charlie Parker."

"That's cool."

Or he tells straight jokes instead of funny stories. Musician jokes. Sitting side by side on the train, bound for home from some night club, the dust smell of cigarette smoke in your suits the way your father used to come home from his job when you first moved to Bountiful.

"What kind of people hang around musicians?"

"I give up."

"Drummers."

And then he says, when you're done laughing, "How can a jazz musician wind up with a million dollars?"

"I give."

"Start out with ten million."

And then he says, "How do you put a gleam in a soprano's eye?"

"How?"

"Shine a flashlight in her ear."

"That's mean."

"So stop laughing."

The difference between Mr. Selby's and Novick's stories is that most of Mr. Selby's were his own, stories he'd been there for, been part of. Novick's are stories he's read or heard.

"You gotta know Bobby Hackett. He played trumpet."

"Yeah. Actually a cornet."

"Yeah. Okay. So he's selling one of his horns. It's a good buy, he tells people. In the upper register, it's practically brand new."

"The upper register. That's funny."

"You get that, right?"

"Yeah."

"Cuz he couldn't play up there. The notes were too high."

You love this big guy. This big dopey hardworking guy who loves jazz and walks with his shoes splayed out.

"Yeah."

CHAPTER 41

THAT SUNDAY, when you knock, a man opens the door. Edith stands next to him in a white blouse and plaid skirt. The same dark bangs and pageboy hair frame a wide face that looks excited this time and a smile that looks playful. You tell him who you are. He tells you he's Herr Goller. His handshake's small but firm. He's not what you expected for someone who fought the Nazis. No Gary Cooper. No Randolph Scott. But you can see someone who makes harmonicas and rubber toys. And another kind of fighter. A terrier. A bulldog. He's short, strong shouldered, his sand-colored hair going thin. His eyelids give his restless pale blue eyes a look between watchful and weary. His face is blotched pink in places. His smile is friendly but quick to come and go. The sleeves of his white Sunday shirt are rolled back to his elbows over forearms as hairless as yours but twice as big around. While he holds the door for you he runs the fingers of his other hand through his hair in a stab at combing it.

Upstairs the long table is set and the air rich with the spiced smell of seasoned meat despite the open window. Hunger rumbles through your stomach. Frau Goller smiles as she comes in from the kitchen carrying a steaming bowl. A light brown apron tied around her waist reaches below her knees just shy of where her dress stops. She's a couple of inches taller than her husband.

Herr Goller sits at the head of the table. He calls his wife Gertrud. She seats you at the other end. Herr Goller holds up an open bottle of wine. Novick tells him sorry but your religion forbids alcohol. Herr Goller grins and says he won't tell. Frau Goller shakes her head and smiles. The dish she serves is venison goulash made from a deer Herr Goller brought home from a hunt. At the head of the table he's mostly quiet while he eats, happy to listen, happy to be provider and host. In the gentle way he regards his wife you can sense the man who makes harmonicas and toys. Novick sits alone across the table. To your right their daughter can't stop blushing every time you smile at her. When you pull a sudden face she jumps and can't stop giggling from behind her hands, her face screwed up, her eyes squeezed almost shut. By the way her laugh lifts into her cheeks. From her chair at the other end Frau Goller directs the conversation. What you like about Austria. Where you've been. If you have a girl back home. What you've seen of Vienna. When you name places she offers historical and cultural details you didn't know. And somewhere along the way Herr Goller says to call him Hubert.

"Then call me Shake."

It just comes out. Across the table, Novick doesn't flinch, but doesn't offer up his own first name.

"Shake," says Hubert. "Is that American?"

You shrug. "I don't know what it is."

Hubert laughs. You're glad Frau Goller doesn't say to call her Gertrud. You couldn't call her by her first name any more than you could have called Cissy's mother Bernice.

The conversation turns to music when she tells the story of the piano piece that brought you to her door. Fruehlingsrauschen. Rustle of Spring.

"My mother always plays it," you say. "I've heard it since I was born."

"In Switzerland!" says Edith.

"Hubert plays piano too," Frau Goller says. "And clarinet. Tell them, Hubert."

"You just did."

"No. Tell them." Turns to you. "He studied at the Wiener Musikakademie. The Academy of Music in Vienna."

The academy. You remember it from a couple of concerts Morgan took you to. The broad red carpeted hallways and staircases. The gold statue of the violinist who had the hair and moustache and furious face of Mark Twain.

"I've been there. You studied there?"

"Yes. Piano and composition."

"His father was a composer," Frau Goller says, "Mostly for the organ."

"Your wife told us you wanted to be an organ maker," Novick says.

"Yes. But like any business it takes, you know . . ." He smiles at Novick and finishes the sentence by rubbing his thumb and finger together. Novick nods.

"So you started making harmonicas?" you say.

He looks at his wife and grins. "Did you leave anything for me to tell them?"

"Is there more?" she says, giving him a teasing look.

He smiles. "Yes. I made harmonicas."

Do you still play clarinet, you want to ask, and he'd probably say not for years, but then they'd ask you what you play.

"Your wife says you have a toy factory," you say.

"A toy factory," he says, and winks at her. "You told them that? Do I look like Santa Claus?"

"Maybe an elf," Frau Goller says.

From there you talk back and forth, fill in holes, as answers lead to questions, stories lead to stories. Hubert talks quietly about the Resistance. His capture by the Nazis and liberation by Americans as the city was bombed away from around his prison cell. You talk about running tanks around Fort Knox and the Mojave. You tell the story about bucking Lieutenant Tanner out of the tank commander's hatch. They laugh. Novick stares at you. There are stories you haven't told him either. You've never felt comfortable talking about yourself for very long. It's always been a matter of what and what not to tell. Or talking too long and ending up where your father starts thinking big shot. But this is different. This is the deep aroma of venison goulash where you can still taste mountain grass in the seasoned meat. This is the meat of a deer that Hubert tells you he killed with a Mannlicher Schönauer 7x57 with a shot to the heart. This is the luminous warmth of Frau Goller's smile while she listens.

At the end of dinner Edith and her mother carry the plates away. Frau Goller asks if you'd like coffee. Novick tells her no. You're not allowed to drink it. The shadow of disappointment and curiosity.

"Who says you can't drink coffee?"

"Our religion."

"No wine, no coffee, what else can't you drink?" says Hubert.

"Tea," says Novick, an apologetic smile in his sad clown face. Tea. Green and black tea. Herb tea's okay. Like Kamillentee."

"Would you like some Kamillentee then?" Frau Goller says.

"No thanks," says Novick. "I'm fine."

"What are you doing next Sunday?" she asks.

Novick looks at her.

"Going to church," he says. "Just like today."

"And after church?"

"Work."

"You shouldn't work on Sundays," Frau Goller says. "Especially missionaries. I have a better idea."

"What, Mama?"

"We make a little drive. Into the Wachau."

Edith squeals.

"What's the Wachau?" says Novick.

"You don't know?" Frau Goller says. "You really do work too hard. It's the valley of the Danube. We'll stop for something to eat at one of the outdoor restaurants. Can you come?"

"Sure." Novick gives you a glance. "We'd love to. Wow. Thank you."

CHAPTER 42

ON THE LAST SATURDAY in May Novick takes you into Vienna to
a jazz concert by a pianist named Friedrich Gulda and his band. A band
called the Euro-jazzorchester. A big horn section. Four saxophones,
two trombones, four trumpets, a French horn. A standup bass and a big
band drummer whose name you know. Mel Lewis. Friedrich Gulda down
in front at a concert grand like the Boesendorfer in the chapel at the
churchhouse.

"Back in the fifties this guy was a famous classical pianist," Novick whispers. "Then he got bored and went into jazz. He's kind of a rebel."

"Cool."

"Hey. Look at that trumpet player. That short one. Satchmo."

"Yeah. Kind of."

"That's not him really, is it?"

"Not even close. Just listen."

The Air from other Planets. Some Charlie Parker bebop. The Veiled Old
Land. Music for Piano and Band. Gulda has astonishing technique. But the
feel is cold and the way he plays is in your face. The horns blare the way a
big horn section always blares. Before he's halfway through you're thinking
back to Lenny and the way the two of you saw eye to eye. The song comes
first. Don't play to impress people. Play to move them. On the way back to
the train there's a light rain falling. Not enough for an umbrella unless you're
a hooker looking to keep your hair puffed and your outfit dry. Novick wants
to know what you thought.

"You could hear his classical training," you say.

"Know what else you could hear?"

"What?"

"His ego."

"Yeah," you say. "Loud and clear."

"Way too much."

You remember what Lenny used to say.

"I like a little melody with my melody."

"A little melody with my melody," says Novick. "I like that."

"It's from a friend of mine. He plays jazz piano."

"What else did you think?" he says.

"Too many horns. I'm not a big band guy."

"How come?"

"I don't know. Probably because I played alone a lot."

He stops cold. "Played what?"

You take a minute to look down at the black shine the light rain gives the sidewalk, understand that you've stepped in something stupid, turn to meet his big expectant face.

"Trumpet."

"Trumpet? Are you kidding? Like in jazz?"

The day you've been waiting for. When you'd need to tell him the truth.

"I used to."

Your eyes skate off to the side where the tires of a passing Fiat rip the skin of the rain off the cobblestones.

"You're kidding." And then he says, "Ever play in a band?"

"A few."

"You bring it?"

"What. To Austria? No."

"Think you could get it sent over?"

"I'm not here to do that."

The resentment and defeat in your father's face whenever he came home from work and opened the garage door and there you were with your horn in the smoke of his headlights. The one time you played in church was for fun. Your father let you know how much fun it was for him.

"You're here to do missionary work," says Novick. "Right?"

"Yeah," you say. "I'm finally doing it."

"You don't think playing a trumpet can be missionary work?"

"That's funny," you say. "Coming from the King of Tracting."

"I'm serious."

"How?"

"Play. Get the word out. Like the Osmonds do. Just plant the name Mormon in people's heads. You any good?"

"The Osmonds. Come on."

"Sorry. I take back the Osmonds. You any good?"

Jazz and church. The troubling wind you've felt whenever they've come too close together. The restless hankering to make that sound take flight. For the ring and the feel in the metal when the sound breaks free. Your father telling you not to play your trumpet like a hypocrite. You look down at your shoes to clear your head.

"I can't do it."

"Why not?" says Novick.

"This is my mission," you say. "Playing's another thing."

"How?"

"It just is."

"Remember what they say about the missing?" he says. "How we need to find them?"

"Yeah."

"Maybe some of the missing hang out in jazz clubs."

"So I should play hymns in a jazz club."

Novick smiles. Then goes serious. "If you've got a gift for playing, it's from God. You should use it to do his work."

You come around a corner. A hooker standing back from a street light against the rain-streaked stone face of a building smiles from under her pale umbrella. A gift, you're thinking, giving her smile back. It was his duty as your senior to say it. He said it like he was almost sorry to have to. It riles you anyway. Mrs. Harding's yard. The winter in the sandpit. The way the cold would lock your knees. A gift. Like it was something you didn't do on your own. Something you didn't earn. God never gave it to you. He tried to take it away. You had to tear it out of his hands.

"I don't know if jazz is God's idea of a gift," you say.

"Well, I wish I'd been there when he gave it to you. I'd of traded you."

"For what?"

"I don't know," he says, smiling off ahead of you. "Football maybe."

"You ever try using football to bring people to the Gospel?"

And now he laughs. "If I could think of a way," he says. "Everyone here plays soccer."

"It's not honest," you say.

"Why not?"

"It's not what people come for. It's like bait."

"It's God's work. It's like your trumpet's an instrument of the Lord."

You can hear him smiling when he says it.

"I can't do it."

"I'm your senior. I can make you."

"No you can't."

"I know. Sorry. Just think about it, though. Okay? Just do that."

You walk the light rain of the half block left to the tram stop. At the corner you wait for traffic before you cut across. Standing with some other people at the tram stop, you feel the easy give of the valves under the fingers of your right hand, make a fist to stop it.

"I love what we're doing," you tell Novick. "I'd like to just keep doing it."

"You mean tracting."

"Yes." And then you say, "My mission didn't start till I got to you."

"We're still gonna do that. Don't worry." Then he says, "Just think about it. Okay?"

"So how would we spread the word in there?"

"That's my job." Then he says, "Just think about it for now."

You look back to the last corner you turned. There's a car pulled up to the curb where the hooker smiled at you. The steam of its exhaust wells up into its headlights. Through the steam there's her silhouette, still holding her umbrella, leaning over, looking into the passenger window.

"Mind if we skip the tram?" you say. "Walk to the train station?"

"Sure."

Chapter 43

IN THE LIGHT RAIN and the halo shine of headlights you leave the tram stop and head off for Franz Josefs Bahnhof and the train back to your room in Klosterneuburg.

"There's another reason I can't play," you tell Novick.

"Lemme take a guess," he says.

"Go ahead."

"That girl you keep writing. Who never writes back."

You walk for a while in silence. Give the truth the time it needs.

"Sorry," Novick finally says.

"What about her?"

"What's going on?"

For a minute you watch the wet street where the moving shine of headlights is mirrored off the glistening backs of hundreds of cobblestones.

"She wrote me a Dear John."

"I got one of those," Novick finally says. "A couple of years ago."

"What'd you do?"

He laughs. "What else? Here I was in Austria. I just had to let it happen." Then he says, "How long since you got it?"

"A couple of weeks before we got together. You and me."

"You've been writing her since then?"

"Yeah."

"And she's never written back."

"Not yet."

Novick stops. You turn around to face him. In the downturn of his open mouth you can see anguish. Put with his droopy eyes he looks like the theater mask of tragedy. You turn away. You're in front of a lighted picture window where three mannequins let you know it's a dress shop.

"What are you trying to do?" he says.

"What do you mean?"

"With your letters."

"Change her mind. Wait for me."

Hearing it out loud shames you.

"So what do you write her?"

"Just how we can make it work."

"She said it wouldn't work?"

"Yeah."

"Think it's another guy?"

"Sometimes I do. Probably not." And then you say, "No."

"She tell you why?"

"Yeah."

"So?"

"She said to be with her I'd have to give up everything."

"How's she supposed to make that happen?"

"It's not like that." You take a deep breath. Let it out slow. "It's just what she says would happen." You hesitate again. The image comes hard. "She said I'd close my eyes and wish for her. When I opened them she'd be standing there. But everything else would be gone."

"That's what she says would happen?"

You look down at Novick's big black shoes. The wrinkles so deep they're out of reach of polish.

"I keep telling her," you say. "Her standing there is all I want."

"What's everything?"

"Family. Church. Where I live. Pretty much my life."

"Trumpet?"

The one song you did together. Out past the gleaming bell of your trumpet you see the fierce curls of her dark hair up the rose honey of her neck. You feel her hands in Yenchik's 40 Ford as you shape her fingers around the valves to show her how to hold it.

"No. 1 could of kept that."

"Your folks don't like her? She's not Mormon? What's the deal?"

You turn to look at the street again. Faces behind the closed windows of passing cars look back at you. State Street back in Salt Lake. Cruising State. Checking each other out. It's not like that here. You look back at Novick.

"She's negro," you finally say. And then you say, "Black. I guess that's the new word."

Novick doesn't say anything for a while.

"Okay," he says. "I understand."

"I can't figure out how to live without her." Then you say, "If I could just talk to her face to face."

"Where does she live?"

"San Jose."

"Think face to face would change her mind?"

"It did once."

"How?"

You tell him. The drive to San Jose. The talking you did in the lamplight of the walkway on the campus where she goes to school now.

"What's her name?"

You tell him that too. How she goes by Cissy.

"Was she waiting for you?"

And you tell him too about the airport. Her pink church dress. Her brother Jeff in his Airborne uniform. Introducing her to your family. How you don't care what you lose.

"Sounds like she still loves you."

"I don't know."

"What makes you think she doesn't?"

"I know she does. She said what we had was a beautiful dream. She just won't write back. I don't know why."

"Maybe she made up her mind. Maybe she's sure."

"Then why can't she write and tell me?"

"Maybe she already did."

"She could she tell me again. So I'd know for sure."

"So what would you do if she did?"

"I'd tell her . . ."

"You'd tell her you could work it out."

"Okay. Probably."

"You ever put yourself in her shoes?"

You come to a another stop. Back off to dodge the umbrella of a man in a raincoat hurrying the way you're coming from.

"How?"

Novick turns down his open mouth again. It plays off his droopy eyes to make him look like this is his heartbreak too.

"Okay," he says. "Don't take this the wrong way."

"I won't."

"She writes to tell you it's over. She's made her mind up. Know how hard that had to be? Knowing she was gonna break your heart?"

You look off down the street.

"She's already broken her own. Now she has to break yours."

"I know."

"Then she starts getting a letter every other day. Telling her no. Telling her we can work it out. Arguing with her. They had to be pretty desperate, right? Those letters? I mean, there's your heart, in every letter, and she's gotta look at it again, the way she broke it."

"It was every day at first," you say. You look down. Wait out the thunder going off inside you. Rocketing through your bones. Rolling up your throat. "I never thought."

"She wants to know you're gonna be okay. She wants that probably more than anything. But every other day you're telling her you're not."

"How do you know this stuff?"

"I wrote some letters too. The same thing. Then I got one from her friend. She told me every time my girl got one she cried."

Tears on her face. You know what they look like from that night in San Jose. You know what put them there. Your open letter in her hand. Your blood on the page. Your latest stupid argument to stay together.

"I get it."

"See where what you're doing might be the opposite of what you think you're doing?"

See her opening yet another letter. Feel her heart go sick as she has to face what she's done to you again. Droplets of water sparkle with the light of the street where they look impaled on the black bristles of Novick's hair.

"What did you do?"

"Wrote and told her I was sorry. I was okay. Told her to be happy. Just dedicated myself to being a missionary. Life got a whole lot easier." Then he says, "Not easier. Simpler."

You start to walk again.

"You must not like this church sometimes," he says. "What it does to people."

You don't say anything. Any other church. Any church but this one. You maybe could have kept her.

"What was her name?" you finally say. "Your girl?"

"Mary," he says. Then he says, "It's still hard to say."

"I need to get back to the room. I need to write her. Let her go."

The massive multi-storied colossus of Franz Josefs Bahnhof raises its two square towers into the rain down the street ahead of you.

"Yeah," says Novick. "Let's get that train."

Chapter 44

Back in your room that night you towel dry your hair and then write her one last letter while Novick lies reading on the bed. You use your good stationery. Not the thin blue stuff that folds in an airmail envelope around your words. Real paper. A real envelope.

> Dear Cissy,
>
> I couldn't let you go. That's why I kept writing. You only broke my heart once. I broke yours every time I wrote you. I'm sorry. I didn't know what I was doing. I wasn't thinking.
>
> Now I know.
>
> I can let you go now.
>
> Maybe it's what you say it is. A beautiful dream. But while it was happening it was real. It will always be real inside the beautiful dream you put around it. I just wanted to keep you.
>
> I'll say goodbye now. Goodbye, Cissy.
>
> Love always,
>
> Shake

And for the last time, after you fold the envelope around the letter, write her name and address on the front. Novick watches you from the bed.

"That's it," you say. "She's gone."

"Okay."

Her photo in the secret compartment of your wallet. Now that she's gone, the promise you made to each other is over too, where you wouldn't use photos to remind yourselves of each other, where you'd remember each other for real.

"Wanna see her?" you say.

In the light of the lamp Novick looks up at you from his open Book of Mormon across the table.

"Sure," he says.

You pull your wallet out. Take a look yourself for the first time since you saw her last, for real, at the airport. The paper worn around the corners. Warped and distressed from its long detention in your wallet. The Fort Ord barracks the first time you saw it. Other times. The parade field the night at Knox when you used your Zippo to illuminate her face. The last time at Hiller before you headed for San Jose where you made your promise to each other. Her image grayed out, faded, and when you think of ghost, you hand it across the table. Novick looks. Then looks back up at you quick without a word before he looks back down. You recognize it. The negro moment. Not just telling him. For real.

"Gosh," he says. "She's a beauty." He shakes his head and looks at you before he hands it back. "No wonder you had a hard time."

You put it away. Not knowing what else to do with it.

"Thanks for setting me straight."

"How did you meet her?"

You tell him about your army buddy Jeff and the weekend he took you home to his family for the backyard barbecue in San Jose. All the food. All the negro people. The spontaneous band. The trumpet her Uncle Paul loaned you and then acted scared to take back because he said you put the devil in it. Everything still as plain as the afternoon it happened.

"That's where you met her?"

"There she was."

"My foster folks used to do barbecues like that," he finally says. Smiles. "I miss them."

"I know."

Novick grins. "He really said devil horn?"

"He did." Then you say, "I need to be by myself tonight."

"I understand," he says. "But I can't leave. You know that."

"No. Here. I mean sleep."

"Where?"

"Just on the floor."

"You sure?: he says. Then he says, "I can take the floor."

"No. That's okay. Thanks."

That night you grab your pillow and take the extra blanket off the closet shelf. The biggest stretch of open floor in the room goes underneath the table. Down between its legs. You pull the chairs out of the way.

"You gonna be all right?"

"Yeah."

"Think about that trumpet."

"I'll think about thinking about it."

"Good enough."

Sleepless. Your eyes get used to the dark. The phantom legs of the table and chairs and bed take form from what light comes through the pale glass of the attic window. The ghost gray hulk of Novick's body under the bedspread. The pattern of the rug this close. The dark underside of the table like the chassis of someone's car on the hoist at Steed's Texaco.

You've been here before. Just in a different time and place and for a different reason. The night of the day you brought your trumpet home from Mr. Hinkle's. The night at Knox, after tricking Cissy into wondering what she ever saw in you, when you had to break your love for her the first time. You know how it works. How to do it. How it's going to feel. What to expect. How to ride it out between now and sunrise. Stay awake. Ride out the howling ache that keeps your knees pulled up and your body curled around your stomach. Ride out the itch of the coarse wool blanket pulled up around your neck. Ride out the ache lodged like a fist in your throat. Your eyes wide open staring while you finally let go. Let go of the aching frantic hold you've kept on her since the morning you came home from Graz to read her last letter. It was a hold on a shadow anyway. On a beautiful dream of a shadow. Let go of every argument you've made since then to keep her. Let go of the chance that a place and life together could have been real. Then keep what nobody can ever take away. Her place in your memory. Her voice from the porch. Her lush black wilderness of hair. Her naked rose gold body. Her shining eyes when she lifts the hoods of her eyelids. Her sudden shining smile in the breathtaking honey coffee beauty of her face. Remember everything. Her heartbeat in your hand. Yours in hers. One hand one heart. Furnish her place in your memory with everything you remember. Her father saying she could be head wife. Her mother telling him to hush. Her brother Jeff. Her circle of Airborne uncles.

The ride north out of San Jose remembering the way she cried out from underneath you. How you crested the Sierras and she cried out again. Oh my God. Shake. Look. All the stars. I've never seen so many up so close. It's like we're out in space with them.

How you can still hear her. You just can't keep her.

You've been here before. Don't want what you can't have. Through what's left of the night you make the fierce and desolate journey not out of love—you wouldn't know who you were without your love for her—but out of the possibility of a life with her. Just you again. You and your garments and your place on the floor surrounded by phantom wooden table legs in the dark. And rage. This cold rage where you drive your rogue black tank through the gate, take position, load up and aim the ninety millimeter gun at a crack between two granite blocks in the wall of the Temple. Point of maximum vulnerability. Adjust the windage and elevation. And pull the trigger. Feel the tank rock back twice. Once from the recoil and then from the blast of the warhead through the granite. Repeat. Load and lock and aim and fire, again and again, until the wall is gone and the sacred rooms behind it are exposed. The Telestial Room. The Terrestrial Room. The Celestial Room. The rooms too sacred to allow her in. Because this is the Church.

Because she's a negro girl. Because the color of her skin is the reason she had to let you go. Howl for every round you fire.

Remember her arrival at the airport. Remember the mirage she came from. The mirage of your disbelief that she could be standing there across the silver lake of polished stone. And then you caught on that she was really there, in a pink Sunday dress, in white Sunday shoes, waiting to be held, to be kissed, to say goodbye for now, to meet your family. Molly's face when you introduced them. And now return her to the mirage she came from. To the beautiful dream inside which everything was real. To the place in your memory inside which everything was touch and smell and feel and see and taste and hold.

Don't want what you can't have. As dawn approaches, she's gone, the way she was gone once you crested the Sierras and started coming down into the desert sunrise, back where she was, someone you thought you had a chance with, someone you could have maybe had except that she was negro and you were Mormon. Gone. Asshole. You need help respecting authority. You might need special attention. Words imprinted in that part of your brain reserved for hurt and rage. Asshole. You remember the first time you called your father one. The night you brought your trumpet home from Mr. Hinkle's. Asshole. How it terrified you at first. When nothing happened how good it felt to have said it. You lie there listening to Novick's clock tick itself toward the setpoint of its alarm while you look up into the wooden chassis of the table. Say it again. Asshole. Your asshole father and his asshole church. Asshole till Novick's alarm clatters and his arm comes out to paw for it and slam it off.

"How'd you sleep?" he says, when his eyes find you.

"Okay. You?"

"Pretty good."

You crawl out from under the table. Toss your pillow across him onto the bed. He pulls the covers back and swings his big legs out and sits on the edge of the mattress in the dingy bag of his garments while you fold the blanket up.

"You think about that trumpet?" he says.

"You know where we can find one?" you say.

He stares at you. Briskly rubs his face with his open hands. Drops them and stares at you some more.

"Are you saying yes?" he says.

"I can't afford one," you say. "I don't want to send home for mine."

"This old guy I know. At church. He should be there this morning."

Chapter 45

"WE'LL NEED to get permission," you tell Novick.

"No. First we're gonna make sure you wanna do this."

"I want to."

He ignores you. "Then we'll talk to Cannon before we talk to President Lindner."

"He's still here?"

"Yeah. He came just before me."

"He hasn't been to church."

"He's probably out touring the mission field. Checking in on everyone."

"Nice job."

That gusty Sunday morning, under white clouds that sail across the atmospheric table of the sky, the train takes you from the Klosterneuburg stop down the river into Vienna. A tram from the station takes you within walking distance of the churchhouse on Boecklinstrasse. That afternoon, when all the meetings are over, the Gollers are taking you on another excursion into the Wachau to see yet another stift or castle or town and have a late lunch at an outside table of another restaurant. On the sidewalk the wind whips the cuffs of your pants around your ankles.

"So far so good?" says Novick, next to you on the sidewalk, the white concrete box of the churchhouse in view up the street.

"Yeah."

After a minute, Novick says, "You know how come negro jazz players started becoming Muslims? You know the story behind that?"

"You mean all the strange names?"

"It's not what you think. I'll tell you sometime."

Your first time back a few weeks ago, Morgan was long gone, transferred to Salzburg, but the rotting picnic table from last summer still stood in the back yard. The widows remembered you. They were excited to hear your accent. You were happy to show them. The elders still gathered around the back of the chapel in breaks between the meetings in the usual groups. You knew a lot of them this time around. They knew you. They called you Elder. You all called each other Elder. Today you don't have much to say. Today you're someone else. They don't know. You don't either. Tracting and jazz.

Missionary and musician. If you can do this. If you can be this lucky. If you can join and then hold them together. Uncertainty and exuberance play like a crazy electric wind in your chest and underneath your skin.

After the last meeting you catch Novick talking to a tall old Austrian with lines of gray hair combed across his scalp, a long gray face, sad but attentive eyes. Novick introduces you. His name is Brother Shlagl. When he talks, in the motion of his gray lips, you can see traces of the imprint left by the steel circle of a mouthpiece. You talk about jazz and his eyes have the eager sparkle of a musician again with lots of stories to remember.

You spend the week tracting and on Friday hit a jazz club where you listen to a trio fronted by a dark-haired singer. You try to see yourself playing behind her. It doesn't come. It will. On Sunday again, after the last meeting, you catch Novick and Brother Shlagl in conversation again, only this time Brother Shlagl has a small brown and tan checkered suitcase in his hand. It's the second time you'll play a borrowed trumpet. The first belonged to Cissy's Uncle Paul. The afternoon of the barbecue he wouldn't take it back because you'd put the devil into it. He called it a devil horn. You let Novick ride the case home on his lap and then carry it through town to your room in the yellow house in Klosterneuburg. Let him lay the case on your shared bed. Let him open it and then stand back without touching it.

"Brother Shlagl said you could keep it as long as you want. Till you go home. He hasn't played it in over twenty years. Since he got baptized."

It's the first thing he's said since church. You cross the room to go look out the window. Think what difference being baptized would make. Maybe he felt that necessary separation the way you did. Maybe he played where people drank and smoked. Maybe he drank and smoked with them.

"He said it's a good one. He's glad someone's gonna use it."

You see the terrible pleading in Novick's big long face and look out the window at the twin towers of the Stift in the distance and remember the first time you brought your trumpet home. The way your mother held it raised with a look of fixed white hate in her face when you came out of the bathroom. The way it looked foreign and malevolent in her fist. This one with the same malevolent feel. Just when your mission was working out. Your father's disappointment. You came here to pay your debt to him.

"Man. I don't know. I thought I was ready."

"Scared you'll put the devil in this one too?" Novick says, and when you don't smile, he's quick to say, "I rushed you. I know. Sorry. I'll get rid of it for now."

In his voice you can hear what Novick's face looks like now. The way his heart feels torn in half for thinking this would work.

"I said I'd do it," you say. "I just need to get used to the idea."

"I didn't mean that crack about the devil," he says.

"I know."

"I think her uncle meant it as a compliment."

"I know."

On Monday you're back to tracting. Novick doesn't say anything about the trumpet. He doesn't bring up jazz. He doesn't even bring his radio out at ten that night. You have to tell him to. You remember the way you kept your trumpet hidden at home behind the Christmas boxes under a bottom shelf on the cement floor of the garage. This time, somewhere in the room you share with Novick, under the bed, in the closet, wherever Novick hid it, there's another trumpet, a foreign trumpet, while you try to get used to the idea that nothing will change if you take it out and play it, that you'll still be doing the work you're here to do.

You take a week to where you can think of playing without seeing Cissy's face and have it take your breath away when she finishes singing Since I Fell for You and turns around in the soft California sunlight of the back yard to watch you play your solo. To where you can think of playing without seeing her hold your horn in Yenchik's Ford and having the feel of her hands and fingers take hold of your heart when you help her weave them into place around the casings for the valves. And then most of another week before you understand that you'll never be able to think of playing without her being there somehow. And then the night is there when you tell Novick okay.

"You sure?" says Novick.

"Don't ask me that."

"You want me to get it?"

"Yeah."

"I'll be right back."

He goes downstairs. You hear the landlady's voice. His big shoes clomping up the stairs. And then he comes into the room again with the case.

"You could have kept it in here," you say.

"That's all right," he says.

He lays it on the bed again. This time he doesn't open it. Just stands back to let you do what you need to. The case is well kept. The brass corners are scratched and scuffed, and the finely checked brown and tan fabric is old and dull, but nothing's ripped up or broken, the frame is sturdy, the latches work. You lift back the lid. Cradled in velvet the color of red wine. In Mr. Hinkle's music shop you couldn't feel the instrument in your hands the first time you looked at it. This time, without touching it, the feel is instantaneous.

"I need to practice."

"I figured."

"A couple of hours a day at least."

"We can do it at night."

You reach down and take the horn off its cradle. It slips without thinking into place in your hands. You look at the scrollwork on the bell. Getzen. Wisconsin. You wonder how it got to Austria. Maybe the war. Maybe an American band. You open a little velvet door to a small compartment. Valve oil and slide grease. A rack that holds a mouthpiece. The snake of a steel spring with a rag through the hook at its end. You can smell its long history. You work the valves, check the slides, look its bruised and burnished finish over.

"He cleaned this up for us. Fresh oil and grease. Action's really slick."

"Guess he's got pride."

"Everything's here," you say. "Even a mute."

"You may want to wash that mouthpiece."

"I'm sure he did that too. I've got my own."

"You brought it with you?"

"Yeah."

"So you were planning on playing anyway?"

"No. Just to keep my lips in shape."

The way it sits in your hands. The heft and balance. Not quite the feel of your own. But close enough. You pull your Samsonite out from under the bed and fetch your mouthpiece out of its cloth pocket. It slips easily into the lead pipe. Novick watches as you barely touch it to your lips and give the valves a silent dry run two octaves up the C scale just to see if you remember.

"We need to find a place to practice," you tell Novick. "I can't do it in the house."

"How come?"

"Know how a trumpet sounds in a room like this?"

"How?"

You wet your lips and set them in place on the mouthpiece. It's been a year but you can feel where your muscles are formed to take the cup. The single note you meant to play takes off and runs a minor scale two octaves up and down again. The hard sharp sound carves the air of the room like a whirling knife. The highest notes are rough. But there it is. The sudden overwhelming pull to keep going. Reach for a song. Set that steel bird free. What you do. Who you are. You'd forgotten. You left it in the Mojave. Here it is in Austria. And now trouble rides a cold wind that sweeps sand off the desert floor. You lower the horn.

"Wow," you hear Novick say. And when you don't say anything, he says, "You okay?"

"Yeah."

"It's pretty loud," Novick finally says. "I never thought of that."

"I know."

"We'll find a place."

"Where?"

"We'll find one."

"I'll need some rope."

"What for?"

"Tie it to my bike rack. If we find a place we need to ride to."

"Okay."

"Guess we should ask President Lindner now," you say.

"I told you. We're not gonna do that right away. You practice. Then check out a club or two. See if you want to do this. He doesn't have to know."

"Okay."

"Looks good on you."

"It feels good."

"You really can play, can't you."

You look at him. See him proud and ready. The way you've seen fathers look at their sons. Bishop Byrne and Mr. Hinkle and Mr. Selby and Lieutenant Tanner at you. The way Novick will look one day at his own kids.

"Tell me after I've practiced some," you say.

"Can't wait."

"Feels good to have an agent," you say.

Shoes on the wood stairs. Whispers. A knock on the door of your room. Novick opens it on your landlady and her beefy dark-haired daughter. They don't come in. Just stand there crowded in the door frame while they contemplate you and your borrowed horn.

"He plays the trumpet too," says the daughter, with a smile she's given you before, swaying slow and lost in some dream in her nightgown to some tune you were playing on the piano downstairs.

"Wonderful," her mother says.

Novick turns back to you. "Agent," he says, and his dopey smile goes wide. "I like that." Then he says, "Man, did I get lucky. This'll be something."

CHAPTER 46

IT'S PRETTY LOUD. The feel where the air flow comes off your diaphragm down above your stomach through the continuous pipe from your lungs and throat out through the long brass pipe to the bell. The feel where you hit the pitch and the metal rings in your fingers and the note breaks free, pure and loud and powerful enough to take you anywhere. And now it's yours again. If you want it. You don't have to long for it. You don't have to miss it. All you have to do is find a place to practice.

Hubert doesn't want to talk or hear about religion but doesn't care one way or the other if his wife does. And so you and Novick are free to visit her at her invitation a couple of afternoons a week while Hubert runs his factory. She and Novick use the dining room table. He gives her a German Book of Mormon and every brochure he can lay his hands on. She reads everything he gives her and with a teacher's diligence prepares her counterarguments. He brings out his flannel board and paper dolls to illustrate his lessons. She brings her Catholic Bible and her notes and the brochures she's marked up in red ink. The dining room table gives them room to spread things out.

You become Edith's buddy. When she opens the door, happiness ignites her face, her eager smile lifts her cheeks into her eyes, and she takes your hand and pulls you up the stairs ahead of Novick and her mother. You keep your suit coat on because your saddlebags would stop her cold with curiosity. What's inside them. She'd want to see your own arsenal of brochures. And then you'd have to find a way to keep from talking religion to her. One afternoon she spots them.

"What are those? Under your coat?"

"Mail bags." You spread your coat to let her see them.

"You have mail in them?"

"Sure do."

"Show me."

"I can't."

"Why not?"

"It's against the law to show you other people's mail."

"Why do you have it?"

"When I'm not here with you, I'm a mailman."

"No you're not. You're a missionary."

"I'm both. When I go from house to house, I deliver the mail too."

"How come you never bring us any?"

"I'm not the mailman for your house."

"Why did you come to our house then?"

Eight years old. The age of knowing right from wrong. The end of innocence. The age of baptism. While Novick and her mother talk and argue religion, their voices sometimes raised but never hostile, you listen to her stories from one of the two big leather chairs in the corner of the room where the piano stands. While Novick tries to take her mother through the script that's supposed to end with her admission that the Catholic Church is false, while she politely but resolutely keeps arguing him off course, her daughter takes the things you tell her and turns them into stories. Of a butterfly that delivers mail to flowers. Of giant sardines that swim in the ocean she makes of your stomach. Of knights who ride gleaming black stallions into battle and the ladies in love with them. Ladies who wait for them. Ladies who are always beautiful and blond.

"Why are they always blond?" you say.

"Because blond hair is pretty."

You think of Cissy. Your sisters who never stood a chance of being blond. The girl in her dark bangs and pageboy cut in front of you.

"What color hair do the men have?"

It takes her a minute.

"I can't tell. They wear helmets."

"I think dark hair is prettier," you say. "On a girl."

Her eyes go wide and her cheeks red.

"You do?"

"More mysterious."

She laughs.

"Mysterious?"

"Like you."

And then she does that little thing you like to tease her into doing. That lag of a second or two while she looks at you, curious and blank, then shrieks and slugs your arm.

"I'm not mysterious! Don't say that!"

She brings out her games. You play them next to the piano on the soft brown rug that covers the open area of the hardwood floor. Her favorite is a simple game called Spinnefix. Thin steel orange rods form a spider-web the size of a plate. At the center of the web sits a moveable button painted with a fly. Arranged around the outer spokes of the web sit five buttons painted like spiders. The end of one spoke is open to give the fly an escape route. One player takes the fly. The other player takes the spiders. You take turns. You follow the paths of the rods. You move from one joint to the next. The spiders try to circle the fly and cut off all escape rods. The fly tries to get to the edge of the web where it can fly away. You and Edith alternate between the spiders and the fly.

"I win!" she'll say, clapping her fists together.

"I let you."

"No you didn't!"

"Then you let me lose."

"I didn't let you lose! I beat you!"

"That's what I mean. You let me lose."

"Mama! Herr Tauffler says I let him lose!"

"Oh Edith! Don't be silly! How can that be!"

Her mystery is the way stories cascade out of her. The way stories grow out of stories. The voices from the dining room, one crisp with a teacher's patience and the other heavy and stumbling with the earnest weight of testimony, fall out of hearing range while this girl takes you away in place and time on the improvisational magic of her imagination. One afternoon she tells you about the summer she spent with her grandmother, in her garden, while her mother recovered from losing a baby in childbirth. You look for sadness, and find it for a moment in her deflected face, before she starts telling you stories that transfigure her grandmother's garden into a luminous wonderland where fish turned to flowers and flowers to toads and toads to birds and birds to grass and grass to butterflies and butterflies to songs and songs to fish again. Purple to green to yellow to brown to blue to pink to red to gold and back to purple. You ask her about her friends. Her school friends. From the quick shy way she looks aside you get it. That there maybe aren't any.

"I have wings in my back," she says. "I can fly away and watch the sun come up from the top of any mountain in the world."

"What kind of bird are you?"

"Bird?"

"A chicken? Can you cackle like a chicken?"

"Yes. But I'm not a chicken."

"Can you quack like a duck?"

"I can quack but I'm not a duck either."

"Can you go gobble gobble like a turkey?"

"I'm not a turkey! They can't even fly!"

"Can you sing like a canary?"

"I'm too big to be a canary."

"Can you caw like a crow?"

"They're too mean."

"Then what are you?"

"I'm just Edith! Edith with wings!"

"What color are they?"

"My wings?"

"Yes."

"All colors." And then she says, "They change colors. They can be any color."

"Can you show me sometime?"

"No. I have to be alone."

"How about when you're flying? Can't I see them then?"

"When I'm flying I'm invisible."

"I have a camera that can take pictures of invisible things."

"No you don't!"

You don't have stories about castles and knights and magical gardens and wings that sprout off your back. What you have are the stories Novick tells her mother in the dining room. How God and Jesus and the Holy Ghost appeared to a farmboy in the woods to tell him every church was false. How an angel came into his bedroom and made it brighter than the noonday sun. How he dug a book of ancient plates of gold out of a New York hillside. Stories you can't tell her. And so you're left with stories about yourself. The ranch you grew up on. The steer they gave you to feed and wash and win a ribbon with but not how you had to give it back at the stockyard you later learned was a slaughterhouse. The chipmunk you caught as a pet but not how it ran away with its string leash still around its neck and got caught and hung itself from the branch of a tree where crows pecked its bones clean. Your horse Rex, how big he was, and how you rode him everywhere like an Indian, without a saddle, but not how he almost crushed you against the boards of his stall one night. Your dog Rufus but not how you had to give him to Manny the sheepherder in the movie your father took. The sandpit up behind your house and how you played soldiers in the dunes and off the cliffs but not how you taught yourself to play trumpet there. About the United States Army. How you chased the German Army out of the desert with your tank. How you had to wear a helmet because your hair was blond back then and it embarrassed you. Blond. It makes her laugh.

"Do you have a girlfriend?" she says.

"No."

She looks down quick.

"Did you ever?"

"Yes."

"Was her hair blond?"

"It was dark like yours." And then you say, "Don't you have a boyfriend?"

She looks at you with open horror.

"No!"

Loud enough to stop the conversation from the dining room again.

"Mama! Herr Tauffler asked me if I have a boyfriend!"

"What did you tell him?"

"No!"

"Oh Edith. He's just having fun with you!"

"A boyfriend isn't funny!" she tells her mother.

"Unless he has purple eyes," you say.

She looks at you.

"And grass hair."

She keeps looking.

"And a bratwurst for a nose."

And she breaks out laughing, showing her father's small white teeth, and punches you in the arm again.

The last game you always play with her, this girl with her ivory face and her dark almost black bangs and short hair and summer blue eyes who sits front and center in a cushioned brown leather chair with her hands folded in her lap and her feet hanging, is the game where she wants to know about your family. Your brothers and sisters. Game is her word. You reel them off for her in the order they were born. She wants to go through them one by one. Ask questions. Hear stories. You tell her Karl has mashed potato brains and piano wire hair but not how he tears the heads off Molly's dolls or sets fire to the feet of her paper angels. You tell her Molly used to wear braids but not how your mother pulled her hair so tight there were tears in Molly's eyes. You tell her Roy had a racetrack for his bike in the field behind your house but not the way he cried at your grandfather's funeral. She laughs and looks astonished and covers her mouth.

Then you get to Maggie. And that's where she wants to settle in. Your kid sister. The closest to her in age. Her questions are shy. Her attention to your answers full. What Maggie looks like. What she wears. What she likes to do. Where she goes to school. What games you play with her. If she rode a horse like you. If she has her own room. If she plays piano. If she has a teddy bear and dolls. If she has wings too. She tells you the stories she wants to hear again. The stories bring Maggie to life. Make her real. While you tell them, while she listens, you see wisps of loneliness and doubt pull at her smile and dim her eyes like fragments of passing summer clouds across the sun. And so you make her laugh. Sometimes you see her look down quick to hide something that threatens to rise to the surface of her face where you could see it. Hunger. Envy. Fear. Hope. Longing. The skittish play between them as she asks and listens to you talk about your little sister. You get it. What she wants to know. What it's like to have a brother. What it's like to mean enough to deserve to have one. Why she doesn't.

You've been here before. Where she stands on one side of the line that says this is her family. Where you stand on the other in your undertaker suit and saddlebags. Where she looks at you and all the feeling in her young unguarded face says it's okay. Where you don't know what to do then. Her family. A line you've never allowed yourself to think of crossing. Because you don't belong. Because you're here to move on. And then one afternoon her face is there, her upturned face, the innocence of her longing on its surface, and you're scared to death to step across, to trespass into this family deeper than you know you ever should. But there's her face. The way you don't care. The way you don't give yourself time to think. The way you just say it.

"I keep forgetting."

"What?" she says.

"I've got another little sister."

"You do?" Alert suddenly to the possibility that you're teasing her.

"I do."

"Who is it?"

"Her name is Edith."

For a few seconds her mouth comes open and her eyes go round. And then she gets off the cushion and crosses the floor past the piano to the dining room where her mother listens intently to Novick. Novick looks at her and stops. Her mother takes an arm off the table and puts it around her waist and asks what's wrong. Her daughter looks at Novick, then at the floor, then whispers in her mother's ear. You stand up. Her mother whispers back to her. Whispers again. Past her shoulder her mother looks through the room at you. Whispers back. Then pulls back from her daughter and looks at you again. This time with a question in her face. This question that coarsens the dark skin around her eyes and collapses her smile. There's kindness in her face. But without her smile, with this grim almost final sadness, it seems more like pity. Pity that you could do something this graceless and invasive to a little girl. The bottom goes out of your heart. This line you've crossed. You should have known. You look back at her with apology. Wait to be asked to leave. And then slowly her face goes soft and light again and her smile comes back warm. You look away. But when you look back she's held it there for you.

"Edith says she has a big brother," she says to Novick.

"Yeah?"

"Is that all right?" she asks him.

"Sure," says Novick. "Of course."

She turns to Edith. "So. You have a big brother."

Edith turns her head to make sure you're still there. Turns to her mother again.

"He can be my brother?"

Her mother strokes her dark hair.

"If you want him."

"It's okay?"

"Yes. It's wonderful."

"I don't have to do anything?"

Baptism by immersion for the remission of sins, you think, and shame burns your face, because that's what your job here is. Baptism into the Church of the Big Brother.

"Do I still call him Herr Tauffler?"

"He's your brother now. He has a first name."

She turns her face to you, shy, her eyes big.

"Shake," you tell her.

"Shake," she says.

Her mother's eyes are bright and shining.

"Welcome to our family," she says.

Chapter 47

YOU KNOW what the air will smell like when you say goodbye, stand outside again, head for home. Soft. Sweet. Easy. A little sister. A family. Somewhere you belong.

"Making any headway with Frau Goller?"

"I don't know," Novick says. "I told her today that she's gonna make me a Catholic before I ever make her a Mormon."

"That's pretty funny."

"She got a laugh out of it. She said no, she'd never be a Mormon, and no, I'll never be a Catholic." Then he says, "She tells me I'll be a bishop someday."

"A Mormon bishop? Not a Catholic one?"

"She didn't say. I figured a Mormon one."

While you're out tracting the next few days you look for a place to practice. A dirt road that leads between fields into a shallow valley hidden in the wooded hills. An abandoned factory with its busted windows gone and its toppled red brick smokestack on the outskirts of town. The tops of steam shovels and graders and hoppers and yard lights off behind the hills that indicate an open place like the sandpit. You need a place at night. Novick won't take time out of tracting during the day. You wouldn't want him to. You've got Morgan and then Paulson to make up for. All the hours you lost. You can earn them back. But you're eager now, restless with the bone deep hunger for that sound to fly, still not sure you should be doing this.

"There's gotta be a place," he says. "Like that place you told me you guarded. All that roadbuilding machinery."

"Maybe they've built all the roads they need."

"You get that feeling too? Like there's nothing left to build here?"

"Yeah. Like everything's done."

"They sure don't need to build any more churches."

Since that first dinner, where you and Novick had to turn down Hubert's offer to take your suit coats off because you both had your saddlebags on, Frau Goller has found one way or another to kidnap you every Sunday afternoon. Usually it's an excursion. Usually they pick you up in Hubert's big Opel in front of the yellow house where you live with the Russian mother and the unbearable silhouette of her daughter Olga when she dances in her nightgown through the lamplight.

You wear suits but leave your ties and saddlebags home. You ride in back with Edith. She rides between the two of you like you're Secret Service guys and she's the daughter of a president. In the beige upholstery of the back seat, Frau Goller just ahead of you and her husband at the wheel, you leave Klosterneuburg on roads you've pedaled on your bike, past houses whose doors you've knocked on, dairy shops in whose windows you've had milk and a buttered roll for breakfast and sometimes lunch. Usually you head for the Wachau, the broad valley that cradles the placid deep blue current of the Danube and serves as home to river town after river town, castle after castle, stift after stift, field after field and hillside after hillside of vineyards. Spitz. Wallendorf. Krems. Schallaburg Castle. Durnstein. Kuenringer Castle. Steiner Tor. While Novick waits outside, still reluctant to enter Catholic property, Edith sometimes takes your hand to wander across the stone floors of churches. In their tribute to Jesus Christ the wealth leaves you bewildered. You take photos in front of statues and along the side of the winding road that follows the Danube. You sit at tables on the terraces of restaurants and eat like just another family in the easygoing air and soft late afternoon summer sunlight. Places you'd never know without this family. Restaurants at whose tables you'd never sit. Always the restless doubt if this is okay. You should be passing through. If you can go this deep, feel this permanent, and get away with it.

One Sunday afternoon Frau Goller announces that you'll be visiting a stift called Melk. In the back seat you thumbfight Edith while her mother talks about the Benedictine stift that sits on a hill above the river and the town. Its library of ancient manuscripts. You listen and ask questions while you let Edith win most every fight and keep her from pulling her thumb from under yours when she loses one. She twists and squirms but keeps it quiet because her father has already told her twice to settle down.

"You mind if I tell them?" Novick turns and asks in English over the top of Edith's head when Frau Goller takes a break from talking about the stift.

"Tell them what?" you say, while Edith takes your thumb down.

"Your horn."

"Nur Deutsch!" Edith says, slugs your leg, looks up at you. Her upturned face is flush with happiness. Maggie. How she could ever dare expose happiness like this. And then you think what Novick's asking.

"They'll want to hear me play," you tell him, still in English, holding Edith's wrist.

"I'm guessing so."

"That okay with you?"

"Why not?" he says.

"Then yeah. Tell them if you want."

"How do you say trumpet in German?"

"Trompete."

He smiles. "Just testing."

And then he tells them. In German. In the front seat Frau Goller turns her head to the side to hear him. In the driver's seat Hubert cocks his head to listen.

"You play a trumpet?" says Edith. "Like this?" And holds an imaginary trumpet to her face and toots to make its sound.

"So, Edith. Leave him alone now," her father says.

"Papa makes trumpets. Yellow ones with red where you blow it."

"They're just toys," Hubert says. "Plastic. For children."

"I have one! I can play with you!"

"So you play trumpet," Frau Goller says, her head turned back, not all the way but far enough that you catch the smile in her profile.

"Not since I came to Austria."

"Why not?"

"I didn't bring it."

"We borrowed one for him," says Novick.

"You borrowed one? So you're planning on playing?"

"What kind of music?" Hubert asks.

Novick grins at you like he can't wait to hear you say it.

"Jazz."

"Jazz," Hubert says, and sits up. "I'm crazy about jazz."

"Did you play jazz?" you ask him. "On your clarinet?"

"I tried. It's not as easy as it sounds."

"Can you play for us sometime?" Frau Goller says.

"Sure," you tell her.

"Do you really play trumpet?" says Edith. "A real one?"

"No. We're just teasing you."

Another slug. This time your arm.

"That's enough now," her mother says.

"He's going to be playing in Vienna," says Novick. "Some of the clubs."

"You play that well?" Turned around in her seat now, her arm up across the backrest, she's looking straight at you. "Do we have someone famous in the car?"

"Not famous," you say. "No."

"I know some of the Vienna clubs," says Hubert. "In Schwedenplatz and along the Donaukanal."

"We've gone to a few of them too," says Novick.

"Fatty's Saloon was the big one," says Hubert. "It was sad when he moved to Berlin."

Fatty's Saloon. The name makes you curious and nervous. You want to know more. Then less. You want to know if the updraft of air will hold you when the notes fly out across open space and you try to follow them.

"I heard about that," says Novick. "Last year."

"He had some famous people. Lionel Hampton, Art Blakey, Ella Fitzgerald. Joe Zawinul." Then he says, "I was there for Zawinul."

Names you've never heard spoken with an Austrian accent except on Novick's radio.

"We'll find places," Novick says. "First he needs a place to practice."

"He can't practice where you live?"

"It's too loud."

"What are you looking for?" says Hubert.

"A place where he won't bother anyone. I don't know. Could be an open field. Anyplace."

"A school?" Frau Goller says.

"A school would be great," says Novick.

"Come play at my school!" Edith says.

"I can only practice at night. You wouldn't be there."

"What about a hall?" her mother says.

"Don't they charge rent?"

"I can ask the Stift if they have something," she says.

"I know a place you could use," Hubert says.

Frau Goller turns to him.

"Where?"

"My factory," he says.

"Your factory?"

"Nobody's there after six. Maybe someone cleaning up. But that's all."

"I don't know," she says. "The Kaserne. It's not very nice. All those cats."

"Why not? I know it's not the Staatsoper or the Konzerthaus. But for practice?"

You look out the open window at the rolling vineyards of a stift you've already visited. Warm wind washes through your hair. Your hand and the rippling sleeve of your suit rest on the sill. A different wind rustles through you. One that sends dead leaves scuttling across pavement in the headlights. The sense of something coming. If this is right. This far from home. If you should do this.

"How does it sound?" says Hubert. "The factory?"

"Are you sure?"

"It's in the old Pionier Kaserne. On Leopoldstrasse. Do you know where that is?"

"Yes," says Novick. "We know Leopoldstrasse." He looks across at you. You've tracted the neighborhood around the Kaserne. You've tracted the upper floors where people live.

Hubert tells you the number. Directions for getting into the building once you get there.

"Tomorrow? Around half past six?"

"Sure."

"Bring your bikes inside with you."

CHAPTER 48

THE NEXT NIGHT, on the ride home from tracting, you buy a couple of handkerchiefs to catch the spit when you blow out the valves, some rope to lash the trumpet case to the rack behind your bike seat. The loops and knots come easy once you remember where you used to start. You and Novick head for Leopoldstrasse.

The Kaserne, an old abandoned barracks, sits back from the street behind a big courtyard bordered by a thick gray wall. You ride through the open gate. You know it as soon as you see it. In front of you, across the courtyard, the building is massive, like other buildings in the neighborhood, heavy and gray and forbidding, four tall stories high, each story marked by a row of windows. In the warm late afternoon most of the windows are open. Hubert told you how the top three floors were converted to apartments when the army left. Because the rooms had to accommodate groups of soldiers, they were big apartments, apartments he told you were rented now to poor people.

You let Hubert describe the place despite knowing most everything he tells you. You don't know how to tell him you've been up and down its hallways. Tracted the three upper floors. Knocked on every door. Been inside two of the apartments. With the way he feels about religion it might embarrass him. Mattresses on the bare wood floors and used tables and chairs and a busted couch the only furniture in the big rooms. Street furniture. Sinks and stoves and small refrigerators along a wall. For a short while you had two families interested. Poor people. One family was young. Four little kids. The husband was a part time laborer. The wife was heavy. Her skin this sick gray. The oldest girl was Edith's age. The other family was older. Two parents and their daughter. The daughter was somewhere around your age, maybe a little younger, sly with her dark eyes, short chopped brown hair and a nice face whose smooth round cheeks and full blood red lips and the defiant thrust she gave her jaw went against her thin pot belly little girl build. You could tell she was trying to be bad. You could feel it when she looked at you. When Novick started to talk religion it was pretty much over. You had them long enough for a couple of visits each. Then they caught on and got over their interest in a couple of young Americans who turned out to be as broke as they were.

And now this is where you'll practice. In this building that knows you as a missionary. With the windows open for the night air so there's no way they won't hear you. They'll come looking. This is what you didn't want. These things you did, these things you were, a missionary and a trumpet player, to ever come this close. The fence you kept between them a fence you could jump across or walk through. A dock and a ramp stand off one side of the building. A detached semi trailer, held level by the struts of its handling gear, is backed and parked against the dock. Hubert's Opel is parked with a couple of other cars to the side of the ramp. It's not the kind of barracks you know. The ones at Ord were modern like new elementary schools. The wooden ones at Knox reminded you of the long shed they used for the churchhouse in the sagebrush up behind the schoolhouse in La Sal.

This is what you didn't want. But you already know you'll take it.

"Cats are still here," says Novick.

Everywhere, like they always were, lounging, running, watching, stalking, sleeping, stepping high, washing themselves, on the prowl, all across the courtyard. While you pedal toward the door a woman throws a bag out of a second floor window that trails garbage on its way down and disintegrates when it hits the ground. Cats race from everywhere. Dart and weave around your rolling bikes. Two come rocketing out from under Hubert's car.

"Sure enough."

Inside the building you take a right and roll your bikes down a dark hall with an arched ceiling like the long upper half of a big pipe cut lengthwise. The main floor, for businesses, is the one floor you haven't seen. Hubert shakes your hand at the open door to his factory. Frau Goller and Edith are there. Edith holds a small yellow plastic trumpet, maybe ten inches long, with a red mouthpiece. Behind them lies the spread of a dark brown hardwood floor stained almost black in places across the vast resonant space of the room to a row of tall windows on the far wall. Under the smell of hot plastic, the shoe polish smell of the room takes you back to the first time you stepped inside Mr. Hinkle's store, your hands scraped and your knee hurt and two dollars in your pocket, not knowing what instrument you were looking for, that it would lead you to this place. The high ceiling is vaulted like the ceiling in the hallway. Long arches that look like the top halves of big pipes run from column to column across the room. Where they differ from the vaulted ceilings of the churches you've seen is that they're blank, not sculpted and painted with cherubs and angels, just this dingy flat gray plaster. Big shaded lights hang from the ceilings. Machines and vats are lined across the floor. You can see patches and paths worn into the hardwood where Hubert's workers stand and work and move from place to place. Two tall open archways lead to two other rooms.

"This is how the ceilings in churches look," you tell Novick, knowing he doesn't go into the Houses of the Devil. "Except they're all painted."

"I've seen pictures."

"Sorry."

"Is that it?" Edith points to the case lashed to the back of your bike.

"What if it isn't?" you say, untying the knots, loosening the rope.

She beams at you. Eager to be teased.

"Then I want to know what it really is."

You lay the case on the table and lean your bike against the wall where Novick put his.

"What if I tell you it's a talking puppet?"

"Then I want to talk to it."

"Okay," you say. "Here goes."

And you snap the latches and lift the lid back. Her excited face is right there. She looks up at you confused and disappointed.

"It's a trumpet."

"I never said it wasn't."

"You fooled me again!"

"So, Edith! Stop hitting him!"

"He's always teasing me!"

"Can we get a tour?" says Novick.

"You're interested in this place?" says Hubert.

"It's perfect," you tell him.

And so he walks you around and gives you its history as you walk. After the war he started making bodies for harmonicas. He made them back then out of tin and wood. In the early fifties he heard of injection molding, a process where he could make a mold for a harmonica body, use pressure to inject it with liquefied plastic, and there the body would be when it cooled and you took the mold apart. He leased this place and started with two hand operated injection machines. In a back corner of the room they look like ancient drill presses, operated by hand, with hand-turned wheels as big as the steering wheels of ships.

"I still use these old soldiers sometimes," he says.

He shows you where the molds fit into them. He takes out a mold and opens it into its two halves to show you how the plastic moves into it. His voice is soft, easy, its pace deliberate, conscious that he's talking technical stuff in German to a couple of Americans. He tells you how over time he started designing and molding other toys. How motorized injection machines came along a few years back that allowed him to make larger and more complicated molds. How he has six of them now, lined up in two rows along with mixing vats, hoses, conveyor belts, worktables, and parts bins, big new machines with gauges and knobs and switches and wire guards that protect workers from the hydraulic shaft assemblies that do the high pressure work.

"These look serious," you tell him.

"Oh yes. Very serious."

He takes you through the open gate of an archway into a machine shop where the smell of oil stains the air and the steel of drills and lathes and other cutting tools gleams with the deep polish of absorbed oil. He tells you how making the molds is the trickiest part of the process. The part that requires the most technical artistry. You have to know where and how to cut holes to allow air to escape as the plastic is pressed into the mold. You have to make sure the mold is designed to separate and allow the molded piece to be extracted. He tells you how they can design and machine the simpler molds themselves but have to hire specialized shops for the more complicated molds. The rest of the process is simple. The toys are trimmed and assembled and painted and finished with other parts made of metal and wood and wire.

So this is it, you realize. How the bodies and wheels and other parts of the model planes and cars you used to build were made.

Around thirty people work for him. Two of them sweep shavings up around the work tables. He introduces you. Walter and Dieter. He takes you through another gated archway to a room that serves as a warehouse. Bags and barrels filled with raw chemicals are stacked on pallets. A forklift is parked next to them. Bins and racks are filled with finished toys. He opens a small box and shows you one of his harmonicas.

"Here," he says, and hands it to Novick. "Try it."

"I can't," says Novick. "It's brand new."

"It's yours," Hubert says. "A little souvenir from Austria." And hands him the box too.

"Thanks. Okay." Novick runs the harmonica across his mouth a couple of times. Does a short blues lick that surprises you.

"Not bad." Hubert grinning. The whine of a big fan starts to wind up somewhere. "Where do you think most of these go?"

Novick shrugs. "Christmas stockings?"

Hubert laughs. "Africa."

"Africa. Wow. Why?"

"I don't know. I don't ask. I just fill orders." He turns to you. "I can turn that fan off if it's going to bother you. When you practice."

In the sandpit you had the sifting roar of the winter and spring winds and the long hoarse whistles of train horns from the valley. At Hiller you had the dirty hammering roar of the night trucks up on the high bank of the freeway. Once you got going everything went away.

"No. It'll be okay. Thanks."

"It's just for fresh air," says Hubert.

On the way back to the door where Frau Goller and Edith wait, you remember the name of the Kaserne. Pionier.

"What's Pionier?" you ask Hubert.

"Why?"

"The name of the building."

"Oh," he says. "Of course. Pionier. Someone who makes a path for others to follow."

"Same as in English."

"Yes."

"Were you a pionier?" you ask. "In the Resistance?"

"I made paths," he says, and smiles. "But nobody followed me." And then he says, "Let me show you the place I think is good to practice."

It's toward the back of the big room. An open place with a couple of tables where boxes and rolls of paper are used to package toys and other parts for shipping. In the wall there's the big garage door you saw from outside. The door that leads out to the loading dock where the semi trailer stands. Set into the big door is a smaller door, a human door, so people can come and go without opening the big door.

"Okay with you?" says Hubert.

The concrete and glass and brick that make up this room the size of a gym. Hard surfaces everywhere. Plenty of room for the notes to fly clean and free and bright between the ceiling and floor and walls.

"It'll be loud."

"Like a cathedral organ?"

You remember going with Morgan to recitals where pieces by Bach came shrieking like the cries of flaming birds down off the high rock ceilings. The hymn he played on the Stephansdom organ while you were in the confession booth. How Hubert wanted to be an organ maker.

"No," you say. "Not that loud."

"That's fine," he says. "The smell won't bother you?"

"I used to practice around heavy machinery."

There's noise. The fan has kicked off but there's a background hum from machines or vats that may need to be kept heated or on turning gear to keep things circulating. It won't bother you either. Now, while Novick and Hubert and his wife and daughter and the guys with the brooms stand back, you take your mouthpiece out to warm it up, skate it up and down, make the buzz that always sounds like the siren of an ambulance for insects. Hubert, his arms folded, wears a satisfied and expectant smile. In her dress and sturdy shoes, Frau Goller's smiling too, but with her teacher's look of worry that you'll do okay. At her mother's side, the plastic trumpet in her hand forgotten, excitement radiates off your little sister's face. You hold some notes. Your pitch is unstable. Wobbly. The top of your range out of reach beyond the thin squeal of the highest note you can get. Your tongue dirty when you use it to chop the air flow into individual notes. You'll get it back. You can feel it. You take the trumpet out and slip the mouthpiece into place in its socket in the lead pipe.

"You take requests?" says Novick, smiling.

"Any scale you'd like," you tell him. "For now at least."

This audience. This dopey guy from California dressed like you in an undertaker's suit who borrowed and put this trumpet in your hands. Two men in work clothes leaning on their brooms. Most of all this family. This Austrian family who've made you their son. This little sister of a girl. You hear your mother's voice. They don't know you like we do. Where this will go from here. Your hands slip into place around the casings of the valves. And then, before you can think of anything, you take a breath, raise the trumpet, touch the steel rim of the mouthpiece to your lips.

CHAPTER 49

Don't come to Mississippi this summer to save the Mississippi
negro. Only come if you understand, really understand, that his
freedom and yours are one.

– Bob Moses to white student volunteers
for Freedom Summer 1964

IT MIGHT BEHOOVE YOU to come up to speed on this stuff some.
Since your girl's what she is. What Bill suggested back at Idlewild Airport
after Clayton told him your girlfriend was a negro. What you'd been doing
all along at Hiller. What you'd done here. Through Morgan and then
Paulson. Stayed up to speed. Since your girl was black. And then her letter
came. You thought of stopping then. They didn't want you. They didn't
want your helpless anger. Your weakness for violence. Your tank. They
didn't want you at the lunch counter. They didn't want your sorry outrage
for a woman being firehosed. They didn't want you knocking on their
doors. They didn't have time or patience to listen to you explain yourself.
Explain this God who made their skin a curse and sent them to Earth
through the loins of a murdering brother to take on their dark fence
sitter birthright. They didn't want you to play their music. On the faces
of magazines you could see their contempt in their glittering black eyes.
Their Miles Davis eyes. Don't come knocking on our doors. We got real
problems. And you and your God are one of them. So don't come to no
Mississippi. If Cissy don't want you then we don't need you either.

You don't care what they think or want. How much fierce contempt
they treat you to. Novick stays up to speed. So do you. When he buys
Newsweek you buy Time. And play their music at the factory the way they
taught you to.

"You know Buddy Rich, don't you," says Novick.

Riding side by side on a one lane road through early summer fields
toward the orange roofs of a village too small to show a steeple. The air

through your socks and on your knuckles cool but the morning sun warm on your back. Pockets of white mist nested in the low hills on either side. You weave your front tire through the steaming puddles from a night rain.

"Sure," you say. "The drummer."

"Yeah. Well, he had to check into a hospital once, and the nurse asked him if he was allergic to anything. Know what he said?"

"Nope."

"Country western music. That's what he told her he was allergic to."

Country western. Laughing, you fall behind Novick single file to let a little red and yellow Fiat get around you. You and Novick lift your legs straight out like circus clowns to keep them dry as the Fiat's flimsy tires shoot water out of the puddles. A thin spiral of white smoke spins out of its tiny tailpipe. A couple of strokes on your pedals and you come even with Novick again.

"Where do you get this stuff?"

"My jazz club back home. I told you. Stuff we read and hear from other clubs and some musicians we follow around."

"My trumpet teacher was like that. All these stories. He was from New York. He played with a lot of those guys."

"How'd he end up in Utah? Someone baptize him?"

The concept makes you smile.

"No," you say. "He just likes it there."

You ride along for a while. Novick says, "I forgot to tell you. I tried to learn another instrument."

"Which one?"

"I took some French horn lessons. Or maybe it was English. My mom, the mom I have now, thought I should play an instrument. So she rented one for me."

"How long?"

"Long enough to learn that I belonged in the audience."

On the Friday in June before you turn twenty your father's thick manila envelope includes a birthday card signed by everyone in the family. Your father writes that you're not a teenager any more. Those years are behind you. This cringing urge to puke stirs the raw cold feel of ash that has made its home in your stomach since you learned what he wrote to President Smith. He doesn't know about Brother Shlagl's trumpet. If he'd write a letter to President Lindner. You'd love to have him try. That Sunday the Gollers have you and Novick up for a birthday dinner for you and little Edith. Nine years old now. You give her a journal with lined pages and an exotic painting of jungle birds on the cover. You've inscribed it. For Edith. To write down all your stories.

"Look, Mama! I can write my stories down!"

And she takes off for her room.

"Edith!" says Hubert. "Wait! We're still having a party!"

"She loves it," Frau Goller says.

"Let her go," you say. "Before she forgets the story."

In a leather case her family gives you an elegant deep blue Pelikan fountain pen with a gold tip and the name Wien engraved in gold in the cap. A bottle of ink comes with it.

"So you can write us when you have to move away," Frau Goller says.

"It's beautiful," you say. "Thank you."

"Do you really like it?" she says.

You used to think anywhere but here. Knocking on doors in some city in the South. Negro doors. Doors that were likely to open. Not like the doors here. That was before you knocked and found a family.

"I've never had a pen like this. I've never even seen one. Thank you."

And on Tuesday, the morning of your birthday, sitting out the cloudburst hammering the attic roof before heading out, you get the manila folder that holds all of Cissy's letters, take your chair at the table, find the card she sent in April with her letter telling you goodbye. Across the table, your latest Time magazine open between his elbows, Novick watches you run a knife under the spine of the envelope. The card is elaborate and filled with poetic love talk. But what you look for is her handwriting.

Dear Shake, she writes. Hope you take time to celebrate your big twentieth birthday. Love always, Cissy.

"Uh oh," you hear Novick say.

He's looking your way. He saw you staring at the inside of her card. Touching what she wrote. She could still ambush you. Take you back to April.

"Yeah."

"She having second thoughts?"

"No." You put the card back in the folder. "She sent this with her Dear John letter. Back in April. She said to wait till my birthday to open it." Then you say, "So I just did."

"Okay," Novick finally says.

"No," you say. "I'm not gonna write her."

"I wasn't asking," he says.

"What're you reading?"

"The Mississippi Freedom Project," he says. "They're recruiting white college kids for Freedom Summer."

Novick's reluctance to venture onto Catholic property doesn't extend to venturing into other territory you're not supposed to. Of the World territory. Territory outside the Work of the Lord, beyond the warmth of the burning in his bosom, out past the fenceline, out from under the gray reach of the iron sky. Sometimes it's jazz. Sometimes it's the South. He can't help himself. The South burns in his bosom as much as his testimony does. Where he stays soft and humble but his face loses its goofy brokenhearted look. He lived in a negro family. He had a negro dad he calls his jazz dad. Like Bill and Jerry, like the magazines have started doing, he calls negroes blacks. It still sounds stark. Just this naked almost defiant word you still can't use for Cissy even though in her last few letters she started using it herself. Negro could be all kinds of colors. Coffee honey chocolate rose. Black was black.

"What's going on?" you say.

"Johnson's supposed to sign the Civil Rights Act any day now. I don't know what the holdup is. Blacks are getting their butts kicked and they can't get Johnson or Hoover to do squat to help them."

"Yeah," you say. "I've read that."

"The Freedom Project guys figure it's because whites don't know how to feel for blacks. I don't mean hate them. Just feel for them. You know. The way they'd feel for a white person. They get white blood. Just not black blood."

"Maybe because blood shows up better on white skin," you say.

"Could be. Anyway, they figure if whites don't feel for what blacks are going through, then the media doesn't have to give a darn. If there's no media, nobody's paying attention, and then Johnson and Hoover don't have to give a darn either. Hoover hates blacks anyway."

"Yeah. I know."

"He's kind of a homo too. They say he dresses up in ladies' clothes. Heels and wigs. Bras and panties. The whole wardrobe."

"He does?"

"Makeup too, I heard."

"Maybe the J stands for Jezebel," you say.

"His initial?"

"Yeah. Or Julie."

"Judith."

"Janice."

"Yeah," says Novick. "Janice Edgar Hoover."

"He shoulda been a showgirl," you say.

Novick's smile is sad. The rain comes down and thunder rolls across the roof.

"Anyway, the Freedom Project guys figure the way to get the feds interested is to get the media interested. And the way to get the media interested is to get whites involved. Maybe shed some white blood. And then Johnson and even Hoover are gonna have to pay attention. And you know what?"

"It works," you say.

"Reporters and cameras follow these white kids everywhere. A white kid with a busted skull draws them like flies."

Novick looks down, closes the magazine, pushes it aside, uses the flat of his hand to draw slow circles on the table, like he's polishing it without a cloth.

"They thought of something else," he says. "They sent their recruiters to the top schools. Because the students were kids with rich and powerful daddies. You know. With some pull in Washington."

White college kids. You tell him about Bill and Jerry. Meeting them at Idlewild Airport. How they were headed for Mississippi.

"I just wonder how they're doing," you say.

"They're veterans by now," says Novick. "Unless they got sent home."

"You ever thought of going?" you say.

"South? I used to think maybe after my mission." Then he says, "But they're not taking just anyone. Forget about a returned missionary."

Only come to Mississippi if you understand that you can never be one of them. Shame sets your face ablaze. You get off the chair and cross to the window as if the rain could cool it through the glass. Cissy's face. Flush with blood while her eyes shine wet and the touch of her hands wanders your naked back and her closed lips express melancholy so deep and indelible in her blood you have to look away. Her poison negro blood. The way they lied when they taught you it could kill you on the spot.

"I guess you were planning on San Jose," you hear Novick say.

You watch a rivulet cut the crooked path of a glass pinball through the drops of rain down the window.

"Sorry," he says. "I shouldn't of said that." Then he says, "I miss my dad. My jazz dad."

"I bet," you say.

"I miss watching and hearing him play." Then he says, "Sometimes I wonder what he makes of this stuff."

"You still in touch with him?"

"No. Wish I was." Then he changes up and says, "Anyway, I'm taking you out tonight. For your birthday. My treat."

You turn from the window. "Thanks." Take your chair at the table again. "I've got a question. A personal one. Okay?"

"You can ask," Novick says.

"The Seed of Cain. The stuff they taught us."

"What I think about it?" he says. "That's easy. I don't believe it."

"You don't?"

"I don't believe it's the Word of God."

"No?"

"I think Brigham Young made it all up," he says. "I think it's a lot of racist crap." Then he says, "I have to believe that."

The last of the rain has ended. Sunlight restores light and color and quiet to the gray room. Novick looks around and slowly gets up.

"Time to get out there," he says, himself again. "Get back into the Spirit."

A few days later, while God stands back to watch, Freedom Summer starts. White Mississippi comes out swinging. Newspapers and political leaders whip up white hate and violence across the state. Hoover tells Mississippi that the FBI won't wet nurse black troublemakers. Freedom schools are outlawed. Churches and businesses that host them are fire-bombed. A day or two before the Klan puts a torch to them the White Citizen Council cancels their fire insurance policies without telling them. Crosses burn across the state. Town officials declare dusk-to-dawn curfews and make it criminal to boycott white businesses. The state trooper force is doubled. Cities and towns deputize and arm white guys. Many of them Klan.

But you get it. Only come if you understand that you can never be one of them. You learned a long time ago from learning how to play from the musicians whose photographs hung on Mr. Selby's wall. The musicians you played along with in the garage. The giants in the sky who took the form of clouds around you, watching over you without you knowing they were there, through that long cold winter in the sandpit. You could bleed like them. You could play like them. You could never let yourself think that you were one of them. Not where you're from.

"Here's what I mean," says Novick. Home from practice at Hubert's factory, you're at the table, the parts of your borrowed trumpet spread across a towel. Novick's lying on the bed catching up on his reading.

"Mean about what?"

"Remember those three civil rights workers who disappeared a while ago in Mississippi? One day they were supposed to drive to a meeting with some local guys about a church bombing. The church got bombed because it wanted to do a Freedom School. The workers never made it back. So their home office called the FBI and Justice Department. Neither Hoover or Bobby Kennedy acted like they cared at first."

"Yeah." Wiping down a valve piston for fresh oil. "They find them yet?"

"No. But here's the deal. Two of those three guys were white."

"I know."

Novick puts down the magazine.

"White. So the news that two white guys have disappeared hits the front page of the New York Times. The black guy, he's a footnote, but he gets his photo in the paper too. Then they find their burned out car in a swamp. All of a sudden Johnson and Kennedy and Hoover wake up. Two white guys missing. Most likely murdered. They send in the FBI and the military. Johnson meets with the parents of the white guys. He tells them everything possible is being done. Meanwhile, back in Mississippi, the black guy's mom waits for word about her son. No White House invitation for her."

And now you stop oiling the piston.

"They just left her out?"

"From what I read. But check out the protests. All over the country. They're all over Johnson to finally do something. They're saying it's the first interracial lynching in the history of the country."

"They were hung?"

"Whatever. Maybe there's more than one way to lynch someone. Mississippi's saying it's all a hoax. To get sympathy. They're saying the guys are hiding out in Mexico." He shakes his head. "Mexico."

You look at him. "Mexico. You're kidding."

"No." Then he says, "You know, Brigham Young passing off that Seed of Cain stuff as the Word of God, I don't have a problem with God for that. That was Brigham Young's doing. My problem with God is that he didn't bother fixing it. He didn't come out and say it wasn't true. He just let it stand."

A new way to look at God. It stuns you. It wasn't his. He didn't fix it. He just left it. It leaves you looking at the pieces of your disassembled horn.

"I hate thinking about God that way," says Novick, from the bed. "But it's either that or thinking my jazz dad comes from Cain. I could never think that."

PART 6

DEVIL HORN

CISSY. THAT VERY FIRST NIGHT at Hubert's factory, that test night, when you imagined water and sent that first note out, a middle C you felt in the pulse of your lips and in the sudden ring of the metal in your hands, she was there, her closed smile wistful and unafraid, her eyes shining, her skin honey in the sunlight of the back yard, right in front of you. It wasn't God. But God didn't fix the way you'd been taught to look at her. You held the note just long enough to let the memory cut through you the way lightning splits the night and then thunder closes over it and leaves things whole again. And then you broke the note to run the melodic C minor scale up two octaves. The last two notes were frayed to not much more than crying air.

You came back down. The breaks between the notes were ragged. You had to get back your tongue and range and air flow and the discipline of your pitch. You had to get used to a borrowed horn. A year without playing. A year since the last time you played at Hiller and came back from San Jose and gave Robbie your trumpet to hold for you. A year. But it was all there. It would take practice but everything was where you'd left it. Where nobody could take it away from you.

Coming back to middle C you realized she'd come with you, for just that short ride of a double scale, and stood there again, serene in the sureness of knowing you'd bring her back, so close that if you held the bell of the trumpet up to her face, she could look through it and see clear down your throat into your heart. You shook your head. Looked down at the stained old hardwood floor you stood on. Looked up at Novick and Hubert and the guys with the brooms. Looked over where Edith and Frau Goller were.

Everyone stood there quiet. Waiting to see what else you had. Something else was there. Standing there, your back to the back wall of the factory, there was the kid again, the kid in the back of the garage while the door pulled open and he stood there caught in his father's headlights, the metronome still going, the bandana still rolled and tied around his head. You weren't supposed to be doing this. You knew that. You couldn't smell hot plastic any more. It was like the air inside the factory had been cleansed by the summer air outside. You couldn't hear the machines on turning gear. As if the notes you'd played, the ringing minor line of the notes you'd sent out to chase around the factory, had quieted them.

You knew then. Devil horn. You weren't supposed to be doing this. Not the way your appetite to play kept trying to run away with you. Not the way the sound inside your lungs longed to spread its wings. Not the way trouble rode a cold wind through your stomach.

Cissy was gone. She would come back. You knew that too. Your first few notes would always draw her out of your dream for her into the open. You looked at Hubert again, conscious of the garage door at your back, then looked down. That was when Hubert clapped. And then the two guys with the brooms. And then Frau Goller let go of Edith's hand so that she could clap too. Her smile was warm and proud. Novick just stood there grinning his dopey sad-eyed grin.

Edith shied back a step from her mother's side. Uncertainty flickered through her face. You knew the look. She wasn't important. She didn't matter. Her eyes were skittish. Her big brother could play trumpet. He could fill her father's factory with sound. How could she matter to him. He wasn't really her brother anyway.

You smiled at her. She was quick to turn aside and shy back farther. She stood alone now. Apart from her mother. The trumpet was a good one. The notes would come clear. It would know what you needed. Where you wanted to go. It would let you play. It had only been a year. You could risk a song. You took the mute that came with Brother Shlagl's trumpet and slipped it into the bell. Looked at her again.

"This is for my little sister," you said.

She stared at you for a second. Turned in shock to her mother.

"Mama!"

You brought the trumpet up again. She finally looked at you. Hesitant. Still doubtful. But she held still more and more while wonder started to flood her face. You held her eyes and winked at her and her hands flew up to hide her face but flew away just as quick so she could see you. You remembered the lady in the red dress at the Indigo that cold night. What you played that she liked. What she gave you. You put the mouthpiece to your lips and started the song out low. Low and light with the intro while you heard the lyrics in your head. There's a saying old . . . says that love is blind . . . still we're often told . . . seek and ye shall find . . . You worked your way to the melody. There's a somebody I'm longing to see. . . With the mouthpiece to your lips you tried with your closed smile and your eyes to let her know. This was for her. You could see it start to dawn in her. I'm a little lamb who's lost in the wood . . . I know I could . . . always be good . . . You knew she didn't know the words. You knew she was too young to know them. Won't you tell him please to put on some speed . . . follow my lead . . . oh how I need . . . And here it was. What you were to her. Someone to watch over me. It was in the melody. When she sensed it her face grew luminous. It beamed wonder and delight. That you were giving her this. Playing her this song. Your little sister. Safe now. Not alone.

And then, when you got to the end of the song, you turned it around, took the mute out, closed your eyes for the solo, and this time stood on the hillside up above the sandpit where the notes you played took flight into the sky across the valley. You started low. Without the mute the pure sharp knifing steel of the sound cut the air. You took it suddenly high. When your little sister's mouth came open you knew she would come with you. A storm was moving in. A wall of clouds. An iron sky. The light beneath it this malignant yellow. The wind kicking up. You sent the steel bird into its lightning teeth. Knowing you could bring her home again. Knowing you shouldn't be doing this. Knowing you couldn't help but do it. Knowing you didn't know where this would go.

CHAPTER 51

"YOU NEVER TOLD ME that Muslim story," you tell Novick.

"The one about the musicians?" he says.

"Yeah."

Back up the gravel driveway behind you a woman who told you Keine Zeit resumes hanging her heavy laundry on the sag of a long rope that stretches from a tree to a hook in the side of her house. A light wind takes the heat of the sun off the back of your suit and makes the thick black bristles of Novick's crewcut quiver. Your bikes are parked against a wood fence where the long driveway meets the road. Across the Danube another massive stift covers the top of a low hill. White houses with red roofs spill from its walls down the flanks of the hill.

"Okay," Novick says. "This is good. When they'd go on the road. You know. Line up a bunch of gigs and dates and get a bus and head out. The South had segregated hotels and restaurants. The white places were downtown. The colored places were out in the sticks. So they'd walk into a white hotel and the clerk would tell them right away they didn't take coloreds. Or a restaurant. Or they'd just get told there weren't any rooms, you know, or tables. Even with empty tables right there in plain sight."

You reach your bikes. Novick looks up the driveway at the woman's back and figures he has time to tell the rest of the story where you are.

"I forget the guy who started it. But word about this Muslim thing started going around. They found out that if they joined the Muslim faith, they could get a new Muslim sounding name, and they wouldn't be colored any more. They'd be white. And then they'd walk into a white hotel and when the desk clerk or manager said they didn't take coloreds, the musician would say, I am not a colored. I am a Muslim and my name is Muhammed or Mustafa something. And the desk clerk or manager would say how do you do, sir, and give them a room. Same thing in restaurants. So they all started converting and getting Muslim names."

"That's crazy."

"It worked," he says. Laughing along with you.

"So it wasn't a religious thing."

"Maybe for others. For them it was practical. A way to get a room in a hotel or a table in a restaurant that wasn't in the boondocks."

"That's one cool story."

"Yeah. It's a shame they had to do it. But they got good at it. Ever hear of Fritz Jones?"

"No."

"Ahmad Jamal."

"His real name's Fritz?"

"Was Fritz," he says. "Art Blakey, McCoy Tyner, Kenny Clarke, lots of them did it."

"Fritz," you say. "Yikes. I'd change mine too."

"From Shake? Sounds like you already did."

Novick looks up the driveway. You look too. The woman's standing there, turned your way now, her back to the sails of her sheets, her balled hands on her big haunches.

"Guess we better go," he says.

Over the first two weeks most all of it comes back. The notes and simple scales you taught yourself in the cold and wind and snow of the sandpit. The triad chords of the air horns from the freight trains in the valley out beyond the hillside. Mr. Selby's living room where you learned modulation, resolution, chord progression, the way a melody skated and soared above the deep moving current of a song's changes. The rascal blues scales. The liberation of a tone from the bars of its note. Arban's fat red trumpet method book that Mr. Selby gave you. You can still close your eyes and see the little grizzly bear statue and the framed army medal on the shelf of his fireplace. The model of the fighter plane hung from the bowl of the ceiling light. Feel the way everything in the room feels old, worn in, here long enough to settle in with all the other things around it. Take your lesson in the smell of fresh-baked cookies from the kitchen. Look into the steady hold of his eyes. Still sense the worry in spite of everything that every lesson might be your last. The way the skin between his eyes would tense into a hundred intricate lines. The always calm and measured smile nested in his beard. The classes at the U. Professor Rodriguez. Professor Fisher. The big rooms of the Music Building that in their architecture, their smell, their walls infused with music made them feel like the Paris Conservatory where Professor Arban taught.

Your lips still need work. But you're doing songs again and taking off on solos from inside them. At Hubert's factory an audience starts building. People who work for him start staying late or coming back once they've had supper. An audience obliges you to play songs instead of exercises.

You find them where you left them. Hubert makes your exercise sessions private and restricts the audience to Thursday nights. His friends show up. Kids start dropping in. Kids whose parents work there and their friends. A couple of monks from the Stift. Some bring the collapsible campstools you and Morgan used on the plaza of the Opera House. Cops come by. All they ask for is no drinking. Hubert doesn't want people drinking around his machinery anyway. He installs barred steel gates across the open doors to his warehouse and machine shop. A drummer asks if he can play. Robbie. He knows a bass player. Jimmy. The bass player knows a singer. Sandy. She's a girl named Ursi with pale yellow hair cut short around her face and combed like a greaser's in fenders up across her ears into a duck's ass down into her neck. She studies voice at the Imperial Academy for Music and Performing Arts in Vienna. She knows a guy who plays jazz guitar. Santos. You remember Jimmy putting International Jazz Ensemble on the bottom of your business cards for the band you called How Should I Know. Here it is. This is it. If Jimmy could see you now. An old guy brings an accordion. You play polkas. A woman brings a flute. You play Austrian folk songs. A girl brings a violin. Carla. And then you're homesick for the kids outside the fence at Hiller's. Walt and Chaz and Jenny and Maria and Luke and Billy. The miner kids from Magna who used to come to Hiller's after midnight with their used instruments and take what you could teach them through the fence. The chainlink fence whose wires cut diamonds across your face in Jenny's sketch of you. How they're doing. If they're doing things the way you told them. If they can see the path from where they are to where you are.

In brown slacks, a white shirt open at his neck and sleeves rolled up above his elbows, Hubert's a happy host. You keep telling him to bring his clarinet. He says he doesn't have it but the way he looks off makes you think he's got it in a closet somewhere. He rents chairs and moves the packing tables back to clear space for a dance floor and whatever form the band takes that night. He gives the factory a name. The Factory. He has a big banner made for the back wall. On Thursdays he welcomes the crowd. Leaves the garage door behind you open so people can use the dock for air and a cigarette and a place to talk away from the flammable chemicals and the music and the crowd. Installs rheostat switches to dim the harsh overhead lights. Hangs a rack of four colored floodlights from the ceiling where you play. Couples dance to ballads out in front of you. People boogie when you sometimes change it up with an Elvis or Beatles or Motown tune. They form up and clap and stomp and holler when you kick a polka off.

The daughter from the upstairs apartment shows up with her chopped brown hair, full blood red lips, a tough attitude in the set of her broad jaw, still as little girl potbelly thin as you remember her. She spends most of her time on the dock. And one night you're surprised to see your landlady's daughter Olga there, in a heavy dark red dress instead of her nightgown, at the edge of the dance floor alone, swaying back and forth the same slow indolent way she does in her mother's piano room no matter what tempo the song you're playing is.

Hubert sets out a table when people start bringing food. Rolls filled with sliced sausages and small schnitzels. Crackers and sliced breads and Liptauer and other cheese spreads spiced with paprika. Buttered rolls. Cookies. Pastries. Bottled sodas named Bluna and Keli. He brings plastic forks and knives and spoons out of his warehouse room.

"I started making these once," he tells you. "A few years ago. Nobody wanted them. So now I'm happy I have them."

Missionaries from Vienna get the word. Start making the trip up the river. Show up saying fuzzin this and fuzzin that. Some start looking to talk to people, try to lead them into the dialogue that leads them to admit their church is false, so they can count the night as investigator time on their weekly reports. Hubert gently lets them know it isn't Sunday and his guests are here for music. Tells them to eat something. One night Brother Shlagl's there in his Sunday suit to hear what you're doing with his horn.

"You play very well."

"Want to take a turn?" you say.

He laughs. "You don't know what you're asking."

There are times when you take a factory full of Austrians to a place they've never been on the flight of your borrowed trumpet. Down State Street in Quigley's ghost black Hudson. Coming south through Vallejo in Yenchik's Ford in a sunset so smoke red it looks like the back neighborhoods of the town are burning. And then you bring them back again to Hubert's factory. And then everyone sitting in with the band understands. The accordion. The violin. The harmonica. The trombone. The banjo. Play together. Play from a common place you can find your way back home to. Everyone gets a solo. Some just play the melody. Others just go nuts. Others know how to skate the changes. Others get lost to where you have to go out and rescue them and lead them home again.

And you play the standards you learned from your mother's Broadway songs and Mr. Selby's records. Older couples dance in the muted light of the dance floor and remind you of the old folks homes you and your band used to play. Before you had a name. Hubert gives the guitarist a cup to set on his amp. By the end of the night it's close to full with coins and bills. You give your cut to Hubert.

"For drinks next week," you tell him. "Utensils. Rent. Anything."

"You earned it," he tells you.

"Thanks," you tell him. "But they won't let me."

Frau Goller shows up with Edith only on practice nights. That way your little sister has you mostly to herself. Hubert sets out two folding chairs for them. Frau Goller sits but Edith stands for the hour or so they stay. Stands with her face beaming and the inward point of her toes giving away the shyness of her helpless pride. The song you play for her. She always knows it's coming. Just not when. You announce it as though the factory is packed. As though every head cranes to see who you're smiling at.

"This next one is for my little sister."

Novick asks Hubert if he can pass brochures out to the Thursday crowd. Hubert tells him sure but only outside the door when they're leaving. He doesn't want people reading during the show. He doesn't want people leaving brochures littered around the factory. That's fine with Novick. He can stand at the door and give them out. You both wear suits because above everything else, above the polkas and the Beatles and the standards and the straight out jazz, you're missionaries. Hubert wears a turtleneck and corduroy slacks. When you're idled by someone else's solo, you look out across the crowd not for the girl Mr. Selby said he always looked for, but for faces whose doors you might have knocked on. Faces that may have told you Keine Zeit or Nicht Interessiert if they've told you anything.

At night, home from a practice session or a Thursday at the Factory, you remove the tuning slides and shake them free of spit and then leave the horn out of its case to dry. You stand it on its bell on a small towel on the table. In the bed you share with Novick you can see its ghost pipes and valves from your pillow where the gold catches the light of the street through the window. In the morning you fit the slides back into place and put the horn in its case again. Every Friday afternoon, while Novick reads his Newsweek and your Time, you spread the towel out on the table and take the horn apart to clean and oil and grease the slides and the valve assemblies.

Novick keeps you up to speed. Fills you in as he reads. While you clean and oil your devil horn he tells you how President Johnson finally signs the Civil Rights Act into law but doesn't back it up with any federal enforcement. How in the absence of enforcement Mississippi goes full throttle after the Freedom Project. How in a place called Moss Point whites fire into a voter registration rally and critically wound a negro woman. How in Jackson the McCraven Hill Missionary Baptist Church is firebombed.

How in Raleigh two churches are torched. How in a place called McComb a Freedom House is bombed. How in Hattiesburg the Reverend Robert Beech of the National Council of Churches is arrested on felony charges because his checking account is briefly overdrawn. How in Columbus three volunteers are arrested for trespassing after stopping at a gas station to buy cold sodas. How in a place called Clarksdale cops spray cleaning chemicals on two negro girls inside the courthouse and arrest a volunteer for taking a photo of them doing it. How in a place called Gulfport four volunteers are arrested for escorting negroes to the courthouse to register to vote. How in Vicksburg young Freedom School students are stoned while walking to class. How in Hattiesburg again the Klan uses pipes to put a rabbi and two summer volunteers in the hospital. How in Canton a firebomb is thrown at a Freedom House. How in Vicksburg again a negro café that served white volunteers is bombed. How in Natchez arsonists burn the Jerusalem Baptist and the Bethel Methodist churches to the ground. How at the Greyhound depot in Jackson again a white man attacks a negro woman and after her injuries are treated the cops arrest her for disturbing the peace. How this is how the story goes. Story after story. How every story takes Novick back to his foster family and his jazz dad. How every story takes you back to Cissy.

You keep knocking on doors with the Glad Tidings of the Restored Gospel. You keep practicing and playing in a factory that used to house the Austrian Army. You keep sharing Novick's plastic radio. On Friday, back from the bathhouse, Novick sometimes hands you a magazine open to a photo. A white cop with the sagging gut of a hog bringing down his club on a negro woman in her Sunday dress in front of her little boy in his toylike Sunday suit, a Sunday suit like Roy would wear, makes you want to puke. Puke up everything they've taught you. Puke up the place where they planted the Seed of Cain and taught you to think that the gout of negro blood on a negro mother's forehead has less the truth of human blood than your blood does. Her blood Cissy's. Cissy's blood yours. You hand him back the magazine.

"I don't think I can take much more of this," you tell him.

"I know. It's tough to stomach."

You look at him. "No. Really."

His face goes apologetic. "Sorry," he says. "I'll try to keep it to myself."

"No. I need to know."

"Sounds like you still think about her."

"Yeah," you say. "Her family too." Then you say, "You must think about your foster family. Your jazz dad."

"All the time." He looks into his magazine. Looks up again. "I'm lucky."

"Lucky how?"

"I don't have to believe that Seed of Cain stuff. I know better. Every other guy on this mission has to believe it's the Word of God."

And then you're at the dangerous edge of the iron sky again. Where you can see sunlight just a step or two away.

"Then I'm lucky too," you say.

He looks at you. His face goes anguished with apology.

"I didn't mean to—"

"No. I'm with you."

And there are times when you take the crowd and the band at the Factory to a place they've never been on the red wings of your devil horn. To Birmingham where a negro kid is shot off the handlebars of his brother's bike, a kid who could have been your little brother Roy, handlebars whose grips could have been in your hands. Times when the place goes quiet. Times when you smell cigarette smoke and know it's because the people outside have come to stand in the doorway behind you and watch as if listening alone isn't good enough.

Novick keeps track of the hunt for the three civil rights workers who vanished back in June.

"Still no sign, huh."

"Nope. But get this. They say that chucking the bodies of murdered blacks into the nearest river is a southern tradition. So the Navy sends out sailors to search the swamps and divers to drag the rivers. Soon they're pulling bodies out. All black. They can still make some of them out. Lynched civil rights workers. Guys suspected of collecting guns for a race war." He shakes his head. "They pulled out a kid wearing a CORE teeshirt."

"A kid?"

"Yeah. Fourteen."

You look down blind at the pieces of your half-assembled horn on your towel. What he was doing wearing a teeshirt that to any mouth-breather is a kill target. What use this is. What the point of breathing is if it's not to take a flamethrower to a Klan barbecue.

One Thursday night, as the crowd thins out, Novick brings you a guy named Peter. A tall thin guy with jewel blue eyes and a long and ravaged face and thick black hair wearing a black teeshirt under a loose gray suit coat. His smile brings into relief the scars and creases in his face. He's friends with the singer from the Imperial Academy. He plays piano in a jazz quartet. He wants to have you play with them. You tell him thanks. He gives you his card. Says to call him. Says he's never heard anyone do what you do.

"Are you busy Thursdays?" you ask Peter.

"Sometimes. Why?"

"That means sometimes you're not," you say.

"Yes. I suppose so."

"Come on up and play."

Peter looks around.

"There's something wrong with your piano," he says.

You look around too. Come back stupid.

"Yeah," you say. "That'd help. I'll see about getting one."

You talk to Hubert. By the following Thursday he's found an old used upright and had it delivered and reconditioned and tuned. Peter shows up and takes it for a test ride. Where his face is long his hands are longer. His fingers burn the keyboard. His changes between jazz and classical astonish you. Like Lenny did. The permanent good time ready laugh. Playing with him in his rented house in the Avenues. What he's doing now.

She's there every Thursday night. At the beginning. That's fine. It gets you started right. And by the end she's gone. That's fine too. But sometimes your father's there instead. Out on the stained hardwood floor in front of you they can clap and holler all they want, polka and waltz and bop and boogie till they blow their hearts out, but your father's there at the end, his hand on the knob of your open bedroom door, the silhouette of his face rimmed with the fire of the hallway light, to let you know the truth. That this was never what he meant. That you're fooling them all in a way you're too reckless and proud and too much of a big shot to start to understand. Big shot. His letter behind your back to President Smith. Look out for my son. He thinks he's a big shot. That's when you tell him Asshole. While you blow your spit valve into a handkerchief. While you take the mouthpiece out. While you put your borrowed trumpet in its case. While you cringe back from his headlights in the back of his garage. Asshole that night, in bed sleepless, your dry hard vigilant eyes on the ghost trumpet standing on the table in the moonlight. Silent now. What danger it holds. What rage. What longing. What ghost song will it play.

"So what do you think?" says Novick, on the way home to supper, the sardines and canned potatoes you've been living on the last few days. "You good to go yet?"

"Go for what?"

"You know. With Peter. That club he plays in Vienna."

The Indigo. The Staircase. The Crow's Nest. The Sojourner. Sammy's. The State Street clubs back home. How you always kept them apart from church.

"I'm still not sure."

"Why not?" says Novick.

"What's wrong with the crowd at the Factory?"

"Nothing," he says. "You can still play there." Then he says, "Sorry if I'm eager. It's just that I'm running out of time."

Time. Flying now that you're tracting by day and playing most every night. Novick's done sometime in August. Heading home.

"Then I'm ready."

"Then it's time to see President Lindner. I already talked to Cannon. He'll help us out." Then he says, "Did you know he loves jazz?"

"Elder Cannon?"

"Yeah. He told me. He even tried to play it. He said he was too much of a mathematician."

Two afternoons later you're standing in President Lindner's office in the Mission Home. Elder Cannon's there to help Novick sell the concept of a trumpet playing missionary to the President of the Austrian Mission. The office is a big rich-looking room in a back corner of the mansion. Heavy drapes frame the windows in two of its walls. The dark polished surface of a massive desk is uncluttered except for a penholder and telephone and flip-top directory like your father's and a couple of standing picture frames with their black velvet backs to you. You wonder whose faces they hold. His kids. Probably not his wife because he sees her every day, this ghost presence in the Mission Home, this old woman with gray hair in a limp servant's dress and a face whose wrinkles give away defeat and not much else. Nobody you know has ever heard her say a word, but if she spoke, what you'd expect to hear her say is let me die. There are chairs but even President Lindner stands.

It's the closest you've ever been to him. In his smooth dark suit and white shirt and silver tie and head of trained white hair he looks, even here, in his office, like what he says will come out as a speech. Glasses rest on his chest from the necklace of a black cord. They look downward as though he uses them to check the polish on his shoes. With his eyebrows brushed up and back in wings of white hair, his face is as unrepentant and commanding as it is from the distance of a podium, but up close, where you expect to see the same clarity of impatient anger, the wild wrinkles in the skin around his eyes are congested with something bitter and finally mean.

"We could use a stronger public relations effort, President Lindner," Elder Cannon says.

"Absolutely not."

"You know what the Osmonds are doing for the Church back in California."

"The Osmonds are a family. Families come to watch them. He's talking about playing in night clubs."

"Right now, up in Klosterneuburg, Elder Tauffler's drawing an audience every Thursday night. In a small factory owned by an investigator. People bring their instruments and join in. People dance. They have a good time. A clean time. There's no alcohol. They're very happy. They enjoy themselves. You should see it."

"How do you know?"

The question on your own face when Elder Cannon turns and looks at you and Novick with an apologetic smile before he answers President Lindner.

"I've been there," he says. "Elder Farnsworth and I went up one night."

"You should come too," says Novick.

President Lindner shoots him a look that could wither him like a kleenex in the flame of a welding torch if he was anyone but Novick.

"What kind of followup are you getting?" Elder Cannon quickly asks Novick.

"People are inviting us to visit them. They want to know about us."

President Lindner lifts his glasses, hooks them on his ears, turns to you. Even through the lenses you can tell he'd like to hurt you more than talk to you.

"I imagine they think they're having someone famous visit them."

You look down. President Lindner turns to Novick again.

"Why do you need my permission for something you've been doing without it?"

"We want to branch out," says Novick. "Elder Tauffler's been asked to play in Vienna. We want to make sure it's okay with you."

"In night clubs."

Elder Cannon steps in. "Not just night clubs, President Lindner. From what I understand, they play concerts too."

"Concerts."

"Jazz concerts." Then he says, "They do have them. In the smaller halls and in the parks."

"If it's such a good public relations idea, why can't he play classical concerts?"

"A trumpet's not really a classical instrument."

"I still say no."

"It's an audience we've never reached. The General Authorities are always interested in spreading the name of the Church. Jazz is popular here in Europe."

"I know what the General Authorities are interested in, Elder Cannon."

"I never meant to suggest otherwise, President Lindner."

"And what does his companion do while he's playing?"

"Missionary work. Whatever form it happens to take. Whatever opportunity presents itself. The Lord works in mysterious ways."

"I'll tell you what, Elder Cannon. If you can get European Headquarters to agree, I'll have to go along. I won't have a choice. But I still don't like it."

"Thanks, President Lindner. I'll call them right away."

President Lindner drops his glasses to his chest, looks through them at his shoes, then looks you up and down before resting his furious eyes on yours.

"You know you represent the Church. You carry the priesthood. Conduct yourself accordingly. Wear a suit and tie. I don't care what the other musicians wear."

"I know, President Lindner. I will."

He looks you up and down again. Leaves you feeling like a mannequin. If you could tell him. How you didn't ask for this. How you're happy tracting all day long.

"I don't want you wearing that Duty to God pin either. People won't understand a silver cattle skull in your lapel. Don't give them an excuse to ridicule the Church."

You don't tell him you haven't been wearing it. Just put it on today for him.

"I won't."

CHAPTER 52

And shake off the dust of thy feet against those who receive thee
not, not in their presence, lest thou provoke them, but in secret; and
wash thy feet, as a testimony against them in the day of judgment.
Doctrine and Covenants 60:15

TRAVEL LIGHT. You remember the way you kept it loose your last
six months back home. The way you understood that you were passing
through on a road you knew would end. The way you knew you could
lift your head too quick and see where it would happen. You're passing
through here too. Now, with more than a year gone and less than a year
and a half to go, with the furious consent of the President of the Austrian
Mission, with the lights all green ahead of you, you could almost do the
same thing. Lift your head too quick, follow your borrowed trumpet out
too far, and see where this would end too. And so you keep your head
down and the headlights low so all you see is the next few doors ahead of
the door you're knocking on. The dance floor right in front of you.

"Cannon's good," says Novick. "He got the European Headquarters
to say yes."

"President Lindner hates the idea," you say.

"Doesn't seem to be much he doesn't hate."

"He's gonna look for payback."

"You don't have to do this."

"If we back out now he'll hate us for making trouble." Then you say,
"Either way. I'm doing it."

"So we'll call Peter."

"Not just yet."

"Okay."

"I don't want to be committed to one band and then get transferred.
Like when you go home. I'd rather just sit in with different bands."

"I get it."

"Anyway, if Peter went on the road, I wouldn't be able to go."

"I forgot about that."

"I'd just like to try it on my own first. You know. Where nobody knows me."

"Okay," says Novick. "That's what we'll do."

At the Factory, where girls watch you in ways that say they're interested, and guys stand back in the shadows and you can sometimes sense them wondering what it must be like, you try not to think what you're really there to do. Try to hide it from Hubert and from the people who bring food and drink from home and the musicians who think they're only there to play. Because then your songs go hollow and your solos taste like the dirt that rides the wind back home. Because then your bright steel bird goes black as a desert buzzard with its hideous head of red scar tissue. Because you've never used your horn for this.

For your first club Novick picks a place you've never seen before. After your practice session at the Factory, after another light supper of sardines and canned potatoes, you grab the train into Vienna with your case on your lap. It's another underground place, down four stairs from the sidewalk to an inset door, café tables and chairs, wine bottles for candle holders, cigarette smoke thick enough to show the colored cones of light from the ceiling over the band. It's a trio, piano and drums and bass, and the woman at the piano sings, so you could almost call it a quartet. You recognize Misty. You follow Novick to a table. People who see your case raise their faces to look at you. The waitress lights the stub of the candle in the encrusted neck of the wine bottle on your table. Novick orders a Coke. Knowing you might be playing, you order water, to keep residue out of Brother Shlagl's trumpet. You wait for a break, then approach the woman at the keyboard.

"Entschuldige."

It surprises you when she turns to you and in English asks if she can help you. You tell her how much you like her trio's sound. How much you just liked Satin Doll. Tell her you play trumpet. Ask if she'd mind if you just sat in for a song or two. She's older. She asks how old you are. Twenty. She smiles and says certainly. She asks if you're American. Tells you she's from Moldavia.

"I am Mirela. Tell me your name."

"Shake."

"Like milkshake?"

Long dark loose hair veined with grey. Dressed in a green long sleeved dress that takes a deep plunge down into her lowslung breasts. Raised into the pale mix of red and blue light, even with lipstick, her smile shows the creases that cross from the skin around them into the skin of her lips. You smile too.

"Or shake rattle and roll," you say.

"You have your trumpet here?"

"Yes."

"Do you always dress like this to play?"

"Yes."

'Like Bill Evans."

The bass player's a young negro guy dressed in a flannel shirt with the sleeves rolled back off his heavy forearms. A thick cloud of black hair rides high and round on his head. When the break ends and you come back up with Brother Shlagl's trumpet, he's tuning his bass, but he steps up and offers you his hand. Ronnie. Nice to meet you. The first time you hear a negro with an English accent. The first time you shake a negro's hand and take the simple smile he offers you and feel this cut of shame for what a lie you are. A lie dressed in a smile and suit and tie. You're safe, you tell him in your mind. I'm not supposed to seek you out. So to you I'm just a trumpet player. It makes you want to puke again. The drummer's an older white guy with a gentle face as round as one of his snares and a blond goatee. He gets off his stool and reaches past his high hat and tells you his name is Willie. He's wearing a white shirt and one of those cowboy ties made out of a cord of braided leather with a silver and turquoise cattle skull for a slide. You think of your Duty to God lapel pin back in your room in a drawer. Out in front the usual people sit at the usual tables. Their faces float in the gold light of the usual candles. Trails of exhaled smoke rise like random leaks of lazy steam from the geyser fields of Yellowstone into the pale haze of yellow light from a couple of chandeliers. Novick sits alone at your table. Ronnie the only negro in the house. Mirela uses her microphone to introduce you.

"Please give a welcome to our young guest Shake. Let's see what he can show us."

The first tune is Killer Joe. You fall back against the deep full pulsing stride of Ronnie's bass, feel the steady whisper of the snare drum catch you, bring the trumpet up and let Mirela lay down the opening chord while you float the first notes of the melody out across the room. Mirela takes the first solo. Then Ronnie. Then you. When you close your eyes there's a second negro in the house. Cissy, at Novick's table, in your chair, wearing the sleeveless yellow top she was wearing that night in San Jose, the way it fit her snug and the color bringing out the glow in the dark honey of her skin, her hair pulled high off her neck and forehead in the same eruption of black curls, her smile closed, the flame of the stub of the candle shining in her eyes. And then you're coming around to the melody again for the landing. When you're done the place stays quiet. Mirela turns on her stool and stares at you. In his English accent Ronnie says Good Christ. You've been here before. In front of Mr. Frank's class the day he asked you to play. Stormy Weather. How you stood there afterward, and nobody moved, and you looked down in bewilderment and shame until this chubby kid named Eddie fired off a single clap that brought your head up.

This time you know different. This time it's Novick who breaks the silence. Two slow claps and the rest of the place joins in. It's respectful. But it goes on and on. You turn to the drummer. He raises a drumstick in salute. Mirela gets off her stool and walks over.

"I forget to ask your last name."

"Tauffler."

"Is there a song you like to play?"

"Stormy Weather?"

"Stormy . . . ?"

You sing her a couple of bars. Don't know why there's no sun up in the sky. Watch her smile break in the red and blue wash of the spotlights.

"Ah! Yes! Of course!" She laughs. "I can even sing it if you like!"

"So did you spread the word?"

Walking back to Franz Josefs Bahnhof in the sweet night air for the train home, you know Novick well enough to tell the question makes him nervous.

"Naw. I just cased the joint."

"I thought you didn't care. I thought you were fearless."

"This is different."

"Just do what you do at the Factory. Hand out brochures."

"The Factory's our gig," he says. "This is someone else's."

"Hard to know how to break the ice, I guess."

"Yeah," he says. "Maybe just make some friends for now."

"That could work."

After a minute he says, "You don't have to do this, you know."

"Well," you say, "They want me back tomorrow. So I guess I'm doing it."

You're passing through. Stay light. Don't let yourself settle anywhere too long. From your two nights with Mirela's trio you move to other clubs where you stand in with other bands while Novick starts working out how to break the news to other customers that you're missionaries for this church back in a place called Utah. Some places are dinner clubs with white tablecloths where the band is there for background and you play low and sometimes with the mute. Some are taverns. Some are dance clubs. Some are modern with vast surfaces of glass and polished stone that make your notes ring hard and brittle. Some are converted from historic spaces in buildings hundreds of years old. Sometimes the bands are too big, too rehearsed, their own trumpets too locked into their own solos to have room for the give and take to stand in. But most of them are trios and quartets and sometimes five piece bands that are loose and open to a guy who shows up with a horn. A mix of white and negro and sometimes

Mediterranean players. Sometimes an American musician. Sometimes a bad look or no look at all from a negro player who doesn't like a white guy in a suit with a borrowed trumpet thinking you can do what he does. Sometimes a flash of the concentrated fury you've seen in the faces of Miles Davis photos. When it happens you understand. You know who the giants are. You know where the music comes from.

In late July the remaining days of Novick's mission count down to single digits. By then you've played several clubs in Schwedenplatz and along the Donaukanal.

"Got plans for after your mission?" you ask Novick one night.

"I want to stop in New York. See some of the legends live."

"Do some tracting in the Village?"

He laughs. "Yeah. Never know who's gonna open that door."

You imagine it. Some second floor apartment in some New York hallway. A thread of smoke rising off a bent cigarette in a glass ashtray. Bill Evans voicing some modal chords on the keyboard of an old grand. An afternoon like the one today outside the open windows. A knock on the door. What the fuck, says Miles, sets down his horn, answers the knock. Two white guys in dark ties and undertaker suits standing in the doorway. You and Novick. There not to show him what you've learned from him but to warn him of the Second Coming. There to tell him not to smoke or drink or whore around while he looks at you and sees the knot in the center of your upper lip for what you are. A big shot trumpet player. The fury gathering in his face while you tell him what you are and what you're there for. You aint supposed to come lookin for me, he says. Aint that what they told you?

"Miles," you tell Novick.

Novick startled. Then laughing softly. "Miles. You bet."

In the heart of Vienna, around the corner from Stephansplatz and the massive cathedral of Stephansdom, there's a place called the Zwolf Apostelkeller. The Cellar of the Twelve Apostles. Down a broad staircase from the lobby its doorways are arches and its ceilings are domes formed of thousands of ancient bricks. You wonder what holds them in place. Keeps them from coming down. Statues and busts of what you guess are apostles appear at random around the brick walls and in alcoves in the bricks. Chandeliers made of wagon wheels with shaded bulbs hang from chains. The place could have housed tombs once. Stored bones and skulls. Sturdy wood tables in different sizes cover the stone floor. Simple wood chairs stand around them. The place is where Peter and his quartet play. He's okay with having you stand in all you want. The place serves food, heaping dishes you and Novick can't afford, but by the time you start to play the crowd is mostly down to customers who want to listen to some jazz with their wine and beer and conversation. Groups of students use the larger tables. Older men and women take the smaller ones as couples or alone. Men who smoke pipes and look like beatniks or professors or musicians. And there's Novick, looking around, for people who've started to follow you, people he's broken the ice with, people he can go and sit with when they show up.

And Cissy. Sometimes with a table of students. Sometimes alone. Sometimes with a couple of girlfriends. Sometimes across a small table from a professor with a green turtleneck and a gray beard. Sometimes at Novick's table. Still other times on stage with you. In the closet she has in your dream hang only the five outfits you've seen her wear. Only five. The white top and headband she wore the afternoon of the barbecue. The mint green dress she wore to church. The turquoise choir robe where you singled out her voice. The yellow top the night you showed up at her door in San Jose. And then the pink church dress when she came with Jeff to the airport. Sometimes which of the five she wears depends on the song. Sometimes the place. Never in her choir robe. Never the one other way you saw her, naked, sheathed only in the blood rose glow of her coffee honey skin.

"Check this out," says Novick. "You're in the newsletter."

Home from tracting late one rainy afternoon to change out of your wet suit coat and pants and head for the Factory for a practice session. Some local players have started asking if they could join you. There's a permanent set of drums there now.

"High hours again?"

"No," says Novick, grinning, holding the pastel blue sheet of paper the newsletter comes printed on. "The whole mission knows about you now."

You look. A new way to do the Lord's work. How you started a weekly live music night in Klosterneuburg. How you've been playing jazz trumpet in clubs around Vienna. How you've got a following. How you're a real "Instrument" of the Lord. Quotes in case anyone misses it. All the times you've dodged the impulse to be stupid enough to put it that way.

"You told them."

"Not me."

"Who did? Who wrote this?"

"I don't know. Not like it was a secret."

"I sound like a fake. A hustler."

"You know they're gonna come out to hear you. All the local missionaries."

"I'll be playing to sixty American guys in suits."

Novick thinks about it. "Yeah," he says.

"President Lindner's really gonna hate me now."

"No he's not, man. It's working. I got some folks about ready to have us come visit them. Hang out. Give them the first discussion."

"Seriously?"

"Yeah seriously. I never thought I'd say this, but I'm not ready to go home just yet. This is as good as my mission's been."

"So they really know we're missionaries," you say.

"Of course. I said leave that to me."

"You tell President Lindner it's working?"

"I'll make sure he knows." Then he says, "By the way, Cannon's going home soon."

"Who's replacing him?"

"This guy Hill." Then he says, "He's a son of a bitch. Excuse me. I just don't get why they'd pick him."

CHAPTER 53

AT CHURCH THAT SUNDAY you're surrounded. Some of the elders knew you played a place outside Vienna. What they didn't know was that you were playing Vienna too. Now they want to know what the fuzz is up. Where the fuzz you're playing.

"I never know. Ask Elder Novick."

"Who do you play with?"

"Pretty much anyone."

"What's it like?"

"Like?"

"Get paid?"

"I can't take money. You know that."

"Baptizing anyone?"

"Ask Elder Novick."

"Going anywhere else? Like on the road?"

"I don't belong to any band."

"Getting any real work done?"

"All day long."

"You smell like fuzzin' smoke. Cigarette smoke."

"Comes with the territory."

They start showing up. Some come in and look around like they don't know what to do. You think of the wide-eyed Mormon kids out cruising the savage river of State in the lifeboats of their father's station wagons. Others come in and walk smack into the middle of the room like the FBI on the hunt for someone to take outside and baptize. They don't stay long. Some dirty looks and they're gone. Others know. In their civilian clothes they invisibly find a place to sit and stay out of the way. Either way. You never meant to be popular. Things are moving. Pulling you along. In a way that feels bad. You remember. Out with your buddies in their cars coming home at night down Highway 89. Dark except where the headlights run. Where the highway keeps coming out of the dark and then vanishing behind you. Dark out the sides. Dark in the mystery just out of reach in the back of your head. The feeling of moving through things too fast again to ever be forgiven for them.

Days before Novick's mission ends the bodies of the three civil rights workers are found. Novick reads about it in Newsweek and passes it along. Someone directs the FBI to a dirt dam. Three bodies are dredged out of the mud of its base into daylight. The body of the negro shows he was brutally beaten before he was killed by gunshot the way the white guys were. Across the table Novick's polishing the grime and water stains out of his big black shoes while he reads. You've got your horn apart. He turns the Newsweek your way to show you a photo of the wife of one of the white guys. White, with short dark hair, her lean young face shows more resolve than grief.

"Listen to this," he says, turning the magazine back. "What she said to the press."

"Go ahead."

Novick starts reading. In his lumbering and humble voice you listen for defiance in the voice of the woman in the photo.

"My husband Michael Schwerner did not die in vain. If he and Andrew Goodman had been negroes, the world would have taken little notice of their deaths. After all, the slaying of a negro in Mississippi is not news. It is only because my husband and Andrew Goodman were white that the national alarm has been sounded."

He finishes reading. Sticks his hand inside his shoe and picks it up. You slide the third valve piston into its cylinder. Work it up and down. This queasy feeling. You're white too. You're here because you're white.

"She just came out and said it."

"Yeah," says Novick. "She worked for CORE too. Like her husband."

"So what they figured was right."

"Yeah," he says. "White blood." Then he says, "I don't get what's wrong with people."

"So where you gonna stay? In New York?"

It brings him back from Mississippi and spreads an eager smile across his face.

"I'll just find a YMCA somewhere. If not, I'll just get a hotel. My dad sent me plenty to cover one and still have a good time."

"Tell me what clubs you're gonna hit again."

"Oh man. Birdland, Blue Note, Vanguard, Village Gate, Five Spot, Half Note. Some I probably never heard of."

"That's a lot of Cokes," you say.

"Well, who knows," he says, with a wink. "I won't be a missionary any more."

"Tell me who you're gonna see again."

"Man." He shakes his head. His smile goes wide with pleasure. "Everyone I can." Then he says, "You're teasing me."

"Tell Miles hello if you see him."

"If he's in New York, I'll see him."

"Nice."

"I ever tell you what happened to him a few years back? Outside of Birdland?"

"No."

"Don't think that racist stuff is just down south."

"What happened?"

Novick sets his shoe down on the table. Pushes back his chair.

"This was a few months after his album Kind of Blue was released. It was a big bestseller. He was doing a gig at Birdland to promote it. Between sets he escorts this white chick out to a cab. Before he goes back in he stops to have a smoke on the sidewalk. It's pretty crowded. Most of the crowd is there for him. This cop tells him to move along. Miles asks what for. He tells the cop he's working in the club. He points up to the marquee and says that's his name up there. The cop doesn't care. Just tells him to move along again and then decides to arrest him. I don't know. I think Miles gave him that stare of his. Some detective passing by sees what's going on and comes charging in and takes his nightstick and starts pounding Miles on the head."

"Holy crap."

"A couple of hundred people are yelling at the cops to stop. They don't care. They finally put him in a car and take him to the station where they book him for assaulting an officer. Then they put five stitches in his head."

"When'd this happen?"

"What year did Kind of Blue come out?"

"Fifty nine."

"So I guess five years ago."

"Maybe that's what he looks so angry about."

"Who wouldn't be. I heard that New York cops used to be some of the worst racists around."

"Be careful."

"I'm not black."

"Glad to be going home?"

His smile gives way to contemplation. "Yeah," he finally says. "I guess."

"You're not?"

"Kinda feel like I didn't do my job."

"What?"

Novick looks down at the palms of his open hands.

"Be nice if I had a baptism to show for it. That's all I'm saying."

Morgan and Frau Kettler and all the strangers he talked to at concerts and operas. Paulson and the 10 Oktoberstrasse 17 Ping Pong Club.

No baptisms. You want to tell Novick that all the doors he knocked on counted for something. He was planting the seed.

"You remember that scripture about shaking the dust off your shoes?"

"Yeah," he says.

"Man, if we shook the dust off our shoes in front of every door that never opened, we'd have sent thousands of people to Hell by now."

He looks up at you.

"What are you saying?"

"I'm telling you how hard you worked."

"That scripture's insane," he says.

"I'm sorry. Look, man. It's Austria."

"Yeah," he says. "Still."

"You worked harder than anyone I know. It felt good. It felt honest. Look at the high hours we kept getting."

"Yeah. I know."

Morgan. Then Paulson. And now this guy sitting here with his hands closed and his sad eyes on the floor between his stocking feet.

"And I got this feeling that anyone who ever beat us was making it up," you say.

"Well," he says, his head down, in a voice that kills you. "I couldn't say."

Chapter 54

THE GOLLERS have known that Novick's going home and you'll be leaving Klosterneuburg. They have the two of you for dinner the night before his last night in Austria. Fresh venison roast and mashed potatoes in deep brown gravy. You can almost taste acorns and grass in the wild meat. You're headed for one of Vienna's outskirts districts. You'll still be close enough to visit and do the Factory if Hubert wants. It just won't be the same. Everyone around the table knows. Frau Goller won't have Novick to debate religion with. She isn't happy where they're sending you. She knows the district. She wonders why they put you there. She wants to call someone. Fix this mistake. You tell her it's fine. It's still Vienna. Close enough to come visit on Sundays and come play on Thursdays. If she calls and complains they might send you out to Vorarlberg instead. And then you'd never see each other. Edith picks at her food in silence.

"What are you going to do about the Factory?" you ask Hubert.

"Keep it going," he says. "Everybody expects it. And you can still come."

"Are new missionaries coming?" Frau Goller asks.

"Yes."

"I don't want new missionaries!" Edith suddenly cries, and jumps off her chair and goes charging toward her room.

You both pack the night before you leave. Novick gives you his plastic radio. The friendly Russian landlady and her sullen Russian daughter Olga offer to wash the bedding and clean the room and cook you a farewell dinner of bratwurst with boiled potatoes. They drink dark red wine while Novick and you have water. You leave the tracting book and a list of addresses for the dairy shop, post office, cleaner, bathhouse, a couple of cheap restaurants on the study table. You write a report on where you're leaving things. Names of the people you've started to call investigators. The right train to Vienna. You leave a note with the address explaining what goes on at the Factory. You leave out the Goller family and their home address.

The next morning the Gollers drive you and Novick to the Mission Home, your suitcases in the trunk, your bikes on a bumper rack Hubert borrowed from one of his workers. Hubert carries your bikes to the steps of the porch. You stand back while they say goodbye to Novick.

"Thanks for everything," he tells them.

"I want you to write us when you become a bishop," Frau Goller says.

Novick laughs through his sad face. You help Hubert put the bike rack in the trunk. Tell his family you'll see them Thursday. You've got Edith's trust again. She hugs you before she takes the front seat between her mother and father. You and Novick watch the Opel make its way down the street before you go inside. Tall and rangy, oily brown hair, contempt in his face and nothing close to patience in his attitude, newly appointed Second Counselor Paul Hill meets you in the lobby and tells you to wait in the conference room.

"I still don't get that guy," says Novick.

"Thanks for making me a missionary," you tell him. You shake his big hand. Return the sad affection in his face. Feel how he wants to stay.

"Thanks for all the music," he says. "Wish it could have been longer."

"Thanks for the radio."

"Sure thing."

The scorn that comes with Hill when he walks into the conference room makes you and Novick release your long handshake.

"Your ride to the airport's coming," he tells Novick. He hands you an address on an index card, a set of keys, directions that are made of tram lines.

"What's the landlady's name?"

"There isn't one. You've got an apartment to yourselves."

"Okay."

"Your junior's name is Daniel Rudd."

"So I'm a senior now?"

"Are you saying you're not ready?"

Thirteen months. Four good months with Novick. You hold Hill's cold glare. See how his lips look halfway gone. Like bitterness has chewed away at them.

"I'm a fast learner," you say.

"This wasn't my idea. It was Elder Cannon's."

"Making me senior, you mean."

"Your junior's coming in to the Sudbahnhof tonight. Around eight."

"I need to leave my bike out front. Come back for it."

"Your choice. Got your saddlebags?"

"Yeah."

"Fill them while you're here."

"Get home okay," you tell Novick. "Enjoy New York."

"I plan to," he says.

"What do you plan to do with your bike?" Hill wants to know.

"Give it to you," Novick says.

"Why would I want it?"

The sudden way Novick goes apologetic.

"I thought maybe you could give it to an elder who can't afford one," he says.

"They're supposed to bring their own bike money."

The sudden way you want to hurt Hill.

"Maybe a member could use it then."

Hill looks at Novick like what he has to say can't be more useless.

"Maybe you could give us a minute to say goodbye."

Hill turns the unbearable burden of his disgust on you, finds there's nothing left to say, and leaves.

———

CHAPTER 55

AND THEN THERE'S nothing left to say. You haul your Samsonite and Brother Shlagl's horn case down the hill to the tram stop where you waited with Morgan your first night here. This time you know more than just the street you're on. This time you know your way around. A long relay of trams takes you through Vienna and out the other side to the outskirts. This time it isn't a pretty little town with a stift at its heart. This time there is no heart. This time it isn't a resort town nested in the shadow of the everlasting Alps. This time there isn't an amusement park and a giant Ferris wheel across the street. This time, as you ride through it, the City of Music mutates into block after block of warehouses and truck and railroad yards and immense apartment buildings with the cold oppressive ugliness of prisons or institutions. The gray streets are empty. You can sense the bleak history of the long monotonous occupation of the last war. Like this is where the old and useless were housed. Like this is where they hid. Like this is where they grew old and defeated and started to lose their teeth.

You find the building with your number on it. In the dark dank lobby the ceiling and walls are stained. Shreds of plaster paint hang from them like leper skin. You climb the stairs. In the dim hallway of the third floor find your apartment number. No landlady. All yours. Apartments must be cheap out here if you and your junior can afford one to yourselves. Inside, in shadow, you look for light switches. In the small kitchen there's a stove with a miniature oven underneath the two gas burners. A small tin-surfaced dinette table and two chairs stand on the brown linoleum at the window. The window looks out on a grim wall whose curtained windows are maybe ten feet across an airshaft. A knee high fridge stands open and unplugged below the sink. Dish towels and washrags are folded on the drainboard. A steel cupboard hangs on the stained wall. On the bottom shelf they've left you a couple of burned aluminum saucepans, a frying pan, a spaghetti pot, a couple of plastic plates and cups. One of the cups holds some table knives and forks. They've been left clean. Two cots stand on opposite sides of the bedroom with sheets and blankets and small flat pillows folded and stacked on their bare mattresses. A small dresser stands against the back wall. The living room holds a study table with its own two chairs, a small bookcase with some brochures and what looks like a tracting book left on the top shelf, the stick frame of a small easy chair with warped thin gray cushions, a floor lamp. A handwritten note on the table like the one you left in your room in Klosterneuburg tells you where to find a restaurant, cleaner, grocery, and dairy shop, and which tram line goes to the churchhouse. In the bathroom there's an open tub, smeared with grime left from a hurried cleaning job, a toilet with a wall mounted overhead tank, a washbasin. The faucets of the tub work. You won't need to find a bathhouse. The mirror in the face of the medicine cabinet on the wall above the basin is clouded black with mold and just big enough to shave in. The hot rooms smell of ammonia and wet wool.

You open the windows. Make up both cots. Choose one, open your suitcase, choose your dresser drawers, unpack, split the wood and wire hangers, tape Maggie's drawing to the wall above your cot where you can see it when you wake up. Find two burned aluminum saucepans and a frying pan in the oven. Plug in the fridge and close the door. In your gut the place has the feel of payback. President Lindner maybe. His California henchman Hill. You don't know. You don't care. You've had your share of better places. You're a senior now. At thirteen months, two months shy of halfway, you're the guy in charge. Ready to make your mark. You feel prepared. You've slogged through the heavy biblical language of the Book of Mormon and cringed whenever you read about the appetite of the Lord for eternal punishment. The Doctrine and Covenants where the Lord talks about places like Nashville and New York and Cincinnati. You've tried the Pearl of Great Price, but it was too cobbled together, too rambling to make sense. You've memorized the dialogues of the six lesson plans. You've only had four months of real missionary work. But thanks to those four months, thanks to Novick, you feel seasoned. A veteran. There's not that much to it. And you're in Vienna. A place you know how to negotiate. You've got a tracting book. Blocks of apartment buildings filled with people who can't go missing. Brother Shlagl's horn. The Factory up in Klosterneuburg. The bands you play with in the city. And maybe Rudd's the kind of guy who can hobnob with an audience. Either way. You're ready. Ready to try on your grandfather's shoes. In the fire you built in your chest so long ago for the Holy Ghost to light, you feel the kindling take flame, the heat begin to spread.

You take the tracting book and the list of local places out for a walk around the neighborhood. Connect addresses to buildings. The streets and sidewalks are empty, but you can sense life in the lifeless buildings you pass, life hiding in the heavy gray of walls thick as prison walls, life watching you through holes in old curtains and from under the skewed slats of venetian blinds raised just a slit above the sills. The sound of traffic maybe two or three blocks away. The high hoarse moaning hum of highway traffic coming and going on the gray air in the canyons of the buildings. Traffic just passing through the outskirts on its way to somewhere else. Above the walls of the buildings the sky is blue. But the blue goes the iron gray of an overcast as the canyon walls of the buildings leach the light out of the air.

You call the Gollers from a phone booth. Tell Frau Goller your new address. While you read a number for some girl named Katya scratched jagged into the front of the phone box, she makes you promise to come on Sunday with your new companion.

After you say goodbye you walk off the last of the worry. You're a senior now. In charge. You think back on times you've told someone else what to do. There aren't many. Mostly musicians. A few blocks away, close to another tram stop where the apartment blocks give way for a street with some stores, you find the small restaurant, the dairy shop, the grocery store, the cleaner they listed for you. You stop in the dairy shop and buy a couple of rolls along with some milk and cheese for breakfast in the morning. Stop in the grocery store for a can of cleaning powder.

Back home again you put the rolls in a wicker basket on the kitchen table and the milk and cheese in the fridge, and feel this impatient reserve of exuberance start to come unleashed. If it's a rathole it's one that you and your junior can fill with the spirit of your calling. In the bedroom you can see the two of you kneeling at your cot. You use the powder and a washrag to clean the grime out of the tub and off the covers for the light switches. The place feels better. The smell something you can get used to. You move the bookshelf closer to an outlet and plug Novick's little plastic radio in. When you adjust the dial the station that runs his jazz program comes in clearer than it did in Klosterneuburg. You take the long relay of trams back to the Mission Home for your bike, ride it back through the city, lock it to a paint-crusted pipe in the lobby behind the stairs you'll climb each day.

And finally, after you've done what you can to make this new adventure as real as possible, when all you're lacking is the junior companion you'll share it with, you sit down to write a letter home. It takes a while to get it right. On the minefield of a sheet of paper, you cross old lines out, scribble new lines in, and then copy what you've written on a clean sheet.

Dear Family,

I have some exciting news to share with you. I've been promoted to senior companion. I'll be working with a junior named Elder Rudd. I'll be in charge of everything we do. I know that the mission has entrusted me with a big responsibility. I'm not only responsible for my own mission but also for his. I'll rely on the Lord to guide us. I'll take good care of him to make sure his mission is the best it can be. I can promise you that we'll work hard to

spread the gospel. I'll do everything in my power to live up to our name and make all of you proud. We're assigned to a district on the outskirts of Vienna. I'll write you more later. I have to head for the train station now to meet him and bring him home. Our new address is down below. I love you all.
Shake

At seven you're out the door. You drop the letter in a mailbox you spotted earlier when you were scouting out the neighborhood. And then you're on your way to the Sudbahnhof to pick up Elder Rudd. He's coming up from Graz. You feel a new kind of freedom in your chest and feet. An exuberant almost weightless freedom. Like Morgan said. It's your turn now. You've done your time shackled to a senior. You needed to before it could be your turn. You're free. Free to show what you can do. Free to prove yourself to your unbelieving father. Free to put a match to his letter to President Smith and turn what he wrote to smoke. Doors will open. On the trams, seats are available, but you're too restless to sit down, and hold the post instead, your legs practiced at moving with the rocking and jerking of the floor. Nobody insulates you now from the other passengers. Through the open windows comes the raw feel of the city. This is you now. Your city. Doors will open. You'll find a way to open them. At the Sudbahnhof you cross the stone floor of the main hall. Along its walls are an espresso place, a travel office, ticket counters, other shops, boards showing arrivals and departures. You're early. Climb the stairs and walk up and down the platform for the trains arriving from the south. There's still blue left across the sky but the platform lights are taking over from the failing daylight while you wait.

This is where Novick came to meet you.

Now it's your turn.

You don't know what instinct makes it so quick to pick the guy you're there for out of a crowd of passengers. If it's a spiritual thing. A priesthood thing. A sense for knowing some guy in the crowd is Mormon. But you know it's Rudd the instant you see him. He's not what you expected. Not some Idaho farmboy or some East or South High kid or some hip guy out of California. Nothing to let you know he's Mormon. You just know. Watching him walk up the platform after exchanging a wave with you, he looks like a regular guy, just older, with a lean build, good looks, black hair cut and combed in an offhand way, a cheap suit this olive drab striped with thin slightly darker lines, a nondescript green tie, big black thick-soled wingtip shoes. He isn't into style. Neither was Novick. But Novick didn't have the throwaway reckless attitude this guy does. Novick was a guy on the way to becoming a man. Morgan and Paulson too. Rudd's a man already. You can tell from the way he walks, turns his head, grins, moves his shoulders, carries his small suitcase. He's a man. He's put style and other guy things aside for bigger things to care about. When he reaches you, he's your height, but the size and force of his hand when you shake goes well beyond yours, and his grin is bold, in your face, friendly but quietly defiant at the same time, an edge to it. Up close you can see cold points in the pupils of his eyes that let you know he's watching from behind his face.

"You're Tauffler," he says.

"Yes. You're Elder Rudd."

"Yeah. Dan Rudd. So you're the guy with the trumpet."

"You heard about that."

"Yeah. You were playing here in Vienna. It was in the fucking newsletter. I went apeshit when I heard I was getting you."

The bottom goes out of your stomach.

"How was the ride?" you say.

"A motherfucker. Some son of a bitch from Turkey sitting next to me was eating this mutton jerky shit the whole trip. I'll be smelling his breath for a month."

"That all your luggage?"

"Yeah. Let's get it to the room. Some broad on the train got me so hot I'm about to explode. Then I want to see this town."

"First time in Vienna?"

"Yeah. Believe it? Time to finally party. You playing tonight?"

"Not planning on it."

"I want to hear you. Sit back and hear a missionary play some jazz. Man. What a concept. A fucking horn blowing missionary."

You stand there and for a crazy instant wish you could get your letter to your family back. But it's gone. Gone on its irretrievable way to Utah. You look at your junior and understand that nothing will be the way you told them it was going to be.

PART 7

ROGUE IN AUGUST

HE SAID IT. The real word. Over and over. Not fuzz or frick. The raw word. That's all you can think about as you get his bike from the baggage car, catch the tram in front of the Sudbahnhof, begin the long ride home to the place you prepared. What you should do. People are getting on and off the tram, and he's talking to you, asking you questions about Vienna, and you're answering, and he's saying the word again, and again, and all you can think about is the time you're going to need to figure out what to do. Call the Mission Home. Report him. You know what they'll say. You need to pray harder. You need to ask the Lord for strength and wisdom. You're supposed to solve problems on your own. Call us if that doesn't work.

In the rocking clamor of the tram, standing among passengers, you hear how he's twenty-eight to your twenty. How before coming on a mission he was a flight engineer for United. How he owns a ranch outside Cheyenne together with a pilot. How his goal was to do a fresh stewardess every night. How he came on a mission to see what it was like. You hear all this, and all you're thinking is your first day as a senior, your first day in charge, and here you are, not feeling like you're in charge of anything, your first junior throwing the real word around like rice at someone's wedding, telling you he's done more stewardesses than you'll probably ever see. He hears that you were in the Army and going to the U when you got your call to serve. That you've been here thirteen months. While he listens you watch him stare at women. Not the way you've seen anyone stare before. Not like he's checking them out. But like he's doing them. You see one of them smile. But the smile's not innocent. It's like the one he's wearing. Hard. Full of heat. Like she's already said okay. Like they're naked. Like they're already doing each other right in front of you.

What you should do. Tell him he's not supposed to use that word. Tell him he's not supposed to look that way at women. Tell him he needs to stop being profane. Right. Tell him something he doesn't know already. You play jazz trumpet. You sometimes gave in to thinking you were something. He's more a man than you've ever let yourself think you'd someday be. He doesn't need a horn. A decent suit. Paulson's attention to his hair. Even a mirror. None of the things guys think they need. He knows who he is. In the cold points in his pupils and the frozen edge in his confident grin there's menace. It says don't mess with him. It says he'll have his way. You hold his bike so he can pretend it isn't his. You hold the bar above your head and look out the window. Vienna sounds and looks the same. But you know it isn't.

"I love this town." He says it like a ventriloquist, without moving his lips, while he holds his do me grin on a girl holding the pole down the tram a ways. "Fuckin' beautiful women."

You tell him which cot and drawers are his. He says thanks and asks where the bathroom is. You try to pretend he's using it to pee or wash his face. You sit at the table in the dingy light of the living room, looking blind through the tracting book, still not close to knowing what to do. He comes in, unpacks, then looks around and picks your trumpet case off the floor next to the stick chair with the flat cushions.

"This your horn?"

"Yeah."

"Mind if I look at it?"

"Go ahead. Be careful."

You watch him open the case, lift Brother Shlagl's trumpet out, turn it over in his hands, the way Cissy did yours in Yenchik's 40 Ford.

"Can't wait to hear you play tonight."

And any crazy comparison to Cissy vanishes.

"Sorry," you say. "Not tonight."

"No?"

"No."

He keeps looking the trumpet over. Works the valves. Turns it around and looks down the bell into the mouthpipe.

"I say we're going," he says.

That quick lizard darts in a crooked path across the surface of your heart again.

"It's not happening," you say.

"This is pretty light. I thought it'd be heavier. Stronger."

"It's easier to hold," you say, playing it straight. "Better sound. Thin metal can vibrate."

He takes it in both hands. You can see black hair on their backs as they tighten up around its pipes.

"All that sound comes out of something this flimsy."

"A violin's the same way."

"Bet I could bend this fucker right in half."

You've seen it coming.

"You probably could."

"I really want to hear you play."

"You will."

"I mean fucking really. Tonight."

He tests the flex of the horn again. The afternoon you brought your trumpet home from Mr. Hinkle's. Your mother right there in the hall when you came out of the bathroom. The trumpet raised in her hand like the rugbeater she never used to beat a rug. The crazy fear.

"So you're gonna ruin that trumpet if you don't."

"That's up to you."

"Then you should know it's not my trumpet."

He looks at you. Puts his grin on hold while he considers what you're saying.

"What is it? Rented?"

"Borrowed. From a member here in Vienna. So go ahead. We'll take it back to him Sunday. You can explain it to him."

"I could say I didn't have a thing to do with it."

"He'd know."

You watch him think about it. Then put the trumpet back and close the lid.

"Just testing you. I'd never have done it anyway." Then he says, "Just thought I could scare you into fucking playing."

You look down at the tracting book again. And suddenly he's got you by the throat, lifting you off the chair, swinging you around to keep you on your feet, slamming you up against the wall. His face an inch from yours.

"You're playing tonight," he says. His teeth clenched. His grin deformed in this grimace of rage. This fierce black glitter in his eyes. He holds you there. Lets you look. Look all you want. And then through his teeth says, "Don't you ever tell me fucking no again."

His absolute strength. Not tempered by anything human. Just this pure crazy adrenalin strength. It's not being hurt that scares you. What scares you is what he is. What scares you is time. To think out how to handle him. Not having enough. You can't breathe. Your face goes hot. Blood throbs in the veins just under your jaw where he's clamped his hand. Time. Stay calm. He'll let go. Let him have his way and you'll have the time you need. Call the Mission Home. For what. For saying the real word instead of fuzz. None of his other seniors had to. Or if they did. If Hill knew what he was doing when he gave you Rudd.

He lets up his hold just enough to let you breathe.

"So you going to hit me?"

"I don't know."

"If you hit me in the mouth," you tell him, "I won't be able to play. Up to you."

His face relaxes. He drops his head in front of your face. You're looking at hair he uses some kind of tonic on. You can smell it. Brylcreem. Lucky

Tiger. You don't know. You're looking at scalp where the hair is thin on top. The start of going bald. He lets you go.

"Sorry," he says.

"We'll go later on," you tell him. "We've got some time to kill."

You grab dinner at the restaurant you found when you were out walking the neighborhood. You can barely eat. You catch a tram and ride into the still night skyline of the city till it wells around you and immerses you in its noise and light and motion. An hour to kill before the band kicks off. By that time you'll be clear of food enough to play. You come across a theater. Rudd wants to see the movie on the marquee. The Silence. A Bergman movie. You say okay. You still need time to think. The movie's black and white and stark and subtitled and somewhere in the middle when you walk in. You sit in the dark with Rudd on one side and Brother Shlagl's case in the empty seat on your other side. You try to pay attention to the movie. Two sisters, one sick and lonely, the other on the make with a young son in tow, have settled in a nowhere town in Eastern Europe somewhere. War's coming. The sister on the make goes out looking for love and finds herself a waiter. The sick and lonely sister is left alone with the son. You turn your head when you realize she's masturbating. Turn it again when a young couple in a theater start making out and maybe having sex. Turn it again where you're looking at a breast or ass or watching someone take a pee or just getting the suggestion that the sick and lonely sister may be trying something with the son. A tank goes past the window of a train.

The movie ends. You shouldn't be here. But you stick around and watch it from the start to where you first came in. You ignore the subtitles. You ignore Rudd. The constant undertow of something nasty going on makes you leave the theater dirty. The Zwolf Apostelkeller's just a short walk off. The band will be cooking by now. Deep into their second set. Maybe on break. You walk up the short tunnel to its side entrance and go in. Take the narrow stone stairs that make a hard left halfway down. The place is maybe half full. A mostly young after dinner crowd. Some you know from when you've played here. The band is getting together for the final set. The bass and guitar tuning up. Jimmy and Santos. The tenor softening up his reed. Eddie. The drummer sliding into the cockpit behind his drums and cymbals. Robbie. Nothing feels the same. Nothing feels real but the electric panic in your chest. Peter standing there. You let him know you're here. Take a small table. Peter announces you. Waves you up. Heads turn your way. Some of the customers clap. Some of the regulars call your name. And then you're taking Brother Shlagl's trumpet out, setting the case aside, slipping your mouthpiece in, hearing the pitch and setting the tuning slide, and Peter's counting down on Girl from Ipanema.

Waiting for your line you take a look across the room to make sure you weren't just seeing her. Wanting her to be there. To help you think this out. But there she is. At one of the larger tables with a mix of six or seven kids who, like her, look like college kids. The negro girl you thought you saw on your way to the stage. She startled you. You looked away too quick and scared. The table she shares with her friends is littered with mugs and glasses and ashtrays holding burning cigarettes. She's smoking too. The kids she's at the table with are white. The kinds of college kids who could have volunteered for Freedom Summer and gone knocking on Mississippi doors. As wild as the night has gone it astonished you at first to see her. But there she is. In the dim light the striking white of her teeth and eyes in the dark honey of her smooth face and bare shoulders. Looking back at you like you could have her after all. Looking while your line comes up and you lower your head, close your eyes, bring up your borrowed horn.

You ignore them. You keep your eyes closed or your face down so that all you see is the blurred rush of the floor at your feet. You're passing through. On your way to San Jose. Every solo takes the audience out of this boneyard basement in Vienna back across the ocean. Every solo brings them north out of San Jose again while Cissy rides with you in Yenchik's Ford, high up the switchbacks into the Sierras, high to where you're among the stars, where your solo cries out for her at how close they are, where you know that she'll be gone when the sunrise out across the desert sets fire to the line of the horizon. Every solo brings the crowd back home across the desert of Nevada, through all the desert towns, the endless highway that endlessly replenishes itself, while the man burns away next to you. Every solo lets the people at the tables say goodbye to her and wipe her cheeks in her pink church dress at the Salt Lake Airport. Every solo lets them read her letter in the early morning dark and lets them say goodbye to her for good. Every solo cries for her. Every solo cries for where this runaway night is going.

Somewhere during the set Ursi shows up. Peter has her stand in. Short hair the color of straw combed like a greaser's, the back of her neck pale, she does Here's that Rainy Day. She does Summertime. She does Ain't Misbehavin. For the last number you ask her if she knows Since I Fell for You. She does. You ask Peter if the band can play it. He says of course. And then while Ursi sings, you stand behind her, your head lowered and your eyes closed so instead of Ursi you can see the fiercely curled black hair pulled off the dark rose honey of her neck, so instead of Ursi you can hear her voice in the sunlight, and when she's done and turns around to you, your solo takes them out of this ancient basement again to the San Jose back yard where she lets you take her again, far away as you want, till dusk makes the light wind restless and the animals quietly start to cry to one another, as far away as you want because she trusts you to bring her home again. Cissy. Where you leave her now, safe with her family, for what you know will be the last time.

Tears blur your view of the floor and cut down your cheeks when you lower your trumpet. For being done with Cissy. For being scared of what could be ahead with Rudd. For something broken. Ursi comes in to run through the verse and chorus one last time. The band brings it in for a landing. Out in front of you the crowd starts clapping. And then keeps on clapping. You keep your face down and let the long applause take you back to the Indian they wheeled out of the blinding sunrise of the parking lot into the Moab hospital the morning you were there to bring your mother and baby Maggie home. The slow unbroken river of vomit out of his mouth onto his pillow where it amazed you how he could even breathe. You take your handkerchief out of your back pocket and wipe your face like it's just sweat. And then open and blow the spit valves into it. When it finally dies down, and you raise your face, you give Ursi a hug. She holds you for a minute. Whispers if you're okay. You whisper yes. You shake hands with Peter and the other guys. Put Brother Shlagl's horn back in its case. Then look for Rudd.

He's not where you left him. Where you find him, waving, grinning his big grin like he's welcoming passengers aboard a United flight, raises the hair off your neck and tenses up your shoulders. The negro girl and her mix of friends are turned your way. Faces come up when you weave through the tables toward theirs. You say thanks but feel the cold again of the troubling night wind. At the one vacant chair, the chair they've held for you, stands a full glass of red wine. Next to you, at the head of the table, Rudd has his own glass, half empty, in his raised hand.

CHAPTER 57

THE NIGHT KEEPS running away. Through hands whose fingers you can't close. Across from you sits a young white guy wearing a dirty gray turtleneck sweater with braids knit into it, slack around his thin neck, his uncombed dark brown hair cut long and ragged, his pale blank eyes set wide on opposite sides of a blunt nose, a ragged little patch of acne on each cheek, his lips like the nasty cut of a crooked scar when he closes them to suck smoke out of his cigarette. A gold pack of Benson and Hedges and a small box of wood matches sit next to his beer mug. From across the table, in the chair next to him, the negro girl smiles at you. Her bare shoulders and arms are thin. The long thin fingers of her hands play with the stem of her glass of white wine. The articulation of their bonework. A sleeveless top colored the baked salmon red of sandstone cuts deep into her chest to show the soft tops of her dark breasts. You remember Rudd on the trams you rode home from the Sudbahnhof and then into Vienna. The way he looked at girls and they looked back. You look at the negro girl to see what he's done to her. If he's done her yet. Nothing there. You glance at Rudd. He's got the look but has it aimed down the table. She could be a guy the way he looks past her.

"Great playing," one of the guys down the table says.

"Amazing," says another guy.

Both of them with accents. You turn their way. A couple of girls there too. One of them Rudd's target. Just from the way she exhales smoke, white like she never sucked it down into her lungs, and looks back in his direction from her hooded eyes.

"Thanks," you tell them.

"Who are you?" the negro girl says. Her dark face is so lean and polished it looks sculpted off the underlying bone of her forehead and cheeks and jaw. Her lips are full and lush when they bare her white teeth in a smile. Under the thinly drawn curves of her eyebrows her eyes are large, luminous, soft like a grazing animal's, the pupils dark. They echo the startling fullness of her lips and the soft lush warmth in her smile. Her hair is pulled back like a ballerina's off the high slope of her forehead. She speaks English but her accent is Austrian. She's from here.

"I'm Shake," you say.

"Jake?"

"No. Shhh. Shake. You?"

"Anna," she says, extending her long thin hand. You barely touch her fingertips to shake. "Short for Annalise." Then she says, "You play so beautiful. I was so moved."

"Thank you."

"You made me cry."

"I didn't mean to."

"Oh no. It was good crying."

You smile at her. Annalise. A smile you keep in place when you turn to Rudd.

"So what's going on?"

He breaks off his naked stare down the other end of the table and turns to you with his Fly United grin.

"You're one motherfucker of a player," he says. "Jesus Christ."

"Thanks. Now what's going on?"

"What you see."

"With the wine."

"We're just getting to know each other," he says. "A little wine helps. I got you one." He nudges the glass in front of you like you haven't seen it. "Here."

"No you didn't."

He keeps his grin in place. But there's that glitter in his eyes. Like this will go his way no matter what it takes.

"Yeah," he says. "I did."

"We can get sent home for that."

"Are you gonna tell?"

"Right now all I'm telling is you."

The grin goes soft. He wants to be your buddy now. The negro girl and turtleneck guy are watching. In your nostrils the smoke of his cigarette carries the sweet stink of burned perfume.

"Come on. Loosen up. Have some."

The way he talks is off. You didn't notice it at first. The inflection forced. The timing and tone of what he's saying wrong. Just off key. The expectation that you'll laugh. And there's his face. Every expression bigger and harder and louder than it needs to be. Like a foreigner who knows American English but doesn't know how to be American.

"That's okay," you say. "I'm not thirsty."

"Hey. Friends. My friend Shake doesn't want to join us."

"What? No wine?"

"Come, Shake. Have some! Drink with us!"

"Yes! We toast you!"

"Here's to you!"

You smile. Look down at the table.

"He says he's not thirsty!" Rudd says.

"Come on! Have some!"

"He's cherry!" Rudd says.

"What is cherry?"

"A virgin!"

"A virgin! Ho no!"

"No virgin can play like that!"

The ribbing goes back and forth along the table. No harm done. You look their way, smile, raise your hand. To buy time. To think this out.

"I don't drink," you tell them. "Thanks anyway."

You glance at Annalise. She's just watching. The trace of a smile looking to see where this will go.

"Pick up that glass," says Rudd, menacing again, holding his own glass up to show you how it's done. "Don't be a pussy."

You look at him. Then his glass. Then smile. "So I'm a pussy."

"Yeah. A pussy. Hey everybody! He's a pussy!"

"Pussy! Pussy! Pussy! Pussy!"

Voices around the table join in with his chant. When he's got them going on their own he downs what's left in his glass and slams it on the table crooked and hard enough to snap the stem. The bowl goes rolling off the side. Shatters on the stone floor. The chanting stops in a startled hush. A waiter hurries over with a mop and broom and dustpan. Rudd uses his Fly United grin to make a grand apology. Like the waiter understands. Like the waiter's his buddy. The waiter smiles, plays along, sweeps up, holds the dustpan for Rudd to drop the broken base into it, shakes his head still smiling like it's been a hoot to clean up Rudd's mess. He asks Rudd if he'd like another. Goes to fetch it. Rudd looks at you again. The menace back in his eyes while his grin tells you thanks for flying United.

"Now have a drink. Pussy."

But the guy across the table in the dirty braided turtleneck has your attention. He doesn't like you. Not because he thinks you're a pussy. Not because you're not thirsty. This deeper hostility. The way your playing made the negro girl cry. Not that she cried. Just that it was you instead of him.

"What's up?" you ask him.

"Your friend says you're a Mormon missionary."

You hear American English.

"Yes. So is he."

"Hey! You guys were great!" Rudd shouts, in German.

You turn and look. Along the far wall of the room, Peter and the band are leaving, headed for the stairs up to the side door with their instruments. They look at Rudd like they've heard the sour note too. "Thanks," says Peter. "See you next time, Shake."

"Maybe Thursday," you tell him.

The turtleneck guy is stubbing the butt of his Benson and Hedges out when you turn back. You smell crushed ash and the ruined perfume the cigarette is loaded with.

"So why don't you tell Anna here what you believe about blacks," he says.

"Blacks," you say.

"Yeah. Blacks. Or do you still call them negroes?"

"Who wants to know?"

"Why don't you tell this black chick here what you believe about negroes."

He picks up his mug. You can see teeth through the glass and the beer, see into the cavern of his mouth, when the scar of his thin lips opens for a swallow. He puts down his mug and lays his arm across Annalise's dark shoulders, his white hand on her dark skin, where his fingertips draw little circles, circles that shine, wet, from the condensation from his beer mug. Black veins of dirt under his fingernails. You see her wince as she reaches for the pack of cigarettes and box of matches.

"What I believe about negroes."

"Yeah. Tell her. Really make her cry."

"I'd rather make you cry."

He glances at your smile. Opens his mouth. You watch doubt flicker in his wet lips.

"The seed of Cain," he says. "Come on. Tell her she comes from Cain."

"You don't need to do this," you tell him.

He's still working on your smile. Not knowing which way to take it.

"Come on," he says. "Tell her why her skin's black."

His fingertips still draw circles on her shoulder. When she lights her cigarette she pulls back her shoulder to let him know. You watch the flare of the match put honey in the dark rose of her face and light up the way the skin between her eyebrows tightens into tiny lines like Cissy's did when something troubled her.

"Why don't you tell her," you say. "Since you seem to know."

"You're the missionary," he says. "You tell her. Tell her how her skin's a curse. That's how God punished her for being a chickenshit in some war in heaven."

Rudd picks up his fresh glass of wine. Yours stands full in front of you. You think of telling him what Novick said. How it wasn't God. How Brigham Young made it all up. But he's not here to have anything explained. You smile across the table with the easy calm your playing always leaves you with.

"Looks to me like God did her a favor." You look at her. "You're beautiful."

"Thank you," she says.

The turtleneck guy shoots her a glance, sees her smile, just as quick looks back at you.

"Tell her black men can't have your priesthood. Go on. Tell her."

"I don't know why they'd want my priesthood."

"God doesn't think they're responsible enough. Someday though. Isn't that it?"

You've been watching his eyes. One of them, his left one, goes just a little sideways when he talks. The other one keeps the hostile focus of its pale almost silver pupil on you.

"Keep going," you say.

"But the thing is, they'll still be black, right? Big lips? Flat noses? Frizzy hair? Still have that old curse?"

He looks at Annalise's now downcast head. Brings his hand off her shoulder to run his fingers across the hair at her temple. Without looking up she flinches away. Fire follows the nerves up your back and through your shoulders down your arms into your hands.

"Hey," says Rudd. "Relax. Let's just have a drink here."

You look the other way down the table. The other kids have fallen into conversations of their own. You look at the turtleneck guy. He's got his hand back on Annalise's shoulder. He checks your smile again. You can feel him want to get it off your face.

"Keep going," you say.

"How long have you had the priesthood?" he says. "Since you were fucking twelve years old. Right?"

"How'd you guess."

"You must've been some responsible little twelve year old."

"Guess I was."

It throws him, you not taking him on, makes him hesitate.

"So the thing is, once God says they can have the priesthood, they're as good as anyone else. Right?"

"Sounds like you had the same teacher I did."

"But they'll still have that old curse. They'll still be black."

"Go on."

"So the day comes where you give a black guy your priesthood. He starts a family. What color are his babies gonna be?"

"You don't know?"

"Think they're gonna be white?"

"What do you think?"

"Answer me."

"I just did."

"They're gonna be fucking black. Black as she is. Meaning the same old shit. You look at a black baby, you think here's another one that wasn't valiant. Another one that needed to be punished. That's always gonna be true, isn't it?"

Annalise pulls on her cigarette. The sudden red burn of the ash glows in the skin of her sculpted cheeks. She turns her head to exhale. You watch her glance at the dirty white hand on her shoulder.

"Pretty much," you say.

"So you can give 'em all the fucking priesthood you want. More than they can handle. It don't mean shit. They're still black. There's still a time when they were chickenshits."

"So they say."

"And they're gonna keep having baby chickenshits."

You just smile at him.

"Yeah," he finally says. "Here's what I understand. You're a sick motherfucking piece of shit for believing this crap. Trying to get other people to fucking believe it."

For a minute you don't say anything. Just watch his eyes skate down a couple of times to see what your smile's doing.

"You don't want to tell me what I believe."

It's what he was looking for.

"You're a racist. You think you're Miles Davis, but you're just a fucking racist."

CHAPTER 58

YOU LOOK ACROSS at Annalise. She's looking down, at her ciga-rette, the white stick between two long fingers, nails painted to match the sandstone color of her top. She was intent on looking nice. She came here planning to be treated nice. You look back at the guy in the turtleneck. He looks edgy. Like he could have gone too far for what he called you. Done something only a grownup could fix.

"You're right," you say. "I'm a racist missionary for a racist church."

His face goes slack. Recovers with a nasty smile and looks at Annalise.

"Hear that?" he says.

You watch her dodge his breath. Direct a lame smile at her cigarette.

"Take your hand off her shoulder," you say.

He looks back at you. Where they were stroking her skin his fingertips stop cold.

"What?"

"Take your hand off her shoulder."

"You serious?" he says.

"You don't know how serious."

He glances at her.

"She likes it."

"Did you think of washing your hands before you touched her?"

He closes his arm around her neck, extends his fingers, looks at them, leaves his hand draped just above her breast. You give him time to look back at you.

"You remember the last time you washed them?" you say.

"Up yours," he says.

"Or the last time you were hurt?"

"What?"

"Hey," says Rudd. "Relax. Have some wine."

"Yeah," the guy says. "Jesus."

Down the table the conversations go quiet. Rudd's got his Fly United grin only half there now, an afterthought, wondering, alert.

"You want me to have some wine?" you ask him.

"Just take it easy."

You reach for your glass. Slug it down. The sweet vinegar taste makes your face want to turn inside out. You set the glass in front of Rudd.

"You feel better now?" you say. "I'm not a pussy?"

"Take it easy."

"What I'll take is another one."

You turn back to the turtleneck guy.

"You really want to take your hand off her."

"I'll let her tell me that."

"I've seen her tell you three times now."

"Fuck you."

"You don't want to say that."

His eyes dart down for another quick look at your smile.

"Fuck you," he says again.

You look down the table again. Back at him. Push your chair back. Smiling like you like what's coming. Get up with a slow shake of your head like you can't believe he'd be this stupid. You've got one arm of your suit coat off when he lifts his arm off Annalise's shoulder and takes his hand back. Annalise sits up, her shoulders straight, an ancient weight off her back.

"Sorry," he says, his grin dirty. "I forgot she was your property."

The night you and Quigley were dragging State and you took a hammer away from a guy in the street and sank its claws into his crotch. Property. The way he'd been using the hammer to rake the side of a station wagon occupied by a young Mexican couple not bothering anyone. Property. The word sends the same ugly hungry electricity racing up your back, into your shoulders, down your arms into your hands. You look at the table to ride it out. Not this time. You slip your coat back on. Sit down and give the turtleneck guy an easy smile.

"You know a lot about my church," you say. "The race stuff, anyway. How come?"

"I studied it."

"In college? A religion class? Some class on race?"

"Just on my own."

"What else do you know?"

"About what?"

"Let's see. Remember that negro church in Birmingham that got bombed last year?"

He takes a minute.

"Lots of black churches are getting bombed."

"This is the big one. Where four little girls were killed."

"I heard about it."

"You know the name of the church?"

"Probably some Baptist church."

"Sixteenth Street Baptist Church."

"I remember it," says Annalise, and it kills you to have her look you in the face, the disturbed choiring of the lines in the smooth skin between her eyes. "So sad."

"Yes it was."

You turn back to the turtleneck guy.

"It's the church where the negro kids in the Children's Crusade would gather last summer to march through Birmingham. Remember that? The Children's Crusade?"

"I heard about it."

"You hear about the attack dogs? The fire hoses? The billy clubs? The arrests?"

The waiter brings your refill and goes to set it down in front of you. You take it from his hand and chug it down again. Feel it warm your stomach again.

"You hear how the jails were flooded with negro kids? How they didn't care? How they just kept coming till they swamped the town?"

"They sound very brave," Annalise says.

"Yes they were," you tell her, and turn to Rudd. "I'll take another glass."

"Maybe you need to take a breather," he says.

"Maybe you need to shut up."

You look around. Catch the waiter's eye, raise your glass, turn back to the guy in the turtleneck.

"You know whose church it was? Where those girls were killed?"

"I'm sure you'll tell me."

Through the calm you start to feel the wine. Quicker than beer. Different from the Boston Sloe Gin you and Quigley sometimes shared on State Street in the Hudson.

"Reverend Ralph Abernathy. Head of the Southern Christian Leadership Conference. Those girls were killed in the basement. They were right through the wall from the bomb."

"Terrible," Annalise says.

You look at her.

"It didn't damage the church much. It's a tough old church. Stone. But it went through the wall and took out those little girls."

"A shame."

You turn back to the turtleneck guy.

"Know what their names were?"

"Who."

"The girls who were blown apart that morning."

"Why should I."

You turn away from him to check out the others at the table. They sit there quiet looking back at you. You smile, shake your head, look at the turtleneck guy again.

"Why should you know their names?"

"Yeah. Why."

"Well, in case someone asks you, like I just did, it'd be nice to be able to tell them. Especially some negro girl you're looking to impress. She might think you actually care."

You turn to Annalise. The way you keep expecting Cissy.

"Addie Mae Collins," you tell her. "Cynthia Wesley. Carole Robertson. They were fourteen. The fourth one was Denise McNair. She was eleven."

She lowers her eyelids. You sit back to let the waiter set a fresh glass on the table. Hear Rudd order another one. Turn with a smile to the turtleneck guy again.

"You know what Freedom Summer is, right? Going on right now?"

He takes a minute again to look you over. Work out which way your smile's going.

"I've heard of it," he says. "Sure."

"Yeah, well, you've heard of it."

You turn to Annalise. Tell her what's going on in Mississippi. Negroes trying peacefully to register to vote. The retribution. Crosses burning. Churches and schools and cafes and houses firebombed.

"They're after that one right," you tell her. "To vote."

"Don't they have it already?"

"The whites won't let them use it."

"Why?"

"They know negroes would vote for their own people. Take their power away."

You watch her take her last sip of wine. Tilt back her head, turn the glass up, expose the tendons and arteries just under the skin of her long neck. The waiter brings two more glasses of red. You point to Annalise's glass. The turtleneck guy lifts his empty mug and hands it to the waiter.

"Know what a Freedom School is?" you ask him.

"I get what you're doing," he says.

"How about the SNCC? Heard of that too?"

"I'm done with this crap."

"Freedom Riders? Bob Moses?"

"Hey," you hear Rudd say. "Take it easy."

It's meant for you. You turn his way. His leering smile edged with doubt. And you were scared of him. You turn to Annalise.

"Student Nonviolent Coordinating Committee. They run most of the civil rights show across the South."

You turn back to the turtleneck guy.

"Know what their logo is?"

"Tell me."

You turn to Annalise again. Reach your hand across the table.

"Here. Just shake my hand. It's clean."

She puts hers out. You hold the handshake still. Skin against skin. Color on color. Cissy floods your blurred head. The still warm ghost of her hand. Your breath catches.

"That's it," you say to the turtleneck guy.

"Shaking hands," he says. "Bullshit."

"Yeah. A handshake." You turn her hand up, and then yours, and then level them again. "Not just any handshake. A black hand and a white hand. To show unity. You ever shake a negro girl's hand before you wash it? Before you think it's okay to touch her shoulder?"

"You know something? Fuck you."

You let Annalise draw her hand back.

"You know something? You really don't give a damn about any of this."

"Hey," says Rudd. "You need to let up."

"You need to stay out of this."

"That an order?"

You stay on the turtleneck guy.

"How come you're here?" you say.

"Here? To watch you act like a fucking asshole."

"Does your momma know you're here?"

"How come you're here?" he says.

"I've got gigs to play. Doors to knock on. People to baptize. Jerks like you to educate on what's happening back home. How about you?"

"None of your fucking business."

"Which means you're not doing squat. So let me guess. You sit around college cafeterias all afternoon, sipping cold coffee with a couple of other losers, bullshitting each other."

You give the waiter time to spread your drinks around. The other end of the table is quiet. Every face turned your way.

"The defender of the negro race when you don't know crap. Acting like you care."

"At least I'm not a fucking racist."

"Putting your dirty hand on a negro girl without asking her? Throwing around profanities without thinking it may bother her? That's not racist?"

"You're the racist."

"And you're a cheap fake. Using me to try to score with what you call a black chick. That's what I call a racist."

The turtleneck guy just stares at you. And then gets up and kicks his chair back.

"I'm outa here. Fuck you all."

Annalise watches him go.

"He never touched his beer," she says.

"He touched you. That was enough."

"Thank you."

You slug down your wine again. How many glasses. You don't know. Just that the calm you had after leaving your heart on the stage is gone. You look at Rudd. This time he gives you his Fly United grin and signals the waiter again.

"I'm done," you tell him.

The waiter comes and tells you it's closing time.

"I have to go too," says Annalise.

You settle up, grab your trumpet, head back up the staircase. The kids from the other end of the table follow. You don't remember it moving this way, the steps playing hide and seek with your feet, when you first came in. You don't remember coming in.

"This escalator's going sideways," you say.

And then you can't stop laughing. Annalise laughs too. Takes your trumpet case for you. Outside again, on the sidewalk, she hands it back. You look down to see what she's doing before you recognize and take it. You watch the other kids from the table walk away in both directions in the dark and become the strangers they were to start with. Rudd stands waiting at the curb.

"Shouldn't they wait for you?"

"I came alone," she says.

"That guy?"

"He's a friend of a friend from school."

"Be careful."

"I know. Don't worry." She gives you her shining smile. You have to stop yourself from thinking you can kiss her.

"Good."

How stupid it sounds to say it so loud. Almost shout it.

"You be careful," she says. "You've had much to drink. Thank you again."

"You're welcome."

"Maybe I'll hear you play again sometime."

"I'm usually around."

"Gute Nacht."

"Gute Nacht."

CHAPTER 59

SHE LEAVES. You watch her go. How thin she is. In the warm early August dark of the street how quick she is to vanish. A phantom. She leaves you wild. Cissy walking back into the ghost of your dream of her. You watch the place where you lost sight of her. It keeps shifting. Blurring. You keep losing balance to some stumbling swaying dance on a moving sidewalk. You look around, try to place yourself among the buildings, start to laugh again. In this hilarious and desperate relief you suddenly know. A street or two off Stephansplatz and the massive cathedral where you confessed and were forgiven for jacking off in the bathhouse. How many times since then. You laugh louder. In the heart of Vienna. Inside the Ring. Drunk. Drunk your first night as a senior. Hitched to this crazy junior. Approaching cars have four headlights. You can't tell which are real and which are ghost.

"You okay?"

You look at Rudd, standing there not knowing where he is, where to go from here, how to get home. That's your job.

"Just dandy!"

"I like the way you took apart that fucking asshole."

Fucking asshole. Two words you didn't think you'd hear till you were home again. You stare at his crazy grin and ride out this wave of hysterical anguish at the sudden sober memory of Cissy's face.

"No. He may be an asshole but he's right."

"What?"

"We're racists."

"The fuck you say."

"Not like Mississippi. We got this little story that makes it all official."

"You really believe that shit?"

"We're supposed to!"

"You're drunk."

"You know how cruel that story is? You ever wonder?"

"Take it easy."

"Know what negroes were doing in the pre-existence? They weren't sitting on some fence while we were fighting some stupid war! They were playing jazz! Blues!"

Rudd's crazy grin goes slack. Fades to a hesitant shadow of a smile. You start laughing again.

"Fly United!"

Jazz and blues. That's right. You're drunk. You don't give a damn. And that's how you know how drunk you are. You can fly. Fly like a trumpet line. Fly right off the street up to a rooftop and perch there like a gargoyle with your stone frog devil face looking out of your bugout eyes down on the street. Spread your lizard wings and fly high above the city laughing. Because you don't give a damn about not knowing how to fly. You can fly. You lay the case on the sidewalk and stumble into it before you take your borrowed trumpet out. Your devil horn. And then you have to wait till you've stopped laughing before you fit the mouthpiece in. Gershwin. Can't Help Lovin Dat Man. Fish gotta swim. The line comes clear. Rudd grins again. You could care less. Birds gotta fly. The notes ring off the hard stone walls of buildings and their windows and the cobblestone street. I gotta love one man till I die. You could give a damn. Cissy. Tell me he's lazy. Rudd wants to know if you're having fun. Tell me I'm crazy maybe I know. You close your eyes. Cissy. Can't help lovin dat man of mine. You veer away from the chorus and go straight full speed into Summertime. Your foot keeping Robbie's easy beat. You could care less. Five or six bars in you can't keep up. The sound starts to gutter and fall apart. You fight it for another bar or two but the song doesn't want you making fun of it. That's fine. You could give a damn. Rudd says let's go. You start laughing. You try to jam the trumpet into the case. Laugh like a tickled coyote, stumbling backward, when you figure out you need to take out the mouthpiece first. You stab it into its velvet hole and fit the horn in its cradle and snap the case shut. You could care less. You can fly. You stand up and have to take two steps back and one to the side and then one forward to stay on your feet and keep from pitching into Rudd.

"You sure you're okay?" he says.

"You already asked me! Look at you!"

And then you're laughing as his grin fades again to an amused smile. Like he's watching a monkey jack off in its cage at Hogle Zoo.

"Who needs United!" you say. "I can fly on my own!"

"You know where we are?"

"Yeah! That's Tulsa down there on the right!"

"You're fucking nuts."

"And you're cute!"

And then you're off and laughing again.

"So where are we?" says Rudd.

"Right where we are!"

"You know the way home?"

"I don't want to go home!"

"I'm just asking if you know the way."

You lose patience. Get hold of yourself.

"Stephansdom's around the corner. Up a couple of streets. That good enough?"

"What's that?"

"The mother cathedral of Austria."

"You can get us home from there?"

"There's a tram right there. I need to walk first. Holy crap I'm drunk."

The hookers are out. You cross Rotenturmstrasse and walk some of the side streets. Come back to Rotenturm and hang a right toward the cathedral. The hookers come out of the shadows smiling. They come off the walls of the buildings and the windows of the shops they lean against. Others stand back and watch you try to keep your feet in front of you. Some look at your trumpet case. Maybe they heard you. Heard that steel sound glide and dive and soar fast and clean and loud through the stone canyons of the buildings. They weren't that far away. You could care less. You could take it out and play it here too. Take requests. Eins Zwei Polizei. Lili Marlene. This close to the wine you drank you'd be blowing red spit into Brother Shlagl's trumpet. You already have. You don't care. You can fly. Back on Rotenturm there's hardly any traffic. A new white Thunderbird with the light of the street flowing like oil and colored water along its bodywork rolls up along the curb. One of the big fat newer ones. Big enough for back seats. You could give a shit. The passenger signals you and Rudd over. Sunglasses. What you can see of his dark-skinned face looks out of the thick black nest of his hair and beard and almost fills the open window. Not negro. Arab. Turkish maybe. You don't know. You've seen guys like him at jazz clubs listening. Looking around. Rudd steps up and leans down. You stand back and wait. The guy takes off his sunglasses. Grins and leaves you staring at his teeth. A couple of words and he's out of English. Starts using his hands. But he speaks a language it looks like Rudd knows.

"They want a couple of hookers," Rudd steps back and says. "They need help."

"From us?"

"Yeah. They can't get any to go with them."

"How come?"

"How come? Look at them. Fucking gorillas."

"What are we supposed to do?"

"Get in back. Go scouting. Talk a couple of hookers into it. That okay?"

Hookers for Turks. How this night could get more nuts than knowing you can fly and not get hurt. You could crap your raven crap on Rudd's head.

"Sure. How about you?"

"Yeah." Rudd takes another look. With his sunglasses on again, except for his nose, the passenger loses what's left of his face. Rudd shows him his Fly United grin.

"I guess."

The passenger gets out, pulls his backrest forward, and you shove your trumpet case inside and crawl in after it. Take a look at the driver. Tell him hi. Same kind of guy. Sunglasses too. He reaches his hand back. It feels plump under its coarse skin. Rudd comes in behind you. The backrest comes back. You feel trapped. And then you're cruising. The passenger points them out. The driver pulls over. Rudd puts his elbow and face out the back window and beckons them to the curb. In the dark behind him you're staring. While your head reels, while you try to hold things still, you watch them smile. Watch them listen to Rudd. Watch them lean down to take a look at you and the guys up front. Watch them stand back, stop smiling, shake their head. The mood in the Thunderbird, the guy mood, looking to get laid, goes quiet and defeated. Soon you're dropped off, saying goodbye, wishing them luck they won't have, back on the sidewalk again. The Thunderbird pulls off. You look around. Still in the neighborhood. Stephansdom close by somewhere. A couple of streets away.

"What's going on?" you say.

"They all said no," says Rudd. "They said they'd go with us but not with them. I told them they were loaded. They'd pay anything. They still said no."

"That's nuts."

"Fuck, man," says Rudd. "Now I want a piece."

You've felt it too. The nearness of the possibility. Smiling hookers saying they'd take their clothes off for Rudd and you. Just ask. Just for money. The warm rousing itch of the possibility that comes to life in your crotch and crawls up your back into your shoulders.

"So you're saying what."

"I gotta find one," he says.

And then you're heading back toward Rotenturm. You turn the corner. One steps forward off the lighted picture window of a shoe and purse shop. In the cut of light she's ordinary looking. A long face and a mane of brown hair. Bare arms and legs. A bare face. The rest of her bare if you want it. Rudd starts talking to her. You step away. This time her smile doesn't go away till he turns his back on her to come talk to you.

"I don't know," he says.

Things moving too fast to be forgiven for.

"What?"

"I've never paid for it."

"First time for everything."

"Yeah. I'm not sure. Maybe we could find a couple of girls."

"Everything's closed. Everyone's gone home."

"I don't even think I've got enough."

"Why? How much does she want?"

He tells you.

"Schillings?"

"What'd you think? Groschens?"

"How much you got?"

He takes out his wallet, opens it, thumbs through the Austrian bills.

"Not enough."

And then you're setting down the case, pulling your wallet out, stepping into the light of the big window, counting out bills for Rudd. Just enough left to pay your own way.

"I got it."

"I don't know."

"Yeah you do."

"I've never had to pay for it."

"You started this. You're gonna finish it."

"Don't tell me what to do," he says.

You look at him. Feel like laughing but know how it would go off on its own, this frog faced gargoyle with its stone fangs, this high screeching bird, this insane hyena, the string to a kite too big and high for you to hold as it burns through your fingers.

"I'm your senior. I can tell you anything."

He looks at you. The bills in your hand. Takes them.

"Okay," he says.

"What about me?"

"Let me talk to her."

The friend she says she has, around the corner a block up on a street called Graben, is small with chopped blond hair. In the blue light of a shop window there are bruises on her young face. Down the street stands a massive statue of tangled human beings who look like they're climbing one another reaching for the sky. You remember it. Morgan showed it to you. The Pestsaule. The Plague Column. Built as a memorial to victims of the plague. You walk past the door of a club called Chattanooga. A place you've played. Suddenly, for an instant, you're sober. Scared. You turn your head toward the street to keep from being seen. A real girl. A stranger. Things are moving too fast again. The highway rushing into the headlights and then under the floor and into the dark behind you. But this is where you want to go. And things have moved too fast for you to know your way back home from here.

And then the four of you are just two couples on the sidewalk, walking with purpose down Graben and around a corner into a street so narrow it feels more like an alley. She asks you what's in the case. When you tell her trumpet she wants to know what you play. When you tell her jazz she looks interested. You're asking her not to hurt you. She keeps telling you she won't. In the bright fast eager rush of the highway in the headlights of being drunk you want to know about her. In the blood-colored wine in its racing mix with blood through your veins there are things you want to know before you see the rest of her and do her. What she has for breakfast. What the bruises are. Her favorite song. If she's from Vienna. She walks with her hand in the crook of your arm like some date to the fair. You keep your arm crooked to let her know she can count on you. You're about to do her and you keep your arm crooked for her. If she bowls or skis or ice skates or plays Ping Pong. Your head sings. Your head races. Your head flies. What her name is.

"Rosa," she says. "You?"

"Fred."

Rosa and Fred. Down the alley the only light is a sign over the entrance of a building just ahead of you. Hotel Rabe. You follow Rudd and his hooker into a lobby where everything is painted this gleaming red. The paint so shiny it looks wet. The hookers take keys from a paunchy old balding guy behind the blood red counter. He looks like he's seen this a million times. The four of you go single file up a narrow stairwell down a narrow hall where you and Rudd split through two adjacent doors. The room is barely big enough for a cot, a nightstand, a washbasin on the far wall, and a chrome and naugahyde kitchen chair for your clothes. The light from the small lamp on the nightstand is dull red. You remember what your mother called the lamp the lady at the Indigo gave you. The lamp of a whore. Rosa holds her hand out for her money. You count it out. She puts it in her bag. Slips out of her clothes before you get your suit coat off. Sits naked on the edge of the cot in the dull red light that illuminates her to watch you undress. You step it up. Fumble with your buttons and shoelaces. Stumble and lurch out of your shoes and pants. She cries out when you get to your garments.

"Oooh! What are those?"

"Just underwear," you tell her. Then, giddy again with hilarity and fear, you say, "It's a new American style."

"You're taking them off."

"I know."

You pull the garments off your shoulders glad to be in the dark enough to where she doesn't see the angled buttonholes of the symbols. Enough to where she can't see the way you're shivering.

"I'm not doing anything strange," she says, wary, at the edge of pissed off.

"I don't know anything strange."

You stumble again stepping out of them. Toss them into a dark back corner to let her know how throwaway they are. Pull off your socks. Head for the cot with your pubic hair stained by the light of the lamp like fuzz the color of rust.

CHAPTER 60

TOO FAST TO be forgiven. Too drunk still, too new at this, to know what she expects. You let her show you what to do. Lie on your back while her unfamiliar hand strokes you till you're hard. She rips open a packet and rolls your first rubber down the length of your boner. Motions you aside to give her room to lie down. Lets you know to get on top of her. You give her the length of your weight but keep some on your elbows. Feel her small breasts under your chest. In the dull light see through the makeup on her shoulders to more bruises. Under the weight of your legs she wrestles her own legs open. Yours fall between them. Her hands are on your back.

Too drunk still to know. Exhausted now, like you've been running, trying to catch up, you lie there, wanting to slow it down, wanting to rest, wanting to lie with her, sleep for a while, hold her still and kiss her. She pushes your face aside. You don't know why. Feel the sting of shame. If kissing is something strange. Against some rule. Worse than having you inside her. You don't know. Her hips are thin when she thrusts them up against your groin. The ridge of bone between her thighs is sharp. She pulls and pushes at your shoulders. Bewegen! Bewegen! Move! Move! A sharp shrill voice like a knife in your ear. You get it. This won't be over till you've done her. Till she's earned what you gave her. So you pay attention. Focus. Remember Katy the night before your farewell when she had you smell her perfumed hair. Beneath you she reaches down and brings your boner back. Too drunk still to know where it goes, you keep stabbing, till she finally reaches under you, slams it home, starts thrusting her hips again. The bone between her thighs bites into you. Bewegen! Bewegen! Move! Move! The rubber doesn't let you feel much. Sensation is elusive. You feel like you're doing air. But you stay focused. You've got to bring this home. Smell her hair. Move! Move! You move on from Katy. Run through memories. Try to surprise yourself with other girls. She needs to get this done. She needs to get back on the street. You think your way through it. A naked girl under you. You inside her. Think it through. Think of faking it. But you finally feel it coming and bring it to the point of no return and let it go. Pain in there with pleasure.

Too fast to be forgiven. She rolls you off onto your back. Strips off the rubber. The sting of some hair comes with it. She gets up, goes on bare feet with her thin butt to the back of the room, tosses the rubber in a wastebasket, slings her left leg over the washbasin, turns the faucet on, splashes water up against her crotch, takes a towel, rubs herself dry. Hurries to her clothes. While she dresses you start to hear hollering from the next room. Rudd. "Motherfucker! I've never fucking paid for it! God damn motherfucker!" His fist hits the wall. Then a piece of furniture. The crash and groan of a cot. Tearing up the room. For the first time this lost and crazy night you're scared. The next door over opens. Sharp quick heels run down the hall, pick their way down the stairs, hurry down the sidewalk out the window. "Motherfucker! Jesus Christ! I can't believe it! Son of a bitch!" Your girl cracks the door out to the hallway.

"Auf wiedersehen, Fred."

"Auf wiedersehen, Rosa."

She doesn't turn her head to you. Just looks both ways and takes off too. Rudd's still in his room, hollering, moaning, throwing things around. You shut the door, find your garments, get dressed, stuff your tie in a pocket of your suit coat. The next door slams. Rudd storms past outside. "Motherfucker! God damn motherfucker!" The hallway shrieking with his voice. You hope he keeps going. Out of your life. Out of what you've done. But he comes back. Bangs his fist on your door.

"You still there?"

"Yeah. Just a minute."

"I fucking paid for it! What the fuck!"

The schillings you gave him. Tell him at least he got a discount. Know he'd come crashing through the door if you did.

"I heard you!"

You grab Brother Shlagl's trumpet case. Open the door. He's right across the hall. He looks nuts with agony and rage. You follow him down the stairs and through the lobby where the paunchy old clerk comes off his stool when he sees you. Then you're outside. You start off down the street.

"You know how to get us home from here?"

You look at him. This brute crazy torment in his face.

"I'll figure it out," you say.

He stops. Looks around. His face goes calm and grim and cold.

"I'll be right back."

From down the street you watch him go back and then into the hotel. Wait shivering in the naked cold of the warm August night. More sober now than drunk. He comes running back out and down the street toward you.

"Let's go!"

You run along with him, your trumpet case under your arm, across three or four streets, around three or four corners, before he stops.

"I bashed his fucking face in."

"Who?"

"That desk clerk."

You remember how gray and tired of life he looked.

"That old guy?"

Rudd's breathing harsh. His eyes points of black glitter. His face rock hard insane. Shiny with sweat. He takes a glance back up the street.

"That son of a motherfucking bitch. I showed him. Making me pay for it. He won't be handing out keys for a while." He stops, drops his head, looks at his fists. "Fucked up my knuckles."

He looks back up. Anguish in his face.

"I've never paid for it in my fucking life. You understand that? I promised myself I'd never fucking pay for it. That god damn cocksucker."

PART 8

HIDE FROM THE LIGHTS

THERE WAS a time, starting at twelve, where you could be the bearer of a bread or water tray to the rows of the congregation assigned to you. Send it on its way along the row to the other end where another deacon waited for it to travel from hand to hand and reach him. Proud once your tray was on its way to step a row forward or back and wait for the tray coming toward you from the other aisle. Stand proud and straight as a Boy Scout while you waited. Hope and sometimes negotiate with another deacon to get the row where Susan Lake was sitting. Keep watch on the paper cup she took and marked with lipstick so that when it got to you it was like she'd sent you a secret kiss.

A time, starting at fourteen, where you could stand with the rank of teacher as an usher at the door into the chapel to welcome your neighbors to church and return the grins of the men and the smiles of the women and sometimes shake their hand and always say their name. Where you could sit in the living room of the Soderstroms while Sister Soderstrom cried about how broke her family was and how far behind they were on tithing.

A time starting at sixteen where you could stand as a priest at the sacrament table and tear slices of Wonder Bread to pieces while your mother played the sacrament song. Kneel on the stool behind the table and read the blessing into a microphone and hear your voice come down as big as God's from the speakers in the sky of the high ceiling.

And a time, starting at nineteen, where you had the power as an elder to baptize people by immersion for the remission of their sins. The power, if they were male and anything but negro, to lay your hands on their heads and ordain them into the priesthood.

You wake up sick. Enough to die. Pain like a hammer pounding nails through your forehead. A knife blade up the back of your neck into your head. Your stomach like it wants to come up your throat and turn you inside out. On a hard cot, under the damp skin of a limp sheet in the dawn of your first morning in this room, this room you don't recognize at first, this nowhere room, you look up at the stained gray ceiling. In the heat that saturates the air you shiver in the sweat of your garments. Your mouth feels caked. Like the last thing you ate was mud. Your teeth feel coated with grime. Slow, like if you move too fast you'll give yourself away, you peel back the sheet, unsnarl your feet from its damp hold, sit on the board hard edge of the cot. Under your feet you feel the hard stubble of the worn rug. You ball up and hold yourself while your head pounds and your body shivers and your stomach wants to puke you inside out. This stink of wine and sweat and smoke and perfume and the makeup she hid her bruises with. In your crotch your own scabbed jizz and the crusted residue of whatever came from her.

Panic makes your heart pound and sends a bolt of lightning that electrifies the pain in your head. Your horn. But there it stands. Its case on end just inside the door. You don't remember carrying it around last night. But you did. Through everything. It makes you want to puke again.

You don't dare brush your teeth. Wash your hands. Wipe down your face and chest and crotch and everything else that touched her. You have to wear what you did last night. Let it come in the dirty waves of its details and wash around you. Blast away every other memory you try to hide behind. Every memory that was good yesterday. Everyone you know. Their names make you want to puke again for everything they hoped for. Close your eyes and their faces blind you. Now, your eyes on the wall above the empty unmade cot across the room, wide open so you won't see anything but the pattern of tiny flowers on the dingy wallpaper, your mouth comes open too, wide open, because you need to howl, howl everything out, howl out what you did. Nothing comes. Just your mouth open, stretched wide like you can't catch breath, like you'll drown if you can't howl. Nothing comes. God doesn't want to hear it. It belongs trapped inside you. You finally hear this moaning whimper, this shivering moaning whimper for the way you've broken everything, for how you sit here now where everything you were was lost last night.

You called him Fred.

In this place. In this room with people in all the rooms around you. These rooms with their freight of old and scared and defeated people hoping for death under the iron sky and flaming rain of the Nazis and their bombers. You know them. You've knocked on the doors of buildings like this one. Their lives no more than the rooms they never leave but only keep their mute watch from. You are what they are now. If they heard you howl they'd start to howl along with you. Howl out everything too. This howling chorus of the dying. This death howl out of this thick gray prison whose windows are barred with defeat and fear and the long slow wait for the howl to exhaust itself. You're one of them. This room is all you are. These nowhere walls that cage you.

Fred. The name she called you. You could have told her any name.

You stand up. You know without checking the other rooms that Rudd's gone. You're alone in this place that fits you now the way it would fit anyone. Alone in this place that doesn't care what you want to call yourself. You want to puke again. In the kitchen you pull out a chair. Its metal legs make tiny shrieks on the floor. Sunlight comes down the air shaft through the window and lays its blinding hard-edged blades across the white enamel of the table. The grimy drips and runs and chips in the white paint of the window frame stand out in bright inescapable relief. The ragged ring of dirt where a flowerpot once stood on the windowsill is tattooed into the white skin of the paint. The floor with most of its yellow skin worn through to its brown underskin is scarred with millions of scratches, millions of veins of dirt, left there by grit brought in on the soles of the shoes of the dead. Nothing can hide in this light. Nothing can be clean. Nothing can hope to be anything but what it is.

Sunlight on the skin of your white knee. So stark you can see where the hairs are worn away. From praying. From pretending God cared. Sunlight on the dingy leg of your garments worn in patches down to threads. It terrifies you to have them on. The way God could use them to punish you. Turn them to fire like the Stetson and suit of the faceless man in the passenger seat of Yenchik's Ford. Turn them to acid that burns your skin to slow white rising smoke. Make them a crawling second skin of ants. You reach for your shoulders to take down the sleeves. You touch them but your hands pull back afraid. Leave them on. Take them off. You don't know what's worse. Leave them on. Wear their stink. The stink you made of them. Their power gone. The shield of their symbols against the power of the Devil gone.

Fred. Like she cared.

Bent over. Shivering again. You know you can't talk to God. Can't tell him how sorry and scared you are. Your mother. She knew where you were headed when she called you those breathtaking names the night of your first date. Fucking beast. Rape artist. Even in the disguise of your Sunday clothes she knew. Your father too. Every time the door came up and his smoking winter headlights caught you with your trumpet in the back of the garage. When he wrote President Smith to tell him you needed watching he knew. Headed where you'd sit nameless in this nowhere kitchen and know what they saw ahead for you. The dark mystery always just out of reach in the back of your head. Now the mystery is there, glaring in the sunlight, the guts of the disemboweled steer they shot and slaughtered every Friday in La Sal.

The wicker basket on the table. How you came home yesterday from the dairy shop with rolls and milk and cheese for breakfast. How you put the rolls in the basket and then remembered the rat trap and put them in the fridge instead. The thought of having one. The choking taste of dust the instant you put your teeth to it.

How you came up with Fred.

Your mind runs looking for another place to hide. It takes the scent of the hard morning light off the kitchen table and follows some trail to other moments of sunlight this absolute. The blank anvil of a dusk sky on the Mojave Desert. You and Lieutenant Tanner on your knees on the blue steel desert floor in your army fatigues while he talks to God in a way you've never been talked about before. His hands on your shoulders. Yours on his. His head bowed. You watch his hair turn white and his tan face turn to chalk and the chalk start to crumble while he prays. The more he prays the more of his face breaks loose. White dust streaks the front of his fatigue shirt. Where they rest on your shoulders his fingers start to crumble too. You run your mind away again. It finds the backyard barbecue in San Jose where you sit across a picnic table and marvel at the rose honey skin where the sun plays its liquid light through the overhead leaves onto her face and shoulders and arms. It was never your business asking what her name was. But through the blush of her smile she tells you. While she does, the skin that is touched by sunlight on her face and shoulders and arms turns slowly white and bruised and the lush dark curls of her thick hair turn thin and limp and blond. Bewegen.

Fred. For the love of God.

Through the window, from across the airshaft, the haggling foreign voice of an old woman brings you back to where you are, on a chair in a kitchen you're renting with money your father sends. You rest your elbows on your knees. Your face in your hands. In this kitchen so far from home your mind goes back to yesterday. To a guy you remember before you told a prostitute his name was Fred. You watch him come down the steps of the Mission Home, down the grass-edged path to the gate, down the street of large established houses to the tram stop at the bottom of the hill. He's happy, light of foot, eager to where the suitcase and trumpet case he's carrying seem weightless. Under his worn blue suit, against his ribs where detectives carry holsters, he carries a pair of frayed cloth saddlebags that hang on straps from his shoulders, filled with a fresh supply of pamphlets. You watch him board the tram and pay his fare. You watch him do it again, on another tram, and then again, as he rides a relay of trams through the heart of Vienna and out the other side, the ugly outskirts side, where a gray armada of apartment blocks houses all the people he has to make sure don't go missing. It's bleak but you know what he's thinking. What he's charged with. This is his shot. His Elder Cannon shot. Nobody can go missing.

This guy you called Fred.

Yesterday he got off the tram and checked the index card he was holding. He walked the sidewalk looking for the address on the card. Yesterday he unpacked the Samsonite on one of the two cots in a shabby room whose mildewed smell he knew he could get used to. Yesterday he found the dairy shop and bought the rolls in the wicker basket along with some milk and cheese for breakfast today. Yesterday he took another relay of trams back into Vienna, to the Sudbahnhof, to pick up his first junior companion. He waited on the platform for an American guy named Rudd. Yesterday and every day before it was a lie. They had nothing to do with who you are today. Nothing. Who you are begins here in this savage morning light and the way it shows you this shabby place where you'll live. You want to cry but know you don't have the right to. Your throat aches the way you've kept it clenched around your need to cry.

In the bathroom you get on your knees in front of the toilet. Rest your elbows on the rim. Lower your face into the bowl. Open your mouth. Convulsions come up your throat and leave you retching. Pain thunders through your head. Drool comes off your lower lip and puddles like yellow oil on the water.

And finally you come to understand what God wants from you. Not your mother and father. They always knew better. But Karl and Molly and Roy and Maggie. Lieutenant Tanner. The Soderstroms. Your home congregation. All the people who believed in you. God wants to hear you ask him to forgive them. They were wrong to look up to you. But in being wrong they were innocent. You get on your knees at the side of your cot this time. You give God back your priesthood. The powers of the ranks you moved through with your buddies. Deacon. Teacher. Priest. Elder. All the keys you were trusted with. Surrender what you're not responsible enough to hold. A white negro. Surrender your baptism.

Maggie. You look up at her drawing on the wall above your cot. She can't see this. You scratch back the tape to take it off the wall, look at her one last time as she holds the hand of a stranger, then put it back in the family envelope for good.

And after that you're done. On your own. You and your borrowed horn. You and your big shot thing called jazz. He won't turn your garments to acid or a coat of ants or some infinitely burning fire. Their symbols won't mean anything more than the cloth they're made of. He'll let you live with what you've done. Live instead of sending you home in a coffin. Live to knock on doors. A quiet howl of anguish tries to rise up from your lungs again for what you've lost. For the guy you were yesterday. For that step he took on faith in his grandfather's shoes out onto air he thought might hold him. For how you've lost him.

A horn blowing missionary.

And then you can open your Samsonite and find the unopened bottle of aspirin you haven't needed till this morning. Wash your face. Open the mirrored door of the medicine cabinet to keep from looking at yourself. Comb your hair by feel. Brush your teeth. Put on your pants and shirt and tie and socks and shoes and the coat of your suit.

Chapter 62

Rudd shows up after nine. You're at the study table looking through the tracting book when you hear the key and watch the door across the room push open. From where he's standing, in the hallway in his cheap throwaway suit, the raw and dirty morning energy of the city comes off him. He steps inside and closes the door. You look down because looking at him, seeing the unpredictable menace flickering under the surface of his Fly United looks, what you did last night comes up into your throat in this naked chaotic need to howl again.

"Where've you been?" you say, looking up again.

"I left my watch at the hotel." He drops his key in a side pocket of his suit. "I just went back to get it."

That he knew the way. Kept track of the trams last night on the way home. Or just on instinct. Or asked people. The Hotel Rabe. On a side street somewhere off a street called Graben. A street called the German word for Ditch.

"You okay?" he says.

The question sounds insane.

"Get me up next time," you say.

"Yeah," he says, half smiling like you're kidding. "Well, I didn't get it."

"Your watch?"

"I couldn't get close to the place."

"How come?"

"There were cops everywhere. I acted like I was just walking by. I asked a cop what was going on."

"What was going on?"

"The desk clerk whose ass I kicked. They had to take him to the hospital." He puts his hands in his pockets. Looks down at his restless shoes. "They don't know if he'll make it."

"You mean live," you say.

"Yeah."

You stare at him. Remember the clerk. How decrepit he looked. It wouldn't have taken much.

"Tell me you're kidding."

"Why would I fucking be kidding."

You look down at the tracting book. Names crowded into columns on the small pages. Names as meaningless as the names of the dead you were baptized for when you were just a kid.

"I don't know what to do about my watch."

You look back up. In the dirty morning light of this place you got ready yesterday for what you hoped for, you watch Rudd rub his knuckles, push back his sleeve, feel his wrist for his missing watch. This guy off the street. This freak. This guy you can't make real. Where he came from. Why he's here. What made him think a mission was a good idea. If United was a lie. If a mission was a game. A way to get away from almost killing someone else. A place to hide. How he got through everything it took to come here. Acting slick. Playing humble. Conning everyone along the way. Even God. In the light that reaches him, standing there not knowing what to do about his watch, you can see him doing it. Ending up here. You just can't see why.

"Yeah," you say. "You do know what to do about it."

"Maybe go back after things have cooled off." Then he says, "He won't be there to remember me."

"No," you say. "That's not it."

"What? I should forget about it?"

"Is that a serious question?"

"I'd hate to fucking do that. Like I'm supposed to throw an Omega in on top of money for a sorry piece of ass."

What he did. How bad it was. His deviant strength. Nobody comes on a mission when they're twenty-eight unless they need to get away from something worse than bad.

"Listen to yourself," you say.

"What."

"You might have killed a guy. And you're worried about your watch."

"Maybe you're right."

"Did it have your name engraved on the back?"

"No."

"Then they can't track you down."

"I guess that's supposed to make me feel better."

The flicker of menace in his face again.

"Count your blessings," you say.

"Yeah," he says. "Fuck you."

"What if he dies?"

"I don't know."

"You don't know? You know what it's called?"

"Why?" he says. "You thinking of turning me in?"

Turning him in. You look around the room. Remember thinking you and your junior could paint and furnish it with the spirit of your calling. Your borrowed trumpet case stands on end in the far corner. Why you took that first glass. You still don't know. But this is it. All this room is. What you are now.

"You're an accomplice anyway," he says.

You see him leading everyone around the table in the chant that you're a pussy. See him naked in the next room on top of his naked whore, doing business, paying for it, while you hear your own whore whisper harsh into your ear. Bewegen!

"I wasn't there," you say, hearing the shiver, trying to cover it.

He goes guarded. "The fuck. You were outside waiting."

"I was? Did I forget something too? Leave something there?"

"You were with me all night."

"I had some wine with you and some kids. I stood in with the band. Then I came home. You told me the rest." Then you say, "I never took my watch off."

He thinks it over. And then his grin goes hard and his eyes glitter. You hold their black shine.

"I could fuck up your mission."

"Too late for that."

"I could fuck you up."

You look at him. Give him time to think through what he said.

"Don't touch my trumpet again," you say.

"I was kidding," he says.

"Don't touch it again."

"You said it wasn't yours."

"You know what I mean."

You watch him pace toward the other end of the room where the sun from the window catches the top of the case. Stop for a minute. You get off your chair. But all he does is turn around and come pacing back.

"How will I know if I killed him?"

"It'll be in the papers."

"Maybe I don't want to know. I just want my watch back."

"We need to knock on some doors," you say.

"You had breakfast?" he says.

"There's a roll for you."

"Where? I'm fucking starving."

The dairy shop yesterday. The guy you were, picking things out, buying food to share with your junior for your first breakfast. The howl comes up your throat again.

"In the fridge." Then you say, "There's milk and cheese."

"I'll need some money."

"I don't have enough left to give you."

You watch it cross his mind again, the sharp flash of a black knife through his eyes, the way he paid for it.

"I'll have my mom wire some."

"Get some breakfast. We need to get out there."

CHAPTER 63

OVER THE NEXT few days you strike a deal with God. Not out loud. He doesn't want your voice. Not face to face. He doesn't want your face. So it's a deal you strike alone. If you can work off what you've done. You've already given back your priesthood. What you offer him now is how hard you'll work if he'll let you stay. You've got seventeen months left. If that will be enough to work off a single night. Spare your family what they'd go through if you came home early with your unforgiven reason why. The deal you strike is desperate and cold. No hand to shake. No eyes to search for trust. A deal without a face. A faceless deal. A deal you strike in solitude in the terrifying silence of the dark.

And in the dark silence of your deal you see the sculpted face of the slender negro girl across the table. Annalise. See Cissy across the backyard table of a barbecue. See the circle of her Airborne uncles. Feel her mother's hands draw the wind out of your face. See her father's hand work the carburetor linkage of Yenchik's engine. See a boy shot off the handlebars of his brother's bike. A kid with his stomach in the teeth of a German Shepherd. A woman with her back to the force of a firehose trying to strip her of her Sunday dress and hat and purse and any dignity she hoped for. Four girls slaughtered by an explosion of fire and shattered rock. Jackson. Birmingham. Everything you've read. Every photograph that ever made you sick. Cissy. The dark giants of your negro heroes. In the deal you strike with God you relinquish all of them. Let them go. They don't want you anyway. Bob Moses doesn't want you in Mississippi. Cissy doesn't want you in her life.

And you try to let go of all the questions. If Brigham Young made everything about the negroes up. Made up the whole insane and awful doctrine, like Novick had to believe, so he wouldn't have to believe his jazz dad was the seed of Cain. And if God just let it stand. If he did nothing for the negroes of the South because he didn't care. If he looked at them like someone else's children. Looked at them like they were born to be whipped and clubbed and hosed and bombed and lynched and jailed and shot and hurt a thousand other ways. You try to let the questions go because you've begun to answer them with anger and distrust. Anger and distrust toward God that flares into resentment when you open a paper or magazine to another story or photograph. And resenting God is the last thing you can do. Because he holds your mission like the fragile glass ball of a Christmas ornament in his omnipotent hand. And so, in the deal you strike with God in the fearful dark of what you've done, you stop reading. Stop staying up to speed. Glance off in a stab of cold shame when you pass a newsstand and see a negro face or headline on an accidental cover.

They don't want you anyway.

From that first morning on you wake up to this new guy you've become. He's there when you open your eyes to the dull beige wallpaper with its pattern of small gray dingy flowers worn and scratched away in patches. This fugitive. This outlaw who harbors the lunatic hope that he'll be allowed to work off a crime for which the only remedy is excommunication and a ticket home. To his family. A family for whom nothing would ever be the same again.

Welcome home, Fred.

And this guy Rudd, this other new guy, is there too, in the cot against the wall across the room. From that first morning on you start living up to your end of the deal you struck blind. Check the tracting book for the last building hit by the elders who were here before you. Start with the next building. Climb the stairs to the airless barely breathable heat of the top floor, wipe the sweat off your forehead, start knocking on battered doors set deep in the thick walls of the dim damp decaying hallways where light barely travels from the few caged bulbs and most of the doors stand in shadow. Move from door to door, hallway down to hallway, to the ground floor, the short reprieve for outside air, one grim building to the next. Have Rudd record each reject in the tracting book. Keep going late into the evening. The next morning you're out again. Earlier this time. And early every morning after that.

You come to accept what you already know. There is no Fred. The guy you wake up to is you. The outlaw secret he carries hidden deep in the back of his head is yours. The dark and desperate intermingling ache of guilt and hope and fear that settles like a steady hunger in your stomach will be permanent.

Rudd tries to call his mother collect from a phone booth. When the second call goes unanswered he slams the receiver into its yoke and steps out of the booth.

"I just remembered. She's on a cruise."

"Where?"

"I don't fucking know. But I'm screwed."

"That makes two of us."

"How about your folks?"

You look for any sign in his questioning face for the way he already owes you.

"They can't afford it."

He looks off across the street. Then slaps his hand flat against the door of the booth so fast and hard the glass shivers.

"Shit."

For the week and a half or two till your check arrives, and a week or so later Rudd's, all you have between you is pocket change. Too broke for tram and train fare through Vienna up to Klosterneuburg. You use some change to call and tell Frau Goller you can't make it for dinner Sunday or to the Factory on Thursday. You tell the lie that you're too busy settling in. The lie leaves you staring at the phone box. The first of how many lies you'll probably have to tell and you tell it to a family who would never lie to you. Frau Goller tells you they'll miss you but she understands. Too broke for the European Cokes you'd have to order at the clubs you play. Not that Rudd would order Cokes anyway. So nights you stay home. The milk and cheese you bought your first time here are gone the first full day. From there you ration out what you can spend on food. For breakfast a roll without the usual luxury of milk and butter. For lunch an apple or banana you can eat while you go on tracting because it doesn't matter. Nobody's going to open a door to see a half gone piece of fruit in your hand. For supper spaghetti. Spaghetti without sauce. Spaghetti where you closely count and ration out a pile of thin gray sticks and then break and boil them in a saucepan every night. You use water to quell your unforgiving hunger.

Rudd doesn't mind tracting. How much of it you do. It surprises you at first. But then you catch on. How he sees it not as a calling but a job. A job he clocks out from at quitting time. The rest of the night is his. You remember how it went at Hiller. The rack of time cards you and the night mechanics used. The whack of the clock that stamped your card goodbye and made your life your own again. Back home at night, clocked out, after another supper of spaghetti, he's restless. The air in the place takes on this static carnal charge. He'll read a lesson plan or some brochure or magazine. Write a letter. Rap his fingers on the table. Get up and stalk the rooms. Open and close the fridge. Look out the window like someone caged. Sometimes use the bathroom and come out with the attitude. The bathhouse attitude. Light on his feet. Relaxed. A little breathless. A load off his mind for now. Ready for conversation. The animal charge out of the air. Even then you can feel the night still pull at him. The street still draw him. Like the bathroom was a warmup. A way to get in the spirit.

And then one night it happens. What you knew from the start was a matter of time. Just not this soon. Not even a week since your first night together.

"I'll be back."

Standing by the door in the uniform of his cheap suit. The skin of his face tensed and gleaming with this appetite he doesn't try to hide. The way it charges the air in the room to where it seems to tremble. In his black eyes and hard grin you can see the dare to tell him not to leave. You weren't planning to. You've broken the strictest most serious rule there is. Holding him to the lesser rules makes no sense. He'd laugh at you. You'd laugh at yourself.

"Where you going?" you say.

"Who knows."

"You're broke."

"Yeah?"

You forgot. He doesn't pay for what he's after.

"When will you be back?"

"It depends."

You don't ask on what. You know. On what he prowls the streets for. What he finds. The smell of some accidental woman on her own patrol for the same thing. A woman he can undress with his eyes while she helps him take his clothes off.

"Tonight?"

"That depends too."

On whether she has a place where he can spend the night. Or if they have to do it on the fly in some alley or basement stairwell. You save yourself the speech about never losing sight of your companion. It's not like you could stop him. And so you strike another silent deal. This time with Rudd. If he does a full day's work the night is his.

Every time he goes the questions he leaves behind are the same. If this is how he was with his earlier two seniors. If they knew what to do to stop him. If they told him they'd report him. Or if this is only how he is with you. Because one fugitive can't report another fugitive. Or if he saw in you the possibility that he could be like this with you. Saw it right away on the platform at the Sudbahnhof. Because you were a horn blowing missionary.

"Heading out again, huh."

Trying to keep the shiver of fear from coming up your throat into your voice.

"Yeah."

"Taking in an opera?"

"An opera?"

"Tosca. Madame Butterfly."

For a minute, standing at the door, his Fly United grin goes guarded.

"I guess you could call it that," he says.

"I guess you could."

"What about those clubs you play?"

You wait. For his grin to lose traction on the slick skin of his face.

"Some other time," you say.

"Thinking of reporting me?"

"The first thing on my list if you ever touch my horn again."

"I could do the same."

"I'm not talking about the Mission Home."

You watch his face go ugly. Then mean. Then form itself around a smile, a real one this time, one that makes your skin crawl, like you're buddies after all, like there's an understanding that he'd never touch your horn and you'd never report him to the cops. And then he's through the door and gone.

Chapter 64

TWO WEEKS into August your check arrives. Rudd's is still a week or so away. He takes another loan. You call Frau Goller to let her know you're settled in. She invites you up for Sunday. Mobile again, money in your pocket, food in your stomach, you can start playing the Factory again, get back to playing the clubs around Vienna. You're not sure you want to. Even less sure you can. But you know you need to. Too many people would ask too many questions if you up and quit. That Sunday you take Rudd to Klosterneuburg for dinner with your family. When you go through the gate of the Stift he stops.

"Jesus," he says. "What is this place?"

"A Catholic cloister. They call it the Stift."

"People live here?"

"They do. Right over here."

Alive with excitement, Edith pulls back the door, but her lively smile goes dead when she looks at Rudd. You open your arms to bring it back. She puts her arms around your waist but her hold is shy. She leads you up the stone stairs while Rudd follows. Frau Goller sets a meal of schweinsbraten and spaetzli on the table where Novick worked so fervently and hopelessly to persuade her of the truth. Now you sense his big ambling humble presence in the room. You shake Frau Goller's hand, and then Hubert's, and then introduce Rudd. You watch Frau Goller for some hesitation, some reluctance, some alarm for his grin when she shakes his hand. It doesn't show. Maybe from years of strictness as a teacher. Or because you've never seen her anything but kind. What shows just for a flicker in her smile is this awareness that you've brought something new into the house. A man when she expected someone more like you. Still more kid than man. If she senses some threat. If she sees on his reckless face the secret of what you did. Rudd shakes Hubert's hand. Then offers his hand to Edith.

"Edith, say hello to Herr Rudd," her mother says.

She finally extends her small hand.

"So you're Edith!" he says, in a voice too young for her, with a loud grin that startles her, shies her back a step. "I'm Danny!"

She slips her hand free. Comes and stands at your side. You take seats around the table. Edith the chair beside you. Rudd a chair across the table. At the head of the table Hubert slices the roast and doles the slices out to the plates he calls for. From the other end of the table Frau Goller passes around the side dishes. While you eat, while the taste of her home-cooked food explodes in your mouth, Frau Goller starts asking Rudd about himself. You remember her schoolteacher's attentiveness. Rudd tells her how he's from Wyoming. How he has a ranch there. How he was a flight engineer for United Airlines when he was called to Austria. She asks him what a flight engineer does. He tells her. Start and shut down the engines. Inspect the plane before takeoff and after landing. Do a pre-flight checklist. Write up a flight log afterward. Manage engine power. Calculate the fuel the flight will take. Test operate all systems. Hubert asks what kinds of systems. Rudd tells him. Fuel, cabin pressure, air conditioning, hydraulic and electrical equipment, overheat and fire protection, wing flaps, landing gear. He knows the German words for all of this. His accent is close to perfect. Like he could be sitting there in a Lufthansa uniform. He sounds almost too legitimate. Like someone who could have read up on it just for the cover of a job.

"Everything except fly the plane," says Hubert.

Rudd laughs. Then puts on a look of remorse. "I didn't mean to bore you."

"I didn't know there was such a position on a plane," Frau Goller says.

"That means we're doing our job," he says.

"Where does this engineer ride?" says Hubert.

"In the cockpit. Behind the pilots."

"What if something goes wrong?"

"We fix it in flight or wait till we're on the ground."

"It sounds very exciting," Frau Goller says.

"It actually gets old," he says.

"But you left a position like that to become a missionary."

"Yes."

You're thinking maybe what got old for him was a different stewardess every night. In the chair next to you, Edith concentrates on her spaetzli, seeing how many noodles she can stab with the tines of her fork at one time.

"You must have given up a good salary too."

"Compared to what I earn as a missionary, yes."

He starts laughing halfway through his joke with the expectation that the rest of you will join him. Frau Goller smiles.

"You have a very good accent, Herr Rudd," she says. "You speak German well."

"Thank you," he says.

You've seen her face change. Draw some distance back. Now it goes patient with the way he pretends to be bashful.

So," says Hubert, looking at you. "You're coming to the Factory again."

The secret you brought here. How you haven't touched the trumpet since that night on a downtown street before you paid a hooker to make you what you are now.

"How's it been going?" you say.

"People keep asking about you. When they'll see you. The musicians too. They're losing their patience."

"Is it open this Thursday?"

"Yes."

"We'll be there."

"The Return of Shake," says Hubert, grinning, raising his wine glass.

"Can I go, Papa?" Edith says. "Please?"

"Ask your mother," he says.

"Mama? Can I please go?"

Her mother smiles at her. "Yes. I'll take you. Don't forget that I'm going to the farm this Saturday for two weeks. And you have to get ready for school to start."

Edith claps her hands and squeals. Looks up at you with a smile so broad it pushes up into her cheeks and almost presses her eyes closed. Rudd watches from across the table.

"I'll play you a song," you tell Edith.

"What?"

"You choose."

She goes serious for a minute.

"Greensleeves?" she says.

"That's a song?"

She looks shocked. Then sees your smile, cries out, slugs you in the arm with a quick strike of her small fist.

"You taught it to me!"

"That's enough," her mother says.

"What's this factory?" says Rudd.

You let Hubert tell him. How it started as a place for you to practice. How people started coming. How he had a banner made. A big one, he says, spreading his arms, one that says The Factory. How other musicians started coming in to play. Local at first and then from Vienna. Friends of yours and then friends of theirs. How people bring food and come to dance. While he talks your stomach goes raw as if you haven't eaten in a week. The way nothing will be the way it was again. The way Hubert doesn't know. The way nobody around the table knows except the guy across from you.

"Every Thursday night?" Rudd says.

"Yes," Hubert tells him.

Rudd grins at you. "Famous, huh," he says, in English.

And then, Rudd out of the way except when he asks a rare question, the conversation turns to the rest of you. The family you've become. How you are. If you're eating well. How you like where you live. If Edith's excited about school starting. If Frau Goller's ready for classes to start again. If you've heard from Herr Novick. You tell them about his plan to stop for some jazz in New York City. Frau Goller reminds you of the invitation you and Novick accepted to join them for a weekend at the farm where they vacation in a place called Rohr im Gebirge.

"Come for the last weekend," she says. "You can ride with Hubert when he comes after work on Friday. We can all come home together Sunday night."

Later that afternoon Hubert drives you through town and down the hill to the train station in his big Opel. You ride up front. Rudd in back. Nobody talks much. You're thinking how it was when Novick was around. Wondering what Hubert's thinking.

"Nice family," says Rudd, pacing back and forth on the platform once Hubert drops you off. The skin up your back goes tight.

"They are."

"So they call you Shake," he says.

"Yeah?"

"Everyone else is Herr Somebody. Herr Novick. Herr me."

"It's their choice."

He doesn't talk again till you're standing aboard the train sharing a pole with him among passengers heading back into Vienna from a weekend in the country. Till he's looked them up and down and come up empty.

"I'll be going out when we get home," he says.

Herr Rudd. He made it through his first look inside your family. He ended up behaving. All you could have asked for.

"Suits me," you say.

Chapter 65

THAT SUNDAY NIGHT, after Rudd leaves, you're left with your promise to Hubert to bring your horn to the Factory on Thursday. You haven't touched it since that night on the street outside the Zwolf Apostelkeller. Since then, in its case in a corner of the living room, it's given life to an old dread, the dread your own horn made you feel the day you brought it home. A malevolent presence you had to hide in the garage to keep from bringing the combustible air your mother breathes to its kindling point. You don't know what to do. You look across the room at it and wonder if you even want to play. Or even can. What you'll sound like. You come back to what you promised Hubert. Finally pick it up. Leave and go looking for a place to practice away from the massive tombs of the buildings where you'd have to keep your playing low in order not to wake your neighbors out of dying in their sleep.

You walk the dark dead streets toward the yards and warehouses you know lie close to the highway. A tear in a wire fence lets you inside a darkened yard surrounded by the black ghosts of warehouses and buildings whose windows are jagged holes in the weak light that reaches their splintered glass from the few high lights of the yard. The highway runs with the dirty river hiss of the freeway that ran the high bank above the yard at Hiller. You wonder if there's a watchman. You look for the kind of office you had, the small shack that housed the two small rooms, light through the dusty windows. Under the moonlight the shadows of the machines in the yards look derelict, crippled, shot, the tires flat where they have tires. Piles of junk parts and rubble give off the smell of soot and oil and the residue of dead fuel. A scrap yard. You listen for guard dogs. Whistle loud. No bark in return. No chain being dragged across dirt. You set the case on the running board of a truck with its tires flat and its hood and engine gone, open the lid, take out the horn and set the mouthpiece. A siren winds up from somewhere in the city. You flinch, duck, look around. A real siren. Not the heehaw heehaw yap of a cop car. A siren that begins low and rises slow and penetrating to a long high whining howl and then comes down again. You wait it out. You hear it follow Rudd down a dark street to a hotel in whose red lobby the tired man behind the counter holds a shotgun in his face. He's wearing Rudd's watch. He's ready this time. Both barrels, At such close range, each barrel takes out one eye, and behind each eye the rest of Rudd's head.

And then, when the siren dies, it takes Rudd with it, leaves behind the dirty hiss of the highway and the low hum of the city's blended energy. You wait. Look at the horn in your hands. Remember back across two weeks to the last time you played it. The drunk and wild and desperate night on the street that marked the end of who you were and became the beginning of who you are now. The night you gave it to the Devil. Put the Devil in it. Devil horn. You put the mouthpiece to your lips not trusting what will happen. Let the sound go on its own. Feel the strength in the lift of its steel wings. Ride it out of the yard, out of the city, west across the ocean, then anywhere but home, some other American city where God and your father don't know where or who or what you are.

On Thursday, after two nights practice at the yard, you're back at the Factory. It hasn't changed. People are happy to see you. Shaking hands, saying hello, you look for signs in their eyes where they can tell you're not the guy you were. That you're the one who's changed. The only thing they notice is that Novick's gone and this other guy, this guy they look at twice when he flashes his Fly United grin, is with you. Musicians ask where you've been. Why they haven't seen you in the city clubs. Just busy, you tell them. You check in with the mostly young crowd out on the dock. The thin girl with chopped dark hair who lives upstairs uses the tough attitude in the pout of her red lips and the slow look sideways in her eyes to let you know you're back. She's wearing a short black skirt with short boots. Her legs are sheathed in long red stockings like the tights you've seen dancers wear. Edith and her mother are there in their usual spot for the last time before they head for the mountain farm where they'll vacation till school starts. Hubert takes the stage to welcome you back. You kick things off with Satin Doll. From the stage, waiting while you ride out someone else's solo, you keep an eye on Rudd. Watch him talk up people in the crowd. Take a bottle of Bluna and a sandwich from the food table. Slip out to the dock now and then. Try to talk to Gabriele, the big chesty farmgirl who flirts around all night but turns all business when the party's over, herds people out, cleans up, and always leaves alone. You don't want him passing out brochures. And so you don't tell him what Novick did.

On Friday you start to play the clubs again. Look for Rudd. Sometimes he's moving around, on the prowl, at the bar, a wine glass in his hand.

You never talk about that night. But you can feel the way you hold each other hostage. Sometimes he stays home through the night. You can feel it in the black air of the room in the cot against the other wall.

Sometimes you hear a muffled grunt when he reaches the fevered end of what you confessed to a Catholic priest. You can feel it in the morning that you've shared the air with him. Or he goes to bed but can't stay put. Waits till he thinks you're asleep while you lie there, turned to the wall, your eyes wide open, the night wind wailing through your head, sleepless yourself with the inconsolable awareness in the dark that everything you ever were is gone, that the only dimensions your life has left are the dimensions of these rooms, that the only thing you live for is your deal with God. Hear him dress in the dark and then turn the door lock from the hallway side. The night hunter. The werewolf. Some mornings his cot is empty and undisturbed and the dismal rooms of the place are yours till he shows back up in the throwaway uniform of his cheap suit, his eyes crazed, his grin dangerous, his attitude loud and swollen, the unshaved skin of his face gleaming like dirty chrome in the morning sunlight.

"I'll catch you later."

"Good luck out there."

From the open door his face goes hard.

"Good luck," he says.

"Yeah."

"What the fuck does good luck mean."

"Have a good flight," you tell him.

He lowers his guard. Slowly gives you his Fly United grin.

"I'll do that."

You make your own evenings when he's gone. Write letters home. Letters to your buddies on their missions. None of them knows the way you've crossed from where they are to where you are. In your letters you give them the face they know. The face that makes sense to them. Sometimes you practice the lesson dialogues you've memorized out loud, using two voices, American and Austrian, one to recite the questions, the other to recite the answers Bruder Braun can't help but give you back. Sometimes you listen to jazz on Novick's plastic radio. Sometimes you take a walk to let the cool night air cut fresh through the black smell that stains the air you pull in through your nostrils. Sometimes you think of practicing at home, soft, the tubes and valves familiar in your hands, the mute in, conscious of the people in the rooms around you waiting to finally die, afraid to bring them back from the distance they've gone toward death. And so keep your practice to the scrap yard. Sometimes you catch your face reflected on one or another window like the gaunt and haunted face you saw on the glass of the window in the bus on the ride with Jeff from the barbecue back to Fort Ord. Sometimes you think of Cissy. None of them know. Only God and Rudd know. And a bruised blond hooker whose whisper to move was sandpaper in your ear.

You like the mornings when you wake up finding you're alone. He'll be back. He knows his side of the deal. Back in time to clock in and go knocking on the prison doors of the colossal apartment blocks in whose hallways you work off your side of the deal with God. In the meantime you've got time alone. Not to think things over. Just time. Time alone to learn how to walk on the updraft of air for another day while the earth falls two thousand feet away beneath your shoes.

ONE NIGHT AT the Factory, taking a break before your second set, you step out onto the dock. People say hello. You know some of them by name. Helmut. Johann. Siegfried. Others have never come forward to tell you who they are. In the half dark, the light dim from the two caged security bulbs off the high back wall of the long dock, the flares of matches and the burning glow of inhaled cigarettes briefly give you their faces, make you think back to the miner kids from Magna who rode in the blind boat of their rocking Pontiac across the dark field with their ragtag instruments to come listen to you and learn how to play themselves through the chainlink fence at Hiller. Frank and Luke and Chaz and Billy. Maria and Jenny. Hands come out. You shake them. Some of them know the Mormon rule about smoking and drop and step on their cigarettes when you approach. The eyes of a girl are sly in the shine of light from the open door behind you. Smiles show teeth.

After a minute, left to yourself again, you look around. Almost out of range of the last light on the dock you can make out a couple. A familiar dread lights off its sick and bitter smoke in your stomach. Dark mostly against the night beyond the dock. Slivers of moonlight off the skin of their faces. The guy in a suit. Pressed together. Her short skirt up. Her hand the last place it should be. You walk through the people across the stretch of bare concrete. They don't look your way. You turn to the edge of the dock and stand there. The trains you've waited for, you stand there thinking, standing like this at the rim of a platform. Villach. Graz. Franz Josefs Bahnhof. The Sudbahnhof where you waited for this guy. Here he is again. The nerves down your arms ignite like fuses racing for your hands. You let them burn themselves out. Then turn their way.

"Hey there."

Soft but loud enough to be heard this close over the voices gathered back behind you around the open dock door. The girl jumps back. Tries to hide her face behind her tousled hair but you recognize her. The girl from upstairs. Her mouth looks puffed and numb and smeared. Shock flushes her face of any trace of what Rudd was making her feel. He gives you his phony buddy grin. The grin that could turn without moving, just by going hard and cold, from buddy to menace. You look away while Rudd puts things back where they belong and the girl turns her back to work her miniskirt and blouse and shimmy her panties and bra back into place. Remember the night you were afraid of him. The first night where he slammed you hard against the wall of some stone building to let you know what was what. Where he had the wine glass waiting and the negro girl across the table when you came off the small stage with your trumpet. You were more scared that night of being a senior companion than you were of Rudd. You know that now. Too late now to change what you can never change. He could have hurt you. But then you never much cared if you got hurt because you always knew you'd get through it and be okay. That night you didn't remember that. You step forward through the dark. He stays put. Her face down, raking her chopped brown hair with her fingers, the girl scurries past you, past the closed doors along the back of the dock toward the open door behind you. Rudd watches her go. Then looks at you. Above the chatter of the people smoking on the dock you can hear someone tuning a guitar.

"Don't ever do that again," he says, the shining white menace of his grin set hard in the dirty stone of his jaw.

"Leave," you say, casual, like this is all about the weather.

"What'd you say?"

"Leave."

"Leave?"

You look away again while he grabs his crotch and shakes his leg. Imagine him in his Fly United uniform. A blue tie and a white shirt with a United logo on the pocket and a blue United visor hat on his head. Sadness cuts through you, sharp and howling, a knife so razor sharp you don't topple apart but stand there like you're still one piece, like nothing happened, as long as you stand still. You smile, stand at the edge of the dock, inhale the night air sharp with the smell of cats. The way it never had to happen. You've never had it ambush you. This startling flight of a sheet of newspaper in the wind like a flapping bird touching down and taking off again across the path of your headlights. You could have let him hurt you. You could have said no and let him try to change your mind. You look back now and see it. The way too many rules for how to deal with your companion stood like crippled branches of scrub oak in the way of making it that simple. You look back at him.

"That's right," you say. "Leave."

"Come on. Leave?" He's got his arms extended, the palms of his hands out, his grin back to being your buddy again, his face like you can't be serious.

"That's it."

"Because of her?"

"You're still here."

The grin goes hard again. Like you're crazy to screw with him.

"The fuck you say."

You keep it casual. Like you're playing. From the vantage point of a solo. An easy solo whose notes you can feel move through your lips.

"Leave now. From here. The dock."

"You think you can tell me to leave."

"It's up to you whether you do or not."

"You know what I can do to you."

Beat your face. Make it so you can't play trumpet for a while. Maybe a long while. Tell the mission president about that night. And then there's what you could do to him. The story about a flight engineer and a hotel clerk. A story the Vienna Polizei would like to hear. A story that would bring their yowling little cars through cobblestone streets to the outskirts place you live.

"I know her folks," you say instead.

It stops him.

"You didn't ask her how old she was?" you say. "Didn't card her first?"

"Don't kid about shit like that."

"Let's go meet her folks."

"Her folks. Not bad."

"They're right inside. I'll introduce you."

"Fuck you."

"Or I can bring them out here," you say.

"Fuck you."

"Or you can leave. Head back to Vienna."

"Without you?"

"You know the way to the station."

Your name called. It's Hubert. You don't turn around.

"Don't think about coming back. Find yourself something else to do when I come up here."

"You're the senior."

"Just trying to keep you out of jail."

He jumps down onto the dirt. Cats leap out of his way and then start to follow him. Hubert's alone on the dock in the light of the open door. You can hear the bass player tuning up now. Licks on the piano. The sax running up and down a blues arpeggio. You watch Rudd go. Reach the gate and turn and look at you. Then put his middle finger up.

"He had to go," you tell Hubert.

At the end of your second set you come back out. Banter with the kids and grownups out there smoking. You look down the dock. A guy in a suit is standing there. Rudd. Back again. This time for you. When you reach him you see the hard black glitter in his eyes. He takes you by the lapels. Turns you slowly around and stands you back against the wall. Glances at the door to see if anyone's spotted him.

"Don't you ever tell me to leave. Don't you ever tell me to fucking do anything again." His knuckles hurt where he works them against your collarbones.

"Here's the deal," you say. "You touch me, you'd better kill me."

"Why?"

"I've got this story the Vienna Polizei are going to love. You touch me, I don't care how bad you hurt me. I'll crawl to the station puking blood the whole way if I have to."

"You wouldn't fucking dare."

"Try me. Or else kill me."

You watch the glitter fade. The buddy grin come back. He opens his fists, lets your lapels go, puts his hands on your shoulders.

"I had you going there."

He waits for you to answer.

"I won't be home when you get there," he finally says. "Don't wait up. I don't know when I'll be back."

And then he's gone.

"What's going on?" Hubert's out on the dock again.

"Everything's okay," you tell him.

He looks at you. Understands. Finally says, "Good."

CHAPTER 67

ON THE FRIDAY afternoon of the last weekend of August, Hubert
takes you and Rudd to the mountain farm where his wife and daughter have been on vacation the last two weeks. Frau Goller told you to
wear more casual clothes. You wear a blue sweater and Levis. Rudd a
short sleeved plaid sport shirt, slacks, a sport coat. Your Diversion Day
clothes. On Sunday all of you will come home together. For now you
ride up front with Hubert. Rudd rides in back, his presence behind you
unwanted, a bad storm the Opel can't outrun, always in Hubert's rearview
mirror. For the hour and a half it takes to get there you don't talk much.
Hubert focuses on driving. Under a deep blue sky, where clouds like clustered feathers ride on their table of air and their shadows glide across the
tended hills of green vineyards and dark forests, you watch the scenery.
Thinking you brought this guy into this family's life. Thinking that to have
you, they had to take him, this flight engineer, riding now behind the pilot
and copilot where he's used to riding, this time without systems to test
and instruments to watch.

Rohr is like other Austrian villages whose doors you've knocked on.
From another century but kept up so that its ancient houses and buildings look like they were built and painted yesterday. As always, you think
of being at the wheel of a used Porsche, a girl you love in the passenger
seat, your trumpet in back. Just that moment. Not the detail work of buying one or who the girl could be. The weather has changed. A light rain
makes the cobblestones shine like polished silver in the steel light. The
higher reaches of the surrounding mountains are skirted by an overcast.
Filaments of mist rise in places like the thin white smoke of small wet
fires from the flanks of the hills. Hubert takes you through the village up
a dirt road that leads to a big farmhouse and a couple of ramshackle barns
around a muddy barnyard. Frau Goller comes out of the house in a light
green summer dirndl and strong black shoes. She turns to the barnyard.
"Edith!" she calls. "They're here!"
She kisses her husband on the cheek. Smiles and says hello to Rudd.
Turns to you and takes your hand in both of hers. You feel their warmth.

"Shake." Her eyes glowing. "It's good to see you."

If Hubert told her about the night on the dock with Rudd. To have you, they have to take him, as if having you alone wasn't bad enough. What you've done.

"It's good to see you too."

Edith comes charging across the grass in a checkered skirt and light blue blouse, falters and slows to a walk when she sees Rudd, then gives her father a hug, then hugs you, then puts out her small hand at the end of her extended arm to Rudd. You look at the ground when he takes it. They've reserved a room for you and Rudd on the second floor just down the hall from theirs. In the large kitchen, where tall wood chairs surround a wooden dining table with the centerpiece of a vase of wildflowers, Frau Goller introduces you to a big stout welcoming woman who owns the house, and gives you a ring that holds two keys.

"This is for your room. And this is for the kitchen door into the house."

"Okay. Thank you."

That night the five of you go down to a restaurant in the village. The sky has cleared above the mountains. Steam rises off the cobblestones. In the shadow of the mountains, the restaurant is small, the architecture from another century, well kept like the rest of the village. Hubert parks out back. You enter through the rear where the branches of a large pine tree have been trimmed to clear the path. A hallway takes you past the restrooms and kitchen into the dining room.

Booths line two walls, tables and chairs stand across the floor, and the back wall is a bar where three men stand and talk among themselves. The mingled smell of vinegar and spiced meat and boiled dough is cut with cigarette smoke. At a side booth a young couple smoke and sip from beer glasses and talk quietly without smiling. Everyone greets the Gollers. Everyone knows them. You take a booth at the front window. Edith sits at your side, at the window, across from her mother and father. A woman comes out from the back and chatters cheerfully with Hubert and Frau Goller while she pulls a chair from a nearby table and sets it at the head of the booth for Rudd. Frau Goller introduces you as two young Americans. The woman's name is Lisa. The owner's wife. Friends of the Gollers for years. She wears her thick dark hair in a loose braid. Her tanned face shines with a light coat of sweat. The cream pudding of her breasts rides high in the deep cradle of her farm dress when she leans forward to shake your hands and fuss with knives and forks and napkins. Rudd locks in his Fly United grin and steals a shot at her cleavage every chance she gives him. Starts taking on that look you've seen him use to strip a woman naked. Turns and watches when she walks away.

"She looks young for an owner's wife," he says.

Frau Goller looks at him. Alarm hardens her smile. The waitress, a young plump blonde whose cheeks glow with the red of fieldwork, brings your drinks and plates. She gets Rudd's attention too. Less than halfway into dinner he asks where the men's room is. Hubert points his fork past the bar. While you tell Frau Goller about a new drummer at the Factory, while you and Hubert laugh, Rudd stops at the bar where the owner's wife is standing and draws her into conversation. A minute later, she frowns, takes a strange look at Frau Goller, moves off to sit with a fat man with a white beard, suspenders holding up his lederhosen, at a table for two against the far wall. Rudd goes past the bar. He's gone long enough for everyone to finish eating. You wonder what he's found back there. He finally comes back. Wolfs down what's left of his dinner. The waitress comes out to clear the booth. Rudd looks at his wrist where he used to have a watch. Asks you for the time. Tells the booth he needs to go. Turns his grin on you.

"I'll need the keys for later," he says.

"You don't want to do this."

"The keys."

"Sorry."

His grin goes cold. He shows you the black shine of menace in his eyes. You put your own grin on. He nods to let you know he gets it. Goes back to the bar where the waitress sits on a stool and leans in close to talk to her. The men at the bar stop talking. With their heads lowered you can tell they're listening. The fat man watches from his table. The owner's wife turns and looks. Rudd pulls back when she gets up and approaches them. You look at Frau Goller. She's watching the bar. Her face is sick with shock and shame and anger.

"Das ist doch allerhand," you hear her say. This is just outrageous.

Hubert doesn't look away.

"Ja."

Edith excuses herself. You let her out of the booth. She goes past the bar into the back. Rudd returns to the table to say goodnight. Thank the Gollers for dinner. Sticks out his big hand. It hangs in the air. Nobody makes a move to take it. He finally folds it up and pulls it back and turns and goes out the back way.

"I'm sorry," you say.

"You have nothing to be sorry for," Frau Goller says, in a quick strict voice that puts you in a school desk in a classroom.

"I should have left him home."

"You can't do that," Frau Goller says.

"I'm glad he's gone," says Hubert. "Now we can enjoy our evening."

He hoists his glass of wine. You raise your glass of water. Your family. If they only knew. You wouldn't be here either. Frau Goller starts talking about Novick. How gentle he was. How he loved jazz. How she could talk to him about the Bible all day long. In the booth against the side wall the young couple act like they're each alone. The girl leans back, lights a cigarette, shoots smoke straight into the air. The guy just sits there, head down, looking into the beer left in his glass.

"Where's Edith?" Frau Goller finally asks.

"I thought the bathroom," Hubert says.

"She's been gone too long."

Your little sister. Rudd out there somewhere with the hand nobody wanted to shake. You start to get up.

"I'll go find her."

"No. I see her now. Here she comes."

You let Edith back into the booth. She doesn't say a word.

"Where were you?" her mother says. "We were worried."

"The bathroom," she says. "And then I went out and looked at the stars."

In the morning you wake up alone. The bed across the room still made. You've been here before. Where a nervous wind tightens the skin on the back of your neck. Now your family's been here too. They're having breakfast in the farmhouse kitchen when you come downstairs. The woman who owns the house sits with them at the table. Asks if you'd like coffee.

"No thanks."

"Would you like some eggs?" Frau Goller says.

"I gathered them," says Edith. "This morning."

"Then I'll have to have some," you tell her.

The woman smiles, gets up, goes to the stove, uses a knife to crack two eggs into the hiss and spit of a frying pan.

"Bacon too?" she says, over her shoulder.

"No thanks."

"It's my job," says Edith, proud. Then she says, "I have to leave one here and there so the chickens remember to lay more."

"Do they forget?"

"I don't let them." Then she says, "Will you come to the stable with me?"

"Sounds like fun."

She claps her hands once and holds her palms together under her chin. "It has pigs and cows and sheep. You can go in the stalls with them. You'll like it!"

Her bright animated face. The striking blue of her eyes. Her impulsive happiness.

"I did that too," you say. "With my horse."

"And they have a bull. But I'm scared to go in his stall. Maybe I won't be scared if you're with me."

"You're not going into a stall with a bull," her mother says sharply.

"Your mother's right," you say.

"But you'll come with me?"

"Of course I will."

You thank the woman when she brings your plate. The eggs are stained brown with grease from the bacon you could smell. You didn't think you'd be hungry. Frau Goller and Hubert sip coffee while you eat.

"We're going home this afternoon instead of tomorrow," Frau Goller says. "I have things to do for school on Monday."

You look at her. Behind her soft smile you can see her hope that you'll believe her.

"I understand," you say.

Rudd comes through the open door into the kitchen, his shirt wrinkled, his hair half combed, the coal dust of whiskers on the hard shine of his oily face, a werewolf still in the process of turning human again. Says good morning too loud, too off pitch, too Fly United. Comes right to the table and takes a chair. Sends his big grin around the table. Frau Goller and Hubert both say good morning back. Then get up.

"Just tell her what you'd like," Hubert tells Rudd, getting up.

"Come, Edith," her mother says.

Edith slides off her chair and leaves the kitchen with them. Rudd takes a roll out of the basket on the table.

"I get the feeling they don't like me," he says.

You watch him chew bread. The way he never gets it. Shaming your family. Bringing the grease and smell of his night into the presence of your family. The woman takes your plate and knife and fork, sets them in the sink, leaves the kitchen.

"You get the feeling," you say.

"So what's going on?"

"For one, we're leaving later this afternoon."

"We?"

"All of us."

"I thought we were leaving tomorrow."

"They did too."

"That little shit," he says.

It takes you a minute to know who he means.

"You want to walk home?" you say.

"She really fucked me up last night."

The real reason you're going to the stable. Not to protect her from a bull. But if Rudd gets it in his head to come looking for a cow or sheep and finds her there.

"That's a hard thing to say about a kid."

"Yeah. But she did."

"What?"

"Nothing." He puts the last of the roll in his mouth and gets up. "Never mind. Is the room open?"

"Yeah."

"Some night," he says. "I need to clean up."

CHAPTER 68

EDITH TAKES YOU by the hand to the old stable off the barnyard. The walls are cinderblock and broken plaster. In the yard, pigs sleep in the sun on a bed of mud mixed with scattered hay, a goat nibbles on a crushed boot, some chickens pick through manure for seeds, and a big white goose stands on a mound of muddy dirt and squawks at you. A pile of old plaster and brick and boards and concrete rubble have the look of an abandoned demolition project. Inside, the smell of dust and hay and animals is overpowering, and takes you back to the stables and stalls at La Sal, where you were Edith's age and her name could have been Sharon or Mary or one of the other girls you played with. Cows look at you from the stalls you can see in the light from the doorway. Three sheep from another. The rear of the stable is dark but you can tell there are animals back there from the way they stirred when you came in and even now make their soft questioning cries. In the light from the door, half her face is lighted, the other half in shadow.

"So what do you do with the animals?" you say.

"I pet them and talk to them. Sometimes I make faces with their faces. Sometimes I try to make them laugh. Sometimes I just sit and watch them. Sometimes I lie down with them when they're sleeping."

Rex. The big workhorse they retired and gave you at the ranch. The way he sometimes shifted and caught your leg or your chest up against the boards of his stall and you could feel how easily and without thinking his absolute strength could crush you.

"You should be careful," you tell her. "Especially with the cows. They're heavy. They can hurt you without knowing it."

"I know. I'm careful."

You smile at her. Her smile back is heartbeat quick.

"I'll never tell anybody," you say.

Her face goes puzzled.

"Tell anybody what?"

"About last night. With Herr Rudd."

You stoop down. Look at her face. Hope to God you're doing this right.

"I just want to know if he did anything to you."

And now her face goes cross.

"I don't like him," she says.

"I don't either."

"So why are you with him?"

"They make us be together," you tell her.

"Who?"

"Don't worry. You'll never see him again."

You let her search your face.

"Ever?"

"Promise." Then you say, "Not after today."

Her face takes on the resolve you know she learned from her mother's face.

"Then I'll tell you," she says.

How upset she saw her mother and father get at the restaurant. How she didn't know why. Just that it was Herr Rudd. How all she knew was that she couldn't let him get away with it. How she excused herself for the bathroom but hurried out the back door instead. How she went past Rudd talking to the waitress. How the branches of the old pine tree that stood outside the door were wet and heavy with resin. How she took some branches and ran them through her hand till her palm and fingers were coated. How she waited there for Rudd. How she called him when he came out. Herr Rudd! How he stopped, looked around, turned to her. Werewolf, you're thinking, seeing the animal hair start to sprout off the backs of his hands. How she smiled and said Auf Wiedersehen and put her hand out. How he said Auf Wiedersehen and took it. How his face went ugly. How he jumped and yanked his hand back. How her hand came with his and almost made her fall because they were stuck together. How they both had to pull to get their hands apart. How Rudd ran back inside to try to clean his hand off.

"It had to take him a long time," she says. "It did me." She puts out her hand palm up and says, "There's still some there."

You stand back up where you can take and look at her palm and fingers.

"Where?"

She takes your finger and places it where you can feel the stick of the sap in her skin.

"See?" she says.

The afternoon when the football jock smashed Doby's new tube of Brylcreem in the parking lot of Dick's Market. The way you picked up the gout of white hair cream and smeared it all over the windshield and driver's seat of the Jeep. You waited till they got inside. And after you were done you ran. Doby, West, Keller, all of you ran. This girl in front of you stayed.

"Yes," you say. "I feel it."

"It'll go away."

"How did you think of such a trick?"

Suddenly she's shy. She can hear it, in your voice, see it in your smile. You're proud. She puts her hands behind her back and shrugs and looks down at her toes.

"I just did."

"How did you know there was resin in that tree?"

"I touched it before."

You look down at her. Your little sister. In the dim light, one of the outside pigs comes in, bumps into your calves, snorts, noses its way around you toward the dark of the stable.

"I'm so proud of you."

In the light and shadow that define her face she looks up from under the dark bangs that fall across her forehead.

"Really?"

"Yes. Don't tell your mother I said that."

"I won't. You don't tell her what I did."

"You're so brave," you say.

"Really?"

"Yes."

Her quick unguarded smile shows the white flash of her teeth and rises high into her cheeks and eyes. She jumps against you, wraps her arms around you, buries her head in your chest. You put your arms around her. Hold her tight.

"I love you, Shake."

Rudd, you're thinking, in the face of this much innocence.

"I love you too, little sister."

"My big brother."

"My funny valentine," you say.

She lets go, steps back, slides out of your arms.

"A funny valentine?"

Her rascal smile. You go to touch her face, catch yourself, brush her bangs aside like they could be crooked. She closes her eyes and raises her face to your hand.

"You."

"Why funny?"

"Because you are."

You smile at her. The flash of her teeth again as she dodges her head to the side and then down. You use her chin to bring her face back up.

"Did he do anything to you?"

Her face goes cross again.

"He said I was an idiot."

You look down at the dirt you're standing in to let the flash of rage cut through you, open you like lightning through night air, keep going while thunder rolls along behind it before leaving you whole again.

You're smiling when you show her your face again.

"You're not an idiot. You're a lot smarter than he is."

"He was angry. His face was mean. It scared me."

An idiot. You've seen what scared her. Coarse hair thickening and spreading down across his Fly United face. The slow mutation of his nose and mouth into a snout.

"Can I sit by the window in the car?" she says.

"Sure you can."

"Will you sit in the middle?"

To keep Rudd away from her. Pinned to the far corner of the back seat where he can sit looking out the window. His last ride ever with your family.

"The whole way."

Her arms reach quick around you. You look into the dark of the stable from where the soft and restless noises of waiting and sleeping animals have been calling. What you've done. What you've brought into this family. Not any more.

"So show me your animals," you say.

You work it out in your head in the grim hush of the drive back to Klosterneuburg. You wanted to tell him earlier, after the stable, but you didn't want to run the risk of the Gollers having to see you with black eyes and a bashed and bloodied face. So you save it for the platform late that afternoon, waiting for the train into Vienna, after they drop you at the station. People scattered along the platform look headed for a Saturday night in the city. In your sweater and Levis you could be one of them. But you're not. Your clothes disguise what you really are. The sun hangs low in the sky behind you. People across the tracks, headed the other way, stand waiting with their faces in the failing light. You're headed home a day early. The Gollers too, in Hubert's big Opel, headed up streets you've walked a hundred times to reach their place on the property of the Stift. The pitch of the afternoon light sets fire to sadness and longing and shame and touches the deep and permanent hunger in your bones.

"You won't see them again," you tell him, fighting the quiver from showing in your voice, the sudden pulse of rage and fear when you turn and find him looking past you down the platform with the familiar lure of a carnal smile in the black stubble of his lower face.

"See who," he says, and in the way he keeps his smile fixed you think of a ventriloquist.

"The Gollers," you say.

He turns to you without changing his expression.

"What do you mean?"

"You won't see them again. Or this town."

"What's the deal?"

"You really don't know," you say.

"I thought you liked them."

"I do. That's why you won't see them again."

You watch his smile go hard. The black glitter come into his pupils.

"But you will," he says. "That's what you're telling me."

"I'm saying you're not welcome."

"They said that?"

"They're too decent to tell you how they feel."

"So it's you."

"All me."

"This town. You mean the Factory too."

"That's right."

"I thought I wasn't supposed to let you out of my sight."

He's serious. It astonishes you.

"You'll be okay on your own," you say. "You've proven that."

You watch him squint into the low sun. Think things over. The black hairs of his stubble lay the tiny spears of shadows in the sunlight on the shine of his unwashed skin.

"Missionaries come to the Factory to hear you," he says.

"What about them?"

"They'll wonder where I am."

"I've thought of that. It's worth the risk."

"What'll you tell them?"

"That you're around somewhere. I don't know. It's a big place. I'm busy playing."

"What about the clubs?"

"The Gollers won't be there," you say. "So the clubs are up to you." Then you say, "Missionaries show up though. They're small places. Nowhere to hide. They'll expect to see you. With a Coke in front of you."

You watch him catch on. How this could be good for him. Under the skin of his face his muscles work for his Fly United grin. He drops his head to where the sun strikes the filaments of shadows again through the thinning hair on the crown of his scalp. If he'll bring up his face and you'll see the black glitter in his eyes just before he smashes his fist into your mouth. Or slams you against the wall of the platform. If he'll wait till people aren't around. On a sidewalk home after the last tram ride. In the apartment. But he raises his head with a different attitude in his face.

"You're right. I fucked things up with them. I'll stay away."

He takes out the box of mints he always carries in his pocket. Faces you straight on. In the breath through his grin you can smell the raw sweet opening burst of the mint in his mouth.

"I'll come to the clubs though," he says, "I don't want to make you look bad."

Fugitive. In the disguise of your sweater and Levis that lets you think you could blend with the people on the platform. Be just another guy waiting for a train. How far you've come from what you thought this would be like. Too far to know the way back. Too far to be forgiven. Too far to lose the constant ache down in your stomach. You've caught that shimmering sound that takes you above the rage and fear, above the sadness and longing and shame, above the stolen time you're living on, above the ache, that sound you can ride through the sky to places he couldn't start to follow.

"That's cool," you say.

"So we've got a deal," he says.

"I'd call it a truce."

He puts out his hand.

"Truce it is."

He looks past you again. Picks up his leer of a smile where he left off.

"I'll wait down there," he says. "See you on the train."

And leaves you where you wanted. Alone. You run your eyes down the platform and then along the platform across the tracks. A young couple, the guy behind the girl, his arms around her while she leans back into him. An old couple where the woman wears a yellow scarf over her hair and the man a flat tweed cap with a short brim over his forehead like guys who drive English sports cars wear. People like you alone. A man reading a paper with a briefcase next to his shoe. A woman carrying a mop and bucket. A cluster of girls. A group of guys around your age. Four of them. And suddenly the yearning possibility that you could just fit in. All the deception gone. All the hunger gone. All the concealed intent of your real purpose here. To harvest them. Gone. Where that August night isn't a ragged piece of shrapnel that lies against your heart, sharp metal waiting for God to twist into your heart when he's finally tired enough of you, but just a story you could entertain them with. Just another guy. A guy who could be their friend. A guy bound for home after visiting his Austrian family. Start from scratch. The way you did the Army. Your accent's good enough. You stand there, just you, on your own in the late afternoon light of the low sun, all the fugitive hunger gone, just the sudden flood of this incomprehensible feeling of release, this feeling that in the common pool of this light the color of tea you belong among everyone around you. The deep spontaneous sense of home in the air you share with them. This is where you're from. Tears pool and start to crest your eyelids. You walk toward the far end of the platform to be alone with them. Alone. Just one of everyone. This is what it feels like. This is what it will feel like from now on.

Chapter 69

YOU WAKE UP every morning to the sound of a lone trumpet. Not from a dream that reaches back to your winter in the sandpit and later on your dirt platform on the hillside high above it. Not through a wall from a neighboring apartment. Not from the air shaft out the window, where you can almost see yourself sitting and playing in the frame of the open kitchen window, setting the notes free to soar on rising air up the vertical shaft toward the square of blue sky. Just the sound, in your head, the sound that soars and dips and weaves and finally breaks the range of hearing and leaves you lying there, lying where you have to acknowledge other kinds of sound, street and highway, the hard cot under the length of your body, the garments you've slept in, the bleak stained moldy prison surfaces of the ceiling and walls whose color has been leached to plaster gray, the way the smell of the place is something you no longer smell because it's who you are, these bleak rooms at any given moment all you are. Thousands of miles away, in Mississippi, it's still dark, the middle of the night, peaceful except for a lone car filled with the hooded mouthbreathers of the Klan, cruising the dirt roads in an old black Chevy looking for someone to bomb, shoot up, lynch. And another couple of thousand miles away is San Jose, a couple of hours earlier at night, where she's probably still up, maybe still out somewhere, the lightning flash of her smile caught in the headlights of an approaching car. She'll be going to bed soon.

The truce with Rudd settles in. He gets used to being left behind when you head for Klosterneuburg, late on Thursday afternoons to play at the Factory, after church on Sundays for another ride into the country. In the siege that your companionship becomes, where mission rules have lost their meaning, you both get what you let each other have. He's free to roam the streets without the sheep's clothing of an Instrument of the Lord. Free to strip women naked where they stand, in their shoes, and have them strip him naked back and then get down to it. You're free to play at the Factory without your stomach roiling with the fear that he's doing some woman in a dark corner of the courtyard while stray cats rub their backs against his naked calves. Free to have the Gollers open the door when you knock and find you standing there alone. Free to make the walk to the scrap yard where you send that steel bird out into the night and like a falcon have it come back home to you. Sometimes you'll come in late and he'll be there. Sometimes you'll open the door on a dark apartment. You turn on lights, avoid the fact reflected in the dull suddenly visible walls of the place that is where the real you begins and ends, that you're alone in this place that tells you what you are. You know he'll be there in the morning to punch the clock when it's time to hit the hallways and the doors again. It's his job.

"What do I put down for Thursdays and Sundays?" him saying.

In the apartment Sunday night, across the table from each other, you're filling out your first weekly report since you struck your truce.

"Same thing I do. Time spent with investigators. Same hours."

Watching a dirty smile crawl slow into his lips.

"I guess I could," him saying. "We do a lot of investigating."

Thinking how far you've come from what you thought you came here for. You remember Morgan. How he logged investigator hours.

"Just tell whoever she is you're a missionary for the Mormon Church."

"Missionary. Yeah. That could make things interesting."

You spend every day in the dim dank hallways of the endless apartment blocks of your tracting area, knocking on doors set deep into the thick walls, while Rudd keeps track of the rejections in the tracting book. Nicht interessiert. Keine Zeit. Sometimes silence once you tell them through the flimsy scarred wood skin of the door who you are and what you'd like.

You remember how it felt to work with Novick. How for the first time on your mission you could feel the Spirit of the Lord around you. How you could breathe in deep and feel his spirit flood your lungs. How you could feel the warmth of the Holy Ghost expand your chest. How you felt safe and protected and serene in the haven of your sacred calling. How you always knew that the Lord would look after you.

How far you've come from what you were. Since that August night you've worked as hard as you ever did with Novick. But you work now on your own, unprotected from the naked fact of these bleak hallways and their derelict locked doors, not safe from the daily accumulation of rejection and futility. The Holy Ghost long gone. Ashes in your chest from the fire he briefly tended. But you keep going. Knocking on doors. The doors of those who can't be missed. The only way the dark wind crying up the cliff will hold you while you keep walking across the enormous space below you to the other side where a jet plane waits for takeoff from the level ground of the Vienna airport. The other side so far away it's still not visible. Every door you knock on one more step on the faith that the updraft of wind, the tide of the ancient lake of air that fills this prehistoric space, will hold you. Every Keine Zeit the right to take the next step to the next door.

You started playing the Vienna clubs back when you got your August check and could afford the trams and Cokes again. You've kept playing them because the bands and musicians you've come to know keep asking you. Because at church on Sundays missionaries keep wanting to be told where you'll be playing. You don't often know but tell them what you can. You keep playing them because it would go up on a neon billboard if you suddenly quit. Because if people asked you why you wouldn't know what to tell them. You wouldn't have a reason good enough. And then they'd start to wonder. If you had some lip or mouth disease. If your trumpet broke or someone stole it. If you got a Dear John. If you lost your testimony. If someone in your family died. If you got drunk one lawless night and took a whore to a sidestreet place called the Hotel Rabe where you did her in a room of dim red aquarium light.

Rudd behaves. He sticks with Cokes. Hangs out with customers and the occasional missionaries who come in. Even hands out brochures. When he talks to a girl it never goes further than getting her number. Under the colored lights of one or another stage, lights that glide in spears of liquid fire up and down the barrel of your borrowed horn, it sets you free, free to play, free to close your eyes and feel the metal ring, free to show how light can taste and sound can fly.

In September you put your fourteenth month in the country you were sent to harvest for the Lord behind you. On your other calendar, the outlaw calendar you track in your head, you cross off your first month. One month that God has let you stay to hope you can work off the unforgiven sin of that August night. If he'll let you stay for another one. And then another. You don't dare ask. You don't dare look. Just run with the headlights low enough to only illuminate the length of a single day. Let each day pass beneath you and vanish into the dark that chases you.

"You love doing this," him saying, out knocking on doors one afternoon.

"Doing what?"

"Tracting like a motherfucker."

"Come on. Not while we're working."

"Sorry," him saying. "Tracting."

"It's what we're here for."

"I'm talking about the way you love doing it."

"Just trying to put distance on things."

Heading for the next door. Stopping when you hear a series of locks click back on some door down the hallway. An old woman appears out of the long wall, short, her back round and her shoulders broad, haunches like an old cow, a colorless dark scarf over her gray head as she turns and looks for keys and works her way down the locks on her door again. You and Rudd standing back against the wall, smiling, while her pale eyes look up at you from their ancient gray nests in her furious face. If you should say something. Not let her go missing. She walks with her shoes apart in the slow stiff rocking motion of the bowlegged old cowboys in La Sal. Rudd waiting till she's down a flight of stairs before turning to you.

"You mean that fucking hooker? That's why we're doing this?"

"Hold it down," you telling him.

"Her? She couldn't understand me even if she heard me."

"This is what we're here to do."

Rudd smiling. Shaking his head.

"You're trying to square it with the Church."

"I pretty much lost the first nine months of my mission. I'm squaring it with that."

"You know there's only one real way to square that hooker," him saying.

"No harm trying a different way."

"I still miss my watch," him saying.

"Still mad that you paid for it?"

"Shit." His Fly United grin. "Don't remind me."

"You still owe me."

His grin goes stiff.

"Damn. I forgot all about that."

"Call it even. On that night anyway."

"You sure?"

You've thought this out. What he did with the bills you counted out and handed him on the sidewalk while his hooker waited.

"Yeah." Then you say, "But I'll take what you borrowed waiting for your check."

And one day, munching on apples, you and Rudd knock on a door and hear an old man's voice demand to know who's there. You tell him through the door. The door opens just enough for a single eyeball and the slice of a shriveled face. You hide your half gone apple behind your back.

"Religion?" he says, shrill and furious, a voice of defeated hate.

"Ja," you tell him.

He yanks the door back. Scrawny and bent, wearing long dingy gray underwear, a nasty raisin of a face, he puts his hand in front of his crotch and rapidly pumps a ghost boner.

"Das ist meine Religion!"

And slams the door. Rudd starts laughing. And then you're laughing too. Hard and hysterical. And then you can't stop. Can't stop looking at each other and starting up again. Rudd imitates him. Pumps his own ghost boner and says what the old man said. This is my religion! Yes it is, you think, still laughing, and there it is, the way it always is, the black points of his pupils, calculating, sizing you up behind all the insane hilarity that keeps coming and coming out of you. How far you've come. How far from how you thought this was supposed to go.

Chapter 70

YOU MOVE into October. Chalk off another month you've been allowed to stay. In the growing cold you start wearing your London Fog raincoat again. Rudd wears a pair of thin wool gloves to mark rejects in the tracting book in the dark mausoleum cold of the hallways of your buildings. On Thursdays, when you come to the Factory alone, people lay their coats and jackets on the injection presses and worktables when they come in, set the platters and bowls they bring on the portable banquet table Hubert covers with brown packing paper. The big overhead door to the loading dock behind you when you play comes down for good. Smokers use the small door set into the big door to step outside. They keep their coats and jackets on a stack of pallets by the door. Edith and her mother show up every Thursday. Like you, without Rudd there, they can relax. It's a school night, so they only stay for the first set, and you always make sure to include a song for her.

"This next one is for my little sister. Edith."

Like you, without Rudd there to have to watch out for, your family can relax. On breaks after your first set, before she has to leave, you take Edith by the hand, introduce her to the members of that night's band.

"I'd like you to meet Edith. My little sister."

"Hello, Edith! So you're the little sister we play for!"

"Ah! The famous Edith!"

"Hello, Edith. I'm Peter. Nice to play for you!"

"I'm Ursi. You must be a very special little girl!"

At first you see her reluctant to extend her small shy hand when they reach down for it. But then you see her start to smile. The trumpet player's little sister. And then shyness give way to pride and pleasure as her smile broadens and lifts her cheeks into her eyes. You watch happiness skip her back in the school clothes of a white blouse and blue skirt to the coat her waiting mother holds open for her. The very special famous little girl. Made of light. Light that always chases back the dark that stays gathered around your heart.

By November you can feel winter start to close its gloved hand in the dark grip you know will hold till March. You zip the thin fur lining into your raincoat to turn it into a winter coat again. Streetlights that didn't come on till after Rudd was gone for the night now start coming on before you've stopped tracting for your supper break. Once you're back home, Rudd starts leaving earlier at night, throwing you his grin on his way out the door to see what's on the other side. From the study table in the living room, you're used to seeing him leave, but this sick black dread still rises toward your throat the way it always has.

"On the prowl again, huh."

"You know me," him saying. "Can't let my meat loaf."

Every time he goes you listen to his footsteps on the stone floor down the hall and imagine hoofs instead of shoes. You imagine the transformation. A misfit in his uniform of a cheap suit. One of those special pigs that root through the night dirt for the rutting truffle scent of a woman wanting the same thing. Sometimes you force yourself to focus on the humor of the image. Sometimes you smile to yourself and wonder what your smile would look like in a mirror or on a window. Sometimes you stand at the edge of the cliff again, scared, weightless, floating, like you've taken that step again onto the cold updraft that rises deep and moaning up the faces of the night canyons. You need to leave too. Leave this place you once imagined you could fill with the Spirit of the Lord. Whose prison walls you thought you could paint with the purpose of your calling. Take your horn and go.

One November night the first snow comes down through the high lights of the scrap yard. Flakes that appear out of the dark to catch fire in the pale incandescent yellow of the lights. Thousands of them fall spiraling in blazing points to the floor of the yard around you. You play into the hush they bring. Watch the flakes land on the brass of the trumpet, warm from your breath, and crumple into water the way they did in the sandpit. Sometimes you feel like the watchman again. Sometimes it feels like it's your job to check the fenceline of the yard. And sometimes when you close your eyes the kids are there from Magna. The big Pontiac lumbering with its headlights off across the field toward you. The dark ghost with the glinting hood ornament of the streamlined Indian chief. The doors opening all around. Walt and his old guitar. Chaz and his harmonica. Billy and his bongos. Luke with an old electric bass like Jimmy played. Maria. You can see her dance through the chain link wires of the fence. The way they saw you back, through the same wires from the other side, in the drawing Jenny did of you. You play this time knowing they won't come. Knowing they don't know where you are. Knowing they've moved on.

Just keep at it, Walt, you saying. It'll happen. You'll see.

What if I can't find a teacher? Luke saying.

Just call the guy I gave you, Luke.

Okay, Luke saying. I'll do that.

You asking if Magna has a music store.

Yeah, Luke saying.

They know teachers too, you saying. Local guys. I found mine at one.

You're really gonna go.

How Maria was always the hardest to face. How she was always honest. How she could always find whatever you were hiding behind and leave you standing there.

Yeah, you telling her.

You broke Jenny's heart, you know.

I didn't know.

That's why she hasn't come back, Maria saying.

I'm sorry.

She can't stand to look at you.

Okay.

I don't mean that bad.

Okay.

She doesn't either, Maria saying.

Okay.

Just that shit keeps getting taken away from her.

I'm sorry, you telling her.

Playing for them now in your raincoat with its thin fur lining zipped in place for winter. Wearing the black rubber shoes that slip over your regular shoes to keep them clean of the slush and mud of the scrap yard where the big machines you used to guard at Hiller have come to die and be picked apart. Songs you played while the miner kids waited in the dark. Laura. Angel Eyes. Over the Rainbow. Songs you play now because the solos you play are solos whose sound can fly you back to them.

<h1>CHAPTER 71</h1>

ONE NOVEMBER NIGHT, coming home from the Factory, the letter you've been hoping for from the Mission Home is there in the lobby mailbox. In the living room, in your London Fog raincoat under the ceiling light, you read that on Monday you're taking a junior named Richard Croft to work in a place called Linz. There's a letter for Rudd too. Later, when he gets home, you learn that he's headed for a town called Kapfenberg.

"You know who this guy is?" says Rudd.

"What guy?"

"Richard Samuelson. My new senior."

"I've heard the name."

"Fuck," says Rudd, dropping his letter on the study table. "Another senior."

Another senior. Saying it like he deserves to be one. Another senior who doesn't know what's coming. What he'll do that you didn't.

"Monday too?"

"Yeah. Kapfenberg. Know where it is?"

"South," you say, remembering the train stop. "Not far."

"I guess you're pretty happy about this," he says, across the study table, that mean shine in his eyes, that hard look in his waiting smile.

"I'm ready for someplace new," you tell him.

You watch him lose the smile. You wait while he runs his eyes across your face.

"Yeah," he finally says. "I can see that."

"Aren't you?"

"I'll have to see." Then he says, "You going to the Gollers Sunday?"

"Yeah."

"Want me to come along?"

"You've already said goodbye."

You watch him run his eyes across your face again. See the black shine flicker.

"I may be gone by the time you get back."

Gone, you think. For the last time. Gone for good.

"Okay," you tell him. "Just leave your keys in the mailbox."

"Good idea."

"We need to clean this place up this weekend."

"I'll help. Don't worry."

That Sunday, your last in Vienna, you bring the trumpet to church to give it back to Brother Shlagl. He puts up the palms of his long hands. He doesn't want it back. Wants you to keep it.

"It was forgotten. Now it has a life again." His laugh is soft. "Like a resurrection."

You remember Cissy's Uncle Paul. The way he scampered off when you tried to give him back the horn he'd loaned you. The way he said you put the devil in it. Made it a devil horn. With a transfer to Linz you were hoping you'd be done. Done with this big shot thing called jazz. Just another missionary. A hide from the lights missionary. In your hand, in its case, the horn you've just been given feels like an orphaned thing, a stray you'll take from place to place, not to play but just to care for.

"Thank you," you say. "I'll take good care of it."

Brother Shlagl smiles. Gives you a father's pat on the shoulder.

"I know you will."

And that afternoon you gather around a dining room table set only with the vase Frau Goller used to hold the flowers you brought her and the journal you gave Edith. You can tell from the bookmark, from how deep the wrinkled pages go, how much of it she's used. You tell them you have to move again. This time out of town. Too far for Klosterneuburg. Too far to make the Factory on Thursdays. Too far for the Sunday excursions you've come to love in the back seat of the Opel. Edith gets off her chair, picks up her journal, goes down the hall to her room, shuts the door.

"Where?" Frau Goller asks.

"Linz."

She keeps her smile but trouble tenses the shadowed skin around her eyes.

"Linz," says Hubert. "They used to make tanks there. For Hitler."

A look from his wife shuts him up.

"It's only two hours or so by train," she says. "You can still come visit."

And so you have to tell her the rule about staying in your district. How you're not supposed to leave except for a mission reason. Like a conference. At the head of the table Hubert comes alert.

"How big is this district?"

"I don't know. Maybe just Linz. If it's a city. Some country around it maybe. As far as you can ride a bike."

"Linz is a city," Frau Goller says.

"A district is how far you can ride your bike?" says her husband.

"I'm guessing."

"Why can't you leave a district?"

"They think we might get in trouble."

"That's silly," Frau Goller says. "You come all the way from America to work for them, for nothing, and they treat you like they have no faith in you."

"I know."

"Austria is a beautiful country. You should be free to enjoy it."

"I know. It's okay."

"Is the Wachau in your district?" Hubert asks.

"Here? Probably not."

"All those trips we took? Did we get you in trouble?"

"No."

"Is Herr Rudd going to Linz with you?" Frau Goller asks.

"He's going to Kapfenberg."

She doesn't say anything. But this quiet satisfaction settles in her face.

"Well," says Hubert, "if you can't come to Klosterneuburg, can we come visit you?"

"Visit me?"

Down the hall a door opens. Edith comes back to the table. "Papa please! Yes!"

There's no lesson plan for this conversation, you're thinking. This family you were sent to Austria to baptize if you found them.

Frau Goller smiles. "Are we allowed to come out of our district?"

"You'd visit me?"

"Of course," she says. "Why not?"

Edith sits next to you. Takes your hand. This family, you're thinking, not knowing where to look. What you've done. What they'd do if you told them. How much simpler your life will be when you don't have to deal with people who think you're someone they love. How much easier it will be to hide.

"And we'll write," Frau Goller says.

"I'll write back."

"That will be nice."

And then you turn to Hubert and ask what you haven't wanted to ask but knew you had to.

"What about the Factory?"

The way he smiles, looks at his open hands, you know it's been on his mind too.

"I'll close it," he says, looking up. "One more week. To let everybody know."

"Why?"

"I don't know your friends."

"I have their numbers. They know you."

"I know them!" Edith cries, coming off her chair. "Peter and Ursi and Stefan! And Jakob! And Markus! And Lara! They're my friends too! They play for me!"

Frau Goller turns a sad smile to her daughter.

"That's true," she says. "They're all your friends."

"They can come! I'll tell them! They don't have to go away! Please, Papa!"

You watch Hubert reach out and put his hand around the back of Edith's head, pull her close, think about it. Then slowly shake his head and shrug.

"No," he says. And looks at you. "It was you and me." Then he says, "Maybe they'll bring you back to Vienna someday. Maybe then."

Rudd's gone when you get home that night. You find the mailbox unlocked and his keys inside. Only one bike stands chained to the pipe behind the lobby stairs. You can feel it too when you first go in the door. The air is different. Calm and still and clear where it felt torn by a nervous dread that always carried the residual smoke of something dirty burning somewhere. Relief you can feel in your shoulders and lungs. The feel of home it never had. This place that did its best to be home the last three months. For the first time now it feels that way.

That night, after packing up, eating some grapes and bread out of the fridge, folding the bedsheets and blankets, washing the tub and toilet bowl and sink, leaving the tracting book and the addresses of places the incoming elders will need, you make the walk to the scrap yard one last time. It's cold enough to freeze the hair in your nostrils when you inhale hard. Cold enough to turn your breath to steam when it escapes the bell as sound.

The sky above the sandpit. You remember wondering if they were there through that secret winter in the hills behind your house, when you had to play alone through all the questions, when all the questions tore through you like wind and went away unanswered. Your negro heroes. Men who taught you everything they knew. Giants in the sky around you watching over you. If they took the shapes of clouds. If the hard bright points of the early stars as the sunset lost its color into night were their eyes, the rings some of them wore in Mr. Selby's photographs, the glitter of their instruments. If you could have seen them in the constellations. If they were even there. You didn't know them then. That they could even be there for you to look for, towering over you, in a circle around you, like Cissy's Airborne uncles the afternoon you fell in love with her.

You don't look for them now. Not this far from home. Not the way you're here to spread the word that their skin is dark because they're cursed. Now, when you play to scavenged trucks and heavy equipment, to jagged heaps of rusting metal, you don't have to look to know you're on your own. Alone with the ache of the fugitive black wind that sifts across the dirt floor of your stomach. Because nothing will ever be the same again. Nothing will ever be the way it was. Motherless Child. Your father's song. You bring your trumpet level, touch the cold steel of the mouthpiece to your lips, because this is what you do and who you are.

PART 9

THE MECHANIC

CHAPTER 72

YOU PICK UP Elder Croft at the Mission Home where Morgan came for you. You don't see President Lindner. But you see Elder Hill, the basketball player who gave up a scholarship to come here, the tall and lanky and sanctimonious always pissed off guy who took Elder Cannon's place as second counselor, the guy who doesn't like you playing jazz. He doesn't shake your hand. Just cuts you a hard thin smile that looks like it hurts his face when he hustles past you in the lobby like he's dribbling fast and hard. Your new junior sits on the far side of the long table when you open the door to the conference room.

"Elder Croft?"

"Hi. Yeah. Are you Elder Tauffler?"

"Nice to meet you."

He comes to his feet and stretches his arm across the table for your hand.

"Same here," he says.

The big Tandberg tape recorder on its steel rack across the room with its microphone cords coiled. The big windows closed this late in November against the cold early winter fog outside. Croft picks his overcoat off the back of a chair.

"Sorry I didn't make it in earlier," you say.

"It's okay."

"Ready to go?"

"Yeah."

"Where's your bike?"

You and Croft take a compartment on the train out of Vienna west to Linz. Your bikes and suitcases ride in the baggage car. Brother Shlagl's trumpet rides in the rack above your head. Croft sits across from you on the facing bench. With the compartment to yourselves you get to know each other as Americans. He comes to you from working the doors of the city of Graz. You know it from going to a conference once with Paulson and other guys from your district. You remember making the train ride home not knowing Cissy's letter, her last letter, was waiting there for you.

He's been on his mission five months. Until today he's had one senior. Now he's got you.

"What's in the case?" Croft looks up above your head and nods.

"Case?"

"In the rack."

"Oh. A trumpet."

"Wow. Okay. You're that guy. I'm sorry. I mean Elder."

"Guy's okay," you say. Through the window the winter fog infuses everything with this bleak indefinite light. It bears the beginning of the cold that will settle in by January.

"You bring it from home?"

"No. It's borrowed."

"Who'd you borrow a trumpet from?"

"A member. In Vienna."

"Wow." Shaking his head.

"Wow what?"

"I read about you in the newsletter."

"Yeah. I remember them saying."

"Playing jazz. In Vienna."

"You like jazz?"

"I haven't heard enough of it to know," he says. "It must be cool to play, though."

"Yeah. It is."

"Did you play back home?"

"Yeah."

"Where?"

"Places up and down State. All over town. North and south. Out west too."

"Do you play any rock and roll?"

Air under your shoes. The updraft of open air for thousands of feet below you to the waiting horseshoe of the Colorado River. The updraft of your father's letter to President Smith. Not knowing what you hunger for.

"I don't play any more."

Croft smiles to let you know his curiosity is friendly.

"So how come you're bringing it?"

"The trumpet?"

"Yeah. If you borrowed it from a guy in Vienna but you're not gonna play it."

"He wouldn't take it back."

"No? A trumpet?"

"Yeah."

"Aren't they expensive?"

"Some are."

"Is his?"

"It's a good one."

"So you're really not gonna play it."

"I'm not here for that. Not any more."

"So what're you gonna do with it?"

"I don't know," you say, smiling. "It's kind of like this stray dog I picked up."

You both laugh at that.

"Let me guess," you say. "You play guitar."

"How'd you know?"

"I didn't. I just guessed."

"Yeah. But I'm just one of those three chord wonders."

"Blues?"

"Blues? No. Just pop songs. Country western."

"Three chords you could play blues." Then you say, "You sing too?"

"Not that you'd want to hear."

"That's the problem with a trumpet," you say. "You can't play chords. Or sing either."

He gets it. You both laugh again.

"I remember something else," he says. "All those high hours you got."

"It's why I'm here."

"Me too. It makes the time go faster." Then he says, "Besides, it'd be cool to see my name in the newsletter."

"You don't mind tracting?"

"Heck no."

"Great minds think alike."

And then, both of you knowing you'll get along, you're laughing again.

He's from Salt Lake. Granite High. Five blocks up from 33rd South where you used to make your turnaround and head back north up State Street. A regular guy. A guy who knows he's no big deal. Humble by intuition. A guy just here to do his mission. Maybe an inch taller than you, slim, straight dark blond hair whose hairline has already cut its way into his temples, a slender face, dark green eyes. The way his eyebrows slant down toward his nose makes him look intense. But he's not. It's just the way his eyebrows are. He takes things as they come. Easy to crack jokes with. In the long moments when the conversation takes a rest and he looks out the window or at his hands you can see him eager to be liked. You can see him look forward to this new adventure. See a guy who'd shine your shoes or iron your socks if you were the kind of guy to ask him to.

In a long lull in the conversation Croft pulls the small black looseleaf of the six lesson plans out of the inside pocket of his suit, opens it, starts reading. You keep watch out the window. Almost obediently, Croft sits back, looks out the window too. So this is what it's like to have a real junior, you think. Someone who puts himself in your hands. Rain and mist dampen the repeating clack of the steel wheels on the slick rails. The horns send their long hoarse cry back along the train. Distance. On that August night. On the months that followed it. On the last time you saw Rudd. Distance.

You remember your old trumpet teacher Mr. Selby. How he had a piece of shrapnel, jagged and sharp from the war, too close to his heart for the doctors to remove. How he always had to remember it was there. How he had to be aware of how he moved, deliberate and attentive, because the wrong quick unthinking movement could twist and cut the metal into the beating muscle of his heart. You carry your own piece of shrapnel now. The black jagged blade of that August night against your heart. The truce you had to make with Rudd. The awareness that you're not the kind of senior the guy across the compartment thinks you are. The fugitive fear that this will end without you knowing when it will, quick but expected, the chrome green flash in the eyes of a deer the instant it leaps into the path of your father's station wagon.

It's over now. The black wind that tore through everything the last few months is gone. The train puts its steady scheduled distance on that time and place. Crossings with gates and flashing lights and waiting cars pass in wavering streaks through the rivulets of rain on the glass. And now the distance lengthens in the dark behind you. God knows you have that black blade there. He knows it's his to take into his fist and twist into your own heart any time he chooses. He's given you three months on the deal you struck with him. Maybe he'll give you four. Or maybe five. Or maybe all of it. It's up to him. You don't ask. It's not your place to ask.

You look back at Croft. His lips moving. Reading then closing his eyes in the exercise of memorization.

"Want some help with that?" you say.

He looks up. "Yeah. That'd be great."

"What lesson are you on?"

"Just the first."

"Okay. I'll be Herr Braun. You'll try to talk me into thinking my church is false."

He looks at you confused.

"But you're Mormon."

"I know. Makes it interesting."

And that's how you spend the rest of the ride. Croft faltering through the German version of a leading question, his accent pure Salt Lake, while you recite the answer you know you're supposed to, the answer designed to lead him to the next question. You think of fooling with him, giving him an answer out of nowhere, a more authentic answer, an answer that doesn't dovetail with such neat imbecilic simplicity into the next question. And then you think no. Maybe later. But not now. Listening to him, watching him get angry and apologetic when he has to glance down at the script, you know the path he follows is too fragile. You want to play it straight for him. Let him lead you into making the admission that the church you've belonged to all your life is false.

CHAPTER 73

AS YOU WALK through the streets, carrying your suitcase and trumpet case in search of an address, the feel of Linz is a mean and exhausted feel. The buildings without character. The facades stained this dingy gray. Your place this time is a room in an old apartment in a grim part of the city. Two low cots with thin mattresses rest against opposing walls with a table and two wooden chairs between them. The woman who rents the room to you works at night mopping floors in a hospital somewhere. Her husband was killed in an accident at the steel mill. She lets you use the kitchen as long as you do it quiet when she's home and sleeping. When you flush the toilet, the wall mounted tank sends thunder through the walls, but she tells you not to worry. She knows you can't do anything about it. There's a small chipped basin in the bathroom where you can shave and wash your face. A bathhouse she says you can ride your bikes to. She showers at the hospital.

"Which bed would you like?" you ask Croft.

He looks at you.

"Aren't you supposed to choose?"

"Why?"

"Because you're the senior?"

"Okay. I choose to let you choose."

"You sure?"

"Positive."

"Okay." He looks back and forth. "This one?"

"Good. That would've been my choice too."

His shoulders drop. "Sorry. I'll take the other one."

"I'm kidding."

"You sure you don't want it?"

"Stop asking me."

"I'm sorry. It's just . . ."

"It doesn't matter to me. Honest."

"Okay. Sorry."

No, you think, swinging your Samsonite onto the cot he didn't choose. Please don't be sorry.

In the morning Croft sits across the study table from you waiting. You've had your prayers. You've washed and shaved and dressed for the day. You slide the tracting book the elders left for you across the table.

"You okay with handling this?"

You watch him thumb through it.

"Yeah. Wow. This writing's tiny."

"There's a city of doors in that book."

He laughs and looks up. "You just check off addresses, right? If people say yes or no? Or don't answer?"

"Your senior didn't have you do it?"

"Naw. He did pretty much everything. All the talking too."

An apologetic side. Like the way things go are because of him. Like he doesn't see the possibility that his senior could have been a jerk. A Paulson with a Schaeffer pen. You take the tracting book and show Croft where the latest entries are. The dates that have to head the columns.

"Okay," you say. "Let's grab some breakfast. Then find where we start and get started. Got your saddlebags loaded?"

"Sure do."

He isn't Rudd. Not even close. With a couple of suits it looks like he put some attention into picking out, shirts he hangs in the closet, striped ties from a real men's department, a tube of Ipana toothpaste he rolls from the bottom up, he's a guy you could talk to about mowing grass or tying boy scout knots. Sometimes you'll see him take a look at your trumpet case. He never asks if he can see what lies inside it.

He's eager and grateful when you start to teach him how sentences go in German, work with him on his accent, take the part of Herr Braun in the dialogue he's trying hard to memorize. He's nervous when he does his first introduction to the peephole of a closed door. As winter moves into the streets and chills the hallways of your buildings it isn't long before he's doing most of them. Sometimes you watch him work and wonder. If you'd had Croft before they gave you Rudd. You would have known what it was like. You would have had some practice. You would have learned from Croft what to expect. How to take charge. But they gave you Rudd cold. When you didn't know. When you'd never been in charge of anything. When most all you'd ever done was what you'd been told to do.

"Have you got a girl?" he asks one night. Then in a hurry says, "I mean back home. You know. Waiting."

On battered plates at the old table between your cots you're splitting a cold knackwurst and two buttered rolls for dinner. In the light from the fixture in the ceiling his eyes are shadows and his face looks gaunt. You hope he's okay. In the cold and slush you've been knocking on doors ten hours a day.

"No." You smile. "Not here either."

"Me neither. Not any more anyway."

"Dear John?"

"Yeah."

"Me too."

"How long ago?"

"A few months."

"How long have you been here?"

"Between sixteen and seventeen months."

"Wow. Just over a year to go."

It takes you a couple of seconds.

"Yeah. I guess so. Seventeen."

"I got mine a month ago." He looks down at the fork in his hand and comes back up with a smile you can tell he doesn't mean. "She lasted a whole four months."

"A month ago?"

"Yeah."

"I'm sorry." And then you say, "You don't seem too suicidal."

He shrugs. "I get over stuff pretty quick."

You remember all the letters to Cissy. The night it took you after Novick made you see how all your letters were only hurting and hurting and hurting her. The night you spent on the floor, under the table, because it was the only floor space in the small room that was big enough.

"Still," you tell Croft.

"Wanna see her?" he says.

"You've got her picture?"

"Yeah. That's all I got, though" he says. That and a Dear John," he says, and reaches for his wallet, slips a photo out, hands it to you across the table.

"She's cute."

"That mole there? She got rid of it. That's an old picture."

"Not many of them last," you tell him, handing the photo back, watching him slip it back into his wallet. "Girls, I mean. Not moles."

"Got a picture of yours?"

You see it the night at Fort Knox, on the empty parade field, her face illuminated in the flame of the Zippo they'd given you, still in your wallet.

"Not any more."

"Too hard to look at, huh."

Your turn to smile. "Actually, she was pretty easy to look at."

"Yeah." A laugh and a nod. "I get it."

There was the Sinatra song you sometimes heard from the kitchen radios of restaurants. The verse about small town girls on the village green. Hide from the lights. You still had Cissy then. That girl is gone. Now, from the dark side of the black road ahead of you, while Croft stays on the lighted side with his high beams on, you can finally hide. Hide from the lights. Hide even from your own face. Shave with it lowered away from the mirror so not even you can see it. Keep your head down. The headlights low where they barely crack the dark ahead of you. Where the road behind you closes on the welcome dark again.

CHAPTER 74

THE MEETING HOUSE in Linz takes up the second floor of an
old building that stands wall to wall with buildings on either side along
the narrow canyon of a cobblestone street. The street floor houses a
flower shop and a hardware store. You stop for a minute to check out the
tools in the window and remember back to working on the cars of your
buddies, all of them on missions now, their cars all waiting. A chipped
porcelain plaque bolted to the stone wall next to the street door tells you
the meeting house is upstairs. By now, after almost a week of tracting,
you're used to the gray haze that sometimes stains the air and makes the
buildings of the city dingy, fallout from the iron mines and coal fired
steel mills on the outskirts.

Up the stairs a big hall serves as the chapel. Folding chairs are rowed
across the floor on either side of an aisle that leads to a shallow stage
and the podium. In the backrest of every other chair is a wire rack that
holds a hymnbook. Off the stage an upright piano stands against the
wall. Against the opposite wall stand a table and bench for the sacrament. The painting of Jesus that hangs on the wall of your chapel back
home also hangs on a side wall here. Tall windows behind the podium are
draped. Light comes from ancient glass fixtures hanging from the ceiling.
Radiators quietly hiss around the walls. Their steam makes the warm air
humid and brings the smell of polish out of the old planks of the floor.
A door opens onto a hallway. If it leads to a bathroom, some classrooms,
maybe a kitchen where they prepare the sacrament. That ancient and deep
and elusive sense of home again. Home before any home you can remember. If this is what the meeting house was like when you were still a kid
in Switzerland.

You and Croft introduce yourselves to the handful of elders who work
the different areas of the city. You know some of them already. A couple
from the churchhouse in Vienna. Another from one of the towns in the
south when you worked in Villach. Others know your name from the
newsletter. They want to know if you'll be playing here in Linz. No, you
tell them, you're here like them to just do missionary work. You introduce
yourselves to the president of the branch who in turn introduces you to

the scattered gathering of men and boys once Priesthood Meeting starts. A thin man with a white beard and a bowed back plays the hymns. You see Morgan when he's old.

In the interlude between Priesthood and Sunday School you introduce yourselves to the women who come in the door with their children. One woman comes in with a teenage girl. Her name is Sister Reiter. She's maybe in her forties. The girl is her daughter Sonja.

Poverty comes in the door with them. Sits down toward the back of the room with them. Pervades everything about them. Their coats and shoes and then their dresses when they take their coats off. The rough and hurried way their dark brown hair looks like they brushed it back without a mirror. This deep fixed sadness in their faces. From the back of the room you keep coming back around to them. How they keep to themselves. How nobody approaches them except with a passing smile on their way to someone else.

"Yeah," an elder named Burnham tells you. He's short, built like a bulldog, with a face and nose and teeth that look to have seen their share of high school fights, thick stiff light brown hair trained in a blade off the side of his head, but with a gentle attitude in his eyes and voice. "They're not real social. The husband's a mechanic. He got hurt bad in some accident. Now he fixes cars. Smokes and drinks and gets rough. He doesn't want to be bothered."

"He's a mechanic?"

"Yeah."

"You know whose area they live in?"

"Yeah. Mine."

"Mind if I try to . . . you know . . . fellowship them a little?"

"Why?"

"I don't know. I just feel bad for them."

"They're all yours."

And so, over the next few Sundays, you fellowship them. You start alone to break them in. Croft understands and hangs out with the other elders. They're shy at first. Pull back from your attention when you say hello and welcome them. You keep the small talk short. In her gaunt face, where worry sharpens the fine lines in her forehead and around her mouth, Sister Reiter's dark eyes keep glancing past you, and you can tell you're making her feel too obvious. Her daughter just looks down to watch her fingers fuss with the buttons of her brown wool jacket. Slowly but steadily their nervous worry goes. They start to come in and look for you and smile when they see you. Call you Elder Tauffler. Let the small talk go a little longer before they break away to take their chairs alone. You introduce them to Croft. They take to his easy way and help him through his broken and apologetic German. Soon Sonja's talking about school. About Ping Pong and gymnastic tournaments while you wonder if every kid in Austria plays Ping Pong. Other members take notice. Start talking to them too. Sit with them. Invite them to sit toward the front of the chapel. A girl around Sonja's age makes friends with her.

The Sunday comes when you can ask Sister Reiter about her husband. How his name's Otto. How he used to work at the mill. How a rack of pipes let go one day and crushed his hip. How they fired him when he wound up too crippled to keep up at his job. How he rented a shop and started fixing cars. How he doesn't have many customers. How he's taken to drinking. How he spends money they can't afford at a bar most afternoons and comes home in this bitter anger to a cold supper she has to heat up again.

"He's a good man," she says. "The accident did this to him." Then she says, "I want to stay with him."

Through her helpless willingness to tell you about her husband you can see her shame. So you tell her about your old Sunday School teacher. Earl Bird. How he worked as a bus mechanic till some of his fingers were crushed and had to be amputated. How he was fired too because a mechanic needed two full hands. How his wife got him a job as a hairdresser at the salon where she worked. Sister Reiter listens to you amazed.

"He can use scissors?"

"He's not bad. I've had him cut my hair."

"Poor man."

"Where's your husband's shop?"

"No, Elder Tauffler. He doesn't want a thing to do with the Church."

"I don't want to go there as a missionary. I just want to meet him. See his shop."

"I don't know. He'll think I sent you . . ."

"I won't wear a suit," you say. "I'm just interested in seeing what he does." Then you say, "I work on cars too."

"What will you wear if not a suit?"

You laugh. "We have regular clothes."

And she tells you the street. A handpainted sign. Otto's Auto. Home from church that afternoon you share what you want to do with Croft.

"We're not doing this unless you agree," you tell him.

"I don't know a thing about cars."

"I do. If this works out, you can keep us company, or study. It still counts as time with an investigator."

"No. I'm all for it. I just want to watch you do this."

"We'll see."

The next morning, wearing your Diversion Day sweaters and Levis under your coats, in your sneakers, you jump on your bikes and go looking for the shop. You find the sign. The hand lettering for Otto's Autos thick rough black paint on a sheet of white plywood hung above a closed garage door. A man sits on an upturned engine block next to the door, having a cigarette, wearing a blue cap without a brim and an old brown jacket over a pair of dark blue coveralls in the cold November wind that scuttles trash along the cobblestones. From the grease on his hands and the black smears on his haggard face you figure who it is. He looks older than his wife. You stand there, holding your bikes, and tell him who you are. Where you're from. He flips his cigarette into the street. Gets up slow, labored, on one leg, and uses his hands to bring his other leg even. He's lean. Taller than you. Half of what you thought was grease are whiskers black as grease. He was good looking once. You can see what Sister Reiter saw back then. Lines etch his skin, thin as paper, stretched over the big bones of his face, loose below his jaw. His blue eyes sit deep and watchful in their sockets. One of them wanders to the side. And so you focus on the eye that looks at you.

"You know my wife," he says. "So you must be missionaries from that church of hers. I'm not interested. She's supposed to tell you."

"She did. So we're not here about any church." Then you say, "She made us promise."

"Why are you here? I don't fix bicycles."

"I've done a lot of work on cars. I just wanted to see how they do things here."

"You're a mechanic."

"I took it in school. I worked on the cars of my friends."

"American cars?"

"I built a racing engine for an Austin Healy Sprite. I kept a Renault going."

"Dauphine?"

"Yeah."

"A joke," he says, with a sneer of a smile.

"I know." Then you say, "I want to get an old Porsche when I get home."

He narrows his eyes. Looks off down the street. Takes out and lights another cigarette with a small wood match that ends up on the cobblestones. Takes a hard drag that puts deep hollows in his cheeks.

"You won't see any Porsches here."

"You do Volkswagens?"

"I get my share."

"They're supposed to be about the same."

"Let me show you something."

He leans hard to his left as he limps the couple of steps to the door, bends down sideways to take the handle, pulls the flat door up into its cradle, leaves you looking at the rear end of Lilly's Renault, the same gray beige, the same cooling grills between the taillights, the same black stain where the exhaust pipe juts out below the bumper, the back hood open over the same dinky troublemaking engine, its cylinder head off. You lean over the engine. A droplight hangs off the hood. Its light shows the black carbon caked to the tops of the pistons. Wind snakes into the small garage.

"This is the one I kept running," you say. "Even the color."

You hear Otto grunt, then say, "New head gasket."

"Could be worse," you say.

You hear a quick hard laugh. "It usually is."

You stand up for a look around the shop. The floor is brick. Heavy wood workbenches stained deep with oil flank the side walls. Tool racks hang from the dark back wall past the nose of the Renault. The light from outside so bright it takes you a minute to see the three bare bulbs hung from the low ceiling.

"Bring the bicycles inside," you hear Otto say.

"Okay," says Croft.

Behind you Croft wheels the bikes in. Otto brings the door down. A radio somewhere in the shop plays opera music through a speaker not up to opera.

"What do you do for a hoist?" you say.

"Look down," says Otto.

Under the rear end you see the edge where the bricks of the floor have been pulled away for a dirt pit narrow enough for the wheels of the Renault to straddle. In the shadow of the Renault it's too dark to see how deep it is. You remember the concrete pits in the maintenance shop at Hiller.

"Wow. How do you get down there?"

"A ladder at the other end," says Otto, taking off his jacket, Croft slipping out of his overcoat.

"Did you dig this?"

"Yes." Then he says, "I used the bricks from the floor to make a floor for it."

Crippled as he is, you're thinking, taking your raincoat off.

"What'd you do with all the dirt?"

"I hauled it down the street to an empty lot," he says.

"Looks like a nice job," you say.

"I felt like a gravedigger."

When you turn and look at him he's smiling.

You smile too. "When I wear my suit I feel like an undertaker."

"We could have started a business," he says, his laugh soft, the rough edge gone.

"I'm Shake." Putting your hand out. "This is Rick. No. Don't mind the grease."

"Otto."

"Can we look around?" you say.

"You boys come to my house. Might as well know all my business."

"Auto shops are my favorite places."

"Not churches?" he says.

You walk around the Renault. A vice and grinder and press bolted to a long side bench, new and used parts kept separate on the shelves below it, a compressor and engine hoist and solvent tank and welding rig along the opposite wall, wrenches and other tools hung on the rack on the back wall. Some of them are too big for any car you've ever seen. The wire coils of a small space heater burn red on the back bench. In one corner a doorway without a door leads to an office just large enough for a desk and chair and filing cabinet. A couple of old rifles, some boots, a rack of antlers, a leather helmet, an old accordion, and other unrelated things are stashed in a corner. Through an open door you can see a washbasin and the edge of a toilet. Back in the shop you breathe deep on the pungent mix of oil, solvent, grease, exhaust, the smell that takes you back to Steed's Texaco where West worked, where your buddies brought their cars, where you sometimes took beers from the small refrigerator with the round top. Against the crude brickwork of the ancient shop it surprises you how clean and ordered everything is. From the front of the Renault you can see the wood ladder that descends to the brick floor of the pit.

"You run a clean shop," you say.

"The only way," he says.

"I saw an accordion. Do you play?"

"Sometimes people don't have money," he says. "They give me what they can." Then he says, "One day I'll see if I can sell that junk."

"Your wife said you worked at a steel mill."

"Maintenance." Then he says," My wife's brother still works there. Philipp."

"What kinds of machines?"

"All of them. Casting and milling mostly."

"You brought some of these tools with you?"

"Yes. Maybe one day I'll get to use them. On a big car. An American car. A Cadillac."

You laugh. "I could bring the tank I used to drive."

"You drove a tank?"

"Yeah. And fired it and everything else. Even maintenance." Then you say, "We used to pretend we were chasing Rommel around the desert."

"They used to make tanks here," says Otto. "For Hitler. And artillery. Big factories."

"I heard that."

"I can tell you the whole story someday."

You end your tour and make it back to where Otto and Croft are standing. See the patch on the pocket of his coveralls that tells you his name.

"Do you need any help?"

Otto laughs. This time it's hard and bitter again.

"I don't have enough work for myself."

"Then just for company." Then you say, "I miss being around cars."

"I can barely afford to feed my family."

"No pay. I can't take money."

He studies you.

"No religion," he says.

"No religion. Just a day or two a week." Then you smile and say, "I'd like to hear that Hitler story."

Otto looks around. Comes back to you.

"You're serious."

"I'd stay out of your way. Unless you needed me." Then you say, "It's easier to bleed brakes with two people."

He studies you again.

"Do you have work clothes?"

"I can get some."

"You can use mine," he says. "They all say Otto. If that's okay."

"That's fine."

"What was your name again?"

"Shake."

"Shake," he says. "Okay." He turns to Croft.

"Rick."

"Call me when you want to come. Let me write my number down."

CHAPTER 75

FRAU GOLLER WRITES once a week. In her schoolteacher's hand she tells you how your family is. How Hubert's been sad since he closed the Factory. Wishes he'd kept it going. Spends his Thursday nights at a local wine bar now, drinking with his friends, the way he used to. How Edith is doing in school and on the piano. How they all miss you. How Edith tells her stories now to the big teddy bear and porcelain doll in her room. It's getting cold, she writes. Winter is coming. Asks if you have a warm coat and scarf and gloves and shoes.

You write back about Linz. About Croft. Put her at ease about winter coming. Tell her to tell Edith you miss her. And you write her about Otto. How you're helping him.

It isn't long before you know what you needed to know about him. He's a good mechanic. As good as you've seen. Meticulous, a step at a time like West but faster, everything clean and ordered, the tools and parts he'll need lined up on a workbench with a fresh shop rag to clean things when he's done with them. He treats his crippled leg like his good leg, without much thought, as though he was born with it. His long hands work the same way. Like they've known from birth that this was what they'd do. He gives you a pair of coveralls. You roll back the sleeves and roll up the cuffs and wear his name on your chest. Do cleanup. Keep him company. Take his surgeon requests for tools and wipe them clean when he hands them back. Take Croft along to ride your bikes to dealers and parts shops with lists of what he needs.

His cars are old. Banged up. The slow erosion of rust along their rocker panels, fender seams, wheelwells, doors, and roof posts, the paint stained and dull and worn in places to the primer, engines crusted with dirt and grease like the one you and Jimmy Dennison took apart in the cellar in La Sal. You watch the curious engine of a three cylinder Saab, the midget transmission of a Fiat, the dinky carburetor of a Volkswagen come apart and go together in his hands. Everything cleaned. Slick with fresh oil. Bolts torqued in the right sequence and torqued again. You go down the ladder into the pit to drop old oil out of an engine or hold things in place while he bolts them together from above. Croft sits on a bundle of clean rags on an empty grease barrel, watches, sometimes talks, moves his lips as he memorizes the dialogue of a lesson plan.

The customers are mostly on the poor side. They take a look at you, then your name patch, then you again. They part deliberately and almost painfully with their bills and coins without acknowledging the deal they're getting. After a thankless day you'd be hitting a bar too. You'd be coming home bitter. The few customers who are better off shake their heads and tell Otto he should raise his rate and charge more for parts.

The Sunday comes when you feel confident about recommending him at church. Before and after Priesthood Meeting, with the persuasive conviction you put behind your testimony, you start to spread the word among the men. Not about the glory of the Restored Gospel. But something men are always on the hunt for. A genius mechanic. A mechanic who can diagnose a problem instantaneously. Honest and reliable and inexpensive. Guarantees his work. You know because you've worked with him. You write down the name and address and number for his shop on pages you tear from the back of your pocket notebook.

"Nobody knows about him. He needs customers. Once people start to find out, they'll be lined up down the street."

"How do you know him?"

"He's Sister Reiter's husband."

"Who got hurt in the mill?"

"Who got fired for getting hurt."

"He's a mechanic now?"

"He's been a mechanic for years. First at the mill. Now his shop."

"I heard he isn't a member."

"Sister Reiter is. So is her daughter. Would you like to help them?"

"Of course."

"Then try him. You'll get a good deal. And do a good deed at the same time."

"Okay."

"Don't talk to him about the Church. Leave that to me."

"Yes. You're the missionary."

"If you like what he does, maybe you could tell your friends."

And then you wait. Wait while you keep talking him up. Wait while you keep spending time at his shop. Wait while he teaches you how to set the timing by the sound of the engine and how to read a meter to chase down a short or lost ground.

The wind has been calm. Smoke from the factories has flooded the air of the streets to where the cloudless sky above the city looks gray and the sun is pale enough to stare at.

"This is a new customer," Otto says. "It needs a new muffler and radiator. Rust. Other than that it runs well. He takes good care of it."

An old red Peugeot 403 stands over the pit in his garage. Ragged lines of brown rust have eaten through the rocker panels and the rims of the wheelwells. Puny, the size of garden hoses, the rotted pipes of the old exhaust stick their broken ends out of the top of the trash barrel. Otto's taken out the radiator too.

"A new customer? That's good."

"The second one this week."

"That's good too."

"I've never had two cars at once. The other one is on the lot down the street. An Opel. I have to find the property owner before he tows it away."

"What does the Opel need?"

"I don't know yet," he says. "An engine problem. I'll look at it this afternoon when I'm finished with this." Then he says, "The parts for this one are on their way."

When you're not at Otto's you're tracting familiar hallways where you can hear howling sometimes come through a door down the hall ahead of you. Croft doesn't mind spending ten hours a day knocking on doors. He doesn't question anything. You see him from this dark place where you've come to live, this place out of the lights in the shadow of the face you wear, back in the dark mystery that was always just out of your reach in the back of your head. Now you know what the mystery is. Not to put into words. But by feel.

"You okay? Tired? Cold?"

"No. I'm fine."

In the snow and slush of late December, gray from the soot of the stacks of the factories, you ride through puddles with your legs high, off the pedals, to keep them out of the dirty spray of your front tire. When it gets to be too deep for bikes you wear rubber galoshes, unbuckled, the legs of your pants tucked in to keep them dry. Toward Christmas the downtown streets and the buildings of the main plaza are bright with colored lights that in the early dark conceal the exhausted gray of the city the way nightfall hides an overcast and lets you imagine the stars are out. People are everywhere, shopping, carrying bags, eating and drinking what the street vendors sell. Walking the streets in the shopping district, passing through on the way home, your open galoshes on, you and Croft breathe deep on the Spirit of Christmas, stopping at occasional shop windows.

"My family told me not to get them any presents," says Croft.

"Yeah. Mine said the same thing."

"It sucks. I got some money. I only got my folks and little sister."

"Yeah. I know."

Sometimes you wander through a shop just to catch some warmth after tracting all day into the night, looking at a thousand gifts and souvenirs all racked out for Christmas, not touching anything, just browsing, lightheaded from the sudden heat on your face and in your lungs and the colored profusion of dolls and marionettes and painted cans of candy and little statues of famous places, smiling at the saleswoman, stopping to pretend you're considering something, moving on, traveling light, taking off your gloves to let your fingers warm. There are Russian dolls that fit inside each other like the set that Keller brought to Scouts one night. You think of getting Molly and Maggie a set. You wonder what Karl would do to them. How he'd deface and ruin them. And then one night you stop cold. On the red velvet of a display rack stands a small box. The wood inlay of its lid shows a uniformed rider on a rearing horse. In tiny puzzle pieces of different colored woods, the inlay of the rider and his boots and hat and uniform is intricate, and the horse's raised front hooves and bridled mouth and eye show the same intricate attention. A handwritten card next to it says Edelweiss. Then Croft is standing next to you.

"Wow. Pretty cool."

"Yeah. It's from the Spanish Riding School in Vienna."

"How come Spanish?"

"What do you mean?"

"Instead of Austrian."

"I don't know. It just is. My first companion took me there."

"Hope I get to do Vienna while I'm here."

"You will."

"Wow," he says. "Pricey."

"It's a music box."

"Oh."

You pick the box up. Turn it upside down. A plastic window in the bottom shows the row of thin gold teeth and the gold pins set in the gold roller like porcupine quills.

"This one must do Edelweiss."

"What's Edelweiss?"

"You didn't see The Sound of Music?"

"Yeah."

"Edelweiss is a song from it. Here."

"You gonna play it?"

"See if you remember it."

The box inside is deep blue velvet. There's room for some jewelry. The childlike pings of the teeth as they're plucked take you back to the Queen Theater where you sit next to your mother in one of the deep cushioned seats in the dark. Julie Andrews. How the movie made your mother cry.

How the changing light from the screen glistened in the tears that wet the skin of her cheek. How she didn't try to wipe them clean. Just sat there wearing them.

"Yeah," says Croft. "I remember it."

"Think I'll get it for my mother."

"May I help you?"

The saleswoman is standing there. The jagged line of her ruby thin-lipped smile tells you what she knows. That you're not here to buy. Just mess around.

"I'll take this," you say.

She looks at you. Startled at first. And then her face takes on a familiar look. Like she could be wishing you were someone else. That you can afford it amazes you. That she'll sell it to you, that you can leave the shop with it, is even more amazing.

"Do you have a box for it? I need to ship it."

"Where?"

"America."

"Yes. Of course. I can package it for you."

"Thank you."

Outside again, the packaged music box in a shiny green paper sack in your gloved hand, heading home.

"It's never gonna get there in time," says Croft. "Christmas is in four days."

"It doesn't matter. It'll get there."

Frau Goller writes to ask if they can come visit the second Sunday in January. They'll take you and Herr Croft to a restaurant for a long Sunday afternoon dinner. You write back how you'd love to see them and tell Croft who they are.

"An Austrian family?" he says. "Wow. That's really cool. A little Austrian sister."

And you tell him about the Factory.

"That's even cooler, man. Like a jazz factory. I'll get to meet them."

At church the members decorate the chapel and throw a Christmas party. They bring instruments and give performances. They bring home-made cookies and salami sausages and socks and mittens. They sing Austrian Christmas songs around the piano. All the Linz elders are there. One brings a guitar and plays and sings Lili Marlene while Croft stands there watching the chord changes. Sister Reiter and Sonja show up. They both wear festive red dresses and bright red lipstick. And then Otto comes in behind them, rocking to his left side as he walks, in a black suit and red tie, his mechanic's cap off for the first time, his black hair combed, his rough face shaved, carrying two colored bags. His wife and daughter can't help themselves from smiling. You can't either as you watch men who are now his customers come forward, shake his hand, pat his shoulder, get into conversations while he wrestles with confusion and surprise to find them here. And then Elder Burnham comes your way.

"What's going on?"

"What do you mean?"

"That's her husband, isn't it? The crippled guy?"

"Yeah."

"So what's going on?"

"You know anything about cars?"

"What's that supposed to mean?"

"I've been helping him out at his shop. Bringing in some customers."

"Have you been working on him?"

"I haven't said a word to him about the Church."

Burnham studies you. There's a slight but permanent snarl in his upper lip that probably got him into more fights than he wanted in high school.

"He's from my area."

"I know," you say. "That's why I got your permission first. You want him back?"

He thinks it over.

"Naw," he finally says. "I don't know cars from Adam."

Otto joins the members when they exchange gifts. A darkhaired teenage girl named Lisa with a librarian's face and thick glasses in round frames gives you a baggy sweater she knit by hand out of blue and brown yarn. A couple of the women wear Santa hats. Otto corners you. His clean hand reaches out for yours.

"So this is where my customers have been coming from," he says. "You tricked me."

"I told them about a good mechanic," you say. "They told their friends. No tricks."

He grins while he studies you.

"I'm so busy now I had to give up drinking."

"Is that good or bad news?"

"Good." He turns and searches the gathering for his wife. Finds her and takes a minute to watch her. Turns back to you. His face serious this time. "It's very good news."

The day after, when the shops open for business again, Christmas is over. Decorations come down. Wreaths come off the streetlamps. Shop windows go back to business as usual. Smoke from the stacks of the steel mills dulls the sky the color of lead again. Soot turns the plowed and shoveled snow gray along sidewalks where occasional young couples walk in the cold from somewhere to somewhere else past the locked doors and dismal walls of the buildings. Linz is quick, almost eager, to shed its fleeting festive spirit and retreat into a city without much spirit or conviction. And then New Year's is behind you too.

On the Sunday the Gollers are supposed to visit a snowstorm settles in and turns the city white and silent. Your family doesn't show up. Over the afternoon you make trip after trip to the phone booth down the street. Finally, toward dark, Frau Goller answers. They just got home to Klosterneuburg. They ran into the storm on the way. The Opel went off the road into a field. They were stuck for three hours. When they finally got on the road it was too late to come. They had to turn around.

"I'm sorry. I'm glad you're all okay. I'm glad you made it home."

"Edith is so disappointed. We all are."

"So am I. Herr Croft will be too."

"I don't know when we'll be able to come again. Hubert's very busy at the factory. He has orders he didn't expect this close after Christmas."

"I understand."

"I'll write you."

"I will too. Is Edith there?"

"Yes. She's in the bath trying to get warm."

"Tell my little sister I love her. Tell her to save a story for me."

"Yes, Shake. Of course."

And from there you can look ahead, like the city, to an uninterrupted winter. Week after week you split your time between Otto's and the hallways of your buildings where you log the tracting hours you've been logging since November. Each week is a reprieve. Another week you've been allowed by God to stay and work off what you owe him.

In early February Croft gets to see his name in the January newsletter. High hours for the month. And you can knock another month off the fugitive calendar you keep in your head. You're down now to less than a year. You can see your last birthday in Austria a few months off. And when you let yourself look up, see a few months further off, your last Christmas in Austria starts to show on the horizon. If it's a mirage. If God will let you get there. The District Leaders come to see you. You and Croft split up and take them tracting. They finally say enough. Let's just find a restaurant and talk. Croft can't stop grinning.

CHAPTER 76

YOU COME UP from the pit underneath an old Volvo where you've let Croft help you install a new set of tie rod ends.

"What's next?" you ask Otto. He's wiping down and hanging tools from replacing a cracked exhaust manifold. You wait with the tools you've used.

"I have three cars to choose from. But let's take a break."

"So what about that Hitler story?"

He laughs. "Hitler." Then he says, "Did you know he grew up in Linz?"

"I thought he was German."

"Most Austrians wish he was."

He shakes a cigarette loose from a flattened pack and lights it with a wooden match he strikes on the side of the small box it came from.

"Austria was the first country Hitler took over for Germany in the Anschluss," he says. "Linz was his home town. When he marched in with his Nazis, people welcomed him as their liberator. Their home town son. He gave a speech. Thousands of people were there to cheer him. I was a boy. My father brought me to hear him speak."

He takes a bitter drag off his cigarette. Shakes out the half burned match and drops it into the ashtray of an oil can with its top cut off half full of water like the butt cans nailed to the posts of the barracks at Knox.

"Within an hour of his speech," he says, as he exhales, "Hitler executed the mayor and other city officials. From there, he took over the mines and the factories, and started using them to build tanks and artillery. He destroyed homes to build new factories. He made Linz the biggest manufacturer of heavy weapons in the Third Reich."

He picks a sliver of tobacco off his tongue and flicks it into the can. Then looks at you.

"You ever hear of Mauthausen?"

"The concentration camp?"

"One of the worst. Their method of extermination was to work their prisoners to death. Starve them. Freeze them. They built Hitler new factories. They built air raid shelters. They died doing it. When they got too weak to work they were thrown into the Danube. You know the Nibelungen Bridge?"

"Yes."

"It was built by prisoners." He drops his half smoked cigarette into the can. You hear the quick extinguishing hiss.

"He took away all the Jews in Linz. He turned on Austrians too. Imprisoned and executed them for small things. One man was executed for stealing a bicycle. My father was reported for listening to a foreign radio broadcast and sentenced to prison. He took his life there."

With his hands in the pockets of his coveralls Otto lowers his head and looks for a long time at the bricks in front of his shoes.

"I didn't know what I was asking," you finally say. "I'm sorry."

"No," says Otto. "You didn't know. It's not your fault."

He takes a deep breath. Raises his head to look across the small shop. Turns to you.

"Can we step outside? You and me?"

You look at Croft.

"Sure," he says. "Go ahead."

With your London Fog raincoat over your coveralls, the winter liner zipped in against the February cold, with Otto in his brown jacket, you stand squinting in the sunlight of a day cleared of smog by a cutting wind. Otto cups his hands, turns his back to the wind, has to use two matches to light a bent cigarette.

"I want you to baptize me," he says, looking with his eyes narrowed across the street. He takes a hard pull on his cigarette and looks at you.

"Baptize?" you say.

He grins.

"I've surprised you."

"Yes you have."

"We're even now," he says. "For the way you tricked me."

"You said no religion."

"I meant it."

Bruder Braun comes to your mind. The six dialogues you've memorized and rehearsed and never had the chance to use. How silly and wrong they seem for Otto. How you'll have to improvise.

"There are things I need to teach you first."

"My wife's done that. Everything about this Joseph Smith, the Book of Mormon, this Restored Gospel, eternal marriage, all the commandments, how much they want from me. Go ahead," he says. "Ask me anything."

"She taught you everything?"

"She's very good."

"She must be."

"I love my wife. I love my family. Nothing would make them happier."

"Have you prayed about it?"

"Of course. With my wife and daughter."

"Do you believe everything?"

"When my wife told me that she knew it was true, there were tears in her eyes. I believe her tears." Then he says, "I've caused enough of them to know they're true."

With a bitter scowl he looks across the street again. In the harsh sunlight a line of grease cuts like a shining knife wound down the side of his face.

"That's good enough for me," you say.

He looks back at you. Then says, "I thought you'd be happy."

"I'm more than happy," you say. "Happy for you. Your family."

"So. When can we do this?"

"Any time you'd like."

"There's one problem," he says. "I quit drinking. I can't give up smoking."

Suddenly you hold the happiness of a family in your hands. Tell them he can't be baptized. Or let the smoking go and baptize him. A fat guy with a black beard come up the street on a struggling moped, pedaling to help the tiny engine, the long tails of his thick gray overcoat riding the wind. You watch him pass. You think of the Mormon guys back in Salt Lake who showed up at the clubs you played, bottles and glasses and cigarette packs on their tables, waitresses emptying their ashtrays. The guys in your Reserve unit who smoked during weekends at Fort Douglas and on summer camp in the Mojave. You think of what you've done. You step off the edge again from level rock onto open air.

"You don't have to," you tell Otto.

"Give up cigarettes? No?"

"You don't have to tell them when they interview you."

"Who's going to interview me?"

"The missionaries in charge of Linz. Before you're baptized."

"I should lie?"

"I used to lie. Every year when we were interviewed. There was one question the bishop always asked. I lied every time. We all did. All my friends."

"What question?"

"I probably shouldn't tell you."

"Sorry. I didn't mean to ask."

"If I played with myself," you say.

He stares at you.

"You mean . . ."

"That's it."

He starts laughing. And laughing starts him coughing, bent over, staggering, grabbing your arm, making you smile at the memory. You wait him out while the wind beats your raincoat around your knees.

"Just don't smoke the day they interview you. Or in front of your customers. You'll be okay." Then you say, "After you're baptized, you'll just be another Mormon who smokes."

"I can do that."

"Maybe someday you'll think about quitting."

"I can't say. Maybe."

You look off down the street. An old man rides high on a tall black bike dinging his bell while a dirty pigeon fans out its wings and scurries out of his path. Here it is. How you should tell him. What reason you should give. This was always the plan if you ever got this far. You look down at your sneakers, brown now with grease and oil and shop dirt, then look back up at Otto, at the eye that looks at you.

"I have a problem too," you say.

"What problem?"

"I can't baptize you. I wish I could. But I can't."

"Why?"

"I don't have the authority."

"You don't?"

"Not in God's eyes."

"Why?"

"I just don't." Then you say, "I broke a rule."

"What rule?"

"A missionary rule. A serious one." Then you say, "All I can say is I didn't kill anyone."

"Then how serious?"

"I shouldn't be here. In Austria. If they knew, I wouldn't be."

"So if they don't know, why can't you baptize me?"

You look off down the street. "God knows." You look back at Otto. "It wouldn't count in God's eyes if I baptized you. I can't do that to you."

He narrows his eyes. Purses his lips like he's about to whistle. Looks away, then down, as a scrap of paper and some dirt twist in a tiny whirlwind past his shoe.

"Well then," he says, looking up again. "I wanted you to be the one."

"Rick can baptize you. I'll be there." Then you say, "I'm sorry."

You watch him think it over. Then smile.

"Want to hear a good story?"

"Sure."

"I told my wife when you first started coming here. A missionary named Shake. She had no idea who Shake was. I didn't know your last name. She didn't know your first. We talked about it for days. Then she remembered. A missionary had asked her for the address of the shop. And we finally put your two names together." He puts out his hands, apart, palms up, cupped like he's holding two apples. "Shake," he says, to the hand holding the cigarette, "and Tauffler," he says to the other hand. He brings them together to form a single cup. "Shake Tauffler."

You both laugh.

"Rick is okay?" he says, "No broken rules?"

"He's clean."

"Rick will be fine," he says. "This is for my family."

"I need to find where we can baptize you."

"The swimming pool," he says.

"What swimming pool?"

"The public pool," he says. "The indoor one. After it closes for the day. My wife and daughter were baptized there." Then he says, "We just have to ask."

"So we're okay. You have a white shirt?"

"Yes."

"Does it say Otto on it?"

"Aha. You're joking."

"Yeah." Then you say, "You'll need some white pants too."

"Okay."

"We've got a baptism," you tell Croft, later that afternoon, out tracting again. He stops cold.

"We do?"

And between two doors in the hallway you're working you tell him the story.

"That's what you guys were talking about?"

"Yes."

"His wife converted him?"

"Looks that way. She taught him everything."

"Wow." Then he says, "Maybe she oughta be a missionary."

"Want to hear the good part?"

"What?"

"You're doing the baptism."

"Me?"

"If you want."

"But you're the senior."

"So?"

"Are you sure? Isn't there a rule?"

"Not that I know of."

"You did all the work. Look at your hands. You should be doing it."

"It's my choice, right?"

"You really serious? You want to give me the baptism?"

"Why not? It counts for both of us."

"Yeah. But it's your first."

All you need out of this, you're thinking, is to tell your father.

"Just say thanks."

"Thank you." Then he says, "This is unbelievable. I'm gonna baptize Otto."

You talk to Elder Burnham. This time he's not happy that you stole an investigator out from under his nose. You remind him that Otto was never under his nose. He's still not happy. You show him the lines of black grease embedded so deep in your fingernails and fingerprints that they can only wear away. And then he's okay.

"You want to do the confirmation? After he's baptized?"

"Cool. Yeah. Thanks."

Otto passes his interview. The guy who runs the pool gives you a date and time. You help Croft learn the baptism prayer in German. Take him shopping for a pair of cheap white pants. Help him practice how to hold Otto, let him down, bring him up again. Otto comes to the pool with his wife and daughter and a guy he introduces as his wife's brother Philipp. Otto and Croft wear white. The pool, a still sheet of turquoise glass, waits for them. The guy who runs the pool looks on from his booth. Otto and Croft go barefoot down the tile steps into the shallow end and wade down the gradual slope toward the deep end where the diving boards are. Otto's rolling walk from his crippled hip leaves a zigzag trail behind him. They stop when the water reaches their chests. Their hands fumble while Croft shows Otto the hold you practiced. Otto holds his nose. You remember the last time you were baptized. It was for the dead. Croft raises his arm.

"Otto Gottfried Reiter, having been commissioned of Jesus Christ, I baptize you in the name of the Father, and of the Son, and of the Holy Ghost, Amen."

Then puts his hand on Otto's back, lowers him backward till the water washes over his face, brings him dripping up again. With the fingertips of both hands to her open mouth, tears shining on her cheeks, Sister Reiter watches her husband become a Mormon. She told you no religion. She meant it. Now you know. She wanted to do it herself. She knew what it would take.

They wade back to the stairs where a metal chair waits for Otto. Water puddles on the tiles below him. Croft and Burnham and his junior and the branch president circle him and stack their hands on his head. In his farmboy German Burnham confirms him as a member of the Kirche Jesu Christi der Heiligen der Letzten Tage. Gives him the gift of the Holy Ghost. Burnham and the branch president dry their hands and sign the form. It's a good baptism. At church that Sunday, when the branch president announces their new member, Otto rises to his feet and takes in the smiling admiration of the congregation with a wave of his hand. The following Sunday, in a classroom, you're asked to stand among the circle who lay their hands on his head while the branch president gives him the priesthood and ordains him to the rank of deacon. In Sunday School and Sacrament Meeting you start to watch Otto pass the bread and water trays. You write your father the long awaited news.

One morning in March you show up for work and find Philipp there in a pair of Otto's coveralls. Otto tells you he hired him away from the mill. He needs full time help now.

"He's a good mechanic," Otto says. "At least as good as me. He'll learn fast."

"So you're telling me we're fired."

Otto cracks a grin. "I can't afford you any more."

You watch Philipp use a hand truck to take the barrel of ruined parts out the door to the trash bin in the alley. What Croft once did. How you'll miss this.

"Otto and Otto," you say, watching Philipp go.

Otto laughs. "His coveralls are coming. With his own name."

You and Croft go back to full time tracting. In her shy Swiss schoolgirl penmanship your mother writes a delighted letter about the music box. And toward the end of March there are letters from the Mission Home.

You're relieved to see Croft get one too. You can open yours knowing it won't be the letter that ends everything. Just another transfer. Croft is going to Leoben. You're headed back to Vienna. An elder named Clark Stover will be your junior. A new companion. Four more months on your calendar. More distance, both time and a new companion, on that August night. Seven months total. If God will let you stay for eight. Or nine. You don't ask. The rest of your mission is out of sight, dark, beyond the low throw of your headlights.

At the bottom of your letter, in someone's handwriting, there's a note that asks if you still have your trumpet. The note chills you. Makes the air beneath your shoes uncertain. From Dead Horse Point, in the blue haze of the distance, across the plateaus that fell away into canyons of their own, you remember being able to see the La Sal Mountains when your father pointed them out to you, the lazy roll of the peaks in whose shadows you were just a kid. If the air will hold you all the way across to their shelter again. You don't know. The last thing you can do is ask.

On your last day in Linz you stop in to say goodbye to Otto. He opens the shop door. Leaves you looking at the smooth round butt of a pale yellow Porsche coupe.

"My first one," he says. "Just a tuneup and oil change."

Right there in front of you. Its rear hood up. Its engine right there. The way everything holds still for you.

"Look at that," you finally say.

"Take your time."

"Can I look at the rest of it?"

"Sure," says Otto.

"Underneath?"

"You know the way." Then he says, "You leave tomorrow?"

"Yes."

"So when you're done looking, let's take a test ride. Let me close it up."

PART 10

THE PLAYER

THE TRAIN WILL get you to Vienna. The rapid unrelenting steady beat of its steel wheels on the rails will get you there. Nothing else feels certain. Nothing you can hold in your hands and call your own. Why they asked about your trumpet. There was only one reason. To play again. And from that reason there were only questions. What. Where. Who for. Questions whose answers they'll only give you once they have you in the Mission Home.

Nothing your hands can hold. Nothing you can trust. Everything feels borrowed. Like it can be taken back. Time has felt that way since that August night. Your trumpet too. But now everything. Otto's baptism. If word gets out you gave it to your junior. Why you'd give away that rare an honor. Why you'd be that generous. If a baptism meant that little. If it meant anything. What else could be wrong with you.

But you'll be able to see your Austrian family. Marvel at your little sister's stories. Tease her into slugging you. Relish Frau Goller's approving smile. Start up the Factory again if Hubert wants. As you approach Vienna, rain mingled with clots of sleet starts to leave its crooked trails across the window, and the glass is cold to the touch. The train will get you to Vienna. And you'll have the refuge of your family.

Sleet and rain are driven by a hard wind along the platform when you get off the train. You snug the scarf a girl in Villach knit for you around your neck. Her name was Ilse.

You leave your bike at the baggage room and haul your trumpet case and Samsonite to the Mission Home. Only one suit remains of the two you brought with you. Its crotch has been patched and needs patching again. The other one, the one you're wearing under your London Fog raincoat, is one you bought off a sidewalk rack the last time you worked Vienna, on a cloudy day when you couldn't tell that the dark green cloth had the sheen of fish skin in the sun. All you could tell was that the fabric was stiff and strong and something that wasn't wool. You tried the jacket on. It felt a little like a musician's suit. On the crowded sidewalk you couldn't try the pants and so you didn't know that they were pegged. That the legs tapered from the waist to narrow cuffs around your ankles like the pants some of your high school greaser buddies wore. You didn't care. It was cheap. It felt like it would last. And nobody would open their door to see it anyway. The man you bought it from was from some country like Hungary or Romania. A gypsy maybe. The crotch didn't stand up to your bike seat. It needs to be patched now. You haven't made the time. You can feel the wind finger its cold way through the holes.

At the Mission Home, you leave your Samsonite and trumpet case in the lobby by the door, head for the small bathroom where you first read Cissy's first letter, use a hand towel now to scrub the sleet and rain out of your hair and comb it with your fingers. You come out and check the conference room. The polished wood of the long table is bare. The room is empty. If the transfer letter was a trick to get you here where they could let you know they had you. Because what you'd done had been revealed to them. Because everything was borrowed. Nothing could be trusted.

Back out in the lobby there's noise from the open door just past the conference room. Wissom's at a desk in the staff office. A ledger book like the ones your father used lies open underneath his elbows. His sleeves are rolled up. His black hair thinning. Still the arrowhead of hair that points down into his forehead, but cropped short now, pretty much on its own on the ghost white scalp around it. He looks up across the tops of glasses he didn't have the last time you saw him.

"Hello there," he says.

His voice is still flat as shale. Two other elders look up from their desks and give you their missionary grins. You know one of them. A tall blond guy named Jensen who came to watch you play one night at the Factory. He gives you a wave.

"You got new glasses," you tell Wissom.

"Yeah." Then he says, "I've been waiting for you."

"Is that still the same pen you came here with?"

"Yeah." Wissom looks at his Schaeffer. Smiles back. "Built to last."

"Mine too. Wanna see it?"

He examines its leather case. Finally opens it. Pulls out the blue and gold Pelikan and rotates it in his thumbs and fingers to where you expect him to smell it the way you've seen guys do cigars. Pulls off the cap.

"Mind if I try it?"

"Be my guest."

You watch him sign his name. Look at the gold tip. Write some numbers.

"Slick," he says. "Balanced. Smooth." He caps it, looks at it again before he slips it back inside its case. "Wanna trade?"

He'd part with his Schaeffer just like that.

"It was a present."

"I didn't think so." Then he says, "Your junior's not here yet. But I need to talk to you. Let's use the conference room."

In the room where you and Wissom and Hatch and Clayton listened to Elder Cannon lay out all the rules, you take off your raincoat and scarf, lay them across a metal folding chair. Wissom takes a long glance at your suit. Slips the door shut. You take a chair across the table. He sets a ring of keys down. You figure they're yours. You ask about Hatch and Clayton.

"Hatch is here in town," he says. "Clayton's another story."

"What other story?"

Wissom looks sideways for a minute. Then says, "This is between me and you."

"Sure."

"He went home. Just after a few months. He wasn't doing well. One night he disappeared. His senior found him in an old warehouse. With all his clothes off."

"What?"

Wissom gives his hands a thin smile. "Wandering around buck naked. Happy as a clam. No garments. Barefoot. Cannon let him go home."

Clayton's impetuous cheerleader attitude. The points of black panic in his eyes. Naked. How nothing feels certain again.

"No. I hadn't heard."

Wissom picks up the keys, looks at them, shuffles them around.

"I see you brought your trumpet."

"They told me to."

"That note on your transfer letter. I wrote that."

"I thought I recognized your Schaeffer."

He smiles. "Yeah." Then he says, "I was told to."

"What's the deal with my trumpet?"

"You don't know that either."

Everything borrowed again.

"So tell me."

"We got some baptisms because of you. Novick and you."

"Baptisms."

"Yeah."

"How?"

"How?" He smiles like you could be dense enough to ask. "Your trumpet."

"You mean from playing."

"No," he says. "From staring at it."

You hold his look for a minute.

"I figured you got some referrals," you say. "The way Novick talked to people."

"Yeah. People who heard you play. Some of them became investigators. Some went all the way."

"You're kidding."

"You never knew?"

"You mean baptisms."

"Yes."

"How many?"

"I don't know. A few. But a few's a lot."

You let it sink in.

"Did Elder Cannon know?"

"Cannon was gone when the baptisms started coming in. But he knew there were some on the way."

"How about Hill? President Lindner?"

"Hill knew." Then Wissom says, "He just didn't tell Lindner where they came from."

"That figures."

"They'll be at church," says Wissom. "Looking for you."

"The new members."

"Yes." Wissom puts down the keys. Takes his glasses off. Checks to see if they're dirty.

"Hill hated what you were doing."

"You mean playing?"

"What Hill hated even more was that it worked."

"Yeah. I can see that."

"He tried the same thing with basketball."

"What?"

Wissom lays his glasses on the table upside down. Light from the window through the lenses leaves elongated haloes on the dark wood. Voices from the lobby make him turn his head to check the closed door. When they recede he looks back at you.

"Hill was a high school basketball hero. He turned down a scholarship for a mission. He came here thinking he was going to convert the whole country. Do it with basketball. Hook up with local teams. Show them how Americans won games. They let him try it. He joined local teams. He won games. All the time."

Wissom picks up his glasses. Wiggles them to play with the light they leave on the table. Smiles to himself.

"Everyone he played with got to hate him," he says. "He'd yell at guys who got the ball stolen or fouled someone or missed a shot. He'd make them cry. Never come back. They'd ask him for tricks from the States but all he wanted to talk to them about was the Gospel. If they didn't want to hear about the Gospel he wouldn't talk to them again. The mission finally put an end to it."

"I didn't know."

Wissom puts his glasses on again. The magnified light hides the dark and tired skin you saw below his eyes.

"He scored baskets. He just never scored a baptism. He never will. Not now that he's stuck in the Mission Home till he goes home."

"I get it."

"The first thing he wanted to do when he made second counselor was send you out to the sticks. As far away from jazz as he could get you."

"When?"

"Around the time you made senior." Then he says, "I went to bat for you."

"How?"

"I handle all the weekly reports. Sometimes your name came up. Referrals. People who heard you play. Sometimes they called here wanting more information. We asked where they lived. I'd let the elders who work that area know."

"That really happened," you say.

"You didn't know?"

"No."

"When Hill tried to send you away," he says, "I talked to Lindner. I told him what I just told you. Showed him proof. He told Hill you were staying in Vienna."

You look down at your hands to ride out the shock of the possibility. If Hill had only had his way. Got you out right after Novick left. A different junior. Anyone but Rudd. How you'd still know and trust when you were going home. How you could have baptized Otto. Wissom's waiting when you look back up.

"I owe you one. Thanks."

"You're welcome," Wissom says.

Standing at the edge of the pool. Watching Croft and Otto. What it meant to Croft. How thrilled he was. His face. You still did the right thing.

"Three months later Hill managed to get you out anyway," says Wissom. "The referrals trickled out. I didn't have much to show Lindner."

Rudd working the crowd at the clubs you played. If he ever told anyone what he was doing in Austria. If anyone ever trusted his Fly United grin. Wissom checks the door again and looks at his watch.

"Maybe your new companion's lost."

"I don't know."

"Anyway," says Wissom, "That's only half the story. Here's the good part."

"There's a good part?"

"Why do you think you're back in Vienna?"

"I guess you're about to tell me."

"Why do you think I wrote that note about your trumpet?"

"I'm listening."

"More people called the last few months. Wondering where you were."

"Who?"

"Musicians you apparently played with. People who came to hear you."

"Called who?"

"Us. All those brochures Novick passed out? The number for the Mission Home's on the back."

"They really called."

"They did," says Wissom. Then he says, "Guess who else called."

"God?"

He winces. "Kind of. The President of the European Mission. Head of all the missions across Europe. France, Germany, Denmark, Finland, you name it."

"Lindner's boss?"

"That's him. It wasn't actually the president. It was Haglund. His second in command. He told Lindner what a great job the European President thought you were doing in furthering the Lord's work."

"What?"

"He said Elder Tauffler deserves a dozen roses for what he's doing. He said the president wishes every mission in Europe had an Elder Tauffler."

"Roses? For a guy?"

"I know. Anyway, that's why you're back. The European Mission got calls too. People from here wondering where you were."

"Really."

"Lindner was ticked. He didn't know you were in Linz. He told Hill to get you back here pronto." Then he says, "You think Hill hated you before."

"They want me to play again," you say.

"Like you'd never been to Linz."

You think of Otto. See his watchmaker's hands rebuild a tiny carburetor. Look at your own hands. At the tiny threads of black that still show the coils of your fingerprints. You remember Morgan's haunting version of Come Come Ye Saints while you were in the dark coffin of the confession booth.

"You can't play hymns in a jazz club," you say.

Wissom stares at you.

"That's a joke. Right?"

"I guess I can't say no."

"Why would you?"

"Just a thought."

"Well, Hill would be happy, but Lindner would have a fit. He'd have to explain it to his boss."

"Did anyone let Novick know?"

"Know what?"

"That he had a hand in some baptisms."

"I don't know. I'd say no."

"I'm gonna need his address in California."

"I can get you that."

"How about the people who called? Or got referred and baptized?"

"Got that too. On a list. I wanted to keep track of how it worked. Let me get it."

Wissom comes back with Novick's address and a list of names and numbers. Brings you some paper so you can copy things over. You look for Peter. The pianist you played with. You find a Peter Strogl listed as a caller. You never knew his last name.

"Recognize anyone?"

"Yeah. I think so."

"Just bring back that list when you're done."

"Thanks for everything."

"That's a swell pen."

CHAPTER 78

HATRED FOR HILL makes everything real again. It rises hot up your back as you copy each name off Wissom's list and find other musicians you've played with. You're not supposed to hate. God can hate you. You can hate yourself. Hate for anyone else is like putting the high beams on when it's God behind the extinguished headlights coming the other way.

You don't care. Not this time.

You finish the list and take Wissom's back to him. Bring your trumpet in from the lobby. Use a towel you find on the metal stand for the Tandberg to wipe down the wet case. Four months of dust comes off with the water and leaves smudges in the towel. You set the case on the table, snap the latches open, lift back the lid, take a slow deep breath. Four months since you've seen it. Croft never asked to look at it.

You lift it out of its cradle now, slip the mouthpiece in, and your hands find their way into place around the casings of its valves. It's legal now. You've been told to play it. Told what its purpose is. But its feel is foreign. No longer yours. A borrowed horn again. You go to a window speckled and streaked with drops of rain and clots of sleet. Your fingers take their positions on the valve caps. You raise the trumpet to your lips. Blow, just blow, not closing them, so that your breath is a hollow rush of air through the pipes. Your lips go tight on the steel kiss of the mouthpiece. What would happen if you played something here in this room. This cream colored room where you sense again the numb sense of death you felt your first time here, the feel of a room where people came to watch each other die, while you waited alone for Morgan. What you would play right now. You think of Taps. Remember the Mojave. The loudspeaker sound of the bugle on the evening wind across the dunes and the sagebrush from the camp. You think of your father's favorite song. Motherless Child. You play through the melody in your head and hear the words and realize it's your song too. A long ways from home. So far from what your father wanted that you don't even know if it's still what you call home.

A knock on the open door behind you. You turn from the window. It's a guy your size, good looking, a steel grin that squares his jaw with confidence, a short brown Air Force haircut frosted with sleet and sparkling with diamonds of rain, wearing a real overcoat like your father wears.

"Hi," he says. "I'm looking for Elder Tauffler."

"You're Elder Stover."

And from the quick light shock that tightens his grin you can tell. He was expecting someone else. He looks at the trumpet in your hands. The open case on the table. Back at you. In your sidewalk suit and your hand combed hair you look nothing like the Elder Tauffler he may have thought you were from the newsletters where he's seen your name. He comes in, takes off his right glove, reaches his hand across the table. His handshake goes with his confidence. Firm.

"Nice to meet you." He takes off his other glove. "Sorry I'm late. I got a little lost."

"It's a big town. I look forward to working with you."

"Thanks. Congratulations on your baptism."

"We'll try to score another one."

He looks at the trumpet again.

"You'll be hearing a lot of this," you say.

"What do you mean?"

"How long have you been here?"

"Four months."

Not long enough to know.

"I used to play jazz with some musicians here in Vienna. They want me to do it again."

"Sounds like fun."

"It's missionary work."

You slip the mouthpiece out, drop it into its slot in the case, lay the trumpet in its cradle, bring down and latch the lid.

"The rest of the time," you say, "we'll be doing real missionary work."

"I know. I've seen you in the newsletter."

"There's a towel in the bathroom right down there if you want to dry your hair."

"Thanks. I remember where it is."

Hill stands in the doorway when Stover turns around. Stover steps back, startled to find him there, rattled by his sudden height.

"Elder Stover. Looks like you've met your new senior."

"Yes. I have."

Hill looks at you. A snarl in his thin lips. You keep the easy smile you've learned in the places you've played.

"Did Elder Wissom brief you?"

"About why I'm back? Yes."

"It wasn't my idea. I want you to know that."

"I know whose idea it was."

"Don't let it go to your head, Elder."

"Nope."

"I want to know every place you're performing. Before you perform there."

"Sometimes I don't even know. Till it happens."

"I want to know," says Hill.

"You'll know when I know."

"I want you wearing a suit."

"I always have."

Hill looks at your case on the table. At the list you transcribed from Wissom's list.

"What were you writing there?"

"Some names."

"Whose names?"

You know where this is going. You take a look at Stover. Thawing sleet has started running off his hair. You look back at Hill. His lower lip is tight across his bottom teeth like his hatred for you is the steel bit of a bridle.

"People Elder Novick introduced to the Gospel," you say. "While I played. It was his idea. I thought he might like to know."

"Know what?"

You pick up your list.

"That he did some good. Got some people interested. Some of them were baptized."

"Where did you get the names?"

You turn to Stover. "Elder Novick taught me how to be a missionary. He went home thinking he hadn't done a thing. Hard as he worked. I think he should know."

Stover nods. Steps back to get out of the crossfire.

"Tell me where you got those names," says Hill.

"How many people called the Mission Home because he talked to them? How many referrals? How many investigators? How many baptisms?"

"Give me that list, Elder."

"The hardest working missionary you had. It's all he did. Made sure nobody went missing. And you let him go home emptyhanded."

"Give me that list."

"How do you think he felt at his homecoming?"

"I said give me that list."

You fold the list and put it in an inside pocket of your suit. Put your London Fog raincoat on.

"Now he'll know." You look at Stover. "You ready?"

"Yes."

Hill stands back to avoid getting cracked in the knees with your trumpet case.

"You need a lesson in humility," you hear him say, as you open the door and push your Samsonite out into the weather.

CHAPTER 79

STOVER DOESN'T talk much on the trams you take to the address
Wissom wrote down for you. You hang onto a post with your trumpet
case in your other hand and your Samsonite between your knees. Through
the trembling streaks of rain and sleet on the windows, the buildings
and the overcast give you the sense again of the endlessness of this city.
Stover rides the tram stiff, like a soldier, not knowing you have to keep
your knees loose to keep from pitching back and forth and sideways like
a stumbling drunk.

Your tracting area is on the outskirts of Vienna again. On the ride
out, the rain and sleet let up, but the overcast holds. This time it isn't
some grim industrial area but neighborhoods of stately two and three
story houses with wrought iron gates and weathered trees whose still bare
branches reach high and spidered over the roofs. Your address is one of
the houses. The woman who answers the door wears a reindeer sweater
and powder blue ski pants and has the comfortable attitude of someone
rich. She's maybe forty. Through the savage red of her tan you can tell
that she's good looking. Her hair is this unapologetic platinum blond that
reminds you of the lady from the Indigo. High ceilings and casual furniture make the rooms of her house feel open. There's a phone in the
foyer she says you can use. Just no calls to Amerika. You thank her and
follow her up two flights of stairs ahead of Stover with your head low to
let Stover know you're not looking at her butt. When you reach the third
floor the slopes of the ceiling tell you it's the attic. And you get lucky. The
room is big, two small beds set against opposite walls, two desks and some
open floor space covered by a Persian carpet. There's a small bathroom
in one corner furnished with a washbasin and toilet and a door. She tells
you there's a bathhouse down a couple of streets and around the corner.

Once you're unpacked and settled in, your suit coats over the backs
of your chairs, you and Stover get to know each other. Stover comes
from a town east of Salt Lake called Vernal in a part of Utah famous for
the vast dinosaur graveyards they discovered there. He has a weary way
of talking about himself like he's reluctant to brag. He taps and twirls
a pencil while he lets you know what he's done. Junior Class President.

Student Body President. Eagle Scout. National Honor Society. Senior Patrol Leader. Honor Roll. Yearbook Editor. Homecoming King. Drama Club, International Relations Club, Key Club, Senior Choir. Clarinet in the school orchestra. Quarterback. Basketball. Swimming. You get the picture of a hometown hero. Everything you never were. Maybe he was the only kid in his school. A guy who had to be everything. The reason, you're thinking, for the overload of confidence in his steel grin with its white teeth.

"Heck of a list," you say, when he finally gets to the end of it.

"How about you?"

"I played jazz trumpet and worked on cars."

You wait for him to talk. He keeps tapping and turning his pencil over on his desk. Maybe if you told him more. In the hallways of the big buildings you and Croft could tell stories all day long. Not this guy. He's guarded. Like he's thinking who comes on a mission to play jazz trumpet. You decide against telling him anything for now.

"You know much about Salt Lake?" you finally say.

"Not really."

You wait for more.

"So here's what we'll do," you finally say. "Knock on doors. As much as we can. That's the day job. The night job is hitting the jazz places here in town."

"You mean with your trumpet."

"Yes."

"Where?"

"Around Vienna."

"Where around Vienna?"

"Clubs. Cafes. Wine cellars. Parks when summer's here."

"What do I do while you're playing?"

"Just talk to people. Make friends. Sooner or later they'll want to know what you're doing in Austria. Let them know. Get them interested."

"Is that what Elder Novick did?"

"Yes."

"In German?"

"If you don't trust your German yet, you can use English. Most people know it. They're always eager to try it out. Especially on an American."

"Do they drink in these places?"

"Most of them."

"Smoke too?"

"Yeah."

"I don't know."

"What don't you know?"

"I don't know if I can do that."

"I'm not thrilled about doing it either," you say. "But we were told to."

"By who?"

"President Lindner. And the European Mission President."

"Elder Hill didn't seem too happy about it."

"He's doing what he was told to do."

Stover stops tapping his pencil. Just looks at it. Keeps what he's thinking to himself.

"I've never been in that kind of club in my life," he finally says.

"It's not the Glee Club," you say.

"What am I supposed to say to people?"

"Sit there. With a Coke. Let them start. They'll talk about the music. They'll find out you're American. They'll get curious. Then you can tell them what we're doing here. It'll happen. You don't need to give them the first lesson. If they'd like to know more, give them a couple of brochures." Then you say, "It works. You heard what I was telling Elder Hill. Some baptisms came out of what Elder Novick did."

"Okay."

"Nobody can go missing."

And for the first time his smile strikes you as the real deal.

"I'll do it," he says, eager now.

"The rest of the time we'll be tracting. It looks like a good neighborhood."

"I look forward to that."

"It's not all work," you say. "We get to count the time I play on our reports. Time spent doing missionary work."

"You're sure."

"They wouldn't ask us to do something we couldn't count."

"Okay."

Late that afternoon you go downstairs and ask the landlady if you can use her phone. Not Amerika, you tell her, just Klosterneuburg. Frau Goller answers. Her voice floods you with its familiar warmth but stirs the uncertain feel you had on the train. You can name it now. Nothing is certain because nothing is permanent.

"It's Shake," you tell her. "I'm back. In Vienna."

"Oh, Shake! How wonderful! When can we see you?"

"Sunday afternoon?"

"That would be wonderful!"

"I'll be with someone new."

Nothing for a minute.

"Do you still have your trumpet?" she finally says.

"Yes."

"Could you bring it? Edith talks about it every day."

"Tell her of course."

"She'll be happy. We all will."

Stover's at the desk you let him choose, writing a letter, when you get back upstairs. On the top right corner are his Book of Mormon and his pocket looseleaf of lesson plans.

"The weather's let up," you say. "We need to fetch our bikes."

He turns and looks up at you from his chair. "Sure."

"We've got a dinner invitation after church Sunday," you tell him.

"Oh yeah? Who?"

"A family I've known for a while."

"Where?"

"A town called Klosterneuburg. Just outside Vienna."

"Investigators?"

"Friends. But we count them as investigators."

"Isn't that outside our area?"

"I used to play there. I probably will again. So I guess it's fine with Elder Hill."

"Okay," he says.

The way he has to question everything. You were a pain like that to Morgan. Just not the first day.

"You're sure," you say, smiling.

He stares at you. As if something new and surprising has entered your companionship. "Yeah," he says. "You're the boss."

That night you write Novick and tell him what he had a hand in doing. Copy the list of names into the letter. Mark the people who were investigators and the people who were baptized. Think of copying the list for your father too. Baptisms you could take part credit for. But how you'd bring the trumpet up. How you'd tell him it was jazz that brought them in. Jazz that hooked them. He'd like that about as much as Hill. You close your letter to Novick by asking him how his time in New York went. What jazz clubs he hit. What musicians he saw in person. If he got autographs.

Later that night, both of you stripped down to your garments, you kneel in prayer next to Stover and ask him to say the out loud prayer. Then both of you say your silent prayers. You pray not to God but to the landlady of the room you now call home. You thank her for the phone. You thank her for two beds. You won't have to sleep with a Student Body President or Homecoming King or Eagle Scout. With someone this close to the kind of son your father would have wanted if he'd had a choice. You don't call it luck. You call it what it is, a blessing, not from God but still a blessing, and you need someone to thank.

CHAPTER 80

A NEW WHITE blinding coat of snow covers the exposed yards and sidewalks of yesterday when you get up Saturday. Late snow in early April. You and Stover go exploring. You take the tracting book to find where the elders you've replaced left off. The list they wrote up for you for the dairy shop, grocery store, bathhouse, laundry, post office. Your landlady has already cleared her porch, her walkway to the gate, the sidewalk that fronts her house. The neighborhoods you'll work are neighborhoods of big houses with gray or pale yellow faces, faded orange tile roofs, yards gated with low wrought iron fences. The drawback is their distance from a dairy shop where you can grab a roll and milk for breakfast, a cheap lunch place where you can take a leak, other places on the list.

"We won't have time to come all this way for breakfast every day," you tell Stover. "We'll have to stock up. Take lunch with us."

"That's fine," he says.

You find the last address the elders marked off in the book.

"Okay. This is it. We'll start next door on Monday."

You keep a lookout for an isolated place to practice. When you're back that afternoon you tell the landlady you play trumpet and ask if she knows of one. Her name is Steffi. You tell her yours is Shake. She asks what kind of music. Jazz. It excites her. She says practice here. She likes jazz. She names places in the Donaukanal and Schwedenplatz. You know them. She's alone. Her journalist husband is off in North Africa through the summer. No kids or dogs. So you can use the music room on the main floor where a big black concert grand stands on a vast Persian rug. You see the old-fashioned letters inlaid in gold in the black mirror finish of the front face.

"Boesendorfer," you say, in the presence of the instrument you used to hear Morgan play at the churchhouse. You've never seen one in a house.

"Yes. My grandfather bought it for my mother. Do you play piano too?"

"When I was young."

"You're still young."

"Okay. When I was a child."

She smiles. "Your mother gave you lessons. Am I right?"

"Yes."

"I didn't have the patience to practice either," she says.

"I didn't want to be tied down," you say. "You can take a trumpet anywhere."

She laughs. "Can I look at it? I've never seen one up close."

You bring it down. Watch her run her hands and fingers over it and look inside the bell. This early into spring, you think, her dark red tan could only come from skiing.

"Miles Davis is my favorite," she says, handing your trumpet back.

"One of mine too."

"Do you know Angel Eyes?"

"Would you like to hear it?"

Afterward you ask if you can use her phone to call a musician friend.

"Are you going to bother me every time you want to call someone?"

"I'm sorry," you say, returning her smile. "I can't help it."

"Will your musician friends be calling you?"

"Only if it's okay to give them your number."

Her smile lingers. "Don't you live here? Of course it's okay. Are there many?"

"I don't know," you say. "There may be."

"I'll tell you when there are too many."

"Okay. Thank you."

You call Peter. Tell him you just moved back from Linz and you're ready to play again.

"Linz? What were you doing in Linz?"

"They sent me there four months ago. But I'm back."

"Good! We're going on tour for two months. Come along!"

"When are you leaving?"

"Next week. Come with us!"

"Who's going?"

"Gunter, Manfred, Franz, a few you don't know yet. A soprano sax and a couple of extra percussionists. We have a bus! Come! We'll have a good time! They'll be out of their minds to see you!"

The stories Mr. Selby and Novick used to tell you. About negro bands loaded into old cars or chartered bus doing towns and cities across the South, the Midwest, the Northeast. Using Muslim names to get into hotels and restaurants. Charlie Parker getting his nickname Yardbird from eating road kill chicken. You ride out the appetite to go with them.

"I can ask," you say. "But I think they'll say no."

The phone goes dead for a minute.

"Peter?"

"Who are these people you work for?" he finally says.

And when you don't say anything, he says, "I called them a few times."

"They told me."

"They said you weren't playing any more."

"They were wrong. Here I am."

"So come on tour with us. We're doing most of Austria. All the way out to Innsbruck."

You close your eyes.

"I don't think they'll let me leave Vienna."

"You can't leave Vienna? Why? Did you break some law?"

"I would if I left Vienna."

"I don't get it. It's just Austria. You're not going to China."

Just Austria. You smile. You remember everything about the test ride Otto gave you day before yesterday. From there you extrapolate. A cheap used beat up Porsche. One you could fix yourself since you have more experience than cash. You don't need paint. Don't mind some dents. Can live with split seats and worn carpets. Otto could help you make it mechanically strong. Just Austria. Your trumpet in the passenger seat, you could drive from gig to gig, on roads you've seen from the windows of trains and the back seat of Hubert's Opel, roads that flow in winding black ribbons across valleys and into hills and through towns of such deep seductive beauty you want to cry for them.

"Shake?"

"I know," you tell Peter. "Nobody gets it."

The next day, at the Vienna churchhouse, you tell Brother Shlagl you're taking good care of his horn, hug the widows who trained the accent out of your German, catch up with elders you know, meet three new members who came to the Gospel by way of Novick's love for jazz. You introduce Stover. And run into Hatch. His face is pale. You barely recognize him without the deep sunburn and fiery red of his acne scars. In the break after Sunday School you go down the hall to talk.

He's just made senior. He would have made senior the day you and Wissom did, the day you met Rudd, but his senior caught him doing laps one day in a pool at a Vorarlberg bathhouse, and they held him back.

"So he reported you?"

"Yeah. I used to wait for him to go back into his shower. Then I'd head for the pool. I had him timed. Then one day he came out early."

"When'd you shower?"

"I didn't need to, man. The chlorine kept me clean."

"Sorry."

"Naw. It was worth it." He shakes his head. "Fuzzin' skinny dipping with these naked old Austrian guys. Nobody cared. Man it felt good."

Remembering, he smiles, looks down, looks up again. "Anyway, what's new with you?"

"I just got back from Linz."

"I saw you got a baptism. What's your secret?"

"His wife. She did all the work."

"I read about you playing too. That had to be cool."

"They want me to play again."

"You don't sound too thrilled."

"Not sure yet."

"Man. I wish someone wanted me to ski." Then he says, "Where you playing?"

"Places around town."

"Okay if I come hear you?"

"If I can come watch you skinny dip."

"Those days are over. Hill said if I did it again, I'd be on the next plane home."

You hear the wind through its engines.

"Yeah. I'll let you know where I'm playing."

That afternoon you catch the train to Klosterneuburg. Remember Novick's reluctance to enter Catholic property when you walk Stover under the arch onto the grounds of the Stift. You knock on the familiar door. Edith pulls it open. Looks at your trumpet case.

"You brought it!"

She throws her arms around your waist and squeals. She looks up at you so happy you start to laugh. She drags you upstairs. Her mother meets you at the top in her familiar apron. Her smile is luminous. Her eyes shimmer in the shadowed skin around them. The air that follows her from the kitchen carries the shelter her cooking has always made of the house. Hubert comes in grinning from a back room with his Sunday sleeves rolled off his forearms. You forgot how small his hand was but still know its familiar strength.

"This is Herr Stover," you say. They shake his hand while you introduce them. Frau Goller. Herr Goller. Edith. You watch their faces. No alarm. No holding back. They know. He's no Rudd.

"Welcome to our home, Herr Stover."

"You can call me Hubert."

"You can call me Edith!"

Frau Goller sets out cold venison roast and potato salad and red cabbage. Back in January, on the phone, she told you what happened when they tried to visit you in Linz one Sunday. Now she tells it as a story. How they ran into a blizzard on the way. How the Opel went off the road into the deep snow of a winter field. How it took three hours to get on the road again. How they finally had to turn around and make their way back home.

"I kept going out to the pay phone," you say. "It was snowing in Linz too."

"We weren't alone," says Hubert. "There were other cars around us."

"How did you get out?"

"I walked to a village and came back with a farmer and his tractor."

"I wish I'd been there to help."

Hubert laughs. "Then we wouldn't have had a reason to come to Linz."

"How worried you must have been," Frau Goller says.

"How many times did you call?" says Edith.

"A hundred thousand."

"No you didn't!"

"Every half hour or so. Till you finally got home."

"We were scared, Mama. Remember?"

"Yes, Edith. But everything was fine, thanks to your father."

Frau Goller gets Stover to talk about himself. His home. His family. You learn things you haven't thought of asking him yourself. One brother and one sister. Their names and ages. What his father does. How his mother teaches school too. High school. No girlfriend. You interpret things like Student Body President, Quarterback, Homecoming King, Eagle Scout, Yearbook Editor, the clubs he belonged to. Your family's impressed. He compliments Frau Goller on her dinner. Tells Hubert he hunts deer too. He accepts their admiration with a smile that looks at home among them.

"So how was Linz?" Hubert says.

You tell them about Otto. Show them the residual filaments of black in your fingerprints. Stover eats and listens. It's the first time he's heard the story too.

"Very nice," Frau Goller says. "You helped him and his family."

"I didn't know you could work on cars," says Hubert.

"It must have felt wonderful to baptize someone," Frau Goller says.

"I let my companion do it," you say.

Stover's head comes up from his fork of red cabbage. Frau Goller's face goes curious.

"Why?" she says.

The story you can never tell this family. The story whose current runs like a riptide deep beneath the surface of their faith that you're still the guy you were on the other side of that night last August.

"He'd just lost his girlfriend. In America. He needed something good to happen."

Frau Goller stares at you. Lowers her knife and fork to either side of her plate. "Was he allowed to go home for the funeral?"

It leaves you smiling. "No," you say. "She's alive. She just left him."

"Then that's so kind of you."

"What mattered was how happy it made Otto's wife."

Hubert turns to you. "So they brought you back to Vienna."

"They want me to play again."

"So we can reopen the Factory?"

"Are you sure you want to do it again?" Frau Goller says.

"Yes!" says Edith. "Please! I want to hear you play again! I want to see my friends!"

Hubert grins at you. "You want to tell her no?" he says.

"What's this factory?" Stover says.

"Herr Goller's factory. Where I used to play."

"Give me till a week from Thursday," Hubert says.

"No, Papa," says Edith, making a prayer fist out of her hands. "Today!"

"I brought my trumpet just in case," you tell her.

"I want to see where the music comes from!"

"Then we'll take it apart and look."

"Can we finish dinner first, Edith?"

And she looks at her plate and takes her fork and starts shoveling potato salad into her mouth.

"The dishes too," her mother says.

"Yes, Mama. The dishes too."

"I can help with the dishes," Stover says.

"Have you been writing your stories down?" you ask Edith.

Her mouth full, her cheeks loaded, she looks up from her plate, nods her head.

"She won't stop," says Hubert. "Her journal's almost used up. She reads them to us."

Chapter 81

YOU REMEMBER Mr. Hinkle teaching you how it came apart, where it needed valve oil and slide grease, how it went back together. You can smell the tuna and then the olive loaf of the two sandwiches he ate while he taught you. See the smooth gold pipes and tubes in his long gray wrinkled hands. Smell the shoe polish smell of his back shop while you sat next to him at his workbench.

This time it's a floor of old dark hardwood planks covered with a towel in the piano room of a house that was once a nunnery. Hubert comes in with a newspaper and takes one of the leather sofas. You sit Indian style with Edith with your trumpet on the towel. You start with the valves. How they make it possible to play different notes. Show her the caps on the bottoms of the casings. Tell her they unscrew.

"Go ahead. Take one off."

She balls up her hands.

"What's wrong?"

"I don't want to."

"You're scared."

"No I'm not!"

"What do you think is in there?"

"I don't know."

"Let me show you."

You screw the cap off the first casing and slowly lift it off. You bring the casing to your eye, look inside, quickly set the cap back over the hole.

"Okay. It's there. It's dark but I could see its eyes."

"What?"

"The Valve Monster."

"No."

"You want to see?"

"No. Yes!"

"Here. Look."

She leans over while you hold the casing up where she can look in through its uncapped bottom.

"See it?"

"It has eyes?"

"Yes. Look harder."

She brings up her hands to shield her eye from the light. You depress the valve to shoot the piston up at her from inside the casing.

"Toot!"

She squeals and yanks her head back.

"See? There's nothing to be scared of."

"That was mean!"

You show her how to take the valve out. Let her unscrew the top cap and extract the valve assembly. Show her the spring barrel and the piston. She holds it carefully. You let her take the remaining two valves apart. She lays the caps and valve assemblies on the towel. You show her the tuning slides and how they pull off the pipes.

"Be careful. They're a little greasy."

She looks inside each slide and lays it on the towel. When she finishes, she looks at the body of the trumpet, its pipes amputated, its valve casings hollow, a horn gutted of its ability to make sound. She looks scared.

"I don't like it like this."

"Did you see where the music comes from?"

She looks at you, failure in her face, her bottom lip between her teeth. You pick up the trumpet, slip the mouthpiece in, try to play a note. A hoarse rasp bursts out of the open pipe where the tuning slide was.

"We'll find it. Don't worry."

"Can we put it together again?" Her eyes look up from her still down-cast face.

"Sure. But let me show you how to grease and oil it while we do."

Eagerness lights up her face again. Her hands briskly rub her upper arms as if they're cold.

"Yes!"

You take the small can of grease and the bottle of oil out of their pocket in the case.

"Grease for the slides," you say, holding up the can. "Oil for the valves."

You use one of the smaller slides to show her where they take grease. The dull ends that slide into their open pipes of the trumpet. Wipe the old grease off. Use a finger to rub them with a thin coat of new grease. Show her how to slide the ends into the waiting pipes again. Gentle. Keep the slide from binding. Don't push too hard, but push it home, then work it back and forth. Wipe down any grease that squeezes out. Frau Goller and Stover, done with the dishes, come in and sit at the dining room table where Novick tried with such failed diligence to bring her around to the Gospel. Stover's smile is relaxed and real as he rolls his sleeves back down. The way he might smile in the company of his own family.

"Want to do the other two?"

Obedient, with a schoolgirl's concentration, her hands pick up a slide, clean and grease its ends, then look for where it goes. You show her. Then watch her match the slide to its receiving pipes, work it back and forth, wipe it down. She looks at you for how she did.

"Perfect. Feel how easy it moves?" you say.

Her smile pushes up into her cheeks. She picks up the remaining slide, the main tuning slide, looks at the tiny rocker valve.

"What's this?" she says.

"The spit valve. To blow the spit out when you play."

"Playing makes spit?"

"Have you ever seen me put a handkerchief there?"

"Yes. I remember. Mama couldn't tell me why."

You show her how to oil a valve piston. Wipe it down. Make sure the holes in the piston are clean. Just a thin coat. Run a couple of drops along the dull gray steel and rub them smooth with a finger to coat it all the way around with the wet shine of the oil. Start to slip the valve assembly into a casing.

"Oops."

"What?"

"Do you remember which one goes where?"

Her hand flies to her mouth in shock.

"Aren't they all the same?"

"No. Look. The holes are different."

She looks at the two assemblies you hold up, then at you, her eyes wide.

"Maybe Papa can figure it out."

"You don't want him to think we're dumb, do you?"

"No," she says, her voice quiet.

"Then it's good that everything's numbered."

"It is?"

"Look."

You show her the tiny number stamped into each casing and each valve. One to one. Two to two. Three to three. Relief and excitement animate her face again. From there you show her the valve guides. The grooves in the casing. The small teeth on the valve assembly that have to slip into the grooves so the holes line up with the connecting pipes and let the air flow through the instrument. Start with the third valve.

"Just turn it back and forth. Slow. So you'll feel it."

You watch her hands again as they slide the right assembly into the casing closest to the bell, turn the stem till the teeth click into place, wiggle the stem to seat the valve.

"Okay. We have to make sure it's not backward. Here." You slip the mouthpiece in for her. "Hold down the valve and blow."

The way she holds the trumpet. Something else you'll show her. Her breath blocked, her cheeks puff out, and air escapes her lips on either side of the mouthpiece.

"Okay. It's backward. Pull it out and turn it half a turn. Make sure it seats again."

And when she does, and pushes down and blows again, her cheeks stay put, her breath rushes unimpeded through the trumpet. Her smile breaks her lips apart. She screws the top cap down. Then installs and seats and tests the second valve and then the first. Watching her puts you back on the stool in Mr. Hinkle's shop when you made your trumpet yours. How the feeling came to you that it belonged to you.

"Good. Now you can screw on the bottom caps."

When she's finished, she looks up, her face flush with pride.

"Good work," you say.

"You never showed me where the sound comes from."

"It's not a piano," you tell her. "I can't show you hammers and strings."

"So where does it come from?"

"From you."

"How?"

"Here."

You take the mouthpiece. Show her how to use her lips to make the sound that feeds the trumpet. Close them tight. Leave just a small opening at their center. She laughs when you show her the insect buzz it makes.

"It's not really music, is it?"

"No!" and she laughs again.

"That's the trumpet's job. To turn it into music. Here. Try it."

She draws her lips wide into her cheeks, pulls them tight, points them into the mouthpiece, blows. Frau Goller and Stover watch from the table. Hubert lowers his newspaper to see how she does. Try after try, bleat after bleat, her face goes red with her effort to get it right. She finally gets a short burst of a smooth buzz. Yanks the mouthpiece away. Rubs her lips.

"It tickles!"

"It does at first. But you did it. Try again."

And when she does you start to hear it. The buzz that the trumpet will purify and distill and amplify. You take the mouthpiece. See where it leaves the center of her lips the flush of bright pink. Drop and twist it into the lead pipe and then hand her the instrument. Show her small hands how to hold it.

"Okay. Let's go. Don't touch the valves."

You watch her put the mouthpiece to her lips. Pull it away from her mouth at the garbled noise that comes loud out of the bell. From his chair you hear Hubert quietly laugh.

"I made those noises too," you say.

"You did?"

"Just keep trying."

She does. And you start to hear sound inside the noise. She hears it too. Her eyes go wide as she goes after it. And finally it comes out clean. So loud it startles her. She brings the trumpet down and looks at you. Her face is radiant. Her mother and father clap. Stover joins them. This little sister, you think, looking at her. This only child. This was your face once. That space of a Saturday afternoon after you made your final payment. After you made it yours. The back shop. The stool at the bench. The smell of olive loaf and tuna. Your trumpet in pieces. Mr. Hinkle's long sure hands and patient voice as they guided you through its assembly. That space of maybe an hour that was the one time it was yours and was also innocent. In the hands of this little sister, this only child, you can sense its innocence again. You look at her. This was your face once.

CHAPTER 82

LIKE RUDD, like Croft, Stover's fine with tracting all day long. The air smells of spring. It's good to be outside again. Houses now. With yards and paths and porches and sometimes driveways. Not monolithic buildings that stood their front walls and doorways flush against sidewalks. Not hallways of apartments where all you could have offered, if you offered anything, was to paint their doors or sweep the hallway floor in front of them.

You're Americans?

Yes.

This is about religion?

Yes. The Restored Gospel of Jesus Christ.

I'm sorry. We're Catholic. We're fine.

We understand. Can we leave a couple of pamphlets with you?

No. That's fine. Thank you.

We understand. Is there anything we can do for you?

What?

Get your flowerbeds ready for spring? Clean your gate?

Are you serious?

Yes.

I don't think so.

You remember knocking on the doors of your new neighborhood when you moved to Bountiful and went looking for yardwork to earn money for your trumpet. People, mostly women, strangers to you then, before they became your congregation, before you went on to serve them the bread and water of the sacrament, before you knew all their names by heart, before you knew the names of their husbands and children too, before you could name their cars. How the women all said no. How they all had sons or husbands who cut their grass and tended to their yards. Until you knocked on Mrs. Harding's door.

We'd like to talk with you if you have a minute.

We're Catholic. We're quite fine.

We understand. Can we leave a couple of pamphlets?

They'd be wasted.

Okay. Is there anything we can do for you?

What do you mean?

Rake out your grass. Wash your car.

Dressed like you are?

Right now. Or we could come back.

I'll take the pamphlets.

You always played to take people away from whatever it was that trapped them. You always watched the tables. A blond woman in a yellow dress at a table with a big bald man in a heavy brown turtleneck sweater. While she looked into her drink and her cigarette burned in her fingers where she held her hand against her cheek you would play to keep her safe. While his face was red in the light of a candle and his glistening eyes seemed to rest their gaze on the floor of the stage where you stood you would play to keep him kind. You would play to take them away for the length of a song from the cages of their lives. Break them through the iron overcast of their own sky and take them on the flight of your solo as far away as you could. Out across the country you know. The Mojave. Monument Valley. Dead Horse Point. The places where God lived. The wild land of vast and savage prehistoric red and yellow rock where at dusk they could feel the restless wind start kicking up and hear the twilight cries of animals. You could always bring them home. They could trust you. Even in Vienna, while Novick talked them up and handed out brochures and Rudd prowled for women, you could sense their trust. You could see them listen. You could feel them come with you. Now, out with Stover knocking on the doors of houses, you don't know.

You're troubled in a dark new way about playing again. Except for the time in Sacrament Meeting, when you played with Sister Avery and Sister Johansen to meet the requirement for your Duty to God award, you've always kept your trumpet well away from church. Pain in one or another form was always waiting there when they were brought together. Your mother bickering when you came home from playing stinking of smoke that wasn't yours. Your father making his disappointment clear when he came home from work and opened the garage to find you back there where the trumpet in your hands caught fire in his headlights. Bishop Wacker. President Lindner. Jazz the Devil's music. Jazz the music negroes played. In church they were always giving you commandments. They were always telling you what they could take away from you if you didn't follow them. Playing was something they could never take away. It was too deep for them to reach. You made sure of that from the start that winter in the sandpit. It was all through you like blood.

Why do you want to do something for me?

We like to help people out.

Sure. I could use some help.

That's why we're here.

Come inside. I'm boxing up my wife's belongings.

Your wife's?

You said you help people out. My wife recently died.

We're sorry.

You can help me put the boxes in the attic.

And now you've got this new commandment. One that puts your trumpet in the service of the mission. That gives this dark truth to the corny joke you sometimes hear. Instrument of the Lord. It was hard enough before. But it was voluntary. You could still play free. You could still break through. They could still trust you. This time is different. This time you feel caged yourself. If the subversive weight of this new commandment will be too heavy for your sound. Too much to give it flight. Because you know this isn't right. You know it was never meant to be used this way. It was never about a dozen roses.

In the open door she's pretty. Her brown hair dark with the water of a shower. Holding a skimpy bathrobe closed with one hand. The belt loose down her legs.

I'm sorry. I was expecting someone else. You need to leave.

Is there anything we can come back and help you with?

Do you go up and down the street asking people that?

Yes.

Nobody has called the police?

You and Stover walk off the porch, away from the click of the closing door, to the front gate. Stover closes it behind you.

"Who do you think she was expecting?" says Stover.

"It sure wasn't us."

"You think what we're doing is illegal?"

"No."

At night you get your lips in shape again. Play all the scales and arpeggios and the exercises you remember. Get your range back. Work your tongue. Practice tunes and solos. The landlady sometimes comes in to sit back in a big leather sofa chair and listen. Sometimes she'll ask for a song. Sometimes you'll look her way and she'll be giving you a smile you can feel in a place you shouldn't.

You take Stover out to look for clubs on Graben, Schwedenplatz, in the Donaukanal where you'll find musicians you've played with. At the first club, Stover waits outside, in his overcoat in the cool night air, his breath steaming in the headlights of cars coming up the street, while you take your horn and go inside. Cigarette smoke finds its familiar imprint in your nostrils. It hangs in the dim air and leaves halos around the ceiling lights. At the second club, people at the back tables look at you, then at

the case in your hand, then at you again. In the third club, in the haze
of the colored lights from the low stage, you find Fritz behind his drum
set, tapping and whacking his skins and cymbals. You remember the way
he played when a piece caught fire for him. Hair like Robbie's, a head of
crazy curls, blond like Lenny's was instead of black. The way you took
off yourself and your trumpet rode the lunatic driving rhythms of his
drums before he brought it down so that you could bring it home and
land it. This time it's slow. Piano and bass and guitar. Room for you. You
go back outside.

"Hey."

"Yeah?" says Stover.

"Found somebody. Come in."

You hold the door. You point him to an empty table, drop your raincoat over the other chair, make your way along a side wall toward the
front. They're playing Waltz for Debby. The tune Bill Evans wrote for his
niece. A tune you and Lenny worked on and played one night at Sammy's.
You listen to the piano player work through the moving chords whose
inversions and substitutions always made you think that if breaking glass
could cry it would sound like this. The guitarist looks at your case and
nods. You nod back. The bass player looks at your suit. The piano player
comes around again and the guitarist steps up for his solo. Fritz looks
your way. Grins and uses his head to invite you up.

By the time the guitarist turns his solo around for the last time, your
trumpet's in your hands. He nods at you again and this time grins. Fritz
brings it back around to one. You bring your trumpet up, look for Stover,
see him alone at the table with his overcoat still on, arms folded across his
chest. You sound okay. You even have moments where the cage gives way
and the sound takes flight. You play the rest of the set with them. Then,
while the applause dies, while voices in the haze pick up in conversation,
Fritz comes out from behind his drums with his hand out.

"The Missionary! How are you?"

He introduces you around.

"I knew it was you," says the guitarist. "The minute I saw your suit.
I'm Jakob."

"Heinz," says the bass player.

"Felix," says the piano player.

You shake their hands. Turn back to Fritz. "The Missionary, huh."

"I called to ask for you. When you just disappeared. A few of us did.
They said you were gone."

"Who'd you call?"

"The number on the pamphlets your friend passed around."

"So they said gone."

"Who knows. Different answers. They got tired of being asked about a trumpet player who always wore a suit. They said you'd gone home. Or the information was confidential. We were waiting to see if anyone would tell us you were dead."

"Did they?"

"No. But they asked me if I'd like to be visited by the missionaries."

"Sounds about right."

"I said I'd like to be visited by one missionary. You. That's why you're called the Missionary now. And see? It's true! You visited me!"

You talk about the Factory. Fritz was one of the regulars. You tell him it's starting up again. Fritz tells Jakob and Felix and Heinz about the sessions every Thursday. You tell them they're welcome too. They know Peter and his band. They can take Peter's place. They can invite their friends. Stover comes up and stands there.

"There's a piano there," you tell Felix.

"Then I'll come!"

"I'll let everyone know you're back," says Fritz. "Hey! The Missionary! Back in town! Hide your children!"

And even Stover smiles.

CHAPTER 83

FOR THE FIRST WHILE, gigs come your way by chance, where you
walk into a club and one or two members of the band are guys you played
with last time you were here. So it's impossible to let Hill know ahead of
time. You call Wissom to explain. Wissom instead of Hill because you
want a witness who can say you called. Soon word spreads that you're
back, and with it the landlady's number, and it isn't long before musicians
are calling to tell you where and when they're playing, asking you to come
sit in. When you get home from tracting you find notes with names and
numbers on the little table for the phone. At night sometimes she calls
upstairs to let you know there's another call for you. You tell them all that
the Factory's opening again. For every gig you schedule, you call Wissom,
tell him when and where. He says okay. He'll let Hill know. You don't tell
him about the Factory.

"I'm sorry about all the calls."
She smiles. "Don't worry about it. It's exciting. I feel like your agent."
"Can I do something in return? Mow the lawn? Help you with chores?"
"That's all taken care of. Haven't you noticed?"
"I can do it. You won't have to pay me."
"I can't let my help go. What would they do? Don't worry so!"
The commandment to play. Where you stand caged on a shallow stage
or a clearing on the floor of one or another club and the sound beats its
wings against the silver wires that confine it. But somewhere along the
way you start to learn. How to summon up your negro heroes. Their
framed photographs on Mr. Selby's wall. How to summon up the music
of their albums on the portable record player in the back of the garage.
How to summon up your place on the hill above your house and surround yourself with a sunset sky where the high clouds take on the shapes
of your dark giants and the stars are the glitter of their eyes. Let yourself
feel home among them. Then there is no cage. Then you play from a
place where you're free. Where the notes too are free of the bars of the
clefs that cage them. Where they become tones. Where they fly free of
the commandments of their names. Where you're nameless too. Where

not even God knows what to call you. Where not even God can find you. Sometimes it works. Not always.

One night you get off the phone with a flugelhorn player named Walter and come back into the music room where your trumpet lies in its open case on the piano bench and the landlady's reading a book in the light of a lamp next to her leather easy chair.

"Shake?"

"Thanks again," you say, reaching for your horn. You're still not able to call her by the name she gave you.

"Are these people all musicians?"

"Yes."

"Like you? Jazz?"

"Yes."

"They're very nice on the phone. Do you play with them?"

"Yes."

"Where?"

"Different clubs around Vienna."

"Places where I could come?"

You see her at a club. Sharing a little round table with Stover.

"Of course," you say. "I'm sorry I haven't asked you."

"Sometimes they ask for the Missionary when they call."

"Yeah. They have fun with that."

"Sometimes they ask for the trumpet player who wears a suit."

"That too."

And she smiles the smile you've seen before, the smile that reaches down and brushes you where you shouldn't be brushed, as she puts the glasses on she wears to read, goes back to her open book again.

It isn't long before you're hooked up with most of the musicians you knew from the last time you played. Guys who remember the way to the Factory. They crack jokes about the Missionary. In their teeshirts, their sweatshirts, their sport shirts, their polo shirts, their old sweaters, they crack jokes about the trumpet player in the suit.

"Actually," you tell them, remembering Earl Bird and his second job at Union Mortuary, "I'm an undertaker."

"The Undertaker," Fritz says, rocking back and laughing. "Even better."

"That's me. Somebody has to give dead people haircuts."

The landlady comes alone. Sits by herself at the bar where sometimes an overhead lamp washes her blond hair the luminous ghost white of an angel's. Stover sits out in the audience, alone at a table for two, an ashtray he's pushed to the far edge, his Coke and your glass of water in front of him, a candle teasing its wavering gold light across the expression on his face. You feel bad for him. He isn't Novick. He doesn't get jazz. He doesn't know what to do with people who do. He doesn't know what to do about the landlady when she shows up. He's not the president or king of anything. Here in the smoky clubs of this foreign city there's nothing to be elected to. Even in a suit Novick could look like he belonged. People could look and know that he was one of them. They could hear it when he said hello. Stover sits among them like a chaperone. A vice principal. A student body president. A homecoming king so far from home he's lost in someone else's kingdom.

Sometimes you try to help him. Come off stage when you break and sit and talk to him to let people know he's cool. He's got a suit on too. When you're back on stage for another set you see people pay him more attention. And sometimes when you're playing you catch him watching you and there it is. The feeling that he'd rather be somewhere else. Home in your room studying after another long hard desolate day of tracting. Home feeling satisfied with another day of the Lord's work behind him. Home instead of keeping his breathing shallow in some smoky club.

Home one night from a gig, you watch Stover shake his suit coat out, put it on the wire shoulders of a hanger, then hook it on the curtain rod in front of an open window. You get it. Ventilation. The point of his demonstration.

"Good idea," you say.

He looks at you for an instant like a stranger. Then looks at you like it's you instead of the senior companion he expected.

"Not much luck tonight?" you say.

He works his tie loose, leaves the knot in, lifts it like a silk noose off his head.

"No," he finally says.

"I saw you talking to a guy at the bar."

"Yeah."

"Want to hear how Elder Novick did it?"

He waits till he's taken a seat on the edge of his cot.

"Go ahead."

"First off, he loved jazz."

"Okay."

"He'd come into a club looking like he loved jazz."

"What did he think about all the smoke?"

You look down at the letter you're writing for a minute.

"You know what else he loved?"

"What?"

"The people in the crowd."

"Are you saying I don't?"

"They could tell that he did. They loved jazz too."

"So I should act like I love jazz," he says.

"He made friends first. He kept it about the music. He did his job. He let people know who he was. He brought up the Gospel if they asked. But they were friends by then."

He unbuttons the cuff of his right sleeve and rolls it back in two folds over his forearm.

"Glad it worked for him."

"You must know how to make friends. All the stuff you did in school."

"That was different."

"I just realized. I never asked if you liked jazz."

"It's what we were told to do."

"What does that mean?"

"It's the Lord's work."

"I'm asking if you like it. You play a couple of instruments. What was the last thing you played?"

"West Side Story."

One hand one heart. The wedding dress shop. Tony and Maria. It cuts through you now like a knife through water. And leaves exposed the still place where you've kept Cissy.

"In school?" you say.

"Yeah. In the orchestra."

You think sheet music. A music stand.

"There's a lot of jazz in West Side Story."

Stover looks away. Then down at the rug. Looks back up, sees that it's still you, looks off across your shoulder.

"You're the musician," he says. "I'll take your word for it."

Your turn to look away. Shake your head. Smile.

"There was an elder here in Austria who danced in West Side Story. His high school did it too."

"Who was he?"

"Nick Paulson. My second senior. He's home now."

You think of telling him more. The way he took you to see the movie seven times.

"So you're saying put the music first."

The cage of the real purpose to your playing. The purpose Novick knew enough to leave alone till someone asked.

"I can teach you some jazz. Enough to make it interesting."

"I'd like that." Then he says, "It's hard to talk about something I don't understand."

"Great guitar solo," you tell him. "Try that line. If you mean it."

You use the landlady's piano because he's familiar with a keyboard and you can show him chords. Show him things you learned from Mr. Selby. Intervals. Chords and their progressions. Tones and how they set notes free from the cages of their keys and the bars that trap them on a sheet of music. How a melody moves on the underlying current of its changes. How a solo will break away from the melody but will usually follow that current. What happens when you sharp or flat a tone inside a chord. How breaking a rule can take a song to a place it's never been. Standing next to the bench, watching your hands the way you watched Mr. Selby's, he nods. He understands some of it. But he's not a rulebreaker. Rules are what he lives by.

"So," you say, when you finish answering his questions and close the lid on the smoothest most responsive keyboard you've ever played. "The rudiments of jazz."

"Thanks," he says.

"You can run for Jazz Club President now."

You look up at him.

"I'm just kidding." Then you say, "Think it'll help?"

"I hope so."

"Just listen for the things I've told you. You'll get it."

"I'll do that."

Chapter 84

Ronnie the bass player calls one night and asks you to come sit in. And says he's heard about this gig you play in a town outside Vienna. Wants to know about it.

"It's in a factory."

"A factory?"

"A small one. Bigger than most of the places we play, though."

"You mean a real factory. Where they make stuff."

"Yeah."

"What's this town?"

"Klosterneuburg. Ten minutes away."

"I know it."

"You want to come up? Fritz and his band will be there."

"Hell yes."

"Bring Mirela. There's a piano. And Willie. There's drums."

You show up with Stover the night Ronnie invites you to his gig. The place is ancient. The bar runs the length of a long dim brick corridor that opens up to a smoke-blurred room of cafe tables and a low stage. You remember Ronnie's flannel shirt and his round cloud of black hair. Old Willie's face is as smooth as a moon hubcap. Mirela still wears the green dress that takes the plunge you remember down into her lowslung breasts. She remembers you too. She hugs you while Stover watches from his table. You tell them about the Factory. No pay. Just tips and a good time jamming for a good crowd. Free food and stuff to drink. No liquor. They might have to play a polka. That's fine with them.

Ahead of time you tell Stover Thursday is a night off. No missionary work allowed. No hours to report. Just relax and enjoy. He can even wear his civvies if he wants. His Diversion Day clothes.

"Elder Hill said to always wear suits when you play."

"Elder Hill's not your senior."

Stover looks off for a minute, squinting like he's looking at the sun instead of the ceiling of your attic room, then looks back at you.

"You're right about that," he says.

"No missionary stuff. Period."

"Why not?"

"Because it's my call."

When you walk into Hubert's factory your first night back, you immediately know the residual smell of hot plastic in the air, the feel of home in the smell of dust and oil off the floor. Hubert has the place set up the way you left it, tables and light equipment moved back to clear a dance floor, folding chairs set out where there's room. Edith and her mother are there to dress up the food and drink tables with paper tablecloths, paper plates and cups and napkins, the plastic utensils Hubert couldn't sell, a dish of sliced sausage sandwiches they've prepared together. Stover helps Hubert hang the big Factory banner on its hooks on the back wall. You ask Edith something you haven't asked her before.

"So what song would you like to hear tonight?"

She stares at you. Goes bashful. Looks up at her mother. Frau Goller stops arranging sandwiches.

"Did you think I'd forget?" you say.

"Tell him, Edith. Tell him a song you like."

She looks back at you. You watch it dawn on her. That you're serious. That she can name a song and that you and the band will play it. She pulls on her mother's arm. Her mother bends down to let Edith whisper in her ear.

"Tell him, Edith. He's your big brother."

She turns with misgiving back to you.

"Over the Rainbow?" she says.

"Do you know it?" her mother says.

"Of course."

"It's her favorite song. She's learning it on the piano."

Fritz and his band show up. And Ronnie and Willie and Mirela. Some lone musicians too. Looking to sit in. Hubert has put out the word to his workers and friends. They've spread it around. The first night crowd surprises you. A good crowd. Frau Goller sits in one of the two folding chairs Hubert still sets out for his wife and daughter. In a pale pink dress with light blue polkadots, a red ribbon tied around her waist, pink socks, red shoes you've never seen her wear, Edith stands beside her. Halfway through the first set you tell the band you want to dedicate a song. You point out your little sister. Mirela takes the microphone.

"I'm going to sing a song for a little girl named Edith," she announces, while you watch your little sister start at the sound of her name. "It's called Over the Rainbow." And then she says, "Because she reminds me so much of Dorothy."

You watch her where she stands next to her seated mother. How she brings her hands together. How her smile goes broad. How her cheeks push up and squeeze her eyes almost closed, to curves, like Manny's when he squinted, like the edges of blue spoons. After the set ends, you go down and take her hand, and this time you don't have to lead her. Her eagerness you both back to where the musicians are setting down their instruments, talking among themselves.

"Guys. This is Edith. My little sister."

"I remember you!"

"Shake didn't tell us how pretty you are."

"How does someone as ugly as Shake end up with such a cute sister?"

"Shake isn't ugly!"

"I'm just joking, little one. But you're too pretty to be shy!"

"Hi, Edith. I'm Ronnie. Hope you liked your song."

She looks long and curious at him. He's used to it. Knows it's probably the first time for her. Lets her look all she wants at his dark face, his big round thunderhead of hair, the dark hand he holds out to her before she smiles and places her own inside it.

"I'm Edith."

"I know. The prettiest Edith I've ever seen."

Week by week the crowd is quick to build. People bring food and drinks again. You still know most of them. One night the Russian landlady you and Novick lived with smiles and waves to you from the dance floor. Her heavy sullen daughter is back with her. She still dances alone, the same slow sway no matter what the tempo is, but in a dress her breasts ride high like helium balloons and move with her body instead of the way they moved beneath her nightgown, loose and pendulous, against the way her body moved. The thin girl from upstairs, the girl you caught Rudd messing with, comes down again, but stays out on the dock. You see her on breaks with her chopped hair and painted lips and black Halloween circles around her furtive eyes.

Before the show starts every Thursday you take Edith by the hand while you mingle with the early crowd and the musicians when they show up. Feel her hand telegraph the possessive interplay of her heart between pride and jealousy.

"This song we'll be playing next is for Edith. From her big brother."

Stover only wears a suit the first time. The second time, unleashed from the harness of a missionary, he comes around. Wears his ironed plaid shirt and beige slacks. Brings a Uintah Utes sweatshirt in case the night is cool. His smile comes back, easy, relaxed, without the steel. He starts to talk to people. Sometimes he stands by the food table as though it needs to be guarded. They talk while they fill their paper plates.

Sometimes he holds their plates for them when it takes two hands to ladle food out of a dish. At first you worry what he tells them. If he bears his testimony. Hubert doesn't come to you with anything from anyone so you figure Stover's minding what you told him. Sometimes Frau Goller keeps him company. You introduce him to musicians and locals you're hanging with. You always wear a suit and tie. You have a reputation to protect. The Missionary. Who cuts dead people's hair.

The Missionary. Sometimes you're ambushed by the night artillery flash of a memory of that August night. And when it happens the convulsion of hate for what you are leaps out and takes hold of you like a beast that feels like it will twist you in two. All you can do is look down, close your eyes, ride it out. And then, when you do, and it's gone, the hate relaxes and recedes into the dark mystery out of reach in the back of your head. But it leaves its stench of human smoke.

One night you come home from a rainout night of tracting, stick your bikes under the shelter the landlady lets you use off the back of the house, go inside. Your shoes and socks and the lower legs of your pants are soaked. Stover grabs the couple of pieces of mail the landlady left for you on the phone table. He hands you an airmail envelope. Novick. Sent to the Mission Home because he didn't know where you'd be. Sent from there to you. Up in your room you sit at your desk and open Novick's envelope. It's written in blue ballpoint on a piece of lined paper.

He tells you thanks, a few times, for letting him know. For writing out the list of names of the people he had a hand in introducing to the Gospel. He remembers some of them. He tells you to say hello if you see them. He hopes they'll remember him.

He congratulates you for the dozen roses from the European Mission President but tells you to look out for Hill. Writes that he's an asshole. Writes that he can say that now that he's not a missionary any more. And writes how good it feels to write it. You can't help from smiling.

And then he answers your question about the musicians he went to see in New York. Zero. How he never saw New York. How the Mission Home routed his flight through some other city. How he didn't know till they handed him his ticket when they took him to the airport. How he'd told them what he wanted. Just a few days in New York. How he'd missed the chance. How it had to be Hill.

You sit there with his letter in your hand. You remember his little radio and the way you used to sit in front of it with him. The animation in his dopey face whenever he told a story about one of his heroes. You remember the stories. You hear his voice when he first presented you with

Brother Shlagl's trumpet. How you could hear the way his heart was torn in half for thinking he could rush you into playing. Now your heart feels torn in half for him. You know what it meant to him to hit the New York clubs. And you remember Hill when you went to pick up Stover. The bitter hate that locked his ugly smile in place. It had to be Hill. Payback from Hill because Novick started off this jazz thing as a missionary tool. Shithead. How good it feels to think it. You don't care if God hears it.

"You say something?"

You turn around and look at Stover.

"Nope." Then you say, "I'm gonna step outside. I need some air."

"I'll come with you."

"I need a few minutes alone."

Him watching you tuck your shirt in. You knowing what he's thinking.

"I'll leave my shoes here. Can't go far barefoot."

"The rule says I'm not supposed to —"

"I'll be right outside."

"You're the boss," he says.

"Just a guy who needs some time alone."

The wet cement of the porch feels rough and cool under your bare feet. It's been a long time. Mist still saturates the air and circles the street lamps in rainbows. He wanted to stay in a YMCA. Wanted to hit the Vanguard, Blue Note, Village Gate, other jazz joints in the Village. Maybe head up to Harlem too for places like the Lenox Lounge and the Apollo. Minton's where Miles got his head cracked up by cops. Maybe he wanted to sit back and have a real drink. Feel like he belonged. It wasn't any-one's business. Just his dream. A dream that pulled him from one door to the next till they numbered easy in the thousands. Maybe the chance of a lifetime.

You miss him. It hits you with the startling sudden rattle of rain through the leaves of a tree as a quick breeze tips and spills what water they hold. You miss him. You step off the porch and feel the sheen of water on the slick surface of the stone. The path to the gate is rough con-crete again but the shallow pools feel so good you spread your toes and step into them on purpose. The soaked cuffs of your pants slap around your ankles. Out the gate on the sidewalk you look up and down the street. At cars whose roofs glisten with raindrops in the streetlights. At houses whose lighted windows fade and are lost with distance in the mist. You remember a conversation from earlier that day with a man who answered your knock on his door.

Yes. I know. You've been here before. Not that long ago.

This is our first time here.

Then your . . . comrades. Maybe another religion.

That's possible.

I told them then I wasn't interested. Not to come back.

We understand.

Try not to come to my house again.

No. We won't. As long as we're here, is there anything we can help you with?

Help me with?

Your yard. Weed your flowerbeds. Anything you need.

It's raining.

I don't mean now. We can come back.

You just told me you wouldn't.

You're right. I'm sorry.

I'm sorry. You can still hear your voice. And then you're crying. You don't know why. But on this foreign street this far from home you're crying. Tears pool in your lower eyelids and then spill down your face. Novick. Home in Bakersfield. Home from a time back on the other side of that August night. Novick. Home from the life you had back then. From the time you were still okay. Novick. You stand there crying. On this foreign street in this foreign city crying. Elder Novick. Home where you could call him John.

CHAPTER 85

AT THE CLUBS you watch Stover man up and try to make friends and put the music first. From the stage you watch him look around. Catch a smile sometimes, sometimes just a look, and return the confident chrome flash of that crazy grin. People turn away. Act like they were looking past him. Just stare. Sometimes he'll get up, the only guy in the audience in a suit, walk back to the bar and stand with his shoulders squared next to a guy on a stool, nod and say hello with the monstrous confidence of that small town grin. He doesn't approach women there alone. Women you used to see Rudd hustling. A minute or two later he's always back at his table.

One night, at the outpost of his table at a club where you play with a quartet called Easy Joe from Budapest, Stover looks more miserable than ever. You've seen him fire off his grin a time or two. You've seen the people he's aimed it at flinch and almost duck. You've seen him wander over to the bar and get a fresh Coke from a bartender who doesn't look up when he sets it in front of him and takes his money. Late that night in your attic room you catch Stover looking at you from the travel iron he's using to smooth out the folds left by the cleaner in his shirt.

"I think I can help you."

"With what?" he says.

"It's not personal. Just a cultural thing. Something I had to learn too."

You expected him to study you before he answers.

"What is it?"

"First," you say, "I can tell you're trying to make friends. That's great."

"What's second?"

"You've got a great smile."

This time he studies you a while longer. When his distrust clears he gives you a private showing. You think of his yearbooks. The way they must be filled with photos of the grin he gives you.

"Thanks."

"I think it just might be a little too great."

"What?"

"Your smile. For Austria. It's okay back home. Here it's kinda strong."
"Strong?"
"It can scare people. Put them off."
"How?"
"Well, for one thing, it can make them wonder if they're supposed to know you."
"How?"
"People smile that way here when they know each other. Not when they're strangers."
"What's another thing?"
"Guys. They could think you're . . . being more than friendly."
"What?"
"I'm serious."
"You're talking about the people in these clubs you play. Right? They're not exactly the friendliest."
"Them too."
"Who were you talking about?"
"When we're tracting. You haven't seen someone open the door and take a step back when they look at you?"
"Nobody at church seems to mind."
"They're used to us doing it. Like back home. They got it from us."
"So I guess you're going to tell me how to smile."
"People don't grin like that here. Except at church. Or if they know each other really well."
"Okay," he says. "You know best."
And shrugs and goes back to ironing his shirt.

From that night on he doesn't even try to take the steel out of his grin. He just keeps the whole thing off his face. Puts it in his pocket. Leaves it home. Stops trying to make eye contact. Stops looking for the chance to say how great a guitar or trumpet solo was. You should have kept your mouth shut. You can't teach what he doesn't have. You can't teach what Novick did. You can only make him feel bad. From that night on he keeps his lone vigil like the out-of-town insurance salesmen who occupied tables alone when you played the Captain's Lounge at the Airport Holiday Inn. For everything he's been, everything he's done, you sense some stiff and brittle weakness at the heart of who he is. Maybe his high school was small enough to where he was the only guy. You don't know. It isn't long before he's bringing his Book of Mormon out to clubs. Sitting at his table turning pages in light you know is way too faint to read by.

MAY COMES AROUND. You've run with the headlights off for nine months now. Linz was an easy place to hide. A grim city made for fugitives. Now, where a club has spotlights that color the floor, you cringe when you first step into the light and raise your horn to see spears of red and blue run up and down the brass. And then that first note cuts the smoke and you're okay again.

Her name is Angelika. The girl who lives upstairs with her father and mother in a derelict place above Hubert's factory. She's kept away from you. On a warm Thursday night she asks if she can talk to you. You're on break before the last set. You've come to the far end of the dock to catch some air and some time alone from the people gathered back around the big door when she shows up in front of you.

Angelika. If Rudd even knew that much.

You remember the way she chews gum from the half hour you and Novick spent in her apartment upstairs talking to her folks. In the rebel outfit of a ragged denim jacket, tight black pants that show how thin her legs are, black boots, with her defiantly chopped hair, her bright red lipstick, the deep dark hollow shadows painted around the luminous whites of her eyes in the light of the caged bulbs high on the back wall of the dock, it surprises you how shy she is. She wants to tell you how she likes your playing. She stops chewing, gives you her face for a minute, then lowers her eyes.

"I'm sorry," she says.

Through her makeup, through the way she chews gum, sadness and resignation are so absolute it's as if she'd washed her face with them.

"Come sit with me," you say.

You sit side by side on the concrete edge of the dock with your feet hanging in air. Cats start to gather below them. Arch their backs to stroke legs they can't reach. She leans forward to watch them.

"Nice night," you finally say.

And let her take her time.

"I'm sorry," she finally says, again.

"Don't be sorry. It wasn't you." She turns her face your way, "I know him. I'm sorry for what he did to you."

She looks down again to watch the moving swarm of cats as they arch their backs to try to reach her feet.

"I was afraid to come downstairs again," she finally says. "But he was never here."

You watch the blinking lights of an airliner descend across the dark toward the airport in Vienna. If it's carrying any missionaries.

"I made sure of that," you say.

She looks straight ahead across the courtyard. How white and velvet smooth the skin of her profile is.

"Sometimes I dance out here," she says. "When you're playing."

"What do you dance to?"

"I like the slow songs." Then she says, "I pretend I'm flying."

If that was when Rudd made his move. While she was dancing.

"Flying," you say. "That's how I play too."

"I can tell."

She pulls up her feet, sets her boots on the concrete, puts her arms around her knees.

"Are the cats bothering you?"

"No," she says. "I'm used to them."

"Have you named them?"

She laughs quietly. Then she says, "There are too many. I'd never remember them."

"I can see that," you say.

"Where in America do you come from?" she finally says.

"A place called Utah. In the West."

"I'd like to see America someday."

"Are you from here?"

"No. From Hungary. My parents left to escape the Russian invasion there. I was nine years old. A child."

"I was born in Switzerland."

She sits up to turn her face your way again. "You're Swiss?"

"I was four when my parents took me to America."

If it hadn't been for Joseph Smith. If it hadn't been for two missionaries who came knocking on your grandfather's door. Where you'd be now. What you'd be like.

"Did they go to America because of the war?"

"No. Because of religion."

"The religion you're a missionary for?"

"Yes."

She turns her face to you again.

"So the religion that took you to America brought you back."

"I guess it did." After a minute you say, "So what does your father do?"

She looks forward again and rests her chin on her knees.

"He was a construction worker. He helped put buildings back together. Ones that were bombed. One day he fell off a scaffold and broke his back." Then she says, "He can't work now. So my mother cleans houses and washes clothes."

"My father's a bookkeeper," you say.

"Do you have lots of friends in America?"

"Enough. How about you?"

She reaches down to scratch her ankle through her boot.

"I have none," she says.

"Everyone needs friends," you say.

"People think I'm a gypsy. Because I'm Hungarian. I'm not. But you can't change their minds." Then she says, "We're not gypsies. We're just poor."

You watch her go shy again. Even in profile you can see her deep surrender to sadness. A quick explosive burst on the snare drums startles her. Makes her look past you toward the open door.

"Do you have to go?" she says.

"No. They're big boys. They don't need me."

"I want to know about the religion that took you to America," she says.

The bass guitar kicks in. And then the piano. Here's That Rainy Day. They start turning the head of the song around. Waiting for you.

"You do?"

"Yes." And then with an edge of impatience says, "I just said so."

"Okay. Mind if I ask why?"

She looks off again.

"I just want to know about it." She looks down at her knees. "I want to belong somewhere. Maybe have some friends." Then she shakes her head and says, "Not boys."

The girls who come to the churchhouse in Vienna. A couple of them around her age. If you could get them together.

"Okay. I can tell you everything you need to know. Give you somewhere to belong. But you need to do something for me."

She raises her head. This face, you're thinking, the same face Rudd saw, the face of this girl he never thought twice about defiling.

"What?" she says.

"Show me your smile."

A smear of lipstick on one of her front teeth. A slight overlap between them.

"It's a beautiful smile," you say.

And then, while you watch, it broadens and turns beautiful. "Really?"

"I couldn't lie to a smile like that."

And it folds, goes awkward, caught between pleasure and embarrassment.

"Thank you."

"Shake! That you? Come on!" You turn. Helmut standing at the open door with his sax hanging off its neck strap.

"Look," you tell Angelika. "He came out here to play for us."

She laughs. "You have to go," she says.

"You take requests, Helmut?"

"Inside, yes."

"I'll sit this one out," you call back.

"Okay."

You turn to Angelika again.

"Can I ask how old you are?"

"I just turned eighteen. Why?"

Seventeen when Rudd was having his way with her.

"If you decide to join, you'll need permission from your parents."

"I will?"

"You're too young on your own."

For a minute her eyes skate back and forth across your chest.

"They don't care what I do."

The lie you told Rudd that night. About introducing him to her folks. About them being just inside.

"They like the music though," she says. "They sit upstairs and listen."

"They should come down."

"They don't like people. Being around them. I think they're ashamed."

The band turns Rainy Day around for Helmut's solo. Angelika lets her legs down over the dock again. Starts weaving her shoulders. You sense someone else on the dock. When you turn and look, it's Stover, just outside the big door, keeping you in sight.

"I think everyone's ashamed of something," she says.

"Maybe."

"Do you dance?" she says.

"I can't."

"Most boys can't."

"I mean I'm not allowed to."

"Is dancing a sin?"

You laugh. "Only for missionaries."

It dawns on you. How you don't work here any more. How this town is someone else's territory now.

"I'll introduce you to the missionaries here in Klosterneuburg."

"You're not from Klosterneuburg?"

"I work in Vienna now."

"But I want you. I don't want anyone else."

"Then we'll have to tell them that," you say. "How about coming to church with us this Sunday? We can tell them then."

"Where?"

"In Vienna. You'll like it. Maybe make a friend or two. I'll come up and get you."

"You will?"

"I will."

On the walk down through town that night to the train station you can smell the smoke of Stover's curiosity like a slipping clutch. He's expecting you to volunteer what was going on. He's finally down to metal. Shredding the plates.

"You spent a long time talking to that girl," he says.

"Yeah. I know."

"What about?"

"We're bringing her to church Sunday."

"Her?"

His tone stops you cold and makes you turn to face him.

"Her," you say.

And stare him down.

"I was just asking."

You hold his eyes a minute longer. Let a car coast past on the drum of the cobblestones and leave his face in darkness again.

"We may be looking at a baptism."

"Really?"

"Really."

"Let me know what I can do to help."

CHAPTER 87

THEY FINALLY START showing up at the clubs. You've been waiting. You've wondered why it was taking so long. You figured from the start, when he told you he wanted to know the places and dates you were playing, that this could be what Hill had in mind. You just had too hard a time believing it. It struck you as crazy.

You remember the way they used to show up last summer and fall when you were playing. Before you were sent to Linz. The guys who came in back then were quiet. Usually with their ties and suit coats off or in their street clothes. They came to hear you. They got jazz or were curious. They mostly laid low. They weren't there to do missionary work. This was their time off. They were friendly. They told people they knew the trumpet player who always wore a suit. If they talked church to people they did it Novick's way. People had to ask them. Things took their natural course. Novick always had brochures if they needed one. Rudd too.

This time the elders are a different breed. In full mission dress. Suits and ties. Sometimes a soft bulge in their coats when they reach for a handshake or Coke that gives away their saddlebags. Sometimes young in looks and attitude, like high school kids out dragging State in their family station wagons, babyfaced, round-eyed, rubbernecking, like dragging State was some jungle ride in Disneyland.

At the start they came in timid. Looked around. Found tables. Ordered Cokes. Sometimes one or two would take a chair at Stover's table. Keep him company. Push your water glass aside to make room for their elbows. Stover would put his Book of Mormon down to chat with them. They'd catch your eye, give you a quick reflexive grin, sometimes wave, but they weren't here for you. You watched their confidence grow. Watched the Holy Ghost light fire in their bosoms. Now you watch them start to cruise the tables and the bar. Walk up cold to customers to tell them who they are and what they have for them. Glad Tidings of Great Joy. Sometimes sit down. Customers act surprised. And then bothered. And then mad. When they send them off there's always a brochure left lying on the table.

And sometimes customers will look at you. Because you're dressed like them. Because they were told. We're with the missionary up there with the trumpet. He's one of us. One night, on a break, you take a couple of them outside.

"What are you guys doing?"

"The Lord's work."

"Who sent you?"

"We heard you were playing here. You know. Captive audience."

And then, from the way their eyes glance off, ricochet off the walls and cobblestones of the street, it makes you sick to know that you were right. Hill. You look off down the street. New buildings built on salvaged cellars.

"These people aren't here for that," you say.

"Are you telling us we can't do the Lord's work?"

"You're making enemies," you say. "Not friends." You look at the younger one and say, "Are you even old enough to be in a place like this?"

"How old do you have to be?" he says.

"We're being quiet about it," the older one says.

"You're up. Walking around. Bothering people when they're here to listen to the music. Keep it up and they'll ask you to leave."

The elder doing the talking looks down sad. Like he's let the Lord down.

"Sorry," he says.

"Me too," says his companion.

"You didn't know."

"How should we do it then?"

"Come for the music. Lose the suits. Be friendly. Let it go from there."

"We were told to wear suits."

"Then let people get used to seeing you that way. Before you bother them."

"Just come and listen?"

"Is that so hard?"

"Sorry."

"Leave a tip for anything you order. Even water."

The Sunday you and Stover first take Angelika to church you're relieved to see her on the platform wearing a simple pale blue blouse and dark skirt under her denim jacket, her makeup softer, her hair smoothed down. At the Boecklinstrasse churchhouse you find the Klosterneuburg elders. The senior's name is Davenport. Tall, thin blond hair, the pale smile in his smooth face pious and forgiving, he makes you think of Elder Cannon. In a new American suit and tie his junior looks like he's still holding on to his last American haircut. A flattop starting to go long. You introduce Angelika. The junior's name is Dastrup. In the territorial way of referrals, she belongs to Davenport and Dastrup, the way Otto belonged to Burnham and his junior. You can see the shine of the spirit in their eyes when you go to hand her over. Explain to her that these are the missionaries who'll teach her everything she wants to know.

"I'm sorry," she says, to Davenport. "But I want Herr Tauffler to teach me."

"But he can't do that, Angelika," Davenport says, with a smile that forgives her candid innocence. "You live in our area."

"Why can't I have who I want?"

The steel that comes into Davenport's smile revokes any likeness to Elder Cannon.

"It's the way we work. He should have explained that to you."

"He did. And I told him I wanted to learn only from him."

"How do you know him?"

You nod when she looks at you.

"He knocked on our door once. My family's. With another American."

"I worked in Klosterneuburg four months last summer," you tell them.

"Now he plays trumpet in the factory downstairs."

Davenport and Dastrup look at you.

"What's going on?" Davenport says, in English.

"I play up there one night a week. Our night off."

"In a factory?"

"In the old Pionier Kaserne."

"Did you explain to her that she's our responsibility?"

"Yes." Her English surprises you. "He did. I still want him to teach me."

"I'm sorry," Davenport says. "That's not how it's done. We have to teach you."

She puts out her hand to him. He looks at it confused before he takes it.

"It was nice to meet you," she says, extracting her hand from Davenport's, shaking his junior's hand. She nods at you. Turns and walks down the aisle toward the chapel door.

"Where's she going?"

You watch her move through the members talking in the aisle.

"I don't know."

"Go catch her," says Davenport.

"She's yours to lose."

Davenport looks down at Dastrup. From his junior's face it's obvious he doesn't have a clue or even understand what Davenport needs help with.

"Well then. See you guys later," you say, looking at Stover, turning to walk away.

"Wait," says Davenport.

"What's up?"

"Okay. You can have her. Go ahead. It's not worth losing her."

"Okay then."

Stover follows you out of the churchhouse. You spot her a block and a half away. Waiting. Like she expected you. Or hoped you'd come. You reach her out of breath.

"They said okay," you say.

"You get to be my teacher?"

"Yes." And then you're aware of Stover standing there. "We do."

Her excited eyes go sly.

"So that's how a poor gypsy girl gets her way," she says.

"You did that on purpose?"

"I took a chance."

Back in the chapel you introduce her to two girls, Doris and Hilde, around her age, the girls who came to mind that night on the dock. Tell them she's learning about the church. They go to work the way members are taught to go to work. Make it their mission too. Make her one of them. Open a friendship of two to a sisterhood of three. Sit on either side of her in Sunday School. Share a single hymnbook. Take her to class with them. Spend the break before Sacrament Meeting introducing her around.

You take her back to Klosterneuburg. In the absence of sadness and resignation, her smile's shy, unsure, skittish. She finally shakes her head.

"I don't know how to be this happy," she says.

At the clubs the invasion of elders gets worse. More and more of them come looking to do the Lord's work in a smoke filled place they don't belong in. Even when they throw their grins around they don't look happy. Some look scared. Sometimes you watch a waitress or bartender or the owner talk to them. Sometimes you take them outside. Some of them don't come back once they've been told. New elders replace them. Some stay anyway. Some who feel like they only have to answer to a higher power.

One morning, leaving the house for a day of tracting after calling on the Lord to be with you, the landlady stops you. She's in the white bathrobe you know will come off in the sunlight of the back yard when the weather's warm enough.

"Shake? Can I talk to you?"

"Sure."

She smiles at Stover. He goes on outside.

"I came to hear you play last night," she says.

"I saw you there," you say. "I wanted to say hello but you were gone."

"I didn't stay long."

"Didn't like the music?"

"Don't be silly," her saying. "I love the music."

There are times when you can see in her the lady in the red dress from the Indigo. Like this was where she really lived. Like this was where she'd finally unpacked everything and filled the house with it. There are times when you can hear her voice.

"You could have made a request," you tell her.

"I get to hear you play all the time. All those wonderful songs! One of those young boys came up to me at the bar. Do you know who I mean?"

"In a suit?"

"Yes." Then she says, "He was very young." She runs her hand across the tanned skin of her lower face. "Still with pimples."

"What happened?"

"He started to talk to me about my church. I said I was only here to listen to the music. He said that what he had to tell me was much more important than music. A boy! With pimples!"

"Okay."

"He wouldn't stop. He kept asking me questions. Did I believe this. Did I believe that. I didn't want to be rude, so I finally paid for my drink and came home. He tried to hand me a pamphlet when I left. The bartender had to tell him to leave me alone."

"I'm sorry."

"I'm telling you because he said he knew the trumpet player."

"Did he tell you his name?"

"Yes. Elder something. I don't remember his last name."

"We're all called Elders. It's . . . it's our rank."

"But you're all so young!"

"I'm sorry I didn't see him bother you."

"It wasn't just me. There were others."

"I know."

"Do they come because of you?"

"Yes."

"It's a shame. They'll get you into trouble."

"I'll make sure they don't bother you."

"No. You just play. Just tell me I can be rude if it's necessary."

Davenport saying you can have her. Angelika works as a cook at a breakfast and lunch place in Vienna. Starting the Monday you first bring her to church, you meet three times a week after she gets off work at three, and use a coffee shop she likes around a couple of corners from her job. At a small table in a back corner of the place, mostly empty that time of afternoon, you're teaching someone from Austria the history of the church and the Restored Gospel of Jesus Christ for the first time. You give her a Book of Mormon. You don't use the memorized dialogues of the lesson plans. She wouldn't have the patience and you don't have the stomach. And so you just tell her. How for hundreds of years Christianity went on without the authority of Jesus Christ. You dismantle the Catholic Church. Neuter all the Protestants. Tell her how Jesus finally restored his authority to Joseph Smith. Let her ask questions. Go back over things she doesn't understand or wants to hear again for how strange they are. If Joseph Smith really wrestled with the Devil. If the plates were really gold. She drinks small cups of coffee topped with frothy milk. You and Stover sip on Cokes. You tell her how the early saints were persecuted. How they built cities only to have them burned. How they were driven from state to state. New York. Ohio. Missouri. Illinois. How they suffered and died but kept the faith. How Joseph was assassinated in a town jail. How the saints finally made their way cross country to a great lake where seagulls would save their crops from crickets. Where they would make the desert blossom as a rose. Sometimes she giggles. Sometimes she listens with her painted mouth half open, the gum she always chews at rest on her tongue, her dark eyes wide. The stories about America captivate her. The Great War in Heaven, between the spirits of Jesus and the spirits of Lucifer, puts suspicion in her smile.

"How do spirits fight a war?" she asks. "Did they have spirit swords?"

Stover can't catch a snort of a laugh in time.

"Sorry," he says.

You smile at Angelika. "There are things we don't know the answers to," you tell her. "Things we accept on faith."

"They used tanks in Hungary," she says. "Real ones. The Russians. I saw them."

"Real tanks can't hurt spirits," you say.

"Lucifer," she says. "That's a funny name."

"Yeah. You're right. The first time you hear it."

"The spirits of Lucifer." She smiles. "It sounds like science fiction."

You stay away from the reason negroes have dark skin. Away from the way she'll need to marry a priesthood holder for all eternity if she doesn't want to be a servant in the afterlife. Away from the promise of having her mother and father for eternity. They'll be in a lower kingdom. In the Celestial Kingdom, her own kingdom in the afterlife, she'll be an orphan. Things she'll learn on her own in time.

The priesthood. The Articles of Faith. Resurrection. Progression toward godhood. The commandments and their penalties. Tithing. The doctrine tends to leave her restless, picking at a fingernail, glancing out the window when someone passes. Chastity. The Word of Wisdom. Her questions remind you of questions you and the other kids in class threw at your teachers on Sunday when you were trying hard to make sense of what you were being taught.

"Smoking is a sin?"

"Yes."

"And coffee?" Looking down at her little cup in its saucer.

"Just a little sin."

Stover listens. Tries to keep up with your German. Smiles when you and Angelika smile. At the end of each lesson in this dusty sidestreet place, where the booths and tables are empty and the big man who makes the little coffees spends most of his time on a stool behind the counter turning newspaper pages, you quiz Angelika to get her ready for her interview with the District Leaders. Then Stover bears his testimony. How he knows beyond the shadow of a doubt that everything you've taught her is the truth. Sometimes you have to translate a word for him. His intensity commands her attention. Stops her chewing. Leaves her staring. After that, you pray, quietly, heads down, hands in your laps.

"I'm a tanker in the Army," you tell Stover, after you say goodbye to her one afternoon on the sidewalk.

"You're in the Army?"

"The Reserve."

You keep walking while another conversation having to do with you dies an early death.

"How come you don't use the lesson plans?" he says.

"I don't want to sound like a lawyer."

"You memorized them, though. Right?"

You stop and look at him.

"You want to test me?"

"I didn't mean anything."

"All you need to know is what's in them," you say. "From there you can improvise."

You walk for a while in silence.

"You brought up tithing early," he says. "It doesn't come till the last lesson."

"Once they're hooked. Right? I don't believe in doing that."

"It's done that way for a reason."

You remember Sister Soderstrom. Telling your father they needed to take out a loan to catch up. Asking your father why it had to be ten percent. Why it couldn't be eight or seven or four. The way she started crying.

"I know," you tell Stover. "The reason is what bothers me."

And on the tram back out to your neighborhood he has another question.

"Is she really a gypsy?"

"No," you say. "She's just from Hungary."

After that first Sunday Angelika shows up at church on her own. A Mormon orphan. But Doris and Hilde are there like sisters as soon as she comes through the door. They show up with her on Thursday at the Factory where they dance together on the open floor in front of you. Where you watch her spread her arms and fly when the songs are slow. Davenport and Dastrup show up in suits and ties. So they found the place. It's okay. It's their town. Davenport, you think, watching from the stage. Saying you could have her. Like she was ever his to give away.

CHAPTER 88

THAT SUNDAY, in the break between Priesthood Meeting and Sunday
School, you and Hatch step out on the sidewalk for some sunlight and
air, take a stroll out to the back yard. The weathered old picnic table still
stands there. Moss has taken over more of its decaying surface.

"I got a sick joke for you," says Hatch.

"Go ahead."

"What do you call a lady missionary?"

"This is gonna hurt, isn't it."

"You wanna know?"

"Go ahead."

"A boxelder."

"I don't get it."

Hatch looks at you like you just invented being stupid.

"An elder with a box."

"Jesus, Hatch! You can't say that!"

In the cloudless sunlight of the back yard, you duck, expecting lightning out of a sky incapable of lightning.

"What's wrong?" says Hatch. "A boxelder's just a tree."

"That makes a difference?"

"I can't help myself."

You watch a young elder you recognize from one of the clubs come
around the corner of the churchhouse, catch sight of you and Hatch,
drop his head and scratch his neck, turn around.

"All these elders are coming to the clubs I play."

"I know," says Hatch.

"You do?"

"Hill didn't tell you?"

"Tell me what?"

"He's been telling everyone where you're playing. He's been telling
them to go because the people there are easy pickings. Maybe he didn't say
that. Captive audience. Ripe for the harvest. That's what he said."

"He told you to go?"

"In church once. Not long ago."

"What'd you tell him?"

"Nothing. I couldn't tell him what I wanted to. A couple of other seniors were there." Then he says, "They didn't know what to say either."

"They didn't."

"He said where you were playing was where the Lord needed us."

"When does he tell you where I'm playing?"

"Usually at church. Or he'll call."

"You know what he's doing."

"I know it ain't good."

"Owners are telling me to make my friends behave."

"Yeah."

"One owner put a sign out. No suits."

"You're kidding."

"No. So they come in their street clothes. Brochures in their back pockets."

"I don't do Hill's bidding," he says, "He's a jock. So am I. I know guys like him."

"Two owners told me to stay out. One said to take my missionaries to Africa."

"Africa. That's funny."

"So this is real," you say. "Good to know."

"Real?"

You tell him the dozen roses story. Why you were called back from Linz.

"I never figured you for roses," says Hatch, smiling.

"Hill's trying to shut me down. So he can tell Lindner it isn't working. And Lindner can turn around and tell the European Mission President."

"You think that's what he's doing?"

"He's using missionaries to do it."

The same table. The same elusive play of sun and shadow through the new leaves of the tree on its mossy surface. On the pages of the magazines and papers you used to sit here reading. The same birds darting through its branches. The noises from the street. The sun warm on your back. The music coming from the chapel. What you can't remember is the guy. The life before the life you have now. When you were hoping for something better.

"What're you gonna do?" says Hatch.

Keep playing but not let Hill know where or when. Stop telling Wissom. Or tell him the wrong places. Send elders crashing the wrong clubs all over Vienna. Or quit. Maybe it's enough. Tell the guys you play with that you won't be playing any more. Tell them quitting is the only way to lose the missionaries.

"I don't know," you say.

"Hill's gonna keep doing it," says Hatch. "He's not gonna quit."

You look at him. Hands in his pockets. The flat jingle of coins where his fingers play with them. Hatch. Caught skinny dipping in a bathhouse pool. Forgiven. A violation small enough to let him stay in the life you used to have back on the other side of that August night. A small gray bird lights on the table. Twitches its head back and forth between you and Hatch, takes a peck at the moss, darts off again. The stuff you used to read here. The photos you know used to make you sick and leave you helpless. Now you can't remember what it felt like.

"No," you tell Hatch. "He's not gonna quit. He's just gotta make it look like it's me."

"How about that factory you play at?"

"He doesn't know about it."

"He will."

CHAPTER 89

PLAYING ONE SATURDAY NIGHT at Chattanooga you know it's finally time to quit the clubs. The dark reason you play, the deceptive reason, has brought its weasel face out in the open now. Its face is Hill. You've felt it coming. The way the guys you play with look at you like you're no longer one of them. You'll play out the coming week and not let Hill know where. To give yourself a clean last week. One face. Your own. Let the musicians you play with know. Let the people know who come to hear you. Let your negro heroes know. You can be trusted again. You can play free. Without the Pied Piper subterfuge while elders scout the room. There won't be any. One week clean.

And then you'll play the next week just to say goodbye. To the places they brought you back from Linz to play. To the musicians you've played with. To the people who've come to hear you.

You don't tell Stover what you're doing. You'll wait till next Sunday to tell him that the week ahead will be your goodbye week. You know he's loyal. He's an Eagle Scout. What you don't know is where he puts his loyalty. In you or Hill.

You hit the clubs where you've been asked to play or hit them on the fly. On breaks you tell them you're playing out the week and then some gigs next week. And then you'll be gone. You play with some of them for the last time.

"The missionaries? That's why you're quitting?"

"Pretty much."

"I don't even see any tonight."

"They don't know I'm here."

"I can think of better ways to get rid of them."

"I don't want to visit you in jail."

"Why don't your leaders just tell them to stop?"

"They don't work that way."

"You really have to quit?"

"I'm causing too much trouble."

"We'll miss you."

"I'll miss you too."

"I meant your horn. We'll miss your horn."

"I won't miss your sax." Smiling. "That's for sure."

Him smiling too.

"What about the Factory?"

"It's still on."

Free now just to play. To spread one gospel. The Restored Gospel of the Music. You didn't know how burdened and dull your playing was. How the ringing sound of steel had gone to iron and then to lead almost. The guilty weight in its wings as the sound lost its way when you tried to give your solos flight. How tame you'd tried to make it. How mindful of the Lord's work. You didn't know. Now you're free to let the devil have your horn. Free to let your devil horn reach down into your lungs and take the breath it needs to give music to what's been out of reach too long in the dark mystery in a back recess of your head. In the night wind that has sifted restless and directionless too long across the desert. Everything you've kept hidden from the lights. Play yourself free.

"Mind if we do some blues this set?" you saying.

"We usually do."

"I'll show you what I mean."

And so you show them. You were obedient before. You didn't know. Now you play raw. Angry, mournful, vexed, defiant, anguished, fearful, sometimes hopeless, half insane. Now you play your devil horn for someone's high school son with his stomach in the teeth of a Shepherd. For someone's mother dressed for church while a firehose tries to strip her of everything but the struggle to stay on her feet and breathe. For someone's kid brother shot dead off the handlebars of his bike. For four girls crushed by shattered rock in the basement of their church while another girl stumbles blind out of the rubble left by a bomb. For Freedom Riders, white and negro side by side like you and Jeff rode back to Fort Ord once, trying to escape the furnace of a blazing bus to stagger choking but at least alive into the bats and rocks and bike chains of the Klan. For a girl at a lunch counter with pancake syrup crawling through her hair across her scalp while her boyfriend tries for all he's worth to stay still. For Miles Davis. For your negro heroes if they'll have you back. For all the people God has turned and walked away from. For Novick. For his jazz dad. For a breathtaking girl with flashing teeth and skin that turns this radiant dark gold in sunlight. Where she sings for her father while you play her uncle's horn behind her. You play your devil horn for what you've long been waiting to. Play through all the questions you were always taught to never ask. Play for the way God never fixes things. When you open your eyes, when you bring things home again, the guys in the band are staring, the faces out in front of you are stilled, all turned your way. The high beams on.

On one of the tram rides back to your room in the attic Stover looks thoughtful. Something on his mind. He finally gives it words.

"No elders showed up again."

"I noticed."

"Did you tell Elder Hill where you were playing?"

You've seen him wave across the tables. Say hello. Keep his grin down to an easy smile. Start to talk to people. It's a shame, you think, watching him catch on, start liking what he's doing.

"I thought I did. Maybe not."

"So what song would you like to hear tonight?"

She looks down at her shoes. "I don't know."

"I don't know? I don't know that one."

Her shy face comes up smiling.

"You choose one."

"I don't know that one either."

Since you've been back, since he's opened up the place again, Hubert's been taking the microphone to open the show, welcome his guests, introduce musicians, crack some jokes. When he's not at the microphone he's been moving through the crowd, talking to the people of his town, standing back to watch them eat, drink, dance or just listen to the music, pleased and happy. He put this together. This is his show. Sometimes he'll step outside to patrol the dock. Accordions, harmonicas, wooden flutes, bongos, other instruments join you on the stage or play from the edges of the crowd. You turn standards like Autumn in Paris and Ain't Misbehavin' into polkas. Lay blues tunes over Latin rhythms. Solos are joyous, jumping, crazy, taking the audience to places you've never known. Dancers form groups. Little kids spin themselves dizzy. Angelika and her sisters swing the skirts of their dresses, crack the floor with their heels, their folk dancing wild and defiant. People applaud the solos and holler and clap and whistle when you bring songs in and let the drummer land them in a crashing finish. Davenport and his junior have been here every week. In their street clothes since their first time here. You'd never have guessed that Davenport loved jazz. That Dastrup could sing the blues with so much down and dirty soul.

Edith and her mother always take the same place, off to your right by themselves, the schoolteacher and the schoolgirl, like it's where they've been assigned. Edith stands next to the folding chair her mother uses. All you have to do is look her way to see her break into a smile, squirm, shuffle her black shoes, point their toes inward, as she waits for her song to come her way. If you lose this too.

"This next one is for my little sister Edith."

That Saturday night you finish the last set of your last club gig. It's a modern restaurant and bar in the hotel part of town. A fancy place for important people who only want your trio there for background to their conversations. The hard echo of the glass walls and polished stone of the floor have made it necessary to play muted. You've fielded occasional requests. Nodded to acknowledge occasional light applause and occasional tips dropped in passing into the big snifter on the baby grand. The piano player gathers up his charts. The bass player zips his gig bag up around his standup bass like he's dressing a mannequin. The house music comes on low again. You clear your horn of spit and take the mute out of the bell. Stover spent the night at the bar because the tables were reserved for people who could afford to order food. For once you're not the only member of the band dressed in a suit. Most of the men at the tables wear suits too. With all the suits it's been hard to distinguish missionaries. You haven't seen any. You've made it through the week without seeing one. Over the week you've felt the guys you play with warm to you again. Felt yourself come back again to just a guy who plays jazz trumpet.

"Excuse me."

You hear the accent in the English words. You turn around. It's a young guy, broad shouldered, red hair, dressed in a gray suit, the look on his freckled face serious enough to put you on alert. A missionary maybe. A native. Austrian or maybe German. You see Stover watching from the bar.

"Yes?" you say, using English too.

"My name is Christian," he says. "Christian Strasser."

And puts his hand out.

"Shake Tauffler."

"I know," he says.

"Thank you."

He hasn't let go of your hand.

"You're American?"

"Yes," you tell him.

"A missionary?"

"Yes."

"I can't believe it," he says. "We just walked in here tonight. And here you were."

"Believe what?"

"Do you remember a girl named Annalise?"

"Annalise."

"She goes by Anna," he says. "You met her last year. At a wine cellar where you were playing one night."

It takes a minute. And then the night that changed everything comes crashing in around you in a wave of memory.

"Yes. I remember her."

"She told me what happened," he says. "She told me what you did for her."

"That—"

"I just wanted to thank you for protecting her."

"She was worth protecting," you finally say.

He still has your hand. But now he turns his head. You look too. See her across the restaurant waiting by the door. The sudden smile in the sculpted face. The thin arm that comes up when she sees you looking. The long fingers she wiggles. The hand you raise to wave back at her. The last time you played Since I Fell for You. Christian turns your way again.

"We're engaged," he says. "We're getting married."

"Congratulations." Then you say, "She'll be a beautiful bride."

He just looks at you. And after a minute, where the grip of his hand has been still, he starts shaking yours again.

"She said you got a little drunk. She was worried."

"Tell her it worked out fine."

And now he smiles.

"She was right," he says. "You play very well. We enjoyed listening tonight."

"Thanks."

And now he lets your hand go.

"Enjoy your stay here in Austria."

"It's a beautiful country."

"Nice meeting you. Nice to have the chance to thank you."

You remember how kind she was. How that reminded you of Cissy too.

"Just be good to her."

"Don't worry," he says. "I know how lucky I am."

At church the next morning, in the break after Priesthood Meeting when women and children are allowed to come in for Sunday School, you watch Hill move among the members, chatting with the men, giving the women his basketball hero smile, bending down to kiss a widow's cheek or shake a kid's hand, playing the Second Counselor of the Austrian Mission for all it's worth. You can't miss him. Not the way his head stands over everyone like a lone cabbage in a harvested field. You watch him shake and then hold Angelika's thin hand in the knuckled monster of his own when her friends introduce her. Let go, you're thinking, let go, and when he does, he looks around and comes your way.

"I need to talk to you," he says, his face grim, the open scar of his thin lips drawn tight across his teeth. "Come with me."

You follow him down the hall. In his long brown scarecrow suit the ambling way he walks makes it easy to see him dribbling a basketball. He turns into the bishop's office, goes around the desk, takes the leather chair behind it, leans back, kicks one leg up on the desk, the clodhopper sole of his giant shoe between the brass nameplate that reads Bischof Tischler and a standing picture frame you figure holds a photo of the bishop's family. He waves his hand at the two wood office chairs that stand across the desk from him. You stay in the open doorway. Lean against the frame to let him know.

"Come in," he says. "Close the door."

"I'm fine here."

The guy who cheated Novick out of his long dream regards you for a minute. Drums his knuckled fingers on the leather padding of the bishop's armrest.

"Tell me what you're up to," he says.

"Closing down."

"What does that mean?"

"Quitting."

"Playing."

"That's right."

"I don't believe you."

"That's your choice."

He looks at you. You can see it. How you're stealing his moment. How he wants to play it out. Leave your dozen roses limp and black and shriveled in your hand. He finally looks down, picks a gold engraved letter opener off the desk, starts slapping the palm of his free hand with the flat of the blade and looks back up.

"You know you're expected to play."

"Expected."

"Let's say ordered."

His fingers close and trap the blade as it slaps his palm. Like a small bird. You look up the hall.

"Ordered," you say.

"President Lindner. The European Mission." His fingers free the blade but he leaves it lying in his palm and looks at you. "It's what the Lord called you to do."

Up the hall the man whose proud brass nameplate sits on the desk is coming your way.

"Here comes the bishop," you say.

Hill doesn't move. When Bishop Tischler reaches you he shakes your hand and asks if he can help you. You step back. He looks inside, finds Hill in his chair, Hill's ugly shoe up on his desk between his picture frame and nameplate, his letter opener in Hill's hand, and his face goes hard and glaring.

"We need another minute," says Hill.

"Take your time," he says. "But do it with your shoe off my desk."

He waits for Hill to consider his request, lay the letter opener on the desk, and with slow deliberation finally take his shoe down.

"Never disgrace my family again."

He holds his glare on Hill till Hill has looked away and can't look back.

"It's his office," you say, after Bishop Tischler leaves back up the hall.

"I know that."

His easy contempt is back. Hot and cold together race up the skin of your back into your neck. You could end your mission here if you let yourself.

"It's his letter opener too," you say.

"That's probably true."

He picks it up again. You step inside the office far enough to close the door behind you.

"So it's what the Lord called me to do," you say.

"Through two mission presidents."

"Did the Lord call you to do what you're doing?"

"What am I doing?"

"Sending a pack of elders to every place I play."

"You and your companion haven't given us a single lead. You obviously needed help."

"We've got a baptism coming up."

It throws him. He glances down, fishes for composure, looks back up.

"Connected to your playing?"

On the wood floor of the Factory you see her dancing with her sisters.

"Very much so."

"So you don't want other missionaries to have the same opportunity."

"That's not what you wanted to happen."

He looks down long enough to lay the letter opener on the desk again.

"Tell me," he says.

"Same thing that would happen in a basketball game if I threw a hundred balls out on the court."

His face goes bloodless white and hard.

"You really think you're somebody."

You look down at Bishop Tischler's nameplate. The letters engraved in the brass respectful of the title.

"Yeah," you say. "Either way, Bischof Tischler, I'm done playing."

How quick he can get to his feet. Just the slam of Bishop Tischler's chair against the wall and he's standing over you. It amazes you. A guy his size to move as quick as a lizard or chipmunk can change direction.

"I could send you home, Elder."

"No. To send me home I'd have to call you shithead."

Shock leaves his face slack. And then this fixed rage in his small eyes.

"You're done when I say you're done," he says.

"Sorry."

"No. I want you out there playing."

You look up at him. Hate trembling like the restless idling of Yenchik's engine in your nerves and muscles. What you said. What he'll tell Lindner. You open the door. Step into the hallway. Leave him standing there behind a desk that isn't his while you head for the solid ground of the foyer hungry for its sanity.

You wait to tell Stover till after church when you're on the train to Klosterneuburg for your usual Sunday invitation. You ride side by side on a bench. Stover has the window. You tell Stover he'll be seeing the last few tables of his last jazz clubs this coming week. You tell him you've already started to say goodbye.

He turns from the view and rests his eyes on your knees as though it's as far as he can turn and lift his head. And then, after a minute, he says the last thing you expected.

"I figured. It's too bad."

"What do you mean?"

"I really got to like it. Listening to you guys play."

"You did?"

He raises his eyes to look at you.

"Yeah." Then he says, "I listened for everything you told me. I heard it. I was ready to start talking to people. We were saying hello and how are you."

You're left staring at him. At the quiver in the skin of his face from the repeating crack of the train wheels on the rails.

"Why?" he says. "What's wrong?"

"Nothing."

"Then all the missionaries started showing up," he says. "I figured the end was coming."

"Have you told anyone about the Factory?"

"Like who?" he says.

"Any missionaries."

"I don't think so. No."

"I need to ask you not to."

"You think Elder Hill would find out," Stover says.

"We'll just keep it going long as we can."

"If they start to show up," he says, "you can leave it to Hubert and me."

You look down at your hands. The way you questioned where this Eagle Scout would put his loyalty.

"I owe you an apology," you say.

"For what?"

"I wasn't sure I could trust you." You look at him. "I'm sorry."

He glances off, out the window, confusion and hurt in his eyes.

"You're my senior."

At your stop you use the pedestrian bridge to cross the highway and then make the walk up the narrow uphill streets that lead to the familiar gate of the Stift in silence. Outside the gate you stop. Still see the residue of hurt in his eyes.

"I think Angelika's pretty much ready," you say.

"To be baptized?" he says.

"We'll need to get her interviewed first."

"Right."

"And then schedule her baptism."

"Yeah." He looks down, shakes his head, comes up grinning. "This is exciting."

"I'd like you to do it."

He stares at you. His mouth slack.

"Wait," he says. "You mean baptize her?"

"Yes."

"Like you let your last junior do?"

"You want it or not?" you say.

"I'd be honored. Wow. Why me? What about you?"

"I've done my part. This is your part."

"Sure I'll do it. I just don't get it. Thank you."

"We'll have Davenport and Dastrup confirm her."

"Okay. Wow. This is the most humbling thing I've ever been asked to do."

"Come on. More humbling than a touchdown pass?"

And now his grin is genuine. No steel.

"What's a touchdown pass?" he says.

Chapter 90

BACK HOME that night, in her music room, you tell the landlady that the coming week will be your last week playing in Vienna. No. You're not moving. Just quitting. But you'll still need to play to stay in shape.

"To an audience of one," she says. "I'll have to get a cafe table and stick a candle in a wine bottle. So I can sip wine and listen."

You both laugh.

"And a spotlight," she says. "Who knows," she says, smiling while you shake your head. "Maybe I'll invite some other musicians over. Maybe I'll start my own club. What do you call it in America? Speak something?"

"A speakeasy," you tell her. "You'll need more than one table, though."

"No" she says. "Just one will do."

"Two chairs?" you say, "In case Herr Stover wants to listen?"

She laughs. "Okay. I'll share my table. Two chairs. But only one glass for wine."

"I'll be saying goodbye to my friends this week," you tell her. "Playing with them one last time. Want to come along?"

"All week?"

"Except Thursday."

"Oh. When you play in Klosterneuburg."

"You can come then too."

"No boy missionaries? No pimples?"

You laugh. "Promise."

"Just once," she says. "Call me by my name."

The three of you, two young guys in dark undertaker suits and a classy blond woman in a casual but elegant looking dress and high heels, walking the streets of Vienna, you hit the clubs where you've been asked to play or know they'd welcome having you sit in. It unnerved you back when you learned that some of the clubs up and down the ancient cobblestone streets of the Donaukanal were often cellars that survived the bombing of the buildings they supported. Cellars on which new buildings came to be built. Buildings that Angelika's father helped build before he fell off a scaffold.

Short stairwells lead down to the doors of the clubs where you can hear the music muted by the heavy wood, then loud, a sudden flood, when you pull back their doors to step inside. Club by club, while Steffi and Stover share a table out in the audience, you play a last set or two with them. Club by club you tell your friends you're playing out the week and then you're done.

"Hate to see you go."

"I hate going."

Every Sunday afternoon you still catch the train to Klosterneuburg for a dinner invitation or an excursion to another stift or castle or town in the Wachau where the low hills that rise from either side of the Danube are striped and crosshatched with rows and rows of vineyards that lift and fall with the pitch of the earth. And every Sunday Edith asks if your trumpet needs to be cleaned and oiled again. You've been bringing it along.

At the Factory, after your last set one Thursday night, Franz steps up with his tenor dangling off the hook of his neck strap. You've capped the set with a blazing uptempo rendition of Green Dolphin Street. The hollering and whistling are dying out.

"I love this," he says, grinning, bouncing up and down, waving a hand out across the crowd.

You watch big chesty Gabriele drop the way she's been flirting around all night, turn all business, take over the way she always does. Start picking up, moving through the crowd, telling everyone in her big hoarse voice the night's over, time to clean up, remember their bowls and trays and pans and leftover drinks. You've wondered why she always leaves alone. What it would be like to leave with her.

"I love it too," you tell Franz.

"A factory." Then he says, "A jazz factory!"

"Yeah. Not bad." Then you say, "Have you seen Hubert?"

"He had to take a kid to the hospital."

"What?"

"You see that crazy kid with the little washboard?"

"Yeah. What happened?"

"He broke the spoon he was playing it with. So he started using his knuckles. He wore the skin right to the bone. He just kept going."

"His knuckles? Didn't he feel it?"

"I guess not. The washboard's covered with blood."

The skin chewed through by the corrugated metal. The shock of the white of the bone. If there's enough left to even stitch together.

"God. I hope he'll be okay."

"Listen," says Franz. "Everyone's asking what happened. Customers and musicians."

"Yeah. I miss them."

"You can't drop in now and then?"

"Not really."

"Why? What would they do? Crucify you?"

"Crucify? Was that on purpose?"

"What else would they do to a missionary?" Then he says, "Let's eat. Before she cleans everything up. I'm starving."

And now you can't get that kid's knuckles off your mind.

"Go ahead."

CHAPTER 91

THE FIRST TWO finally show up. You warned Hubert they'd be coming. He told you not to worry. He knew how to spot them. Sure enough, during your first set, you watch them come in, fold their dripping umbrellas, set them against a wall where other umbrellas stand, lay their raincoats where other coats lie across a table, look around. Dark suits, hairtrigger smiles, the nervous look that they don't belong here or anywhere else in Austria. While you play Don't Get Around Much Any More you watch Hubert talk to them. From there they leave people alone. They talk briefly to Stover, listen to a couple of tunes, gape at Gabriele, gather their coats and umbrellas, look for your eyes, nod as they pass the pallets and plywood of the low stage on their way out. Just two. You wonder if the rain kept more of them away.

You decide to wait till the following week to see if they showed up by accident or for a reason other than Hill. It turns out they were scouts. The next Thursday, the evening warm and cloudless in the dry courtyard off the dock, fourteen of them show up, in seven pairs of two, wearing full missionary dress, working the dock and the loose edges of the crowd inside where people are easier to split away and be cornered for an introduction to the Gospel. Hill's Army. Hill's Avenging Angels. Who actually believed Hill when he told them he was sending them here to do the Lord's work. Davenport and Dastrup, regulars now in their street clothes, look around confused, wondering what's going on. It's their town. Hatch and his junior are there, faces in the crowd in their street clothes, interested in them too. You see people listen, polite at first, then shake their heads, then look annoyed, then walk away. You see Hubert shadow them. Try to talk to them. A few take him seriously. Others look down at him, smile while they listen, then turn around and keep going. Like he's nobody. With his shirt open at his throat, sleeves rolled back, just another face in the crowd, some kind of joke thinking he can stand in the way of the Lord's work of telling his neighbors their church is false. Shame and fury crawl like slow fire up your back into your shoulders. It's not Hubert's job. They're here because of you.

You kill the band at the start of your solo, set down your horn, take the microphone. The instruments die off. You raise your arm. The momentum of dancing idles down and stops. Couples come apart to look your way. People come in from the dock. You speak to the crowd in German.

"We have some American guests here tonight. The young gentlemen in suits. Excuse me for a moment while I welcome them in English."

Faces look around. You speak with an easy smile.

"Welcome to the Factory, Elders. I need to tell you a couple of rules the owner asks everyone to follow. First, there's no drinking, and smoking is only allowed out on the dock behind me. I know those don't apply to you, but this one does. No missionary work."

You watch some of them look around.

"Then why are we here?"

"To hear some music. To have some food. Make some friends. Enjoy yourselves. But there's no missionary work allowed."

"We were told to come do the Lord's work, Elder Tauffler."

"You were told wrong. I'm sorry."

"Aren't you a missionary?"

One of the younger ones. This redheaded freckled kid who looks like he's fresh out of the sunshine of an Idaho potato field.

"This is everybody's night off. As long as you're here, it's your night off too."

"You're telling us we can't do the Lord's work?"

An older one you recognize, one who's been around, with brown hair he doesn't know how to comb and a blue Austrian suit too big for his shoulders.

"It's not my rule. It's the owner's. These are his friends and neighbors."

"They're God's children too."

"What does he have against us?" another elder says.

You start to lose the smile you've worked to keep in place.

"You'll have to stop or you'll have to leave," you say. "That's the rule. Respect it."

You look at Edith and her mother. This open shock on Edith's face. A smile on her mother's. You go back to German to speak to the waiting crowd.

"I want to thank the man who makes this night possible every week. Who gives us this place to play. The boss. Hubert Goller. Come up here. Please."

He waves you off. But people break out hollering and clapping and whistling, shouting his name, till he makes the stage and stands in front of them, grinning in spite of himself, running his hand through his hair. The band plays a crashing salute. You give the crowd a minute. Then raise your arm. Turn to Hubert.

"I want to thank you too," you say. "For me and my friends behind me. Thank you for giving us a place to play. And wonderful people to play for."

You shake his hand. The crowd explodes again. Starts to chant his name. Hubert! Hubert! Gabriele, in back, hands cupped like a megaphone around her mouth. The landlady's daughter Olga. Hatch and Davenport. All the names and faces you've come to know. Stover at the food table, arms folded across the chest of his plaid shirt, smiling. You wonder where Angelika and her sisters are. The drums and bass pick up the cadence of the chant. The guitarist jumps in with a riff. You look at Hubert.

"I think they want to hear from you."

Hubert takes the microphone. Clears his throat. You watch the elders. Some of them surprised. The man they treated like a joke. You feel his hand on your shoulder and turn to him.

"Thank you for the music," he says, and faces the crowd. "Last year a young man from America told me he needed a place to practice his trumpet. This is what came of it. Not only is he my partner," he says, and looks at you again, "he's a member of my family."

This time, while you stand there stunned, the applause and burst of music are for you. Hubert waits it out.

"Without my wife Gertrud and our daughter Edith, this would also not be possible. Stand up, Traudi. Let them see who you are."

A modest half embarrassed smile on Frau Goller's face as she stands. Surprise on your little sister's. Hubert waits for the applause and the music again.

"So let's all enjoy!"

You pick up your horn. Take the song from the top again. Hatch catches up with you on break.

"We brought bananas tonight. They're almost gone."

"Thanks. That's cool."

"That took balls," Hatch says.

What you've done. Put the lights on high beam.

"I had to," you say.

"You know Hill's gonna hear about it."

"Yeah."

"He'll be ticked."

"I think I've got a transfer coming."

"You think he'd do that?"

"It's all he's got left. Get me out of here."

"Who's the big girl with the killer chest?" says Hatch.

"You dog."

"Come on. Who is she?"

"Her name's Gabriele. Want me to introduce you?"

"She'd eat me for breakfast," he says. "There wouldn't be enough of me left to excommunicate."

After four weeks, with something to believe in, somewhere to belong, new friends, a student's knowledge of the history and doctrine of the church and a beginner's testimony of the truth of the Restored Gospel, Angelika's ready. You've set an interview appointment with the District Leaders. You've talked to Bishop Tischler to schedule her baptism. That night at the Factory, while Hill's Army gradually retreats out the door, you play through the second set without seeing her and her sisters Hilde and Doris on the dance floor. You've started to wonder. Her interview's tomorrow afternoon. If they're helping her cram. Quizzing her somewhere. If she got cold feet. Hilde shows up at the end of the second set. Takes your hand and leads you out onto the dock.

Angelika's wearing a simple pink dress. A wide pink ribbon keeps her hair back off her forehead. Her makeup is muted. Her lipstick pink. The black death stare gone from around her eyes. Her jaw still. Not working a wad of gum. New white shoes. Doris is there with her. She and Hilde can't keep from smiling. They did their job.

"Wow," you finally say. "You look nice."

"It's a new dress for my interview. I wanted to show it to you to make sure it's okay."

She backs away. Pulls the sides of her dress away from her legs in a fan and does a twirl. You catch a couple of guys with sneers in the nests their pimples make of their lips. She doesn't see them.

"Do you like it? Doris and Hilde helped me pick it out."

Pink with white shoes. The Salt Lake Airport two years ago. The mirage across the polished and blinding stone of the floor. It takes you a minute.

"It's perfect. You look beautiful." It takes you another minute. You look at Doris and Hilde. "I need to talk to Angelika alone."

They both nod. "We'll be inside," says Doris, as they turn and leave.

"Let's get away from this crowd," you say.

You take Angelika toward the far end of the dock.

"Doris and Hilde showed me where I'll be baptized," she says.

"At the churchhouse?"

"Yes." She smiles. "A little swimming pool." Then she says, "First I have to pass my interview." She laughs. "Then I have to practice holding my nose."

What you've known almost from the start. How her heart is set on giving you the honor. How hard it will be to tell her you can't. How you still don't have a reason for this girl whose open smile you can't lie to. A reason other than the truth.

"You'll pass," you say. "They want this as much as you do."

How she looks down the dock. How she crosses her arms and huddles her shoulders together. Like a blade of cold wind has found and cut through only her.

"Will it really wash all my sins away?"

"Every one of them." Then you say, "You'll be good as new."

And then she just looks at you, quiet, her face an open question she can't bring herself to ask. You get it.

"That was someone else's sin," you say. "Not yours. Don't be scared. Or ashamed."

"But I—"

"No."

"Do I have to confess tomorrow?"

"No."

From inside the Factory you hear the bass guitar. Deep throbs of a quick progression. You look back at Stover where he keeps his vigil just outside the door.

"Tell them to start without me," you say. "I'll be in."

He nods and disappears. You turn back to Angelika.

"You'll need a white dress too. For your baptism."

"I know. Hilde and Doris told me. I already have it."

"It's not too thin, is it?"

"No. Doris told me that too. I can't wear anything under it, so it has to be heavy, because it will be soaking wet."

"Okay," you say. "Interview tomorrow at three. Baptism Saturday at three."

"Do you have white clothes?" she says.

How it's time to tell her. From inside come the rattle and thud of drums. The pianist striking and holding the note the guitarist needs to tune his strings.

"I won't be the one to baptize you."

Shock leaves her searching your face.

"What are you saying? You don't want to?"

"More than anything."

"So why not? Can't I have who I want? Does that other missionary get to do it? The one who said I lived in his area?"

You can't lie to her. Not to her face, her dress, the ribbon in her hair, her pink lipstick. Not to her eyes. Dark, intent, naked. Like an animal, she expects the truth, the truth of what she sees, what she listens for, what she hears.

"That's not it." And then you say, "I don't have the power."

"You're not strong enough to hold me?"

"Not that. The authority."

"But you're a missionary," she finally says. "You told me missionaries have authority."

"I did something wrong," you finally say.

She lowers her eyes for a minute. When she looks back up she says, "With the man who did some—"

"No."

Rudd. You don't want him anywhere near her again. Anywhere near this. Not his name. Not his face. Nothing. Not his memory. You try to hold her eyes. Tell yourself you told the truth. It wasn't with him. He was in a different room. But she can tell. You can see it in the eyes you finally have to look away from.

"Maybe it was his sin," she says. "Not yours."

Two streetwalkers. Two rooms. Two beds. One of each of them yours.

"No. It was my sin."

"So get baptized again," she says. "Wash it off."

"It's not that easy. Not for a missionary."

"Why not?"

"What's important is you."

"Would they excommunicate you?"

The first time you hear the word you taught her.

"If they knew. They'd have to."

"Nobody knows?"

"God knows." Then you say, "Now you know too."

"So if nobody else knows . . ."

"In God's eyes your baptism wouldn't count. Not if I did it."

"So who will do it?"

"Elder Stover. But I'll be there. You know that."

She studies you again.

"Did you murder someone?" she says.

The desk clerk at the Hotel Rabe. If he lived. You look out across the courtyard. In the night sky are stars that were always there. You look down at your shoes.

"No."

"Did you dance with someone?"

You look at her and laugh. "No."

"You won't tell me what it was."

You smile. "Do you want a confession?"

And now she laughs. "You're not Catholic," she says. "And I'm not a priest."

The District Leaders do their interview at the corner table in the coffee shop where you taught her everything. She wears the outfit she wore last night. You and Stover wait outside with Doris and Hilde in the warm air of a blue sky above the rooftops of the downtown buildings till she comes out the door with the District Leaders.

"I'm ready," she says, her smile shy but her face luminous in the sunlight.

"She's more than ready," says Bangerter. "Good work. She's good to go."

Stover the Eagle Scout came to Austria prepared. With a pair of white pants. Just in case. There with you on the tile floor of the font room are Bishop Tischler, Doris and Hilde, Stover, and Davenport and Dastrup. Dastrup sports a new Austrian haircut. They'll do the confirmation when Angelika takes the folding chair on the exit side of the font. Stover enters the font first. Turns and stands in the center waiting while Angelika descends the stairs into the waist deep water. She lets her hands float on its surface. Looks at you. In the water, in her white dress, her smile is hesitant. She wades into Stover's waiting arms. He shows her how to hold his arm while he holds hers. Her free hand holds her nose. With his arm raised Stover recites the baptism prayer. Then lowers his hand to the small of her back. She looks at you and smiles again, then lets her knees give, and then Stover lets her down, down till her hair floats away from her head, down till every hair of her head is immersed, till water washes over the entirety of her face.

In your place, in the place you would have occupied before that August night, Stover brings her out of the water again. Water floods off her face as she breaks the surface. Water rushes to fill the hole her body left. When she's on her feet again, Stover releases her. She shakes her head and uses her hands to clear her face and wipe her hair back. Her soaked dress clings to her as she comes up the tile stairs of the font. Bishop Tischler lays the large white towel he's holding around her shoulders. Davenport and his junior wait behind the folding chair to lay their hands on her head and confirm her a member of the Church of Jesus Christ of Latter Day Saints. Die Kirche Jesu Christi der Heiligen der Letzten Tage. She pulls the towel around herself but has something else in mind. An angel on bare feet, hair glued to her head, her body more slight in her soaked and clinging dress than you imagined, trailing water, she turns and hurries your way, opening her dripping arms. The towel falls open with them. You open your own arms. Hold her tight. Feel the wet of her dress come through your shirt. Feel the wet of her hair against your face. Feel it in her back and shoulders. She goes to Doris and then Hilde. Like you, they don't shy back from her wet embrace, but step up and take her in their arms too. She closes the towel and goes to the chair where Bishop Tischler has joined the elders who stand behind it. Cleansed of sadness. Cleansed of loneliness. Somewhere to belong now.

"Okay," she says, fanning her open hands, taking a deep excited breath, letting it go, sitting down, holding her head erect to receive the power and the glory through the palms and fingers of the waiting hands. "I'm ready."

Stover stands in his soaked white pants on the top step of the font. You bow your head, fold your hands, close your eyes. Davenport starts his confirmation prayer. You've taken her through it to keep her from being surprised or scared. What to expect and not expect. You hear Davenport give her the Gift of the Holy Ghost. You've left out the burning she's supposed to feel in her bosom because you don't want her to blame herself when the Holy Ghost takes a look at the fire she's built for him, laughs, and keeps on going, like he did for you.

With the official stuff behind him, Davenport launches into the blessing part of the confirmation, the part he can improvise. His solo. It's long, elaborate, devout, borrowed from speeches you've also heard. You don't mind. Angelika's strong for her size. Her neck can balance and hold the shifting weight of six hands. You hear the chair creak as she adjusts her position now and then. You've put out of your head the way you should have been in Stover's place. Put out of your head the way Angelika wanted you to be the one. What matters is you brought her here. You didn't take her all the way. But you brought her to this threshold. And then you sent her on. You did this right.

Chapter 92

On Sunday the weather shifts between mist and drizzle from the time you go to church to that afternoon for dinner with the Goller family. After dinner Edith loses herself in cleaning and oiling your trumpet in the other room. You take Hubert outside to apologize to him. Tell him what happened. Why all the missionaries. The twin towers of the Stift are ghosts in the low mist.

"What do they have against you? That I won't let missionaries ruin things?"

"No. It's me. Personal."

"Personal? Who?"

And so you tell him about Hill. Why you had to give up the city clubs. How you might be transferred. While he listens his face goes young. The blotched skin tightens and clears and his eyes narrow and his mouth takes on a closed frown. Like he's squinting. Maybe aiming. Trying to catch a shadow deep in the mist of the distance. If you're looking at the resistance fighter he used to be.

"I learned a word from the Americans who liberated me," he finally says.

"What word?"

"Not a word for a missionary."

"What is it?"

"Motherfucker."

The word burns, reminds you of Rudd, but you laugh because it fits.

"The Factory stays," he says.

"What do you mean?"

"If you go. I know the musicians. We're friends now. They'll come."

"You're keeping it going."

"You have phone numbers?"

"I'll bring them."

"I need to make a sign." He uses his hands to show how wide he plans on making it. "No missionaries," he says.

"You won't need to. If I'm gone, they'll be gone."

"Then we just need a trumpet player."

"You've got one. Kurt."

A smile relaxes his face.

"We just need a trumpet player," he says again.

And now you smile too. Look off into the mist gray of the distant woods for the enemy Hubert was looking for.

"Well," you say, "I'm not gone yet. It may not happen."

"Ja. We will see."

The transfer letters are there on Tuesday on the little table for the phone when you get back from tracting. They're typed on Austrian Mission stationery with the usual talk about being called by the Lord to labor in another part of the field. You're going to Knittelfeld. The last town Morgan worked before he came to work with you. Stover's being called to Innsbruck. You're surprised. Knittelfeld's not that far, a couple of hours, while Innsbruck's clear out west, close to the end of the country. No hope of sneaking back to Vienna to play for a night. You wonder if they got your transfers backward from the way Hill wanted them. You'll work with an elder named Barry Butterworth.

"I'm supposed to be there Thursday," says Stover. "Day after tomorrow."

"Me too."

"So we don't even get to say goodbye at the Factory."

Stover shakes his head slow. From the look on his face you can see him saying the word Hubert learned from his American liberators. You can hear yourself saying it with him.

"Looks that way."

And then you read the real surprise. You'll be District Leader. You'll visit the missionaries who live and work in your district. So you'll be provided with a car.

"They're making me District Leader," you tell Stover.

Stover stops with one arm out of his suit coat. "That's great," he says, slipping the rest of his coat off, leaving his saddlebags hanging in the open. "Congratulations."

"No. Here. Maybe I read it wrong."

Stover looks up from the letter grinning. "Nope. You're a District Leader."

In the morning, once the office opens, you use the landlady's phone to call Wissom. You can hear guys talking in the background. A typewriter going.

"Yeah," he says. "It surprised me too. I mean the guy hates you."

"So why?"

"I think a couple of things. First, he needed a good reason to get you out of Vienna. Something legitimate for Lindner and the European Mission. Second, your track record. Two baptisms. The times you made the newsletter. The people your trumpet brought in. The name you made for the Church."

All you thought about was staying out of sight while you worked on nothing but the hope of paying off your deal with God. Always knowing you could never do enough. Now you see yourself through Wissom's eyes.

"And don't forget those dozen roses," Wissom says.

"A record," you say. "I never saw it that way."

"Well, it is. You made it easy for Hill. He could point to it and say look at this. If anyone deserves a promotion, this Elder does. And good-bye Vienna."

"Yeah. I get it. Thanks."

"Did I say congratulations?"

"I don't remember."

"Well, congratulations then."

"Thanks."

"I wish they'd transfer me. Some sleepy little place where I could serve out my last few months in peace. Away from Hill."

"I know," you say.

You hang up. Wissom knowing when he's going home. His end date. Yours still elusive, uncertain, in the dark. This menacing apprehension in your stomach. God with your stomach in his hand. If you should tell your father. If he'll write you back the way he did about your first baptism back in Linz. This pride that left you staring blind at the floor of your room. This overblown pride he followed with a short scripture about not letting your own pride go to your head. To start working on the next one. You haven't told him yet about Angelika.

You call the trains for Innsbruck and Knittelfeld. Then Frau Goller. Then come back upstairs. Stover is dressed, ready to go, slipping the tracting book into a saddlebag, smiling to himself.

"What's the smile for?"

"That woman yesterday. When we asked if we could mow her grass for her and she told us she just mowed it."

"Yeah. Next time I guess we should look before we ask."

"What's wrong?" he says.

"Why?"

"You look . . . I don't know . . . like something's wrong."

"I'm not so sure I want this," you say.

"District Leader?"

"Yeah."

"That's nuts."

"I like being on the street." Then, hearing yourself, you say, "Working the field. Just doing my job."

"District Leader's a job too."

"Wanna trade?"

"Trade?"

"I'll go to Innsbruck. You go to Knittelfeld."

Stover smiles. "You were my leader," he says. "You did darn good."

"I'll throw in the car," you say.

He laughs. "I'm gonna miss you."

"I called the Westbahnhof. That's where you're leaving from. It's a five to six hour ride out to Innsbruck. Trains run every couple of hours."

"How about you?"

"Knittelfeld's only a couple of hours."

"Guess I'll have to get an early start."

"Ready to hit some doors?"

"We should call the Gollers."

You tell him you did. They won't be home today.

"Tell them goodbye for me." Then he says, "Tell them thanks for everything."

"I will."

You take a look at Stover in his suit. Dark blue against the stark white of a shirt split in half by a blue and green striped tie. Saddlebags keeping his arms from hanging straight. Ready to ask strangers if you can mow their grass, bring their trash cans off the street, just to be looked at strange and sent away. Why you're doing this to him his last day. Why you're making it as useless as every day before it.

"Get your street clothes on," you say. "Let me show you the city."

"You already have."

"I mean in daylight. So you can take some pictures."

His grin goes broad.

"You've got a deal."

You tell the landlady that night. She's wearing the kind of robe you saw Madame Butterfly wear at the opera, lavender with big black flowers, the sleeves so huge they drape off her arms, the robe folded carelessly deep across her chest. You tell her you'll be gone tomorrow.

"But I'm so used to hearing you play almost every night."

"I'm sorry. It wasn't my idea."

The way she pouts brings deep lines and puckers into relief around her lips and in her chin.

"First the clubs," she says. "And now this."

"I wish I was staying."

"I know. I'm just disappointed."

"Thanks for letting me practice here."

"Of course. Where else?"

"Nowhere."

You return her smile.

"Herr Stover's leaving too. He's going to Innsbruck."

"Innsbruck. That's nice." And then she says, "Will new missionaries be coming here?"

"I'm pretty sure."

"But no trumpet player."

You look down. Catch yourself looking into the paper skin where her breasts meet. Look down quick before you look back up to find her smiling.

"Probably not," you say.

"Maybe you can get me a piano player then."

Morgan. All day long, while you showed Stover the city he showed you, there was the longing for your time with him.

"I knew one," you say. "A good one. He's gone home by now."

After a minute she says, "I'll give you back the balance of your rent."

"That's okay."

She puts her hand up to your face. You feel the hand of the lady in the red dress in the parking lot that night at the Indigo.

"There's something in your music much older than you," she says. "I don't know what it is. But it moves and stills me. It's wonderful."

CHAPTER 93

THREE MONTHS. How long you and Stover lasted. June. Three more months since that August night you can add to your calendar. Ten months total. Seven left. If God will let you make it. Go home clean. Having worked it off. You're getting real headlights now. Real roads you can't run at night without them.

In the morning you push Stover's bike for him, haul it on and off trams, while he lugs his suitcase to the Westbahnhof for his train.

"Good luck," you say, on the platform, extending your hand.

"I learned a lot from you."

"From me," you say.

"Yeah. About being a missionary." Then he says, "Elder Hill was wrong about you."

"How?"

"When he said you needed a lesson in humility."

The day you and Stover met. You were on your way out the door of the Mission Home into the sleet and rain and wind of an April storm.

"I remember."

"You're one of the most humble guys I've ever known."

It startles you.

"Humble?"

"Yes," he says.

"Is that good or bad?"

"In my book, it's as good as it gets."

"Then thanks. You were a pleasure to work with."

"Thanks again for the baptism. And everything else. Goodbye, Elder."

Insane that you have to call each other Elder.

"I look forward to the day I can call you Clark."

"I look forward to calling you Shake."

"Take care."

"You too."

It's hot. Wet. The sky pale white. You're soaked when you get back home to grab your own stuff. You write the landlady a thank you note and tell her the key's in the mailbox. For the first time you use the name she gave you. You tell her you're leaving your bike for her to give away. You leave the note on the rack of her Boesendorfer like a piece of music she could play. At the Sudbahnhof you pick a late afternoon train and use a pay phone to call Butterworth to tell him when it's scheduled to arrive in Knittelfeld. A little girl answers. You leave a message with her and hope for the best. You leave your Samsonite with the baggage clerk. Head across town with your horn to Franz Josefs Bahnhof for the train north up the Danube. People look at the case that stands on the floor between your knees and then at you with the usual question in their eyes. That feeling again that you're just one of them. One of everyone. At the Klosterneuburg station there's a light breeze off the river that dries you of sweat as it follows you up the steep cobblestone streets and through the Hauptplatz and then to the place inside the arched back gate of the Stift. The way they were that day last summer, that first day, all the second floor windows are open. This time there's no piano music. You don't need it. You know who plays it. You know who lives inside. You know your family.

Hubert lets you in. Upstairs, down the hall, the door to Edith's room is closed.

"She knows you're going," Frau Goller says, arranging torn leaves of washed lettuce in four large shallow bowls. A cold roast stands on a cutting board on the counter.

"I think she blames herself," says Hubert.

"It's not my decision. Like Linz."

"Yes. We told her. Don't expect a young girl to be logical."

"Can I talk to her?"

In her apron Frau Goller picks up a long slender carving knife and drives the tines of a carving fork into the dark brown roast.

"I told her Knittelfeld isn't that far. We could visit you. It's summer. We don't have to worry about getting stuck in a snowy field."

"I think she'll miss you at the Factory," Hubert says.

This family. This family who lives on the second floor of an old nunnery to a vast and wealthy abbey. Who let you in and made you one of them. In the absence of a companion you feel almost like a real son. Like a family of three is now four. You reach into the inside pocket of your suit coat and take out the list you put together.

"Here. Names and numbers for all the musicians."

"Ah," Hubert says. "Thank you."

"With the instruments they play."

He arches his eyebrows. Unfolds the list. You watch his eyes do zigzags back and forth across the paper. "This is excellent."

"I hear voices," you say.

"It's Edith," says Frau Goller. "She's talking to her big bear."

"And her doll," says Hubert.

"Let me try to talk to her."

"Hopefully she'll listen to her big brother," Frau Goller says.

You go down the hall. Stop at her door. Listen to her eager melodic voice for a minute before you knock.

"Dorothy?"

Her voice goes silent.

"Who is it?" she finally says.

"Your big brother."

The door comes open.

"I'm not Dorothy," she says, to your shoes. "I'm Edith."

"I know who you are."

She looks up. This face. Your little sister. You reach down your hand for hers. She looks at it. Then takes it. She'll be fine. She'll play her song for you if she's not too shy. Or read you a story she's written in her journal. Then you'll play for her. Over the Rainbow. The way you'll come in, minor and dissonant from out of nowhere, will rattle her, but she likes being rattled, and she'll stay spellbound on the edge of the leather chair. You'll play the melody through. Then come back to the front, touch down for a measure, long enough to pick her up, and then take off with her. Edith. Dorothy. Toto. We're not in Klosterneuburg any more. If you're the Tin Man. Or the Lion. Or the Scarecrow. Or the Wizard. Or just the Big Brother and the Little Sister. On the steel bird sound of your horn you're off to find out. There was the life you once had where this was okay.

PART 11

EISENERZ

YOU ASK HUBERT to tell the crowd at the Factory that night goodbye for you. Especially Angelika. Tell her you're sorry. You didn't have time. It came up too sudden. He tells you he'll know what to say. That afternoon the train to Knittelfeld takes you south on the same tracks that took you to Villach last year to mark off the bleak days through the long claustrophobic winter in the attic room with Paulson. Here at the first of June the passing countryside has started its slow explosion out of the dormant white of winter. The late afternoon sky is flocked with puffs of clouds. Their dappled shadows glide across dark forests and greening fields. You ride with this quiet ache for having to leave the Gollers and the Factory. This relief to be out of Vienna. Free again, the way you were in Linz, from playing for a lie.

Ten months now since that August night. Seven left till you've done the thirty you were called here for. If Knittelfeld is where you'll run your mission out. You'll have a car. In the reach of its real headlights you'll be able to almost see it now. The elusive end of your stolen road. If he'll let you get there. You don't ask. Try not to wonder as the train rolls you toward a town where everything you want, everything you still fear, waits for you.

Elder Butterworth meets you on the platform. A round sweet pudgy face and a smile of spiritual bliss with the blue eyes and silk blond red wavy hair of the cherubs you've seen in the cathedrals of Vienna and the Wachau. He's shorter and heftier than you. You shake hands. He welcomes you to Knittelfeld. Asks how your ride was. Helps you pick up your Samsonite. You look for any sign that Hill has talked to him. Asked him to keep an eye on you. You search his face but can't get past the bliss. It mystifies and troubles you. Where you've seen it before.

"Is that your trumpet?" he asks.

"Yes."

"I read about you." Then he says, "How about your bike?"

"I gave it away. Should I have kept it?"

"I guess not. So then we're ready."

He leads you out of the concrete bunker of the station to the parking lot. In the soft red steel of the sunset, your car's a Beetle, beige with a beige interior. You can go places now. You and Butterworth. Take roads that lead into the woods and through the hills and fields to other villages where other elders live. You remember going from pedaling a bike to driving when you turned sixteen. The sudden new reach of your world when you traded the safe range of your legs for the dangerous distance of an engine. You load your Samsonite and horn in the back seat.

"Okay," he says. "All loaded up?"

Across the roof of the Beetle his smile takes on more bliss. Enough to recognize where you've seen his face before. Frau Kettler. Listening to Morgan play in her darkened living room where the closed red drapes never let you know the weather or the time of day or where you were.

"Sure am," you say. Then you say, "Wow. A car."

"Would you like to drive?"

"I'd like to just get used to riding first."

"Oh. Okay. It's really not hard."

"I haven't driven in almost two years."

Butterworth takes the Beetle through town. You draw fresh air into your lungs from the breeze that comes in through your open window. The mutter and growl of the engine back behind you comes off the walls of the old well-tended pastel buildings that border the cobblestone streets. It sounds tired. But in the passenger seat you feel charged. Free. You and a buddy going somewhere. Like back home. You and Robbie maybe. Your trumpet in back. You cross a bridge over a small river.

"How long have you been here?"

"In Knittelfeld? Not long. Almost two months."

"How about your mission?"

"Just over twenty months. You?"

"Twenty three. What's the river?"

"The Mur."

"Okay."

"You want to look around a little?" he says.

"Thanks. If it's okay I'd just like to unpack."

Out past the buildings of town the rolling hills are rimmed with the soft fire of the sunset. The hills lay long shadows over the fresh green of fields carved out of the dark woods.

"How about hungry?" he says.

You look at him. In the sunset light you wonder if his smile is permanent. If bliss is his response to everything.

"Not really. But are you?"

"I can wait too," he says. "I've got some food in the room. And there's a dairy shop downstairs."

"Sounds good."

"Congratulations on your baptisms. I've seen your hours in the news-letter. You earned them." Then he says, "I'm still looking for my first one."

"We'll see what we can do."

Your room is on the attic floor of a house again. A stucco house where the landlady runs a dairy shop out of the ground floor. It stands on a nar-row road a few blocks out of town together with some other big pale yellow houses. You meet the little girl who took the message of your arrival time and thank her. Long light brown hair in two ponytails and dark brown eyes when she looks up at you. She tells you her name is Rachel and she's five. Her mother is tall, large boned, cheerful, with a thin face, large eyes set close to each other against the flanks of her sharp nose, thick loose dark hair lined with gray. Underneath her housedress she moves like a man. Her name is Susi. She tells you her husband's name is Jasper. Along with the small cigar she's smoking you can smell cabbage cooking with the heavy fat of ham. She wants to know if the case you're carrying holds an instrument.

"A trumpet."

"What do you play?" she says.

"Jazz mostly."

"My God. I love jazz."

Before you head upstairs with Butterworth she asks if it's possible to play for her sometime. You tell her sure. On the stairs, carrying your Samsonite, Butterworth says he'd like to hear you play too. Tells you he used to play a tuba. You tell him okay. In the attic the slope of the roof cuts low into the ceiling over your cot. You'll have to watch your head. You're relieved to see another cot across the room.

"Do you know how long we've had this place?" you ask Butterworth.

"No. It was here when I got here. Why?"

"My first senior worked here. I just wondered if this is where he lived."

"I don't know," says Butterworth. "Oh. I forgot to ask if you have a license."

"Yes. An Austrian one."

"Austrian? For real?"

"Yeah. I've never used it, though."

"Can I see it?"

"Sure."

"Wow," he says, unfolding it. "A photo. All I've got is my Utah one."

"I've still got mine from Utah too."

He hands it back.

"You should do the driving then."

"I'd be happy to."

In the morning you send your new address out to the people who need it. You haven't stored away your father's letters since Morgan told you what he wrote to President Smith. Read them and thrown them in the trash. Now, in your letter to your family, you finally tell them about your second baptism. Butterworth directs you to the post office through cobblestone streets still wet from an overnight rain. The beige paint of the little Beetle is dull as dust except where it's wet along the doors and quarter panels with water and a film of winter dirt. Dark red veins of rust show in the skin of the metal along the joints where the round fenders are bolted like ears to the body. Pools of rain, collected in depressions in the cobblestones, explode under the narrow tires. The rear bumper hangs loose and cockeyed off its brackets and rattles like a dull wind chime off the back of the fenders. The chrome is stained with the hard black residue of smoke from the two thin tailpipes. From the gap in the hammering stutter of the engine you can tell that one of its four pistons is mostly along for the ride.

"Mind if I do a little work on this?" you ask Butterworth. "The car?"

"Do you know how to?"

You tell him about Otto.

"That's great."

It takes a couple of days. You replace the spark plugs and the distributor points and rotor and clean and rebuild the carburetor and set the timing and adjust the valves. Replace the caked air filter. Change the thick black oil for the honey of fresh oil. Get new bolts for the rear bumper. Buy new wiper blades. Make sure the bolts for the fenders will hold the rust. Replace a dead brakelight. Take off the wheels and check the drums and replace the front shoes. Take almost half a turn of slack out of the steering. Make sure the muffler's good. The tires look okay for now. Jasper, a tall skinny guy with a bald head and a bush the color of sagebrush for a beard, lets you use his tools in trade for playing some tunes for him and his wife in their living room. They like a song called Green Dolphin Street. They like a song called Nature Boy by Nat King Cole. Susi lets you use the hose and a bucket and soap to wash the car. You scrub the black residue of exhaust off the pitted chrome of the bumper. Have Butterworth help you give the car a coat of wax. Borrow Susi's vacuum to clean up the interior. Wash the film of grime off the inside surfaces of the windows. The engine runs smooth on all four cylinders. Responds to the pedal. Revs free as its parts ride on their fresh coat of new oil. You remember the engine you and Jimmy Dennison found and took apart in the potato cellar of your house on the ranch. Like new inside. The slick shine of the pistons. The bearing journals and counterweights of the crankshaft. Connecting rods. Wrist pins. Names you didn't know then.

"Try it out," you tell Butterworth. "Let's take a ride."

"Wow. What a difference. This is amazing."

"Good."

"It feels happy."

While he drives you look down at your hands. Threads of black still have to wear out of the tiny whirlpools of your fingerprints, the wrinkles of your knuckles, the grooves where your fingernails meet your fingers.

"I want to pay for half the stuff you had to buy," he says.

"I think they're supposed to pay us back."

"That's right. I forgot."

"Try letting the engine rev a little higher before you shift."

"Why?"

"It helps it stay clean. Circulates the oil better."

"Okay."

He's from Salt Lake, from South High, the massive old three-story school set back from State Street around Fifteenth South, the bold vault of its tired sand-colored face stained gray from years of exposure to the four lanes of exhaust and tire smoke you used to join on Friday and Saturday nights in Porter's Hudson or West's Pontiac or Snook's Chevy. Sometimes in your father's Valiant station wagon. It was a school that drew its kids from the poor neighborhoods that stood back behind the used car lots and repair shops and tire outlets and diners and other ragtag single story businesses that lined State. You remember its gym where you once did battle with other high school bands.

That he went to school there, that he briefly played tuba in the marching band, that he has an older sister is about all you know of Butterworth. He doesn't volunteer much else. So you're left to imagine his cherub cheeks puffed out around the big cup of a tuba mouthpiece. No girls come up in conversation. So you're left to imagine one yourself. Shy and modest in a dress with a small collar buttoned to her neck and the same spiritual blush of chastity to shield herself in a part of the city known to be rough. It's okay with you. Because then you don't have to tell him much about yourself. Because you don't know what to tell him that he'd either like or be scared off by. The fights on State and in high school parking lots. The clubs you worked in his South High neighborhood. Like the Indigo.

After a few days you start to realize that his constant bliss is something he wasn't born with but had to learn. From men he knew from church. Returned missionaries with this smiling benevolence that could surround and trap you if you let it. The feeling in their presence that you could do no wrong because they held you in a constant state of being forgiven. You think back to Cissy's brother Jeff and the look in his best friend's eyes when he came home from his mission. Like there was nobody home but the goldfish. The look of bliss that let Jeff know he was loved despite the curse of the color of his skin and the consequence that he couldn't have the priesthood. In Butterworth you can tell it hasn't set its roots deep yet. That it still takes practice. Sometimes you can see the strain of holding it pull at the tips of his smile. Trouble in his cherub cheeks.

He likes the passenger seat. In the driver's seat you fall in love with the Beetle. With its simplicity. Its innocence. Its eager doglike obedience. It doesn't matter if it looks a little scruffy. It just matters that it runs okay. That mechanically it's reliable. The first thing you do is drive out to introduce yourselves to the missionaries who knock on the doors of the villages in your district. Spend the day with them. Switch companions and either go tracting or visit members or any investigators they may have. Give them the benefit of your experience. You've converted two people to the Gospel. How you did it. What you found that did the trick. You tell them about Otto and his shop. You tell them about Angelika. The lonely girl looking to belong to somewhere safe that wouldn't hurt her.

Your father types a letter back about her baptism. By golly. A second baptism. It reminds me of the wonderful opportunity I had to baptize all five of my children. So I know what you must have felt to take a new convert into the waters of baptism.

If he's bragging. If he has to put himself ahead of you. Each of you was eight. It wasn't like you had much choice. You skim the rest of his letter and toss it in the wastebasket.

He doesn't know that all you did was watch.

In the meantime you fall in love with everything around you. The late spring early summer air. The rain that moves in from across the hills and settles in the valley. The cobblestones that make the Beetle tap dance on its tires and the steering wheel shiver in your hands. The tended fields and winding roads and lush dark forests when you and Butterworth drive out to visit the missionaries in your district. The orange roofs and pale yellow stucco walls of the farmhouses. The handful of members whose warm adoring faces pull fiercely on your heart in the little meeting hall where you and Butterworth bless and pass the sacrament and give the speeches. If you could serve out your mission here.

CHAPTER 95

THE LAST of your district visits is a small iron mining town called Eisenerz. The landlady tells you about it. A town that Hitler occupied and used to feed iron and steel to the heavy weapons factories of Linz and other towns where tanks were made to do battle against the tanks you trained on. Your landlady tells you it sits deep in a valley surrounded by isolating mountains. Ore is mined off the surface of one of the mountains that overlooks the town. She tells you the mountain is gradually being carved away. You think of the vast bowl carved by Kennecott Copper into the heart of the Oquirrh Mountains. The smelter and the black spike of its smokestack and the yellow smoke that stains the air of the valley and makes the sunsets start in late afternoon. You think of Magna. The town at the foot of the Oquirrhs where the miner kids were from who used to come at night to the fence at Hiller to hear you play and learn from you. Luke. His old Pontiac lurching and rocking with its lights off across the field.

Two elders work the town of Eisenerz. Doug Bateman and Ron Wolfe. Eisenerz. You translate its blunt name for Butterworth.

"Iron ore."

"That's what it means?"

"Eisen. Iron. Erz. Ore. Ever been there?"

"Not yet."

Butterworth calls and sets up the day of the visit and gets directions. You take off early in the morning in weather that goes from rain to drizzle to mist to rain again. A two lane road leads through valleys of fields and then starts to climb into the hills and then the mountains. When you reach a small village called Vordernberg the road narrows and becomes a tight cobblestone street that threads through old buildings before it opens up again and starts to climb for real.

"Know what it means? Vordernberg?"

"Not really."

"Split it up. Vordern Berg."

"Vordern Berg." Then he says, "I know berg is mountain."

"Vordern means the front of."

"So it means there's a mountain ahead."

"You're looking at it."

The blind engine of the Beetle only knows the change in load as it starts to push you up the road that climbs out of Vordernberg. You shift down. Rain and wind start to come out of the drizzle hard and whip across the windshield. You turn the wipers on. As you climb into the fog of the overcast toward the summit you hear soft hail on the steel of the roof and see it burst like insects where the wind drives it against the windshield. You crest the summit. You start down the other side. The storm turns fierce. In the howl of the wind the hail builds up on the windshield where the wipers keep pushing it back. You see snow now in the hail. Ahead of you the steep road down goes gray and in places white.

"Just stop," says Butterworth. "We can wait it out."

"I can't stop."

"Why?"

"It won't stop."

"It won't stop?"

"It's too slick."

And then you don't hear anything from him. You feather the brakes. Feel the tires lock up and let them go again to keep from skidding off the road or going sideways. You shift to a lower gear to brake the back tires with the engine. The tires break free and the Beetle starts to go sideways again. You shift back up. You can't see either side of the road. The side that falls suddenly off down the steep slope of the mountain or the uphill side where you'll run the Beetle into the jagged wall of blasted rock. The buildup of hail and snow on the windshield limits the reach of the straining wipers. You search for a place between the brakes and clutch and gas pedal, a balance between letting the tires slide and then roll and then slide again, where you can hold the speed of the Beetle down and try to steer it. Slide and roll. Slide and roll and steer and work the curves. Butterworth hasn't said a word since you told him you couldn't stop. You'd like to look at him now to see if the ride has wiped the smile off his face and fear has driven out bliss as his one expression. But you can't. The road seems endless. A long stretch of straight road ends in a sharp switchback that wants to pull the rear end of the Beetle off the mountain. It finally starts to level off. And then you drop through the blinding overcast of the storm and the hail is rain again and then you're in the town of Eisenerz. You pull over and get out to stretch the fear out of your arms and legs and back. The wind whips your suit and tosses the blade of your tie back across your shoulder. You look back up behind you where wind has started to strip the clouds off the walls of the mountain you could have died on.

Butterworth's out of the car too. Across the roof from you.

"You have directions to their place?"

You can hear the shiver that fear and relief put in your voice.
"Yes." Then he says, "That was quite a ride."
"It was."
"The Lord was with us the entire time."
He narrows his eyes to the wind and smiles and looks away. The bliss is back. Now you know what keeps it there.
"Somebody was," you say.
"The Lord," he says. "I made sure. I prayed the whole way down."
"That's how the Lord was with us? Because you prayed?"
The wipers. The plugs. The points. The brakes. The carburetor rebuild. All the things you bought and installed and fixed. And finally the driving. It took everything you knew. Everything you could guess and try and hope would work.
"I always thought the Lord helped those who helped themselves," you tell Butterworth.
"What do you mean?"
"We had a good car," you say.
"We did. Thanks to you."
"Thanks," you say. "The driver did okay too."
"Yes you did. You did great."
"Thanks."
"I just think the Lord was here to guide you."
You've heard it before. This interpretation of humility that has always made the word a synonym for anonymity. You smile across the roof of the Beetle into the face of his bliss.
"You ready to go?" you say.
"Yes."
"You have the directions?" you ask again.
In the car he searches through the inner pockets of his suit coat. You start the engine.
"Here they are."
"Good. Let me know where the turns are."
You start the engine.
"I'd like to say a prayer first, if that's okay."
You're parked off the side of the road. The rain is over. Sun has started breaking through the increasingly ragged clouds. A couple your age come your way along the sidewalk. As they pass they look inside at you.
"Okay," you say.
After Butterworth thanks the Lord for taking the Beetle in his hands and bringing you safely out of the sky, his directions take you down a road that appears to lead out of town through a shabby outskirts neighborhood. Weeds two feet tall, dense with spring growth, line the sidewalk on the left side. Long homely buildings that look to be in decay stand

four stories high along the right. Foundations made of stacks of dark flat stones. Walls made of eroding blocks of some other stone. The colors that mottle them, like the scars of fires or the wear of too many winters or the residue of smelters, range from orange to yellow to rust to brown, veined here and there in black. They could be schools or hospitals for the wounded in the Second World War or prisons or apartment buildings. They could have been all of them.

"Look at that," says Butterworth.

You look up. Pull over. Leave the Beetle running in neutral but ratchet up the handbrake. Get out into the wind. Out of town ahead of you, over the roofs of buildings and low hills, stands what was once a mountain among the other mountains that surround the town. Scalped now of the forests and meadows that cover the mountains around it and carved now into tier after horizontal tier of naked rock and dirt that the shovels and trucks can use as roads to come and go and dig and haul the ore away to smelters. Rust red, gray, shades of brown and yellow, almost white in places, the naked colorations of the rock and dirt make the mountain look skinned, skinned like the steers they used to shoot and gut and butcher once a week to feed the ranch. You can still see the shape of the mountain because the tiers follow the serpentine contours of its slopes and ridges and valleys like the elevation lines you learned to read in the Army.

"There they are," you hear Butterworth say from the passenger seat once you're driving again.

You've seen them. Two guys in dark suits waiting in front of one of the buildings on a thin strip of concrete sidewalk barely wide enough to walk along. They look new, stylish, out of place, like insurance salesmen against a backdrop of buildings where a suit would be the last thing you'd expect to see. You pull up, get out, shake hands and introduce yourself.

Bateman's the senior. You know him. You like each other. He was a street guy back home. He came to hear you play a couple of times while you both were in Vienna. Wind lifts his thin brown hair to show more scalp than you remember. He looks just a second too long at your own hair, long in need of a haircut you haven't made time for, and at your synthetic sidewalk suit.

"You still need that haircut," Bateman says, smiling.

"I always need a haircut." Remembering the way he used to tease you in Vienna.

Taller, younger, skinnier, his curly red hair trimmed short, still raw from home in an American suit and shoes, Wolfe's the junior. He smiles when he shakes your hand. But there's this helpless trouble in his pale eyes that keeps him from holding your look for long. The skin around his eyes is dark.

"You Elders had breakfast?" Bateman asks.

"Yes."

"How was the ride?"

"We ran into hail and snow coming down the mountain. Pretty much slid all the way."

"Yeah," says Bateman. "That happens a lot."

"The Lord was with us. He had us in his hands."

Bateman looks at you. Then at Butterworth.

"Who was driving?" he asks.

"Elder Tauffler was," Butterworth tells him.

"That was my guess."

You like Bateman all over again.

"That's some mine," you say.

Bateman throws a look over his shoulder.

"Yeah. It keeps the town going. Like Kennecott does Magna." Then he says, "So. What would you Elders like to do?"

"We thought we'd pair up and do some missionary work," Butterworth says. "Tracting, seeing investigators, visiting members."

"We got two members. Widows. One's at work. The other's in the hospital. Zero investigators." Bateman smiles. "Plenty of doors to knock on, though."

"We could go visit the sister in the hospital."

Bateman looks at Butterworth.

"She can't have visitors. She's pretty bad off."

"We're her priests," says Butterworth. "They let priests in."

"For last rites. If you're dying."

"Okay." Butterworth's smile stays in place. "Tracting it is. Where should we start?"

"We could drive into town," says Bateman. "Get out of this wind. Split up from there. Meet for lunch later. There's a cafe right there that serves cheap food."

You turn the Beetle around and head for the center of town. Bateman gives directions. With the extra weight of back seat passengers the Beetle chatters less on the cobblestones of the streets. You could have used them coming down the mountain. The narrow streets are hilly. The valley is tight. Little of the town is built on level ground. When you reach the central plaza Bateman tells you where to park. Butterworth wants another prayer. From the back seat Bateman takes his turn.

You get out. Let Wolfe out of the back while Butterworth lets Bateman out. In the protected heart of town the wind is down to a breeze. The buildings around the plaza are bold and strong and painted the rust red and iron gray and forest green and pale yellow of the mine and the mountain it lays bare. Bands of old scrollwork run the length of a couple of the larger buildings. More scrollwork runs around the frames of the windows and doors. People wander the cobblestones in the sun and sit at the tables of the terrace of a cafe. Some of them look for a moment at four young guys in suits.

"This is nice," you say.

"Yeah," says Bateman. "How do you want to do this?"

"Not what you'd expect for a mining town."

"Yeah."

"The scrollwork is something."

Bateman steps up and looks himself.

"You know how they did it?" he says.

"No."

"What they do is put down a layer of plaster the color they want the background to be. The black there. Or you could use green or blue or whatever. Then they put a coat of plaster over that. The color they want the scrollwork to be."

Suddenly he stops. Goes stiff. Pain clenches his face like a fist that has hold of it from the inside.

"You okay?" you say.

He lifts his hand to hold you off while he rides it out. Then he relaxes again. "I'm fine. Anyway," he says, "then they carve the scrollwork out of the top layer down to the first layer underneath. So the first layer shows through."

"Cool," you say, watching him.

"Yeah," he says.

"So how old is this place?"

"Centuries."

"They take good care of it."

"Yeah."

"I'll take Elder Wolfe," you say. "That okay with you guys?"

"Fine with me," says Bateman.

"Sure," says Butterworth.

"Which way do we go?"

"You guys go that way," says Bateman. "We'll go this way."

"How long?"

"A couple of hours?" says Bateman. "We'll meet back here."

CHAPTER 96

YOU WATCH Butterworth and Bateman walk off across the plaza for a minute before you turn and walk with Wolfe down the street Bateman indicated. Wolfe doesn't say a word. His head down.

"You're a legend," he finally says.

"I am?"

"Aren't you the trumpet player?"

"Oh. Yeah."

"Elder Bateman said you were pretty good."

"Thanks."

"Playing all over Vienna. That had to be something."

"Yeah. You play anything?"

"Not really. Play around. My mom's old cello. My dad's clarinet from high school."

You walk a ways farther. Where the buildings are apartments and houses now and the only businesses are small ground floor shops.

"We can start here," says Wolfe.

You're in front of a women's clothing shop. In the window three mannequins in dirndls look with sculpted faces and sightless eyes out at the street. To the left of the window an arched dark green door leads into the building to the apartments on the two floors above the shop.

"Tell me how you're doing," you say.

"Me? I'm doing fine."

"Tell me. That's why I'm here."

Wolfe's eyes go wild in their dark sockets. Rebound back and forth off the buildings and cobblestones down the street. He finally presses them shut. His chin puckers up. He opens his mouth and draws breath and then exhales. His eyes come open.

"Nothing's wrong," he says. "We're fine."

"Can you tell me why Elder Bateman's limping?"

"He's limping?"

"It looks like it hurts him to walk."

"No. He's okay."

"I knew him when he didn't limp," you say.

"Then I don't know. He doesn't talk about it."

In the way his voice rises and becomes insistent you can tell it bothers him to lie. Maybe you're rushing things.

"So where are you from?" you say.

"Spanish Fork."

"I used to have a girlfriend in Spanish Fork. She was a cheerleader. Me and a couple of buddies used to go down for the games. It's nice down there."

"Where are you from?"

You tell him Bountiful.

"I've never heard of it."

"It's a town a few miles north of Salt Lake."

"It's called Bountiful?"

"I know. Kind of strange."

"I didn't mean that," he says.

"How long have you been here?"

"In Austria or Eisenerz?"

"Austria."

"That was stupid," he says. "It's the same answer. Four months."

Four months. You were still with Morgan. About to be transferred. About to have him tell you what your father wrote to President Smith.

"So this is the only place you've worked."

"Yes."

"How was winter?"

"Pretty rough."

"Tell me what's wrong."

Wolfe turns and looks hard at the building behind you. "Shouldn't we be tracting?"

"Just between us." Then you say, "I'm just a trumpet player. You can tell me."

"Geez!" Wolfe suddenly says, and whirls away. You look. In the window of the shop a guy has undressed one of the mannequins and taken off her dark wig. She stands there bald and naked.

"Let's keep walking," you say. "I feel like a window peeper."

"Yeah. Man. Me too."

"I'm not going to report anything you tell me," you say. "Unless you want me to."

"It's your job to report me."

"It's my job to help you. What's wrong with Elder Bateman?"

"It's pretty bad," says Wolfe.

"What is it?"

"He's scared they'll send him home if he says anything."

"Why's he limping?"

"He made me promise not to tell you guys."

"Then don't tell me."

"I'm scared he could die."

The warble in his voice makes you look at him.

"Then tell me."

"He's got this huge sore on his tailbone. It's all infected. Pus and blood. He can barely sit down. Forget riding his bike. He takes his clothes off and there's this stain in the back of his garments. Watery yellow and red."

"Has he seen a doctor?"

"That's a long story," says Wolfe.

"My favorite kind."

"He got it a few months ago. He was scared to tell the mission. Scared they'd send him home. But he wrote his dad about it. His dad the bishop. His dad ended up calling the Mission Home. They told him thanks for letting them know. They'd take care of it."

"Who's they?"

"The Second Counselor."

"Hill."

"Yeah," says Wolfe. "Elder Hill."

"How long ago?"

"I guess it's been a couple of months. He's still waiting to hear from them. It just keeps getting worse."

"Maybe he should write his dad again."

"He did," says Wolfe. "Cuz his dad wrote and asked. Elder Bateman wrote back and told him they'd taken care of it and he was fine now. He was scared to tell the truth. He didn't want his dad to call the Mission Home again."

"So he's not doing anything," you say. "Not going to a doctor on his own."

"He's scared they'll find out."

"The Mission Home? How would they find out?"

"I don't know," says Wolfe. "He says they just find stuff out. So we just keep praying for it to get better."

"So he's just living with it."

"He pops aspirins like peanuts."

"Aspirins don't fix anything."

"I know," says Wolfe. "I tell him that. He just gets mad. He'd kill himself before he'd go home early. With his dad being a bishop."

"I'll figure something out," you say. "Nobody's going home."

"I'm scared the rats will get to his sore."

"What rats?"

"In our place."

"You guys have rats?"

"Yeah. Pretty bad."

"How do they get in?"

"It's a basement apartment. We think where the sewer pipes come through the walls." Then he says, "I sleep on the kitchen table so they can't get to me."

"The table?"

"Yeah." He looks away. "I see people in the halls. Where we live. They must have rats too. They can live with them. I have to sleep on a table."

"Where does Elder Bateman sleep?"

"On the couch."

"Why?"

"No beds," says Wolfe.

"No?"

"Nope."

"Did you let the District Leaders know?"

"The ones before you? Not right away. We didn't want to look like complainers. Elder Bateman says the mission doesn't like complainers. It means their testimony's weak."

"Rats are real," you say.

"We finally told them. About the rats. They saw that we didn't have beds."

"What'd they do?"

"They said they'd tell the Zone Leaders. And the Zone Leaders would tell the Mission Home. They said to pray about the rats. Keep our faith strong and it would protect us."

"From rats."

Wolfe's face goes red.

"We didn't want to complain," he says.

"Rats and no beds isn't complaining."

"Elder Bateman thinks it is."

"What did the Zone Leaders say?"

"They told the District Leaders it wasn't the mission's business to furnish apartments. The mission relied on local members to help with that."

"Two old widows?"

Shame makes his face go red again.

"How long ago did they tell you this?"

"Back in late winter," he says. "Maybe three months."

"Nothing else, huh."

"No. That's why Elder Bateman won't tell them about his sore. He doesn't think they'd do anything about it. Except maybe send him home."

"And you've still got rats."

"We trapped some. It didn't help."

"You guys need a new place."

"Right."

"Tried finding one?"

"We've asked around."

"We'll come back tomorrow. Help you guys find one. It'll be easier with a car."

"Okay."

"We'll see what we can do about Elder Bateman."

"Good luck." Wolfe's quick laugh is bitter. "Maybe he'll listen to you."

"Have you told your folks?"

"No. They'd just get upset." Then he says, "We keep waiting for word from the Mission Home."

You start walking again. Make way in the narrow street for a small truck to pass. Return the driver's wave. Next to you Wolfe feels restless. Like he wants to go on now with what you started.

"How else are you doing?"

He stops walking. Looks down. You can see his face working. Not knowing between courage and desperation.

"I'm not cut out for this," he finally says.

"We all get that way sometimes."

"Yeah. I figured you'd say that."

"It's true."

"I'm that way all the time."

He raises his head and looks at you eager to correct himself.

"I mean the last two months or so. I was okay at first."

"I know."

"It's not just rats. It's having people treat you like you're crap once they know what you're here for. Never seeing anyone. We pray and pray and everything stays the way it is. Nobody wants us around. I'm sorry. Except a couple of sweet old ladies. One of them dying." Then he says, "The weather's the only thing that changes."

He narrows his eyes and looks off down the street.

"And Elder Bateman's sore," he says. "It changes too. It gets worse. I mean when's he gonna get blood poisoning? When's a rat gonna nibble on it? Give him some sewer disease?"

Three teenage girls walk past the other way on the opposite side of the street. In the sunlight on their faces you can see them check you out. Wolfe doesn't notice them.

"I can't go home either," he says. "I'd be a quitter. My folks would look like they failed. My girl would find some guy with the guts to stick his mission out."

You remember Yenchik. His mother dying. The brutal ride down the road where Robbie lived and the pavement ran out. Raising the hood of the Ford to show you the gleaming engine that was his mission money. The crazy itching hurt he couldn't get rid of.

"What would your mom do if she knew you lived with rats and slept on a table?"

"She'd go nuts. She'd raise holy heck. My dad would tell her calm down and not rock any boats. She'd tell him to go fly a kite." He shakes his head. "Oh boy. Would she ever."

"You know Bateman's folks?"

"I know his mom's always writing him and he's always writing her. His dad's a bishop."

"He is."

"Yeah."

"Want to know how to make it work? Being here?"

"Like you playing trumpet?"

"I found a family."

And you tell him. How you heard piano music from a window and knocked on the door. How you just wanted to say you liked the music. A mother and father and little girl. How you made friends from there. How they took you in.

"Wow."

"They made me feel like I belonged here. Had a home here. You know?"

"Where?"

"This little town outside Vienna."

"Wow," he says.

"Other missionaries do it. My first senior had this woman in Vienna. He'd play her piano. We'd sit there and drink tea and listen. My second senior had this Ping Pong club for teenage kids. My third senior, well, I was with him when we met the family."

"So you don't tell them you're a missionary?"

"No. You've gotta be honest. But let them know you care about them. Not just making Mormons out of them. Respect them if they say they're not interested."

"So how do you end up converting anyone?"

"You don't ask that question. Just be a friend. I knew this mechanic in Linz. I helped him work on cars. Later on he brought up being baptized on his own."

"My dad and me souped up a 55 Chevy and took it racing."

"Drag racing?

"What else is there?" says Wolfe.

CHAPTER 97

THAT LAST NIGHT in the Mojave. How Lieutenant Tanner took you out in a Jeep across the desert to the place that was the vast floor of some prehistoric lake. How the setting sun set bright lines of fire to the rims of the low black distant mountains all around you and gave the desert floor this sheen of metal blue. How he got you to talk about yourself while the vast sky went red and bronze and copper. How easy it was. How you got out of the Jeep and walked. How he asked if he could pray with you. How you brushed the small sharp rocks away to make yourselves a place to kneel in the dirt. How you put your hands on the saddles of each other's shoulders. How he prayed. Talked to God like God was just some regular guy. Told God you were in his hands now. Told God it was his job to take care of you while you were gone and keep you safe and bring you home again. Because the vast place where you knelt in the dirt and held the weight of Lieutenant Tanner's hands on your shoulders was the place where God lived.

Lieutenant Tanner didn't know that God didn't care. That God didn't fix the things he was asked to fix. That he let things stand that weren't his word. That in the mix of fear and hope and faith you felt for God would come resentment that could boil sometimes into disgust. That what you would do one August night would leave Lieutenant Tanner crumbling on the desert floor like a kneeling statue of a soldier made of salt and dirt.

Drag racing. What else is there. You smile at Wolfe's answer. And then start getting him to talk about himself. Tell you things. About racing with his father. About the work they did on the engine and suspension. About his girl. High school. What he did. Track and field. Broad jumping and throwing a javelin. How he tried an old clarinet his father still had from high school but it made his lips burn. His big sister and little brother. His Individual Achievement Awards. His Duty to God Award. The way Lieutenant Tanner got you to tell him almost everything about yourself.

"Know what you want to do when you get back home?"

"No. I did a year at BYU. But I knew I was going away."

"I'll make you a deal," you say. "Stay. Give Austria a chance. There are better places than this. You'll work them. Let me talk to your Zone Leaders. Get you guys a transfer. Four months here is long enough."

"I don't want to rock any boats."

"Don't worry. I'll rock them for you."

"Elder Bateman too."

"Nobody's going home."

"Maybe you should talk to him."

"I will tomorrow. When we come back."

"Okay."

You stop. Look down the street where three men work through a hole they've made in the cobblestones.

"Mind if we go back to your place?"

"Why?"

"I'd just like a look at it. I've got the car. We've got time."

The basement apartment is beyond shabby. The windows are small, mounted high, their sills barely above street level. But once your eyes get used to the dark it surprises you how clean it is. The old wood floor of the living room is stained in patches that look like used oil but gleams deep with polish. A desk and chair and lamp and a brown swaybacked couch with lifeless cushions and ripped armrests worn through to wood occupy the room. Stains that look as old as the building darken the cloth. Where Bateman sleeps. When Wolfe closes the door a massive old upright piano stands against the wall behind it. The top and bottom panels that hide the hammers and strings and soundboard are gone. Half the keys are dirty sticks that have lost their ivories.

"It was here," Wolfe says. "Somebody just left it. It's pretty shot."

"How come it's open like that?"

"We figured one less place for the rats to hide."

Wolfe switches on the ceiling light in the windowless kitchen. His bedroom. His bed, a table with a scratched and dented metal surface, stands on chrome legs in the center. A leaf extends the table maybe another eight inches to give Wolfe more room. It's not enough. You can see how he'd still need to pull his knees up. A chair with split green plastic upholstery stands on its own chrome legs at either end on blue cracked linoleum worn through to black in places. On the clean linoleum counter next to the empty sink, a wire rack holds a couple of plates, cups, utensils, a dented aluminum saucepan. Above and below the counter the cupboards and cabinets have screw holes where the hinges were. The doors are gone. One less place for the rats to hide, you figure. A lone box of spaghetti occupies one of the shelves. Off to one end of the counter stands a hot plate.

"The stove doesn't work?"

"It's been disconnected."

"How about the fridge?"

"Just to keep food away from the rats."

"You guys sure keep things clean."

"Every day. The rats again."

"This is where you sleep."

"Yeah."

"Do you have a pad? An air mattress?"

"I use the cushions off the couch."

You look at him. He looks down at his hands.

"Elder Bateman just sleeps where the cushions go. Where the springs are."

"How do you keep from falling off?"

"It's tough. My back hurts in the morning."

"That a bedroom?"

"Yeah."

The bare wood floor of the room is stained but sleek with polish like the living room. Two suitcases stand against a wall. On the dingy rose paint of another wall hangs a framed portrait of a middle-aged man in a gray suit and silver striped tie with groomed gray hair and a muted smile you've seen on a thousand self-satisfied men.

"The bishop?" you ask Wolfe.

"Yeah. Bishop Bateman."

"Where do you guys keep your bedding?"

"In there." He points to a tall dark armoire with the varnish wrinkled and peeling like sunburned skin. "On a shelf. We keep our clothes in there too. The rats can't get in as long as we keep the doors closed."

"So every morning you fold your bedding up."

"Yes."

"The District Leaders saw this."

"Yeah."

"You told them how you guys slept."

"Yeah."

"The mission told them it wasn't their business to see that you had beds."

"Yeah."

"Do you know who told them that?"

"I guess the Mission Home." Then he says, "They told us what we really needed was a phone. So we got one."

You look at the portrait of Bishop Bateman. Not to see him. Just for a place to look while you ride out the searing rush of anger and revulsion you feel for God. Lieutenant Tanner didn't know.

"Would you mind if we prayed?"

"Sure."

"Where do you guys usually pray?"

"In the living room. At the sofa."

"Mind if we use the kitchen?"

"No."

You take the chairs at opposite ends of the table he uses for a bed. Fold your hands on its metal surface. Wolfe follows your lead. You close your eyes. You don't bow your head.

"Dear God," you say.

And then, the way Lieutenant Tanner waited on the desert floor, you sit at the table and wait for God to show up. It's been a long time. But then you see him there. His broad back turned. You know it's him. You've seen his back for so long now you've stopped counting. His long and wild hair this luminous almost fluorescent white.

"This is Elder Tauffler."

You wait to hear his voice. He doesn't turn around.

"You don't have to look at me," you finally say. "You just need to hear me."

He doesn't say anything. Just a twitch of his head as if he thought for a second about looking over his shoulder.

"I want you to do your job," you say.

The table jerks slightly under your hands and elbows. Come on, Wolfe, you think. Stay with me.

"I know," you say. "If you did your job, you'd start with me. But I'm here about another job. There's an elder here with me. Elder Ronald Wolfe. Know him?"

He doesn't answer.

"I'm here about him and his companion. Elder Douglas Bateman." Then you say, "You may not know him either."

Nothing.

"Well, in case you don't, they're missionaries. For you. All their lives they've done everything you ever asked of them. When you called them to Austria to serve you, they came."

You wait for him to speak. In the face of his silence you go on.

"They put their lives on hold to do this job for you. They trusted you to do your job for them. See after them."

In the small creak of his chair you can sense Wolfe's nervousness again. You know the feeling. You wait for a truck to rumble and bang past the building. Wait for God to speak.

"Do you take time to listen to their prayers to you?"

You wait for God to answer. For revulsion and fear to run their course again.

"I didn't think so. So I'll tell you what they pray about. They live in a place infested with rats. No beds. One sleeps on a couch without cushions. The other sleeps on a kitchen table to stay out of reach of the rats. One of them is sick and getting sicker. Help us. We're in your hands. That's what you'd hear if you listened to their prayers."

In the place where God lives, where he stands with his back to you, a wind starts kicking up as the unforgiving sun descends toward the line of mountains in the distance. You watch it disturb his glowing hair as it starts to take on the pale red of the air.

"If you cared enough to listen," you say.

You stop to give Wolfe time to deal with what you said.

"You know what they live with. Doing your work. Shame for the way they're looked at. For the way they're treated. They think it's them. You could let them know it's not. It's what you called them here to do."

You watch God cock his head again. Watch the wind play with the folds of his robe and the hair of his naked calves.

"You know what I mean. Lead people to say their religion is false. Forsake everything they love. Harvest them. For you. Like they're wheat or corn or apples."

Except for his whipping hair, except for his robe in the wind, God doesn't move.

"So maybe you could let these elders know that when they get rejected, when they're looked at like they're lepers, it's not them. It's the job you gave them."

Don't be afraid, you think. You've been here before. Here on the steel blue dirt of what you thought was the floor of the earth. Here where the earth falls suddenly away through thousands of feet of open space and the next step you take will walk you out onto the rush of air up the vertical face of the rock. You wait for another truck to pass. One you can tell is empty from the loose jangle and hollow bang of its bed and suspension. You try to calm the cold wind that howls raw up the canyon walls. Don't be afraid. Don't let God see you afraid. Take that step. You've had nothing to lose since the night he brought Rudd into your life.

"Another next thing you could do is lead these elders to a family that will take them in and love them. A family where they can just be themselves. Where they can feel like they belong here."

On the floor of the desert you remember the small sharp rock that bit into your knee. In the uptick of the sunset wind you feel afraid again. The way you're in the place where God lives. Where God could kill you a thousand different ways if it weren't for Lieutenant Tanner's quiet hands on your shoulders and the steady voice of his prayer. Keep going. Stay steady for Wolfe. Your throat hurts. Nothing to lose. God still stands there with his back to you. The wind is stronger now. Whips his glowing hair off his head, lashes his robe around his legs, picks up the dirt around his naked feet.

"These elders know that you expect humility. They've been humble enough to put up with rats and live with being sick. You've let them keep believing they don't deserve your help. And that's been okay with you because you haven't done a thing to change it."

The table jerks again beneath your hands and elbows. Stay with me, you think. We're almost there.

"Show them some humility for once. You should be on your knees to them for the way you've left them twisting in the wind."

You give God time to strike you dead or answer you.

"Too hard? Here's something easy. Lead them to a new place to live. Give them beds. See that Elder Bateman sees a doctor. Let him know he won't be sent home."

You watch the broad back of God again. The wind send ripples through the cloth of his ancient robe.

"You say faith without works is dead. They've got faith. They've done their job. Maybe you could show them some faith. Do the job of looking after them."

You watch God turn his head aside. Far enough that through the whipping strands of his windtorn hair you can see the profile of his ancient face. He turns forward again and starts to walk away. Smoke from the scorched dirt of his footsteps is caught and torn apart by the wind.

"Do your job," you say, your anger and fear apparent in the ache of your raised voice. "Just do your job."

He keeps walking. Against the fire along the rim of the distant mountains that sets fire to his wild hair, against the red steel of the sky, you watch him go, a silhouette now as he moves across the windswept steel of the desert floor. A sudden gust makes him stumble. Take a quick step to the side. God. Who should have known the gust was coming.

"Show them something." you say, to his departing silhouette, its windblown head of raging fire. "Show them anything. They're your children. Not someone else's. Soften your heart. Fix something for a change."

And then, once he's gone, once you're back in this kitchen at the table Wolfe sleeps on, once you cool down, you say, "In Jesus name, Amen."

You open your eyes. Unlock the bones of your fingers and separate your hands. Wolfe doesn't looked up. You wait. Remember the way you felt at the end of Lieutenant Tanner's prayer. How you needed to be still till everything around you, the whirling vastness of everything around you, the vastness of the steel blue desert and the line of fire that rimmed the distant mountains, the first pale points of the stars in the vastness of the sky, everything found where it belonged again. Became something you could trust again. You let Wolfe sit. His hands flat on the table. His head down where you're looking into the blond field of his curly hair and his shoulders hunched so that the padded shoulders of his suit rise off his back like the beginning shoots of wings. He finally brings his head up.

"Who are you?" he says.

"Your District Leader," you tell him.

"I mean to talk to God like that."

"When he doesn't do his job?"

"Were you really talking to him?"

"That's what prayer is."

Wolfe lifts his hands and covers his face with them.

"Wow," he says. Slow to drop his hands. "What did he say?"

"Nothing." Then you say, "Are you okay?"

"Yeah."

"I'll fix this for you. I'll figure something out."

Tears find their way down his cheeks.

"Okay."

"We should get going. Hook up with our companions."

"Just . . . just. Okay. Give me a minute."

"Take your time."

"I want to stay," he says. The skin around his eyes is red. "I want to do what you did. I want to find a family."

On the ride out of Eisenerz back up the mountain late in the afternoon, in clear weather and on a dry road, you and Butterworth compare notes. You tell him what's going on.

"Wow. Elder Bateman didn't say a word."

"Thanks for saying yes to coming back tomorrow."

"I thought we were going to recommend a transfer."

"Yeah. Who knows when. The elders who replace them will need a new place anyway."

"Right."

"I want to talk to Elder Bateman."

"We could give him a blessing."

"Elder Wolfe's done that." Then you say, "He may feel like his wasn't good enough."

You wonder what Butterworth's thinking behind the meditative smile you can hear in his voice. He reaches inside his suit coat and comes out with a small notebook. On one of its pages he writes down how you spent your time that day.

"How much tracting did you and Elder Wolfe do?"

"A couple of hours." Then you say, "We report to the Zone Leaders, right?"

"Yes."

"And they report to the Second Counselor? Is that how it goes?"

"As far as I know. Why?"

"That's what I thought."

Your mouth and teeth feel dirty. On the arm you're steering with you see grime in the white cloth where the sleeve of your suit pulls back to reveal the cuff of your shirt. Your throat hurts. Nothing to lose. You crest the summit and come off the other side through Vordernberg again. Then you're off the mountain and following the meandering line of the road between the fields of farms again. The clouds that covered the valleys and kept them in rain all day have lifted and broken in time to reveal the last of the sky before the coming sunset. Beyond the road, on either side, the soil of the fields is almost black with rain. Fragile rows of seedlings run like mint green stitchwork across the soil. The pale yellow stucco walls of the farmhouses are still mottled from the rain. In the distance ahead of you stand the orange roofs and the steeples of Knittelfeld. Nothing to lose. White tendrils rise like weightless silk from the pools of mist that lie in the pockets of the hills.

PART 12

NOT INTO NIGHT

YOU ENTER KNITTELFELD and follow the puddled streets with steam rising off the cobblestones shining in the last light of the sunset to the house in whose attic you live. Park off the side of the house. Butterworth goes into the dairy shop on the first floor for a roll. Through the window, in the light inside, you watch the landlady look up and give him a smile from behind the counter. You head upstairs. The room is hot. The air warm and thick enough to wade through. You open the windows you closed this morning against the coming rain. Cool air spills in on the light sunset breeze when you open the second one. You take off your suit coat. In a couple of minutes Butterworth is there. Half the roll is already gone. You hear the quick hammering of the landlady's little girl Rachel chasing up the bare wood stairs to knock on your door. There's a phone call for you downstairs. Amerikaner. You put your suit coat on and follow her back down. In the shop where you smell fresh bread and milk and cheese the black receiver of the wall phone hangs by its cord. Amerikaner. You already know. You pick it up and say hello while the landlady tells her daughter to stop standing there staring up at you.

"Elder Tauffler?"

"Yes."

"It's Elder Hunsacker. From the Mission Home."

So they had the Public Relations Director make the call. You thought it would be Hill. You thought he would relish the call enough to make it himself.

"Hi."

"How are you?"

"Fine," you say. On the wall above the phone hangs a poster for Gauloises Disque Bleu cigarettes. A pack the size of a man's torso lies in a striped beach chair. "How about you?"

"We're fine." Then he says, "Something's come up. We need you and Elder Butterworth to come to Vienna right away."

"Tonight?"

"Yes. It's a three to four hour drive. So you'll need to leave as soon as possible. President Lindner wants to see you."

"Tonight."

"Yes. When can you leave?"

"Now."

You look at the big shop window. The light outside isn't strong enough to see through the reflection of the shop interior where you can see the landlady watch an old woman slowly count out coins on the glass countertop.

"One more thing. We need to ask you to bring your belongings."

"How about Elder Butterworth?"

"Yes. Elder Butterworth too."

"He needs to pack too?"

"Yes."

"We'll be there."

"One more thing. You probably know what this is about. Please don't tell Elder Butterworth."

You wait till the woman leaves with her bottle of milk and bag of bread and then tell the landlady. You have to leave for Vienna. They want you to bring your belongings.

"Why?" she asks.

"I don't know. They didn't say."

"Is there an emergency?"

"I don't know."

"They just tell you to pack and come to Vienna but not why?"

"They said they'd tell us when we get there."

"My god. So mysterious. Like Interpol."

You laugh. "Close."

"What about the room? It doesn't sound like you're coming back."

"If we don't," you say, "they'll send someone else."

"Oh well. Then have a safe trip. Don't forget your trumpet."

You've rehearsed this moment a thousand times. Staged it in a thousand different settings. Made up a thousand different ways the call would go. Maybe that's why it feels like another rehearsal. Where you go outside into the twilight and around the corner of the house out of sight of the shop and the landlady and her little girl. Where you stand in the parking lot and feel the gravel through your shoes while you look at the lights in the windows of the houses along the road in shadow now. Where you see the soft red gold of the sunset line the lush green horizon of hills above the rooftops and realize you've lost this too. Where you think the sudden insane thought that you were once a little kid with a yard somewhere in Switzerland to play in. Where a whimper lodges in your throat. Where you know it's finally over but it's too brand new for anyone to tell you what to feel or how. Where this is how a razor blade is sharp enough to work.

Where for a minute you know you're cut but can't feel anything yet. Cut through. Cut through so clean you stay together and feel like the minute before you feel anything, before you see blood, before you fall apart, will never end. Roy. Maggie. Molly. Karl. If they feel anything. You raise your hands to your face. It's still there. It still has skin.

Back in the attic Butterworth's got his suit coat off and his sleeves rolled up. He's washing his face with water he brought up from the bathroom to fill the porcelain bowl on the dresser. You wait for him to reach blind for the towel on the dresser and dry his face and hands. Your stomach feels raw. Your legs won't stop shivering. You expected fear. Felt it in your knuckles every time you've raised your hand to knock on a door. Heard it in your voice when you've raised it slightly to carry through the wood or metal panel of a door when you've introduced yourself to the questioning voice from the other side. But the fear you expected dances now on something you hadn't known would be part of this. Something wild. Something made of surrender and relief. As though what lies ahead of you from here is what needed to happen all along.

"What's wrong?" says Butterworth, looking at you.

And for once the smile is gone. You've questioned it. If a smile that blissful could be sincere. Now you know it was.

"They want us to come to Vienna."

"Vienna? Who? Why?"

"The Mission Home. They didn't say."

"When?"

"Tonight. Now."

"Right now?"

"As soon as we pack."

Butterworth looks bewildered. And then scared.

"Is it a transfer?"

"All they said was come to Vienna and bring everything."

"Everything?"

Where it doesn't take long to pack everything you own into your big gray Samsonite. Where Butterworth finishes right behind you. Where you fold up your bedding and give all the drawers and the closet and under the beds another look. Where you're down the stairs and out the door. Where you load your suitcases and Butterworth's briefcase and your trumpet case into the back seat. Where little Rachel and her mother Susi stand in the doorway of the shop like they're made of painted glass. Where you start the Beetle with the key and pull it back and then forward and switch the headlights on and and turn out on the street. Where you give the horn two beeps and a little girl and her mother wave at you. Where you stop in town to fill the tank. Where your legs start shaking when you hold the clutch and brake down. Where this is what it will be like when you finally get the call. Where you'll head north anyway into the gathering night with the mutter of the engine back behind you. Where you'll feel yourself bleeding but can't find where you're cut. Where you'll follow the headlights north. Where you can run with the high beams on again. Where this is the way it will happen when your time as a fugitive comes to the end God always had in mind.

And sometime during the ride north you wonder why Butterworth has to ride silent next to you and be kept in the dark. In the turmoil of guessing why he's going where he's going. What you have to lose if you tell him. If you don't obey what Elder Hunsacker said. Nothing. Not a thing to lose. Not now.

"I can't let you sit there and wonder."

Where he turns his face your way.

"Why? Do you know?"

"Yes."

"What is it?"

"I'm going home."

Home. Where the word will let you know that the relief you felt was temporary. Because this is far from over. Because only the fugitive part will lie behind you. Still ahead of you as it plays out will be all the people this will hurt.

"What?"

"I'm going to be excommunicated."

"What?"

"I'm pretty sure."

"Why?"

Getting drunk one stupid terrifying night and taking a prostitute to bed in a fleabag place called the Hotel Rabe. Her bruises. Her harsh whisper. The way she turns her face aside. Your garments in a corner of the room while you lie on top of her. Bewegen.

"Something I did last August. I'd rather not say."

Where Butterworth looks out the windshield again.

"Okay."

"I'm sorry."

"I am too." Then he says, "Thanks for letting me know."

"I wasn't supposed to."

"Thanks. They won't know."

Where in the long dark of night you understand that your father was right to send the letter to President Smith. That your mother was right in calling you the kind of beast she called you.

"We'll need to let Bateman and Wolfe know we're probably not coming tomorrow."

"I'll try to get hold of them."

"Thanks."

"Do you know what they plan on doing with me?" he says.

"No. I'm sorry. I wish I did. Send you back to Knittelfeld, I guess."

"Do you think they'll interview me? About you?"

"Maybe."

"I don't have anything to tell them."

Where you get lost in Vienna but find the tram lines you used to take to get to the Mission Home and follow them. Follow the transfers you used to make to different trams. Where you follow the hill you used to climb to get to the Mission Home on Fuerfanggasse. Park the Beetle. Hear the ticking of the hot engine and smell the oil steaming off the exhaust as you pull your suitcases and Butterworth's briefcase and your trumpet case out of the back seat. The porchlights are on. The front door is unlocked.

Where Elder Hunsacker will greet you in the lobby. Look at your hair. Look at your suit. Where two other elders will greet Butterworth, ask him if he's hungry, take him down the beige carpet of the hallway, in the direction of the kitchen past the bathroom where you read Cissy's first letter to you. Where one of the elders will carry Butterworth's suitcase and briefcase and the other will carry your Samsonite and trumpet case. In his clean white hands they'll have the alien and dirty look of things picked off the street. Where Butterworth will turn for one last look at you. Where Elder Hunsacker will touch your elbow and escort you to the office where the President of the Austrian Mission waits.

CHAPTER 99

ELDER HUNSACKER LEAVES and closes the door behind him.
The last time you stood in this office, on this rich looking rug you can feel
now through the worn soles of your shoes, Elder Cannon made the case
to President Lindner to allow you to play in the clubs and cafes around
Vienna. Novick was here too. It was back a year ago. This time it's just you.
President Lindner stands behind his massive King Somebody desk. He's
dressed like he's coming back from speaking from a high pulpit to a vast
multitude of people. The harvest of Austria. A black suit that shows off
the big shoulders of his short carpenter build. The bright white chest of a
dress shirt. The bold silk sheen of a tie striped gray and silver. The bloom
of a matching handkerchief in the breast pocket of his suit coat. The bright
white waves of his hair combed back off his forehead and ears. Under his
flared white eyebrows you've seen the placid contempt in his eyes before.
The last time you were here. At church. At a conference in Graz. In his
broad face the contempt is ice cold as he takes in your finger combed hair
and your cheap suit and stained shoes. Nothing to lose, you're thinking.
Nothing you haven't already lost. A couple of leather armchairs stand in
front of his desk. Portraits of Jesus Christ and Prophet David O. McKay
hang on the paneled walls of a room that wears its quiet wealth and expects
your reverence. Over your head hangs a chandelier with a ring of dangling
crystal teardrops. You think of where you were just a matter of hours and
miles ago. The apartment back in Eisenerz where rats roamed the night
floors and sniffed at the stain of mingled pus and blood in the back of
Bateman's garments. You can still hear the muttering engine and the road
noise of the tires and the night wind of the drive here. Still feel the thin
plastic steering wheel in your hands. Still look across and see Butterworth
with his eyes set straight ahead in a face naked of bliss. Still see the river of
blurred asphalt in the high beams rush underneath the Beetle.

And still hear the sound you listened to. The sound you made sure that
long winter in the sandpit could never be taken away from you. Because
you'd practiced each single note till you owned it. Till it was deep inside you.
Deep inside your lungs and mouth and lips and fingers. Where they couldn't
reach it. Because even then you knew they'd try. All the way from Knittelfeld

it was there, clear and free, with the night sky through the windshield all to itself. And you knew. It would get you through this. It was the one thing you had. It was the one thing you were.

President Lindner comes out from behind his desk and stops across the rug from you. Nothing to lose, you think, not moving, watching him.

"Did you bring everything with you?" he says, in his German accent and a voice unnecessarily big for the room.

"Yes."

"Do you know why you're here?"

You see full on the studied cold contempt you felt when God turned his head and you briefly saw his profile through his flailing hair.

"I'm not sure."

"Did you tell your companion why?"

About the possibility. Not the reason why.

"No."

Nothing to lose but the thing they can't take away from you. How easy it is to lie to this retired carpenter. He keeps his face dead still while he studies you and runs you through some truth test in his head. His blue eyes are flat, the blue as blank as solid turquoise, not veined and filamented like regular eyes where you can see through them. You wonder how he can hold the hundreds of muscles in his face fixed in place that long. He finally turns and walks off toward a window where the only thing to look at is the black of night outside. The black of the night and his reflection on the glass.

"We had your friend Elder Rudd in here earlier this week," he says.

Rudd. The reason this is happening right now, today, not a week or month from now. Hearing his name, remembering him, your throat goes tight, and you can't remember when you've felt this ragged, this much road in a room like this.

"He's not my friend."

"That's how we learned about you."

"What did you learn?"

"I'm sure you can guess. But I'll tell you anyway. Where you did what you did only once, at least as far as we know, he was only getting started when he was with you. He never stopped. His last companion finally had enough and called us."

And you went into action right away, you're thinking, watching President Lindner. While two elders in Eisenerz gave up waiting to hear from you. Blamed themselves for complaining.

"What did he tell you?"

"We asked him who else was involved. Any companions. We persuaded him that it would be in their best spiritual interest. He tried to protect you. It took us two days to get him to give us your name."

Rudd. He would have coughed up your name like he was being asked about the weather. You wonder if Lindner turned his back and went to the window to make it easier to lie to you. In the window now you can see your own reflection back behind his. If that's what he's watching now. Hair you combed with your fingers. The sheen off the shoulders of your synthetic suit.

"Is he still here?"

President Lindner shifts his feet and puts his carpenter hands behind his back while he stays facing the window.

"Rudd? No. We've sent him home."

"When?"

"Two days ago. We wanted to make sure he was home before we called you."

Lindner turns from the window and levels his contempt on you.

"Yes," he says. "We excommunicated him. If that's what you'd like to know."

You look down at the rug. Persian. Oriental. You don't know. Just how the quiet elegance of its patterns and colors makes your shoes look dingy.

"We haven't decided what to do with you," Lindner says. "We know that he was the ringleader that night. That it was his idea. That he took charge."

And this is where you could lie to him again. The way he lied to you. How you don't know what night he means. Spare your family. But now this has to end the only possible way it could ever end.

"I was his senior," you say. "It was my doing as much as his."

"We'll be the judge of that, Elder Tauffler."

"I was his senior."

"You know you should have come forward right away."

"Yes."

"Why didn't you?"

"I thought if I worked hard I could start to make it up to God."

"You weren't worthy to do God's work."

"I didn't do anything official."

"You desecrated your calling. You defiled the priesthood. You had no authority to do his work."

"I hoped—"

"You hoped you wouldn't get caught. The Lord knows that. I know that."

You remember the cold. The rain and snow. The endless doors. Walking the slush of the streets at Christmas. Playing trumpet when it made you sick to play. Letting go of everything to just keep working. Your calendar. Time served against time left. Hoping you could make it.

"I worked hard."

"You deceived and cheated the Lord."

If you could have stood here almost a year ago. If you could have confessed that you'd gotten drunk and gone to bed with a prostitute the night before. You don't know.

"You have two baptisms," President Lindner says.

"I converted two people."

"Who?"

"A nineteen year old girl. A mechanic in Linz."

"Since that night?"

"Yes."

"You baptized them."

"I let my juniors baptize them. I knew I couldn't. I didn't confirm them either." Then you say, "I told you. I've avoided doing anything official."

"Do you think that matters?"

"Matters?"

He looks down. Smiles at the elaborate rug you both stand on.

"Did you teach them the Gospel?"

"Yes."

"Did you take them through the lessons?"

"Yes."

"Did you bear your testimony?"

"Yes."

"Did you pray with them?"

"Yes."

"You don't see?"

"See what?"

"You had a hand in converting them. So their conversions are worthless. Defiled by what you did. They don't count. Neither do their baptisms."

Otto dressed in white in a public swimming pool in Linz. Angelika in white too. In the font in the churchhouse.

"I don't believe that," you say. "That their baptisms don't count. I'm sorry."

"What you believe doesn't matter. Those baptisms don't count."

"I'm the one who did wrong. They were innocent."

"They were deceitfully converted by someone unworthy of teaching the Gospel. I don't care if the President of the Church baptized them. It still wouldn't count."

"They didn't know that. They had faith."

"Their faith was misplaced."

"It was placed in the Gospel."

"It was placed in you. That's where they were wrong."

"With all due respect, President Lindner, it was placed in the Gospel. I know. I was there."

"They trusted you."

You look down at his gleaming black shoes. If he had someone polish them just for you. If he got so immaculately dressed just for this. If he's lying. You look back up.

"Okay," you say. "Then they'll have to be told."

"Told what?" the president says.

It astonishes you that he hasn't thought this through.

"That their baptisms are no good," you say.

He says nothing.

"They can't go through life thinking they're members. Living the commandments. Paying tithing. Baptizing their children. Hoping they'll enter the Celestial King—"

"Yes," he says. "They'll have to be told."

"How about the elders who baptized them?" you say.

"They'll have to be told too," the president says.

"You think God's that cruel."

He stares at you. You watch what you said strike home. His face go slack to where it's almost boneless. He takes two steps away across the rug, turns back to you, his contempt in place again.

"This is your doing," he says.

"Then I'll be the one to tell them."

"No. You're not to contact them in any way. We'll take care of it."

And then you know. He was lying. Otto and Angelika are fine. A retired carpenter, dressed for a speech he's probably carried in his head for years, just looking to hurt you.

"Okay," you say.

"I'm going to tell you this in confidence, Elder. I'm sure you know that I've never thought too highly of you."

"Yes."

"You've always been a little rebellious. Less than spiritual."

You hear your father's accent in the voice of the retired carpenter they made your mission president.

"I've heard that," you say.

"Even with your famous grandfather." Then he says, "You thought you could ride on his coattails. You thought you could fill his shoes."

Nothing to lose, you think.

"Seriously," you say.

The president flinches when you smile at him and shake your head.

"Oh yes," he says.

"Do you know how many times I got high hours? Not in my grandfather's shoes. In my own. Have you kept track?"

He glances down at your shoes before he catches himself.

"You never should have asked if you could play in night clubs," he says.

"I didn't ask. Elder Novick and Elder Cannon did."

"They asked on your behalf."

"They asked because they thought it was a way to meet investigators."

"In night clubs," he says.

If he forgot that he said okay. That he had you transferred back from Linz when he heard from the European Mission that you deserved a dozen roses.

"It worked."

"What do you mean?"

"We got referrals. They went to other missionaries. A couple were baptized. Some are still probably investigating. Elder Hill didn't tell you?"

Lindner's face loses its fierce bonework again for an instant.

"Elder Hill told me it was a failure. Especially the second time."

"Ask Elder Wissom. He'll tell you."

"My point is this. Those clubs led you to what you did. You put yourself in evil places. In immoral situations."

"That's not what happened."

"Yes it is."

"No. I was put with Elder Rudd. That's what it was. Rudd wasn't my idea, President Lindner. He was someone else's."

"Other missionaries had no problem with him," the president says.

What he would have done if Rudd had grabbed and slammed him back against a wall and held him by the throat. If he could have seen Rudd's eyes and kept his pants clean.

"I don't think you have any idea what they might have gone through. Just because you didn't hear from them."

"And yet you're the only one who went along with him."

"Once. And I'm here to pay for it."

Lindner turns back to his desk, walks around behind it, uses the armrests to lower himself as the leather chair catches and takes his groaning weight. You have a feeling this is over. A feeling he won't be offering you a chair. He leans back with his retired carpenter hands still on the armrests.

"I tried to transfer you to another mission once. Because I had a feeling something like this would happen."

"I'm sorry it didn't work out," you say.

"What I'm leading up to is this. In my opinion, you should be excommunicated. But the General Authorities are bending over backward to show you some leniency. Not for your sake but for your parents. And your grandfather."

"I don't deserve leniency."

"You're right," he says. "Any leniency you're shown will be meant for your family."

"I don't want leniency."

"Not even for your family."

"It would be worse if I came home a liar."

He looks at you. Shakes his head. Lifts his arm, pulls his sleeve back off his wrist, looks at his watch.

"How late is it?"

He falls for it. Looks at his watch again.

"Almost midnight."

"Thanks for talking to me."

"We're convening an Elder's Court in the morning at nine. Get some sleep. They have a room for you."

He looks you up and down where you stand on the rug that spreads its ornate pattern across the wood floor. You don't move. In your cheap synthetic suit with holes worn through the patches of older holes in the crotch of your pants, you don't move. With a rug you could never afford soft and lush where you can feel it through the hole worn through your shoe, you don't move. Unable to remember the last time you had your hair cut, or even looked in a mirror, you don't move. You don't know how to move except to wait him out.

"Come to court with your hair combed," he finally says.

"Anything else?"

"Wear a better suit."

"Anything else?"

You stand there on his fancy rug and let him search your face for disrespect. In Eisenerz, Bateman's in bed on the springs of a busted couch, and Wolfe's on a kitchen table trying to keep two cushions under him.

"I wouldn't know where to start," he finally says.

A young elder you don't know takes you to the back of the big house to a small room behind the kitchen. On your way through the kitchen he asks if you'd like anything to eat. You see a bowl of apples and oranges and bananas on the table but tell him no. In the small back room stands a narrow cot with a nightstand. On the nightstand a handout Book of Mormon, Das Buch Mormon, lies next to a small lamp. If you opened it you'd see your grandfather's name. The sheets are made. A nubbled blue blanket lies folded on top of a small pillow at the foot of the bed. A small oval rug made of a braided coil of rags lies alongside the bed on the light wood floor. A chair stands in the back corner to hold your clothes. In its straightforward simple utility as a place to sleep the room reminds you of the room in the Hotel Rabe. If this is where Rudd slept when he was here. If they changed the sheets. If he jerked off the way you used to have to listen to him in the dark. The room smells fresh. A small high window cracked partly open lets a cascade of night air into the room.

"There's a small bathroom in the lobby," the elder says.

Where you read Cissy's first letter the day you got here. You can still see the pattern of the wallpaper. Tiny blue tulips with stems like the tails of kites.

"I know," you say. "Thanks."

"Goodnight."

You float the blanket across the bed. Lay the pillow at its head. Use the chair to hang your suit and shirt and tie. Keep your garments on because you don't know what to do with them except what you've always done with them. Switch off the light in the ceiling and get in bed in the dark. The pillow and sheets feel cool where your skin is naked. You're finally alone. You wonder where Butterworth is. If he's okay. In a room of his own somewhere in this vast house. They wouldn't have sent him back to Knittelfeld if they had him bring his suitcase. In the morning, before your trial starts, you'll talk to Wissom. Tell him you need home addresses for a couple of elders. Douglas Bateman and Ronald Wolfe. He'll give them to you. He'll wonder why you're here. Or maybe he'll know. He was here when they did Rudd. Maybe he figured out that you'd be next.

Slowly the small high window reveals itself by the faint light that comes through it from the random lights of the neighborhood. Your legs start to shiver. Not the shiver you get from being cold. Not convulsive. Just light and rapid and uncontrollable deep inside your legs. While you lie there you can feel it move through your stomach and up your back into your chest. You lie on your side and bring your knees up. In La Sal there was the prairie dog that you wounded with a twenty-two but had to shoot again to kill. The same quick involuntary shiver in its fur while it looked up at you and waited. What it will be like. How they'll strip you of the priesthood. Lay their hands on your head and reverse what your father did when he gave it to you. How they'll take away your membership. Walk you into an empty font and have you hold your nose while they dunk you backward into air and let you fall a thousand feet through open sky off Dead Horse Point. You don't know. What will happen from here on out, what this will be like, is up to them.

And with that thought, that this is finally in their hands, you're in the cab of the cattle truck again, riding on a stack of gunny sacks between Manny and Hidalgo, cresting Soldier Summit, hearing the flight of that steel bird sound for the first time. That line of music that came out of the radio and took you through the windshield out into the vast exhilaration of the open sky. Safe between them. Everything your family owns in their brown hands. Calm spreads through your body the way light and warmth spread from a sunrise. A calm you've never known lays its hand on the way you're shivering till the shivering stops. Lets your legs stretch out and your back relax and takes you into sleep.

CHAPTER 100

VIENNA. SOMEWHERE in June. In the morning you open your suitcase to check out your other suit. The last of the two you brought from Utah. Wrinkled. Worn. Old and tired. Musty when you hold it to your face. Holes through the patches in the crotch of the pants. The shirts wrinkled. And so you put what you wore to Eisenerz back on. Then remember. Undress again to take your garments off. Before the day is out you'll be stripped of everything their symbols mean. Without the right to wear them. You pull on your pants and shirt over your naked skin. You go to the lobby bathroom to throw water on your face, brush your teeth, wet and straighten your hair with your hands without looking at your face in the mirror. Steal back to your room where you make the small bed, fold the blanket, lay it on the pillow like it was last night. Like you hadn't been here. You sit out breakfast. The chatter of elders and clink and scrape of forks and spoons and plates. Stay in the room off the kitchen where your travel alarm clock ticks its way toward nine.

And then it's time.

Voices come from the conference room. American voices. Low but unmistakable. The voices of missionaries. In the open door you stop cold. For the instant you stop, you suddenly wish for a better suit, a haircut, a cleaner shirt, shoes without holes. For the instant your glance takes, before you look quickly down, you memorize everything. Four rows of folding chairs in the always empty back half of the room. More chairs lined along the walls. Most of the chairs taken. Every head turned your way. Every voice killed. Faces you know or recognize or haven't seen before. The sweet sharp metallic mix of early morning aftershave, deodorant, mouthwash. For the instant you stand there before you find your legs again, before you look up at the sound of your name, you feel your stomach knot up, your heart convulse in the cage of your chest, your face burn with disbelief and shame.

You didn't know that this would have an audience. Nobody told you.

"Elder Tauffler. Sit here, please."

Gerhardt. The elder with broad shoulders and muscular neck, the blond hair around his balding head cut short and the sleeves of his shirt rolled back off his thick and hairy forearms, the elder who always tends the Tandberg. The big tape recorder sits off to one side of the center of the conference table. At either end of the table rests a microphone, its head propped up on a couple of books, the wrinkled black vein of its cord trailed back to the Tandberg.

You take the chair he indicates, at the foot of the table, alone, the stilled audience of elders behind you. You won't let them see your face. But what you can't hide is the disregard that rises off of you in this well-tended room like something they could breathe.. With your arms on the armrests, your head lowered, you don't move, aware of their eyes all over you, where your hair has started to shag around your ears and down across the collar of your shirt, where slush and mud off the back tire of your bike have left a faded strip that won't come clean up the back of your cheap synthetic suit, a sidewalk suit whose color and sheen look false in their play of blue and olive, whose fabric has started to fuzz from wear, whose shoulders fit loose the way you sit hunched forward, your head drawn down between them. On the armrests of your chair, where the sleeves of your suit pull back, light grime lines the cuffs of your white shirt. You want to pull them forward, hide the cuffs, but you don't move. Through the holes in the crotch of your pants the wood of the chair is cold at first. More elders come in. Chairs creak and groan. Street noise comes through the tall windows that are open to the early summer air. Gerhardt threads brown tape through rollers and guides from the feed reel to the takeup reel. Takes a stool away from the table, back against the wall, to wait with the rest of you.

You try not to think back to the first time you were in this room. But there it is. Fresh off the plane, in a new American suit, a new American tie, new American socks and shoes, your German lousy but your testimony strong. How pumped with purpose you must have been. How ready you must have been to open the doors of Austria. How eager to harvest the mission field. How full of it you must have been, looking up at Elder Cannon while he took you through the rules, thinking you could be like him.

This room. Where this began. Where it will end.

President Lindner comes in and goes past you to the head of the table where his chair and microphone wait. From his position against the front wall he can preside over the room while he conducts business with you. He wears a scowl whose lines cut deep and permanent into his broad German face. His calm blue eyes are hooded by the brushed wings of fierce white eyebrows. His full head of thick hair is sculpted in waves as white as snowdrifts. You can see distaste and impatience in his face for what lies ahead.

He clears his throat and looks to your right.

"Elder Hill? Elder Hunsacker? Are you ready?"

"Ready here," says Hill.

"Ready, President Lindner," says Hunsacker.

You saw them too in that frozen instant you stood at the door. Side by side in chairs against a window with pads and pens and clipboards. Hunsacker wears glasses with round rimless frames that ride so low on his small nose that the lenses leave his soft eyes naked. Hill, thin and tall and rangy, with his small hard hostile eyes, bitter mouth, hair that looks like it was cut with a Boy Scout hatchet. The smooth German accent in the voice of the president. The diction too practiced and precise for a carpenter to ever need. A carpenter, you think, who spent time rehearsing for something bigger than making cabinets.

"Are you ready to record, Elder Gerhardt?"

"Just need a sound check."

"Good. I need to explain some things first. Then we'll begin. Elder Tauffler?"

"You don't have to call me Elder," you say.

"You'll have to speak louder. I didn't understand that."

"I said you don't have to call me Elder, President Lindner."

The president studies you. "We'll call you Elder for now. Elder Hill will be your prosecutor. Elder Hunsacker has agreed to act as your defender. Is that all right with you?"

"I don't need to be prosecuted or defended. I know what I did."

At the edge of your vision Hill sits up.

"What does that mean?" he says. "You know what you did?"

Lindner raises the palm of his hand.

"I've got control of this, Elder Hill." He looks back at you. "What are you saying?"

"I'd just like to confess."

"First I need to know if you're satisfied with Elder Hunsacker as your defender. Even if you don't plan on using him."

"Yes. I wouldn't want anyone else."

"It's the right of the court to appoint the prosecutor."

"I understand."

"Would you like to meet with your defender before we go on?"

"There's no need to."

"You should know that I'm supposed to appoint a prosecutor and defender. If you plan to confess, and that leaves them with nothing to do, that's fine. But I'm bound by the rules of the Elders' Court."

"I just don't want to waste anyone's time."

"That's not how it works," says Hill.

Lindner shoots Hill a look of fierce impatience. "Are you that eager to prosecute this elder? He's willing to confess."

"I just thought . . ." He holds up his legal pad. "I put in time preparing for this."

"It doesn't look like you'll need it."

"Then I'd like to ask if I could leave. I have things to do."

"You'll be staying. Sit back."

The president looks down the length of the table again.

"Do you have any questions before we start?"

"Yes."

"Go ahead."

"All the elders here. Are they the jury?"

"I don't know," the president says. "Elder Hill? You put this together. Why are all these elders here?"

"They're here as witnesses."

"This many?"

"It seemed right, President Lindner."

"I don't recall this many for the trial a few days ago. I recall two or three."

"This is a special case."

"There weren't this many witnesses to the Golden Plates," Lindner says. "Don't think for me, Elder Hill. Ask me."

He looks at you again.

"We can start any time you're ready. Anything else?"

"No."

"Start the recorder now."

Gerhardt looks at you.

"Say something into the microphone. Don't lean forward."

You sit up straight.

"Hello."

Your amplified word barely finds its way out of the speaker. Gerhardt fiddles with the Tandberg.

"Again."

"Hello."

The word comes wailing out of the speaker this time on the high howl of feedback. The mission president's hands lift off the table.

"Sorry, President Lindner. Once more, Elder Tauffler."

"Hello."

"Your turn, President Lindner."

"Hello."

"Again. Only this time just sit back."

"Hello."

"Okay. All set. Recording."

CHAPTER 101

THE REELS OF THE TANDBERG begin their lazy but relentless rotation. You don't know how this will go. All you know is that everything happening around you is happening because of you. Everyone in this room is here because of you. The last time everything around you was because of you was your farewell almost two years ago in Bountiful. This is the negative of that. Not where your mission began but where it will end. You dismiss the audience of elders seated behind you because you have to. Because if you didn't it would be too hard. Fear and shame and humiliation would ride ahead of you on the story you're here to tell. The story they came to listen to. You dismiss Gerhardt. You dismiss President Lindner. You don't know how this will go. You haven't cried since the morning after that August night when you tried and quickly knew that crying wasn't for you. It was for the innocent. The people who would be hurt because of you. How this will go. You don't know. From now on the Tandberg will record everything you tell it. The elders gathered behind you will hear what it's like to commit the sins of intoxication and fornication in the wild desolation of a single night. Because of you they'll know what it's like to witness an excommunication.

Lindner puts on a pair of half frame reading glasses, introduces himself, and reads from a sheet of paper to tell the Tandberg and the elders seated behind you that this is an Elders' Court convened on this day in June of 1965 in the headquarters of the Austrian Mission. That he, as President of the Austrian Mission, is presiding. That the defendant is Elder Shake Wilford Tauffler. That the sins under investigation and disposition are intoxication and fornication committed by the defendant on a night in August of last year. That preceding this recording, the court conditionally assigned a prosecutor and defender, in the event that Elder Tauffler entered a plea of not guilty and wanted to pursue a formal trial. That the elders appointed to those positions are Second Counselor Paul Hill and Public Relations Director Roger Hunsacker, respectively. That they are present. That also assembled here are elders called as witnesses. That the defendant is also here. That he has been presented with the choice of a defender and has chosen not to use him.

"He will now confirm that choice for the record."

Gerhardt looks at you.

"Elder Tauffler?" Lindner says.

"Yes."

"Would you confirm your choice?"

"I've chosen not to use a defender."

"Okay." Lindner pushes the sheet of paper aside and sits up. "Elder Tauffler, do you understand the charges against you?"

"Yes."

"Would you state them for the record?"

"Shouldn't I be doing this?" Hill says.

"This is a confession, Elder Hill. Not a prosecution. I can handle it. Sit back."

Lindner looks at you again.

"State the charges, please."

"Intoxication and fornication."

"Are you aware that you committed these acts as an elder in the priesthood while serving as a missionary of the Church of Jesus Christ of Latter-Day Saints?"

"Yes."

"Are you aware of the penalties for these acts? As an elder and a missionary?"

"Yes, your Honor."

"This isn't an American courtroom, Elder. I'm not a judge."

"I'm sorry. I'm new to this."

You hear a couple of stifled laughs from behind you.

"Were you aware of the penalties at the time you committed them?"

"As aware as I could be."

"What does that mean?"

"I was intoxicated."

"But you had previous knowledge of the penalties."

"Of course."

"Please tell us what you think they are."

"For intoxication you can be disfellowshipped. For fornication it's excommunication."

How smooth you are in giving voice to the two most punishing words in the language of the Mormon Church. How long you've been saying them to yourself.

"The penalties are that severe, Elder, because the work of the Lord is a holy undertaking, and the calling to baptize people requires the utmost worthiness."

"Yes. I know."

"The record now shows that you understand both the charges against you and the penalties for those charges. Do you still wish to plead guilty?"

"Yes. That and confess."

"We'll get to that. Do you plead innocent or guilty?"

"Guilty."

"We all need to hear you."

"I said guilty."

"Witnesses, if any of you didn't hear the plea, raise your hand."

Lindner looks out across the room. And then goes on.

"You understand that we'll need to hear everything," he says.

"I'm prepared to tell you everything."

"He could confess to anything," you hear Hill say. "How will we know he's telling the truth without being cross examined?"

"He's already admitted his guilt. Elder Gerhardt. Do we have enough tape?"

If you'd wanted to lie you could have lied yesterday. Told Lindner you had no idea what Rudd was talking about. Left Hill with a roomful of elders wanting to know what they were doing here. But lying was never your deal with God. Your deal with him was always to pay for what you'd done. One way or the other.

"Enough tape for now," says Gerhardt.

"Whenever you're ready, Elder Tauffler."

"Where would you like me to start?"

"Well, wherever you think the beginning is," the president says.

You look at your hands on the armrests. You're finally here. You look at the screened silver head of the microphone. The times you've played your trumpet into one. Muted and open. You gather your breath and then look up at Lindner.

"I met Elder Rudd at the Sudbahnhof late in the afternoon. He was coming in from Graz."

"Was there anything unusual about him?"

"He was older than me."

"How much older?"

"Eight or nine years. I wasn't expecting that. I was supposed to be his senior."

"If I'm not mistaken, he was your first junior."

"Yes."

"And this was your first day as a senior."

"Yes."

"Did anything else seem out of line?"

A fucking horn blowing missionary. Rudd saying that. His grin and the way it scared you.

"He liked to curse."

"Like what?"

"The real word for fuzz." Silence from the elders behind you. "He used it pretty much all the time."

Lindner's expression tells you he doesn't know what you're talking about.

"Fuzz. The way hell is the real word for heck."

"I've never heard that word used that way," the president says.

"You can ask any elder in this room."

"Did you tell him to stop?"

"I was too shocked at first. Later I did."

"What happened next?"

"I took him to our place. I wanted to show him around the neighborhood and tracting area. He wanted to see Vienna. He wanted to hear me play. I told him not tonight."

You look down at the microphone and then up again.

"That was when he took my trumpet and threatened to twist it in half."

"What did you do?"

"I told him it wasn't mine. It was borrowed. It belonged to a member."

"What happened then?"

"He grabbed me by the throat and slammed me back against a wall and told me never to tell him no again."

"He did what?"

"He slammed me into a wall. By my throat. With one hand. He told me never to tell him no again." Then you say, "I've been in fights. Never with anyone that strong. I knew I didn't stand a chance."

"He never told us that," says Lindner.

"Then he didn't tell you everything."

"So Rudd forced him. That's his confession."

The president turns his fierce impatience on Hill again. "You need to restrain yourself," he says. "Don't do that again." He looks back at you. "Keep going."

"I took my trumpet and we headed for downtown Vienna."

"You didn't think of calling us?"

"Of course I did."

"Why didn't you?"

"I knew he would have stopped me."

"You could have come straight to the Mission Home."

"I would have had to come alone." You look at the president. "I hoped I could handle him if I had time to figure out how."

"So you showed him around Vienna."

"I took him to the Ring to show him some tourist places. He saw a movie theater. It was showing a movie he wanted to see. The Silence."

"What's it about?"

"Two women and a boy."

"Was it promiscuous?"

"There was sex in it."

"Did you know this?"

"Not before we went in."

"Did you leave?"

"No."

"You stayed for the whole movie."

"It gave me time to think."

"Did you ask the Lord for help?"

"I prayed all the way through it."

"What happened then?"

"He wanted to hear me play."

You look at your hands again. The welter of sweat and used deodorant rises from under your suit and becomes the air you breathe. This is where you have to start to leave things out. Things that are yours. Things that won't matter anyway in the way this will play itself out.

"There was a place close by where I'd played before. So we went there. Friends of mine were playing. I played with them. When I finished, Elder Rudd was at a table with a group of students. Drinking wine with them."

"He was drinking wine?"

"Red wine. There was also a glass where they'd saved a chair for me."

"Where did it come from?"

"Elder Rudd ordered it for me."

"Did you pick it up?"

You don't tell the Tandberg about the negro girl. How she brought Cissy front and center out of your past. About the skinny acne riddled guy beside her with teeth like the shards of a broken Coke bottle and a mouth like a ragged wound who kept calling the Church racist. About proving him stupid with everything you knew. The girls killed in Birmingham. Their names. About letting the negro girl know he was a fake and a huckster.

"Not at first. I told Elder Rudd we were leaving. He said no we're not. He kept egging me on. Calling me names. He got the students to join in." You look at the president. "There's no good reason. I picked it up. That's what matters."

"Did you have more than one glass?"

"Yes."

"How many?"

"I don't know." Then you say, "One was too many."

"Then what, Elder?"

"We said good night and left and started walking toward the tram stop. There were prostitutes all over. Not all over. But they were out."

"Prostitutes," says Hill.

"Ignore him," Lindner says.

You don't tell the Tandberg about taking your trumpet out and playing like a lunatic up and down the street. About the Arab guys in the Thunderbird who couldn't get prostitutes to talk to them and asked Rudd and you to help. About the brand new rousing feeling knowing you could get a girl to take off all her clothes just by giving her some money. That it could be that easy. That you were drunk enough to think that way. To want to try it out.

"We found a couple of girls. They took us to a hotel a few streets away. We went inside and they got keys to a couple of rooms from an old man behind the desk. Then they took us upstairs. I went into one room. Rudd went into the room next door."

You don't tell the Tandberg about asking her, over and over on the walk to the hotel, not to hurt you. About the garish blood red paint that covered every surface of the lobby, ceiling to floor, except the old man at the desk. About the bare red bulb in the cheap shadeless lamp on the nightstand next to the cot in the small room. About remembering the lamp the woman in the red dress gave to you and you in turn gave Molly. About your mother calling it the lamp of a whore. About thinking no. This is the lamp they give a whore.

"Had you paid her yet?"

"I paid her then."

"How much did she cost?"

Lindner glares hard at Hill. "He paid her. How much doesn't matter. One more time." He looks back at you. "Go on."

"She took her clothes off." Then you say, "So I did too."

"Were you wearing your Temple garments?"

"Yes."

You don't tell the Tandberg about the way she looked at you when you stood there in your garments. About the way she asked you, curious and a little scared, what they were. About the way you told her they were just American underwear and then threw them in a corner to show her they meant nothing. To keep her from running.

"That didn't stop you? When you looked down and saw what you were wearing?"

"I was drunk, President Lindner."

"Go on."

"I got into bed with her." You hang your head. Look at your hands again. Reach down to wipe them on your pants legs. Then leave them in your lap. Wish you had something to wipe the sweat and oil off the armrests with. When you look back up the president hasn't moved. "Afterward I got dressed and left. Then we went home."

"You got into bed with her."

"Yes."

"You'll have to tell it, Elder."

You look at the Tandberg. Back at the president. Try to pretend there's nothing behind you but some empty folding chairs where an occasional creak can be blamed on an imagined wind that blows across the room.

"I had sexual intercourse with her," you say. "I committed fornication."

The rasp of a throat clearing. And suddenly the weight and desperate humiliating heat on your back of all the elders listening.

"Are you sure?" the president says.

"Sure?"

"That you had intercourse."

"Yes. Of course."

"You were drunk. You may not remember correctly."

"I know that we had intercourse."

"We need to be sure that you penetrated her. We have to know exactly what happened."

"I just told you."

"Let's go back to when you got into bed with her. Were you wearing anything?"

"No."

"I mean to protect yourself."

"She had a condom."

"A prophylactic?"

"Yes."

You don't tell the Tandberg about the mechanical way she got you stiff and then put it on for you.

"Tell us how you know you had intercourse. We have to be absolutely certain."

"What do you want?"

"Everything you remember."

"I know I had intercourse with her."

"That's fine. But I have to know it too. Beyond the shadow of a doubt."

"She was on her back. I was on top of her. We had intercourse. I remember doing that. What else do you want to know?"

"Everything you can tell me to persuade me that you either did or didn't penetrate her."

"I was inside her. I don't know what else to say."

"This is very important, Elder Tauffler. We have to be certain of that. You were drunk. It was almost a year ago. It's possible you imagined it."

You stare at him. If this is what he wants. You to tell him you're not sure. The Tandberg to record it.

"She had to show me where it went," you say. "That's how I know."

The metal groan of a couple of chairs behind you. You're ready for the recoil of humiliation. You've faced it on your own a thousand times. Your eyes wide open in the dark. Committing the sin of sins and you didn't even know how it was supposed to be committed.

"She what?" says Lindner.

"She had to show me."

"Look at me, Elder. Tell me."

You don't tell the Tandberg how you could have gone back to your memory of Cissy to remember how it went. How you wouldn't let yourself. How hard you tried to shield your memory of her from what you were doing. You look up at the president.

"She had to take and show me," you say. "I couldn't feel anything. Is that enough?"

"You couldn't feel anything."

"No. I couldn't. Because of what I was wearing."

"The prophylactic."

"Yes."

"And you were intoxicated."

You don't tell the Tandberg how you just kept jamming it against her groin like something blind. How she finally had to take and put it in for you. Raise her hips and take it in the thin fingers of her small fist and guide it home beneath this bone you hadn't known was there.

"Yes."

"If you couldn't feel anything, then how can you be sure you penetrated her?"

"I'm positive, President Lindner."

"You're certain. You didn't just imagine it."

"I'm sure."

You don't tell the Tandberg about the way you wanted to just lie there. Hold and kiss her. Go to sleep. How she had to keep telling you to move.

"Excommunication is very serious, Elder. Especially for a servant of the Lord. We don't want to make a mistake here."

"I'm telling the truth, President Lindner."

Why. What he's after. Why he won't take your word. His face gives away nothing beyond placid contempt. Why he wants you to keep repeating the most intimate and damning part. If he wants to give you the opportunity to back out. Give you an opening to doubt yourself. You were drunk. It was almost a year ago. No. You can't. The rest of your life would be this lie that has been your life since then. You think of Lieutenant Tanner. What he would want you to do. If Tanner would just get up and say enough. Enough of this. In his friendly way, with his grin, but in a way that Lindner and everyone else in the room would know that it was over. He penetrated her. No more of this inquisition. Come on, Shake. Let's go.

And you would have to tell Lieutenant Tanner no. I have to stay.

The president studies you. "Let's go back one more time. She helped you put on a prophylactic."

"She put it on me by herself."

"Then she had to show you."

"Yes."

"How did she show you?"

"She took it in her hand."

"What did she do with it?"

"She put it where it was supposed to go."

"You're absolutely positive."

"Yes."

"You felt yourself penetrate her."

"Yes."

"But you said you couldn't feel anything."

"I could feel it go in."

"How do you know it wasn't just her hand?"

You stare at him.

"I know what a hand feels like."

An abrupt cough from an elder behind you.

"You weren't too intoxicated to know the difference."

"If you'd like me to lie, President Lindner, I can. I can tell you nothing ever happened. Whatever you'd like. Because I don't know what you're asking."

"What you need to understand, Elder Tauffler," the president says, "is that we don't like hearing this any more than you like telling it. In fact, we're disgusted by it. You were a servant of the Lord. You were doing the Lord's work. Some of the elders in this room may have worked with you. What we're being forced to hear is the Devil's work. What we're listening to goes against the conscience of every elder in this room. But we're doing this because we want to help you. We want to give you every opportunity to explain yourself. We're trying to find if there's any doubt in your mind about what happened. If there's any doubt, then we have something to work with. I'm sorry if you're embarrassed about the details, and I'm sorry Elder Hill thinks we need all these witnesses, but whether you penetrated her and actually committed fornication happens to be the deciding factor. That's why we keep going over this. We have to be absolutely sure that you don't harbor any doubt."

"Please, President Lindner. I'm positive of what I did. I know how this has to end. I was wrong to think I could work it off. I just want it to end the way it has to."

"Then you'll still have to convince me."

CHAPTER 102

YOU GLANCE AT his hands where they hang off the armrests. The fingers thick. Not plump but thickened by real work. When he had to depend not on position or title but on what his hands could do. The retired carpenter using the sacred protocol of this Elders' Court to quench his long resentment. The still calm with which he contemplates you is opaque. You can't see through to what he could be thinking. You know retaliation is in there somewhere. You've been alone like this before. You thought you had nothing left to lose. But you were wrong. You have fear and shame and humiliation left. You can't lose them. You can only live with them. Make friends with them. And then they give you courage. To tell the Tandberg everything. Take it where it's never been before. Play it a solo. Not on the sound of your trumpet but on the sound of your voice and what it has to tell. An ugly solo. A death solo. The death solo of an ugly song. A solo out of a wild and ugly night that will take Lindner and his audience of elders out of this blank dream of a room across the City of Music to the shame of a desolate room in a side alley hotel. Not a solo you'll bring them home from. Because you haven't found your own way home from it. Out of reflex you adjust the position of the microphone. Look at the Tandberg to see if there's enough tape on the feed reel. Look at the waiting face of the president again. Welcome the fear and shame and humiliation because without them you won't exist.

You feel your trumpet in your hands. Hear the bright ringing shimmer of its sound. You wonder if the president will come with you on its wings. If Gerhardt and Hill and Hunsacker and the guys behind you will have the stomach to come along.

"Are you sure you want all of it," you say.

Gerhardt has his hand up. "Not so soft," he says. "A little louder."

"Are you sure you want all of it," you say again.

"Enough to convince me," the president says.

"Okay. The wine cellar. I came off the stage and sat down to the wine glass in front of me. Red wine. Rudd started pushing me to drink it. When I refused he started calling me a pussy." You give the sudden creak of chairs behind you time to quiet down again. "Soon the whole table was calling me a pussy. Chanting it."

"We get the picture, Elder."

"Just let me know when you're convinced, President Lindner."

"I will."

"I didn't touch the glass. There was a guy across the table from me. Acne. Dirty. Broken teeth. Long hair. A dirty old gray turtleneck. Smoking. Benson and Hedges. He—"

"Benson and what?"

"Hedges. A cigarette brand. He was American. He found out we were missionaries. He started talking about negroes and the Church. He called the Church racist. He called us racist. He knew the doctrine. The Great War in Heaven. Fence sitters. The seed of Cain. I tried to defend what we believe." Then you say, "He got pretty ugly."

You lower your head. Look down at your legs. At the cheap sidewalk fabric worn thin and shiny by your knees. Raise your head again when you realize that looking down could expose the grime in the collar of your shirt.

"Ugly how?" says the president.

"Foul mouthed. Nasty. It was hard to listen to." Then you say, "It's not an easy doctrine to defend."

"It's the Word of God. That's the only defense it needs."

"I was in the Army. I've looked negroes in the face."

The president studies you. You watch the calm contempt leave his face. Congestion move in. A storm gather in his head while the sculpted white waves of his thick hair take on the menace of thunderheads the way you used to watch them move in from across the desert toward the sandpit. The only sounds are a bird outside the window and the steady hum of the Tandberg and the music of your solo.

"What was Elder Rudd doing?" he finally says.

"Sitting there watching. Smiling."

"He didn't say anything?"

"No."

"Go on."

"There was a negro girl next to the guy arguing with me. Thin. Pretty. Nicely dressed. He was showing off for her. Acting like he was defending her people. At some point he put his arm around her shoulders. He didn't ask. Her shoulders were bare. His hand was dirty. Dirt under his nails. It was on her skin. Drawing circles with his fingers. Like he owned her."

You feel the anger rise again. You look at the Tandberg, the methodical cold turning of its reels, to give it time to pass.

"She looked scared. I could tell she didn't want it there. She didn't know what to do. It bothered me too. I finally told him to take his hand off her.

He laughed. He said I'd have to make him." Then you say, "That was when I picked up the glass. And emptied it. And got up."

"You got up?" the president says.

"To take his hand off her shoulder. To hurt him. I lost control for a minute. I told Elder Rudd to order me another glass."

"Did you hurt him?"

"No. He knew I was serious. He took his hand off the girl. I sat back down again."

"And Elder Rudd? He ordered you another glass?"

"Yes."

"Go on."

"I knew the guy was a phony. I started going after him. To see how much he really knew or cared about negroes. Their struggle. I started asking him if he knew this or that. He didn't know a thing. I ended up exposing him."

"Exposing him."

"To the girl. To the other students at the table. For the fraud he was. He finally got up and swore at the table and left."

"How did you know so much about it?" the president says. "This struggle?"

"Magazines. Newspapers." Then you say, "It's everywhere."

You look down at your hands on the armrests. Silence behind you. A mute choir of maybe thirty elders. You wonder crazily how many of them would sing tenor and how many bass.

"Why was it your business to defend this girl?"

You stare at the president. The placid face that can ask that question. "Why?"

"Did you forget that you have a higher purpose here?"

"I told you. I lost control."

"What is this word you used?" he says. "Racism?"

"A word for prejudice. Against negroes."

"You think the Church is prejudiced?"

You remember Novick. His jazz dad. The seed of Cain. How you had to believe the way Novick did. How Brigham Young just made it up. How God just let it stand. Another reason to excommunicate you.

"I don't believe what they say about negroes is the Word of God."

It takes the president a minute. A passing truck with a bad exhaust draws his blank glance to the window before his attention comes back to you.

"You don't," he says.

"The girl thanked me," you say.

After another minute, he says, "How much did you drink?"

"I'm not sure. Two or three more glasses. Four."

"Go on."

"We left at closing time. Once we were outside I took my trumpet out and blew it up and down the street. Then two men in a white Thunderbird came along. I think they were Turkish. They were looking for prostitutes but all the girls they approached said no. They wanted us to help them. Because we were white, I think. I don't know. Elder Rudd was doing the talking. Anyway, we got in back, and Elder Rudd tried talking to a few girls, but once they got a look at the Turks, they walked off. We finally gave up and got out."

"Turks in a Thunderbird," you hear Hill say. "We're supposed to believe that."

The president shoots him a fierce look.

"Where was this?" he says.

"Close to Stephansdom," you say. "Am Graben. You know where the Plague Column is."

"Yes."

"Elder Rudd was . . . worked up. He wanted a girl for himself. I went along. I was drunk. So we ended up looking for our own. Elder Rudd found one first. She had a friend." Then you say, "She was thin. Blond hair. There were bruises on her face."

Gerhardt sits off the side of the long table, his thick arms folded high across his chest, his head down, watching the needles on the two dials of the Tandberg.

"They walked us down a side street to a hotel called the Rabe. I remember being scared. The whole lobby was painted this shiny red. The desk, everything. The girls got keys from a man behind the desk. They took us up these narrow stairs to two rooms next to each other. There was a cot and a nightstand with a dim red lamp on it. There wasn't a shade. Just the bulb was red. She asked for her money. She got—"

"You had enough?"

"Between us we did."

You wait for the president to ask how much.

"Go on," he says instead.

"She got undressed. I finally did too. I took off my coat. I took off my tie. I took off my shoes. I took off my pants. There was a small chair for my clothes. I took off my socks. My garments scared her. I acted like they were nothing just to let her know to not be scared."

"Go on."

Where you sit naked now in your wooden chair at the end of the table.

"Could I have a glass of water, please?"

"Elder Hunsacker?" President Lindner says. Hunsacker gets up and leaves. Gerhardt puts the Tandberg on pause. You keep your eyes on the head of your microphone till Hunsacker sets a glass in front of you. Maybe asking for it was a bad idea. Maybe everyone in the room sees a wine glass.

"Thank you."

"You're welcome," you hear Hunsacker whisper.

The liquid wets and cools your mouth and loosens the fist clenched around your throat. You didn't know how good it could taste. How thirsty you were. You try to keep your gulping quiet. Half the glass is gone when you set it down again.

"When you're ready," the president says.

Gerhardt starts the Tandberg up again.

"I got on the cot with her. She put the condom on for me. Then had me lie on top of her. I couldn't find where it went. She finally put it inside her." Then you say, "I've already told you that."

The audience of witnesses behind you. If they've come with you this far. Where they can look at the faint light stripe of dirt up the back of your suit, at your neglected hair, at the grime in frayed collar of your shirt, where they can stand now in the back of the room where you've stripped and witness your naked back, raised into the dim red air while you poke around till the bruised girl underneath you finally takes you in her hand. You wait for another truck go past outside. You raise your eyes to the president's waiting face.

"Take your time," he says.

"I just wanted to hold her. Kiss her. She kept pushing my face away. I just wanted to go to sleep. She kept saying bewegen."

You feel Gerhardt watching you and glance his way. Embarrassed, distressed, disgusted maybe, he lowers his eyes. You don't know.

"If she kept saying bewegen," you say to the president, "I think that's pretty good proof that I . . . was where I was supposed to be."

The president glances down, looks back up, leans back, folds his arms across his chest.

"Is that what you wanted?" you ask him.

"We'll see. Keep going."

And now you've brought them where you've been before. They've come with you. Where they can stand now and watch her work her thin legs on either side of you and her hands pull on your naked back to urge you into moving. Where the night wind starts to kick up. Where they too can hear the night cries of animals. For the first time you're scared. You can feel it in the tremble wanting to come into your voice. Hear it in the waver of your solo. Hear it want to skate high and out of the reach.

"For the new elders here," you say, "bewegen is the German word for move. So I moved. I couldn't feel much. I was drunk. But . . . I finally made it happen."

"Made what happen?"

"What happens at the end."

"So you saw it through."

"She wanted to earn her money."

In Lindner's face you can see the bitter German carpenter in a kitchen listening to some housewife tell him she's changed her mind about the cabinet knobs again. She wants to go back to the first ones. From his face, the skin hardened into fine ledges of eroded sandstone, you can tell he hasn't come with you. You've taken yourself beyond the reach of his power to shame you. Like the pulse your trumpet makes in your lips and hands when that sound takes a leap an interval of five notes higher. Free. Taken your solo high enough through fear and shame that you've reached where they end and let you break free of them.

"Would you like me to keep going?" you say.

"Yes."

"She rolled me off her. She took the condom off. She threw it in a wastebasket. She put her leg over the edge of the sink and turned the water on and splashed herself clean. She dried herself with a small white towel. She was dressed again before I had my garments on."

"Okay." The president unfolds his arms and lays his hands on the table. "I'm convinced."

"But this is where it gets good."

"I don't think—"

"You asked for everything," you say.

"If there's more."

"I was getting dressed and I heard Elder Rudd start yelling through the wall. Loud and angry. It sounded like he was throwing furniture. I heard his door open and slam. It was his girl. I heard her heels run down the hall and then the stairs. My girl ran out the door. I met Elder Rudd in the hall. He was punching the walls. He was out of his mind."

You pause to give the sudden vivid power of the memory time to sink back to the place it came from.

"I followed him down the stairs. He was yelling when we went through the lobby. He kept saying how he'd always promised himself he'd never pay for it. We got outside and started down the street. He said wait. He went back to the hotel. He came out running a couple of minutes later. He said let's go. I said what's going on. He said he'd just beat the shit out of the desk clerk. He said he may have fucking killed him." Then you say, "I'm quoting him."

The president flinches. Then looks at Hill before he looks back at you.

"He never told us about the desk clerk," he says.

"It happened," you say. "And that was what he said."

"Why should we believe you?" Hill says.

Elder Cannon. The first time you were in this room in your new American suit and tie and shoes. The gentle way he fielded questions Hatch and Wissom and Clayton kept asking him. Hatch skiing. Wissom living on sixty bucks a month. Clayton having his girlfriend visit. You not asking anything.

"Rudd forgot his watch," you tell the president. "He went back for it in the morning. The police were there. The clerk was in the hospital. They didn't know if he'd live."

"You should have told us," says Hill.

"What would you have done?" you say.

"Sent him home so fast his head would spin. We could have been liable."

"Isn't that against the law?" you ask the president. "Helping someone who maybe killed someone escape the country?"

"Elder Hunsacker?" says the president.

"I'm not a lawyer yet, President Lindner. But I know it wouldn't look good."

"Anyway," you say, "it gave me a way to control him. I could turn him in."

The president looks at you. You're not sure if he recognizes you or could even tell you where you are. You feel light, in the clear, out beyond shame and fear, out beyond their crushing gravity, where you took that step that took you out on open air and you learned that for the sound of your trumpet there is no gravity, only the ability to fly, fly clean and free at last in the vast reach of all the sky around you.

And then you bring it home. Because you know where home is.

"Now you know everything," you say.

Your voice breaks the hold of the president's trance.

"Excuse me," he says. "Elder Gerhardt, you can turn that off till I get back."

CHAPTER 103

THE PRESIDENT uses the armrests of his chair to push himself up from the table and goes past you again as he leaves the room. Your part in this is over. You could sit back now and see how the rest of it will happen. But you don't sit back. Just bring your hands up from the armrests, fold them under your chin, look straight ahead at the far wall, clear of Lindner's head till he gets back to do his part. The creak and groan of chairs return you from the memory of that night to the fact that the audience of elders you took with you are back behind you, stretching their arms, flexing their hands, checking their watches, glancing back and forth without looking directly at each other. Some will be looking out the windows. Looking down at their knees. Picking lint off their sleeves. Nobody talks. They've seen you naked. Watched you do it. Off to your right, Gerhardt sits still, arms folded, eyes on the Tandberg.

The haggard weariness you heard in your voice is all through you. Nothing left to hide. Nowhere to hide it. The dark mystery in the back of your head, the mystery that was always out of reach, is out in the open now. This is what you are. What they heard, what the Tandberg recorded, is what you are. You look for fear. Gone. You look for humiliation. Gone. You look for the fugitive you've harbored. Gone. Shame is still there. But the shame is clean. Aware suddenly of the grime in the exposed cuffs of your shirt, you lower your hands to the armrests again, lower your eyes to the long table without seeing the grain or polish. You hear a whisper. Someone getting up. Moving. Murmuring excuse me.

"Elder Tauffler?"

Your name this close to you. You flinch, pull your arms and shoulders in, then turn your head to look up. Two elders stand there. You know one of them. McQueen. Tall, an athlete's build, quietly sure of himself, his groomed black hair trimmed close, always immaculately dressed, so unbelievably good looking he could almost pass for beautiful. You've heard him play Schubert and Chopin on the Boesendorfer grand at the churchhouse. You've heard he works hard. You've never seen it show. In his dark blue American suit and fresh white shirt and blue and silver tie he looks better than brand new elders do when they first get here from the men's shops of their home towns.

"Yes?"

"I'm sorry this had to happen this way."

"It's okay."

"I'm sorry you were asked to keep repeating yourself," he says. "President Lindner didn't need to be persuaded," he says gently. "He knew from the start."

"It's all right."

"None of us needed to be here."

"Sorry."

"No. Elder Hill needs to be sorry. But then he already is. As sorry as they come." You watch him look across the room. "Aren't you, Hill. This was sadistic. You're a sadistic son of a bitch."

It startles you coming from McQueen.

"You need to watch yourself," you hear Hill say.

"You don't do this to people."

"We needed witnesses."

"You needed to humiliate this elder. You should be reported."

"Says the elder who never made Second Counselor."

McQueen contemplates Hill with a poised and quiet smile. "You're right. Not that I didn't try to get my head up President Lindner's ass. But yours was always in the way."

You hear Hill jump off his chair.

"You fancy pants queer."

You hear the door open and turn to look. The president walks in, stops when he sees Hill and McQueen and his companion on their feet, closes the door behind him. There's a sheet of paper in his hand. You look back down at the table where your hands have left accidental swirls and patches of oil and sweat on its polished wood despite your effort not to touch it.

"What's going on here?" you hear the president say.

"We're talking about the spectacle that was made of this."

"What did you say?"

"None of us needed to be here to witness this. Maybe two or four at the most."

The way McQueen talks to the retired carpenter, a quiet smile evident in his voice, lets you know that the title of president is meaningless to him.

"That's not your business."

"You knew he was telling the truth the first time," you hear McQueen say. "We all did. But you couldn't get enough of it."

"How dare you talk to me like that."

"Excommunication would have been enough."

"You don't know what you're talking about."

"Whose idea was it to give him a madman like Rudd? As his first junior?"

"That's confidential."

"That's the real sin."

"That's enough."

"We're leaving," you hear McQueen say. "I hope you feel good about what you did here."

"We're not finished yet."

"We are. Excuse us."

You hear McQueen leave with his companion. Hear the handle of the closed door lift back into place when McQueen releases it from the other side. Lindner walks slowly past you to his chair. You hear the front door of the Mission Home open and then close. The scuff of shoes on the front steps and then the sidewalk. You raise your eyes to see Lindner take his chair and lay the sheet of paper he brought in with him on the table.

Gerhardt leans forward to turn the Tandberg on. The president raises his hand and shakes his head.

"Elder Hill?" the president says. "Is that why all these elders are here? A spectacle?"

"Of course not."

"Then tell me what the real reason is."

"I told you, President Lindner. They're here as witnesses."

"Show me where an Elder's Court needs two dozen witnesses. Show me that rule."

"I don't have it with me."

"Then go get it. We'll go on without you."

You feel him on your back as Hill walks behind you on his way to the door.

"Anyone else who wants to leave is free to go."

"If it's okay," you say, "I think everyone should stay."

"They don't have to be here, Elder."

"They should see how this is done. So they'll know."

The president looks across the room. "Okay," he says. He looks at you. "I've just spoken with Apostle Gordon Hinckley. He wanted to be informed about the outcome of the trial. I told him I had no doubt that you'd committed fornication. He said in that case, he's sorry, but we can't make any exceptions."

"I know."

"That was why I kept questioning you. I kept looking for doubt. I kept trying to make you an exception."

"I appreciate it."

You watch the president put his half frame reading glasses on and pick up the sheet of paper. Then nod at Gerhardt. The reels of the Tandberg start turning again. You watch the president read.

"Shake Wilford Tauffler. I hereby revoke your membership in the Church of Jesus Christ of Latter Day Saints and all rights and privileges of membership. You are no longer a member. I hereby revoke your keys to the Aaronic and Melchizedek priesthoods and the power associated with those keys. You are no longer a priesthood holder. You no longer possess the Spirit of the Holy Ghost. I also divest you of the covenants and endowments and blessings you made and received in the Temple. Do you understand?"

"Yes."

"You'll have to turn in your Temple Recommend. You may attend church meetings such as Sunday School and Sacrament Meeting. You may not attend Priesthood Meeting. You may not take part in any class discussions. You may not hold any callings or positions. You may not perform or participate in any ordinations, appointments, confirmations, or associated responsibilities that require the priesthood or membership in the Church. You may not wear Temple garments."

Over the tops of his reading glasses the president looks at you again.

"Do you understand?"

"I'm not wearing them."

The president looks at you a moment longer.

"You may not perform missionary work of any kind. You may not partake of the sacrament. You may not bear your testimony. You may not pay tithing or make monetary offerings of any kind, including fast offerings, building funds, and contributions to departing missionaries. Do you understand?"

"Yes."

"You may choose to pursue reinstatement. If you choose to do so, be advised that it is a long and arduous process. It can take years. You'll be required to confess what you did to your congregation and ask for their forgiveness. You'll be required to demonstrate your faithfulness to the Restored Gospel of Jesus Christ and your obedience to all commandments except those you'll be prohibited from following. You'll submit to interviews on a regular basis to confirm that your contrition for what you've done is absolute and that you haven't engaged in any activities that run counter to the teachings of the Church."

The president looks up again.

"I understand."

"You're not simply someone seeking to join the Church for the first time. You've deeply betrayed and offended God. You've desecrated the priesthood. You were once trusted with the sacred rites and responsibilities of membership and the priesthood and you showed that they meant nothing to you. So you have much more to prove. Do you understand?"

"Yes."

Over your shoulder the door opens but doesn't close. From the flash of cross impatience in Lindner's face, you know it's Hill, holding his place in the doorway till Lindner finishes.

"Your name will be erased from the records of the Church. In the eyes of the Church it will be as though you never existed. You were never baptized or confirmed. You were never ordained into the Aaronic and Melchizedek priesthoods. You never served as a deacon, teacher, priest, or elder. You never performed the sacred duties of those ranks. You never received any Individual Achievement Awards. You never received a Duty to God Award. You never made covenants with God in the Temple. You were never called on a mission. You never served in the mission field as an Instrument of the Lord."

The president continues for a long moment to look at the paper in his hands. Then lays it aside, carefully takes the loops of his reading glasses off his ears, folds them, puts them back in the chest pocket of his suit, looks with some reluctance down the table at you.

"Did you hear everything I've said?"

"Yes."

"Do you understand everything?"

"I do."

"Then I hereby declare this trial concluded."

The president looks at Gerhardt. Gerhardt leans forward to turn the Tandberg off.

CHAPTER 104

YOU'VE BEEN ALONE like this before. The kids with their instrument cases in the halls at school while the instrument you brought into your house stayed caged and hidden like some blind malevolent brass rodent in the garage. The winter afternoons in the sandpit with all the questions you didn't know to even ask before you found Mr. Selby. After that the giants filled the sky and the stars were their instruments and diamond rings. The bike rides out of your neighborhood once you learned that you could outrun God. After that your head was clear and you were on your own. Out where everything Lindner took away from you, one thing after another, only unburdened you, took away weight, let you soar higher and lighter than you could remember ever having soared.

From the other end of the table the president looks at you. What he sees. Who you are. What you look like. You don't care. For once his face is clear of contempt. Not soft. Just easy. If it's because you're the one guy in the room without the priesthood. The one guy not a Mormon. The one guy with his past erased.

You've been alone like this before.

Hill comes in, tries to latch the door in silence in a room ruled by the shared held breath of silence, then crosses behind you again to his chair. Lindner watches him. You watch Lindner.

"Well?" says the president.

"I'll have to look for it later," you hear Hill say.

The president drums his fingertips on the table while he looks at Hill.

"That's what I thought," he finally says. "Until you can bring me that rule, Elder, you're suspended as my Second Counselor. In the meantime, Elder Hunsacker, I'm calling you to act as Second Counselor. Is that clear?"

"Yes," you hear Hunsacker say. "But—"

"I won't tolerate unnecessary cruelty," Lindner says to Hill.

Unnecessary cruelty. It makes you sick to look at him. As if there's something in the mind of this retired carpenter he calls necessary cruelty. You hear Hill gather up his clipboard and pen and the legal pad you figure listed the questions he never got to ask or hear you answer. This time the tail of his suit coat brushes the back of your head when he crosses behind you.

Lindner looks at you, looks down when he finds you looking back at him, looks back up, ready this time.

"Okay," he says. "Do you have any questions?"

"I'll need some underwear," you say.

"We'll see that you get some. Anything else?"

"Yes. It's not related to this court, but it's important."

You hold the president's eyes while he studies you. Searches for what you could still have left to say. Finally looks at the room behind you.

"Then court has been adjourned. You elders are free to leave. Elder Gerhardt, you can get rid of these microphones. Elder Hunsacker, I'd like to see you in my office afterward."

Chairs behind you groan. A startled bird bursts chirping off a bush outside the window. Elders start heading for the door. The president waits. You can't call yourself an elder any more. What you should call yourself now. Tanker. Student. Mechanic. Dishwasher. Night watchman. Yard worker. You've been all of them. Trumpet player. What words on a sheet of paper, words recited in the German accent of a retired carpenter, can never take away from you. Elders pass behind you on their way out. If they look down on you. If they hope to catch your eye to let you see contempt, hate, forgiveness, curiosity, whatever they've been made to feel. If they hope to get a look at the face that for the last hour or so has never turned around to show itself. You sit at the end of the table with your head down. You don't move. A couple of elders jostle you. Bump your chair in what feels like deliberate disgust, then pause briefly, hoping you'll turn and look up to face what they want to show you. Two elders pat you on the shoulder. When the traffic dies you finally glance around. It startles you to see a scattered handful of elders still in their chairs. Elder Hunsacker's there too. You turn forward. Glance down at the table before looking up at the president.

"You elders are staying?" he says.

"If it's okay, President Lindner," you hear an elder say.

With placid indifference the president watches Gerhardt pick up the microphones, roll up their cords, take away the books that propped them up, speed the reels forward till the feed reel is empty, take them off the Tandberg, put the reel containing the record of the trial in a pancake flat box. When Gerhardt sits down the president finally looks at the elder past your shoulder again.

"Stay if you so desire," he says.

Then looks at you with the same indifference.

"What is it you want to say?"

You sit forward. Rest your folded hands on the table.

"Yesterday, when I was still a District Leader, Elder Butterworth and I visited a pair of elders in our district. They work in an iron mining town. Eisenerz. In a deep valley surrounded by steep mountains. Hard to get to. They've done four months there alone."

You hear your own voice, quiet and earnest, with recognition for your lack of standing.

"Go on," the president says.

"I know I'm not their District Leader any more. But yesterday I was. So I feel responsible for reporting what I saw there. They're in bad shape. They're good missionaries. They work hard. But they need help."

And now the president's indifferent eyes have started going hard.

"They live in housing for miners and their families. The basement's infested with rats. They don't have beds. The rats are so bad the junior sleeps on couch cushions on the kitchen table to stay out of their reach. The senior sleeps on the couch. Without the cushions."

"The kitchen table," the president says.

"They keep the place spotless. They don't dare keep much food. They've tried traps. The rats get killed but keep coming. They told their old District Leaders about it. The District Leaders told them they passed the information up to the Zone Leaders."

You hesitate, lower your head, look up, to the window to your right, then back at the president.

"They were left to think that they looked like complainers."

You watch the word leave its mark in the president's face.

"There's a more serious problem. The senior has this infection on his tailbone. This open sore. Pus and blood. It's so bad it hurts to walk. He limps. He needs to see a doctor. But he's afraid he'll be sent home. He can't do that. It would kill him. His father's a bishop."

The president's look has hardened further, back toward contempt, to where the skin of his face looks like thin shelves of pale eroded sandstone again.

"So they just keep asking the Lord for help. With the rats and the sore and no beds. Elder Butterworth and I were going to go back today to help them find a new place. It's easier with a car. Especially since one of them has trouble walking."

You lower your head and study your hands. The way your thumbs can bend at the knuckles. Then separate your hands and look up at the president again.

"What they really need is a transfer. I know. Everyone wants a transfer. But four months is a long time to be that isolated and live that way. It's the only place the junior has worked since coming here. It's all he knows. He told me he wasn't sure he was cut out to be a missionary. He's wrong. He'll make a good one. But he needs a change." Then you say, "A bed instead of a table."

The elders behind you are dead still. A big dog starts to bark from a neighboring yard. You lift your head again and look straight into the contempt of the president's face.

"Who are these elders," the president finally says.

"The senior is Doug Bateman. His junior is Ron Wolfe."

In the withering glare of the president's eyes you don't move.

"Do you know what just happened?" the president says.

"Just now?"

"You were excommunicated."

"Of course I know. Right now these two elders are more important."

"You were excommunicated. Do you understand what that means?"

"Is that a real question?"

"Don't you think you have enough to worry about without these elders?"

"With all due respect, President Lindner, I was responsible for them. I'm just finishing what I started."

"You're not a missionary any more. Let alone a District Leader. Those elders are none of your business."

"They were my business yesterday."

"Yesterday isn't today."

"Yesterday they were my responsibility," you say. "Today they're yours." Then you say, "Now that you know about them."

The president's expression gradually relaxes back to indifference. You understand what he's doing. Erasing any meaning you ever had. Reducing you to a stranger. Someone without significance or consequence. Someone less than real. You watch him use his armrests again to lift himself to his feet.

"Elders, this meeting is over. You're all dismissed."

You push back your chair and get up from your end of the table.

"Excuse me, President Lindner. The elder with the back sore?"

"Yes?"

"Elder Hill spoke to his father once. His father called the Mission Home."

"What's his name again?"

"Bateman. He's a bishop. Bishop Bateman."

"He called here?"

"Yes."

"I don't remember a call like that."

"He called about his son's infection. Elder Hill told him the mission would take care of it. The bishop called his son and told him he'd be taken care of."

"The mission isn't responsible for the medical needs of its missionaries."

"Then Elder Hill's fine. Because he did nothing."

It catches the president off guard.

"Elder Bateman waited," you say. "He's still waiting. He ended up telling his father the mission had taken care of it."

"He lied to his father," the president says.

"He was afraid his father would call again. He was afraid to make more trouble. Afraid he'd be sent home. So yes. He lied to his father."

The president looks down for a moment, at the table, before fixing his impatient gaze on you again.

"There's never an excuse to lie," he says.

"I have his home address."

"What does that mean?"

"It means I'll visit Bishop Bateman and correct the record when I get home. Make sure his father and mother know the truth."

And now the retired carpenter who became the president raises the fierce wings of his eyebrows and gives you the cold fury of his full attention.

"Elder Wolfe?" you say. "The elder who sleeps on the kitchen table? He was told that it isn't the mission's business to provide beds. The local members are expected to help with those needs."

"That's the policy of every mission. Yes."

"The local members are two old widows. One's in the hospital."

"Then members from other towns in the district should contribute," the president says.

"I have his home address too."

"So you're threatening me again."

"That's really how you see this," you say.

"There's no other way to see it."

"With all due respect, President Lindner, you just excommunicated me. You did what you needed to do. I'm just doing what I need to do."

The president looks down again, at the table, at the sheet of paper in his hand.

"Elder Hunsacker, see that he gets some underwear and a plane ticket. See that he doesn't leave the Mission Home."

You watch Lindner walk past. Now you know how this goes. What you're left with. His legs are thick in his creased pants. Filaments of lint from the cream carpet fleck the black heels of his polished shoes like tiny white ants. Someone touches your elbow. Elder Hunsacker. Through his rimless glasses his eyes look sympathetic.

"How are you doing?" he asks.

"I don't know."

"Yeah. Dumb question."

"So what happens now?"

"Like President Lindner said, I guess. Some underwear and a flight. The flight might take a couple of days." Then he says, "What size shorts do you wear?"

"I don't remember. I think thirty."

"Thirty it is. Boxers or jockey shorts?"

It was always jockey shorts. Now you're used to having things hang loose.

"I'll take boxers."

"White okay?"

"White's fine."

"Got it. Thirty, boxer, white. I'll get you a couple pair."

"Let me give you some money."

"That's okay. They're on the house."

"Thanks." Then you say, "So what do I do now?"

"Just lay low, I guess. Wait here. The conference room's good. Nobody uses it. We have to get you a flight."

"What happened to Elder Butterworth?"

"He's gone. We reassigned him. Gave him an elder from the staff for now."

"I hope he's okay."

"He'll be fine."

CHAPTER 105

HUNSACKER BRINGS YOU two pairs of boxer shorts that afternoon. Back in your room, you take off your suit, pull a pair up your legs, take a minute to look down. They're big. They fit your waist loose and billow out around your thighs. Maybe Hunsacker figured wrong when he translated thirty inches to its Austrian size. Maybe two years of biking and walking and climbing stairs and the permanent hunger you learned to ignore have cost you some weight. You pull your pants up over them, put on your coat, head back to the conference room.

Still later that afternoon Hunsacker comes in again. This time with a big jock looking guy named Price with thick brown shining hair and the dull good looks of someone who could have had any girl he wanted but whose themes and book reports you'd have had to write if you'd been buddies back in high school. Elder Price. One of Hill's guys. You could know just from the way he looks at you if you didn't know already.

"Brother Tauffler?" Hunsacker says.

So that's what they call you now. Like Brother Brown in the dialogues of the lesson plans. Like an investigator.

"Yes?"

Hunsacker sits down across the table. Price stands next to him. A rumble rolls like distant thunder through your hollow stomach.

"Have you had anything to eat today?" Hunsacker says.

"I'm okay."

"There's sandwiches in the dining room. And soda."

"I'm fine. Thanks."

"Your flight's in three days. Sorry we couldn't get one sooner. There's a stop in Montreal but you won't need to change planes."

You don't exist. And yet there's enough of you here for Hunsacker to talk to.

"Okay. Thanks."

"We'll get you to the airport."

"Thanks."

He takes a small notebook and pen out of the inside pocket of his suit. Tries to look at you for a minute.

"I'll need all the cash you have," he finally says. "To put toward your ticket. The Church will loan you the rest. You can pay it back when you get home."

"Pay it back?"

When Price shifts his weight you know why he's here. Hunsacker looks around like he'd rather be somewhere else before he looks back at you.

"Yes."

"They flew me here. They're not flying me home?"

"They're not in the habit of . . ." His face goes red. "You know. Only when you're honorably released." Then he says, "I'm sorry."

"It's okay. I just didn't know."

You get up. Reach into your pocket for the few bills of Austrian cash you have left. Start to reach across the table.

"Can I keep some of it? I was thinking of buying some souvenirs. At the airport. For my brothers and sisters."

Hunsacker looks at you for a moment, surprised, like you're bringing home enough of a souvenir yourself for your family to deal with.

"I'm sorry," he says.

You hand them to him across the table. Reach back into your pocket for change while you watch him count the bills. Somewhere around forty dollars. He writes the amount in a notebook.

"I have this too," you say, extending him the few coins in your open palm.

"No," he says. "This is fine."

You drop them into your pocket and sit back down.

"You didn't need to bring muscle," you say, smiling.

Behind him Price shifts his weight again.

"I know that," Hunsacker says. "Not for you."

"For Rudd."

"Yes." Then he says, "I'll need your Temple Recommend too."

You find it hiding behind your Austrian license.

"Anything else?" you say, gently, when you hand it to him.

"That's it," Hunsacker says. Then he says, "You doing okay?"

You don't exist. And yet you have the presence to have him ask you.

"I'm fine. Thanks for asking." Then you say, "How about you?"

Hunsacker looks surprised. "Me? I'm fine."

Three days. You eat breakfast and dinner in the dining room with the mission staff. Wissom's at the table. So are Gerhardt and Hunsacker. You keep your head down. Hear how occasional the conversations and awkward the banter are with you at the table. Hear the stretches where the only sound is the dull chime of silverware on ceramic. You don't exist. And yet you occupy a chair. And yet at the end of the table a plate and knife and fork and spoon define a place for you. And yet dishes of food are passed your way. You don't exist. And yet you put food into your mouth. Around you, you can feel the elders wrestle with the presence of a guy who's been excommunicated, with the fact that you're not supposed to exist where they're concerned. You're relieved that Hill's not at the table. You wonder where he is. If he eats with the president. For lunch, the kitchen staff leaves fruit, cans of soda, a pile of sandwiches cut into triangular halves on a platter in the dining room. You remember the sandwich halves. Clayton, Hatch, Wissom, the four of you, fresh off the plane, eating around the conference room table, talking about your briefing with Elder Cannon. The first thing you ever ate in Austria. You don't remember their taste because your sense of taste is numb to taste except for the taste of dirt. Ham could be tuna. Eggs could be spinach. Roast beef cardboard. Water blood. You can look at your plate, at your glass, see what things should taste like, but all you taste is dirt.

What real dirt would taste like. If it would taste like this.

You don't exist. In the back half of the conference room the chairs have been folded up and leaned against the walls again. Where there was an audience of elders, listening as you took them through a night to a place they'd never been, a place where they watched you naked do the unspeakable thing you did, the plush cream carpet is bare like the first time you were here with Wissom and Clayton and Hatch. The nap of the carpet is crosshatched with the broad stripes left by a vacuum cleaner. The Tandberg is back on its metal stand. The deep chestnut surface of the table is polished except where the oil and sweat of your hands have left it smeared. And yet you don't exist. In this numb dream of a room that struck you almost two years ago as a place where people came to watch each other die, where you imagined a closed casket on the table, you don't exist. When you get up to stretch your legs, to walk around, to look out the window they've left open, you stay close to the table, away from the fresh nap of the vacuumed carpet.

Hour after hour. Broken only by an occasional car or truck on the cobblestones, the passing voices of a conversation between adults, the rapid musical babble of children in a language you now understand, broken only when you open the door and check the lobby to use the bathroom a few steps away, broken only by the hunger that takes you down to the dining room for a couple of sandwich halves and a soda long after the noise of lunch has died away, broken only by a knock on the door to let you know it's dinnertime. You don't exist. Keep your head down in the lobby when an elder comes the other way to save him the indecision of smiling and saying hello to someone who doesn't exist except as a drunk and naked guy in the light of a red bulb. Retreat after dinner to the conference room again till sunset. Then make your way to your room behind the kitchen where you lie on the cot in your boxers and start the long vigil of waiting for sleep.

One night a knock on your door brings you to a sitting position on the edge of your cot. The room is warm from the heat of the day. The open window won't bring in cool air till late. It's Wissom. He doesn't wait for you to answer. He looks embarrassed to find you in shorts.

"Got a few minutes?" he says.

"Yeah. There's a chair. Let me move my pants."

"Just checking in," says Wissom. "Hope you don't mind."

"No. Thanks."

"You doing okay?"

"Just waiting for my flight."

"You're sweating."

"Yeah."

"I made your reservation. Took care of your ticket. It's waiting for you."

"Thanks."

"There were earlier ones. I don't know why they told me Friday."

If other stuff has to be put in order first.

"You taking this okay?" says Wissom.

You smile. "It's not supposed to be easy."

"You should have seen Rudd. He acted like he didn't give a . . . you know. About it. Talking and laughing at dinner. Yukking it up. Going around the place like he owned it. He even disappeared a couple of times. Showed up later."

"I know that one," you say.

"He knew they couldn't do anything to him. Not more than they'd already done."

"I know that one too."

"Did Rudd really beat that old guy up?"

"Yeah."

"He almost died?"

"He may have. I don't know."

"Everyone says this is all on Rudd. Most of the guys feel bad for you. Like Lindner should have cut you a break."

The failing light from the window reflected on Wissom's glasses keeps you from seeing his eyes.

"Still got that Schaeffer?" you say, smiling.

He pats his shirt pocket. "Always," he says.

"It wasn't Lindner's call. It was Apostle Hinckley's."

"Yeah. Anyway. If you're wondering why you haven't seen Hill, he's gone."

"Where'd he go?"

"He didn't go. He got sent."

"Where?"

"You'll like this," says Wissom. "Eisenerz."

"Eisenerz?"

"Yeah. I wrote up the transfer."

"What about Bateman and Wolfe?"

"Don't worry. They're okay now. Bateman's in Graz. He'll see a doctor. Wolfe's in Salzburg. Beds," he says. "No rats."

"That's good news."

"I wanted you to know."

"Thanks," you say. You look down at your bare knees. After a minute you say, "You're serious. Eisenerz."

"You won," says Wissom. "Everyone's glad that jerk is finally out of the Mission Home."

"I won. That's a strange way to put it."

"Not the war," says Wissom. "The battle."

"I need a favor."

"Name it."

"I need to call someone. This family. Let them know I'm going home."

"I can't," says Wissom. "I'd really catch crap. Rudd ruined that for you too. We let him call and found out he was calling girls."

"They really need to know. They've treated me like a son."

"I could call them for you."

"Would you?"

"You got rid of Hill. I owe you."

You get up. Find your lesson plan looseleaf and tear a blank page out of it. Use your fountain pen to write down their name and the number you know by heart. Tell Wissom about them. Tell him to be gentle. No detail. Just that you broke a rule and have to go home.

"That's still a sweet pen," says Wissom, watching you put your Pelikan away.

"Please tell them I'll write them as soon as I get home."

Wissom uses his Schaeffer to write a note.

"I'll do it tonight." He folds up the paper, gets up. "Sleep well. You've got it coming."

"One more thing. Please tell Hubert to let the musicians know I've gone home."

"You want the paper back? Write down some names?"

"No." Then you say, "Just one more thing." It takes you a minute. "Tell them I'm sorry. Tell them I love them."

"Sorry and love them," says Wissom as he writes.

"Thanks."

"Listen. If you want to get out, take a walk, let me know. It's okay as long as someone's with you."

"I'll think about it. Thanks."

Hate for what you did came looking for you the morning after that August night when you woke up by yourself in the place you shared with Rudd. Hate for what you'd made of who you were. You've held it off the last eleven months because there wasn't room for it. There were fear and hope instead. There were doors to knock on. There were gigs to play. There were Otto and Angelika. Now, hour after hour, in the void of who you are, in the open void that was left when they took away everything you were to them, hate has started to settle in. In your chest, where the Holy Ghost resided, hate has started moving in and sits down now. Hate has started to take the seat of power vacated by the priesthood. To leach and set like wet cement around all your memories of church. Your blood carries its ice cold slurry everywhere. Into the secret place where the towering clouds above the sandpit take on the forms of your dark giants in the sky. Hate looks down now from the clouds. Hate numbs your mouth when you think of touching it to the steel kiss of the mouthpiece. Because you've betrayed them too. You've played everything they taught you for the church of a God who calls the color he's given their skin a curse.

In the morning, for breakfast, the same young girl and shaky old man who brought sandwiches and sodas into the conference room two years ago leave platters of scrambled eggs and sausage and toast and oatmeal along the white cloth runway down the center of the table. Steam rises off the platters into the light falling from a chandelier. Hunsacker presides from his new chair at the head of the table. A crystal water pitcher and a crystal vase of yellow flowers at the center of the table frame your view of his face. You spoon sugared oatmeal into your bowl when the platter comes your way.

With his sleeves rolled back off the thick blond hair that covers his forearms, Gerhardt tells the story of an elder whose front bike fork broke off from the constant pounding of the cobblestones, sending him flying while his open saddlebags scattered brochures all over a busy street. The elders around the table laugh and groan. You smile into your oatmeal. It was in Linz. It was winter. The way you tore up your knee and scraped your hands. The honking of traffic while you dragged the bike and the wheel off the street. The way you had to leave the brochures in the slush while the tires of traffic rolled over them. How Otto welded the fork together for you again.

"Brother Tauffler," you hear Wissom say. "Wasn't that you?"

The spirited ring of forks and knives on plates comes to a stop. By the time you raise your head, for the first time at the table, everyone but Price is turned your way.

"Yes."

"How'd the fork break?" says another elder.

"Cobblestones," you say.

"I'm sorry," says Gerhardt. "I didn't know."

"No. It makes me laugh too."

"What'd you do for a bike?" says another elder.

You catch Wissom watching out for you.

"I had it welded back together."

The elders go back to eating. One by one they finish up and leave the room.

"I made that call," says Wissom, when it's just the two of you. "Wanted you to know."

You look up again.

"Thanks."

"I talked to the wife. Nice woman." Then he says, "You really mean a lot to her family."

"They mean a lot to me."

"She called you her son. She was really upset to hear you're leaving."

"They treated me like a son."

"She said her daughter would be heartbroken."

"I was her big brother."

You sometimes used to think what it would be like to call another American city home. You used to think Birmingham or Jackson. You used to think San Jose. In the numb dream of the conference room it comes to you again. This time not as a thought but as a possibility. How it could be real. And now it doesn't matter where. Any American city other than Salt Lake. A city where you'll feel like you still exist. Where you'll be just another guy in Levis and a teeshirt walking down a sidewalk somewhere. Chicago. Philadelphia. Where you'll have a face that can feel the warm hand of the sun. Where food will taste like food again. Where you'll have arms and hands that can feel what it's like to hold a girl who's never heard of the Mormon Tabernacle Choir. Where the negro guys you play with will never have to know that you were Mormon once. Los Angeles. Where you'll never have to try to figure out the arithmetic of being in but not of the world. Because you'll be of the world then. Where you'll have lips, and lungs and breath and a horn, and what you do with them will be who you are.

Your family. Your mother and father. Karl and Molly and Roy and Maggie. You'll set them free. From having to deal with having you around. From calling you a son or brother. From having you sit in the congregation. They could cut your face out of the photos of the family.

They too could act like you don't exist.

You used to think Switzerland. How you could start your life over where it started the first time. Let them draft you. Serve in the Swiss Army. Get an official knife. How close it is. You could hitch there.

Lately you used to sometimes think Vietnam. How you could volunteer yourself for active duty. They were using your tank there now. The M48 Patton. The tank you knew like you knew any song and what you could do with it. If you came home in a coffin at least it would be with honor.

And you used to think San Jose. Now you think San Jose again. You're not a Mormon any more. You're free of Brigham Young and his racist lie and the God who let it stand. If you could win her back. If she would have you now. And then shame burns hot in your face as the permanence of losing her sinks in and leaves you stupid. She's gone. She lives her life in the life you had before that August night. The life you can't go back to.

But how it could be real. Tomorrow they'll drive you to the airport. Maybe Gerhardt. You'll tell him thanks when he drops you off. Say goodbye. You'll go into the terminal, get your ticket, cash it in for a ticket to another city. One not as far from where you are as Salt Lake is. Boston maybe. New York. That way the flight will be cheaper than the ticket you're cashing in. That way you'll get some money back.

In the conference room, where you've spent two days now, you reach for your pocket and count the Austrian coins Hunsacker said they didn't need. About thirty-seven cents in American change. You'll need more while you look for work and a place to live. While you search for clubs and look for gigs. While you start a life you've never had. A life where all the hate would turn back to blood and flesh and skin and bone again. Because nobody would care. Because the story about a missionary and a hooker in Vienna would only be another funny story like the story Gerhardt told about your bike at breakfast.

Sometime that afternoon there's a knock on the door. It's Hunsacker again. With Wissom this time. They both sit down. Hunsacker in a suit. Wissom in a shirt and tie.

"Well, all set for tomorrow morning?" Hunsacker says, smiling his new Second Counselor smile.

"Pretty much still packed," you say.

Hunsacker and Wissom both lower their eyes to the tie and suit and shirt you've worn since Eisenerz. And now through all of this.

"That's good," says Hunsacker. "Doing okay?"

You watch Wissom look off at a wall. His Schaeffer in his shirt pocket. Hunsacker keeps his smile on but you can tell what he's thinking. How he'd face his own folks. How he'd never let this happen. How he'd rather come home dead.

"Yeah," you say. "I am."

"Did those boxers fit?"

"Just right." Then you say, "Still getting used to them."

Wissom looks down and glares at his hands. Hunsacker pulls a small envelope out of an inside pocket and hands it to you. There's nothing on it. No name, no address, no stamp.

"What's this?"

"I think it's from your father."

The bottom corner of the flap is taped. You work it loose, reach in, pull out a small piece of folded paper. It's handwritten. Your father's. Neat, strong, practiced, you know it instantaneously from the times you've seen and admired it. Not in a letter but in the ledger books you've seen open on the door he uses for a desk in the furnace room. Ever since the Army his letters have always been typed.

Dear Son,

   I want you to know I love you. Come home and we'll get through this together.
With all my love,
Dad

"Maybe we need to leave," you hear Wissom say, thousands of miles away.

"Are you okay, Brother Tauffler?"

"We need to go," says Wissom. "Now."

CHAPTER 106

SIX MISSIONARIES escort you to the airport in a Volkswagen bus like the bus that brought you and Wissom and Hatch and Clayton into Vienna almost two years ago. Two in front, two on the center bench with you between them, two on the bench behind you. Gerhardt does the driving. The broad shoulders and sleek square head of Hill's boy Price ride next to him. Because taking you to the airport is an errand more than real missionary work, they're not required to wear their suit coats, and they make the ride in the warm wind blowing through the windows in their white shirts and ties, leaving you the only one in a full suit. You know the buildings now. You know the streets and trams. Where the jazz clubs are. The opera house and parks and concert halls and palaces and train stations. The grim outskirts. A town named Klosterneuburg. And a hotel on a side street off a street called Graben. The scope of a city that seemed infinite to you that first time through. You know the language now. Nobody says much.

At the airport you still remember the vast room that constitutes the terminal. The long bank of windows below the high ceiling through which bright daylight falls and illuminates the room and turns the polished stone of the floor almost into a mirror. The white expanse of the walls and the signs that hang on them. You approach the ticket counter in the company of six elders. At the counter you set your trumpet case on its end and hand your passport, faded and warped and worn around the edges now from carrying it around, to a smiling woman in a uniform on the other side of the counter. She looks through its stiff pages, compares your face to your photo, hands it back to you.

"We hope you enjoyed your stay."

"It's a wonderful country."

She raises an eyebrow and smiles again.

"Yes," she says. "I have your ticket here. You're flying to Montreal and then to Salt Lake City."

The elder who carried your big gray Samsonite in from the Volkswagen bus passes it through the counter where the woman ties a luggage tag to the handle. Another elder reaches for your trumpet case.

"No," you say. "I'm taking that on the plane."

The woman tucks your baggage slip into the sleeve of your ticket and goes to hand it to you. Price steps up with his hand out.

"I'll take that," he says.

She looks at him confused. Draws the ticket back.

"You'll have to wait till I'm finished with this gentleman," she says.

She looks at you with a question in her smile now.

"I'll take it," you say.

She puts it in your hand. You give it to Price.

"Are the rest of you flying too?" she says.

"Just him," says Price.

The terminal speakers crack with the high melodic thunder of a woman's voice.

"Have a good flight back to your country," the woman at the counter says.

"Thank you."

You pick up your trumpet case. Traffic across the terminal is light. With your escort of elders you walk across the vast mirror of the stone floor toward the turnstile that leads to the gate where you'll board your plane home. Ahead of you, at the turnstile, a short man in a uniform stands behind a small podium and checks what you guess are the passports and tickets of a small cluster of people waiting to be passed through. A dark-skinned woman in a long bright yellow robe with a carpetbag on the floor next to her feet stands in the middle of the terminal reading the overhead signs. An old couple, the man in a Tyroler hat and suit, stand looking at the window display of a small shop. A policeman watches you and your escort. As you approach the turnstile you can make out a man and a woman and little girl standing gathered together maybe thirty yards to your left. The fierce bright sunlight through the windows high above them lets you see them only in silhouette, but from an imprint deeper than sight, you know who they are. You stop. If they're real. If this is another mirage of sunlight and longing off the trick of the polished stone floor like Cissy was at first at the Salt Lake Airport. A stranger turned her real by walking in front of her. No stranger this time. Just the silhouette arms of the woman as they open and reach out. The silhouette of the little girl as she steps away from her mother. Standing where they can't miss you. The elders who went on ahead of you come back.

"What's up?" you hear one of them say.

The excursions. The dining room table. The piano room where you played with her and listened to her stories. The Factory. Now to see them standing there alone. In this foreign place you made necessary. It takes you a minute.

"I need to say goodbye to this family."

"Those people? They're here for you?"

Those people. "Yes," you say.

"Who are they?"

"I told you. A family I need to say goodbye to."

"Members?"

"What difference does that make?"

"I guess none."

"If you want to write it down, no. They're not members."

"Keep it short."

And now you turn to face the elder doing all the talking. Young, flexing his spiritual muscle, he stands back a step.

"Keep it short?" you say. "Really?"

And then Price is there.

"What's going on?"

"He wants to say goodbye to those people."

"Who are they?"

"He says a family."

Price turns his dull jock face on you. "I don't know if you're allowed to do that."

"I don't know if I need your permission," you say.

"They're not members," the young elder says.

Price looks across the floor at them. Gerhardt comes in.

"Let him go," he says.

"Make it quick."

You cross the floor. Hubert stands next to his wife in a familiar short-sleeved shirt and slacks and sunglasses. In a dress you know, chocolate brown with small beige flowers, its small collar buttoned, Frau Goller lets her arms down. In a red and blue plaid skirt and pale blue blouse you've seen before, dark short lively hair and bangs you know so well, Edith huddles up against her mother holding the cloth of her dress. She's got her red shoes on. The pull this family has on you wants to reach through your ribs and take your heart. Her shimmering eyes and the wet skin around them are red. Her bottom lip and chin are quivering. The broken heart of a girl who has to go back to being an only child. This time not for Linz, not for Knittelfeld, but for good. You set your trumpet down. Drop to one knee on the polished stone in front of her and look up into her face.

"Please don't go," she whimpers.

"I'm sorry."

"Please stay. You're my brother."

"I know."

"You're my brother."

"Always."

"You're my brother."

"You're my sister."

"Mama," she says, turning her face up. "He's my brother."

"Yes, sweetheart. He is."

You look at the floor. At the tips of her red shoes and the thin red straps across her pink socks.

"Tell him to stay, Mama. Please."

She looks back at you. Fear in her wet bewildered face. How you tell her this.

"I'll always be your brother."

"Why can't you stay?"

"I have to take care of something. I'll be back someday."

"He has to go," Frau Goller says, her hand on her daughter's shoulder. "It makes us all sad."

"Why won't he stay, Mama?"

"He has to go."

"Why?"

"He just has to."

Edith looks at you again.

"He doesn't look like he wants to go, Mama. He looks unhappy."

"I know. But he has to."

"Why can't you come home with us?"

"I wish I could."

You watch her face screw up as she starts to cry again.

"Then come with us. Please."

"I can't right now."

"Why? You belong with us."

"I know."

"Don't you like us?"

"I love you."

"Then why? If we love you?"

"He has another family, Edith."

"Can't they share?"

"Maybe."

"Please stay."

"I need to talk to your mother and father."

"Please stay."

"Give me your hand."

Holding it, you rise, face the woman who's treated you like a son, the woman you've let yourself look to as a second mother.

"You really came."

"Of course," she says.

"Brother Tauffler."

You recognize Price. His dead voice out of the loose huddle of elders waiting back behind you.

"How did you know about the flight?" you say.

"I asked the missionary who called us."

She takes your free hand in both of hers.

"Don't worry," she says. "We're here."

"I'm sorry."

"It wasn't you," she says.

You asked Wissom to not go into detail. You wonder what else she may have asked. What else he might have told her.

"It was," you say.

"No," she says, firm for an instant. "We know."

Your little sister Edith suddenly pulls her hand free of yours. Something has made her suddenly look off. Go alert. Bring up both hands to busily wipe her eyes and cheeks and nose of any sign of crying. You turn and look.

The last few times you saw her, she was in a dress, her hair tamed, her lipstick muted, her jaw relaxed with an easy smile, even at the Factory where she danced in graceful circles with her arms raised and waving like the wings of a bird. Back to her old outfit, back to the gypsy rebel outfit of laced brown boots, pink tights like you've seen dancers wear, a short pink skirt and loose red blouse, back to her bold red lipstick and darkened eyes, back to her chopped dark hair, back to the outfit you've always liked, it takes you a second to recognize the girl you schooled in the Gospel in an empty afternoon coffee shop. And then it's because of her thin almost childlike build. The one thing gone is the tough girl pout of her painted lips. She stands maybe twenty feet off, a brown cloth purse that hangs off a long strap across her shoulder, on her way back from a bathroom or shop or somewhere else, waiting to give you time with your family, waiting to see what you'll do. What she's doing here. You look at Frau Goller.

"She asked Hubert if she could come with us," she says, her smile kind. "We thought you'd like to say goodbye to her."

"Yes. Thank you." You turn to Hubert. "Thanks for bringing her."

"I thought you'd like to say goodbye yourself," he says.

Mindful of your little sister, her jealous fear of losing her big brother, you reach down and take her hand again, feel her fingers tentative at first, then tighten around your own.

"Angelika," you say, turning her way again.

"It's me," she says. "I hope it's okay."

"Come here."

She approaches, gives your little sister a gentle smile, offers you her hand.

"I'm so sorry."

That night on the dock with her. Where cats arched their backs for your dangling shoes and you told her you couldn't baptize her. Where you told her this could happen.

"You look good," you tell her.

"This is how I want you to remember me."

"It's how I do remember you."

"I've been helping Gabriele at the Factory," she says. Then she says, "I'm making my own friends now."

"That's good to hear."

"Brother Tauffler."

The dull flat voice of Price again. Angelika looks the way of your escort. The flash of her tough girl attitude is quick to bring a pout to her painted lips and focus her face for just an instant.

"They're here for you," she says.

"They thought I'd like the company."

"They're not going with you."

"No." You smile. "You're stuck with them."

"I wish they were going instead of you."

"They did nothing wrong."

"May I hug you again?" she says. "I'm dry this time."

The way she rose dripping from the water of the font and made her way for you. The way Lindner tried to tell you it didn't count.

"Of course."

And keeping hold of your little sister's hand, you hold her with your free arm, feel her arms around you, smell the perfume in her ear, feel her kiss your cheek. She pulls away and looks at your face alarmed. Pulls a hanky from her purse, wets it with her tongue, rubs what you guess is lipstick off your cheek. Your little sister tries to pull her hand away. Angelika smiles down at her.

"Frau Goller said I can call you Shake now."

"That's true."

"Can I write you? Frau Goller says she has your address. In Utah."

"I'd like that."

"Goodbye, Shake."

"Goodbye, Angelika."

And she steps back again to leave you with your family.

"Are you all right?" Frau Goller says.

"Yes."

Sadness flickers through her face, like light through troubled water, but she holds her tender smile and takes your hand in both of hers again.

"Tomorrow you'll be with your family."

You glance down at her schoolteacher's shoes.

"I'm with my family now."

"I'll write you today. I'll write your mother too. To tell her what I think of you."

"I'll write too."

"We'll miss you."

And she drops your hand and takes your face in both of hers. You let yourself relish their soft feel. In the shadowed skin that surrounds them her eyes hold the sad tenderness of her smile.

"Brother Tauffler."

Her expression goes momentarily to anger as she takes a glance across your shoulder.

"We'll be fine," she says. "So will you."

"Thank you."

Her eyes start to shimmer. She lowers her hands and takes yours one last time. And then it's time for Hubert. You know from when you've seen him moved that he'll try a joke to get out of showing it. This time his face is grim. He gives you his hand.

"Goodbye, Shake." His voice is rough. "Come back to us sometime."

"I will."

He clears his throat.

"We'll miss you."

"Thanks for everything."

"We enjoyed it as much as you."

"Angelika says the Factory's still going."

He grins. "Oh yes." Then he says, "It'll be waiting for you."

"Tauffler!" Price again. Loud. A command voice. "Time to go!"

Hubert looks past you. "There goes our gypsy."

Heading in her tall boots across the floor toward the loose huddle of elders. Going straight for Price where he stands with his big fists on his jock hips. You hurry after her. She still has something to lose.

"Leave him alone!" you hear her say, in English, before you reach her. "He's not your business any more! He's ours!"

You take her gently by the shoulder. Move her aside. Step in front of Price as he lets his hands down from his hips.

"Time to go?" you say to Price, your easy smile in place. "That's what you said?"

"That's right," he says.

"Don't ever tell me what time it is," you say. "Unless I ask."

Surprise takes time to register in the dull hate of his blue football player eyes.

"Don't get smart," he says.

"Don't tell me what to do."

"Let's go."

"I'll say when that happens."

He grabs your arm. "Come on. We're going."

The elders huddle close around him. Angelika steps forward.

"Take your hand the fuck off me," you tell Price.

His hand comes off your arm like the word electrocuted him. He steps back. Stumbles into another elder. Stands there with his mouth in a crooked sneer.

"What did you say?"

"I said fuck. I can say that now."

"President Lindner will be happy to hear that."

"Try to understand this. I'm not an elder. Not a missionary. Not even a Mormon. Just a guy in an airport you don't have any business even talking to."

"I was told to put you on the plane. I plan to do that. Let's go."

"You really don't get it."

"You're under our authority till you get home."

"I was excommunicated. That ended your authority."

"We're still responsible for getting you home."

"I can go home with this family right now. Interrupt me one more time and I'll do that. They'd love it. Especially their little girl. Want to see me put a smile on her face?"

Price grabs your arm again. As if he could drag you across the floor past the cop to the man at the turnstile. As if you couldn't tell the man you're being forced onto the plane against your will. Kidnapped. As if the man would say okay. Go ahead. Force him on the plane. As if you couldn't tear your ticket up when Price has to hand it to you to show it to the man. As if, after what your father wrote, you wouldn't get on the plane for home yourself.

"Let go or I'll call that cop over. You can explain your authority to him."

"You've got a ticket home."

"You're making me reconsider."

Gerhardt steps up.

"He's right," he says to Price. "He's under Austrian law."

Price glares at you but lets you go.

"Get your goodbye done with," he says. "It's time to go."

"It's time to go when I hear my flight announced."

"We've got better things to do."

"Then leave and go do them!" Angelika says.

You keep your eyes on Price. "I mean it," you say. "One more time and I go home with her and this family."

You watch quiet fury work the muscles in his football jaw. Watch him look across your shoulder at the family waiting back behind you.

"You deserve what you got," he finally says.

"That's enough," says Gerhardt.

"Yeah," says another elder. "Let up."

Angelika walks with you across the stone floor where your little sister waits close to her mother's side again. A couple of steps away your trumpet case stands on end alone. The way she made it clean. The obedient way she disassembled it, oiled the valves and greased the slides as you instructed her, then reassembled it, cleansing it of the dirty use you'd made of it. The way her small unknowing hands took the devil out of it. Restored its innocence with her own. The girl who calls you her big brother still cries behind the heartbreak that deforms her face, quiet but not cried out, just short on tears as you drop to one knee in front of her again. You look at the floor to catch your breath and let your racing heart calm down before you look up into her face. You hear the high rough moaning cry that sounds like sandpaper in her throat. You put your arms around her. Hold her tight while sobs wrack her small shoulders. When you let her go, stand her straight again, you stand your trumpet case in front of her.

"This is for you."

She looks at it. Curiosity and wonder are enough to clear her face of heartbreak for a moment.

"Why?" she says.

Why. You haven't thought this through. Because you need to let it go. Because of the places you've taken it. Because it belongs in cleaner hands. You don't know.

"Because I want you to have it." Then you say, "Because it's yours."

"Why?"

"Because it's a magic trumpet."

"What's magic about it?"

Your stomach hurts as you look at her.

"You know. How it takes your breath and turns it into sound."

"So do Papa's harmonicas."

"They're magic too. But there's more."

"What?"

A gift she can't make sense of. One she's heard you play. Over the Rainbow. One that has carried her on its steel bird sound to places far away and brought her home with her face luminous and her dark hair tousled from the wind. A gift that has played Greensleeves for her. What child is this. The late Sunday afternoons and evenings coming home from an excursion where she fell asleep holding your arm and resting her head on your shoulder.

"But I don't want your trumpet. I want you."

You lay your hand on top of the case.

"But this is me. You can take it out and close your eyes and there I'll be. That's what makes it magic."

You take her hand.

"Inside this case—"

A woman's voice announcing your flight breaks and cracks like thunder again so close you can almost smell the air burned by the lightning. Edith jumps.

"Inside this case is me. Your big brother. Every time you open it, there I'll be."

"You will?"

"Yes. You'll hear me. And see me. And talk to me."

"You'll still be my big brother?"

"Always," you say. "I promise."

You set the case aside and reach for her. Draw her in and hold her tight. The skin of her face is damp against your face. You feel her start to cry again.

"I love you." A whisper into her ear.

You let her go when you feel her want to step back. Rimmed in red, wet, uncertain, her blue eyes skate back and forth and up and down across your face.

"It's really mine?"

"Yes. Till I come back. To see my little sister."

"Mama! He said he's coming back!"

"Then he will," her mother says. "Say thank you."

"Thank you," she says. "My big brother."

This child, you think, as her eyes search your face again. You lay your open hand along her damp cheek.

"My little sister."

You stand up. Feel tears pool and tremble now on the crests of your own eyelids. Feel them break across and come down your cheeks as you look at this family you're leaving.

"I'm sorry. I wish I could stay."

"We do too."

You turn and start across the floor toward the turnstile, emptyhanded now, looking aside to wipe your cheeks. You still feel Edith start to cry again, this shivering moan, the cry of a child who's been chosen to take the undeserved brunt of the punishment for what you did that August night. And then your own tears won't stop coming. Hate doesn't cry. And so your tears aren't meant for you, but for her, for her heartbreak, for the consequence that falls on her for what you did. Your escort catches up with you. Around you they feel changed. Muted. Even Price. At the turnstile, behind the small podium, the man's eyes are set wide across deep vertical lines in his forehead, and his cheeks hang like bags filled loosely with stones. He looks at paperwork for two people ahead of you. Around you the elders whisper among themselves.

"I don't think they'll let us through without tickets."

"President Lindner said to put him on the plane."

"What if they won't let us through?"

"We can always say they did."

"Where can he go anyway? All he's got is a ticket."

The people ahead of you go through the turnstile. You turn to Price. Tell him you need your ticket. He hands it to you. Together with your passport you hand it to the man.

"Amerikaner," he says.

"Yes."

He raises his head and looks at you. His expression sharpens.

"Are you all right?" he says.

"I'll be fine." Then you say, "I'm just afraid to fly."

"That's why you're crying?"

"Yes."

He looks at the elders clustered behind you in their white shirts and ties.

"Are you together?"

"Yes. We're missionaries." Then you say, "They're here to help me on the plane."

"Help you on the plane?"

"Yes. Once I'm on the plane I'll be okay."

"Missionaries," he says. "For a church?"

"Yes." Then you say, "They all live in Vienna."

"They're not going with you?"

"No. Just as far as the plane."

"So no tickets."

"No. They're not going anywhere."

"Then I can't let them through."

"I won't be able to board without them."

He studies you. Then looks at your escort again.

"Johann!" he calls.

The cop comes across the terminal floor. They whisper back and forth while the cop looks you and your escort over. The man at the podium turns to you again.

"They can go if they have passports. Only as far as the stairs. And they need to come right back. The policeman will come with you."

"Thank you." You turn to your escort. "You just need to show your passports."

"I left mine back in the Mission Home," an elder says.

"You can wait here," says Price. "Jensen. Wait here with him."

The man checks your ticket. Opens your passport, compares your face to your photo, stamps a page with a stamp that puts an end to your right to be in Austria. An official end to the road behind you now. To any possibility that offered you a road ahead by staying here. You push through the turnstile. Four elders come through behind you. While you wait for them you look back. Across the polished stone of the floor Angelika and your family stand where you left them. You raise your arm. Watch theirs come up. Out of reach now. No turning back. From the way they wave back at you they know it too.

Chapter 107

THERE WAS THE STORY they told you in the Salt Lake Mission Home before you came to Austria. About the mother who told her departing son she'd rather have him come home in a coffin than dishonored.

On your ride to the airport you could turn your head and see, in the humid haze of the distance, the city you were leaving. The steeples and domes of cathedrals that rose above the rooftops of Vienna. Now, in the harness of your seat on board a plane again, you look out the window at the airfield, the view of the city gone. Passengers still come down the aisle, holding their sacks and bags high above the heads and backrests of the seats, waiting for people ahead of them to put their belongings in the overhead racks and sit down, looking down the length of the plane for their own seats. The aisle seat next to you is empty. The passenger holding its number is still a mystery. On the ride out the towering steeple of Stephansdom rose undisputed above the skyline. You remember the booth where you kneeled in the dark and confessed to a nameless and faceless priest with a weary but gentle voice. You remember hearing Morgan up in the organ loft play a haunting arrangement of a common hymn. It was an arrangement where the organ pipes gave individual human voices to the pioneers as they struggled and died and grieved and prayed and hauled their wagons and their handcarts across the Great Plains to their promised land where the Rockies came down and met the barren floor of the great American desert. The arrangement brought to life their hope and doubt and anguish as though they'd come back from the dead to voice them. They took your breath away. Made you start to cry while the priest heard your confession. You remember how he could only forgive you for sins you'd already committed. He couldn't forgive you of your future sins because neither of you could know what those would be.

In the neighborhood of the cathedral's steeple you remember a street called Graben and a hotel called the Rabe. In the coffin dark of the booth you cried for the first time on your mission. You cried for the pioneers. You cried a second time for Novick. And a third for a heartbroken little girl. Don't you like us any more, she asked. No, you say. I love you. But I have to go home for now. I found the sin I need to be forgiven for.

Except for your new boxer shorts, which you swapped for your garments, you haven't changed clothes since Eisenerz, now close to a week ago. You reach up and twist the nozzle till you feel the fresh bath of cool air on your hand and face and chest. Enough to clean away the stale smell that rises from under your suit coat. The dark-skinned woman you saw in the terminal comes down the aisle behind an old man in a blue herringbone suit. She waits for him to lift a backpack into the rack over your head, take out a book, settle himself in the seat next to you. When he thanks her for waiting she smiles and continues past you. When he turns and nods you nod back. When he lays the book in his lap you see the title. Schokolade und Stein. German. A language you no longer have a reason to speak. The door closes. A stewardess comes down the aisle looking into people's laps. You sit back and look out the window as the engines fire up and send a shudder through the plane and then settle down to a steady whistling roar.

Another American city. Any city where you could start to exist again. Los Angeles. Saint Louis. Yesterday you sat in the conference room and let them cross your mind, let yourself imagine a guy in Levis and a teeshirt walking on their summer sidewalks, sometimes alone, sometimes with new friends you'd made, sometimes a girl's hand in yours the way you'd seen couples on sidewalks in the cities and towns of Austria, sometimes with the trumpet Brother Shlagl gave you. Any American city. A city where you could pick up your life and go from there. Atlanta. Houston. It didn't much matter. The cities themselves were nebulous when you tried to see them beyond the sidewalk underneath your feet, the brief stretch of a street ahead of you, shops and buildings you were passing. Brooklyn. Portland. Baltimore. What mattered was a place where you could just exist. Where you could start, day after day, sunrise after sunrise, friend after friend, street after street, conversation after conversation, with a job and a place to play, to build a past again. A past that would give you presence. Nashville. Albany. It didn't matter. It would be a place you'd come to know the way you came to know Vienna. A city where you could play and set that steel bird free again, free of the underhanded purpose you'd been asked to play for, free of the way you'd used it to betray your heroes, unburdened of everything, only the freedom to fly. Any city but Salt Lake. Any town but Bountiful. A place where you wouldn't have to live like someone who didn't exist except as hate for what you did and shame for what you are. Where you wouldn't have to hate yourself to live.

And then Hunsacker came in and handed you the envelope that held your father's note.

Come home and we'll get through this together.

The way you read that line and reached the word that ended it.

Together.

The way it left you numb. The way you sat there staring. A word you'd never heard your father use that way till now. Just you and him. Nothing in the way. Nothing between you. You stood before him stripped of everything you thought he ever hoped for, everything you thought he ever cared about, and he wanted you to know he loved you. And then that word. Together. Written with his hand. And in this sudden rush you were done waiting. Done wondering what it was you could never satisfy. You were his son. The way you stood before him now, stripped of everything you'd done for years to make yourself the son you thought he wanted, everything you ever used to measure who you were. And he wanted you to know he loved you.

And signed it Dad.

Dad. A word your friends had called their fathers. A word they'd used when they talked about your father. Your dad. A word other men had used. Tell your dad hello. Your dad should be proud. A word you'd even used yourself when you talked about him. My dad. A word you'd never called him to his face. A word you'd never heard him call himself. You looked for signs of hesitation in its three handwritten letters. Flaws that gave away any reluctance. There were none.

You had questions. Who told him. How his note got here so fast from Utah in the four days since your trial. How it made it to the Mission Home without stamps or an address on the envelope. If it came bundled with his usual magazines and clippings. The difference between his letter to President Smith two years ago and his last brief note to you is as vast and terrifying now as the space between the edge of Dead Horse Point and the distant mountains where you came from. If the only way to cross that space was to understand that this is what he long expected. How the questions didn't matter. The simple message of his note made smoke of them. And wind of the answers you knew you wouldn't have.

What he expected.

You don't remember Wissom and Hunsacker leaving while you sat there staring at the note, first to trust it, then to ride out the turmoil stirred by its words. They were simply gone. You sat there and felt the pull of those words as they did away with every other possibility you'd let yourself imagine. Gone along with Wissom and Hunsacker was the possibility of another American city. There was only one possibility. Home. Home where your dad and you will get through what you've done together.

Now, in the confining harness of your seat on board a plane again, you want to cringe away from what you've done to him, away from what it had to take for him to brush everything aside, everything between you, and call himself your dad.

You're my dad.

Yes. You're my son.

Hi, Dad.

Hello, Son.

I'm sorry, Dad.

It's okay, Son.

On the highway that leads from the airport back to Vienna, and then from there to Klosterneuburg, an Opel sedan carries a small family and a girl made up like a gypsy revolutionary home again. A nunnery on the grounds of a Catholic Stift. An apartment in an abandoned barracks building. The gypsy revolutionary rides alone in back. The father drives. The mother watches the highway from the passenger side. Between them in the front seat, a little girl rides in tears, an only child again. You look quick down at your knees. You had that possibility. To stay here. To ride home in the back seat with your little sister, to dry her eyes, to bring that shining smile to her face, to be her big brother for good. Go to work for her father. Keep playing the Vienna clubs and the Factory. Tour with Peter. Make this city home. You weren't a missionary any more. You could live clean of any hidden motive. You could do away with the barrier of subterfuge that always stood you apart from them. You could immerse yourself among them. You could just be one of them.

Together, your father wrote. And closed that possibility too.

In your shoes you feel the brakes of the plane release. The engines wind up to slowly start moving the trembling plane away from the terminal toward the runway. The man in the seat next to you pulls at his nose, scratches his jaw, opens his book to its bookmark. He's shy of halfway through. Chocolate and Stone. You wonder what it's about. Then your father's words are there again, where you can see them, almost touch the hand that wrote them, even though his note is out of sight in the inside pocket of your suit.

Out your window the lanes of the airfield pass slowly under the wing as the engines of the swaying plane are revved and lowered and revved again. You feel their wind across the dark floor of your stomach. As you reach the runway, swing around to line up for takeoff, the window sweeps across the back face of the terminal, and sunlight cuts a quick bright slash across your eyes. Karl and Molly and Roy and Maggie. Their scarce letters in your suitcase with Maggie's drawing. They come to you the haunting way they have so many nights since August, you lying in one or another cot, your eyes wide open, staring at one or another dark wall just inches from your face. You remember the ride home from San Jose when you crossed into Utah and they became your reason for coming here. They'll be new to the kind of brother you are. New to the shaming bewilderment you'll cause them. The example you wanted to set for them, the path you wanted to show them out of the fear and hope that were always mingled in their faces, will be gone. You'll have to set a new example now. One that shows them what happens when you fail. One that shows them how to make restitution when you break a rule like the rule you broke. One that shows them the path you don't yet know yourself out of hate and shame. One that shows them how hate and shame can turn back to blood and flesh and skin and bone. You don't know how. But you'll find a way. While the man in the seat next to you turns a page, reads again, you open the palms of your empty hands and look at them.

You didn't need an escort. Just a ride.

The engines come on hard and fast and roaring. Their thrust is absolute in their power to hold you back against your seat. The plane rocks back and forth as the wings reach for air and the tires start to lose their grip on the runway. Then suddenly rides smooth as the wings lift the tires off and the engines pull full throttle for the sky. Vienna starts to fall away below you. Cathedrals become model railroad miniatures of themselves. You don't look for the Donaukanal, Schwedenplatz, other places you once played. You don't look for the Opera House or the Zwolf Apostelkeller. You don't look for the roof of the Mission Home. You don't look for the bell towers of the Klosterneuburg Stift. You don't look for your grandfather's shoes. You don't look for the streets where your mission lies dead like yesterday's puddles in the cobblestones. The City of Music, the city whose majesty and beauty Morgan wanted you to see and hear and feel, starts to lose itself in haze. Haze that will immerse everything you once did here. You remember the prehistoric sea that seemed to close over the space and time you occupied when you lifted out of Salt Lake two summers ago. How that sea won't open for you now, won't give you back the space and time you left behind, because where you're going is a place where you won't exist except as hate and shame. Hate for what you did. Shame for what it made of you.

But you exist.

You start to feel it, hidden deep, hidden almost from yourself. You exist. In the holes in the soles of your shoes and in the crotch of your pants. In the sidewalks you've walked, the streets and roads you've pedaled, the doors you've knocked on. In a Catholic priest who took your anonymous confession. In the Russian landlady and her daughter. In a kid named Herbert. In Novick and his plastic radio where you sat at the table listening together. In the musicians you played with. In the people who are free now to remember just your music. In the City of Jazz. In Bateman and Wolfe. In Otto and Angelika. In your small family and your little sister. And now in the presence of your fellow passengers. You exist. To the old man seated to your right.

"Excuse me," you say, in German.

He turns and looks at you surprised. A large mole on the far side of his nose looks like a blister full of old blood.

"Yes? Do you need to get up?"

"No. No. I just noticed the book you're reading. It has an intriguing title."

Using his thumb as a bookmark, he closes the book enough to read the title, stroke the cover illustration with his other hand.

"Yes," he says. "It's the reason I bought it." Then softly laughs. "I wanted to know how chocolate and stone go together."

"Does it tell you?"

"Ah," he says, turning to you. "Yes. I think it will."

"Can I ask where you're going?"

"Yes," he says. "To Columbus. To see my daughter and her family."

And after you ask about them, and he tells you, he says. "May I ask the same of you?"

"Salt Lake City."

"Yes," he says. "I've heard of it." Then he says, "Vacation?"

"Home," you say, extending your hand. "My name is Shake."

"Jakob," he says, taking your hand. "Nice to meet you, Shake."

You exist. To Jakob and among the passengers around you. One of everyone. You wonder where they're going. What cities they're headed for. If some of them are going home like you. You exist. You don't know what you'll face there but you'll do it. Everything they want. The way you always have. Ease your mother's sorrow by coming home alive instead of in a coffin. Give your father what he wants. Karl and Molly and Roy and Maggie. Show them this new path.

We'll get through this together.

This. In your father's offer you knew what he meant that word to mean. He meant the path to reinstatement. He meant come home and face the music. Repentance and restitution and in the end forgiveness and baptism and the restoration of your priesthood. Your long debt to him used to end when your mission did. Now there is no mission. Just the debt. And now it extends like the highway across the Nevada desert into the shimmering distant silver mirage you never reach, the mirage from which the asphalt and the crosses of the telephone poles keep replenishing themselves.

But you exist.

And in a bird made of aluminum and steel you fly this time not into night but west into the sun.

ACKNOWLEDGEMENTS

Edi Goller, a native of Austria, a girl when I met her decades ago as a missionary, now the author of the novel *Schokolade und Stein* and a prolific short story writer, for her detailed recollections, lifelong knowledge of her country and its towns and cities, and other resources, support that was instrumental in bringing this book to life, giving it the heart it needed, and ensuring its authenticity.

My agent Michael Strong of Regal Hoffmann & Associates for his committed literary and marketing guidance in shaping and promoting my books.

My kid sister Margie for her always inspiring cheerleading. My kid brother Marv for his tireless and always defiant support.

Maurice Stacey, native of Bountiful, for his freely offered advocacy and promotional support in arranging readings, reunions, and public notices during and following my Utah book tour for *Journey* and *Of the World.*

Anne Juenger for inspiring the title of this novel.

The Boys from Bountiful—George Baty, Bobby West, Roger Jensen, Mike Flowers, Johnny Rasmussen, Harold Zesiger, Steve Derbyshire, Bob Gardiner, and Johnny Greenwell—for giving Shake the fictional buddies to make the journey with.

Diane Cole for her two wonderful and enthusiastic reviews of *Journey* and *Of the World* in *The Salt Lake Tribune* that made it possible for me to reach a broad audience across my home state of Utah.

Steve Williams of KUER public radio for an hour and a half of conversation on fiction and jazz on his popular program.

King's English Bookshop, Bountiful Music, Golden Years Activity Center, and First Unitarian Church for hosting readings from *Journey* and *Of the World.*

Sue Emmett, founder and leader of the Exmormon Foundation, for the opportunity to tell my story at the Foundation's annual convention.

The magical circle of poets and writers—Nik Gruswitz, Melissa Montimurro, Carlo D'Ambrosi, Chase Talon, Bryan Straube, and others—who made up the workshop that met at my house each week for much of the 1990s into the 2000s. It was in the circle of this improvised family that Shake Tauffler had his genesis and spent his formative years.

The people who offered to read *Not into Night* as a manuscript in progress. More than twenty people of all ages, from all walks of life, religions, backgrounds, interests, reading tastes, and regions of the country, stepped up to volunteer. In completely random order, these remarkable and good people are Susan Horton, Paul Mossberg, Marian and John Murray, Kelly Frazer, Anne and Eileen Juenger, John Eastman, Kathy Layton, Marvin Zimmer, John Sparks, Ed Selby, Diane Cole, Marjorie Zimmer, Toni Zimmer, Sophie Zimmer, Helen Tobler, Fred Simpson, Lane Anderson, Jeni and Cory Drake, Danny Piperato, and Michael McKelvey.

Reviewers on Amazon, Goodreads, and other online venues, as well as those folks who've written me, who were conscientious and kind enough to articulate and let me know what they thought.

Mrs. Whitaker, Miss Johnson, Ruth Jones, Blanche Cannon, Steve Raab, Franklin Fisher, David Kranes, Hal Moore, Richard Schramm, and all the other teachers who guided, encouraged, and championed me.

Grace Paley, Ray Carver, E.L. Doctorow, Lewis Turco, John Gardner, John Cheever, Jack Cady, and other established writers who saw promise in my work.

All the people—all my students and all my friends across more than four decades—who have had to wait and believe in me so long to finally see this happen. I hope you'll think it was worth it.

All the faithful followers of a kid named Shake Tauffler for their patience and faith in waiting for this third book to finally see the light of day.

My parents who raised me and loved me and, in the end, supported me and gave me a story worth telling.

My wife Toni for her gifted and dedicated editing and for everything else I could not have done without.

 Max Zimmer was born in Switzerland, brought across the Atlantic at the age of four, and raised like his young protagonist in Utah in the take-no-prisoners crucible of the Mormon faith. He earned a B.A. and M.A. from the University of Utah and was teaching fiction, working on a doctorate in writing, when he was invited east for a summer at Yaddo, the writer's retreat in Saratoga, New York. He never intended to stay in the East. But from Yaddo he took a job teaching fiction in the Writing Arts Program at SUNY Oswego. It was there, in the summer of 1978, that *If Where You're Going Isn't Home* was first conceived, as a long love story. From Oswego, Max gravitated toward the city, lived and tended bar in Manhattan, and eventually moved to the northwest corner of New Jersey, where he married his wife Toni and settled in to write *If Where You're Going Isn't Home* from the beginning. The East had become home now. Utah had become a place he wrote about.

Among Max's published works are poems, stories, reviews, magazine articles, short biographies, and liner notes for jazz albums. He was an immediate success as a writer. Following its nomination by Ray Carver, his first published story "Utah Died for Your Sins" was awarded the Pushcart Prize, and singled out in *Rolling Stone* magazine as a raw new voice in American fiction. Max has read at venues ranging from coffee shops to SUNY writer conferences to the Pen New Writers Series. Jack Cady, Grace Paley, Lewis Turco, and John Gardner are among other established writers who have expressed their high regard and admiration for his work. E. L. Doctorow called Max's writing the best he'd seen in a coast-to-coast college tour following the release of *Ragtime*. After meeting him on a similar tour after the publication of *Falconer*, John Cheever championed Max's work for the last five years of his life.

Following *Journey* and *Of the World, Not into Night* is Max's third novel. He has also published a collection of 47 human interest / humor columns he wrote for an automotive magazine under the title *Actual Mileage*.

www.maxzimmer.com